First Edition

I would like to thank the following people whose assistance has
been integral to the creation of this work:
Julia, for her invaluable help and guidance with the text.
Dr Kaveh Farrokh, for his great knowledge of the Parthian Empire.
'Big John', for designing the cover.
Holly Martin, for the cover image.
Ardeshir Radpour, for his help regarding sourcing the cover image.

Chapter 1

'He may be old but his mind is as sharp as ever. I don't suppose you refused his generous offer, did you?' My father, King Varaz of Hatra, was far from happy. He paced up and down the council chamber while everyone else sat at the large rectangular table looked decidedly uncomfortable.

'No, father, I accepted his most kind gift.'

My father, now in his late forties, had a smattering of grey in his short-cropped hair. But he still looked every inch the warrior he was – tall, muscular and imposing – his hands clasped behind his back as he continued pacing up and down in front of the large hide map of the Parthian Empire on the wall. The veins in his neck were bulging and his face was red; he was indeed far from happy. He eventually sat in his chair and began rapping his fingers on the table, which only added to everyone's feeling of unease. He looked at me across the table.

'You are the heir to Hatra's throne, not the commander of some ramshackle desert outpost across the Euphrates.'

'Hardly that, majesty,' interrupted Addu, Hatra's royal treasurer, a rather gaunt man in his fifties. 'Dura Europus is a prosperous commerce centre at the junction of both the east–to–west and north–to–south trade routes.'

Dura Europus was a city built on a high rock escarpment on the west bank of the Euphrates. It overlooked the great waterway, which formed the western frontier of the Parthian Empire, and controlled a strip of land on the western side of the river for a distance of one hundred miles north and south of the city, as well as all ferries and bridges across the waterway for an equivalent length. The revenues raised from the endless trade caravans that passed through Dura's lands were considerable, as were the dues raised from the charges levelled on the aristocratic landowners who farmed the rich Euphrates plain. And now the city belonged to me.

If Addu had sought to soothe my father's temper he was sadly mistaken.

The king banged his fist on the table. 'Dura Europus is on the west bank of the Euphrates, Lord Addu, which means that if an enemy attacks from the direction of Syria, then Dura Europus will be the first the fall.'

'We have heard of no threat arising from that quarter, lord.' It was the first time that Vistaspa, the commander of my father's bodyguard and the head of Hatra's army, had spoken. Five years older than my father and treated like a brother by the king, he had a lean, bony face and dark, cold eyes. He had always treated me with a detached aloofness bordering on disdain and had made little effort to garner my affection. He was utterly loyal to my father and absolutely contemptuous of everyone else, but his qualities as a commander ensured that Hatra's army was one of the finest in the Parthian Empire.

My father leaned back in his chair. 'Perhaps not yet, but they will come, of that I am certain.' He shot me a glance. 'The more so when they learn that the new King of Dura Europus is none other than the man who fought beside the leader of a slave rebellion in their own homeland.'

He spoke of my time in Italy with Spartacus, gladiator, slave and for three years the master of all Italy, and a man I was proud to call friend. Before that I had been raiding in the Roman province of Cappadocia under the command of Lord Bozan, at the time leader of Hatra's army, but Bozan had been killed in battle and I and many other Parthians had been captured by the Romans, then put in chains and sent in boats to be slaves in Italy. It was there that we had been rescued by Spartacus and his men on the slopes of a sleeping volcano called Mount Vesuvius. Thus began a three-year campaign in Italy where I had led Spartacus' horsemen, and where we had defeated the Romans on many occasions.

'I do not fear the Romans,' I said.

My father laughed. 'You should, because when they hear that King Pacorus, formerly the friend of a slave general who terrorised Italy, is now the ruler of a small city within touching distance of their eastern provinces, they might be tempted to send an army to the walls of Dura Europus.'

'I've beaten Roman armies before, father.'

'Ah, yes, I forgot, you laid waste to their homeland. But correct me if I am wrong, they defeated you in the end, did they not?'

'I am made king by Sinatruces, father. That is now law. What is done cannot be undone.'

My father stared at the table before him. 'No, indeed. Vistaspa, you will take five hundred of Hatra's garrison and camp them across the river from my son's new kingdom, just in case he needs to call upon additional troops.'

Lord Kogan, garrison commander at Hatra, raised his eyebrows at this. In his mid-fifties, his shoulder-length hair and thick moustache streaked with white, his broad frame was still impressive. Tall and serious, he guarded his garrison with the tenacity of a hawk keeping watch over its nest.

'That is many soldiers, majesty.'

'I agree, Kogan,' replied my father, 'but I fear that many covet Dura Europus and I want Pacorus to enjoy his new position, at least for a while.'

'I have troops enough to garrison the city, father.'

My father smiled. 'Really? And who would they be?'

'Those who came with me from Italy.'

'A hundred and twenty, including the women?'

My father was referring to the twenty women horse archers who had fought beside me and were led by a Gallic princess named Gallia, the woman who was soon to be my wife. She had called her women warriors Amazons, named after a race of martial women who had lived on an Aegean island called Lemnos. Many people, including most in this meeting, thought they were ridiculous. But I had seen them fight in Italy and knew that they had earned their right to bear arms. I would trust them with my life; indeed, Gallia herself had saved my life once in southern Italy with her proficiency with a bow. It seemed like another life to me now.

'Yes, father, including the women. And Gafarn, if he will accompany me.'

My adopted brother smiled at me. Two years younger than me, he had, since the age of five, been a slave in my father's palace at Hatra. Taken as a captive in war, he had become my personal servant. He too had been captured in Cappadocia, subsequently freed by Spartacus when we had joined his cause, and then fought alongside me in Italy. During that time he had become like a brother to me, and I was glad that he been formally made so by my parents upon our return to Parthia.

'Of course, who else is going to watch your back?'

'Not so hasty, Gafarn,' said my father. 'You are the brother of Pacorus, no longer his slave. You must discuss the matter with your wife first. And I may not allow you to leave. You are, after all, second in line to Hatra's throne and I do not want both my sons embarking on a fool's errand.'

Gafarn smiled at me. 'As you command, majesty.'

My father shook his head. 'No, Gafarn, you must call me "father" now.'

'Of course, my apologies, majesty.'

My father waved his hand at him. 'It doesn't matter. But talk with Diana. She may not want to leave Hatra now that you that have quarters in the palace. How is the child?'

My father was speaking of the infant son of Spartacus and a promise that I had made to his wife, Claudia, to take her son with me to Parthia in the event the slave rebellion was defeated. Gafarn and Diana, formerly a Roman kitchen slave in the gladiator school where Spartacus had trained, now a princess of Parthia and a close friend of myself and Gallia, were now bringing him up. How strange fate was.

'He thrives, majesty, er, father.'

'When you take up residence in Dura, Pacorus,' continued my father, 'you will only have a handful of Parthians to protect you and your new wife, plus the soldiers led by that Roman.'

'You mean Domitus, father.'

'You trust this man?' enquired Kogan.

'With my life,' I replied.

Lucius Domitus was formerly a Roman centurion who had struck a senior officer. As a result he was condemned to live out the rest of his life working in a silver mine. When Spartacus had captured that mine he had been freed, and had subsequently served in the slave army. He had risen to a high rank for he was a formidable warrior. He was also a forthright, loyal and brave individual, and I was delighted that he had elected to come to Parthia in the aftermath of Spartacus' death. Now, he was busy raising a legion that would be in my service.

'His encampment outside the city resembles a host of refugees,' grumbled my father. 'They need to be moved on.'

'That may be difficult, majesty.' It was the first time that Assur, high priest of Hatra, had spoken. Lean and possessing a somewhat severe countenance, he was now in his sixties but still commanded great respect. The guardian of the souls of the city's population, he was the representative on earth of the god we all worshipped in Hatra, Shamash, Lord of the Sun.

'Why is that, Assur?' asked my father.

'It is well known that the individuals you speak of are here for one reason only, to enlist in the service of your son, Pacorus. They believe, rightly or wrongly, that he is beloved of God, since a sage in the service of King Sinatruces foretold his return. Moreover, that he returned to us with the Lady Gallia by his side, whose coming was also foretold, has only added to the lustre that surrounds your son's name. I would advise against making any move against our new guests.'

'How many have graced us with their presence thus far?' asked my father sourly, looking at Kogan.

'My men have counted over five thousand thus far, majesty. And may I add that they are proving a heavy burden on the city's resources. Most brought little or no food with them and Prince, er, King Pacorus has insisted that they should all be fed.'

'Of course,' I added, 'otherwise they will starve and will be of no use to me.'

'This matter needs attending to, Pacorus,' said my father, 'especially since visiting dignitaries will soon be arriving as your wedding guests. It is inappropriate that the first thing they will see of Hatra will be your band of beggars and thieves that have decided to make you a god.'

The meeting over, I made my way to my quarters in the palace to collect my weapons. I took Gafarn with me, walking through corridors teeming with clerks, servants and guards, Kogan's soldiers, who stood like statues in front of white stone pillars.

'I will be glad to get to Dura Europos.'

Gafarn was surprised. 'You wish to leave Hatra?'

'In truth, though I love my parents, I find the atmosphere in the palace suffocating. My parents are watching over me like hawks. I want to get married and then be away.'

'Then it was fortunate indeed that you have been given your own city to rule.'

I bristled at this. 'Fortunate! It was the least that Sinatruces could do.'

Gafarn laughed. 'He could have had you killed and taken Gallia for himself. No one would have thought any less of him had he done so.'

I did not answer because he was right. Gafarn had a gift, which I found very irritating, of being able to sum up most situations succinctly. The Parthian Empire was made up of eighteen separate kingdoms, each one ruled by a king, but each of these kings elected one of their number to be the 'King of Kings', to rule over them all. In this way the empire had one voice and the likelihood of civil war breaking out between ambitious kings or factions was reduced. Sinatruces, now over eighty years old, had been King of Kings for fifty years. The great length of his rule had meant that all the kings of the empire naturally deferred to his decisions and accepted his authority without question.

'Your father seems annoyed at your appointment. But then, hardly surprising as you are only twenty-five and he had to wait until his father, your grandfather, King Sames, died before he could wear Hatra's crown. He was in his thirties then.'

'Thank you, Gafarn, I know my family history.'

'If you know it, then you must realise why he is so peeved. Add in that you have become a messiah, and you can understand his annoyance.'

'I am not a messiah.'

He nodded. 'Indeed you are not, but you are to those who have made the trip to Hatra.'

We picked up our swords, bows and quivers from our quarters and then walked to the stables adjacent to the sprawling royal barracks next to the palace, where my father's bodyguard and the army's other cavalry were quartered. The royal bodyguard consisted of five hundred of the finest sons of Hatra, all personally selected by either my father or Vistaspa, men who had been trained for war since an infant age. Like me, their whole lives were devoted to becoming expert in the military arts – riding, shooting a bow from the saddle, using a sword on foot and horseback, and a lance from the saddle. The royal bodyguard looked down on the members of the city's professional army – a thousand heavy cavalry and five thousand horse archers – who in turn looked down on the city's garrison: Lord Kogan's two thousand foot soldiers, who in reality were a force for maintaining law and order in the city. God knows what they all thought of the ragged wretches who had come to Hatra with the sole intention of enlisting in my service.

The palace, a large limestone building in the north of the city, stood next to the city's royal square, which was normally empty save for special occasions. Opposite the palace was the Great Temple, a massive colonnaded structure erected to pay homage to Shamash. The royal stables were thronged with soldiers, grooms, farriers, veterinaries and blacksmiths. Horseshoes were being hammered on anvils and horses were being saddled, exercised or groomed. The mounts of the royal family were housed in a separate block, a whitewashed stable with a tiled roof and running water. But in truth all of Hatra's royal stables were luxurious, for to a Parthian his horse was the most precious thing that he possessed. Then I thought of my darling Gallia; perhaps not the most precious.

My horse was a pure white stallion called Remus, named after one of the founders of the city of Rome. He had been named thus by his master, and I had 'liberated' him when Spartacus had captured the city of Nola. I had ridden him from that day on, and he had been my trusty steed in many battles. When I escaped from Italy he came with me. During my time with Spartacus Remus had been quartered either in the open or under canvas, and he had got used to it. As I walked into the stables he kicked the door of his stall. A stable hand, a man in his late forties, frowned.

'He still dislikes his stall, I see.'

'Yes, highness. Most of the time he displays a grudging calm and remains aloof from us, but in the mornings, just before you take him out for his daily exercise, he becomes highly irritable.'

'Like his master,' quipped Gafarn.

Once I had entered his stall Remus calmed down, so I led him out, threw a red saddlecloth on his back and then strapped on the saddle itself. This comprised a wooden frame with four horns reinforced with bronze plates at each corner. The horns and the saddle were padded and covered in leather, and once in the saddle the horns held the rider firmly in place. Items of equipment could also be hung from these horns. While I was checking Remus' straps and bridle, Gafarn saddled his horse, a white mare named Sura who had formerly been my horse before I had been captured in Cappadocia. Whereas Remus was headstrong and feisty, Sura was calm and determined. She was a fine horse and I was glad that she now belonged to my adopted brother. We slung bows in hide cases fixed to our saddles, while our quivers hung at our left hips, secured to a leather strap that ran over our right shoulders. For our ride we wore wide-brimmed hats, long-sleeved shirts and baggy leggings.

It was mid-morning now and the sun was beginning its ascent in a clear blue sky. There was but a slight breeze, and already the day was very warm. We left the city via the northern gate, one of four that gave access to Hatra, and then rode across the causeway over the wide, deep moat that surrounded the whole city. Hatra was in the middle of a desert, but the city itself was fed by many springs that produced cool, sweet water. These springs kept Hatra green and the moat full, but my father kept the surrounding area deliberately parched. When I asked him why he did not build watercourses that would make the desert bloom he had smiled and replied. 'If an army lays siege to Hatra, its troops will die of thirst before they breach the city walls.'

It took us half an hour to reach the encampment of my followers, a vast collection of tents, temporary canvas shelters, dogs, horses and camels. It was not difficult to find, as there was a steady stream of traffic going to and from the city carrying food, shelters and water to the site. My father was right: it was an unsatisfactory situation and had to be resolved quickly. It was also costing his city a small fortune to maintain this desert army.

At first glance the mass of dwellings resembled total chaos, but closer inspection revealed that, slowly, a sense of order was being established among the disorder. The architects of this transformation were Lucius Domitus and Nergal. Domitus, ex-Roman centurion, was busy forming the disparate throng into new recruits. To this end he had called upon his training and had begun to organise the camp along Roman lines. Thus instead of haphazard groupings of tents, the shelters were now being arranged in neat lines and rows, with tents grouped into symmetrical blocks. And I noticed that many men were employed in digging what appeared to be a dirt rampart around the whole assembly. Gafarn and I dismounted and walked our horses through the camp. Men stopped what they were doing to stare at us, or rather me, and I felt slightly uncomfortable when they began to clap and cheer. The shrill sound of a whistle being blown, followed by a stream of curses, soon diverted their attention back to their duties.

'It's beginning to resemble the camps we had back in Italy,' remarked Gafarn.

'Old habits die hard for Domitus,' I added.

'I doubt that they die at all,' he replied.

Domitus stomped towards us, the sun glinting off the round steel discs on his mail tunic and his metal greaves. Thickset with a lean face, his Roman helmet sported a white transverse crest and his tunic was also white.

'I wish you would send word when you intend to visit the camp,' he said, 'your presence can have a detrimental effect on some of the more impressionable ones we have here.'

'Impressionable ones?' asked Gafarn.

'The dreamers and mystics,' replied Domitus, his muscular arms now turned brown by the Mesopotamian sun, 'those who believe that your brother is a god.'

'And you don't believe that I am a god, Domitus?' I teased him.

'The day you can fly around the battlefield instead of riding upon it, then I'll believe that you're a god.'

'Quite right, Domitus,' added Gafarn,' we don't want his head getting any bigger than it is.'

At that moment a column of recruits marched past, about two hundred in twenty ranks. They had no weapons, shields or armour, but they did seem to be marching in step. At the head of the column marched one of the Germans or Dacians who had served with Spartacus in Germany, his long black hair spilling out from under his helmet. He wore a mail shirt and carried a shield and sword at his hip. Two of his comrades brought up the rear. Domitus eyed the recruits as they passed, and suddenly hit one of them across the back of the shoulders with his vine cane.

'No talking in the ranks,' he bellowed in Latin.

The recruits, being from various Parthian provinces or runaway slaves from Egypt, Syria and a host of other places, would not have understood his words, but they would have discerned the sentiment behind the blow. When I had been in Italy I had learned that the favoured instrument of a centurion, the men who were the backbone of the Roman fighting unit called a legion, was a vine cane around three feet in length, with which they used to beat recruits for even minor infractions, plus anyone else unlucky enough to earn their wrath. I used to think that it was part of a centurion's training to learn how to use these accursed things, but I now knew that each vine cane was created in the underworld and possessed of an evil spirit, and once on earth it searched out its owner, who always happened to be a Roman centurion.

'You don't have to strike the recruits, Domitus. You are not in Italy now.'

He looked at me and shook his head. 'No, Pacorus, I need it more than ever, especially as I don't speak the lingo.'

He was right about that. I and other members of the royal household had been taught Latin and Greek at an early age to enable us to converse with foreign monarchs and envoys when we were older, but Domitus had as yet only a smattering of our language.

'You are surrounding the camp with a rampart?' I enquired.

'Yes,' replied Domitus.

'Who do you think is going to attack you?' asked Gafarn.

'No one, but I need to keep this lot,' he waved his cane around the camp, 'busy so their minds don't wander. So when they're not marching they are digging, and at the end of the day they are too tired to cause any trouble.'

'Have any deserted?' I asked.

'One or two, but most are determined to stay despite my best efforts to dissuade them. That being the case, I decided that they might as well start their training.'

We continued to walk towards the centre of the camp where Domitus had set up his headquarters, a large Bedouin goatskin tent that had two guards at its entrance.

Domitus took off his helmet and wiped his sweaty brow with a cloth. In true Roman fashion he had a short-cropped scalp.

'It's hotter here than in Italy, that's for sure. Will you stay for something to eat?'

'No, thank you, Domitus. I just came out to see how things are progressing. My father is eager for us to be away. After the wedding we will move everyone here to Dura Europos.'

11

Domitus nodded. 'Makes sense. Your father has been very generous so far, feeding and watering us out of his pocket. How far is it to your new kingdom?'

'Around two hundred miles due southwest.'

'Think they can march that far, Domitus?' queried Gafarn.

Domitus smiled. 'Soon they will be able to march twenty miles in five hours, and after that forty miles in twelve hours. They'll be able to get there, have no fear.'

Gafarn looked around. 'If you and the men that came with us from Italy don't speak our language, how do you transmit your commands to the recruits, apart from using your cane?'

'Oh, Nergal lent me some of his boys, the same ones that fought with you and Pacorus in Italy.'

Nergal was a Parthian who had been captured with me in Cappadocia and transported to Italy as a slave. Tall, gangly and a year older than me, he was originally from my father's kingdom, had been my second-in-command in Italy and now commanded the fifty Parthian horsemen that had survived the defeat of Spartacus. Like him, they were now all fluent in Latin as well as Parthian.

'Well, Domitus,' I said, 'it looks as though you are well on your way to raising your legion, but you can't be a centurion any more.'

A look of hurt spread across his face. 'I can't?'

'Of course not, you must become a legate. They command Roman legions, do they not?'

He flashed a smile. 'They certainly do.'

'Good, I will have your commission drawn up, with commensurate pay. I don't suppose I could persuade you to retire your cane?'

'It would be like losing an arm.'

'Mm, well, we must be away. If you need anything send word to the palace.'

We left the camp in the capable hands of Domitus and rode back to the city. Leaving our horses at the stables we made our way to the palace, to find my father and mother entertaining Gafarn's wife, Diana, the young son of Spartacus and the woman who had become the centre of my world. We found them in the small 'secret garden' that my mother Queen Mihri, liked to tend as a hobby. The garden was part of the much larger walled royal gardens that abutted the palace and which covered several acres. It was termed 'secret' because only my mother was allowed to arrange the growing of flowers, plants and fig, pomegranate, nut and jujube trees that provided shade. In reality a small army of assistants – slaves – kept her garden and the larger ones tidy and lush, but my mother fancied herself to have a gift for making things grow, and so most days she could be found in a simple white dress and apron, tending to her shrubberies. In the 'secret garden' was a white marble fountain, with four water channels leading off it, signifying water, fire, earth and air. Larger, more ornate fountains were spread throughout the royal gardens, all fed by the springs that watered the rest of Hatra.

Peacocks walked free in the gardens, and there were also a number of dovecotes that had their own keepers. The doves had pure white plumage matching that of the white horses of my father's bodyguard, and so the belief grew that as long as white doves flew above the city and white horses carried its warriors, Hatra would be invincible in the face of its enemies.

Goldfish and koi swam in large ponds beside small copses of date palms and sycamores. The gardens were filled with an explosion of colours from blooming daisies, cornflowers, mandrakes, roses, irises, myrtle, jasmine, mignonettes, convolvulus, celosia, narcissus, ivy, lychnis, sweet marjoram, henna, bay laurel, small yellow chrysanthemums and poppies. They were certainly places of serenity and sweet fragrances.

My mother and her guests were in the shade of the white-painted wooden pagoda that had been built near the marble fountain. Slaves fussed around with trays holding pastries and fruit, while others poured wine. I walked over to my sensual future wife and kissed her on the cheek. Gallia looked happy and relaxed, her long, thick blonde hair framing her oval face, with its high cheekbones and narrow nose, and then cascading over her shoulders and breasts. Today, like every day, she had spent the morning riding on the training fields, practising firing her bow from the saddle. Despite wearing boots and leggings she looked as femininely beautiful as ever, her blue tunic highlighting her lithe figure. By contrast, her friend, Diana, wore a simple white dress that covered her whole body save her pale arms, in which she held the infant son of Spartacus.

'Ah, the general of the desert army returns,' the gently mocking tones of my father came from a sofa opposite to where I had entered the pagoda.

I kissed my mother, Gallia and then Diana. 'Father, I did not realise you were here.'

'Are you going to kiss me, too?'

'Alas, I have used up all my kisses for today.'

'Leave him alone, Varaz,' said my mother, 'sit down next to Gallia, Pacorus, and Gafarn, you sit beside Diana. This is very pleasant.'

I sat beside my darling on a double seat and held her hand. 'Gafarn and I have been visiting my army. Domitus and Nergal have everything in hand.'

'Good,' my father waved away a slave who had been serving him wine, 'can I take it that your followers will be leaving shortly?'

'After the wedding, father. I promise you that after the ceremony we will be a burden no longer.'

'You are not a burden,' stated my mother, her brown eyes glaring at my father.

'Really? I've had Addu boring me to death about how much your followers are eating.'

Out of the corner of my eye I saw a slave fill Diana's cup, and I heard her say 'thank you'. My mother heard her too.

'You don't have to thank the slaves, Diana.'

'No, sorry, majesty.'

My mother shook her head and smiled. 'You must call me "mother", Diana, for now that we have adopted Gafarn, you have become our daughter. And of that we are most pleased, are we not Varaz?'

My father was obviously bored by all this women's talk. 'What? Yes, of course.'

My sisters, Aliyeh and Adeleh, appeared, adorned with gold in their hair, on their arms and around their ankles, looking every bit the Hatran princesses they were. Aliyeh, in her mid-twenties, was tall and thin and possessed of an aloof, serious nature. Adeleh, on the other hand, was two years younger and had a happy disposition. They embraced Diana and fussed over the infant. Their appearance contrasted sharply to that of Diana, who wore no jewellery and was dressed in simple attire. In truth Diana was unremarkable when it came to looks, but such was the kindness in her heart and the goodness in her soul that everyone loved her, from the slave who broke a jug and received an arm round the shoulder instead of a beating, to the fiercest warrior in my father's bodyguard, who was disarmed by her smile and charm. Gallia was far more beautiful, though her reputation as the woman who could shoot a bow as well as any man (I would say better than most), and who was also handy with a sword and a dagger, made some wary of her. She was called 'fierce beauty' by many, though none dared say it to her face, and people's awe of her was further increased by

14

the rumour that she had been sent by the gods to save me from the Romans. No such reputation was attached to Diana, but the magic she possessed to make people love her was just as powerful. It was a strange destiny that had made a kitchen slave a Parthian princess, but no stranger than my own, which had taken me to the side of a former gladiator who had conquered all Italy, if only for a while.

'Your father says that you want to take Gafarn and Diana away from us,' said my mother.

Aliyeh and Adeleh squealed their protests, causing the baby to cry. Aliyeh scooped him up in her arms to calm his distress.

'I merely sought to ask them to come with me, mother.'

'Well,' she replied, 'I would like them to stay, and it's nice having an infant in the palace again. If you want to go and play kings then that's your business, but don't drag Gafarn and Diana along with you. Besides, I've heard that Dura Europos is a dismal place. I don't know why you want to be king of such a city.'

'Because he doesn't want to wait to be king of Hatra,' replied my father, 'besides Dura Europos is closer to the Romans in Cappadocia.'

'Why should I wish to be close to the Romans?' I asked.

'Because your hatred for them burns bright still,' he said, 'and you strain at the leash like a ravenous hound to strike at them.'

'Nonsense.'

'Is it? Gafarn, you know your brother well, what say you on this matter?'

'I think Pacorus has not forgotten the insults he endured at the hands of the Romans.' He was talking of my being chained, beaten and whipped when a slave. 'But his love for Gallia is greater than any thirst for revenge.'

My father clapped and Gafarn bowed in mockery at him. 'A most politic answer. Obviously all your years in the palace did not go to waste. But I stand by my words.'

'In any case,' I added, 'it would have been unwise to refuse Sinatruces, who is the King of Kings after all.'

'Most convenient for you.' My father, like a dog with an old bone, was refusing to give up the argument. 'He was certainly out-manoeuvred by you and that sorceress of his. He sought to entice Gallia to his palace to make her his wife, and then give you the crown of Dura Europos in compensation. But instead he ended up making you a king anyway and he failed to entrap Gallia.'

'No man imprisons me,' snapped Gallia.

'Well said, daughter,' said my mother. 'And now we shall have an end of all talk of politics and Romans. Nothing will happen before the wedding anyway.'

Chapter 2

Hatra, city of one hundred thousand people, was a glittering jewel in the desert the day I married Gallia. Perhaps it was because I was madly in love with my tall, blonde-haired princess from Gaul, or perhaps it was because the city was filled with kings and princes and their gaudily dressed entourages, but whatever the reason the limestone walls and towers of the city seemed to sparkle that day. From every one of its one hundred and fifty towers flew scarlet banners bearing white horses' heads – the royal symbol of Hatra, after the famed whites ridden by every member of the king's bodyguard. Today, though, the men of the bodyguard had been given leave to attend my wedding. Only those who were of Hatra's nobility were allowed to serve in the royal bodyguard, and now they were in the Great Temple with their families and friends, along with hundreds of others who had been invited. The massive temple, its exterior walls surrounded by high stone columns, was filled to the brim. Assur stood impassive at the high altar while his priests fussed and panicked as they tried to get everyone seated in the correct order. Father, my mother and myself were in the front row on the right side of the great aisle that ran down the centre of the temple. Also in the front row were Gafarn, Diana, the infant child of Spartacus and my sisters. Immediately behind, and much to Assur's disapproval, were those who had come with me from Italy. I called them the 'Companions', for that is what they were. And so there was Nergal, my brave and loyal second-in-command who had taken a wild-haired Spanish girl as his wife. I turned and looked at them both, the grinning Nergal who always seemed so optimistic, his brown, shoulder-length hair almost as long as that of his wife. Praxima smiled at me and fixed me with her big round eyes. I smiled back. She leaned forward and laid a hand on my shoulder.

'I am happy for you, lord.'

'Thank you, Praxima. And I am happy that you are both here to share this day with me.'

She had been a Roman slave in a brothel. Now, in her white flowing dress, it was hard to believe that she had fought like a man in Italy; indeed, she had been and was Gallia's subordinate when my love had formed her own band of women warriors. I looked beyond Praxima to where a score of the Amazons sat at my wedding, the survivors of Gallia's command. They were all young and some were beautiful, and as I turned to face the altar I remembered that they were also deadly. I had seen Praxima slit men's throats with a dagger and shoot them down without pity with her bow.

The other Companions were a mixed bunch – Parthians, Dacians, Germans, Thracians and Greeks – former Roman slaves who had laughed and shed blood together, who were united by an unbreakable bond of comradeship forged in the cauldron of battle. They shared jokes with the cropped-haired Lucius Domitus, the Roman whom they loved like a brother. But the man whom we all regarded as a father figure was on the other side of the aisle, to the left of the woman I was about to marry. His name was Godarz and he too had been a Roman slave. In his late forties, tall, lean with cropped hair, he was actually a Parthian who had been a slave in Italy for many years. So many, in fact, that he dressed like a Roman. Curiously, he had served in the Silvan army under Vistaspa long ago, the same man who now commanded my father's army. I can only surmise that it was the hand of God himself who had led me to a town in Italy called Nola, which Spartacus had captured and where Godarz had been a slave. We had released him from his bondage and he had subsequently become the quartermaster general of the slave army, and a man I respected hugely. Now he was going to give Gallia away, for her own father was dead, killed by Gafarn, now my brother.

A large hand slapped my shoulder. 'Not a bad crowd, Pacorus, should be a good day. Mind you, there's still time for Gallia to change her mind and marry me instead.'

Vata planted his stocky body beside me, his big round face wearing a grin. My friend since childhood, his father had been Bozan. During my time away he had become sullen and withdrawn, but today some of the old Vata – happy and carefree – had returned. My father had made him governor of Nisibus, a city in the north of his kingdom, but today he was in Hatra as an honoured guest.

I laughed. 'My friend, you delude yourself, she only has eyes for me.'

He leaned forward and caught Gallia's eye, then waved at her. She smiled and waved back. He put his arm round my shoulder.

'You see,' he said, 'women can't resist a hero.'

'When I see one,' I replied, 'I'll let you know.'

He laughed aloud, prompting Assur to frown at him. Vata ignored the high priest and pointed at the silver Roman eagle standard that lay at the foot of the high altar.

'You remember that day, Pacorus, when you took it?'

He was referring to the battle four years ago when we had defeated a Roman legion and I had captured the legion's eagle.

'Like it was yesterday, my friend.'

Assur suddenly beat the end of his staff on the white marble floor and gradually the hubbub died down. His voice was deep and solemn.

'Marriage is the chief concern of human life, as from it arise the nearest and most endearing relationships which go to form the comfort and happiness of existence in this world: husband and wife, parents and children, brothers and sisters. Marriage may be designated the hinge of all kindred, the strongest link in the chain that binds mankind together. Hail to Shamash.'

As one the congregation answered, 'Hail to Shamash.'

He motioned to me and Gallia to come forward and sit in the two chairs that had been placed before him. Between the chairs two priests held a large white cloth. The marriage ceremony has strict rules, and both of us had been tutored in the proper procedure beforehand. I had fought in many battles and come close to death on many occasions, but today I was more nervous than I had ever been in all my life. And all the while I was aware that Shamash, the god of the sun whom I revered, was watching me from heaven. Were my dead friends, Spartacus and his wife Claudia, also observing me? I liked to think so.

I took my seat on the right side of Gallia and then the two marriage witnesses stepped forward, those who were the nearest relations to bride and bridegroom. Gafarn was standing by my side, while Godarz stood arrow straight beside Gallia. Assur nodded and the priests raised the curtain to allow Gallia and me to hold hands, after which the priests released the cloth to fall over our linked hands. Thus was it indicated to all present that the separation that had hitherto existed between Gallia and myself no longer existed, and that we were now united.

Then the two priests passed a long piece of twine around both of us seven times, a process that indicates union between man and woman. One strand can be broken easily enough, but not seven.

Assur raised both his hands, his eyes to the ceiling.

'May Shamash, the Omniscient God, grant you a progeny of sons and grandsons, plenty of means of provision, great friendships and a long life.'

Turning to Gafarn, Assur spoke solemnly to him. 'I ask you, in the presence of King Varaz, in the presence of the invited kings of the Arsacid dynasty, and in the presence of all who have come to Hatra to witness this marriage, if you have agreed that King Pacorus will take this maiden, Princess Gallia, in marriage, in accordance with the rites and rules of the Great Shamash?'

19

'I have agreed,' replied Gafarn.

Assur's stare was then transferred to Godarz.

'Have you, with righteous mind and truthful thoughts, words and actions, and for the increase of righteousness, agreed to give this maiden to King Pacorus to be his bride?'

Godarz nodded. 'I have agreed.'

Assur then gave his staff to one of the two priests who stood next to him and walked forward, indicating to Gallia and me to kneel. He then placed a hand on my shoulder and the other on Gallia's, fixing us both with his stare.

'Have you preferred to enter into this contract of marriage up to the end of your life with a righteous mind?'

We both replied. 'I have preferred.'

Assur stepped back and once again raised his hands.

'Know all that Shamash has now blessed this union and has decreed that King Pacorus and Princess Gallia, who is now queen, are married, and that no mortal man may question this union. May Shamash bless them. Hail to Shamash.'

The assembly replied 'Hail to Shamash', and then Assur gestured for us to rise. The two priests stepped forward and gathered the twine that had been wrapped around us, which was given to Godarz. The white cloth curtain they gave to Gafarn, then Gallia and I turned and walked down the aisle towards the temple's main entrance. This faced east to greet Shamash every morning when the sun rose to begin its journey across the sky. The temple echoed with the sound of applause as I walked beside my wife, now also my queen. I glanced at her. The thin gold strips in her hair glinted in the light. On her head she wore a gold diadem inlaid with diamonds and large and small emeralds. Around her neck she wore a gold and diamond necklace. She was so beautiful and in truth I could not keep my eyes off her. She glanced at me with her eyes of the purest blue, eyes that could entrap a man as a spider's web catches its prey.

'Well,' I whispered, 'how do you like being a queen?'

She dazzled me with her smile. 'I hope I can be a good one.'

We left the temple and walked across the Great Square to the palace quarter. Our route was lined by troops of the city's garrison, soldiers armed and equipped in the Greek fashion, with full-face bronze helmets surmounted by white crests, leather cuirasses fitted with iron scales and leather greaves around their shins. Their large round shields were made of wood with an outer bronze facing, and their weapons comprised swords and six-foot thrusting spears. Many kings and princes surrounded themselves with guards who looked pretty in their brightly coloured baggy leggings and tunics, armed only with spears and wicker shields, but the troops of Hatra's garrison were trained to fight on the battlefield as well as patrol the city's streets. Their commander, Lord Kogan, a dour, serious man of the same age as my father, drove his men hard, as Vistaspa did with my father's horsemen. Parthia's strength was her cavalry, but the garrison's two thousand men were a useful reserve for my father to call on. It was Kogan who met us outside the temple and escorted us into the palace, walking a few steps behind.

'Your troops look splendid, Lord Kogan,' I remarked as behind us my mother, father and the wedding guests filed out of the temple.

'Thank you, majesty.' His voice was crisp and emotionless.

It was past noon now and the day was hot, the sun beating down from a blue sky. There was no wind and even though I was wearing only white flowing robes, I could feel sweat running down the back of my neck. I looked at the soldiers sanding like stone either side of us. They must have been roasting under their helmets and in their leather cuirasses.

The banqueting hall of the palace was a spacious, airy room with a high ceiling supported by stone pillars. White marble tiles covered the floor and the walls were also white, against which stood more of Kogan's soldiers. At the far end of the hall was the high table for the bride, groom and their immediate families. In front of the high table, which sat on a stone dais, were arranged the feasting tables for the hundreds of guests that were now being shown to their seats as servants served us sweet wine. My father, a gold crown atop his close-cropped head, bent down and kissed Gallia on her cheek, as did my mother, who also wore a crown. As the level of chatter increased, people took their seats and were also served wine. My Companions sat either side of a long table that had been arranged directly in front of me, at right angles to the high table. My father and Assur had disapproved strongly to their being placed in such a prominent position in the seating order, but I had insisted. These were the individuals I had fought beside, shared dangers with and counted as my dearest friends. I smiled as I looked at them: long-haired Thracians and Germans, wild-looking Dacians, leather-skinned Greeks, Parthians from Hatra and the feared Amazons, all of whom had earlier walked onto the dais, ignored my father and embraced Gallia warmly, each one warning me that I had better protect her otherwise I would have them to answer to. My mother sat open-mouthed at their contempt for protocol, the more so when they also embraced Diana, for she too was one of this strange sisterhood. And then they sat with the rest of the Companions, former slaves who now took precedence over Parthian kings and aristocrats.

The banquet lasted hours as a horde of sweating servants brought the guests silver platters heaped with cooked lamb, chicken, camel, goat, stews flavoured with cinnamon, mint and pomegranates; elaborately stuffed fruits and vegetables; skewers of barbecued peacock; apricots, artichokes, eggplants, lemons, oranges, pistachios and spinach. Others filled silver cups with wine or water, and as the former flowed freely the volume of chatter increased markedly. My father and mother fussed over Gallia, while a steady procession of guests made their way to the top table to pay their respects to her and myself. Courteous to me, they focused all their attention on my bride who looked radiant and was clearly enjoying herself. I had seen Gallia wear a stern and cold visage on the battlefield, but today she was carefree and inviting, quick to laugh and eager to return the affection of those who were introduced to her. I could only watch and admire her, and swell with pride as I saw her conquer those kings, my father's closest allies, who had made the journey to be at our wedding.

Parthia was a great empire made up of a number of separate kingdoms, but each of the kings who ruled those kingdoms realised that there was strength in unity, and so they elected a King of Kings to rule over them and the whole empire. In this way the empire remained strong in the face of its external enemies, such as the Armenians to the north, the Romans in the west and the Indians in the east. The aged King of Kings Sinatruces rarely left his capital at Ctesiphon. His son, King Phraates, had made the journey to Hatra in his father's place. He now stood before us and bowed his head. We stood and bowed to him.

'Thank you for honouring our wedding, majesty,' I said.

He smiled, white teeth showing in the middle of his neatly trimmed short beard and moustache flecked with grey, like his shoulder-length black hair.

'The honour is mine, Pacorus. Much has happened since we first met, and now you have brought a beautiful bride from a foreign land to grace the empire.' He suddenly looked sheepish. 'My father sends his regards and hopes you both have long and prosperous lives.'

His eyes averted mine. He was obviously embarrassed that Sinatruces, after Gallia and I had arrived at Hatra from Italy, had lured us both to Ctesiphon with the sole intention of stealing Gallia from me and making her one of his concubines. He had sought to assuage my wrath by making me king of Dura Europos, but his plan had unravelled, not least due to the threats of eternal damnation heaped upon him by his foul old sorceress, Dobbai. The upshot had been that I still had my beloved but had also come away from Ctesiphon with a kingdom.

'Majesty,' I replied, 'your father is both gracious and wise, and the empire is indeed fortunate that he rules over us all.'

The answer obviously dispelled any discomfort Phraates may have felt, for a wide grin showed itself beneath his bulbous nose.

Behind Phraates came King Aschek of Atropaiene, a land many miles northeast of Hatra that bordered the Caspian Sea. He had thick, black wavy hair and a hooked nose. King Farhad, lean, severe and dark-eyed, came next. He ruled Media, a land to the southwest of Atropaiene that also lay on Hatra's eastern border, on the eastern bank of the River Tigris. King Gotarzes of Elymais was similarly stern looking, though his gaunt features resembled a worn-out scholar rather than those of a warlord. However, his eyes were alert and his grip formidable. Elymais was a kingdom that lay to the east of Hatra's lands, the western border of which lay on the coastline of the Persian Gulf. It was also directly south of Phraates' own kingdom of Susiana.

King Vardan, by comparison, was barrel-chested and round faced, with a hearty laugh and hands like a bear's paws. He almost crushed me as he wrapped his arms around me in an iron embrace, grabbed Gallia's hands and kissed them, then embraced my father. Vardan ruled Babylon, once a mighty city but now fallen into decay, though the kingdom's lands were still rich in agriculture and supported a large population. Vardan had brought with him his daughter, Axsen, a woman about my age who unfortunately resembled her father in appearance, being rather sturdy. Years ago, before my destiny took me to Italy and Gallia's side, there had been talk of a marriage between Princess Axsen and myself. Those plans had come to nothing, but much mirth had been had at the princess's expense. We had called her Princess Water Buffalo, and I was now ashamed that I had been so cruel. She embraced Gallia and then me, and was plainly happy to be sharing our day. She told Gallia that she looked beautiful and that she would like to be her friend. My wife took her hand and promised that she would be, while all the time I could feel my cheeks colour. She told Gallia that she was still looking for her own prince, and my discomfort increased. When Axsen and her father had regained their seats I sighed with relief, thinking my embarrassment had gone unnoticed. I was wrong. Gallia jabbed me in the ribs.

'I remember, long ago in Italy, you, Gafarn and Nergal taking great delight in making fun of that young girl.'

I tried to bluff it out. 'Do you? I don't really remember...'

She jabbed me even harder. 'Don't try to squirm out of it. I saw you avoiding her eyes. I think she is charming, and you should be ashamed of yourself for your childishness.'

'Yes, my love.'

She caught Gafarn's eye. 'And you too, Gafarn.'

My brother looked at her, then me, in confusion. I pointed at Axsen and then shrugged. I think he was going to laugh, but then saw the disapproval on Gallia's face. He looked down at his plate and began picking at his food.

King Balas was the last monarch to pay his respects. Sixty if he was a day, he had a kind, round face with hazel eyes and a bushy beard and moustache. He was dressed in a simple light blue robe and plain leather sandals on his feet. He could easily have been mistaken for a carpet salesman rather than a king. Balas ruled Gordyene, a kingdom on Parthia's northeastern frontier, bordering Armenia. I knew he had been a great warrior years ago, and had defeated the Armenians many times, plus anyone else who had been foolish enough to invade his territory. He embraced me.

I bowed my head to him. 'Thank you for honouring my wedding, majesty.'

'You don't have to call me majesty, Pacorus, you're a king as well.' He looked at Gallia.

'Make an old man happy.' He embraced her and then kissed her on the cheek, which made my mother frown and my father laugh. He next embraced my father and then bent over the table and kissed my mother on the lips.

'You are still my sweetheart, Mihri.'

For once my mother blushed and was lost for words and then waved Balas away, suppressing a grin as she did so. He came back to me.

'As I'm staying in Hatra for a few days, you must tell me how you managed to win the heart of such a beauty.' He winked at Gallia.

'Varaz, perhaps we can have an archery competition. You can try and win back that money you lost to me the last time we pitted our bows against each other.'

My father raised his cup. 'I look forward to it.'

'Is the competition open to all?' asked Gallia.

Balas eyed her. 'Can you handle a bow?'

'Better than Pacorus, majesty,' said Gafarn.

Balas threw back his head and laughed. 'Looks like we have some competition, Varaz. I look forward to seeing if what they say about you is true, Gallia. What about you, Pacorus, are you in?'

I shrugged. 'I will take no pleasure in beating you, majesty.'

He slapped me hard on the shoulder. 'We'll see about that.'

It was a happy occasion, as were the days that followed, a time of laughter and joy, of new friendships made and old ones reaffirmed. All thoughts of the outside world receded from my mind as I walked arm in arm with Gallia in the royal gardens, among strutting peacocks and ornamental fountains.

'We could stay here, you know,' I said as we stood on a narrow bridge watching the giant goldfish gently swim in one of the ornamental ponds below.

'Stay here, in Hatra?'

I leaned back on the stone rail and gazed at her. 'Why not? You like it here, do you not?'

She kissed me tenderly on the lips. 'I could be happy here, but you have your own kingdom to rule now. What would happen to it if you stayed here?'

'No doubt Sinatruces would give it to someone else.'

'But he gave it to you, Pacorus,' she said softly. 'What do you want?'

I grabbed her by the waist and pulled her close. 'I want you.'

'You have me forever, you know that. But it is time for you to move on. There is an old saying among my people – you can never step in the same piece of water twice.'

'What does that mean?'

'It means, my love, that you have outgrown Hatra and can never go back to your youth. It is time to spread your wings.'

I pressed my body into hers. 'I never knew you were a philosopher.'

'If you take me back to your bedroom I will show you how a philosopher makes love.' Her voice was sultry and my loins stirred at her invitation.

And so the days passed making love and sharing time with friends. Balas did not forget the archery competition, and so my father arranged for a target to be set up in the gardens, a large round bale of straw packed tight and covered with hide. On the front had been painted a number of rings with a small black circle in the centre. Set on a wooden stand, the target was chest high. A score of servants arranged tables upon which were placed jugs of wine, cups, and platters of meats, bread and fruit. Balas was in a mischievous mood and had gathered a group of supporters to cheer

25

him on. These included my mother and sisters, King Farhad of Media, his son Atrax, who was more cheerful than his stern father though just as tall, King Vardan of Babylon, Princess Axsen and Diana. I competed against Gallia, Balas, my father and Gafarn.

Balas took a large gulp of wine and stood before those assembled.

'Welcome everyone. Now today I am going to give a demonstration of archery to show how it should be done. Obviously I will win, so this competition is to determine who will come second. Has everyone got a bow to shoot?'

A Parthian's bow was one of his most precious possessions. And all Parthia's aristocrats and royalty learned how to shoot one from an early age, most before they could walk.

I held up my bow and nodded to Balas. Like all Parthian bows, ours were double-curved, with recurve tips at the end of the upper and lower limbs, and a set-back centre section that was grasped by the left hand. The limbs, thick in proportion to their width, were fashioned from several pieces of maple, birch or mulberry, with sinew from the hamstrings or tendons of cows or deer on the outside of the limbs, and horn from a buffalo, long-horned cow or ibex on their inner side. All the parts were fastened to each other with glue made from bitumen, bark pitch and animal grease. The whole bow was then wrapped in fibres made from the tendons of slaughtered animals to protect it from the elements. The bows of my father and Balas were covered in lacquer to make them totally waterproof. Gallia, Gafarn and I had bows that had no lacquer covering, which came from China, because we had made our bows in Italy when we had fought with Spartacus.

'Shall we put the target at fifty paces, Varaz?' Balas asked my father.

'You sure you can see that far, old man?'

'Old man?' Balas turned to my mother and feigned mortification. 'Do you hear that, Mihri? He uses any opportunity to insult me, I who have been like a father to him all these years.'

Balas may have been old, but he was still a big, thickset man and his arms were still muscular.

A group of servants hauled the target into position and then scampered away.

'Well, father,' said my father, 'you can shoot first.'

We all hit the target with ease, a servant holding up a small red flag to indicate a centre hit; a white flag denoted a strike outside the bull's eye, and a green flag a hit on the target's outer edge. All the flags were red, so the target was moved back another twenty-five paces.

'So, Pacorus,' said Balas, hitting the bull's eye again, 'when do you leave for your new kingdom?'

I released my bowstring. Red flag. 'One or two weeks, majesty.'

Gallia shot. Red flag.

'Good shot, my lady,' said Balas. He watched her pluck another arrow from her quiver and placed the nock in the string. At our wedding she had been a picture of feminine beauty, flowing blonde locks, white dress and gold jewellery, but today she was dressed in leggings, leather boots, blue tunic and her hair ran down her back in a long plait. I had seen her dressed thus most of the time when she had fought in Italy. Balas was clearly intrigued by her.

'I have heard,' he continued, 'that you have fought in battle, and that you led a fierce band of women warriors.'

She fired her arrow. Red flag. 'It is true, lord, that I have fought my enemies, and others joined me in that fight. Some of them are with me still.'

He smiled at her. 'Well, hopefully you will not have to fight any more now that you are in Parthia.'

My father waved at the servants, who moved the target back another twenty-five paces. Gallia fired another arrow. Red flag.

'While there are Romans in this world, lord, there can be no peace.'

'And yet,' Balas continued, 'is not one of Pacorus' commanders a Roman?'

'You are well informed, lord,' said Gallia. 'And, yes, you are right. His name is Lucius Domitus and he is a Roman.'

'And you trust this man?'

'Of course,' she replied.

Balas pressed the matter. 'Why?'

She looked him in the eye. 'Because we have fought together in battle, and because I know that he would lay down his life for me, and that makes him my brother, and I will fight anyone who says otherwise.'

There was an awkward silence for a few seconds and then Balas roared with laughter. He put down his bow and wrapped his thick arms around her.

'You have got yourself a lion as a bride, Pacorus. Would that I had a hundred like her for my palace guard.'

My mother and sisters smiled, and even Farhad looked momentarily less severe.

'Indeed, majesty,' interrupted Gafarn, 'I heard that Spartacus once said that if he had a thousand like Gallia he could take Rome itself.'

'Spartacus?' Farhad looked at me, clearly intrigued.

'The general I served with in Italy, majesty,' I said. All eyes were on me now, the happy Axsen and her father Vardan, the old rogue Balas and my sisters and parents. I could see that my mother was looking into the distance, perhaps wishing that the subject had not been raised.

'It's no secret,' I said. 'I was taken captive by the Romans in Cappadocia, that much you know at the very least. I and others.' I put down my bow, walked over to Gafarn and laid a hand on his shoulder, then on Diana's, who smiled at me.

'We were to be slaves forever,' I continued. 'To be worked like dogs until we died. But one man saved me, saved all of us, and led an army of us, an army of slaves. And he led us to victory after victory over the Romans, and I was proud to serve under him and even prouder to call him friend.' I moved to be beside Gallia and took her hands in mine. 'And in Italy, hundreds of miles from my home and my family, I found the most beautiful and bravest woman that God put on the earth. She then fought by my side and we defeated the Romans, beat them until we became masters of their land, former slaves turned into invincible warriors by a gladiator named Spartacus.'

Farhad drew himself up to his full height and folded his arms in front of him. 'If this slave general, this Spartacus, was so excellent a warlord, why was he defeated and killed, for I know that he is no more and that Rome still stands?'

'Rome still stands, yes,' I agreed. 'But only because he lost the one thing that was precious to him above all things, and which made him long for death.'

'What was that, Pacorus?' asked Vardan.

'His wife, lord, his beautiful, wise wife, the Lady Claudia. For they were soul mates and where she went he was determined to follow.' I saw that Gallia's eyes were cast down to the ground as she remembered her dead friend. Diana clasped Gafarn's hand tight. I continued, for it was a story that deserved to be told and I wanted to talk of my friend and lord, Spartacus. 'And so, the morning after she had given life to her son at the expense of her own, he marched out of camp to do battle with the Romans, one man against an army. And I walked beside him, not because he commanded me to but because I loved him as a brother, and behind us thousands of others did likewise for the same reason. For we cared not about glory or riches, but only wanted to die with honour beside the man who had given each of us our freedom, perhaps the most precious thing that a person can hold. And so we fought at his side all that day. He was cut down by his enemies, as were hundreds of others, but we beat them again, beat them until they retreated. Then we carried the body of our lord from the field of battle and laid it upon a great pyre, and then laid the body of his wife beside his. We stood and watched the flames consume their bodies and their spirits ascend to heaven. And that, my lord king, is why Rome still stands, because of the death of one woman.'

Farhad nodded his head at me. 'Well said.'

Axsen had tears in her eyes. 'That is the most romantic thing I have heard. Pacorus, you and Gallia must come to Babylon and tell me more of your time in Italy. Father, tell them they must come.'

Vardan smiled. 'Of course, they will be honoured guests.'

My mother had a look of relief on her face. 'You are all very kind, I thank you.'

Balas embraced her. 'Nonsense, we're all here because we like and respect you and Varaz, and this young stallion,' he tilted his head at me, 'is a worthy son. Now, put that target back some more so I can show you all who's the master archer here.'

Gafarn won the archery competition.

Several days later Vardan, his daughter, Farhad, Gotarzes and Balas requested that I take them to see my legion that was being trained in the desert. I gladly acquiesced, and was soon joined by Gallia, my father, Gafarn and my sister, Aliyeh. I found this odd as she had never taken an interest in my followers before, but then I noticed that Farhad's son, Atrax, had also come along and that Aliyeh made sure she rode beside him. My sister was always serious, but today, in the late afternoon's pleasant light, she smiled much and seemed carefree. Gallia noticed them too.

'It would seem that your sister has found an admirer.'

'An alliance between Media and Hatra would please my father. Atrax seems agreeable enough.'

'Hopefully, if she does marry, it will be for love.'

'Princesses usually marry for political reasons.'

She was indignant. 'I didn't.'

'No, because you are an exception, in every conceivable way.'

When we reached the camp it had the ordered appearance of a Roman legionary outpost more than ever. Occupying a large rectangular space on the baked ground of the desert, it was now surrounded by an earth rampart. We rode on the track up to the main entrance, a wide gap in the middle of the rampart, which was guarded by two of my legionaries, men in helmets and mail shirts and equipped with shields and javelins. They could have been

Roman soldiers, were it not for their white tunics and shields rather than the red favoured by the legions of Rome. They snapped to attention as I rode at the head of the column into the camp. As Remus walked slowly towards the centre of the camp I looked around at the neat rows of tents and was reminded of my time with Spartacus. His camps had been laid out in a similar fashion and his army had mirrored the organisation of Rome's legions.

'They have conquered half the world,' he once told me, 'so I see no reason not to employ their methods.'

Gallia reached over and grabbed my hand. 'For a moment I thought I was back in Italy.'

I nodded. 'I know. I still miss him.'

On we rode, to the centre of the camp where Domitus had pitched his new commander's tent, a large beige structure built around a rectangle of poles with two flaps for an entrance, each tied back with leather straps. Two guards stood at the entrance, and one shouted inside as we approached. Seconds later the muscular form of Lucius Domitus strode out into the sunlight. He squinted at us as his eyes adjusted to the light, then raised his vine cane to me in salute. He was dressed in a simple white tunic, leather belt, sandals on his feet and his Roman short sword at his hip. He caught sight of Gallia and bowed his head to her, who nodded back. He ignored the Parthian kings, prince and princesses behind me.

I dismounted from Remus and clasped his forearm, he responded with an iron grip.

'All is well, Domitus?'

'All is well, Pacorus.'

'I have brought some guests who have expressed an interest in seeing your legion.'

'It's your legion.'

'How are you, Domitus?' asked Gallia.

'Well, lady, thank you.'

I turned to my guests. 'This is Legate Domitus, who will be our guide today.'

The horses were taken to the stable area and then Domitus escorted us through the camp and then outside to the training fields, where hundreds of men were practising throwing javelins, marching in units of eighty men called centuries and honing their skills with wooden swords and wicker shields.

Balas, dressed in a simple flowing robe and leggings, a battered turban on his head, was intrigued by the latter activity. He pointed at the men crouching in front of large wooden posts driven into the ground, wicker shields tucked close to their bodies while instructors bellowed orders at them to jab at the posts with their wooden swords.

Balas looked at the sharp-featured Domitus. 'So, you are a Roman?'

'Yes, sir.'

'And what is a legate?' enquired Farhad, who unlike Balas was dressed like a king, with an expensive gold tunic, silver belt and a beautiful sword hanging from it in a silver-edged scabbard.

'The commander of a legion, sir. Don't slash with those swords, stab with them. Slashing is for cavalry and other useless bastards.'

Domitus' outburst at those at the posts made Gallia and Axsen jump, while the others stared at him in disbelief.

'Begging your pardon, but if they don't get it right at the beginning then they won't be much use when it comes to the real thing.'

'My palace guards carry wicker shields,' mused Gotarzes. 'I did not realise that Roman soldiers are also armed with them.'

Domitus suppressed a smile. 'They aren't, sir. They only use them for training.'

'Why?' Farhad was clearly intrigued, while I noticed his son was totally disinterested, paying close attention to Aliyeh, who was clearly delighted with the adoration of a handsome young prince.

Domitus pointed at the recruits sweating under the sun that was now making its descent into the western sky. 'Those shields are weighted with iron strips on the inside, making them heavier than their proper shields, and the swords are similarly weighted. Toughens up the men, you see, strengthens their arms and shoulders. Battles can be long affairs. Isn't that right, Pacorus?'

I saw my father frown at Domitus' familiarity, but those of us who had fought together in Italy shared a bond that was stronger than iron; indeed, any of those who had come with me from Italy was free to address me thus.

'That's right, Domitus.'

'I remember when we fought all day in north Italy, near Mutina,' added Gallia. 'It was hot that day.'

'That it was, lady,' said Domitus. 'But we didn't falter. Hard training, you see.'

'Train hard, fight easy, you remember Bozan's words, father?' I said.

Bozan had not only been the commander of my father's army, but also his friend. 'I do,' he said.

Domitus approved. 'He was obviously a sensible man.'

31

Axsen linked arms with Gallia. 'You are truly an intriguing woman, Gallia. I have never met a woman who has fought in battle before.'

'I would like to know what one of those shields and swords feels like,' Balas said.

'I would advise against it, majesty,' I said. Domitus was shorter than the Parthians present, as were most Romans, but Domitus did not have an ounce of fat on him and his frame was packed with muscles. I had seen him fight in battle, and knew him to be a master with a Roman short sword.

'Nonsense,' said Balas. He pointed at Domitus. 'What do you say, Roman, fancy your chances against an old campaigner?' Domitus shrugged.

'If you wish, sir.'

Moments later Domitus stood with a wicker shield held tight to his left side with a short wooden sword in his right hand. Balas, who unbuckled his sword belt and handed it to my father, was similarly equipped and waved the sword around in front of his body. Domitus crouched low and held his sword close to his body. All his life Balas had fought from the saddle, and though he might know how to battle on horseback he was hopelessly outmatched against an ex-Roman centurion. Balas tried to fight as he would from the saddle, with great scything attacks with his sword, but Domitus easily anticipated these moves and countered them with very effective feints and thrusts. It was over soon enough, as Balas shouted and tried to slash at Domitus' head, but the latter ducked and smashed his shield into the king's body, knocking him to the ground. Then Domitus pounced and was standing over Balas, the point of his sword at his throat. Domitus then stood back, threw down his sword and offered his hand to Balas, who accepted and was hauled to his feet. Balas roared with laughter and clasped Domitus' muscled forearm. My father gave Balas his sword back.

'A most expert display, Roman,' said Farhad, nodding towards the men training at the posts. 'Are all your men as proficient?'

Domitus shook his head. 'They've got a way to go yet, but they're shaping up nicely. Mind you, we need a few thousand swords, javelins, helmets and mail shirts before they can fight.'

'That will be settled when we get to Dura, Domitus,' I said.

'Dura is a small city,' said my father, 'and to equip thousands of men thus will be expensive. It is not Hatra.'

'Perhaps it can be a second Hatra,' I offered.

He smiled. 'Perhaps.'

Farhad continued with his quizzing of Domitus. 'So, Roman,

what qualities do you look for in recruits?'

We began walking back to the centre of the camp as the sun began turning to a red ball in the sky. 'Quite straightforward, sir, I'm only interested in those who are single, have good eyesight and decent characters, and we don't take any who've had their balls lopped off, begging your pardon, ladies.'

On the way back to Hatra, I rode between Balas and Gallia as the sky turned a deep red with the approach of the evening.

'I like your Roman,' said Balas.

'He's a good man,' I agreed.

'Does he miss his home?'

'No, majesty,' I said, 'when we found him he was condemned to be a slave in their silver mines.'

'He has no love of Rome,' added Gallia.

'Does he love Parthia, then?'

'No, lord,' replied Gallia, 'he has a love for Spartacus.'

'But Spartacus is dead, is he not?'

Gallia looked directly ahead. 'Not his memory, or his son, and I think that we are the only true family Domitus has ever known.'

Balas nodded. 'When I heard that you had returned, Pacorus, and listened to the tales that were spreading about you and your wild woman from a far-off land, I thought that they were stories to impress children and old women, but now I begin to think otherwise. I have seen many things in my life, some great, most terrible. But I have never heard of a slave general such as this Spartacus. I have seen the loyalty that he engenders still, and I marvel that an army has appeared in the desert, an army that follows you because its soldiers believe you to be beloved of the gods, an army that is led by a Roman, your most hated foes. And you, Gallia, you who are so beautiful yet fight as fiercely as any man and who leads a band of women warriors, who has fought and killed without mercy. We live in strange times, I think.'

'Let us hope we also live in peaceful times,' I said.

Gallia scoffed at this. 'Pacorus is a dreamer, my lord. He dreams of a world that will never be. The avarice and corruption of men will ensure that there will always be war.'

'I fear you are right, my lady. What can be done?'

Gallia looked at him, then me. 'We can keep our bowstrings tight and our sword blades sharp.'

Balas laughed. 'Forget Dura, Gallia, come back with me to Gordyene and be the commander of my bodyguard.'

In the days following Gallia grew very fond of Balas, the old warhorse who liked to have a pretty woman to impress. He would tell us how he had fought the Armenians and made his capital, Vanadzor, a stronghold that no army could take. We were walking in the royal gardens through a long arch formed by palm trees, Gallia linking her arm in his.

'There were so many of them that they were like an army of locusts, masses of infantry, plus cavalry, chariots and camels. It seemed as though they had brought every animal in Armenia to lay siege to my city. But we threw them back, and then I led my cavalry out onto the plain and scattered them. It was a long, bloody day, but at the end of it we stood triumphant and they skulked back to their homeland.'

'Then you had peace?' asked Gallia.

Balas shook his big head. 'Not for many a ycar, because they kept coming back, tens of thousands of them. And each time we gave them battle and threw them back, but it was hard and I lost a lot of good friends. And then they sent their secret weapon, their most terrible adversary.'

'Who?' I too was enthralled.

'A woman. Isabella her name was and she was the eldest daughter of the Armenian king. She was tall, beautiful, proud and strong, and she told me that her father wished for an alliance between our two kingdoms, and that he offered the hand of his daughter in marriage to cement our alliance.'

'And you refused his offer?' I asked.

'That was my initial intention, but you see her father was clever. He realised that Isabella was more formidable than any army he could throw against me, and so it proved. I fell in love with her and we were married, and so I became my enemy's son. And thus we had peace and I had Isabella, and it was the happiest time of my life. She had a big heart and my people took her into their own hearts and Gordyene seemed blessed.'

'Why didn't you bring her to the wedding?' asked Gallia.

'Because she died over ten years ago, child.' A mask of sadness came across his face. 'Taken by a plague that ravaged my city.'

Gallia rested her head on his shoulder and tightened her grip on his arm. 'I'm sorry.'

Balas shrugged. 'It was the will of God, but I know that she is waiting for me and that we will be together again. Actually, you remind me of her, all zest and fire.'

'What about the Armenians, majesty?' I enquired.

'Their border is quiet these days. Their eyes are on the west, where the Romans will come from.'

'What about Mithridates?' I asked. Mithridates was the King of

Pontus, a land that lay to the south of the Black Sea and a kingdom that had been at war with the Romans for nearly twenty years.

'Who's Mithridates?' asked Gallia.

Balas sighed. 'A great warrior and a man who has held back the Romans for a generation, but now his armies are largely scattered and he is all but beaten. And Armenia is next to Pontus, and when Pontus falls the Romans will be on the Armenian border.'

He said no more. There was no need, for he knew that if Armenia fell then the Romans would be on the borders of his land. But I comforted myself with the knowledge that he did not stand alone, for Gordyene was a kingdom in the Parthian Empire and behind Balas stood the other kings of the empire.

Balas took his leave of us two days later, his lion banner fluttering behind him as he led a column of horsemen out of the city's northern gates back to Gordyene.

'I would like to go to his homeland and see him,' said Gallia.

'It's all mountains and trees,' said my father. 'Good country for hunting.'

'We will go, my love,' I took her hand, 'I promise.'

The next day Farhad and Gotarzes also left Hatra for their homelands. As we said our farewells I caught sight of Farhad's son, Atrax, giving Aliyeh a brooch. He then took her hands in his and kissed them. We all pretended not to notice the tears in her eyes as his father's retinue of armoured-clad horsemen, one carrying his king's banner of a white dragon on a black background, trotted away to Media. The last of the kings to leave was Vardan, along with his daughter Axsen. She was a hopeless and incurable romantic, but we liked her all the more for it. She saw love and hope everywhere, and did not have a bad bone in her whole body. She made Gallia and me promise that we would visit her in Babylon, and gave Gallia a ring with an inlaid ruby gemstone.

'It is the stone of life and energy, and also of wisdom.'

'Really?' Gallia looked at me.

'Perhaps you should give it to Pacorus, he could do with some wisdom.'

Axsen hugged me, a big smile on her face. 'I hope one day to have my own king and I hope he will be like you.'

'I will pray for your happiness, lady, for you truly deserve it.'

'And we promise,' added Gallia, 'that we will come and see you in your home soon.'

'I will look forward to that day, my friends.'

We watched Vardan, Axsen and their royal guards trot away

from the palace, and we waved when Axsen turned in the saddle and raised an arm to us both in salute.

'I like her,' said Gallia.

'So do I.'

Chapter 3

The departure of Vardan and Axsen was the signal that we too had to prepare for our journey to our new home. The training of the legion went on apace under the watchful eye of Domitus, while Nergal took his horsemen out of the city every day to keep their skills sharp. As well as the fifty Parthians of the Companions, there were sixty others who had volunteered to come to Dura with us, mostly the younger sons of the landowners of my father's kingdom. Hatra's kings originally owned all the land in the kingdom, but over the years tracts of it were given to vassal lords in return for military service. These lands were mostly along the fertile banks of the Tigris and Euphrates rivers. The lords in turn granted small plots of their territory to their servants and others who were landless, in return for which they paid a portion of their yearly crops to their lord. The rest of their crop they used for food or sold in the markets. The areas around the two rivers are fertile, made more so by the irrigation ditches, dams, canals and dikes that are used to control the spring floodwaters that come from the mountains far to the north. This results in great surpluses of wheat, barley, millet, beans, sesame seeds, dates, grapes, figs, melons and apples. As well as working his land, every farmer has to maintain his skill with a bow and practise with it on a regular basis. Every Parthian boy is given a bow before he can walk, and so by the time he becomes a man at sixteen he is an expert archer.

Most farmers were able to purchase their own horse, and when their lord called upon them for military service they rode off to war on their own mounts. The lords, of course, had their own herds of horses for themselves their sons and their guards. And when the call to arms came from my father, thousands of horse archers answered that call.

Horse archers could harry and wear down an enemy with their incessant volleys of arrows, always remaining beyond the spears and swords of opposition cavalry and infantry. But the most highly prized cavalry in the Parthian Empire were cataphracts – fully armoured men riding on armoured horses. Cataphracts were organised into formations called dragons, which numbered a thousand men divided into hundred-man companies, but very few of the empire's kingdoms could muster a dragon of cataphracts.

Each cataphract wore a rawhide, thigh-length coat on which was fastened dozens of overlapping iron and bronze scales, the different coloured metals glinting and shimmering in the sunlight. On his head he wore a steel helmet with steel cheekguards, and nose and neck guards. His arms and legs were protected by rings of overlapping steel plates, while his horse also wore a rawhide coat covered in armour. In this way the beast's whole body and neck were protected from enemy spears, swords and arrows. Even the horse's head was covered in armour, including its eyes that were protected by metal grills.

The primary weapon of the cataphract was a long lance called a kontus with a shaft as thick as a man's wrist and tipped with a heavy steel point. When levelled, the lance required both hands to hold it secure either on the right or left side of the saddle. Upon impact the momentum of horse and rider could propel the lance through two enemy soldiers. The rider released the lance and then went to work on the ranks of the enemy with his sword, axe or mace, the latter a brutal weapon that could cave in a man's skull even if he was wearing a helmet. The cataphract was truly a fearsome warrior and my father had fifteen hundred of them. But weapons, horses and armour for both man and beast were expensive and required constant maintenance. Thus the royal stables and armouries at Hatra were staffed by hundreds of squires, craftsmen, blacksmiths and armourers, all working constantly to ensure horses were groomed, fed, watered and shod with iron shoes, that armour was repaired and new suits made, plus the fixing and production of swords, axes, maces, spears, lances, arrows and bows. Any kingdom would find such an endeavour financially crippling, but Hatra was fortunate that it was beloved of Shamash, who had gifted it the Silk Road.

The Silk Road was the name of the trade route that connected China in the east with the kingdoms on Parthia's western frontiers, including Rome. It was so named because the most precious commodity that was transported along the route, and which Rome had an insatiable desire for, was silk. And so great quantities of the precious material were transported by caravan from China through the Parthian Empire, and the Silk Road ran straight through Hatra, to the city itself and then north and west to the city of Antioch. From there it was transported by sea across the Mediterranean to Italy and Rome. The kings of the empire guarded the Silk Road jealously, establishing military strongpoints along its whole length across Parthia, and in return for their safety the merchants who used the Silk Road paid customs duties levied on their goods. In this way they profited handsomely when their wares arrived at their destinations unmolested, and Hatra grew rich from the unending number of caravans that traversed the kingdom each year.

'But Dura is not Hatra,' said my father.

38

He had asked me and Gallia to attend the weekly council meeting that was held in a small antechamber at the rear of the palace's throne room. It was a plain room with a large table and chairs with a hide map of the Parthian Empire on one wall. Those present were my father, Kogan, Addu, Assur, Vistaspa and Vata in his capacity as the governor of Nisibus. Gallia's presence was most unusual as women were forbidden to attend the royal council, at least until today. The expressions on the faces of Kogan, Addu and Assur conveyed their disapproval of this blonde-haired foreigner being seated among them, but Gallia ignored their frowns. Vistaspa wore his usual cold, aloof expression.

'I know that, father.'

He lent back in his chair and regarded me for a moment. 'Do you? Then what do you know about Dura?'

I shrugged. 'It is a city on the west bank of the Euphrates. The opposite bank belongs to Hatra, so we shall be neighbours, father.'

A thin smile creased his lips. 'While you have been here I took the trouble to find out a little more about Dura, and as Gallia is now your queen I thought it fitting that she hears what I have discovered.'

Gallia smiled at him, Assur frowned again and my father nodded at her. 'Dura occupies a thin strip of land along the western bank of the Euphrates, as you say. The city was originally established by the Greeks over two hundred years ago, by the followers of Alexander the Great. It has been part of the Parthian Empire for less than fifty years, and in that time it has been more like a fortress outpost than a city. It was captured by Sinatruces when he was much younger than he is now, and ever since that time it was the domain of the King of Kings, to do with as he saw fit.

'No one wanted to live in Dura or along the western bank of the Euphrates, so Sinatruces sent adventurers, exiles and those he wanted to be rid of to settle this new land. The result is that those who are now landowners view themselves as a separate people from the rest of the empire. They are sullen and resentful, and you, my son, are their new king. And if that was not bad enough, the desert that borders Dura's lands are the territory of the Agraci.'

There was a sharp intake of breath from those around the table, and I had to admit that my heart sank at hearing that name.

Gallia looked confused. 'Who are the Agraci?'

Assur stroked his beard and looked at her. 'They are pestilence, my child, sent by God to remind us that the world is a dangerous place.'

'Thieves and beggars mostly,' added Vata, winking at her.

'Nomads who roam the desert and prey on any unfortunate enough to stray into their territory.'

He was right. The Agraci were fierce nomads who inhabited the northern part of the Arabian Peninsula. The southern part was inhabited by the Bedouins, Gafarn's people, but they kept themselves mostly to themselves, though they were not averse to raiding other people's territory should the opportunity present itself. But the Agraci were a constant thorn in our sides. They were disliked, feared and hated, and everyone in Hatra was glad that the Euphrates separated us from them.

'Well,' continued my father, 'the power of Haytham grows, which is most unfortunate for both of you.'

'Who is Haytham? I asked.

'The king of the Agraci. He has united the tribes of his people and now controls most of Arabia. He sends raiders north to Antioch and Damascus and west to the border of Egypt. It cannot be long before his gaze turns towards Dura. At the moment Prince Mithridates sits on the throne of Dura.'

'Prince Mithridates, who is he?' I asked.

My father smiled. 'The grandson of Sinatruces. The wily old fox sent him to Dura either because he wanted to be rid of him or because he is a capable commander who can keep the Agraci at bay.'

Vistaspa refilled his cup from a water jug on the table. 'Still, when your legion is fully trained you can send it into the desert to undertake pest control duties against the Agraci.'

'That's being unkind to pests,' mused Kogan, which drew chuckles from those present, all except Gallia.

'No wonder they give you so much trouble if you treat them so badly.' Her words produced a stunned silence. Vata was no longer smiling. 'If all they can expect from you is death and persecution, then you will have nothing but war with these people.'

Assur put his hands together. 'My child, I fear you speak of things that you do not understand.'

'I am not your child, I am a queen, so kindly address me as such.'

My father raised his eyebrows at her words, while Kogan and Addu looked down at the table. She continued, undaunted. 'I know everything about persecution and severity and treating people as animals for sport. Even an imbecile knows that if you continually beat a dog it will eventually bite you. If you slaughter the men and women of this tribe, the Agraci, do you think that their sons and daughters will not thirst for vengeance? For supposedly wise men,

40

you appear to be unable to see the simple logic in this.'

Assur cleared his throat loudly and glared at her. Vistaspa, meanwhile, was leaning back in his chair and rubbing his chin with his right hand. He was also looking at Gallia, but was that admiration in those cold, black eyes? I thought it might be.

My father raised his hands. 'Thank you, daughter, for your most eloquent words. But we must move on. My point is this: you are both going into a most uncertain, perhaps dangerous, situation and I want you to think hard about what you are about to undertake.'

'I will go to Dura,' Gallia's words were like arrows shot from a bow.

'Where you go, I follow,' I said.

My father merely nodded. 'Well, then, it is settled. To more practical matters. I have arranged for Addu to issue two million drachmas from the treasury, enough money to pay each man of your legion for a year. They may serve you now for ideological or religious reasons, but eventually even fanatics need food in their bellies.'

I was astounded. It was a huge sum.

'You are most generous, lord,' Gallia's words were sincere and she bowed her head at my father, who smiled at her. Addu fidgeted in his chair.

'You have something to say, Lord Addu?' queried my father.

Addu, gaunt with thinning brown hair, cleared his throat. 'I would merely wish to point out, majesty, that the treasury will miss such a generous amount.'

When my father selected Addu to be the royal treasurer it was an inspired choice. He was truly a man who knew the value of everything and the worth of nothing, an individual who had a large parsimonious streak coursing through him. He believed that taxes and customs duties were for one purpose only – to fill the treasury. But while he was happy to see great amounts of money pour into the treasury, he was loath to see any going out. He viewed any expenditure as frivolous waste, especially any resources spent on the army. He could see the value of Kogan's garrison, though only if his soldiers were protecting the treasury, but to him all other expenditure was a waste of valuable resources.

'Is not the money mine, to do with as I see fit?' asked my father casually.

'Of course, of course, majesty,' Addu's voice became even higher pitched. 'I was merely pointing out that Hatra may need such a sum in the future.'

Vistaspa looked up and fixed Addu with his black eyes. 'Are

you saying that I will have more money to spend on the army, Addu?'

Addu looked alarmed. The conversation was not going the way he wanted, not at all. 'No, no, no. Of course not. The expenditure on the army is already exorbitant. I fear that if we spend any more on it the result could be the city's bankruptcy.'

This was nonsense, and Addu knew it.

My father sighed. 'Lord Addu, Hatra is strong because her army is strong, you know this. The army ensures peace and peace means trade, which means crops grow, taxes are collected and customs duties are charged on caravans that pass through Hatra's territory. In the same way, a strong Dura,' he nodded at me, 'means that Hatra's western frontier is secure, so money spent on promoting that security is an investment in Hatra's future, do you not agree?'

Addu did not, of course, but he merely smiled and politely bowed his head to my father.

'Good, that's settled, then. Pacorus, when do you leave?'

'In a week, father.'

'Then may Shamash protect you both.'

'May He indeed,' said Assur, eyeing Gallia warily. All nodded gravely in response.

The meeting concluded, all went their separate ways to attend to their duties. Assur stomped past Gallia and me without saying anything; clearly still angry at the way he had been spoken to.

'He is arrogant,' hissed Gallia.

'He, my love, is the high priest of the Great Temple and a man who is used to others listening to him. He is wise and severe.'

'And full of himself,' she sniffed. 'How much is two million drachmas?'

'More than enough to pay five thousand soldiers for a year.'

The drachma was the currency within the Parthian Empire. A soldier was paid on average a drachma a day, so I would have enough to pay the legion and buy some weapons to equip them with. It was a good start.

Addu passed Gallia and bowed to her, then scuttled back to his tally sheets and ledgers. My father joined us and we walked to the gardens.

'Thank you, father, for the money.'

'It was your mother's idea, she thought it inappropriate for a prince of Hatra to be unable to pay his soldiers.'

'Will not the taxes of Dura be able to pay for his men?' queried Gallia.

'Perhaps, daughter, but five thousand men is a lot of boots to suddenly descend on a region.' He cast me a glance. 'You could always use your men to extract more taxes from the locals at sword point.'

'That would make me a tyrant, father.'

He shrugged. 'Kings must do what they must to hold their kingdoms.'

'Even if it earns them the hatred of their subjects?' Gallia shot back.

He linked his arm in hers. 'Not every ruler has the love of his subjects. You two will find that Dura is not Hatra.'

'But it will have the same respect for the law as Hatra does, father.'

The days following went in a blur, and in that time Domitus prepared the legion for its march south, while Nergal collected wagons, mules and camels to carry the hundreds of tents, tools and food that we would need on the journey. The royal ovens baked thousands of hard biscuits that would last for weeks, while boxes of dates were dispatched to the legion's camp. While this frenetic activity was going on I went to find Vistaspa. I located him putting two companies of cataphracts through their paces ten miles north of the city, on a baked stretch of flat ground. The earth shook as the armoured horses and their riders galloped behind the figure of Vistaspa, the horsemen carrying their levelled lances with both hands. It was late afternoon and the fierce heat of the day was abating somewhat, but it was still warm and the men would be sweating profusely in their armour and helmets. I watched the men maintain their formation as they halted, turned around and then charged again.

Afterwards I rode over to the men as they dismounted and drank greedily from their waterskins.

'Don't gulp it down,' shouted Vistaspa, sweat pouring down his bony face. 'Take small mouthfuls and give your horses some. They are thirsty as well.' He saw me and saluted.

'I would have a word with you, Lord Vistaspa.'

We walked away from the tired, sweating soldiers and their mounts, whose heads were down. The men would have a long walk back to the city to save their horses further fatigue.

'I have a favour to ask you,' I said.

His face remained expressionless, as it always did. 'Of course.'

'I wish to ask Godarz to be the governor of Dura, with your permission.'

'He is yours to command, majesty, you do not need my permission,' replied Vistaspa, ever the observer of protocol.

43

Godarz had once served under Vistaspa many years ago, before Godarz had been captured and enslaved by the Romans, and I knew that his return to Parthia had delighted Vistaspa. I therefore felt a pang of guilt that I was making this request, but Godarz was a friend and had been the quartermaster general in the army of Spartacus. I needed his administrative abilities at Dura, and more than that I respected and trusted him.

'But I would prefer to have your permission.'

I thought I detected a slight look of contempt on his face. 'You have my permission, majesty.'

I knew that I was a king only by dint of a strange turn of events, and that in normal circumstances I would not have inherited Hatra's crown until my father's death, which hopefully was many years away. Vistaspa knew this too, just as he knew that I had fought in a slave army. He had once saved my life when I had let my guard down around some Roman captives, and soon afterwards I had been captured by the Romans. No doubt he believed that going to Dura was a fool's errand that would lead to disaster, but if he did he kept his council on the matter.

And so, with Vistaspa's permission, I asked Godarz if he would accompany me to Dura.

'I do not wish to drag you away from Hatra if you do not want to leave. It must be your decision.'

Godarz now busied himself with finding the best horses for Hatra's army, especially pure whites; indeed, while a slave in Italy he had assembled a fine collection of horses for his master. One of these beasts was a white stallion with blue eyes that I took and named Remus. I had ridden him thereafter.

'I would have to ask Prince Vistaspa for his permission, Pacorus.'

'I have already done that, for I know that you are friends and so I sought his permission to approach you and he consented.'

He nodded his head thoughtfully. 'And what do you want of me?'

'To be governor of Dura,' I replied, 'to ensure that taxes are spent wisely and the city's defences are strong.'

'I know nothing of Dura.'

'You know what Godarz, neither do I. But perhaps we can learn together.'

He accepted my offer.

There remained one more task to fulfil before I could leave Hatra. Years ago, in another lifetime, my father had sent a raiding column into the wild country of Cappadocia in reprisal for Rome's aggression against Hatran territory. I was part of that raiding party, as was the man I now sought out in Hatra, a guide named Byrd who had also been enslaved by the Romans, and who had subsequently been the leader of a ragged band of scouts in the army of Spartacus.

I went into the city the next morning, walking through the bustling streets bursting with Hatra's citizens and foreign visitors. The air was hot and filled with the smells of pungent spices from the East. The markets were heaving with people buying and selling garments, animals, pottery and exotic foods. The stalls were packed full of wares, customers haggling, shouting, cursing and laughing. Kogan's guards kept order, but in general the atmosphere was good-natured although frenetic. I walked down to the southern part of the city, past brothels, inns and along litter-strewn streets. Beggars, their limbs distorted and their faces diseased, pot-marked and ugly, held out their filthy hands for money. I reached into my leather pouch and gave them some drachmas, for I too had been a penniless wretch once. I walked under an arch into a small square, around which more stalls were arranged. This was the poorer quarter of the city, and the wares on sale reflected that – coarse garments, poor quality utensils and thin loaves. Around the square were shops, mostly one-roomed affairs that opened out on to the square, their owners placing benches to separate the square from their abodes. I had consciously dressed in a simple white tunic, brown leggings and leather boots, but the sword hanging at my hip marked me apart from the dozens of others, some barefoot, all haggard, who were there to buy products.

I walked up to one of the shops on the south side of the square, which like the others had a wooden bench placed in front of its entrance. The bench was piled high with earthenware pots, and behind it a scruffy man, tall with dark, shoulder-length hair, his face lean, was arguing with a portly man with thinning hair.

'You no like, then don't buy.' The seller's eyes, narrow and brown, fixed the customer with a cobra-like stare. The man threw his arms into the air and walked away.

'You won't become rich with that attitude, Byrd.'

He recognised me instantly. 'Lord, I not expect to see you in this part of the city.'

He smiled, one of the few times I had seen him do so in the years that I had known him. He still looked the same as when I had first clapped eyes on him before the fateful raid into Cappadocia. He had been hired as a guide and my first impression of him was far from positive. Dressed in scruffy clothes, I had, I am ashamed to say, looked down on him. But he proved his worth in Cappadocia and afterwards the more so when he became the chief scout in the army of Spartacus. He collected a ragged band of like-minded and similarly attired individuals, fifty in all, who became the eyes and ears of the army. They operated in small groups, riding ahead and reporting back on Roman garrisons and any armies that might be heading our way. And then, after that terrible spring day when Spartacus fell in battle, the scouts had simply melted away like they had never existed. All except Byrd, who elected to travel back with me to Parthia. Since my return to Hatra I had seen him little.

'I close early today, lord. Come inside.'

He threw an old brown blanket over the pots on the bench and beckoned me to enter his shop, which in reality was a small space with a table on one side. A drawn curtain barred the entrance to what I assumed was a bedroom. He gestured at one of the stools tucked underneath the table. I pulled it out and sat down and he did the same. He filled a cup with water from the jug on the table and handed it to me.

'You want to buy some pots, lord?'

I laughed. 'Not quite. I have come to see if I can interest you in coming on another journey.'

He drank some water. 'Journey?'

'I have a new kingdom to go to.'

'I know, lord. You travel to Dura soon.'

'So, I see your old skills have not deserted you.'

He looked disinterested. 'It is common knowledge.'

'I would like you to come with me, to be my chief scout, or anything else that you might like to be.'

'You very kind, lord, but I have a new life.'

I looked around his miserable quarters and his threadbare clothes. I could not believe that he was happy living such an existence, and then I remembered that the Romans had killed his family in Cappadocia when he had been away on the road selling pots. Perhaps he felt guilty that he had lived and they had died. Maybe living in misery was his way of atoning for the wrong that he felt he had committed, but perhaps I was thinking gibberish.

'We miss you, Byrd,' I said absently.

'Who "we", lord?'

'Well, Gallia for one, and Diana and Gafarn.'

A smile spread across his lean face. 'They are fine people. And the child, it thrives?'

'He thrives. He is strong, just like his father.'

'And Gallia, she is well?'

I drained my cup. 'Strong, proud and defiant as ever, Byrd, just like in Italy.'

'I came to temple when you were married. She very beautiful woman.'

'You were at my wedding, why didn't you come to the banquet afterwards?'

'I stay at back of temple, lord, make no fuss.'

I laid a hand on his arm. 'There are no barriers between those who served Spartacus, my friend, always remember that. It matters not if you are a king or a pauper; those of us who were in Italy are brothers. Nothing will ever change that. Please think about my offer.'

I took the purse hanging from my belt. 'Take this. There is enough money for you to purchase a good horse and a saddle. We leave for Dura the day after tomorrow. I would feel a lot safer knowing that you are with us.'

He shook his head. 'Hatra not like Italy, lord, no Romani here.'

I stood up and we shook hands.

'Please give the matter some thought, Byrd. If you decide to stay, then please go to the palace and see Gafarn and Diana from time to time.'

'They stay in Hatra?'

'Yes, my mother likes having a young child in the palace, and everyone loves Diana too much to see her go.'

'It will be hard on Gallia to leave her friend.'

'It will.' I pointed at him. 'That is why your presence is all the more important. She will want as many of her old friends around her as possible.'

I walked back to the palace not knowing if I had convinced him, but hoping I had said enough, if only to give him a better life. But then, perhaps he was contented.

'So, will he come?'

Gallia was checking her bow and the arrows in her quiver and her mail shirt was hanging on a wooden frame by the side of our large bed.

I shrugged. 'You know Byrd, he's a law unto himself.'

She pulled her sword from its sheath. Like mine it was a Roman cavalry weapon called a spatha. Its blade was straight and each edge was sharpened. My spatha had been a gift from Spartacus and was one of my most treasured possessions. My most treasured possession was standing next to me, examining the razor-sharp edges on her own sword.

47

'You said he was selling pots.' She gingerly stroked one of the edges with a finger, smiling in approval at its lethality.

'That's right, down in the south of the city, in one of the less salubrious districts.'

'You should have commanded him to come.' She slammed her sword back in its scabbard.

'And you think he would have obeyed?'

She looked at me. 'Of course not, but it would have got you used to issuing commands. Isn't that what kings do?'

I ignored her jibe. 'In any case, I don't want anyone who doesn't want to be with us. How do you feel about Diana staying here?'

She pulled her dagger from its sheath and examined its blade. 'I will miss her, but she likes it here and everyone adores her, especially your mother. I think she sees the baby as a sort of grandchild. And knowing that Diana is happy and safe is a weight off my mind.' She giggled. 'Who would have thought it, a Roman kitchen slave who has become a princess? It's a strange world.'

A loud knock on the door startled us. 'Lord king, a courier has arrived with a package for you. He awaits you in the throne room.'

We followed the guard from our bedroom, through the palace's private chambers and along a long corridor that led to the rear of the throne room. Kogan's guards stood around the room at intervals of ten paces, looking like bronze statues in their breastplates and helmets. My father sat in one of the high-backed chairs, my mother in another. Assur stood to one side of the marble-covered dais, along with Kogan and Vata. Gafarn, Aliyeh and Diana were standing on the other side, all of them looking at a distinctly nervous soldier who held what appeared to be a large bundle of hides in his hands. The silence was oppressive as we entered the room.

'Ah,' said my father, 'perhaps now the mystery can be solved.'

I was bemused. 'Mystery, father?'

'Indeed. This man,' he pointed at the soldier stood in front of him, 'has brought a gift for you. Tell him.'

The soldier wore red leather boots, red leggings and a yellow tunic. He cleared his throat.

'Thank you, majesty.' His eyes darted between me and my father, who began drumming his fingers on the arm of his throne, until a disapproving look from my mother persuaded him to desist. The soldier continued. 'This package is to be delivered to King Pacorus in person.'

My father pointed at me. 'Here he is, so you may deliver it, finally.'

48

The soldier bowed his head at me and laid the bundle at my feet. He then reached into his tunic and pulled out a tightly rolled parchment, which he handed to me. 'I was also instructed to give you this, majesty.'

I took the parchment, which had a wax seal. 'Instructed by whom?'

'The sorceress of King of Kings Sinatruces, majesty.'

My father suddenly looked interested, as did everyone else. He waved the courier away.

'Open it Pacorus,' said my mother.

I broke the seal on the parchment and unrolled it. The writing was in a language I did not recognise. 'I do not know these words.'

'Let Lord Assur take a look.'

Assur walked over to me and took the scroll. He peered at it for a long time.

'I believe it is written in ancient Scythian, majesty, though I recognise only a few words. However, there is a clerk in the temple who is an expert on languages. I will bring him.'

He then handed me back the parchment and marched from the room. My father pointed at the bundle on the floor.

'Perhaps Dobbai herself is in there, ready to spring out at you. While we wait for Assur to return, we will see what's in it.'

'It is Pacorus' gift, Varaz, so he should open it,' said my mother.

I pulled my dagger from its sheath and cut the cords wrapped round the hides.

Inside was a rolled piece of cloth. I gestured to Vata and Gafarn to give me assistance as I unrolled it. It was a large square standard, white in colour with gold edging. Vata held one corner and Gafarn the other as they held it aloft in front of me. It was as high at both of them, and Gafarn was over six foot in height. In the centre of the banner was a red mythical beast, with the head and talons of an eagle and the body of what looked like a lion. It also had wings.

'How magnificent,' remarked my mother.

'There's enough gold in that edging to pay for a palace,' noted my father.

'How long do we have to hold it here,' complained Gafarn, 'my arms are aching?'

'What is it?' asked Gallia.

'It is called a griffin if I am not mistaken.' Assur re-entered the chamber with a small, portly man scurrying beside him, who walked over to stand beside me and peered at the banner. He smelt of old scrolls and leather.

'Mm, yes indeed. A griffin. Head of an eagle and the body of a lion.'

Assur handed him the scroll that came from Dobbai. 'And this?'

The archivist held it close to his face and started mumbling to himself.

'You were right, holiness. It is ancient Scythian. I haven't seen this language written in an age.'

'Would you care to read it to us,' requested my father.

'Read it?' The archivist looked up and realised where he was. He blushed. 'Yes, of course, majesty.' He bowed awkwardly, and then bowed again to my mother. My father waved his hand for him to continue.

'Can we put it down?' asked Gafarn.

'Lay it down on the floor in front of me,' said my father. As they did so the archivist read the letter. His voice was crisp and a little high pitched.

To Pacorus, King of Dura Europos and son of Hatra, greetings.

Just as you have ended one journey, so you and your bride are about to begin another. Those who are beloved of the gods do not know what path has been set for them, and those of us who are close to the gods are given only glimpses of what they have in store for you. So it is with you, son of Hatra. The gods have given you a great gift in the form of your new bride, and to prove that you were worthy of her you had to throw off your chains and defeat your enemy in the heart of his kingdom. You have fulfilled that part of your quest, but know that it is only one part.

Behold your banner, which is the image of the Griffin, a creature that inhabited the land when the world was young, and when life and death were but a dream. I saw you riding upon this beast in a vision, and knew that it had been chosen for you. The Griffin makes his nest on the high peaks, overlooking his kingdom, safe from his enemies. He has the head and front talons of an eagle and this is appropriate, for your destiny is entwined with the eagles of Rome. You fight them but they are a part of you. The Griffin has the body of a lion, for you will be a lion of the desert when the time of troubles comes. The Griffin has wings to carry him far and wide, just as you will be called upon to go hither and thither to assist those who have need of you. Let the Griffin be your symbol to show the gods that you honour and respect them, so that you are allowed to keep your queen, who has been sent by them to be by your side.

Know you this as well. The white of the background is a symbol of the purity of your cause, and the red of the Griffin will be the blood that will be spilt in your quest. Heed these words, son of Hatra, and obey the gods. For they are watching you.

The archivist handed me back the parchment, then shuffled nervously on his feet. Assur waved him away, leaving us all in silence. All eyes were on me now. My mother looked alarmed, my father bemused, while Assur stared at the banner intently, almost as if he expected it to spring to life.

My father spoke first.

'It would appear that Sinatruces' sorceress still takes an interest in you.'

'So it seems.'

'You should send it back,' urged my mother.

'It's just a piece of cloth, mother. Besides, I like it. I shall have Domitus inform the legion of its arrival.'

Assur nodded in approval. 'A wise choice, majesty.'

'Soldiers are a superstitious lot,' offered Vata, 'they'll see it as a symbol of luck.'

'Then let us hope that it brings you luck, my son.' My father stood up and held out his hand to my mother. 'We are finished here, everyone is dismissed.'

Afterwards I wrote a short letter to Domitus telling him of the banner and instructing him to pass on the information to his centurions, who would inform their men. Then I took it to the armouries to have it fastened to a lance, and afterwards it was rolled around the shaft and covered by a waxed canvas sleeve.

As Gallia fell asleep in my arms I stared at the furled banner propped up in the corner of the bedroom.

In the morning it and we would be marching to Dura.

Chapter 4

We rose before dawn and said our goodbyes on the steps of the palace. The legion would already be packing up its tents and workshops and marshalling into its centuries and cohorts, Domitus barking curses and issuing orders as his subordinates organised their men into their ranks. Gallia was dressed in her war gear of mail shirt, leggings and boots, her spatha in its scabbard hanging from her belt, with her dagger tucked into the top of her right boot. Her bow was safe in its case hanging from her saddle, quiver at her hip. Her Amazons, similarly attired, were mounted behind her as she said farewell to my parents, sisters, Gafarn and Diana. The latter was in floods of tears as she hugged her friend. They had been together since the gladiator school in Capua and were now to be apart for the first time in years. Gallia embraced her friend tightly, kissed her on the cheek, put on her helmet and then vaulted onto Epona, her mare that she had brought with her from Italy. If there were tears in her eyes I did not see them, though I noticed that she quickly closed her helmet's cheekguards, then dug her knees into Epona's sides and trotted from the square without looking back, followed by her Amazons. My Parthian horsemen, Nergal at their head and my new banner carried behind him, waited on the far side of the square. A guard held Remus' reins.

My father, dressed in a simple white tunic, sandals and beige trousers, had his arm around my mother's waist. 'Try not to get yourself killed down there.'

'I will try.'

Tears streamed down my mother's face as I embraced her. 'May God protect you, Pacorus.'

'Don't be sad, mother, I'm only going to Dura not the end of the world.'

My words did not convince her. I kissed Diana and embraced Gafarn.

'Keep your eye on our parents,' I told him, 'see that mother doesn't get too morose.'

'I will, and you look after yourself and keep Gallia safe.'

'Always.'

Vata suddenly appeared, running down the steps as he buckled on his sword belt.

'Apologies, too much to drink last night.' He belched loudly, causing my mother to cast a disapproving look at him. He locked me in a bear hug.

'Farewell, my friend. Keep safe.'

'You too, Vata, and come to Dura soon.'

He released me and looked round. 'Where's Gallia?'

'You missed her.'

'That's a shame. I was going to persuade her to come to Nisibus with me and leave you on your own.'

'Same old Vata.'

We clasped each other's forearms. I turned, mounted Remus and rode from the square and the palace of Hatra. We rode out of the city via the northern gates and then wheeled left to meet up with the legion as it marched southwest, towards Dura. It was not hard to find – five thousand men plus dozens of carts and mules moving across baked ground kicked up a big dust cloud. The men marched six abreast along the road that snaked south towards the Euphrates. Unlike Roman roads it was little more than a dirt track, seldom used by the trade caravans that headed west or east to and from Hatra. The day was bright and warm, with a slight easterly breeze that failed to blow away the dust kicked up by the horses.

We joined the long column of foot soldiers a short distance from the city. At the front marched Lucius Domitus, his helmet topped by a large transverse white crest, as usual his vine cane in his hand. He raised it in salute when he saw me and I reined in Remus beside him.

'All is well, Domitus?'

'All is well. It's good to be on the move at last. Gives the boys a purpose.'

Gallia and her Amazons rode a hundred paces or so in front of Domitus, with my Parthians ahead of them. Galloping up with Nergal, Godarz fell in beside me looking up at the sun.

'It is going to be a hot day. The nearest oasis is sixty miles away. Three days' march. I hope you and your men can cover such a distance, Domitus.'

'Have no fear of that. They can march that distance and fight a battle at the end of it.'

'Hopefully they won't be fighting any battles in the next few days,' I said.

Domitus pointed at the griffin standard fluttering up the road.

'Is that the banner that the witch sent you?'

'She's a sorceress, Domitus,' I said.

'Mmm. I think the boys would appreciate a look at it.'

I agreed. 'Good idea. Nergal, ride ahead and have it shown to the men.'

At that moment I heard shouts behind me. Turning, I saw a figure on a horse riding towards the head of the column. As he drew nearer I could see that the horse was a mangy beast, dark brown in colour with a long mane and tail, and on its back was an equally dishevelled figure – Byrd.

Those men who had fought in Italy and who now marched behind us recognised him instantly, the man who had been their eyes and ears and the chief scout of Spartacus. Some shouted his name and others banged their javelins on their shields in salute, those that had them. He rode up and halted beside me, nodding his head in acknowledgement.

'I'm glad you decided to come with us, Byrd. Welcome back.'

'Thank you, lord. Where is Gallia?'

'Up ahead.' I looked at his horse. Its hoofs needed filing and its whole body needed a good brush.

'Was not the money I gave you sufficient to buy a decent mount?'

He reached into his tunic and pulled out a pouch, then threw it to me.

'No need money, lord. I sell my pots and buy beast with what I had.'

Godarz halted on the other side of Byrd. 'That horse looks disgusting.' Then he reached over and placed his hand on Byrd's shoulder.

'It's good to see you again, old friend.'

I thought I detected a glint of happiness in Byrd's eyes, but he just nodded.

'You too.'

Everyone was delighted to see him, none more so then me, and word quickly spread through the legion of his arrival, which raised morale even higher. Very soon the men were singing as they marched, mostly ballads about seducing young girls and slaughtering their enemies, but I was happy that they were in good spirits as it made the burden they had to carry lighter. Each man carried around fifty pounds in weight on his back – food, water bottle, cloak, spare clothing, a spade and eating utensils – all strapped to a furca as the Romans call it. This is a wooden pole with a crossbar at the top, to which the pack is strapped.

Among the loads carried by the legion's mules were wooden stakes. These stakes became part of the palisade around the camp that was created each night for both men and beasts, a place of safety and a stronghold, not that we would face any enemies in Hatran territory. Three hours before dark each day the vanguard laid out the camp with poles, and as each cohort reached the site its members would fall out to dig the ditch that would surround the whole camp. The earth that was dug was used to create the rampart upon which the stakes were planted to form a palisade. Thus were our tents, wagons, mules, camels and horses surrounded by a ditch, rampart and wooden wall. And in the morning the stakes were removed and loaded onto mules until the evening, when the laborious process would begin again.

Every night I walked among the campfires to sit with as many of the men as I could, and every night they wanted to hear the same stories, of how I had been a slave, had fought with Spartacus and had found Gallia. How we had fought and defeated the Romans. And all the time they asked me about Dobbai's prophecies. Had she foretold my enslavement? Yes. Did she predict my meeting with Gallia? Yes. Was my becoming a king her doing? Yes. All these things they knew already, but they listened in awed silence as I told them the tale again. One night I happened upon a group of Thracians, now all centurions, who were Companions and formerly soldiers under Spartacus. That night they did the talking and I listened. The glow of the brazier cast us all in a red light as we wrapped our cloaks around us, for the desert nights were cool.

'That night when we attacked the Roman camp at the foot of Vesuvius, that was the first time I saw you.' The speaker was big and solid, with broad shoulders and a thick neck. 'You and the rest were in chains.'

'I remember,' I said.

'That was good sport that night. We slaughtered them all. At the end I was standing behind Spartacus as he watched you killing some Roman. You were hacking at his corpse like a mad man. Then you stopped and we all thought you were going to have a go at Spartacus.'

'You looked like a wild-haired demon, Pacorus,' remarked another. I might have been a king, but all the Companions were allowed such familiarity.

'Anyway,' continued the big one, 'next thing you passed out and we had to carry you back to camp.'

'You carried me?' I asked.

'Me and another one. Though we had to break your manacles first.'

'I've still got the scars on my back from when that bastard centurion flogged me,' I spat.

Before I knew it they were all showing off their battles scars with pride. One showed me a nasty white line that ran across his chest.

'One of Crixus' Gauls gave me that when he ran his dagger across my skin for saying something that upset him. Can't remember what it was now.'

Another man looked up. 'That's the thing about Gauls, you don't need a valid argument to get into a fight with them.' He suddenly realised that I had married one. 'No offence, sir.'

'None taken, and I agree, they are a testy race.'

'Good fighters, though,' said the big Thracian.

I thought of Gallia in her war gear sat on Epona's back shooting down her enemies without mercy. 'Good fighters, yes.'

'Hopefully,' I said, 'we won't be doing much fighting from now on.'

They looked at each other and then burst into laughter.

'What is so amusing?' I asked.

The big one spat into the brazier.

'The gods have a purpose for you, and it isn't to sit on a throne growing old in the middle of the desert. All we know is fighting and war, just like you. It is our destiny.'

'Can a man not change his destiny?' I enquired.

He shook his head. 'No.'

The trip to Dura was uneventful. The legion maintained a steady pace each day and the cavalry walked beside their horses along the dusty road. Byrd, as was his wont, disappeared for hours on end, riding ahead of the column to scout. I told him there was no need, as we were in Hatran territory and my father had established small strongholds throughout his kingdom – forts with a garrison of twenty or thirty cavalry – to both keep the peace and alert him to any threats. It was over two hundred miles from Hatra to Dura, and we had passed two of these forts already on our journey, half a dozen men plus their commander riding out to present his compliments, and to take a look at my new bride no doubt. But Byrd would have none of it, every day leaving camp before dawn to return again just before nightfall. The first thing he did was to report to me, and declare that he had seen nothing untoward.

'I could have told you that, Byrd. Now go and get yourself something to eat, and get your horse seen to.'

The state of Byrd's horse had been a constant cause of friction between him and Godarz when we had all been in Italy, but now Godarz did not bother to confront my chief scout over the neglect of his mount. Instead, he made sure that there was a groom waiting when Byrd rode into camp, who was instructed to take his horse to the temporary stables where it was watered, groomed and fed. All this happened while Byrd was reporting to me, and I made sure that he stayed long enough in my tent to allow the horse to be properly attended to after its long day.

At the end of the ninth day, as the sun dropped into the west and red and purple hues filled the sky, Byrd appeared at the entrance to my tent. As usual, he was covered in dust and grime, his hair lank around his shoulders. It had been a hot day, and both Gallia and I had taken off our boots, armour and helmets and were stretched out in chairs.

Seeing him I pointed to a jug of water on the table. 'Help yourself, you must be thirsty.'

Gallia raised her hand in recognition, and then closed her eyes. It had been a long, tiring day.

'Your kingdom about to break out in revolt, lord.'

I jumped up. 'What did you say?'

He walked over the table and poured himself a cup of water, then drank it down.

'The lords in your new kingdom very angry, lord.'

Twenty minutes later Godarz, Domitus, Nergal and Byrd were gathered in my tent, their faces illuminated by two oil lamps that hung from the centre poles. Gallia stood beside me. Byrd then proceeded to tell them what he had learned that day. He had ridden to the eastern bank of the Euphrates and had crossed the river forty miles upstream from Dura. There was a bridge there, which was held by Hatran troops, giving access to the western side of the river. A toll was imposed on every traveller wishing to cross the bridge, though in truth there were few, as the bridge had originally been built by Sinatruces to facilitate troop movements across the river. My new kingdom had only been a Parthian province for a short time, having been conquered to create a shield for the western edge of the empire and, according to my father, to be a dumping ground for malcontents. Byrd crossed the river and learned from farmers on the far side that the kingdom was seething with resentment.

'Why?' asked Godarz.

Byrd shrugged. 'They say Prince Mithridates is a tyrant.'

'Who's Prince Mithridates?' said Domitus, yawning.

'He's the eldest son of King Phraates of Susiana, who in turn is the son of the King of Kings,' I replied.

I could see that this meant little to Domitus, who looked at me blankly. 'The point is,' I continued, 'that he has been ruling Dura and its lands, not very well by the sound of it.'

'Will he not present himself to you at the river tomorrow, Pacorus?' asked Nergal.

Protocol demanded that the prince should present himself to me in person, though as yet I had received no word from him. In any case if what Byrd said was true, then I decided that etiquette would have to take second place to realities.

'He should, but tomorrow I will take all the horse and ride straight to Dura. Domitus and Godarz, you will stay with the legion and continue its march.'

'I and the Amazons will come with you, Pacorus,' said Gallia.

'Very well, we leave before daybreak.'

In the cold half-light of the pre-dawn I saddled Remus and checked my quiver was full. My bow was carried in a leather case fastened to my saddle, my quiver holding thirty arrows hung from a belt that ran over my right shoulder. My armour comprised a black two-piece leather cuirass. A good friend, a German named Castus, who had been a general in the army of Spartacus, had given it to me in Italy. The cuirass had been taken from a dead Roman officer following one of our many victories. It was muscled and embossed on the upper chest with a golden sun motif, two golden winged lions immediately beneath it. It also had fringed strips of black leather over the thighs and shoulders, which were also adorned with golden bees. On my head I also wore a gift from Castus – the dead Roman's helmet, a superb steel piece that was padded inside, had large, hinged cheek plates and a brightly polished brass crest, in which was secured a plume of white goose feathers.

'You look very much the Roman,' remarked Gallia as her face disappeared behind her helmet's cheekguards.

'Castus gave me this armour.'

'I remember. Do you think you will need it today?'

I vaulted onto Remus. 'Let us hope not.'

We moved fast, one hundred and twenty riders striking hard for the Euphrates. The great river began in the high mountains of Armenia, and then ran south for nearly two thousand miles before it emptied its waters into the Persian Gulf. Like the Tigris that bordered Hatra's eastern frontier, the Euphrates was mightiest in the spring after the winter snows had melted in the mountains. The melt waters flooded south, raising the depth of the river along its whole course and always threatening to break its banks. Spring was now upon us and the river would be deep and fast flowing, the more so at Dura because another river, the Khabur, joins the Euphrates around forty miles north of the city. The Khabur dries up almost completely during the summer months, but in the spring it adds to the Euphrates' torrent. The bridge that we headed for spanned a shallow section of the Euphrates; indeed, in the summer a man could wade across on foot, though now the waters would be twice the height of a man at least. But the bridge, over five hundred feet in length, had reinforced stone pillars that could withstand the flow.

We reached the bridge two hours after leaving camp and then rested the horses. I had the guards at the bridge fetch water for the beasts while their commander told me what he knew about what was happening on the other side of the river.

'Very little, majesty.' He was a lean man in his late thirties with thinning shoulder-length hair and a gaunt face. He wore scale armour over his tunic and an open-faced helmet with a white plume on his head. He commanded fifty men, half a company, whose task was to guard the bridge and also patrol up and down the riverbank to prevent unwelcome guests – thieves, enemy scouts, Agraci – from entering Hatran territory. This mission was extremely easy at this time of the year when the river was swollen. I looked at the fast-flowing brown water heading south. I saw him looking at Gallia and her women, who had taken off their helmets and were wiping the sweat from their necks and brows. Gallia had her hair tied into a long plait, though Praxima always liked to have her red hair hanging loose at all times.

'There used to be guards on the far bank, but two months ago they disappeared and since then we have heard little of events at Dura.'

'Has there been much traffic across the river?'

He shook his head. 'None, majesty.'

I did not doubt it. The farmers ate what they grew and no trade caravans came to this part of the kingdom any more. For to head west was to enter Agraci country, and certain death.

We continued our journey, across the bridge and then into the Kingdom of Dura, my kingdom. Riding south from the bridge, we travelled through country made lush by irrigation ditches and dams. I ordered my banner to be unfurled and carried behind me, for it was right that I should proclaim my presence as the new ruler of this land. We trotted past farmers working in the fields. They watched us for a few moments then continued with their work. In the distance I saw the fortified mansion of one of the kingdom's landowners, a great walled residence with a high mud-brick tower. The tower provided an eagle's eye view of the mostly flat terrain, and would give warning of the approach of hostile forces. The mansion also provided a safe haven for those who worked the land. Each lord would have his own retinue of soldiers, mostly horse archers, and in times of war these men would be reinforced by the farmers who worked the land. Dozens of soldiers riding behind a large white banner would not have gone unnoticed, but no riders emerged from the mansion. We rode on.

We at last came to Dura. My first impression of the city was its strength. Perched on a rocky outcrop above the banks of the Euphrates, any attacker would need a mighty army to take it. The only approach that could be made to the city was from the west where a large, flat plain of rock and earth led to the city's western wall. At least half a mile in length, this wall was made stronger by high, square towers positioned at regular intervals. At a mid-point in the western wall were the main gates – black-stained wood studded with iron plates. On the north and south sides of the city's walls were deep wadis, so the only way in was via the gates that were shut in our faces.

Our column halted on the road about three hundred yards from the gates. There was no sign of life anywhere on the plain or on the walls. In the distance and looming over the city stood the Citadel, which was built on the highest part of the outcrop.

'Everyone stay here, out of arrow range,' I commanded, nudging Remus forward. 'Nergal, you are with me.'

We walked our horses towards the gates, and were soon followed by Gallia on Epona.

'You should keep back, lady,' said Nergal, clearly worried that we might be felled by a volley of arrows at any moment.

'Nonsense,' she snapped. 'What sort of queen stays behind while her husband rides into danger?'

'A sensible one,' I suggested. She ignored me.

We reached the gates unharmed, to find them still shut. The gatehouse itself, which I later learned was called the Palmyrene Gate, was impressive. The two towers that flanked the gates were square and at least fifty feet tall, with arrow slits cut high in their walls. There was a great stone arch over the gates themselves. From a distance the walls and gates had looked impressive; up close they appeared even more formidable.

'Is the city deserted?' queried Gallia.

Nergal pointed to our right, to a part of the wall from which hung three rotting corpses. Our approach had temporarily scared off a host of ravens that had been picking at the cadavers, the bloated birds now sitting on top of one of the towers, watching us.

'Someone put them there. I wonder what their crimes were to deserve such a punishment?'

Before I had chance to answer the gates began to creak and then slowly open inwards. Nergal instinctively drew his bow from its case and strung an arrow from his quiver.

I ordered him to put down the bow as the gates opened fully to reveal a man in his fifties, of average height and build, standing in the middle of the road. He had shoulder-length brown hair, a round face and wore a flowing white gown. At first I thought he was a priest. Two soldiers, each armed with wicker shields and spears, stood by the gates. Aside from their spears they wore no armour and carried no swords, and their only head protection were cloth caps. The middle-aged man knelt before us and bowed his head.

'Greetings, King Pacorus. My name if Rsan and I welcome you to your city.'

'Get up. Are you the governor?'

'No, majesty, I am the city's treasurer.'

My anger towards Prince Mithridates was beginning to rise. To have failed to greet us was bad enough, but to send a mere treasurer was an insult. I leaned forward in the saddle.

'Does the governor have something better to do than meet his new king?'

Rsan shifted nervously on his feet. 'The governor was executed several weeks ago, majesty. His body, along with that of the garrison commander and the high priest, is currently hanging from the walls.'

'On whose orders?'

'Those of Prince Mithridates, majesty.'

I turned to Nergal. 'Ride back and get the others. Well, Rsan, let's go and meet your Prince Mithridates.'

He looked even more uncomfortable and averted my eyes. 'I'm afraid that the prince and his retinue left the city yesterday.'

'What!'

'Apologies, majesty.' He once again knelt on the ground and bowed his head. 'He just left without any warning, boarded a boat and headed downstream. That is why the gates were shut.'

'Get up. So who is in charge?'

He looked round and then at me. 'I think I am, majesty.'

I was seething inside, but there was no point in taking out my anger on the poor fool standing before me.

'Well, show me to my new palace so I can wash the dirt from my body.'

He bowed his head again. 'Of course, majesty. But where is your bride, Queen Gallia? We were told that she would be accompanying you.'

He had not cast the rider sitting beside me a second thought; after all, 'he' was just another soldier dressed in a mail shirt with a helmet on his head. Gallia pulled off her helmet.

61

'She is here. Take us to our home.'

Rsan, momentarily stunned, bowed once more and led the way from the gates to the Citadel. On the way I noticed that the city appeared to be divided into rectangular blocks of houses and shops separated by straight roads perpendicular to each other, much like the layout of Roman towns. I also noticed that the shops were closed and there were no people on the streets.

'Where are the people?' asked Gallia.

'Prince Mithridates ordered a curfew.'

'Why?' I asked.

'He, er, well. He told everyone that you were going to take the city by storm and burn it to the ground.'

'He is obviously insane,' remarked Gallia. Rsan said nothing.

The Citadel lived up to its name, a walled stronghold with a gated entrance in the southwest corner. The walls were high and thick with a firing step all along their length and square towers at each corner, also with firing platforms on top. Archers and spearmen lining the step and towers had the protection of a high stonewall with slits in it at regular intervals. Inside the Citadel, barracks were sited along the southern wall. These were fronted by verandas. At the northern end of the Citadel were workshops, bakeries and a granary. The latter was set up off the ground on a grid of short stone pillars to deter pests and allow air to circulate, preventing the food inside from spoiling. Fronting the granary was a raised timber platform where goods could be offloaded from carts.

On the eastern side of the courtyard was the palace, flanked by the large armoury on one side and stables on the other. There were more stables and barracks along the west wall. Finally, standing directly opposite the palace steps, stood the treasury and a squat building that I assumed to be a headquarters building, the place where the administration of the garrison took place. Except that there was no garrison.

'Where is the garrison?' Sitting on Remus in the stone-paved courtyard I looked around at what appeared to be an almost deserted stronghold. Two guards carrying spears and wicker shields were standing at the top of the palace steps, two more were either side of the gates.

Gallia halted Epona beside me. 'Where is everybody?'

'I do not know. Rsan, where is the garrison commander?'

'Dead, majesty.'

'Call assembly,' I ordered.

Rsan ran over the front of the headquarters building and rang a large brass bell that hung from a wooden stand outside the main entrance. A few moments later fifteen soldiers were standing to attention in the courtyard. They included the guards on the steps and at the gates. I dismounted as Nergal and the rest of my horsemen trotted into the courtyard. I waved him over.

'Get the horses in the stables, then find the kitchens so we can all eat.'

Nergal saluted and looked at the short line of soldiers. 'Is that the whole garrison?'

'It would appear so.'

As I dismissed the soldiers I ordered Rsan to follow us into the palace. Like the rest of the Citadel it was a functional building, with a colonnaded porch that led into an entrance hall with white walls and a low ceiling. We walked through the hall into the throne room, at the far end of which was a high-backed chair on a stone dais. White stone columns around the sides of the room supported a low ceiling. There was a corridor to the left of the dais and a large red door on the opposite side.

I pointed at the corridor. 'Where does that go?'

'To the banqueting hall, kitchens, guardroom and slaves' quarters, majesty,' answered Rsan.

'And where does that door lead?'

He walked over and opened it. 'To your private apartments, majesty.'

The day was fading by the time my horsemen and their horses were settled into the barracks and we finally sat down to eat. Like the other rooms in the palace, the banqueting hall was functional and not over-large. Compared to its equivalent in Hatra it was positively tiny. Light came in through the high windows cut in the wall, though the afternoon was dying by the time servants brought us wine, bread, fruit and cooked lamb. At least the kitchens were still staffed. I asked Rsan to dine with Gallia and me. We were three figures huddled around the end of a long table later joined by Nergal and Praxima. They both took off their sword belts and laid them on empty chairs, sitting down beside us eager to begin eating. As servants scurried around lighting oil lamps hanging from walls I saw Rsan eye Praxima warily. Nergal's Spanish woman was certainly a wild one, her long hair tumbling unkempt down her back. She used her dagger to cut slices of meat from the side of lamb that lay before her. I had seen her slit men's throats with that dagger.

'There is room for two hundred horses and five hundred men, Pacorus.' Nergal filled a cup with wine and took a large gulp.

'So where is the garrison?' I asked Rsan, who picked at the food without enthusiasm.

'Dead, majesty.'

'From what?' queried Gallia.

'Alas, majesty, they were killed in battle.'

I finished my wine and stretched back in my chair. 'Please enlighten us, Rsan.'

We had finished the food by the time he had finished his sorry tale. When he had been placed in charge of the city, Prince Mithridates had fancied himself as a great warrior, the equal of Alexander the Great and Hector of Troy. He had decided to put an end to the Agraci once and for all, and had ridden out of the city at the head of most of the garrison plus his own retinue of cavalry given to him by his father, King Phraates. The force totalled three hundred foot and five hundred horse, and most of it was slaughtered when it was ambushed by the Agraci two days' march from the city.

'Apparently,' continued Rsan, 'they were overwhelmed by huge numbers of Agraci, who descended on Prince Mithridates and his men like a plague of locusts. The prince did not lack for courage, but there were simply too many of them.'

'And who told you this?' I asked.

'Prince Mithridates himself, who managed to escape the slaughter and make his way back to the city unscathed.'

'A true hero, obviously,' remarked Gallia dryly.

Rsan continued. 'The prince, with what few forces he had left, attacked the Agraci again a while later, and captured Haytham's young daughter.'

Rsan shook his head, his brow furrowed. 'The Agraci king, majesty, is a most cunning individual, and when his daughter was taken from him he started raiding the prince's, er, your kingdom. Prince Mithridates called upon the local lords to give him men to punish Haytham, but they refused.'

I was surprised. 'Why?'

'The prince had raised the taxes considerably to pay for his household here, and they resented it. So he invited each lord to send his eldest son to a great feast here, in the Citadel, as a sign of his contrition towards them. And when they came he had them all put in chains.'

This was outrageous. I stood up. 'And have these men have been returned to their fathers?'

Rsan looked down at the floor. 'No, majesty, they are locked away in one of the store rooms next to the armoury.'

'Go and get them, now!'

Gallia pointed at him. 'Wait, where is the daughter of this Agraci king?'

Rsan held out his arms in a gesture of innocence. 'In one of the kitchen store rooms, I believe.'

Gallia stood up. 'Find her and bring her here too.'

'Majesties,' said Rsan, 'these prisoners may be dangerous, and you have no guards. May I suggest...'

'Enough!' I shouted. 'Go and fetch the prisoners.'

Rsan scuttled away. I told Nergal to go and fetch some of my horsemen just in case we encountered problems. He came back with a dozen men who stood around the hall with their bows beside them. First to arrive was the Agraci prisoner, who was a mere girl of eight or nine years. She had big brown eyes and shoulder-length brown hair. Her feet were bare and her clothes torn, and manacles were around her ankles. She shuffled slowly into our presence, shaking and obviously frightened. Gallia was enraged at her treatment. She walked over to the girl, knelt down in front of her and tenderly embraced her. 'You are in no danger.'

Whether she understood or not, Gallia's words were spoken in a soft tone which the girl would have noticed. Gallia looked at me while still holding her.

'Get these chains off her.'

I told Nergal to go and get an armourer or blacksmith, and ordered that more food be brought from the kitchens. The girl looked as though she could do with fattening up. Gallia took her hand and then sat her down at the table while I waited for the other prisoners to arrive. They did so ten minutes later, a sullen group of young men, unshaven and also clapped in irons. Their eyes burned with resentment as they stood before me.

'My name is Pacorus and I am the new king of Dura. You will all be released immediately and are free to go back to your families.' Though they said nothing, I detected a palpable feeling of relief in the room. Some of them looked at each other and nodded.

One of them, about my age with a dark complexion, held up his manacled wrists. 'What about these?'

'What about these, majesty, I think is the correct term.'

He looked me with narrowed eyes, then relaxed. 'Apologies, majesty.'

'No apologies are necessary. The chains will be removed now, though I hope that you will all stay tonight as my guests.'

My offer was met by silence, but their mood improved when

two anvils arrived and two burly blacksmiths with thick forearms broke their fetters, attending to the Agraci girl first. And the room slowly filled with chatter as they sat down at the table and helped themselves to the food that was ferried from the kitchens. Most of them cast glances at Gallia, who was feeding the girl small pieces of fruit and bread from a plate. The girl still said nothing.

'Is she mute?' I asked.

'I doubt it,' she hissed, 'she's probably terrified. I'm going to take her to our private apartments, give her a bath and get her into some clean clothes.'

'What about me?'

'What about you?' she sniffed. 'I'm sure you are capable of finding a place to sleep tonight.' I kissed her on the cheek and she led the young girl from the hall.

Once the former captives had had their fill, Nergal escorted them to one of the barracks where they could sleep for the night. Afterwards he came back and we sat together at the table while the servants cleared away the mess. Praxima had disappeared with Gallia and the child, but not before she had threatened to 'cut the balls off Prince Mithridates' if she ever met him.

'I apologise for Praxima, Pacorus.'

I passed him a cup of wine. 'Why? I feel the same way, spoilt little brat. He has created a disastrous situation and now he has run back to his father. I should send Praxima to fetch him back and then she can carry out her threat.'

'Not how you expected to begin your reign.'

I shrugged. 'No matter, tomorrow is another day, and Domitus and the legion will be arriving.'

Nergal finished his wine and stood up. 'You might be needing them. Goodnight, Pacorus.'

'Goodnight, Nergal.'

Rsan approached wanting to make conversation, but I bade him goodnight and he left me alone with my thoughts. My limbs ached from the journey and I realised that I still had my armour on. I took off the cuirass and laid it on the table along with my sword and belt. Collecting them up I went to find a room to sleep in while my wife attended to the daughter of an Agraci king. It was a strange start to our new life.

The next day, having slept in one of the bedrooms in the palace's private chambers, I rose early and took breakfast on a large terrace overlooking the Euphrates more than a hundred feet below. The palace was sited on the eastern edge of the Citadel atop the cliff that rose up sheer from the riverbank. There was a small, narrow island in the middle of the river, and on the far side the other bank was Hatran territory. At the foot of the cliffs was a small harbour, from where Mithridates had made his flight no doubt.

Gallia and our young guest joined me soon afterwards. My wife wore a simple white gown with sandals on her feet. Her hair, unplaited, shone in the morning light. Slaves fussed around us, serving us fruit, pastries and cool water. Gallia sat beside me with the child next to her. The little girl looked far healthier than last night, with her hair combed and her face washed. She too wore a simple white dress, though I noticed she still bore red marks around her ankles where the fetters had been.

'You two look well.'

'Yes,' Gallia smiled at the child, 'she is pretty, don't you think?'

'I suppose.'

The child nibbled at a peeled orange as Gallia stared out over the river. 'Our bedroom also has a terrace with a similar view. Magnificent, isn't it?'

I cut a slice of melon with a knife. 'Hopefully tonight I can see for myself.'

'It's a very large room,' said the girl.

'So,' I said, 'you can speak.'

The girl smiled to reveal perfect white teeth. 'Of course.'

Gallia put an arm round her shoulders. 'What is your name?'

She finished the orange and picked up a wafer smeared with honey. 'My name is Rasha.'

'That's a lovely name,' replied Gallia.

'It means young gazelle.'

'My name is...' I did not finish my sentence before she interrupted me.

'You are Pacorus and your wife is called Gallia, and you rescued her from a fire-breathing dragon in a land on the other side of the world, and you got back home on a white stallion who has wings.'

Gallia laughed. 'Who told you such things?'

Rasha finished eating her wafer and picked up a fig. 'The slaves told me. They used to sneak me food even though I wasn't allowed any. Was the dragon big?'

I nodded gravely. 'Big and ferocious, and he had huge claws and breathed fire that singed my hair, and my battle with him lasted all day and all night, but I jumped on his back and killed him with my sword.'

Her eyes were alight with excitement. 'And was Gallia chained to a rock?'

I faked sorrow. 'She was, chained and helpless. But fortunately I came to her rescue.'

'What a gift you have for fairy tales, Pacorus.' Gallia observed with a raised eyebrow.

'Did you ride your horse here?' asked Rasha.

'Yes, he's in the stables. Would you like to see him?' She nodded enthusiastically.

So after breakfast we walked through the palace to the stables, Gallia jabbing me sharply in the ribs on the way.

'Helpless was I?'

Rasha helped to groom and feed Remus, though she was disappointed to discover he had no wings. I told her that he had taken them off as they were very heavy, and in any case he didn't need them now he was home.

While Gallia took Rasha off to meet her Amazons, who were grooming their horses near the stables, I had the sons of the lords given back their mounts. They assembled in the courtyard as I stood with Nergal on the palace steps and bid them farewell. I told them that I was sorry for their mistreatment and hoped that we would meet again in happier times. I also told them that their fathers would not have to pay any increased taxes. There was nothing else to say. The gates were opened and twenty unhappy and resentful young men rode from Dura.

'At least you freed them,' said Nergal.

'I had hoped to meet them and their fathers in more auspicious circumstances.'

'Well, I'm sure their ire will subside once they are back with their families.'

'Let's hope so, Nergal, let's hope so.'

My mood failed to improve as Rsan briefed me on the state of the royal finances. The treasury was empty due to Mithridates' failure to collect any taxes and his penchant for extravagance. I saw no evidence of this in the palace, but Rsan informed me that the prince had had all the gold ornaments and statues shipped back to Susiana before my arrival along with his harem.

'His harem!'

'Yes, majesty, a dozen women he had purchased from slave traders. They too went back with him to Susiana.'

'Talking of slaves, all those in the Citadel are to be freed immediately.'

Rsan looked alarmed. 'Freed, majesty?'

'That is correct. They can stay if they wish, in which case they will be paid for their services, but they are all free to choose.'

'I do not understand.'

'It is quite simple, Rsan, I was a slave once, and I will not have any man or woman endure what I have experienced. See to it.'

In the afternoon the legion arrived and Domitus and Godarz presented themselves at the palace. And as they took nourishment on the palace terrace where I had taken breakfast earlier, I briefed them on what had happened thus far.

'You let me take a couple of centuries and hunt the bastard down. We'll bring him back and you can have him crucified on the far bank, over there.' Domitus was as blunt as ever. He spoke in Latin, a language Rsan could clearly understand, for his mouth was open, aghast at such a proposal.

'Believe me,' I said, 'I am sorely tempted. But I like his father and his grandfather is King of Kings, so I will forego that pleasure.'

Domitus belched loudly. 'Pity.'

I gestured for Rsan standing by the door, to sit.

'Rsan here is the treasurer, though he tells me the treasury is empty. Rsan, this is Godarz, who is the new governor of the city.' Rsan bowed his head to Godarz, who nodded back.

Rsan became less sombre when Godarz informed him that a large sum of drachmas would be filling the treasury forthwith, just as soon as it was offloaded from the carts. I instructed Domitus to house two centuries in the Citadel, with a further cohort stationed in the city itself. There were some twenty-five towers on the circuit wall surrounding Dura. Each was capable of holding a dozen men. In addition to the large gatehouse at the Palmyrene Gate, all of them needed to be garrisoned.

The legion's camp was established half a mile west of the city among the rock and iron-hard earth of the desert. As it was to be a permanent fixture, I ordered that a mud-brick wall be erected around its perimeter. The men would still be living in tents, but each cohort would be rotated between living in the camp and garrison duties in the city and Citadel, which would provide a variety of living conditions. The score of men from the original garrison I gave to Rsan as a treasury guard. They were under the overall command of Domitus, who took up residence in the headquarters building in the Citadel, but I did not want to dismiss them lest they took to banditry, and in any case I wanted to assure Rsan that he still had a place in the new regime. It was not his fault that the city's former ruler had been a tyrant.

The city curfew was abolished and life for Dura's citizens began to return to normal. Brick-making for the legion's camp provided immediate additional employment for the citizens and trade in food and animals showed signs of recovery. This was most important, for without markets there would be no taxes for the treasury, and without taxes there would be no money to provide weapons and armour for the legion. Blacksmiths, farriers, veterinaries and armourers all had to be fed and housed.

Five days after our arrival at Dura I was returning to the city from the training fields – a barren stretch of earth near the legion's camp – in the company of Gallia. While the legionaries practised drills, throwing javelins and becoming proficient with their swords, the horsemen honed their archery skills. The Amazons trained with them. We were both covered in grime and our tunics were soaked in sweat as we walked our horses back to the city. It was approaching noon and the heat of the day was stifling with a raging sun in a clear blue sky.

There was no traffic on the road west from Dura that snaked past the legion's camp and out into the desert, to where the Agraci waited.

I drank from my waterskin, the liquid warm and unedifying, and then passed it to Gallia. Epona was lathered in sweat, as was Remus, and they were both breathing heavily from their exertions.

'I would like to chop off the hands of Mithridates,' she said casually.

'Praxima wants to cut off his balls, you want to slice off his hands and Domitus wants to crucify him. There won't be much left of him afterwards, that's for sure.'

'Arrogant little puppy, he has caused us many problems.'

'He certainly has,' I replied, 'but at least I can put one thing right. I think it's time Rasha was returned to her father.'

'I agree,' she said, wiping sweat-matted hair off her brow. 'But who will take her back. Everyone fears these Agraci.'

'I will,' I said.

She turned to look at me with those blue eyes I loved so much. 'Are you mad?'

'I don't think so, but I want to meet this king, so perhaps if I take his daughter he will not kill me outright.'

'And perhaps he will.'

'It doesn't matter,' I said, 'it's decided.'

'Then I am coming with you.'

'What?'

'Either we go together or Rasha stays here'

I looked away from her into the empty desert.

'There,' she continued. 'now it's decided.'

Rsan was appalled at the idea of us going into the desert without an army, as was Godarz, while Domitus advised against it. Nergal just looked shocked and shook his head continually, but I told them that the matter was not up for discussion.

'I will take Gallia and Byrd, and the child.'

'You will not return, then,' announced Godarz.

'If that happens, my friend,' I said, 'you will become king. All those present will bear witness to my wish.'

'At least let me go with you, Pacorus,' said Nergal, his eyes full of pleading.

'I will think on it. We will leave tomorrow.'

I told Nergal that he would be staying at Dura.

Chapter 5

The new day dawned bright and sunny with a light breeze blowing from the west. Rasha was in a good mood and was even more talkative than usual. There was now no resemblance to the frightened, haunted little wretch we had first seen when we arrived at Dura. In her place was a pretty, inquisitive and intelligent girl who skipped around the palace. She always accompanied me when I went to the stables to groom Remus, and in truth I became quite fond of her. But it was Gallia who was the focus of her affections, and whenever she and her Amazons rode out of the city to the training fields Rasha went with them. As to be expected of a child of nomads, she was at ease in the saddle and could ride as well as any adult. She had her own room in the palace, next to ours, and everyone liked having her around, even the normally stern Domitus. So it was quite poignant when the morning came for her to leave us. After the garrison had mustered just after dawn Gallia, Byrd and I mounted our horses in front of the palace steps alongside the waiting Rasha. Byrd was his usual seemingly disinterested self, though his horse looked remarkably well tended and fed – no doubt Godarz's influence. When I had asked Byrd to accompany us into the desert he had accepted in a nonchalant fashion, and merely shrugged when I told him that we might not be coming back. Those who were assembled to see us off – Godarz, Nergal, Praxima, Rsan and Domitus – appeared not the least calm. Even the iron-hard Domitus was frowning with concern.

'Are you certain about this, majesty?' queried Rsan.

'Quite certain,' I answered.

And so we trotted from the courtyard, through the Citadel's gates and west down the main street of the city through the Palmyrene Gate into the desert, Byrd out in front. Many people fear the desert and in truth it is an unforgiving environment, hot during the day and bitterly cold at night, the abode of snakes and scorpions. The parched white bones of dead animals lying in mute testimony to the desert's harshness. But the desert is also beautiful and serene. The wide-open spaces and lack of people allowing one to think and be at peace with its vastness. Its yellow and brown hues, the lush green of its oases and the stark outlines of the many outcrops give the desert a unique appearance that I always found invigorating. In truth I loved the desert and found journeying through it gave me an inner calm. I think it was the quiet, the absolute silence that pervades the desert that made me react to it the way I did. Even Rasha fell silent after the first morning.

We encountered no traffic on the track that wound its way west towards the oasis settlement of Palmyra, once a thriving trade centre but now the capital of the Agraci. This would have been the same route that Mithridates had taken during his abortive campaign against them, and the road the few survivors used in their flight back to Dura. I prayed to Shamash that we would not suffer the same fate.

That night we cooked and ate a brace of rabbits that we had brought from the city. Byrd found us some firewood from an abandoned wagon that we passed during the afternoon, and we sat around the fire as it cast our faces in an eerie red glow. Byrd had questioned us lighting a fire, but I told him that we were not on a scouting mission. The night was cool and so Gallia wrapped Rasha in a blanket and put a woollen cap on her head.

Rasha gnawed the meat from a small thighbone and then looked at Gallia. 'Can I visit you again?'

Gallia smiled. 'Of course, if you wish.'

'Good. I like my room, and when I visit you I can put some of my own things in it.'

How innocent the world seemed through the eyes of a young child. I saw Byrd staring at Rasha. I wondered if he was thinking of his own family, now long dead, and his former life. If he was he never said. The next day he rode beside me with Rasha between Gallia and myself. On our right, in the distance, sat a long, squat limestone plateau, while on our left was an expanse of sand and rocks. A glint of light caught my eye and I squinted towards the plateau.

'We are being watched,' said Byrd casually.

'By whom?' asked Gallia.

Byrd nodded towards Rasha. 'By her people.'

We saw nothing untoward for the rest of the morning and by noon it felt as though the sun was cooking us in a giant stone bowl, so we laid up in the lee of an outcrop forming part of a granite ridge extending to the north. We unsaddled the horses and used the saddles as back supports as we rested in the shade. I caught sight of a lizard scurrying between the rocks while overhead a buzzard glided effortlessly in the sky. After two hours we saddled the horses to continue our journey. The first hour was uneventful. Once again we appeared to be the only people in the barren landscape. But then I caught sight of a group of riders that suddenly appeared on our left flank, around a quarter of a mile distant. Their black shapes on black horses shimmering in the haze. Byrd rode up to me.

'Our escort has arrived, lord.'

'So it seems. You had better stay close.'

'What do we do now?' asked Gallia.

'We carry on, my sweet.'

As we continued our trek west another party of horsemen, six in number, appeared on our right flank, at a similar distance to those on our left. The terrain was becoming hillier now, great sandstone slabs rising out of the ground. We ambled around one such pillar of stone and were confronted by line of at least a score of warriors on horseback. Remus, sensing danger, whinnied in alarm and we halted.

Each warrior was armed with a spear and sword at his waist. On their heads they wore turbans that covered the lower half of their faces. Only their dark eyes were visible. They carried large round shields on their left sides and wore black flowing robes covering their arms and legs. They were mounted on horses that could only be described as beautiful. Parthians love their horses, but I could see that this group of Agraci also held their mounts in high esteem. Their horses were big and powerful, deep chested with short heads, broad foreheads and wide jowls. They were a mixture of greys and chestnuts. Each one was wearing a red halter decorated with cowries and other adornments, finished with two groups of tassels, one on each side of the noseband. The tassels were braided, with the tops gathered and secured by gold threads. The horses' chest sets were also decorated with coloured beads, cowries and golden silk threads, while red and gold tassels adorned each rider's saddle.

One rider had halted in front of the group. He was a large, broad-shouldered individual who carried no spear or shield; his only weapons a curved sword with a white horn handle in a black sheath with a gold tip. He nudged his horse forward until he was around twenty paces from mine, fixing me with his black eyes as he did so. He halted and looked at Rasha then removed his turban to reveal a big, square-shaped face with a long nose and a thick, close-cut black beard. He dismounted from his horse and smiled at Rasha.

'Have you no greeting for your father?' His voice was deep, his coarse accent typical of the desert peoples.

'Father!' Rasha jumped from her horse and ran over to him. He scooped her up in his long arms and held her close. Then putting her down he examined her closely, no doubt to make sure she had not been harmed. Thankfully the marks on her ankles where she had been chained had disappeared. He stood up to face me, his right arm around her shoulder. He said nothing as he regarded us, while behind him his men eyed us menacingly. I decided to break the silence.

'My lord, my name is…'

'I know who you are, Pacorus, King of Dura, but I am intrigued as to why you would bring your queen with you?' He glanced at Byrd. 'And you bring so few warriors. Where is your army, your famed legion?'

'I did not think it proper, lord, to enter your kingdom with an army at my back.'

His face betrayed no emotion as he no doubt weighed up our fate. 'And now you expect me to let you return to your city unmolested?'

'That is your prerogative, lord. My only thought was to return your daughter to you and therefore atone for the injustice done to your family by my predecessor.'

'A Parthian army rides into my kingdom, attacks my people and steals my daughter. Parthians are not welcome here.'

'I am not a Parthian, King Haytham' said Gallia, 'so what will you do with me?'

Haytham was taken aback. No doubt a woman had never spoken to him thus, or indeed anyone. Then the semblance of a smile creased his lips.

'So, you are the famed Queen Gallia, the beauty from overseas who fights like a man. You too we have heard of. No doubt you have heard that we are savages.'

'I have heard much, lord,' she replied, 'but I judge people according to how I find them. I hope you are a man who does the same.'

He said nothing for a while but just stared at us. It was Rasha who broke the silence.

'Where is your camp, father?'

Haytham looked at his daughter and smiled. 'Not far. Shall we invite your friends to accompany us?'

'Oh, yes,' she replied, 'we have had a very tiring day.'

He looked up into the sky and then at us. 'Come, you will enjoy my hospitality tonight.'

Rasha walked back to her horse and Gallia helped her into the saddle. Haytham vaulted back into his saddle and led the way to his camp. His warriors rode all around us, though their demeanour was not threatening. An hour later we trotted into the Agraci camp, a sprawling collection of black tents grouped around one of the many oases that dotted the desert. The camels and horses were tethered among the throng of date palms growing around the waterhole. After we dismounted our horses were taken from us.

We were then shown to a large rectangular tent made of strips of woven camel hair laid over a wooden frame. The front section was tied open to allow air to circulate in the interior, and there were rugs on the floor. Moments later Rasha was at Gallia's side, tugging at her hand for her to go and see her father's camels. So off they went, leaving me alone with a tall, lean man about my age who had black tattoos on his cheeks. He had removed his turban to reveal long, straight black hair and no beard. He had olive skin and dark brown eyes.

'My name is Prince Malik, the son of King Haytham.' His voice was deep like his father's.

'I am pleased to meet you, Prince Malik.'

'Can I get you anything, lord king?'

'No, thank you.'

He bowed in a perfunctory manner and then turned to leave, stopped and looked back at me. 'Thank you for returning my sister to us. My father has missed her greatly, as have I.'

With that he was gone. I took off my sword and laid it on the rug, then stretched out beside it. I closed my eyes and listened to the sounds of men talking and laughing and camels bellowing and roaring. Despite being in the midst of the Agraci I felt no sense of danger or threat, just relief that we had made initial contact with their leader and that he had spared our lives thus far. I must have dozed off, for I was rudely awakened by Gallia throwing herself onto the rug beside me.

'That child has boundless energy,' she said. I opened my eyes and saw that she had closed the tent flaps.

I was suddenly alarmed. 'Where's Byrd?'

'Oh he's all right. Last time I saw him he was deep in conversation with one of their warriors concerning a camel.'

'Byrd, deep in conversation? Perhaps you were seeing a mirage.'

'What's a mirage?'

I propped myself up on an elbow to look at her. 'An illusion created by the heat. Perhaps this is all an illusion and we are actually lying dead in the desert.'

'Shut up, Pacorus. I need to get some rest before the feast tonight. It's being given in our honour, apparently.'

'Feast?'

'Oh yes,' she motioned for me to lie back down and rested her head on my shoulder. 'You know, for a king you sometimes know so little.'

It was dark by the time we had rested and refreshed ourselves,

76

and when Gallia opened the tent flaps two black-clad warriors were waiting to escort us to our feast. We walked among groups of warriors sitting around fires mostly ignoring us, though one or two did act with surprise when they saw Gallia's blonde locks shimmering in the firelight as she passed. Haytham's tent, a cavernous black structure, was pitched beside the water among the date palms. A guard took our swords before we entered the tent. Six warriors sitting in a circle momentarily halted all their talk as Gallia unbuckled her sword belt and handed it to the Agraci guard. We bowed our heads to Haytham and entered the tent. He rose when we entered and invited us to sit on his right side, the place of honour. Also present were Rasha and Malik, the young girl rushing up to Gallia and throwing her arms around her before pulling her by the hand to her place. I saw Byrd chatting to a man who looked as sullen and unkempt as he did. He raised a hand to me and carried on talking. Clearly he had found a kindred spirit. Rugs covered the floor and we sat down cross-legged in the circle.

Haytham clapped his hands and food and drink were brought in and served. This comprised jugs of water and large flat dishes piled high with stewed lamb served on a bed of rice and bread and sprinkled with pine nuts. While we ate I noticed that Haytham took only morsels from what was served, all the time looking at Gallia and me. After we had eaten, washed our hands in bowls of warm water and dried them, Haytham clapped his hands once more. The servants disappeared and the flaps of the tent were closed, leaving us alone with our host and what I took to be his senior commanders.

'A most sumptuous meal, lord,' I said. 'I thank you for your hospitality.'

Haytham nodded. 'It is given freely. But now, King Pacorus, we must talk of things more serious. What do you want of me?'

This Agraci king was clearly no fool. He knew that I could have sent his daughter back to him with a lowly escort of a few guards. I did not need to bring her myself. He knew this, as he also knew that my mission had a dual purpose. I decided to be direct and not insult his intelligence.

'I desire peace between our peoples, lord.'

As a tired Rasha fell asleep in Gallia's arms, Haytham said nothing for a long time. I could feel my heart beating in my chest. Eventually he spoke.

'For years your people, the Parthians, have hounded and killed the Agraci, driving them from their lands and treating them no better than animals. Even your own father, King Varaz, has led raids against my people. And now you, his son, sit in my tent and ask for peace. As a father I thank you for giving me back the life of my daughter, but as a king this is an irrelevance. So I ask you, why should I should be interested in peace with you?'

I knew that what I said in reply would determine whether my reign at Dura would be a success or failure. In my mind I had formulated a plan that I had not even told Gallia of. Now was my chance to put it into action. But only if the right words came from my mouth. I said a silent prayer to Shamash that He would assist me.

'King Haytham, everything you say is correct. Your people have been wronged by mine, and there is nothing I can say that can change that. However, I would ask that you look to the future rather than the past. If we can have peace between the Agraci and Dura, then the result will be mutual benefits.'

'What benefits?' I knew that I had pricked his interest.

'As you know, the trade caravans that travel between the Orient and the west bring great wealth to those kingdoms they journey through. Hatra, my father's kingdom, is the richest in the Parthian Empire because of the duties it charges on the non-stop traffic that goes between east and west.'

One of the warlords present interrupted me. 'Wealth that Hatra has used to purchase weapons and men with which to murder the Agraci.'

'Silence!' Haytham's shout caused me to jump and Rasha to open her eyes.

'Please continue, King Pacorus,' he said, more quietly, freezing the man who had spoken with his iron-hard stare.

'It is five days' ride from Dura to your capital at Palmyra, and another five west to reach the coast of the Mediterranean. The owners of the caravans would gladly pay to have access to the coast through your territory. There are many in Egypt who crave the spices, silk and riches of the East, and would pay handsomely for them.'

Haytham smiled. 'So you wish to become rich.'

I saw no reason to lie. 'Of course, why not? We can both become rich. Is that not more desirous that butchering each other and having the vultures pick at our bones in the desert?'

'I propose a peace treaty between us. Dura will make no further encroachments upon your territory. Your people can have access to Dura's markets, and you will be able to levy customs duties on all trade caravans that pass through your territory. In return, I ask that your raids upon my territory cease immediately.'

I pointed at the man who had spoken out. 'You talk of Hatra being able to purchase weapons and men and you are right, but peace makes trade possible and trade brings wealth. And with wealth you too can purchase weapons, horses and armour to remain strong.'

Haytham nodded thoughtfully. 'You speak with a maturity far in advance of your years, young Parthian. Some say that you are favoured by the gods. I do not know of such things and in any case your gods are not mine. But I do know that you do not lack in courage, for to venture into an enemy's lands with only two companions is brave indeed, if a little foolhardy.

'I will think on your proposal. In the meantime, know that you are free to return to your city and your people. I will send my answer to you in due course. I will say no more on the matter. I bid your goodnight.'

He rose, smiled at Gallia and then picked up his sleeping daughter from my wife's arms. Everyone stood up and bowed their heads as Haytham headed for his sleeping quarters. The evening was at an end and so we were shown back to our tent, Byrd to his.

In the morning we took our leave of Haytham, Gallia and Rasha embracing as they parted from each other. Byrd was sitting emotionless on his horse and Malik was standing next to his father. Haytham's face was a stone mask as we rode from his camp escorted by a dozen of his warriors. They followed a hundred paces behind us, then around noon wheeled away and disappeared into the desert. Byrd rode ahead, leaving me alone with Gallia.

'Do you think Haytham will accept your offer?'

'I hope so, it will make things a lot easier.'

'What things?'

'The defences of Dura need strengthening, the legion needs to be fully equipped and I need to have a force of cataphracts. All this will be possible if Haytham agrees to peace.'

'For someone who wants peace, you sound as though you are preparing for war.'

'If Dura is strong then enemies will think twice before attacking it.'

'You are speaking of the Romans?' she said. 'You think they will attack us?'

'I think the Romans have an insatiable desire to conquer the whole world. You know them; they will come. And I will be ready when they do.'

But thoughts of the Romans had to be put aside for the moment as I waited for Haytham's answer to my proposals. There was much rejoicing when we got back to the city, not least because everyone thought that we would die at the hands of the Agraci. In the days following I travelled to the estates of all the landowners in my kingdom. Though their failure to present themselves upon my arrival at Dura could be construed as an insult, I decided to ignore their slight; after all, their sons had been prisoners in the city. And so I met them one by one. I took Nergal and fifty horsemen, plus my griffin banner, and was in truth well received. I was honest and forthright with each one, telling them of my trip into the desert to meet Haytham and my desire for peace with the Agraci. I also told them that I had said that his raids upon their lands must stop and that I was waiting for his answer. The expressions on their faces told me that they remained sceptical that I would receive the answer I desired, but I think they were pleasantly surprised I had bothered to visit them and inform them of my plans. Each one asked if it was true that Gallia had accompanied me on my mission, and I told them it had been so. I think they were disappointed she was not with me during my visits to them. I told them I would be inviting them all to a banquet in due course, and assured them the gates of the city and Citadel would be open the whole time during their visit.

'Do you think you have won them over?' I sat with Gallia on the balcony of our bedroom perched high on the cliff overlooking the Euphrates below. She was combing her hair, which sparkled in the light of the late afternoon sun.

'Who?' I said. 'The Agraci or the lords?'

'Both.'

I shrugged. 'We will know soon enough.'

I looked at her. Her fine features and perfect skin making her every inch the queen she was.

'I know Dura isn't Hatra.'

She looked at me quizzically. 'What do you mean?'

'I know that Dura is a fortress city and doesn't have the gardens and grand palace that you were used to at Hatra. I'm sorry if it is a disappointment.'

She put down her comb and fixed me with her blue eyes. 'Sometimes, Pacorus, you are a complete idiot.'

'What?'

She gestured at the balcony with her arms. 'This is my home, the place where I hope to raise a family, the place where I want to grow old. Why should I care if it does not have ornamental ponds or exotic animals wandering around in lush gardens? I would not wish to be anywhere else.'

Of course, she was right. I was a fool. All her life she had never known a home. She had grown up in her father's berg in northern Italy, was then sold into slavery, had lived in tents during her time with Spartacus, and finally had spent time in my father's palace in Hatra. Now, for the first time, she had a place that was hers.

'I'm sorry.'

'Quite right, too.'

In truth our home was far from lavish, frugal would be the correct word to use. All my father's money had been deposited in the treasury where it was watched over by Rsan, who displayed the same reluctance to part with any of it as Addu had at Hatra. Every drachma was itemised and locked in a vault below the treasury. Nothing was spent on furnishings for the palace, my only concern being the equipping of the legion. Aside from the Companions who had brought their arms and armour from Italy, most of the men had no equipment.

'I need five thousand mail shirts, shields, swords and helmets,' said Domitus, 'plus another five thousand javelins to start with.'

Rsan was shaking his head. 'Impossible. Such an expenditure would empty the treasury.'

Now that Domitus has settled the legion into its camp, he was impatient for it to be fully equipped. All three of us were standing in the armoury, a squat, thick-walled building that had grills on its small windows and one small wooden door faced with iron. It was filled with rows of empty stands that used to hold spears and swords, though there were a few bundles of arrows stacked on shelves.

Domitus drew his own sword, a Roman gladius with razor-sharp edges. He moved closer to Rsan and held the point of the blade only inches from his belly.

'This, Lord Rsan, is the type of sword I desire, very useful when you want to get cosy with your enemy.'

Rsan's eyes were wide with alarm.

'No slashing with this little fellow, just three inches into an enemy's guts a few times will spill his innards without any fuss.'

'Thank you, Domitus,' I said, 'there's no need to alarm my treasurer.'

Domitus smiled at Rsan and sheathed his blade. 'Just stressing that my legion needs weapons if it is to keep the city, and your treasury, safe.'

His smile disappeared when he heard the bell in the courtyard being rung frantically. I followed two paces behind him as we raced from the armoury and onto the flagstones. I saw Nergal on

81

his horse with a dozen of his men behind him and one of the guards beside him ringing the bell. Around us other soldiers were spilling out of the barracks to form up, while the gates of the Citadel were being closed. Gallia and Praxima appeared on the palace steps, followed by Godarz.

Nergal saw me and saluted. 'Agraci war band approaching the city. I was returning from the training fields when a party of Domitus' men alerted us to their approach. I have ordered the Palmyrene Gate to be closed.'

The garrison had formed up by now – a hundred legionaries and fifty Parthians, the latter on horseback armed with bows. Gallia's score of Amazons formed the end of the line.

I pointed at Domitus. 'Stay here with your men. Nergal, we will ride out to meet them.'

I ran towards the stables to saddle Remus. Gallia followed me.

'I'm coming too.'

We rode through the city and out through the reopened Palmyrene Gate west towards the approaching foe, all of us armed with bows and swords. I was wearing my helmet and leather cuirass. Gallia's Amazons were clad in their mail shirts and helmets, while Nergal's Parthians were similarly attired. We galloped past the legion's camp, the men standing to arms, and saw a great mass of black-clad horsemen in front of us. So Haytham had chosen war instead of peace. As we slowed and riders to my left and right rode forward to form into line, I must confess that I was greatly disappointed. No matter, we would soon scatter these Agraci. Then I reached behind me, pulled my bow from its case and extracted an arrow from my quiver. The others did the same as we slowed our horses to a walk and then halted them. The Agraci were about a quarter of a mile distant. They also appeared to have slowed. In fact they had halted. They made no move to get into any formation. No doubt they would attack us in one great, disorganised mass.

I raised my bow in the air to signal the advance; everyone responded in a like manner. Gallia was at my side, arrow in her bowstring. I nudged Remus with my knees and he began to move forward. Ahead I saw that one of the Agraci was also moving towards us, though he appeared to be the only one. We continued our advance, moving into a trot, when Gallia suddenly called out.

'It is Prince Malik.'

I instinctively halted Remus.

'What?'

Gallia had taken off her helmet and was pointing at the lone horseman approaching, with his hand raised.

'It is Prince Malik, Pacorus.'

'Halt, halt!' I screamed, and my riders pulled up their mounts. Gallia was right, it was Prince Malik, and the fact that he was riding alone ahead of his men indicated that he was not here to fight. I rode up and down my line of riders.

'Stand down, stand down.'

I put away my bow as Malik approached. Gallia was advancing to meet him as I joined her until we halted a few paces from the prince.

Malik removed his turban and bowed his head. 'Greetings, King Pacorus, Queen Gallia.'

I raised my hand to him in salute. 'Greetings, Prince Malik. You come well accompanied.'

He looked back to his group of riders, who must have numbered over three hundred. 'Indeed, my apologies if we appear warlike. My father thought it wise to send me with a strong escort. There are those among your lords who are still at war with us, I think.'

'How are your father and sister?' asked Gallia.

'They are well, and Rasha sends you her greetings.' He looked at me. 'I bring a message from my father, lord king, that there shall be peace between you and him.'

At that moment I could have soared like an eagle. 'This is most excellent news, Prince Malik, you must come back to Dura with me to refresh yourself.'

He suddenly looked solemn. 'And my men?'

'They are welcome too, as are all Agraci in my kingdom.'

So we rode back to the city, three hundred Agraci warriors following us. When we entered the city people fled in terror at the sight of them, women scooping children up in their arms and racing back to their homes. Malik diplomatically ignored their shrieks of alarm and some curses. When we reached the Citadel he looked back at the city.

'I fear it will take a long time before old enmities are forgotten.'

'We have made a start, Malik,' I assured him, 'and that is the important thing.'

He stayed for two days, though most of his men rode back to Palmyra that afternoon. The next day I showed him round the Citadel and then the city. He had a keen mind and an agreeable manner, and did much in his short visit to dispel many old prejudices about the Agraci being bloodthirsty, mindless barbarians. In any case his race meant nothing to Domitus, who was a Roman, or to Godarz, who had spent many years as a slave in Italy and who had only a distant recollection of the Agraci. I noticed that Rsan made himself scarce, but no matter. And of course Gallia admired him greatly. We gave a feast in his honour that night. Malik sat on my right side at the top table. Also in attendance were Domitus, Godarz, Nergal and Praxima. Malik was fascinated by the notion of Gallia's Amazons.

'And are the stories about you true, majesty, that you and your women have fought in battle?'

'Of course,' replied Gallia. She pointed at Praxima sitting next to Nergal. 'Praxima over there is my second-in-command and is a fearsome warrior on the battlefield.'

'And you do not mind your wife being placed in such danger?' he said to me.

'When I first met her we were always in danger, surrounded as we were by our enemies.'

He looked down at his cup. 'You were slaves.'

'It's true,' I said, 'and I have never forgotten that time.'

'Do you burn to avenge the wrongs committed against you, by the Romans, I mean?'

'We killed our fair share of Romans in Italy,' said Gallia casually.

'And if they stray near my kingdom we will kill some more,' I added.

He looked at Domitus. 'And yet a Roman is one of your trusted commanders.'

'Yes,' I said, 'I trust him with my life.'

'It is most curious.'

'They were curious times, Malik. But tell me,' I said, 'why did your father agree to my proposal?'

He considered for a moment. 'Because you gave him back his daughter and because you treated him as an equal. And I think that made a great impression upon him.'

'And so he is,' I said, 'for he is a king.'

'Not all Parthians think like you do, majesty.'

Chapter 6

With peace agreed upon Malik returned to his people and I began to plan for the future. The first task was to equip the legion. To this end, two large brick buildings were purchased on the other side of the Citadel's northern wall. Each building was rectangular in shape and gradually filled with workshops, furnaces, anvils, tools and quenching troughs. I told Godarz to send word far and wide that Dura was looking to hire the best armourers and blacksmiths that money could buy. Soon men from Syria, Judea and a host of Parthian kingdoms were presenting themselves at the Citadel. Godarz organised their hiring and Rsan their pay. When my treasurer complained about the cost I told him that the taxes from the markets would help pay for them. In this I was proved correct, for with the cessation of the Agraci raids commerce began to return to the city. Anyone was free to come to Dura and trade their wares, as long as they paid for the hire of a stall in the market. The latter was held in the city's main square, halfway between the Citadel and the Palmyrene Gate, and was open every day. Domitus' men kept order and Rsan's clerks collected duties from each stall. The treasury began to fill. The generosity of the kings who had attended my wedding also helped to equip my army. As wedding presents Gotarzes sent iron, Farhad and Aschek bronze, while Balas sent me two hundred tons of wood to make shields and javelin shafts. The load was floated down the Tigris and then transported on carts via Hatra to Dura. Finally, Vardan sent me two thousand hides.

But commerce within the kingdom was only one half of my plan to swell the kingdom's revenues. To really fill the treasury, Dura needed the caravans from the East. So I instructed Byrd to ride to Palmyra and then to Judea and south to Egypt and spread the word that I needed bridge builders. A month later he returned with a bald-headed man with black make-up around his eyes who presented a scroll with Greek writing upon it from his king, called a pharaoh. The scroll attested to his skills as a builder of bridges. The man also spoke Greek. I showed him the Euphrates from the palace's terrace. Though the river was wide at this point, in the middle of the waterway, just north of the city, was an island shaped liked a spear blade. The Egyptian pointed at the island. 'Bridge should go from this bank to the island, then from island to the far bank, divinity.'

'The water is deep at this point.'

He shook his head. 'No matter, divinity. I build pontoon bridge, lay planks across a row of boats. Easy to maintain and safe, and when the wood rots you can replace it quickly.'

We obtained material for the bridge from the many riverine woods, called huweijat, that hugged the banks of the Euphrates. Domitus sent his centuries far up and down river armed with axes to cut down the trees. The wood was loaded onto barges and floated downstream or rowed upstream to Dura, where carpenters under the Egyptian's watchful eye constructed the road of planks and the vessels that would support them. The caravans would be able to cross the river immediately north of Dura and then take the road to Palmyra. If they so desired they could camp for the night near the city before continuing their journey.

Domitus' legionaries unloaded the wood and carried it to the workshops. The barges for the pontoon bridge were assembled along the riverbank, a host of carpenters sawing, planing and hammering the beams and planks into place. As the spring gave way to early summer I liked to lend them a hand, unloading tree trunks from barges and hauling them by rope to the benches that the Egyptian had set up under canvas roofs a hundred paces or so from the water. Nergal also liked to pitch in and the two of us, stripped to the waist and covered in sweat, would struggle to lift a thick log from a barge and pull it to where it could be stacked with others to dry out before it was worked on.

'Come on, your majesty,' bellowed Domitus, dressed in helmet and mail shirt, his cane in his hand, 'put your back into it. You too, Lord Nergal. Otherwise the both of you will be pulling extra guard duties for the rest of the week.'

The other legionaries around us grinned to each other as their commander took great delight in pouring scorn on our efforts.

'You see boys, years in the saddle makes you soft.'

We pulled another thick log from the barge and let it fall onto the bank. Unfortunately it fell into the mud and splattered us. We got into a worse mess when we had to manhandle the log out of the grime, which caked our leggings and torsos in mud. We secured a rope around one end and then the two of us hauled it to where the others were stacked. We stood panting, bent over, our hands on our knees.

'Only another few dozen to go, majesty.' Domitus was having great fun.

I looked at the river, where at least a dozen barges were waiting to be unloaded, each one piled high with wood.

The appearance of Gallia and Praxima interrupted our work, the two of them riding to the water's edge. Domitus raised his cane in salute.

'You look disgusting,' said Gallia.

'Have you had a mud fight?' added Praxima.

I walked over to a table holding water jugs and filled a cup, handed it to Nergal and then filled another for myself.

'Honest toil, ladies, good for the soul.'

'You had better come to the Citadel,' said Gallia, 'there is something you should see.'

'Oh, what is it?'

'You should see for yourself,' she replied. 'And clean yourself up first.'

'You too, Nergal,' said Praxima.

We washed ourselves in the river and then we all rode back to the Citadel. The courtyard was filled with horsemen, all on well-groomed mounts fully armed with bows, quivers and swords. Their tunics were a multitude of bright colours and their saddles were trimmed with silver and gold strips. Their harnesses were made of fine red and black leather, and the tails on their horses were all plaited. They numbered a score and they looked magnificent. As I halted Remus I suddenly recognised them. Of course, they had been the captives, the sons of Dura's nobles. I also saw the look of disbelief on their faces as they stared at my appearance. Then they dismounted and knelt before me.

Gallia had halted Epona beside me. 'They have come back to serve you.'

'Get up, get up all of you,' I shouted. 'You are all most welcome.'

Nergal organised their stabling and accommodation in the barracks and that evening we all ate in the banqueting hall. Each one presented himself to Gallia and me. They certainly looked much changed since I had last seen them. They were aged between the late teens and early twenties. I told them that I intended to create a force of cataphracts and they would thus become armoured horsemen. They seemed very pleased with this as they already had their horses. All that was required was the armour.

'That will be difficult, Pacorus.' Godarz was scratching his head, which I noticed was going bald. 'The armouries are already at full capacity making mails shirts, shields and helmets for the legion, and now you want more armour.'

'The sons of the nobles brought money with them, did they not?'

'Oh yes, enough to keep them and their horses for a year, but not enough to purchase suits of armour for themselves and their horses. And another thing, we will have to obtain leather vests for the legionaries to wear between their mail armour and tunics.'

'Why?'

He looked at me with a knowing look in his eye. 'When you decided that you wanted your own legion, you forgot that we are no longer in Italy.'

'Of course I didn't,' I said irritably.

'Oh yes you did. This is Parthia, and in Parthia and the East in general horse archers are more prevalent than mail-clad foot soldiers.'

'So?'

'So, my young king, if the legion goes into battle it will be subjected to heavy arrow fire from horse archers. Mail armour is very good as protection against slashing or blunt weapon attacks, but not as effective as a defence against arrows. Give your legionaries leather vests under their mail and they will have maximum protection.'

I sighed loudly. 'I see.'

He rubbed his head again. 'Indeed. So five thousand leather vests are needed as well. So you see, armour for your cataphract project is quite out of the question, even with Vardan's generous gift. And each cataphract will also need two squires to serve him.'

In fact, Godarz had been too pessimistic when it came to leather. It proved easy to obtain, as the royal estate, my estate that was located south of the city, had vast herds of pigs, goats and sheep. The mail proved more difficult and expensive to produce. Not only did we have to purchase the bronze and steel from which the armour was made, but also hire the armourers and metal workers to create the mail shirts. Watching the latter being made was truly a wondrous experience. Each suit comprised around twelve thousand riveted links alternated with a similar number of punched rings. On average it took forty hours of labour to produce one mail shirt that reached down to mid-thigh. Godarz had two hundred metal workers and a hundred armourers working in shifts night and day.

The one thing that would decide whether I could raise and finance my army would be the willingness of the trade caravans to risk the trip through Agraci territory to Syria and then south to Egypt. The economics made perfect sense, for to undertake such a trip would save at least a month in time. Most caravans came from Ctesiphon and Seleucia and then headed north to Hatra, thence to Antioch and then Syria, before making the long journey south via Damascus and Tyre to Egypt. I sent messages to the trade envoys based in Hatra that if they wanted to do business with Egypt, then Dura should be their destination. This would not be taking revenues from my father's coffers, for the caravans would have to pay duties to Hatra anyway before they reached Dura.

The pontoon bridge was finished now. The Egyptian was most pleased with his project, as was I.

'Bridge very strong, divinity, will last a thousand years.'

'Just thirty of forty will suffice,' I said.

A month passed and I was growing increasingly concerned that my efforts had been in vain, but then one morning, as the sun shone on the blue waters of the Euphrates, a row of camels appeared on the horizon. Though word was sent to me at the palace I had already spotted it from the terrace, and both Gallia and I raced to the stables to fetch our horses. Like excited children we rode to the bridge, followed by Godarz and Rsan, who were also in an agitated state.

The merchant who owned the camels was a small wiry man of Oriental appearance, with a thin moustache that had waxed ends. He wore a black cloth cap on his head and red sandals on his feet that rose into a point at his toes. His steps were short and quick, and when we were introduced to him he held his hands clasped to his chest and smiled a great deal.

'My name is Li Sung and I have a consignment of silk to sell to the Pharaoh of Egypt,' his Parthian was impeccable.

I stood before him with Rsan and Godarz. 'Greetings, Li Sung,' I bowed my head to him, 'you are most welcome.'

As his thirty camels, their attendants and guards crossed over the bridge, I walked beside him.

'I have heard that you have opened a new route to Egypt, one which can save me much time,' he said.

'That is true.'

He nodded his head. 'I have also heard that this route goes through territory that belongs to bandits.'

'I have reached an agreement with the people to whom you allude. You will have safe passage through their territory. You will be able to use their watering holes, and they will offer you protection, subject to the usual customs duties, of course.'

'Of course. I have travelled through your father's kingdom for many years, and because you are his son I have decided to hazard this journey. Many eyes are upon me, King Pacorus.'

He was right in that, for if he reached his destination safely then many caravans would follow his. I knew what he was intimating at. His eyes did not blink as he looked at me. I blinked first.

'Of course this one passage, this passage through Dura, shall be free of all charges, Li Sung,' I said.

He smiled and bowed his head. 'You are a most gracious king. I shall tell the emperor of your generosity.'

I allowed Li Sung to quarter his beasts and their valuable cargo inside the legion's camp that night, and in the morning he moved out two hours after dawn. The previous afternoon I had sent a message to Haytham alerting him of Li Sung's caravan, but I was still nervous as I watched the line of camels fade into the distance.

'They will be quite all right,' Gallia reassured me. 'There is no reason why Haytham won't keep his word.'

'I know, but still.'

I had toyed with the idea sending an armed escort to protect the caravan, but that would be interpreted by Haytham as a sign that I did not trust him. It all came down to trust. Gallia laid a hand on my arm.

'Have faith, Pacorus. Haytham will keep his word.'

And so he did, for after three days Byrd returned with news that Malik had met the caravan with a hundred warriors and was escorting it to Palmyra. Li Sung had paid the agreed tolls and nothing appeared untoward. Upon hearing this news the stress left me like the waters of a burst dam, and I hugged Byrd in gratitude, leaving him somewhat mortified.

'I would like to go back and accompany caravan to Egypt, lord.'

'Of course,' I said, 'I would like to know that it has reached its destination safely.'

Gallia watched him go the next day.

'He has his eye on a woman,' she said.

'Byrd? I doubt it. He's a solitary individual.'

'That's the image he portrays to the world, but underneath he craves love like all of us. Why else would he want to get back to the land of the Agraci?'

'To reassure me that all is well with the caravan. He knows how important it is to me.'

She raised an eyebrow. 'Did not you see the look in his eyes when he was talking about going back?'

I had no time for such trivialities. 'I doubt Byrd even notices women, and anyway what sort of woman would want his life?'

Life went on at Dura. Weapons production in the city continued apace, though we established the leather tanning centre a few miles to the south of the city walls, as the stink in the Citadel would have been unbearable. Leather was something we all took for granted, though I for one was ignorant of how it was actually produced. So one day I rode to the tanneries to see for myself how animal skins were turned into leather. The foul odour of dung and urine greeted my nostrils about half a mile away. The overseer, a huge fat man

90

who panted the whole time, showed me round his empire of filth.

The animal skins were first soaked in water to soften them, and then scoured to remove any flesh and fat. Afterwards they were soaked in urine and then scraped with a knife to remove any hair. The material was then bated in huge vats of animal dung mixed with water, the workers using their bare feet to knead the material. After this is was ready to be made into sandals, boots, vests, armour and waterskins. I watched the process until I was about to retch, then hastily thanked the overseer for his valuable efforts and fled the scene.

Far more enjoyable was observing the increasing number of mail shirts and weapons being manufactured. With production in full swing it was possible to fully equip one cohort a week, not only with mail shirts but also helmets, leather vests, swords and shields. The helmets had a reversed brim at the rear, cheek flaps and a forehead cross-brace as added protection against downward sword strikes made by a rider from the saddle. I had to confess that Godarz and Domitus had thought of every eventuality.

Domitus rotated each of his centuries through guard duty at the Citadel, and at the end of their week of standing at the gates and patrolling the walls the men were issued with their new weapons and armour. Then the century, resplendent in its shiny helmets, shields and mail shirts, would march back to camp. It was a clever ploy, for every man actually looked forward to guard duty at the Citadel. In this way the legion began to shape into a formidable-looking body. And every day the men were drilled relentlessly. 'Train hard, fight easy' was our motto. Learn drills until they become second nature, so when the fighting starts battles become nothing more than bloody drills.

Gallia and I allowed ourselves no indulgences; we didn't even have crowns.

'What use is a crown if your quiver is empty,' she told me, and she was right.

And then, nearly two months after he had left Dura, Li Sung and his camels appeared out of the western horizon. Nergal himself brought me the news and I rode out of the city to meet the wily old fox. Once his men had watered and fed his beasts I invited him to the palace to eat with us. He sat next to me as a guest of honour as he told us all about his journey.

'Palmyra is very green,' he said, picking at the roast lamb that was laid before him, 'a lush green island that stands like an emerald in the desert.'

'And you encountered no trouble?' I said.

He looked at me with narrowed eyes. 'I know that the Parthians and Agraci have been foes, but you and Haytham are wise, I think. He accepted me as an honoured guest.'

'And what will you tell your guild of merchants, Li Sung?'

He nodded and smiled, for this was the crux of the matter. He took a sip of his wine. 'That we have a new route to Egypt.'

I personally led the escort that rode beside Li Sung and his camels across the pontoon bridge and into Hatran territory.

'I hope to see you again, my friend,' I told him.

'I think that will be likely. The Egyptians have a great desire for our products. They pay handsomely for them.'

I did not doubt it. The rolled silk that he had carried in waxed leather tubes on his camels' backs were literally worth a king's ransom. And now his camels carried gold on their backs, gold for him and for his emperor. The last piece of the mosaic was now in place, and over the succeeding weeks an increasing number of caravans crossed the bridge at Dura on their way west. Prince Malik visited us often, occasionally bringing Rasha with him. As Gallia had promised, she had her own room in the palace, next to ours, with its own balcony overlooking the river. Malik was greatly interested in the legion and he would spend hours talking with Domitus in his headquarters in the Citadel, the ex-centurion, crop-haired and muscular, sitting opposite the long-haired desert warrior swathed in black robes. To my surprise, Malik could speak Latin, a consequence of his father having had him tutored in Alexandria as a child, and the two formed an unlikely friendship. Malik was always full of questions. He had an enquiring mind, and I thought would make a good king when his time came.

After a particularly hard training session, during which my horsemen had been learning to work with a cohort of legionaries, we had all retired to the legion's camp to rest the horses and ourselves. I wanted my cavalry to be able to fight closely with the foot, which meant learning to ride between cohorts, reforming behind and between lines of centuries as well as protecting the legion's flanks. The legionaries were at first nervous about having dozens of horsemen thundering around them, kicking up clouds of dust and obscuring their view. But confidence grew with practice. Train hard, fight easy.

'On the open plain your foot soldiers would be swept away by my horseman and camel riders,' said Malik as he removed the saddle from his sweat-lathered grey horse.

Domitus, his face streaked with lines of dirt and sweat, took off his mailed shirt adorned with silver discs and then unstrapped his metal greaves that protected his shins. He pulled an arrow from my quiver and snapped it in two.

'A lone man on the plain is helpless, I agree,' he said to Malik.

Then he grabbed a bundle of arrows from my quiver and handed them to Malik.

'Now break those.' He could not.

Domitus took them from him and replaced them in my quiver. 'You see, strength in numbers. Five thousand men standing shoulder-to-shoulder and in all-round defence cannot be broken by horses or camels. The beasts will not run into a solid wall of shields.'

'The Parthians can stand off and shoot you to pieces,' said Malik.

Domitus handed me a ladle of water from a bucket; I emptied it, refilled it and passed it to Malik.

Domitus wiped his face with a cloth. 'Not if we lock shields in front of us and over our heads. They will run out of arrows before our discipline breaks.'

'There are some who have broken a Roman legion,' said Nergal.

Domitus rested a hand on my shoulder and looked straight at Malik. 'Only a handful, and Pacorus here is one of them. But even he needed a bit of luck.'

'And a few thousand Thracians and Germans,' I added.

'I do not understand.' Malik was confused.

'At a place called Mutina in northern Italy,' I told him, 'my horse fought all day under a hot sun against a mighty host of the enemy. Though we shot and cut down many, at the end there were still Romans standing in their ranks, undefeated.'

'I used up all my arrows that day,' said Nergal, splashing water on his face.

'We won because the horse and foot worked together, Roman and Parthian tactics working in harmony, so to speak,' added Domitus.

'Like you are doing now,' said Malik.

I nodded. 'Like we are doing now.'

'You were the commander of the army at this place called Mutina, lord?'

I shook my head. 'No Malik, I fought under a great general named Spartacus.'

As the weeks passed, the number of the caravans travelling through Dura increased markedly. In addition the city's market thrived, so much so that a new one had to be established to the north of the city, just off the road that the caravans used to travel east and west. The harvest was good, with the local farmers producing an abundance of onions, radishes, beans, lettuce, wheat, barley, millet and sesame seeds. There was also a healthy trade in wool and leather. The tolls from the markets flowed into the treasury, as did the taxes paid by the lords of the kingdom whose sons now served in my army. No Agraci raids meant a peaceful frontier, and a peaceful frontier meant crops could be harvested and cattle, sheep, goats and pigs raised and slaughtered for meat and skins. The canals and irrigation ditches of the whole kingdom were owned by the king, whose responsibility it was to build and maintain them, and so whenever one needed repairing or a new one dug, I sent a century of legionaries to do the work. And if it was a large project I sent a cohort. In return the men were kept in the peak of physical condition and more money poured into the treasury, for everyone who drew water from the king's irrigation system had to pay for the privilege of doing so. The sums were small, but thousands of farmers paid these water duties so the cumulative amount was large.

Rsan was a very happy man, and I realised that he was in fact a conscientious and able administrator who above all was honest. Under him was a small cadre of tax collectors who rode up and down the kingdom on mules, ensuring his system was working smoothly. And the jewels in the crown of the kingdom's finances were the trade caravans that crossed the pontoon bridge over the Euphrates each day.

With royal finances so healthy I could now raise my cataphracts. I now had two hundred cavalrymen – Gallia's Amazons were a law unto themselves so I did not count them – requiring armour for both horse and man.

Domitus and his legionaries wore mail armour, but thick rawhide coats that reached down to their knees protected my cataphracts. Split below the waist at front and back to allow the wearer to sit in the saddle, the rawhide was covered from top to bottom with overlapping iron scales. Each scale had to be riveted onto the rawhide, a process that took a week's work in total. In addition to the scale armour, each rider's arms and legs were encased in overlapping rings of steel that gave protection against sword and axe blows but allowed full freedom of movement. Helmets were also made of steel, with steel cheekguards, long leather neck flaps and facemasks. A ring for holding plumes topped each helmet. My father's cataphracts wore open-faced helmets with a long nasal guard, but I wanted my men to ride into battle with their faces covered, so they would look like steel-clad killers sent from the underworld.

Each rider's horse was also covered in a coat of scale armour to protect his sides and neck, with additional armour on its head.

Once the men and their horses were fully armoured, they spent much time learning to charge holding the kontus – a heavy, thick lance nearly fifteen feet long that was tipped with a long steel point and had a steel butt spike.

Rsan complained that the cataphracts were an expensive drain on the treasury. He was right, for as well as the weapons and armour, each rider required two squires to accompany him on campaign to help him dress in his armour and get on and off his horse, as well as to mend and maintain the armour. In return the squires would learn to become the next generation of Dura's cataphracts.

Rsan shook his head. 'The expense is considerable, majesty.'

He was sitting in his office behind his desk, scrolls neatly stacked on his work surface and tally sheets filling the pigeon holes along one wall. I was opposite him, having spent the afternoon in the city at a company of embroiderers, explaining to the owner the design I wanted for the pennants that would be fixed to each kontus, just below the blade. This was to be a red griffin on a white background, exactly the same design on the standard hanging in the throne room.

Rsan was reading the parchment I had handed him, shaking his head as he did so. 'Pennants, majesty, are extremely expensive. Are they entirely necessary?'

'Of course, Rsan. I cannot ride into battle without the enemy knowing whom they are fighting. Besides, has not the harvest been most excellent this year?'

'Indeed, majesty, but the expenditure of your legion, your cataphracts and her majesty's horse are proving significant.'

'Her majesty's horse?'

We were sitting on our bedroom balcony enjoying the late afternoon sun. 'If you can have your toys, Pacorus, then I can have mine.'

Her hair, framed by the light, had the appearance of molten gold.

'I have decided to increase the number of Amazons, as several women have come forward who want to serve me.'

I was sceptical. 'What women?'

She shot me a disapproving glance. 'You attend to your business and I shall attend to mine. Besides,' her tone changed to one of the seductress, 'you want me to be safe, don't you, to have a bodyguard.'

'You are protected, there's five thousand legionaries out there to keep you safe, and threats from whom?'

She waved her hand in the air. 'It's been decided now. I ordered Rsan to furnish me with three score of bows and quivers, an equal number of mail shirts and helmets. In addition, I require white cloaks for us all.'

'Is that all?'

When the cataphracts and Gallia's increased number of Amazons had been fully armed and armoured, I decided that it would be a good time to visit my parents at Hatra. I asked Godarz to accompany us since I knew he was keen to see his old friend Vistaspa again. I also asked Malik to come.

'Me, majesty?'

We were eating our evening meal on the terrace overlooking the river. I found the banqueting hall too large for when Gallia and I took our meals together, as did she. The palace terrace was much more comfortable and intimate.

'Yes, Malik, you. And I wish you would call me Pacorus. We are, after all, friends, are we not?'

'I fear that the Agraci are not welcome in your father's kingdom.'

I wrapped some roasted lamb in a pancake and dipped it into a yoghurt sauce. 'My father welcomes all my friends Malik, have no fear of that.'

'Who will you leave in charge of the city?' asked Gallia.

'Domitus, I think. Command sits easy on his broad shoulders.'

Malik raised his eyebrows. 'How strange that you would leave a Roman in charge of your city.'

I bit off a chunk of the pancake. 'Of course, why not?'

'Malik, Domitus was a slave, like Pacorus and me,' said Gallia. 'He fought beside us in Italy and we both trust him with our lives.'

'Some say,' I continued, 'that the Parthians and Agraci are mortal enemies. And yet here we are, sitting together and enjoying each other's company.'

He looked thoughtful. 'You are not like other Parthians, majesty, er Pacorus. In fact, you two are unlike any others I have met.'

Gallia looked at him. 'In what way?'

He shrugged. 'I know not, only that you have brought peace when there was war, and trust where there was distrust before. Perhaps what they say about you is right.'

'And what do they say?' I asked him.

'That you are beloved of the gods.'

The Citadel was almost bursting on the morning when we left

for Hatra. Two hundred mounted cataphracts were in the courtyard, their faces hidden behind steel masks so that only their eyes could be seen, but only up close. From a distance only two black holes stared out. Gallia's Amazons, now numbering fifty, were formed up in a block on their left, dressed in brown boots, baggy tan leggings, mail shirts and helmets with closed cheekguards. Praxima sat at their head. Behind the cataphracts were four hundred squires, each holding the reins of a camel loaded with food, tools, spare quivers, a tent and the weapons of his master.

We rode down into the city and through the Palmyrene Gate, then swung north to take us over the pontoon bridge and into my father's kingdom. I rode in my Roman helmet, cuirass and spatha at my hip. I left my cataphract armour behind as I was not riding to war. Gallia rode on my right side and Godarz on my left, with Nergal and Praxima behind us and a long column of horses and camels behind them. A short while after we had crossed the bridge we were met by a detachment of my father's army – a dozen horse archers dressed in white tunics and red leggings. Their commander paid his respects and then left us, riding back to his fort.

We halted several miles from Dura to allow the cataphracts to take off their heavy scale armour and that of their horses, as it would have been torture for the riders to travel the whole day under a merciless sun in full armour. We then road north across country avoiding the roads, which were full of traffic – caravans, merchants and people on foot – all kicking up a choking dust that found its way into the eyes and lungs. The heavy traffic was a good sign as it indicated trade was thriving in Hatra.

It took us seven days to reach Hatra, my father and Vistaspa linking up with us five miles from the city with an escort of cataphracts. Vistaspa said little aside from a curt greeting to me and Gallia, though I detected a look of approval as he observed my own men behind us, who were now again dressed in their full war gear. My father, wearing his crown on his helmet, rode at the head of his men, Hatra's banner of the white horse's head fluttering in the breeze behind him. He greeted us warmly.

'It is good to see you both, your mother has missed you.' He looked at Malik, who laid a hand on his heart and bowed his head. My father shot a glance at me but said nothing, but he must have known that the black-robed warrior was an Agraci.

Hatra was as big, bustling and loud as I remembered it, the streets packed with people going about their business. We moved slowly through the throng, some of Kogan's guards clearing a passage but not with violence. Many cheered my father and his men, and then myself and Gallia even more as they recognised us. Some reached over to touch my leg or stroke Remus. I also noticed that more than one frowned and shied away when they caught sight of Malik, his cheeks adorned with black tattoos and his black robes indicating his Agraci heritage. To his credit he kept looking ahead, though riding through a sea of potential enemies must have been uncomfortable for him. When we got to the palace my mother and sisters were waiting at the foot of the steps, as were Kogan, Assur, Gafarn and Diana. Our reunion was long and tearful; Gallia hugged Diana for an age and they linked arms when my father insisted that everyone must go inside to their rooms. Nergal led my horsemen and the Amazons to the royal stables as we filed into the vastness that was Hatra's palace.

As we strolled though the great stone columns Gafarn put an arm around my shoulder. 'It's good to see you, brother. I see that you have widened the circle of your friends.'

Malik was trailing behind me. 'Prince Malik, this is my brother, Gafarn.'

Malik bowed his head to Gafarn. 'An honour, lord.'

Gafarn burst into laughter, which startled my parents and sisters and caused Assur to frown deeply. 'I'm not lord, though some call me that. I am a Bedouin, taken captive as an infant and raised a slave in this palace.'

My mother was most upset. 'Gafarn, you should not say such things.'

Gafarn shrugged. 'Why not? It is true. I am not ashamed of who I am.'

'You are a Bedouin?' Malik was most surprised.

'Yes, and my wife, Diana, once a Roman kitchen slave, is now a princess of Hatra. So you see, Prince Malik of the Agraci, nothing is ever as it appears to be.'

Assur made his excuses and left, as did Kogan and Addu, clearly made uncomfortable by Malik's presence, but my father had him shown to a luxurious room in the royal apartments and that evening at the banquet held to celebrate the return of myself and Gallia to Hatra, he was placed on the top table. I sat next to my father with Gallia beside my mother as the hall echoed with the chattering of three hundred of the city's lords and their wives invited to attend. A small army of servants ferried food and wine from the kitchens to the tables.

'I like your heavy cavalry, Pacorus.'

'Thank you, father.'

'Horsemen armed and armoured thus are expensive.'

'Very.'

'Dura's finances can stand such an indulgence?'

'Now we have opened up the trade route to Egypt, they can.'

'I heard about your trip into the desert to meet with the Agraci,' he said, looking at Malik.

I nodded at Malik sitting next to Nergal and Praxima. 'That is King Haytham's son, father, a man whom I esteem a friend.'

'I know who he is.'

I looked at my father. 'You do not approve?'

He smiled and laid a hand on my shoulder. 'You have brought peace and prosperity where there was war and financial ruin. How could I disapprove? There are some,' he tilted his head towards Assur, 'who disapprove of you making peace with the Agraci.'

'And you?'

'I say that kings have to be above all practical. You have the reputation of being a great warlord, and now you are earning yourself a reputation as a wise king. I am proud of you. How is Gallia?'

I looked at my love, deep in conversation with my mother. 'Happy. She likes Dura.'

My father suddenly looked serious. 'I heard that you took her into the desert when you visited the Agraci. That could have been dangerous.'

'I told her that, but she insisted on accompanying me.'

'And you let her?'

I grinned. 'I could have forced her to stay in Dura, but I only have five thousand legionaries and two hundred cavalry. Too few for such a task, I fear.'

My father roared with laughter.

It was good to be back at Hatra, albeit for a short while, and to see my parents again. Those were the happy times, and even Vistaspa seemed to have mellowed somewhat, though perhaps it was because his friend Godarz was back with him. Gallia and Diana spent much time together with the young Spartacus, now grown in size and taking his first steps. Gafarn beat me with depressing ease in the archery competitions we held in the gardens and on the training fields and Addu was most impressed when I told him about Rsan and the treasury at Dura. Those were special days. It was not paradise, for people still died of sickness and disease, thieves still had their hands cut off and murderers were still executed, but peace and contentment reigned over Hatra and Dura.

But peace never lasts, and two days before we were due to head

99

back to Dura, a courier arrived at my father's palace. It was late afternoon and we were all relaxing in the shade of my mother's summerhouse when the courier presented my father with a sealed scroll.

'Where are you from?' said my father, breaking the seal.

'Ctesiphon, majesty.'

My father read the words and frowned.

'What is it, Varaz?' asked my mother.

My father waved away the courier and breathed a deep sigh. 'Sinatruces is dead.'

I had to confess that this news came as no great shock to me, for the King of Kings had been over eighty years old and most people died well before that great number. But had I known what this one event would lead to I would have shown more concern, for the passing of one old man was to be the catalyst for tumultuous events that threatened to destroy the empire and would again bring me face to face with my old enemies – the Romans.

Chapter 7

My father convened his council the day after we had received the news of Sinatruces' death, and as I was in the city he asked me to attend as well, along with Godarz. Gallia was not invited, much to her chagrin. As usual, the council met in a small room next to the throne room. Around the table sat my father, Kogan, Vistaspa, Assur, Addu, Godarz and myself. My father opened proceedings.

'So, the day has finally come when we have to turn our thoughts to a new King of Kings. Lord Assur, I believe that your scribes have been researching the archives concerning the correct protocol in this matter.'

'Yes, majesty,' his voice was deep and serious. 'There are very few who remember the days before Sinatruces since he has ruled for over fifty years. But now the kings of the empire must gather in Esfahan to elect another of their number to rule over them.'

Isfahan was a city located in the heart of the empire, a place of water and greenery in the middle of a searing desert wasteland.

'Who will have your vote, sire?' asked Vistaspa, 'assuming that you do not desire it yourself.'

'Indeed I do not,' replied my father. 'Sinatruces had respect because he was old and everyone had got used to him sitting in Ctesiphon. I think Phraates, his son, would make a logical choice. If nothing else, his taking the office would provide continuity and hopefully a peaceful transition of power.'

Assur said nothing, Vistaspa the same, though my father's general began to drum his fingers on the table.

'If you have something to say, Vistaspa, then out with it,' said my father.

'The empire will need a strong hand, lord, and there are some who say that Phraates lacks strength.'

'He is a good man,' replied my father.

'Good men do not necessarily make good kings. The empire would be better in your hands.'

My father shook his head. 'I do not desire such a thing, and that is my final word on the matter.'

But Vistaspa would not give up. 'You would have the support of Babylon, Gordyene, Atropaiene, Media and Elymais if you put yourself forward.' He looked at me with his cold black eyes. 'And Dura, I assume.'

'Of course,' I replied.

'No!' barked my father. 'One crown is sufficient. The matter is at an end.'

After the meeting Vistaspa sought me out, which was unusual as he rarely had time for my company. It was hard to earn the respect of Vistaspa, who was totally loyal to my father but seemed to eye everyone else with a cool detachment at best, though mostly with open disdain. Today he was most talkative.

'Is your legion ready?'

'Almost.'

'Good, and how many cavalry do you have?'

'My cataphracts you have already seen. In times of emergency they will be reinforced by the horsemen raised by the lords of my kingdom.'

'Farmers on horseback,' he sniffed.

'These farmers can fight; they have been battling the Agraci ever since they crossed the Euphrates to work the land.'

We were walking down the corridor that led towards the palace's royal apartments. I stopped and turned to face him.

'Is there a point to this, Lord Vistaspa?'

He was momentarily nonplussed, and then regained his icy demeanour. 'There are clouds gathering beyond the empire's frontiers, and perhaps within the empire itself. We will need all the bows and spears we can muster, I fear.'

I confess that I was slightly alarmed to hear Vistaspa, a man who had less compassion than a cobra, use the word 'fear'.

'The Romans are gathering their forces in the northeast, to threaten Armenia, while their garrison swells in Cappadocia like the belly of a pregnant camel.'

'I've beaten Romans before,' I remarked casually.

'Then be prepared to fight them again, for my spies have told me that our friend Darius intends to defect to Rome.'

I clenched my fists. Darius was the King of Zeugma, a kingdom on Hatra's northwest border. The Romans had, several years ago, sent a legion to the city of Zeugma, which had strayed into Hatran territory. My father had intercepted and destroyed it, and during the battle I had captured the legion's eagle. That day was the beginning of my long association with the Romans. It was an open secret that the fat, idle Darius wanted to become a client king of Rome; only the fear of Parthian retribution, especially Hatra's large standing army, prevented him from doing so.

'Darius might use the uncertainty around Sinatruces' passing to swap sides.'

'My father can have troops in possession of Zeugma faster than the Romans can,' I said.

'Not if his attention is focused elsewhere.'

I was becoming confused. He took my arm. 'Hatra is rich. There are kings within the empire who would like nothing more than to see us humiliated and reduced in strength. With your father as King of Kings the empire is safe, but Phraates....'

His voice trailed away and an ominous silence was left.

'I'm sure the meeting at Esfahan will resolve all uncertainties,' I said without conviction.

He looked away. 'Perhaps you are right. By the way, your cataphracts are a credit to you. Well done. Perhaps I may visit Dura some time to see how your legion is shaping up.'

It was a most strange conversation and somewhat unnerved me, but I shrugged it off as a case of Vistaspa being unduly alarmist.

'I don't like him,' remarked Gallia of Vistaspa on the second day of our journey back to Dura.

We had enjoyed our time in Hatra immensely and were now making our way leisurely back to our home. Gallia had invited my parents, my sisters, Gafarn and Diana to Dura, and if they all came at once we would run out of rooms to put them in, but they all accepted her invitation so that was that. Her hospitality did not extend to Vistaspa or Assur.

'He reminds me of my father, always scheming.'

'He's a good soldier, but I agree his character is a little foreboding.'

'That's putting it mildly.'

'He thinks the death of Sinatruces presages war.'

'And what do you think?'

'I know not what the future holds.'

But in truth conflict seemed far away as we rode back to Dura, through Hatran territory that was well-protected and thriving with commerce. I comforted myself with the fact that Hatra had, unusually among the empire, a large standing army in addition to the tens of thousands of horse archers my father could summon in times of conflict. Who would be so foolish to make war upon it?

When we arrived back at Dura, a letter similar to the one delivered to my father was awaiting me. All the kings were being informed of the death of Sinatruces. It was signed by his son, Phraates, whom I assumed would be elected to replace his father, notwithstanding Vistaspa's forebodings. A week later another courier arrived, this time from the elders of Esfahan inviting me to attend the Council of Kings that would elect a new King of Kings in two months' time.

Esfahan was part of no kingdom but was situated in the dead centre of the empire, and was recognised by all the kings as a neutral city, owing allegiance to no one kingdom or faction. In the time of civil strife before Sinatruces, when war had riven the empire, Esfahan and its elders had been a place where disputes between rival factions could be settled without recourse to war. That was the theory at least. The long reign of Sinatruces had made Esfahan's purpose largely irrelevant, as Sinatruces had resolved the problem of rivals by defeating and then executing them, though in the last twenty years of his reign he had used his son to resolve disputes. Phraates was of an amicable disposition and had the tongue of a diplomat. His words helped to soothe the tempers of proud kings, and in any case the longevity of Sinatruces' reign had earned the respect of even the most hot-headed rulers, though some liked to think that because of his great age the King of Kings' wits had gone. I had met him more than a year before his death, and his mind and cunning were as sharp as any man's.

'Each king is allowed to take a retinue of thirty, equivalent to the number of arrows held in a quiver, no more,' I said.

'I will be one of them,' announced Gallia, 'and Praxima will also want to go.'

'Do I have a say in the matter?'

'Of course,' she wrapped her arms around me. 'You do want to take me, don't you?'

So that was that. I also took Nergal, Domitus and twenty-five Companions. It was the first time I had seen Domitus on a horse and he looked like a fish out of water. I would have taken Godarz instead but he expressed no interest in going, especially after travelling to Hatra. In any case, he was happy being governor and had little wish to see the rituals of the empire.

Before we left Dura I had sent a courier to Hatra to arrange a rendezvous with my father along the way. We met up with him ten miles west of the Tigris and about fifty miles from Ctesiphon. Accompanying him, and much to Gallia's delight, was Balas of Gordyene, a big man on a big horse with an escort of over a score of horse archers dressed in blue tunics with steel helmets on their heads. Like me they were armed with swords, bows and full quivers.

Balas jumped down from his horse and enveloped Gallia in his bear-like arms.

'I'm glad he,' jerking his head at me, 'decided to bring you along. I need a pretty woman to liven up the journey.'

'I told him I was coming,' said Gallia, 'he had no choice.'

Balas roared with laughter. 'I bet you did.'

That night we camped on the other side of the Tigris in the territory of King Vardan of Babylon. We pitched the tents in a large circle and then set a raging fire in the middle, over which we roasted pig and lamb.

'Whom will you propose at the meeting, Varaz?' asked Balas, sitting on the ground using his saddle as a backrest.

'Phraates,' replied my father.

Balas raised an eyebrow.

'And you, lord?' I asked.

'Varaz of Hatra, of course,' replied Balas. His warriors and those of my father applauded this suggestion.

My father held up his hands. 'I have made it clear that I will not put myself forward.'

'More fool you, Varaz,' said Balas. 'Phraates makes a good errand boy and that's about it. Vardan, Farhad and Aschek would support you. I know, I've asked them.'

'The matter is closed, Balas,' said my father irritably, 'now stop making trouble.'

Balas threw the leg of pork he had been gnawing into the fire. 'So be it, but there will be trouble anyway, you mark my words.'

'It is a pity,' remarked Gallia, 'that there cannot be a queen of queens to rule over you all.'

'Ha,' barked Balas, 'you hear that, Varaz? If she's allowed in the council meeting I'll warrant we'll be bowing down to Queen Gallia at the end.'

'Women are not allowed to vote, daughter,' said my father.

'What if some of the kings do not abide by the decision of the council?' she asked.

'A good question,' said Balas, looking at my father. 'Then, my dear, whoever is King of Kings must enforce his will and show to everyone in the empire that his sword is the sharpest, and Phraates is not the man to do that.'

'Enough, Balas,' my father was growing irritated. 'I know what you are trying to do and it will not work.'

Balas tried a different approach. 'What say you, Pacorus? Who will you vote for?'

'My father first, but if he declines to be put forward, then Phraates.'

Balas nodded his head in resignation. 'What about you, Roman, what is your view on this matter?'

Thus far Domitus had been sitting in silence, eating his food and drinking water from a cup. Now he looked directly at Balas. 'I know nothing of the workings of the Parthian Empire, but I do know that men only respect strength. They may say that they obey the law, but they only do so if the person who enforces it is

105

stronger than they. If this Phraates is strong then you have no fear.'

Balas looked smugly at my father. 'And if he is weak?'

Domitus stared into the fire. 'Then he will be like a lamb among lions.'

My father would hear no more on the matter and so we talked of other things over the next ten days as we rode to Esfahan. Domitus gradually got used to riding on horseback, but declared that he would always prefer to fight on his feet. He and Balas got on well; they were both forthright in their opinions, though Balas was rowdier. Gordyene shared a border with Armenia and we all knew that Rome threatened the latter. And if Armenia fell then Gordyene would be in danger.

'So, Domitus, do you think Rome will attack Parthia?'

Sweat was pouring down Domitus' face even though he was wearing a wide-brimmed hat, for we were travelling across the desert that led to Esfahan, a barren, sun-bleached wasteland that had one east–west road.

'Hard to tell, sir. I was just a lowly centurion and know nothing about what is decided in Rome. But there is a garrison in Syria and eventually they will push east, to the Euphrates at least.'

'You hear that, Pacorus,' said Balas to me, 'Dura is on the wrong side of the river.'

'It will take a large army to batter down Dura's walls,' I replied.

Domitus looked at me. 'Pacorus, that is King Pacorus, is clever. He makes Dura strong so it will not fall easily, and he has the support of his lords who can come to his aid. And across the river is his father's army. Rome will think twice before starting a war with Dura.'

'And there is your legion,' observed Balas.

'Yes, sir, there is my legion. And...' His voice trailed off.

'And?' asked Balas.

'I know that your people do not like them, but there are also the Agraci.'

'The Agraci?' Balas was shocked. 'They will stick a knife in your back when you're not looking.'

'They are our friends,' said Gallia sternly.

'It's true, lord,' I said. 'Prince Malik, the son of the Agraci king, comes often to Dura and has travelled with me to Hatra.'

Balas shook his head. 'We live in strange times.'

My father had said nothing during this intercourse, adding only. 'We certainly do.'

Esfahan was a beautiful city, located directly south of the Zagros Mountains and built on both sides of the River Zayandey.

Surrounded by a high circuit wall of yellow sandstone, it had squares towers at regular intervals along its whole perimeter. Access was via four gates located at the four points of the compass, all of which led to the city's massive central square, a space of grass that was normally filled with traders every day but which for the Council of Kings had been cleared. In place of the market stalls and animal pens was a large circular tent at least three times the height of a man.

Esfahan was a sprawling city with very few tall buildings, its streets wide and airy. The northerly breeze that came from the mountains was refreshing and had the added advantage of dispelling the stench of humans and animals that infested even the grandest of cities. An armed escort from the garrison – spearmen dressed in bright yellow tunics, baggy red leggings and open-faced helmets, met us at the western gates. They carried wicker shields, long daggers in sheaths on their belts and wore brown leather shoes that rose to a point at the toes. Their long hair was plaited like Gallia's when she rode to war, though unlike her they had yellow ribbons in their plaits. Their beards were also plaited and each man wore two gold earrings. They certainly looked pretty – even their oval-shaped spear blades were polished bright, glinting when they caught the sun's rays. Beside them we must have looked a sorry sight, our clothes and faces covered in dust and our horses weary – in need of a good groom.

The guards' commander, a tall man in his thirties with gold rings on his fingers, saluted. 'Majesties, welcome to Esfahan. If you would care to follow me I will show you to your quarters.'

Esfahan was bustling, its streets filled with traders, customers, mystics, holy men, beggars and soldiers of the garrison. There was no king or ruler of Esfahan; rather, a council of elders who were drawn from the most influential members of the aristocracy. The council numbered eighteen to mirror the number of kings in the empire – though technically there were now nineteen upon my accession to Dura's throne. In the old days each king had sent his own man to sit on the council, but after time this had lapsed and the council was drawn from those who lived in the city itself. It jealousy guarded its reputation as a place that favoured no one faction, and its remote location, thick walls and large garrison acted as deterrents should anyone wish to attack it. Not that anyone did, for its great distance from any other city of significance meant that it was largely forgotten, though it formed an important part of the Silk Road. As we had travelled east to the city I had observed in wonder the mass of traffic on the road – the living lifeblood of

107

the empire.

But now there was much excitement in the city, not least because the Council of Kings was such an unusual event on account of the last one having taken place over fifty years before. My party was met at the gates of a villa by its steward, a dark-skinned man in his fifties who had a long black beard and who was dressed in an immaculate white robe with cuffs edged in silver. He had long fingers and his nails were painted red, which earned him a frown from Domitus.

'Greetings, King Pacorus.'

Each of the kings was shown to his own villa – large two-story buildings surrounded by walls and guarded by a detachment of the garrison. Inside the compounds were stables, luxurious private apartments overlooking a marbled courtyard complete with central fountains, the whole residence surrounded by well-tended gardens. A small army of gardeners, kitchen hands, grooms and house slaves kept each villa spotless and the gardens immaculate. Our horses were taken from us to the stables where they were unsaddled, groomed, fed and watered. We were shown to our rooms on the second floor of the villa, each one adorned with enamelled tile floors, doors inlaid with gold leaf and ivory, plaster walls painted with mythical beasts and a large bed over which hung a canopy of the finest white linen. Twin cedar doors led on to a spacious balcony framed by two marble columns, with another pair of columns directly below. The corridors and entrance hall of the villa were adorned with yellow and blue tapestries.

After we had washed and changed into new clothes, an invitation arrived from the residence of my father for Gallia and me to dine with him. It was early evening before we arrived at his residence. Like ours it was a well-appointed villa surrounded by a high brick wall. Guards paced up and down outside the gates and around the wall; clearly the city elders were taking no chances when it came to the security of their royal guests. We were not the first to arrive, for in the large dining hall were already seated Farhad, his son Atrax, Aschek, Vardan, his daughter Axsen and Gotarzes. They all rose when we entered, and Gallia immediately went to Axsen and embraced her as we took our places at the table. Moments later Balas arrived, complaining that he was too old to be dragged from his couch after a hard day's ride.

My father ate little, and only a short while after we had started the meal he began to speak to us.

'I have asked you all here tonight because the issue of the election needs to be settled.'

Balas put down his silver cup. 'You mean you want to make sure that we all vote for Phraates?'

'Yes,' snapped my father.

'He is a good man,' said Vardan, 'but does he have the steel to enforce his will?'

'With our bows and swords behind him he will have enough strength to secure his rule,' retorted my father.

Aschek screwed up his lips. 'It would be better to have an overlord who has the respect of all, and if not all then at least the majority.'

My father was already showing signs of exasperation. 'My friend, who among the kings has that?'

'Varaz of Hatra,' offered Balas casually.

My father held his head in his hands, and then looked up. He suddenly looked old. I had never thought of my father as old before. 'I support Phraates because he offers continuity and stability. He is known to all the kings, and has been his late father's voice in the empire for many years. Parthia must have unity for the troubles that are to come.'

'What troubles?' asked Gotarzes

'The Romans,' I said.

'Yes,' reiterated my father. 'Darius has, as expected, defected to Rome. Word reached me of this but two hours ago. The Romans menace our frontiers, and for that reason alone we must have stability within the empire.'

'We all knew the old admirer of young boys would do so, it is of no consequence,' said Balas.

'The Romans will have heard of the death of Sinatruces,' I said. 'They will try to exploit any opportunity to increase their domains at our expense.'

Balas shrugged. 'If you want Phraates so badly then I will vote with you, Varaz. But only because there is not a more suitable candidate.'

My father smiled, then looked at the other kings. 'And you, my friends?'

They all fell into line, as did I of course. In the few times I had seen Phraates he had always struck me as a conscientious, earnest individual who took his responsibilities very seriously. I was sure that the other kings would feel the same way.

Before we attended the council there was time to visit one of the holiest places in the Parthian Empire, the resting place of Arsaces, the first Parthian king and the founder of the Arsacid dynasty. The tomb itself was a granite sarcophagus set in the middle of a high-domed mausoleum near the centre of the city, a mile to the north of the great square. The mausoleum was surrounded by a high wall and had a small square in front of its main entrance, which was flanked by two white stone lions. The flagstones of the square were also brilliant white, and we had to shield our eyes from the glare as we walked across them to enter the tomb. There were five of us that day – myself, Gallia, Nergal, Praxima and Domitus, who had taken a keen interest in the history of his adopted homeland. We wore baggy leggings and loose-fitting tunics, though Domitus wore his customary white tunic and mail armour and had his helmet on his head. With its white plume he looked like a king and we his retinue. We all wore swords and daggers at our hips. The entrance was flanked by spearmen, with more guards posted around the grey sarcophagus. The interior of the building was quiet and cool, with a white marble floor and white marble columns around the sides. Domitus took off his helmet and we all walked over to the tomb, the sides of which were adorned with carvings of archers on horseback fighting and hunting. It was a most peaceful place.

'Arsaces was the first Parthian king,' I said in hushed tones. 'His blood flows through my veins, so I like to think.'

'Do all Parthians come here to pay homage, lord?' asked Praxima.

I shook my head. 'Unfortunately, most Parthians are too busy facing life's hardships to make the trip here. But all have heard of him and I am glad that you, my friends, are here with me.' I reached over to hold Gallia's hand.

'A most touching scene.'

There are very few men who I dislike when I first see them, for I like to think of myself as a fair-minded individual. But with Mithridates it was different. I disliked him on sight. No, that is incorrect; he invoked my animosity when I heard his voice, before I had even clapped eyes on him.

I turned to see a man about my age with long, shoulder-length black hair that was as straight as an arrow. He was tall and slim, though certainly not gaunt, his face long with wide cheekbones. His neatly trimmed beard came to a point just beneath his chin accentuating the narrowness of his visage, so that he resembled a snake. As I was to discover, it was a most appropriate analogy. He was dressed in a rich black tunic with silver edging around the neck and cuffs, black leggings and black boots studded with silver. He wore a black leather belt, from which hung a sword in an expensive scabbard, also adorned with silver leaf.

His soulless black eyes glinted with mocking arrogance as he bowed his head to me. 'The whole empire has heard of King Pacorus. I salute you. How are you finding my kingdom?'

'Your kingdom?'

'Of course, did I not introduce myself? How rude of me. I am Prince Mithridates, former ruler of Dura.'

He had five companions with him, all men about his age and all wearing expensive clothes and haughty expressions, save one at the end who seemed embarrassed by it all.

'Long have I wanted to meet the hero of children's stories and the friend of slaves.' His voice was condescending and I felt an anger rise in me.

'So, you are Prince Mithridates,' I said.

He smiled, revealing a row of perfect white teeth, the serpent's fangs. 'Indeed, majesty.'

'It would have been good manners to have handed over your kingdom to me when I arrived at Dura, do you not think?'

His smiled disappeared, to be replaced by a mask of contempt. 'My grandfather was old and robbed of his senses when he saw fit to give you my throne.'

His effrontery was breathtaking. 'And you earned the throne through merit, did you?'

'I certainly did not win it by consorting with slaves and other low-borns.'

'Have a care, prince,' I snarled, 'your words may lead you into trouble.'

He ignored my veiled threat and leered at Gallia.

'So this is your queen. For once the street talk and brothel gossip do not lie. A rare beauty indeed. Such a waste to live in the scorpion-infested frontier outpost of Dura, though. A queen deserves a proper palace and kingdom befitting her great beauty.'

Gallia smiled and glided towards him, stopping inches from him. His eyes were alight with lust.

'And would you give me such a palace, lord prince?' she purred.

His eyes darted from hers to her long blonde hair, to her breasts and then back again to her blue eyes.

'I would make you a queen among queens.'

She moved her face slowly towards his, her full lips parting ever so slightly as if to kiss him. Time seemed to slow as we all stared, transfixed, by the scene. Then her right hand shot forward into his groin as she grabbed his genitals and held them in an iron grip. Pain contorted his face. Praxima squealed and burst into laughter while Nergal and the companions of Mithridates looked stunned.

Gallia's face was a mask of cold contempt as she held the

prince's most precious possessions firmly in place. 'I have heard lots about you, little boy, and none of it is good. You are not fit to be called a prince, let alone a king, you who makes war upon small children. Did you think that I would be interested in such a poor specimen of a man?'

Now his friends had recovered from their shock and moved menacingly towards Gallia, hands on their sword hilts, except for the embarrassed one, but like lightning Domitus whipped out his gladius and had the point at the throat of the foremost man, a youth with a large nose and gold bracelets around his wrist. He looked alarmed as this cropped-haired barbarian pressed the point of his Roman sword into his neck.

Gallia released Mithridates and he slumped to the floor in great pain. I stepped in front of my wife and folded my arms in front of me.

'You defile this holy place with your presence, Mithridates. Leave us and go play with your toys.'

Wincing, he staggered to his feet. I thought he was going to skulk away, but at that time I did not know his capacity for hate. He glowered at me, drew himself up to his full height and then drew his sword. I likewise drew mine, but before either of us had a chance to cross blades the embarrassed companion of Mithridates with the kindly face was between us. He grabbed Mithridates by the shoulders and pushed him away.

'You cannot fight here, in this revered place.'

'Get out of my way, brother,' hissed Mithridates.

So he was Mithridates' brother. They were utterly different in looks and manner.

As Mithridates sulked but made no attempt to attack me, his brother turned to face me.

'Lord king, please forgive my brother's intemperance. I would beg that you do not fight him for I have heard of your prowess in battle, and if you kill him then my honour will demand that I must avenge his death, and I would much rather get to know you as a friend rather than as an enemy.'

He then went down on one knee before me and bowed his head.

'Get up,' I said, 'and take your brother and his pets away.'

Mithridates and his companions stood in a group behind the one with a sword at his throat. Their eyes still burned with hatred towards me, though none of them made any threatening moves.

'Release him Domitus,' I ordered. The commander of my legion sheathed his gladius and stared at the man with the gold bracelets, daring him to draw his sword. He did not.

112

Mithridates' brother bowed his head at Gallia. 'Your beauty is truly stunning, majesty. Please accept my apologies for any offence my family has given you.'

'I accept your apology,' replied Gallia, 'yet I do not know your name.'

He bowed his head again. 'Princes Orodes, majesty.'

'Well, prince,' I said, 'we are pleased to make your acquaintance.'

Behind him Mithridates and his other companions were striding from the mausoleum, leaving his brother alone with us. Around us, nervous-looking guards had gathered into a group and approached, led by a young officer with a wispy moustache.

'Majesty, forgive me, but it is not permitted to draw weapons inside this place.'

'Of course, officer, please accept my apologies. We shall be leaving now.'

His face wore the expression of a man who had been reprieved on the gallows.

'Thank you, majesty.' He waved his men away, who returned to their stations around the room. I linked arms with Gallia.

'Walk with us, Orodes.'

As we ambled from the dimly lit mausoleum into the bright sunshine I probed Orodes about his brother.

'Were you with your brother at Dura?'

'No, lord. Being the younger brother I stayed at Susa with my father.'

Susa was the capital city of the kingdom of Susiana, which was the domain of King Phraates. The palace at Ctesiphon is the capital of the empire, reserved as the grand residence of the King of Kings, but Phraates was the King of Susiana, though these past years he had spent most of his time at Ctesiphon running errands for his father, Sinatruces.

'I was sorry to hear about the death of your grandfather,' remarked Gallia.

'Thank you, majesty,' said Orodes, 'he lived long and in peace, what more can one ask for?'

A wise answer, I thought. 'Indeed,' I remarked. 'Let us hope that the reign of the next King of Kings is likewise blessed.'

'I hope so, lord.'

'The council sits tomorrow, so we shall soon know.'

Orodes had an agreeable nature, which made it hard to believe that he was the brother of Mithridates. As he said farewell to us and made his way back to the villa of his father, an uncomfortable thought crossed my mind.

It was Domitus who articulated my thoughts.

'So that Mithridates was the little toad who ruled Dura before you.'

'Indeed.'

Domitus pulled out a cloth from his tunic and wiped his neck, for the day was hot and there was no wind. 'When I served Rome I saw a lot of his type during my days as a centurion. They were mostly tribunes, the sons and grandsons of important people, and all spoilt, arrogant little bastards, begging your pardon ladies. We usually sorted them out, though.'

'How did you do that, Domitus?' asked Gallia.

'Well, if we were on the frontier then they would be ordered to lead punitive raids against bandits. They always relished the chance of slaughtering a few locals and earning some glory, but they invariably went too deep into hostile territory and came back with their tails between their legs, that or a few arrows in their backs.'

'And what if you were not on the frontier?'

Domitus shrugged. 'They they would spend time drinking, gambling or whoring, anything to keep them out of camp.'

'That Mithridates, he's the eldest son of Phraates?'

'Yes,' I said.

Domitus shook his head. 'So if Phraates is elected head king, the toad becomes king in his place?'

'I'm afraid so,' I answered.

Domitus turned to Gallia. 'You should have cut his balls off, lady, for that one's going to cause a lot of trouble.'

The day of the council was hot and still. Again there was no wind, and though the tent was large and all the side flaps were open, inside the heat was oppressive. Slaves brought great jugs of cool water for us to drink but it was still uncomfortable, and it was only early morning. There were many fine buildings in Esfahan, but tradition dictated that the Council of Kings be held in a tent, just as the first one had many years ago.

'Tradition? My aching back says tradition can go hang.' Balas was already in a bad mood, and though everyone was seated in high-backed wicker chairs with cushions, he took a dim view of the assembly. All the kings were arranged in a wide circle, each monarch in front with his followers behind. I was seated between Balas and my father, with Aschek, Vardan, Farhad, Gotarzes and Chosroes to his left. It was the first time that I had clapped my eyes on Chosroes, the King of Mesene, a land to the south of Babylon.

He was a strange-looking individual with a bald head and a long, thin face that was dominated by a huge long nose. His eyes, cold, calculating and narrow, were almost obscured by thick black eyebrows. Dressed in a red flowing gown adorned with strips of gold, my instincts told me that he was untrustworthy, but he was cordial enough if a little curt. Phraates, his hair greyer now and his expression serious, sat on Balas' right side. He was clearly nervous as he continually looked to his right and left and smiled at anyone who caught his eye. Immediately behind him sat Mithridates, looking daggers at me, and Orodes, who nodded his head in greeting. I smiled and nodded back, which earned him a look of fury from his brother.

Balas leaned towards me and then looked at the kings opposite. 'First time I've seen most of them. Ugly looking lot, aren't they?'

He was referring to the kings of the eastern half of the empire, who were mostly descended from oriental races, with their narrow eyes and flat faces.

'I know him, though.' Balas was pointing at a large man opposite with Asiatic features – narrow eyes, a long nose like a hawk's beak, skin like an old leather pouch and a long white moustache and a white pointed beard. He wore leather armour and a leather pointed cap on his head. His followers behind him were similarly attired. They looked like fierce nomads.

'Khosrou, King of Margiana. You don't want to mess with him. He's as tough as he looks.'

Margiana was located in the northeast corner of the empire and had the unenviable task of holding at bay the vast horses of nomads that occupied the endless great northern steppes.

A blast of trumpets got everyone's attention as a procession of the city's elders entered the tent and stood in the circle in front of us. There were eighteen elders to match the eighteen kings present, each one bareheaded and dressed in a long yellow robe edged with gold. One of the elders, who I surmised was the head of the council, raised his arms and began a long and tedious thanksgiving to the gods, thanking them for delivering us all safely to Esfahan and asking them to give us all wisdom to make the right choice this day. He must have waffled on for at least half an hour.

Afterwards the elders sat in chairs reserved for them on the north side of the tent, thereby completing the circle of attendees.

The chief elder rose again and addressed us all, his voice deep. I thought I saw a look of disdain in his eyes as he caught sight of Axsen, Gallia and Praxima, but no one had said that women were forbidden to attend, only prohibited to vote, and in any case Gallia had come as my queen.

'Majesties, today you choose a new King of Kings to rule the empire. May your choice be a wise one. Which one of you will begin by naming a candidate for this most august position?'

He had barely taken his seat before my father was out of his chair and standing in the middle of the circle. Clearly he was intent on taking the bull by the horns.

'I am Varaz of Hatra, and I propose Phraates, son of the late Sinatruces, as a suitable candidate to be King of Kings.'

My father looked at each of his allies in turn.

Balas rose from his chair. 'I, Balas of Gordyene, support my friend Varaz in his choice.' He was followed in turn by Aschek, Vardan, Farhad, Gotarzes and a somewhat unenthusiastic Chosroes. Finally, I too rose from my chair and offered my support.

'I, Pacorus of Dura, also support the election of Phraates.'

It was an impressive endorsement of Phraates' claim, as eight kings of the empire had voiced their support for him. Though as a candidate he could not vote himself, Phraates still had half the kings of the empire behind him. I assumed that the others would fall into line. I was wrong.

As we took our seats, one of the kings opposite rose slowly to his feet. Tall, powerfully built, he had a large round face with a broad forehead. His skin was almost white and his light brown hair was cut short, as was his neatly trimmed beard. He wore a rich purple tunic edged with gold, yellow leggings and red leather boots. His belt and scabbard holding his sword were both black leather inlaid with gold leaf decorations. He indeed looked like a great king.

'I am Narses of Persis, and I would like to propose another candidate for the throne at Ctesiphon.' His voice was deep and powerful, his manner very assured.

The chief elder rose. 'Of course, majesty. Whom do you propose?'

'Myself,' replied Narses.

Balas laughed out loud and even my father smiled, though I noticed that the eastern kings did not seem surprised by Narses' announcement. Narses himself stood impassively.

'There may be some among us who thinks this is amusing. Well, more fool them.' Silence descended on the assembly. Narses strode into the centre of the circle.

'Fellow kings, we all know that Hatra,' he held out a hand towards my father, 'has grown rich during the long reign of

Sinatruces, and King Varaz lists King Phraates among his allies. We also know that other western kings,' he gestured with his hand towards Farhad, Vardan and Balas, 'perhaps intimidated by Hatra's mighty army, are loathe to disagree with King Varaz.'

My father sprang from his chair. 'Have a care, Narses.'

The chief elder was appalled. 'Majesty, please. Threats and violence are forbidden in this assembly.'

My father held up his hands by way of an apology and regained his seat, though I could see that he was struggling to control his temper.

Narses smirked and continued. 'Well, I now understand why kingdoms close to Hatra's borders may be reluctant to antagonise their more powerful neighbour.'

This time my father did not take the bait but regarded Narses with a detached amusement.

Balas rose from his seat and pointed at Narses. 'What makes you think that you have the talents to be King of Kings?'

Narses smiled at him. 'Lord king, if you were a candidate I would not propose myself, so great is your fame. Yet I have to ask King Phraates himself why he thinks he is a suitable candidate, for we have heard nothing from him. Indeed, I find myself asking if he really wishes to be King of Kings at all.'

'Of course he does,' barked my father.

'It is quite obvious, King Varaz,' continued Narses, 'that you wish him to be, but what does he say on the matter?'

Narses took his seat and stared at Phraates, who rose from his chair and cleared his throat.

'Majesties, most of you have known me for many years. I have always had the best interests of the empire at heart and have striven to maintain security and prosperity within the empire and peace with our neighbours. If elected, I promise to follow the same policy as my late father.'

Narses rose from his chair once more. 'A most admirable aim, lord king. For a diplomat.' Several of those around him laughed at this. 'But we are not diplomats, we are kings. Many years ago your father united the empire by force of arms, foreigners respected him because he was strong. I would be a strong king, for I think that ambassadors make poor rulers.'

The words of Narses were impolite but they were also true. Phraates was a good and able man but he lacked ruthlessness, and his inaction at this moment spoke volumes.

'Enough, Narses,' snapped my father. 'We are not here to bandy words but to elect a king. If you are confident of being elected then let's have the vote now and have an end to it. This is a not a debating chamber.'

'No, indeed,' quipped Narses.

The chief elder rose from his chair.

'Majesties, let the vote then be counted. Who wishes Phraates, son of Sinatruces, to be King of Kings?'

Ten of us raised our hands. Phraates, being the candidate, was not allowed to vote, but it did not matter. Two kings who had not spoken sided with Phraates. They were Khosrou of Margiana and Musa, his neighbour to the west, the ruler of Hyrcania, a land that rested on the southern shores of the mighty Caspian Sea. Thus it was decided that Phraates would follow in his father's footsteps. Narses sat with his arms folded, staring at the ground. Gallia leaned forward and whispered in my ear.

'That one has not taken defeat lightly. I fear your father has made an enemy this day.'

'I think you are right, my love, but he has the decision he wanted.'

The chief elder brought the council meeting to an end with another long and tedious sermon, and afterwards I offered my congratulations to Phraates, bowing my head to him.

'Thank you, Pacorus. Your allegiance means a great deal to me.'

Gallia also bowed her head to him and he took her hand and kissed it.

'Queen Gallia, truly you become more beautiful each time we meet. Parthia is indeed fortunate to have you as one of its queens.'

Ever the diplomat. My father embraced Phraates and slapped him hard on the back. As they parted Narses and King Porus of Sakastan stormed from the tent. It was the height of ill manners to do so without paying homage to the new King of Kings, though Phraates did his best to lessen the offence.

'He is hot-headed, I fear. He will calm down.'

The reptile Mithridates was suddenly before his father, bowing deeply.

'Hail, great king.'

'You are now King of Susiana, Mithridates,' said Phraates. 'I hope that you have learned from your mistakes at Dura and will be a good king to your people.'

I doubted that, but Mithridates was clearly stung by his father's rebuke.

'My only regret is not dealing with the Agraci harshly enough.'

'To say nothing of alienating your own people,' I added.

Mithridates turned sharply to face me. 'You dare to speak to me so.'

'I do,' I replied.

He was now incandescent. 'This is an outrage,' he bellowed, drawing the attention of others nearby.

'Go and play with the other children, boy.'

His eyes flashed hatred. 'And you attend to your whore.'

That was it. The time for talking was done. I drew my sword; he did likewise.

'No!' shouted Phraates, and within seconds my father and Balas were pulling me away, while Orodes and Phraates were berating Mithridates.

'Are you mad?' hissed my father. 'The penalty for drawing your sword in the presence of the King of Kings is death.'

I felt anger coursing through my body and restrained myself with difficulty. Gallia stood in front of me.

'You are a king, Pacorus, so act like one. If you want to brawl then go into the street and spare us the sight of such indignity.'

I looked at her, and then at my father. I breathed deeply and put my sword back in its scabbard. I held up my hands in submission and then made my way to Phraates, going down on one knee before him and bowing my head.

'Great king, I have offended you. I await your punishment.'

'Nonsense, nonsense. Get up, Pacorus. The day has been hot and long and we are all tired and our nerves frayed, and when the senses are dulled one says and does things that are out of character. I want you to embrace Mithridates and that shall be the end of the matter.'

He gestured with his arms that we should embrace. And so we embraced, and as we did so he whispered 'slave' into my ear, and I responded by calling him 'boy' ever so quietly so only he would hear. Then we parted, all false smiles and pretended affection.

My father was livid with me and refused to talk as we made our way back to our quarters, though Balas was as jovial as ever.

'That went as well as expected. Reckon you've made any enemy for life, Pacorus.'

That much true, though I gladly accepted the hatred of Mithridates as it was nothing compared to the contempt in which I held him.

Khosrou had followed us, outside and now he called after me.

'Hold, young king.'

I stopped and faced him. Up close he was even more intimidating, with clear grey eyes that had no mercy in them.

'I have heard of you,' his accent was strange, clipped and exotic.

119

He looked at Gallia standing beside me, and a look of admiration suddenly appeared on his face. 'And you, you whom they call "the blonde angel of death".'

Gallia gave him a most dazzling smile and bowed her head ever so slightly towards him.

'You honour me, sire.'

'I would walk with you,' said Khosrou.

'Of course, lord,' I replied.

Domitus and Nergal looked at me but I waved them ahead.

I thought Khosrou was a like a silent assassin but I was wrong. He was friendly and generous, at least on that afternoon.

'Even in my kingdom, which is many hundreds of miles from Dura, people talk of Pacorus and Gallia, of how they defeated armies together riding on a white horse that has wings. And how he is the conqueror of eagles, who has gathered a mighty army around him that will make the world tremble. All this I have heard of you, so I decided to see for myself whether it was true.'

'There is some truth in what you have heard, lord,' I said. 'Though my horse does not have wings.'

Khosrou looked at the sword hanging at Gallia's waist.

'I have heard that you fight like a man, lady.'

Gallia's eyes narrowed. 'You have heard wrong, lord, for I fight like a woman.'

Khosrou smiled. 'And you have a band of women warriors who fight with you?'

'Yes, lord,' she said proudly. 'They are called Amazons.'

'And yet you possess a rare beauty that would grace the finest palace. And you, Pacorus, do you like your woman fighting on the battlefield instead of warming your bed?'

'We met in the midst of war, lord, and ever since I was glad that she could protect herself from danger.'

'And you,' added Gallia.

'It's true,' I said. 'Once she saved me from being run through by a Roman.'

Khosrou nodded and then looked ahead at the arrow-straight figure of Domitus walking beside Nergal and Praxima.

'He is a Roman, is he not, for I have heard that one of your generals is a man from Rome?'

'Yes, lord, he is the commander of my foot soldiers.'

'And you trust him, this man from the race of your enemies?'

'With my life, lord.'

'Mine too,' added Gallia.

It was a while before Khosrou said anything further. 'And I have also heard that you have made peace with the Agraci, the sworn enemies of your father's kingdom.'

'They were only enemies because no one had thought to ask them if they wished to be friends, lord.'

'You two are a curious pair, that much is true, but I like you and I like what you are trying to do. I learned the hard way that it's impossible to subdue barbarians with the sword. You may kill many, but there is an endless supply that will come back like a flood and sweep over the land. They don't stay, but they cause enough damage when they do visit.'

'They have attacked your lands, lord?' asked Gallia.

'Yes.' He said harshly. 'A few years ago I led a great raid into the northern steppes and found nothing, but while I was gone a mighty host of the nomads attacked my capital and set fire to it.'

'Merv,' I muttered.

'Merv, yes,' replied Khosrou. 'You know it.'

'Only the name, lord.' But my mind went back to a feast I attended years ago at the court of Sinatruces at Ctesiphon, where the old king's sorceress, Dobbai, had told the King of Kings that while he sat stuffing his face Merv was burning.

'So now,' continued Khosrou, 'instead of waging war I have treaties with the barbarians.' He smiled at Gallia. 'We still keep our quivers full and our swords sharp, but in general the peace holds. Indeed, some of the rascals serve in my army.'

'They fight for you, not against you,' said Gallia, 'just like the Agraci at Dura.'

'Exactly,' said Khosrou. 'You appear to have a wise head on your shoulders, Pacorus.'

'I hope so, lord.'

'Well, I must bid you both farewell. Perhaps you might come to Margiana when you have the opportunity. You will be made welcome.'

He bowed his head, turned smartly and marched off with his men trailing behind him.

'A good judge of character, that one,' mused Gallia.

'Let us hope that our peace will endure as his has,' I said.

Chapter 8

My father's mood improved in the days following as we headed back west to our kingdoms. Couriers were sent to every corner of the empire to announce the election of Phraates as King of Kings. He would officially move from his capital of Susa to the royal palace at Ctesiphon, though in realty he already had apartments there from his time as his father's envoy. Ctesiphon was the capital city of the Parthian Empire, a huge collection of dwellings clustered around a large palace, the whole enclosed by a rather ill-maintained circuit wall. The palace complex had several throne rooms and a grand banqueting hall befitting the residence of the empire's chief monarch. The thought of Mithridates becoming King of Susiana did not fill me with relish, but I hoped that his father and brother would have a restraining influence on him. In all, though, the Council of Kings had turned out to be a worthwhile occasion for now the empire had a new ruler and peace would be maintained.

A month later we were back at Dura, which had continued to prosper under the expert rule of Godarz and the eagle-eyed Rsan. Gallia recruited more Amazons and Domitus went back to training his legion, which was now fully armed and equipped. Five thousand men had helmets, mail shirts, leather vests, white tunics and shields. The latter comprised three layers of wooden strips glued together and reinforced with wooden strips on the back. A hole was then cut in the centre of the shield, across which was fastened a horizontal metal bar, by which each legionary held the shield with his left hand. To protect his hand, and on the side of the shield that faced the enemy, there was a bulging steel boss over the grip. Each shield was faced with fabric painted white and decorated with red griffin wings. The armouries then began to work on the production of javelins. Ever since my time in Italy I had been fascinated by this particular item of equipment, and was determined to acquire it for my own army. Every spear I had previously encountered comprised a long, straight shaft topped with a blade. But the Roman javelin was entirely different. It comprised a four-foot length of ash onto which is riveted a shaft of thin, soft iron which ends in a tiny triangular tip. Heavy and somewhat cumbersome, the beauty of the javelin is that when it is thrown at an enemy the iron shaft bends upon impact, and cannot be thrown back. In addition, if it gets stuck in an enemy's shield it cannot be wrenched free, thus making the shield useless. The javelin was an ingenious weapon and I was determined to have thousands of them.

'How many, majesty?' asked Rsan, his face illuminated by the oil lamp that sat on his desk, the only light that broke the darkness of night-time.

I stretched back in the chair opposite his desk.

'Ten thousand. To begin with.'

He stopped writing and looked up. 'Ten thousand? But there are only five thousand men in your legion.'

'I know that. But javelins break and you can never have enough, Rsan.'

He was shaking his head. 'Yet more cost, majesty. May I ask a question?'

'Of course,' I said.

'You have raised five thousand foot soldiers, a further two hundred cataphracts, and the lords of your kingdom can furnish you with hundreds more horsemen in times of emergency.'

'That is correct.'

'But we have peace, majesty. You have won over your lords, come to an agreement with the Agraci and have opened up a new trade route to Egypt, which brings in revenues for my, er your, treasury.'

'What is your point, Rsan?'

He sat back and brought his hands together in front of him. 'Why do you then spend so much on soldiers that have no employment?'

I stood up and smiled at him. 'That's a very good question, Rsan. In reply I will tell you the words that someone once told me, and which I have remembered ever since – if you want peace, prepare for war.'

Through Li Sung I obtained the services of Chinese apothecaries who knew how to make a white, sticky liquid which, when alight, was impossible to extinguish until it had burnt itself out. When it was doused with water the flames and heat actually increased in intensity. It was also most terrible because when it hit a surface and ignited it stuck fast, like glue, so any poor wretch covered by it would burn to death despite all efforts to save him. The fearsome liquid was stored in a cool basement under the armoury in the Citadel and was placed under a heavy guard, for it could be as dangerous to a user as to an opponent.

One non-martial indulgence I did allow myself was the hiring of a stonemason to carve a large griffin to be placed on the arch between the towers at the Palmyrene Gate. Squat, barrel-chested and balding, his name was Demetrius and he was a Greek. He had a large round face, piggy eyes and came highly recommended by

King Vardan of Babylon. I visited his workshop one day, a large tent beside the barracks in the Citadel that had been erected for his convenience. He had been in Dura for three days, during which time Gallia had visited him and he had informed her about the statue and how he intended to carve it, after she had shown him my griffin banner that hung behind our thrones in the palace. He had even let her begin the carving.

The large block of sandstone was resting on a wooden pallet in the centre of the room, his chisels and hammers arranged on a long bench beside it. Demetrius was busy marking the stone with chalk when he noticed me picking up a chisel from his bench.

'Kindly leave the tools alone, they are not toys,' he remarked without looking at me.

'How long will it take to finish the statue?'

He sighed deeply. 'As long as it takes, longer if I am continually interrupted, that's for sure.'

He walked over to me, took the chisel from my hand and put it back on the bench in exactly the same spot where it had previously been.

'I was wondering,' I continued, 'if I might try my hand at carving.'

A look of horror spread over his face. 'Certainly not.'

'You let my wife have a go.'

A sly smile creased his face. 'Your wife is a beautiful woman. Besides, it is good luck to have one so fair and beloved of the gods to initiate the carving.'

'I see, and am I not beloved of the gods?'

'I have no idea, but I do know that while you waste my time with idle chatter my work gets delayed and your fee increases.'

'Do you always talk to kings and princes in this manner?'

He was indignant. 'Of course, they hire me for my skill at creating works of art that will last for hundreds of years, not to inflate their feelings of self-importance. If you want flattery, go and talk to your courtiers.'

'I don't have any.'

He looked reflective. 'Then perhaps you are wise like your wife. Such a charming lady.'

'You talked to her?'

He shook his head irritably. 'Of course, we had a very long conversation.'

'You didn't mind wasting time talking to my wife, then?'

'Of course not, why should I? She is beautiful and intelligent. Any man would be a fool to pass up such an opportunity to share the company of one so possessed of grace and charm. Very unusual lady, I have to say. Very different from most of my clients, who for the most part are dim-witted warriors who want statues of themselves waving a sword around. They have some absurd notion that they will live forever if I make a stone carving of them. Laughable.'

'You don't believe that their memories will be preserved for posterity?'

He regarded me for a moment. I think he was trying to work out if I was clever or an idiot.

'The world is full of statues of men who are now long dead. Who remembers them? Not me, and I carved statues for many of them. After a few generations even their families have difficulty remembering who they were. A few, a tiny few, are remembered. We all know who Alexander of Macedon was, and Leonidas of Sparta and Hector of Troy. But the rest?'

'Lucky for you that kings have such vanity.'

He shrugged. 'A man has to earn a living.'

I went over to the sandstone and ran my fingers over its course texture. 'If you think it is a waste of time, why do you carve statues?'

He sighed irritably. 'I did not say I do not enjoy it, I merely commented on the mentality of my clients in wanting to preserve themselves in stone. I love working with stone, metal too for that matter. For one thing, metal and stone do not ask ridiculous questions.'

He turned and stood before my griffin banner that hung on the wall. 'Interesting standard, designed by a sorceress your wife tells me.'

'Yes,' I said. 'A gift.'

'Mm, you are man who knows some interesting women, that's for sure. Now, you really must leave to allow me to get on with my work.'

The new year dawned and brought with it a happy occasion, for my sister Aliyeh was to marry Atrax of Media. Gallia and I travelled to Irbil for the ceremony with a small retinue of fifty horsemen and another fifty horsewomen, half her contingent of Amazons. We travelled north to Hatra and stayed in the city for a few days to await Balas. The old brawler was as roisterous as ever, and it was a happy party that headed east into Media the following week. My father had made Vata the commander of his bodyguard for the trip, the only reason being that I could once again be in the company of my oldest friend. My mother, dressed in leggings, leather boots and a bow hanging from her saddle, a quiver slung over her shoulder, rode beside my father. She wore a loose-fitting white tunic and a wide-brimmed hat on her head, but she would not have looked out of place among my wife's female warriors. It was one of the few times that I had seen her in the saddle, and despite her middle age she still cut a dashing figure. Her long, curly black hair was tied with a black ribbon behind her neck.

My father brought a hundred of his bodyguard and Balas another hundred of his warriors, so our column of horses and camels stretched for five miles along the road behind us. The banners of the kings made an impressive sight, the lion of Gordyene, the white horse of Hatra and the griffin of Dura, the latter carried by Vagharsh, a trusted Companion. Vata rode beside me. He had regained some of his joviality, though he still wore a haggard look that had aged him beyond his years. But now at least he appeared happy and carefree.

'Gallia, I heard that you met Prince Mithridates at Esfahan and that it was a painful encounter for him,' he said, winking at me.

'Prince?' she sniffed. 'He is not worthy of that title.'

'He's a king now, unfortunately,' I remarked casually.

He grinned at me. 'Is that how you greet princes in the land you come from?'

'He got off lightly. I was in a good mood that day,' she said, 'I should have lopped them off with my dagger.'

'Like we did in Italy,' added the grinning Praxima behind us.

Vata looked shocked and glanced at me. 'You don't want to know,' was all I said.

He changed the subject. 'So, your sister is to be a queen.'

I looked ahead to where Aliyeh rode beside my mother, who was being entertained by one of Balas' tall stories.

'Yes, I'm happy for her, and it will be a good alliance for Hatra.'

'She is marrying for love, Pacorus,' said Gallia, 'not because of politics. Or would you prefer that your sister marry a fat old beast who will abuse her.'

I knew that she was talking about her own experiences as a slave in Italy, and her tone dared me to contradict her. I did not. She had grown close to my sisters during our time in Hatra and wanted to see them both happy, as did I.

'It is a good match,' I said.

Irbil was a city that was situated across the Tigris. We reached it in ten days, Farhad himself riding out to greet us on the final leg of our journey. He was an affable enough man and was genuinely delighted that his son was marrying well. The truth was that Media needed Hatra more than Hatra needed Media, but my father had not forgotten that Farhad had supported the election of Phraates and was pleased enough to have him as a relation. Indeed Phraates himself had come to the city, officially to bless the wedding, though I suspected the real reason was to thank those who had voted for him at the Council of Kings. I was pleased to see that Orodes was with him, and the prince greeted Gallia and me warmly. As an added bonus, there was no sign of Mithridates.

Irbil was once a major city in the ancient Assyrian Empire. Indeed, its Assyrian name means 'Four Gods' – Assur, Ishtar, Shamash and Sin – and it was a great centre of learning, science, knowledge and art. The city's citadel was positioned on top of a great circular stone mound a hundred feet high, on top of which had been built high stonewalls, yellow-ochre in colour. The city's shops and houses were grouped around the mound, though there was no outer wall for their protection. Access to the citadel was via a long ramp that had been cut into the side of the mound, which led to a huge gatehouse on its southern side. We rode up to and through the gates, then along a short paved road that led to the central square, around which were grouped Farhad's palace, temples, barracks and stables, the whole enclosed by an inner circuit wall. I estimated that the citadel had a diameter of around a quarter of a mile, no more. It was certainly a strong position, though any attacker could destroy those buildings around the mound with ease. All the buildings inside the citadel were brick, with a myriad of narrow alleyways cutting through the entire settlement. Our quarters were extremely pleasant and had an open courtyard planted with trees, the kitchens, servants' quarters, stores and stables on one side and our rooms on the upper storey opposite. The doors were painted cobalt blue, the courtyard walls had marble facings and the arcade had three stone arches that supported a terrace overlooking the courtyard. Our room had a timber ceiling and plaster walls that were decorated with depictions of wild horses.

The wedding ceremony itself was a grand occasion held in the city's main temple, a cavernous stone structure surmounted by twenty domes resting on arches and columns. Afterwards I embraced Atrax as my new brother and wiped the tears from the eyes of my sister, for her time as my parents' spoilt little girl was now over and she was beginning her new life as a woman. Hatra would no longer be her home for she was now a princess of Media. Yet Atrax clearly doted on her and she adored him, and dressed in his scale armour cuirass and steel helmet he looked every inch the warrior. The day after the wedding feast my mother bade Aliyeh a tearful farewell as she and Atrax rode off to spend some time alone together in one of Farhad's mountain-top retreats in the north of his kingdom. A hundred horse archers dressed in blue tunics and grey leggings escorted the couple.

As we watched the newlyweds ride from the stronghold and waved them goodbye, little did we know that we were also bidding farewell to peace and happiness. For at that moment a chill wind from the north blew in our faces, heralding the dawn of the hard times though we did not know it. As I held Gallia close I heard shouts behind me. I turned and saw an exhausted horse, dirty and lathered in sweat, hobble through the palace gates. The rider on its back, bent forward and hugging its neck, suddenly fell from his saddle onto the ground. A guard held the horse's reins as another knelt beside the rider. I saw Phraates and Orodes looking concerned, and then suddenly we were all running towards the fallen rider.

'He wears the colours of the city of Susa,' said Orodes.

Reaching him, I looked down and saw that the right side of the soldier's tunic was soaked in blood. Phraates knelt beside him as the man, his face deathly pale, tried to rise.

'Highness,' he uttered weakly.

'Do not try to get up,' commanded Phraates. 'Someone get this man some water. What has happened?'

I could see the shaft of an arrow lodged in his side.

'King Mithridates, majesty. He has rid Susa of your allies, killed all those who were loyal to you.'

A look of alarm crossed Phraates' face, but then he smiled. 'Talk no more. We will get you well first.'

The man grabbed his king's arm feebly. 'Others loyal to you have fled west to Ctesiphon. They await you there, highness. Narses.....'

His arm fell to the ground as he passed out.

He was carried to the garrison infirmary as we all stood around in a state of shock.

'I must get back to Ctesiphon,' said Phraates, 'and find out more about what has happened.'

But as he walked off to his quarters with Orodes by his side we all knew the sad truth of what had happened. Mithridates had used the opportunity presented to him by his father's absence to tighten his grip on Susa. But his reasons remained obscure. He was King of Susiana because his father was King of Kings and now lived at Ctesiphon, though technically Phraates still ruled his own kingdom

Susiana as well as the whole of the Parthian Empire. As we all stood in a circle staring at each other, it was Balas who spoke first.

'It would appear that King Mithridates has decided that he should rule Susiana.'

'His head will be adorning Susa's walls soon enough,' said my father.

'You think so, Varaz?' replied Balas. 'I think our young upstart king has allies.'

'What allies?' snapped my father.

'Narses,' I said.

'He's right there,' said Balas. 'You heard him at Esfahan. He wanted to be King of Kings and now he's decided to take the throne by force.'

My father shook his head. 'Just because a dying man utters a name does not mean anything.'

'Yes it does,' insisted Balas, 'and you know it.'

'Perhaps we should withdraw to the palace for further discussions,' offered Farhad.

And so we did, and after more fruitless discourse, which involved my father and Balas arguing some more, I made plans to return to Dura. I wrote a letter to Godarz and sent it by courier. The postal system throughout the empire was extremely efficient, with horsemen riding between way stations located every thirty miles on all major roads. At the stations fresh horses and riders stood ready at all times, so that a letter could cover up to ninety miles in one day. I watched the rider gallop down the road south from the walls of Irbil. Gallia stood beside me.

'We leave at dawn,' I said.

'Mithridates has joined with Narses, hasn't he?'

I turned to face her. 'It would appear so. The question is, how many more kings have joined Narses, if any?'

'He is powerful?'

'Persis is a large kingdom, that much is true, but how many men he can raise I know not.'

She laid a hand on mine. 'You know, Spartacus once told me that it's not the size of the gladiator in the fight that makes the difference, but the size of the fight in the gladiator.'

I smiled and pulled her close. 'That is just the sort of thing he would say. I thought we had done with fighting.'

'While there are men in the world armed with swords there will always be fighting, Pacorus.'

The next morning, before the first rays of the sun lanced the eastern sky, we said goodbye to my parents, Vata, Phraates,

Orodes and Farhad and rode from his city, leaving the camels and ten of our riders to follow us. We rode hard for the Tigris, crossed the river and then travelled south along its western bank, before swinging west to cross the desert, heading for the Euphrates and home. We slept during the hottest part of the day – two hours either side of midday – and journeyed until it was dark, then rose again after two hours of sleep until the sun was roasting our backs once more. We ate hard biscuit, drank tepid water and rested under what shelter we could find. After five days we galloped across the Egyptian's pontoon bridge and rode into Dura. Godarz was on the steps of the palace to greet us, flanked by Rsan, Domitus and Nergal. Their faces registered surprise at our appearance, for we were covered in dust, our dirty faces ran with sweat, the men with stubble on their faces and our hair matted with grime. Our horses were sweating and tired, their heads drooping as we halted them and slid off their backs. My limbs ached from the journey and my eyes stung with sweat.

'We received your letter,' said Godarz as grooms took away our horses to be unsaddled and cooled down.

'Trouble?' asked Domitus.

'Yes,' I replied. 'Council of war in ten minutes.'

'There is something you need to attend to first, lord,' said Godarz.

'What?'

Godarz shifted nervously on his feet. 'In the throne room. She insisted and no one dared contradict her.'

'Her? What are you talking about?' I was tired and in no mood for games.

I marched into the palace with Gallia following and then walked into the throne room. At the far end, in my seat on the dais, was seated an old woman. As I drew closer I recognised her. The ragged robes, lank hair, bony fingers and haggard face made me stop in my tracks as I stared in disbelief at Dobbai, the wizened old crone who had been the sorceress of Sinatruces and who now sat on my throne.

'They say that I am old and ugly, but you two make me look positively radiant. You look like you have been to the underworld and back,' she cackled, revealing a mouth of discoloured teeth. 'Is the burden of kingship proving too burdensome, son of Hatra?'

'No,' I said irritably.

Dobbai ignored me and beckoned to Gallia. 'Sit beside me, child.'

'May I sit on my own throne?' I asked.

'Would you deprive an old woman of the chance for her to rest her weary body?'

Gallia embraced Dobbai and sat on her throne, leaving me standing like some sort of servant in front of her. Behind me, Rsan, Nergal, Godarz and Domitus filed into the room.

'She arrived two days ago,' said Godarz, 'and was insistent that she see you.'

'Ha,' bellowed Dobbai. 'They quaked with fear when they saw me, for they knew who I was.'

I ordered some water to be brought to us and after Gallia and I had slated our thirsts I had chairs brought in and placed around the dais. I was tired, and by the look of the black circles around Gallia's eyes so was she, yet some strange force compelled me to hear what Dobbai had to say, though not before she had ordered a servant to fetch her some wine.

'A hard ride, lord?' asked Nergal.

'Yes, we had to get back here as quickly as possible, for trouble stirs in the east.'

'You only know the half of it,' said Dobbai, gulping wine from a cup and then holding it out to be refilled. 'The eastern half of the empire stirs, son of Hatra, and only you and your father stand between order and destruction.'

'You speak in riddles,' I said, for all I wanted to do was close my eyes and rest.

But Dobbai was not to be silenced. She rose from my chair and walked up and down on the dais.

'You have prepared your defences well, and that is good for they will be sorely tested err long. There are those who would tear the empire asunder, while his people,' she pointed at Domitus, 'wait like hungry vultures to pick over the bones.'

This was too much for Domitus, whose bemusement at Dobbai's words had turned to anger. 'Are we to listen to an old hag whose brains have been addled by the desert sun?'

Dobbai scoffed at his words. 'Addled am I? Well, Roman, if that be so, why is it that I know of a mighty army marching towards you and you are ignorant of such a fact?'

'What army?' I asked.

'It gathers at Persepolis under the bird-god banner of Narses. Thousands of horsemen and foot soldiers, the warriors of Tiridates of Aria, Phriapatus of Carmania, Porus of Sakastan, Vologases of Drangiana, Cinnamus of Anauon and Monaeses of Yueh-Chih. I have seen them in dreams, and soon they will be marching west to destroy the kingdoms that side with that fool Phraates.'

131

'Dreams?' I said with disbelief. 'Those kings were at the council meeting that elected Phraates.'

Dobbai sat down and looked at me, all the while tapping the fingers of her left hand on the chair. 'You still have much to learn, son of Hatra. Narses has been plotting for months, perhaps years, to become King of Kings. He has gained the allegiance of other kings and now intends to take the crown by force. He has already captured Susiana without a fight, for Mithridates has Susa and Narses will already be on the march there. And in between stands poor, defenceless Elymais. Gotarzes will be crushed like an ant beneath a giant's foot, and after him Narses will take Mesene, Babylon and Hatra.'

She leaned forward to fix me with her black eyes. 'You have little time left, son of Hatra, so little time.'

I did not want to believe what she had revealed to me, but my instincts told me that her words were true.

'I can believe that Mithridates would be party to such treachery,' said Gallia. 'He is a snake.'

'And a dangerous one,' added Dobbai. 'If Phraates had any sense, which he doesn't, he should have had his eldest son strangled at birth. I had the misfortune to see him grow up, for he visited his grandfather at Ctesiphon often. I have seen his malice and ambition grow with him. The loss of Dura served only to fuel his resentment and hatred further. It would have been easy for Mithridates to betray his father and brother; how much easier will it be for him to take revenge on you, then, son of Hatra.'

That night, despite my tiredness, I slept little as Dobbai's words went through my mind. I rose before dawn, saddled Remus and then rode to the legion's camp. The cohorts were already assembled on the parade ground in front of the camp and the roll call was being taken in front of Domitus and his officers. Most of the latter were men who had fought with Spartacus in Italy, former slaves who were now leaders of their own cohorts and centuries. Afterwards, sitting in Domitus' command tent, I shared a breakfast of porridge with him.

'Old habits die hard, I see,' I said, pointing at the porridge.

'Rome has conquered half the world feeding its soldiers this,' he said, 'reckon it'll do for my boys.'

'And how are your boys?'

'You mean are they ready for battle.'

'Yes,' I replied.

'Oh, they're ready. Itching to prove themselves. If that old hag is right, then they won't have long to wait.'

132

'You may disapprove of her, Domitus, but I'm afraid to say that she is usually right. We will be marching soon. I will leave a cohort behind as a garrison, the other five thousand of your men will be marching.'

'To where?'

I shrugged. 'Across the Euphrates, then east to link up with my father's army and whoever else will support us, there to await the command of Phraates.'

Domitus finished his porridge and then shoved his wooden plate aside. He placed his elbows on the table, rested his chin in his hands and looked at me. His face could have been carved by Demetrius from a block of granite, so hard were its features. I was glad Domitus was a friend and not an enemy.

'You have something to say, Domitus?'

'I am an outsider in these lands and that makes me look at things differently from those, such as yourself, who have grown up in these parts. When we were at the council meeting at Esfahan, I had a chance to see all the kings who rule the Parthian Empire.'

'It was the first time I too had seen them all gathered in one place.'

'The one they called Narses, he was bold and confident. I've seen many legates like him. They are bold because they have powerful supporters, usually rich and influential parents or sponsors. Same with that Narses. He obviously has great strength behind him and the ruthlessness to implement his ambitions.'

'Now your father, he reminds me of Spartacus – courageous and strong, and a man who knows bullshit when he smells it. Now that friend of his, the big brawler.'

'King Balas?'

'Yes, that's him, now he's smarter than he lets on. And he was correct in what he said about your father becoming head king. Because the one that was elected.'

'King Phraates.'

'He's weak, Pacorus. You may all like him but he lacks resolve. And he's fatally wounded already.'

'How so?'

'Any man who lets his son steal his kingdom will receive no respect, and without respect he will not be able to command other kings.'

'Technically,' I said, 'when Phraates became head king, as you say, Mithridates became King of Susiana.'

Domitus shook his head. 'No one will see it like that. Unless Phraates marches to his capital, takes it back and executes his son, he will be seen as weak. And who follows weak leaders?'

Domitus had done wonders to turn a bunch of former slaves, misfits, thugs, itinerants, drifters and idealists into a body of fighting men, and I knew that what he said was true. He was a simple man, really, an individual who was brave, loyal and forthright. You knew where you stood with Domitus, this ex-centurion whom I had come to like and respect immensely. He said little and never complained, but he was harder than the steel of the gladius he wore at his hip. Every man of his legion respected him, even though he had had many of them flogged and allotted extra fatigue duties to those who were sloppily dressed on parade or inattentive during training, but they knew he was fair in his punishments and he never asked any man to undertake something that he himself would not do. He never spoke of his parents or if he had any brothers or sisters, and I assumed that his mother and father were long since dead. I often thought that he might be lonely, but he never let the mask of professionalism slip. That said I tried to make sure that he was at the palace as often as possible, despite the fact that he disliked sitting behind his desk in the headquarters building. He preferred to be pacing around the legion's camp with his officers, cane in his hand, or leading a cohort on a twenty-mile route march during the heat of the day. I rose from the table.

'The die is cast my friend.'

He leaned back in his chair and placed his hands behind his neck. 'Then let's hope that we can kill Narses quickly.'

But the army would have to wait for the moment, for a more pressing matter had to be attended to.

Despite Demetrius' brusque manners he was not averse to earning extra money on the side. Not that he needed to as he was being paid a king's ransom to carve my griffin statue.

'Nonsense,' he snapped, 'I have given you a very reasonable rate for my services, which, incidentally, are most sought after. I could be in Egypt working for Pharaoh, who would pay me much more and provide me with a harem for my entertainment.'

He really was a most taxing individual. 'Then why don't you?'

He stopped his chiselling and looked at me. 'Well, for one thing, your wife is a most charming lady. And your mother is also intriguing.'

'My mother?'

'Yes, the one who gave you the banner in the first place. I must say that I have never met such interesting females. Most queens and princesses are as dull as ditch water, but they are certainly not.

And for that reason I stay.'

'She's not my mother.'

'Really? Pity.'

'Anyway,' I continued, 'will you take on a new commission?'

'Of course, I have already promised your mother. She was most insistent, said it would bring you luck. Working with metals is slightly different to stone, of course, but my skills are extensive and I dare say I will manage.'

'Dobbai commissioned you?'

He frowned at me. 'That is what I said. Is your hearing impaired?'

But how did she know? Every Roman legion had a silver eagle as its principal standard, which became like a religious icon to the men. It was revered, loved and the legionaries would lay down their lives protecting it. I was determined that my own legion would have a similar standard, though it would not be the eagle design of my enemies. I was going to explain to Demetrius exactly what I wanted but had apparently been beaten to it.

'But how do you know what to cast?' I asked.

'Your mother was quite specific. Now if you don't mind I have a lot of work to do.'

I gave up trying to reason with him and left him to his stonework. A week later he sent a message saying that the new piece was finished. I took Gallia and Dobbai with me to his workshop to inspect it, and was truly awe-struck by what I saw. A golden griffin, about foot and a half long, lay on Demetrius' bench. The expert casting had produced a piece that showed every one of the beast's features, its talons, wings, head, body and tail wrapped around its hind quarters. It was made of metal but it seemed alive, ready to fly from the bench, for Demetrius had gone to work with his tools to expertly refine its features.

I stood in wonder, and even Dobbai for once appeared to be lost for words.

'He's beautiful,' was all Gallia said.

'A beautiful beast for a beautiful lady,' retorted Demetrius.

'It is to be the standard of my legion,' I said.

Demetrius sighed. 'A great pity, a beautiful woman should surround herself with precious objects.'

I looked at Dobbai. 'How did you know?'

She shook her head. 'You are easy to read, son of Hatra. Perhaps too easy.'

I knew that the griffin would become a sacred object to Domitus and his legionaries. It was late afternoon when I had the legion

135

assembled outside the Palmyrene Gate. What a sight – five and a half thousand men fully armed and equipped standing in their centuries and cohorts! The day was still warm as the shadows grew longer, the men silent in their ranks. Domitus was in front of them with his officers, shiny metal discs on the front of his mail shirt and a white transverse crest atop his helmet. I rode out of the city with Gallia beside me. Behind us were my cataphracts in full armour and steel masks, together with Gallia's Amazons in mail shirts and helmets, carrying their bows. Immediately behind me rode Vagharsh carrying my griffin banner and Nergal holding a thick ash shaft, on top of which, wrapped in linen, was the gold griffin. The cavalry deployed into a long line facing the legion and halted, while I nudged Remus forward until he was level with Domitus. His men stood to attention as I raised my right arm.

'Men of the Duran Legion, I salute you. In a short space of time you have gone from being civilians to soldiers. None know what fate has in store for us, but I do know that you will not let yourselves or me down. Some of you fought in Italy with Spartacus. Know you that I hold true to what he believed in, that each man should be judged on his own merits regardless of his position at birth or race. You stand testimony to that belief. I thank you for your faith in me, and as a small token of my gratitude I present you with your standard.'

I dismounted and took the wrapped griffin from Nergal, then walked over to Domitus and handed it to him. He looked surprised, for I had kept this project a secret from him. I took my dagger to the twine wrapped around the linen and cut the threads. The same dagger that had once belonged to a brutal centurion who had been my jailer before Spartacus had liberated me. I yanked the linen cover away to reveal the gold griffin fastened to a small steel plate atop the pole. Domitus smiled with pride as he regarded the work of art, and though his men remained silent I sensed a surge of elation course through their ranks like a lightning bolt. The orange rays of the early evening sun caught the griffin and for a moment it seemed to stir, angry, restless and fierce before the soldiers who would come to love and revere it. Thus did the Duran Legion receive its griffin standard.

Afterwards Domitus selected ten of his best men to be its permanent guard, and it was housed in its own tent in the middle of the legion's camp. Wherever the legion went the standard would go with it. Each night it would be kept under guard in the same tent in the same location in camp. During the days that followed I heard that every man under Domitus' command lined up to see the griffin at close quarters, believing it to possess magic, for they had heard that its creation had been under the supervision of Dobbai. I smiled at this, but perhaps they were right and perhaps it did possess supernatural qualities.

Two days later its stone companion was finished, being moved from Demetrius' canvas workshop on its large wooden pallet by placing logs underneath and hauling it down to the Palmyrene Gate. Tingling with excitement, myself, Gallia, Dobbai, Nergal, Rsan and Godarz followed behind on foot. Demetrius fussed around the load as fifty legionaries sweated and cursed as they pulled the statue through the city, others placing logs under the pallet as it inched its way towards its destination. Domitus bellowed orders and sent for another cohort of men, for word soon spread through the city that the magical statue was finished and people wanted to see it up close. Soon there were hundreds of individuals crowding round the griffin, trying to touch it and generally getting in the way. When the new cohort arrived Domitus used it to line the street and keep people away from the statue. He also had to detail some men to keep others from trying to touch Gallia's hair, for many believed that it was a gift from the gods and thus sacred and charmed.

By the time the griffin had reached the Palmyrene Gate thousands had gathered to see it hoisted into position. The next hour and a half was very fraught as an agitated Demetrius shouted and pleaded with the operators of the giant winch erected above the gates to take care of his work. Godarz had supervised the construction of the winch and the reinforcing of the arch above the gates, and he was bemused by the Greek's behaviour.

'He'll give himself a heart attack if he's not careful.'

'He's very protective of his creations,' I said, as Demetrius fell to his knees and placed his head in his hands as the statue swayed slightly in its rope cradle.

Eventually, and thankfully before Demetrius' heart gave out, the statue was placed on its plinth between the two towers of the Palmyrene Gate. We walked up the steps inside one of the towers and stepped onto the top of the arch. It was wide and strong, allowing the plinth to be safely positioned a few paces behind the battlements. On top staring west with unblinking eyes, was placed the griffin. I had to admit he looked magnificent and would be guarding the city long after I had left this world, Shamash willing. Demetrius fussed around the plinth, using a small trowel to apply a symbolic layer of cement around the statue's base. He gave the trowel to Gallia to apply the last dash of cement.

137

'Surely I should seal the plinth?' I jested.

Demetrius and Dobbai both rebuked me.

'Don't be absurd,' he said, 'it requires a woman's touch, otherwise he will get annoyed.'

'He?' I said.

'Don't interfere with things you cannot comprehend,' added Dobbai. 'Take the trowel, child.'

With all eyes on her, Gallia took the trowel from Demetrius and applied the last piece of cement to seal the griffin to its plinth. Everyone then clapped politely and Gallia smiled radiantly.

Demetrius stroked the griffin. 'He's happy enough.'

'And he can't fly away, either,' said Dobbai, nodding approvingly.

I looked at Nergal, who shrugged, then at Godarz who just grinned. Demetrius was paid his fee and left the city a few days afterwards a rich man, and strange to say that on the first morning after the griffin had been put in position, I rose at dawn and made my way to the Citadel's walls, then looked west to the Palmyrene Gate. And between the towers, sitting on its plinth, was the griffin.

'You decided to stay, then?'

A guard overhead me. 'Majesty?'

I shook my head. 'Nothing.' I left the wall and went back to the palace. It is just a piece of stone I told myself. And yet...

The next few days witnessed a feverish passage of letters to and from Hatra as my father coordinated the response of those loyal to Phraates. The latter, ensconced at Ctesiphon, gathered what forces he could from his own kingdom of Susiana and fortified his royal residence. The plan was for all the kings to march with their forces to Ctesiphon, and then to strike at the rebels quickly before the infection of their treachery spread. Thus far Khosrou and Musa stood on the defensive as the rebel kingdoms lay directly south of their borders.

Byrd returned to Dura with Malik, and I greeted the Agraci prince warmly for he had become a good friend. That night he dined with us and told us the news from his lands.

'My father and sister send their greetings,' he said.

'How is Rasha?' asked Gallia, her beauty now fully restored after our journey from Irbil.

'Well, lady, thank you,' replied Malik, looking sideways at Dobbai, who had now seemingly become a permanent resident of the palace.

'And you, Byrd,' she continued, 'is life being good to you?'

Byrd shoved another piece of meat into his mouth and nodded

his head. 'Good, lady. I like the desert.'

Malik grinned. 'He likes one piece of it, that occupied by a young widow whom he visits often.'

Gallia looked at me with a triumphant smirk on her face.

'That is excellent news, Byrd,' she said. 'We are pleased for you, aren't we Pacorus?'

'Of course,' I said.

Malik stared again at the old woman in black rags sitting at the table, apparently invisible to us. She saw his stare.

'You have something to say, desert lord?'

'Forgive me, Malik,' I said. 'This is Dobbai, who was once the sorceress of King Sinatruces and now...'

'And now I have returned from whence I came to make sure Pacorus does not deviate from his path.'

Malik was intrigued. 'And what path is that?'

She wiped her hands on her robe, stood up and walked from the room.

'It is not for you to know,' she said. Then she stopped, turned and pointed a bony finger at Byrd.

'What of the Romans?'

'Romani troops marching north from Syria,' was his reply.

'Marching to where?' I asked.

Byrd shrugged. 'North, not know where.'

'As long as they are not marching towards us I do not care,' I remarked.

'Keep one eye on Rome, son of Hatra,' said Dobbai ambling from the room.

'I would come with you, Pacorus,' said Malik suddenly.

'This is not your fight, Malik,' I replied.

'Yet I offer you my sword.'

I nodded. 'Then I accept it.'

Some say war is all glory, battles and slaughter, but I learnt long ago that organisation is the key to victory. Dull attention to detail is what gives an army success. Godarz had once been the quartermaster general in the army of Spartacus and now he made sure that my horsemen were fully prepared for the trials to come. Camels were hired and loaded with spare saddles, horseshoes, bridles, harnesses, saddle clothes, brushes and veterinary implements. Others were loaded with spare arrows, thousands of them, plus replacement bows, quivers and food – hard-baked Parthian bread that Domitus swore was worse than the equivalent in the Roman army. The legion marched with its tools, tents, spare weapons and clothing packed onto carts pulled by mules, ill-tempered beasts that Domitus nicknamed 'Dobbais'. He thought this hilarious, until an old and grizzled one snatched his vine cane and chewed it through. He would have slit its throat had not Godarz, who was with him at the time, threatened to make sure that Rsan charged Domitus for a replacement. My two hundred cataphracts had their own camel train, but during the march they rode as spearmen armed with lances and round wooden shields. Their bows and quivers were carried in large hide cases stored on the camels, for no Parthian warrior went to war without his bow. But these men were the steel fist of the army, trained to smash through an enemy in combat. Before battle they would don their scale armour and then encase their horses in similar attire, but to march for a whole day under a Mesopotamian sun was more than even the hardiest warrior could endure. I sent the sons of the nobles who served as cataphracts back to their fathers in the days before we marched, for I still needed horse archers to complement my heavy cavalry. I did not order that the lords present themselves, for the memory of the insults dealt to them by Mithridates would still have been fresh in their minds. So I requested that they release a small number of their men to serve with me for the campaign. In this way I left it to them to decide how many they would furnish, if any. I have to confess I was nervous about their reply. They owed me allegiance, but these men were frontier warriors who had carved out their domains from the unyielding desert, and had then defended them in the face of Agraci aggression. The Agraci threat had now gone, but after their ill usage at the hands of Mithridates would they be willing to send men to serve under another upstart king?

I was pacing the palace terrace as these thoughts coursed through my head. Perhaps they would insist that their sons should stay with them, and then I would have even less cavalry.

Gallia shook her head at me. 'Why do you torture yourself so? What will be, will be.'

'Indeed it shall, child,' said Dobbai, shuffling onto the terrace and seating herself next to my wife on a large wicker chair stuffed with cushions. I really wasn't in the mood for one of her lectures.

'They will come, have no fear.'

I was looking across the river, at a large camel caravan about to cross the pontoon bridge. 'Who?'

'Your lords, of course. That is why you pace like a caged lion, is it not?'

She reached over and grabbed Gallia's hand. 'I hope he is less predicable on the battlefield.'

'How do you know, have you talked to them?'

'Such a petulant outburst. You should have more faith in your talents. They have sent their sons, their most precious possession, to serve with you. Why then do you not think they would send other mothers' sons to fight and die beside you? They will come.'

And she was right. Three days later my men returned and their fathers with them. They had obviously discussed the matter between themselves because each lord brought a hundred horse archers. Thus did I gain another two thousand cavalry.

We had a feast in the banqueting hall that night, a happy gathering of the lords of Dura, their sons and my Companions. It was the first time that the lords had met those who had fought in Italy and they were intrigued by their strange accents and appearance, but everyone got on well enough. Two women stole the evening – Gallia, whose beauty lit up even the darkest of rooms, and Dobbai, whose ugliness was in stark contrast but who had a powerful presence nevertheless. The lords had certainly heard of her and thought it very auspicious that she had come to Dura. And behind where I and my queen sat at the top table hung her griffin banner, the same banner that Dobbai had sent me all those months ago. They knew this, too, and one by one they came up to the table and asked permission to touch it, believing it to have magical powers. Men are superstitious beasts no matter how great their fame or grand their titles, and they put great store in relics, charms and artefacts that they believe will protect them and give them supernatural powers. None more so than warriors who want to go into battle with magical protection. Dobbai looked in amusement as these hardened frontier warlords gingerly extended their hands and held the corner of the banner for a few seconds, before turning sharply, bowing to me and then regaining their seats.

None had seen Gallia before but their sons must have told them about her, this blonde-haired, blue-eyed vision who was Dura's queen. She never wore much jewellery or make-up; she did not have to. That said, tonight she wore a pale-blue gown that reached down to the floor. Her lithe arms were bare and adorned with gold bracelets and she wore slivers of gold in her hair that caught the light and made her blonde locks glint. Her earrings were also gold inlaid with small diamonds and on her fingers she wore gold rings. At the start of the feast the lords had bowed their heads to me, but they had gone down on one knee to Gallia. When the first man did so I gestured for her to extend her hand, which she did, whereupon he took it gently and kissed it. Gallia smiled with amusement, but every one of them, and their sons, insisted on the same ritual. Thus did Gallia once again conquer with her charm and beauty.

Dobbai, sitting on the other side of Gallia, was watching me as a steady line of individuals approached the banner to lay their hands upon it.

'You are not going to hold the standard, son of Hatra?'

'It would be unseemly for a king to prostrate himself before a piece of cloth,' I answered stiffly.

She raised an eyebrow at me. 'Of course.'

But in a private moment, when there were no eyes to see, I had already knelt before my banner and grasped it with both hands and prayed to Shamash that it would bring me luck and bless my kingdom and all those who lived in it. I knew this and Dobbai knew this, and I knew that she knew. She looked knowingly at me but said no more on the matter.

As the evening wore on and the wine flowed freely, some of the lords wanted Dobbai to touch their sword blades for luck, asking my permission for her to do so, because the penalty for drawing a sword in the presence of your king was death. I consented, and so the keen edges of their blades were held before her to touch. I don't know what they thought this would achieve, but they each looked at their swords in awe after she had touched them and as they returned them to their scabbards. I was surprised to see Domitus offer his gladius to her, though when I cornered him afterwards he thought nothing of it.

'Any bit of luck is welcome before you set off on campaign, especially if you're in a tight spot.'

'You think we will be in a tight spot, Domitus?'

He looked unconcerned. 'You know how it is, when the fighting starts there's always a few nasty surprises, and there's always some young warrior on the other side who wants to make a name for himself by spilling the guts of a great warlord.'

'I had no idea you thought of yourself as a great warlord, Domitus.'

He grunted. 'I don't, I was talking of you.'

I slapped him on the shoulders and returned to my wife. But his words had been prophetic, for not half an hour later a courier appeared at the doors of the hall, his face smeared with dirt and his clothes covered in dust. He wore a worried expression, and as a guard escorted him to the top table the babble of voices began to ebb as others caught sight of him. By the time he had reached my table and bowed there was silence. All eyes were upon him as he reached inside his tunic, pulled out a letter and handed it to me. I

142

cut the wax seal with my dagger and opened it. I recognised my father's handwriting. I finished reading it and gave it to Gallia, then looked at the host of expectant faces.

'King Gotarzes of Elymais has been defeated outside his capital by Narses. What is left of his army has taken refuge with him in the city. Some of the rebels have ringed it, the rest, the majority, are marching west.'

There was a murmur of concerned voices. I held up my hands. Silence returned.

'We march to link up with my father in two days.'

Chapter 9

The following day brought worse news when a rider arrived at Dura with another message from my father that a Roman army had invaded Armenia and Gordyene, and that Balas had been killed in a great battle near Tigranocerta in Armenia. I was stunned by this thunderbolt. It was true the Romans had been fighting the Armenians led by King Tigranes and Mithridates of Pontus, the kingdom to the west of Armenia, for years. But these disputes had nothing to do with Parthia. Now, a Roman army had invaded Parthian territory and had seized one of the empire's kingdoms.

I read the letter to an ashen-faced Gallia, who had grown very fond of Balas since their first meeting at our wedding. It related that Tigranes had called upon Balas for his help when the Romans had invaded his kingdom, and Balas had agreed to offer aid. But Tigranes and Balas had been soundly beaten and Balas killed. Tigranes had escaped, though what forces he could still muster was unknown. But now my father was forced to send more of his army north to reinforce Vata at Nisibus, for the Romans were now on Hatra's northern border.

'That lovely man,' was all Gallia could say.

'What are you going to do now, son of Hatra?'

Dobbai was beginning to annoy me. She was like an old crow sitting on a post, cawing away to no purpose.

'Whatever I shall do will be no business of yours,' I snapped.

We were on the palace terrace, overlooking the river, and Dobbai rose from her chair to stand leaning on the stone balustrade, looking south.

'Of course an old woman has no business telling a king what to do, though perhaps in this instance you might like to listen to my advice.'

I handed Gallia the letter and she began reading it, perhaps thinking that if she saw the words they would tell a different tale.

'What advice?' I said coolly.

'The Romans are settling scores with their old enemies, Armenia and Pontus. They have no quarrel with Parthia. Yet.' She raised her arm and pointed towards the south. 'That is where the greatest immediate danger lies.'

I waved my hand at her. 'The greatest danger lies to the east. Narses has Ctesiphon surrounded. That is why we are marching to its aid. I do not need a lecture on strategy.'

Dobbai smiled at me. 'Perhaps Narses is marching upon you, son of Hatra.'

I was just about to order her from my presence when a guard walked on to the terrace and bowed.

'Messenger in the throne room, majesty.'

I followed him, and moments later was confronted by a tired and frightened soldier who had obviously ridden hard to get to Dura. His face was caked in dirt and his shirt soaked in sweat. He was panting hard and barely able to speak, so I ordered that a chair be brought for him and water to relieve his thirst.

'Calm yourself,' I said. 'You are no use to anyone if you collapse and die.'

He drank greedily from the cup, which was refilled from a jug held by one of my guards. He sat with his hands on his legs for a few moments, then rose and bowed his head.

'Thank you, majesty,' he said as I sat down in my chair on the dais, Gallia and Dobbai joining me. The latter had her own chair beside mine, now that she had appointed herself my official adviser. The messenger looked admiringly at Gallia, who wore a mask of solemnity, and alarmingly at Dobbai.

I leaned forward. 'Please continue.'

'I was sent by King Vardan, majesty.'

'King Vardan is marching north?' I asked him, suddenly feeling that things were not that bad, for if Babylon's army was heading north then I and my father could link up with it and our combined forces could then march to the relief of Ctesiphon.

'No, majesty,' replied the messenger. 'Part of the army of Narses has marched south towards Babylon. King Vardan will not be able to aid you until he has defeated this force.'

'I see,' this was news that I had not wished to hear. Still, the army of Hatra and Dura combined would still be a force to be reckoned with.

'There is something more, majesty.'

I had a feeling that I was not going to find what he was going to say agreeable. 'Continue.'

'There is another army marching north to Dura.'

I stood up in alarm. 'What army?'

'The army of King Porus of Sakastan, majesty.'

I immediately sent riders to the lords summoning them to Dura. After they arrived I convened a council of war. Before he had left us, the soldier from Babylon had told me that Porus was just over a hundred miles from Dura, marching along the eastern bank of the Euphrates.

'Ten days' march from us then, give or take,' said Domitus, his arms folded across his chest as he looked at the map of the Parthian

145

Empire on the wall of the antechamber. Sitting around the table were Rsan, Godarz, Nergal, Domitus, Gallia and Dobbai, while the score of Dura's lords stood around the walls. I had my back to the map, while Malik and Byrd were standing beside the door. If any of the lords had an objection to Malik being present none said so, though the looming threat of Porus probably diminished any prejudice any of them felt towards him. From the map all could see that Sakastan was on the eastern borders of the empire, north of Carmania and to the east of Persis.

'How many in Porus' army, majesty?' asked one of them, a man in his forties with a scarred face and pale grey eyes.

'Vardan's man estimated around thirty thousand.'

A murmur went round the room then all eyes were upon me. I stood up.

'It seems we have two choices. We can either stay here and wait for Hatra's army to reinforce us.'

'By which time Porus might be banging at Dura's gates,' said Dobbai.

I ignored her. 'Or we can march south and fight Porus before he reaches us here.'

'You will be outnumbered four to one,' said Godarz, rubbing his chin. 'Tough odds.'

There was silence. I saw that several of the lords were looking down at their feet, no doubt weighing up our chances in their minds. I caught Domitus' eye, who smiled at me. I knew what he was thinking – fight a defensive battle and let the army of Porus break itself on the cohorts of his legion. But it had not yet been tested in battle, was it good enough? Then I remembered who had trained it. I nodded back at Domitus.

'Very well,' I said, 'this is my decision. We will march south and fight King Porus. We leave at dawn.'

Byrd had recruited a handful of Malik's people to act as scouts, and they and their prince left the city while it was still dark, galloping across the pontoon bridge and then south towards our enemy. I watched them go for I managed to sleep only a couple of hours that night. I shared breakfast with a withdrawn Gallia dressed in mail shirt, leggings and leather boots on her feet, her dagger tucked into her right boot. Her sword lay in its scabbard on the table where we picked at bread and fruit. I would have preferred her to stay in the city with Godarz, but arguing would avail me nothing so I did not try. In any case I needed her hundred Amazon archers, and I knew that she would never agree to them going without her at their head. I kept going over the numbers in

146

my mind – five thousand legionaries, two hundred cataphracts and around two thousand two hundred horse archers against thirty thousand. Long odds indeed.

Gallia stood, buckled her sword belt and picked up her helmet.

'Time to go.'

Her Amazons were waiting in the courtyard, mounted and fully armed with bows and swords. Praxima held the reins of Epona as Gallia embraced Dobbai and then mounted her horse. My cataphracts did not wear their armour and neither did their mounts, for a long march would serve only to tire both man and beast. Instead they carried lances, round wooden shields covered in leather sporting a red griffin and wore their full-face helmets. I wore my Roman helmet, cuirass and spatha. I mounted Remus and nodded to Godarz, Rsan and Dobbai standing on the palace steps, then trotted from the Citadel. Vagharsh was carrying my standard behind me. The city's streets were beginning to stir with activity as we rode under the stone griffin at the Palmyrene Gate and wheeled right to take the road that went over the pontoon bridge. Already the legion was snaking south along the road that ran parallel to the eastern bank of the River Euphrates.

We covered twenty miles on the first day, the legionaries marching six abreast and the cavalry covering their flanks and the rear. Nergal organised an advanced guard of horse that rode five miles in front of the army, and beyond them rode Byrd and Malik and their scouts, returning to us each night as the camp was being erected. They saw nothing the first day, nor the day after when we had covered a further twenty miles. The lords thought it most amusing that Domitus and his men built a camp at the end of each day, into which was crammed the wagons, mules and men of the legion. I ordered that everyone, including their lordships, should also camp each night within its earthworks, which made it very cramped but very safe. And each morning the wooden fence that was erected on top of the earth rampart was dismantled and the individual pieces of wood loaded onto mules to carry them to the site of the next camp.

On the third day, as the evening sun was dipping in the western sky, Byrd and Malik thundered into camp and rode up the main avenue to halt before Domitus' command tent, which I had taken over for the purposes of the campaign.

'Enemy ten miles to south,' was all Byrd said as he splashed his face with water from a metal basin on the table.

'Thousands of foot soldiers, plus many horses and elephants,' added Malik.

'Elephants?' I said.

Byrd wiped his face with a cloth. 'Fifty or sixty at least, all with towers on top of them carrying soldiers.'

Twenty minutes later the war council convened in my tent.

'What's an elephant?' asked Gallia, who looked pale and tired.

'A big ugly beast, lady, with a long nose that looks like a snake and huge white tusks either side of it,' said one of the lords.

'Twice the height of a man,' added Nergal. 'Horses do not like them.'

'Don't worry about them,' said Domitus nonchalantly.

'Are they marching this way, Byrd?' I asked.

'Yes, but pace is leisurely, like a stroll.'

'Very well.' I looked at all their faces. 'Tomorrow we will stand and fight them. We will anchor one of our wings on the river. That way they will not be able to outflank us where the water is, and the Euphrates is too wide and deep for them to cross, so there will be no chance for them to attack our rear. When we get to our position tomorrow I will explain our plan of battle more fully.'

They were in high spirits as they filed out of the tent. Domitus pulled me to one side as the others left.

'I'll need a few dozen pigs and some tar.'

'Pigs, tar?' I was confused.

'Yes, you know, bitumen. Send Byrd and his scouts to go and buy some from a local farmer. Think you can arrange that?'

'Yes, but why?'

He winked at me. 'Trust me, it will be worth the effort.'

He departed, whistling, while I sidled over to Gallia and put my arm round her waist.

'Are you sure you're well. You look pale.'

'Of course I'm pale, I've got blonde hair and blue eyes. Or would you prefer a dark-skinned eastern woman to warm your bed?'

She removed my arm and marched from the tent, back to her women. Before battle she preferred the company of her fellow female warriors, and as their leader she wanted to ensure that they were fully prepared for the next day. Tonight was no different, though when I visited her as she was sitting round a fire with her Amazons, she was still in a snappy mood.

'I'm fine, Pacorus, just pre-battle nerves.'

Whatever it was, it certainly was not that. Before and during battle she had ice-cool nerves. I let the matter rest, kissing her tenderly before I left her with her warriors.

The new day dawned slightly humid, and even before his

legionaries had started to form up into their centuries Domitus was at my side, reminding me about the tar and pigs. So I gave Byrd two leather pouches full of money and told him to scour the immediate vicinity and purchase what Domitus required. They were easy enough to find as the area was littered with farms, though many farmers were taking their families and livestock north to avoid Porus and his army. Those that Byrd came across that morning were richly rewarded with silver for their pigs.

I walked to the river with Domitus, Nergal and Dura's lords. The day was overcast but pleasantly warm for the new year was still young. The river, deep and wide at this point, flowed gently towards the Persian Gulf. Around us, the legionaries were being marshalled into their battle positions. There was much joking and coarse language as centurions shoved and cajoled their men into their places. Their faces showed determination not alarm, and I was confident that they would perform well in this, their first battle. Standing fifty paces or so in front of the five cohorts extending from the riverbank, I looked south. Still no sign of the enemy.

The ground where we were standing was a patchwork of fields and shallow irrigation channels, though these would offer little impediment to elephants or foot soldiers. On our left flank, beyond the last cohort, there were no irrigation channels and the ground was flat and largely featureless aside from a few isolated poplar trees. It was good cavalry country. To extend our front, Domitus had deployed his legion in two lines, with five cohorts in each line. The cohorts in the second line were standing behind the gaps between the cohorts in the first line, thus the last cohort on the left flank in the second line actually extended beyond the end of the first line. In this way, should the legion's left flank be threatened, this cohort could turn and form a line at right angles to the first line to provide flank cover. On our extreme left flank, beyond the legion, the horse archers of Dura's lords and my cataphracts, both men and horses now fully armoured, were leading their horses into line on foot, for there was no point in sitting in the saddle for hours until the enemy came into view.

'What is your plan, majesty?' asked one of the lords.

'To beat the enemy,' I replied, grinning.

There was a ripple of laughter. 'The plan,' I continued, 'is simple. We let Porus attack us with his elephants, then once we have beaten them, the horse,' I pointed towards our left flank, 'will attack their cavalry.'

The lords looked behind them at the legionaries checking mail shirts, swords and javelins. Then they looked at each other.

'Speak freely,' I said.

The one who had described to Gallia what an elephant was did so. 'Years ago, majesty, I fought with Sinatruces against the Indians and their elephants. The beasts wear armour and steel covers on their tusks. They only use bull elephants in battle, and they are big and aggressive. They will punch through your legion and trample the men underfoot.'

I looked at Domitus, who now spoke. 'Don't worry about the elephants. We'll use an old Roman trick against them. They won't even reach my boys.'

'Very well,' I said, 'to your positions.'

The lords walked to their horses, vaulted into the saddles and rode away to their men. Vagharsh held Remus' reins as I picked up my kontus lying on the ground and with Domitus' assistance hoisted myself into the saddle. My scale armour felt heavy and I was already sweating. Unlike my men, I did not wear a full-face helmet but retained my Roman helm with its white goose-feather crest. I placed it on my head and looked down at Domitus, who also sported a white crest on his helmet.

'You're sure you can stop the elephants?'

He grinned. 'Quite sure, you just make sure you stay alive.'

'Upon you the battle rests, Domitus. You have to beat off those elephants.'

He raised his vine cane. 'We won't let you down.'

I raised my hand at him and then nudged Remus forward. I rode in front of the legion, raising my lance as I passed the men. They began cheering and banging their javelins on the inside of their shields, shouting 'Dura, Dura', as I rode past them and joined my cataphracts on the left flank. Most of them were lying on the ground resting, as were the lords and their horse archers behind them. Squires fussed around, offering waterskins to men and horses. I too dismounted and took a waterskin from Nergal. Its contents were warm, but I drank some and then gave the rest to Remus. His head, neck and body were covered in scale armour, and fine steel grills protected his eyes. The Amazons sat on the ground in groups immediately behind the cataphracts, Gallia walking among them with words of encouragement. She wore leather boots, leggings and a white blouse under her mail shirt. And like me, the rest of my cataphracts and her Amazons she wore a silk vest next to her skin. If an enemy arrow pierced her mail armour it would fail to go through the silk, a material that is difficult to tear. Instead the arrow would carry the silk into the wound with it, wrapping the material around it as it did so for arrows spin when in flight. Thus by gently lifting the twisted silk and turning the arrow by the same route that it had entered the body, the shaft could be extracted, leaving a small entry hole, though I prayed to Shamash that no arrow would strike her.

She walked over to me with Praxima by her side. Nergal embraced his wife tenderly.

'Well,' I said. 'Here we are again, dressed for battle. I thought we had done with war when we left Italy. It seems I was wrong.'

'Do not worry, lord,' said Praxima, the thought of imminent carnage sparking a glint in her eyes, 'we will beat the enemy once more.'

I walked over and kissed her on the cheek. 'With you beside me I don't doubt it.'

Praxima may have been the wife of my second-in-command, but she had never lost the semi-feral nature of character. She revelled in war and thought nothing of killing. I had to confess that she still unnerved me.

'Keep your women close behind my cataphracts,' I said to Gallia, 'just like we have practised on the training ground.'

Around me individuals suddenly began to stir and stand up. I looked round and saw two figures on horseback galloping in our direction. I signalled assembly to be called and seconds later horns were being blown and men were mounting their horses. The two figures slowed as they approached and I saw that it was Byrd and Malik, who halted yards from me and raised their hands in salute.

'Porus come,' was all Byrd said, before swivelling in the saddle and pointing in the direction he had ridden from. I peered into the distance but could see nothing, but then I heard what seemed like distant thunder, a low, thudding noise.

I turned to Gallia and held in her my arms.

'Shamash be with you.'

She smiled. 'And with you.'

We kissed and then her perfect visage disappeared behind her helmet as she closed the cheekguards and vaulted on to Epona's back. My cataphracts formed into two lines as once more I mounted Remus and scanned the horizon. I still could see nothing, but the rumbling noise was getting louder.

'They are about eight, ten miles away, marching this way,' said Malik, sounding alarmed.

'Many elephants,' was all that Byrd added.

Nergal rode up and saluted. He would lead the horse archers this day, who were grouped in a solid block behind my own men.

And so we waited until the opposing army came into view, though by the time it did so the area was engulfed by the unrelenting din of its kettledrummers on horseback, drummers on foot, trumpeters and horn players. At first the army appeared as a long black line on the horizon, but as it got closer I began to identify its various elements – foot soldiers, horsemen and, towering above everything else, elephants. It took around an hour for the enemy to come into view and a further hour for them to deploy into battle array. And throughout that period we did nothing but wait, for I did not want to interrupt their careful preparations. It was certainly the most colourful army that I had ever seen, a profusion of red, orange and yellow flags and pennants. And all the while the cacophony of noise filled our ears. The captains of the opposing host saw the legion drawn up and deployed their foot to face them, all the while their cavalry – armed with long lances and protected by helmets, hide shields and leather cuirasses reinforced by iron plates – filing into position opposite my horsemen to prevent us launching a charge before their foot was in position. The latter comprised two groups – archers equipped with long bamboo bows the height of a man, which required one end to be anchored on firm ground before they could be fired, and swordsmen dressed in baggy leggings and loose-fitting tunics carrying ox-hide shields. The archers deployed into a dense mass behind the swordsmen, while in front of the foot soldiers lumbered the elephants. I counted at least sixty, each one with its own guard of ten spearmen who walked on either side of the animal.

The elephants were certainly magnificent beasts, their foreheads protected by large polished bronze plates and their tusks encased in gleaming steel armour. On their backs, secured in place by ropes that ran under their bellies, were wooden boxes holding three archers, with a driver sitting on the elephant's neck immediately in front of the firing platform. The elephants seemed unconcerned by the deafening noise, unlike our horses that were beginning to get panicky by the commotion and the sight of the elephants. Remus grunted and began to shift uneasily beneath me, requiring me to constantly reassure him. Eventually the elephants were in position in a long line facing the frontline cohorts at a distance of around five hundred paces. Directly opposite my banner was the standard of Porus, a great yellow flag with braided gold cord hanging on a wooden dowel and attached to a long pole. It carried the image of an elephant's head, the symbol of Sakastan.

After the enemy had finally moved into their positions, I ordered Byrd to ride to where Porus was mounted on his horse amidst a great gathering of his commanders. I told him to convey a message to the king that I requested a parley. So Byrd tied a white cloth around his wrist and held his arm aloft as he trotted across no-man's land towards the king. When he reached the mid-spot between the two armies a rider came from Porus to meet him and the two halted but feet apart. I saw Byrd gesturing with his hands, nod and then turn around to return to me.

Moments later Porus, escorted by a retinue of a dozen lords, emerged from the front ranks of his horsemen. I signalled to Byrd and Nergal to follow me as I urged Remus forward. Both parties slowed as we approached each other, halting to leave a gap of ten paces between us. I recognised Porus from the Council of Kings, a dark-skinned, handsome man with a neatly trimmed moustache but no beard. In his mid-forties, he had dark brown eyes and a slightly bent nose. He looked magnificent dressed in his cuirass of overlapping square silver scales, open-faced helmet, bright yellow silk shirt, red leather gloves inlaid with silver, yellow leggings and red leather boots. A sword with an elaborate silver cross guard hung from his belt, encased in a red leather scabbard with gold leaf decoration. His horse was an immaculately groomed black stallion, its coat shimmering in the sunlight.

I held my hand up to him.

'Hail, King Porus.' He raised his hand in return but said nothing.

I continued. 'You are a long way from Sakastan. This is Hatran territory, therefore I request that you turn your army around and take it home, for it has no business here.'

'Where are your father and his army, King Pacorus?' His tone was sharp, mocking. 'Is he hiding behind his high walls in fear, and sends his son to do his business?'

'The affairs of Hatra are my business,' I replied, 'so I say again, turn your army around and take it back to Sakastan.'

He said nothing but peered past me to my cavalry deployed behind me, then looked south at the legion standing silently in its ranks. Then he looked directly at me.

'I do not think that you are in any position to dictate terms, boy. Have you not seen my army and how it dwarfs yours?'

'It makes a loud noise, I'll grant you that,' I sniffed. 'But this is as far as it goes.'

'Brave words for a whelp,' he said. 'If you prostrate yourself at my feet I will let you live, otherwise we will sweep you aside, just like we did Phraates and his rabble.'

'Phraates is the rightful King of Kings,' I reminded him. 'And all those who take up arms against him are traitors and deserve a traitor's death.'

His eyes flashed with rage. 'You dare insult me, boy?'

I laughed at him. 'I dare. I see that you are not going to surrender after all.'

An evil grin crept over his face. 'Is she here?'

'Who?'

'Your wife, of course, the one who fights like a man? Or is she skulking back in Dura?'

Now it was my turn to be angry. 'Where my wife is concerns you not, though she has killed better men than you.'

He pointed at me. 'When your head adorns my city walls, I will make her one of my harem. Or perhaps I will give her to my men as a plaything tonight.

'The time of Phraates is over. The Parthian Empire has a new leader now. The new age has dawned. I am but the vanguard of Narses, the rightful King of Kings.'

I laughed in his face. 'He and you are traitors, and will live to regret your insurrection. We are done talking, Porus.'

'So be it, boy. Tell your woman to be ready to warm my bed tonight.'

He then wheeled his horse away and galloped back to the safety of his army. I did the same, and just as I had taken my lance from Vagharsh the accursed trumpets and drums of the army of Porus echoed across the battlefield. And as the noise increased in volume his elephants, magnificent and terrifying, began to advance towards the locked shields of the legion.

It was the shortest battle that I ever fought in.

The drivers of the elephants kept their beasts under tight control until they were within three hundred paces of the frontline cohorts, and then Domitus sprang his trick. He had distributed the pigs among the centuries of the first line, immediately behind which stood braziers cooking tar. When the elephants approached each pig had its back covered in hot tar, and was then prodded with javelin tips towards the tusked behemoths. Terrified and enraged, the pigs ran towards the elephants squealing loudly as they did so. The elephants immediately stopped and roared with terror as the pigs approached them. Some reared up on their back legs and tipped the drivers and archers on their backs onto the ground, others swerved violently aside and crashed into the elephant next to them, while others turned around and charged headlong into the mass of swordsmen formed up behind. Within minutes those swordsmen were fleeing hither and thither for their lives as all semblance of order and discipline among their ranks evaporated. Then the legion's trumpets blasted to signal the advance and ten cohorts marched forward. As they did so I turned in the saddle and shouted at my cataphracts.

'Kill Porus!'

I screamed at Remus and he sprang forward. I held my kontus with both hands on my right side as the four horns of the saddle held me firmly in place, the lance tip aimed at Porus directly opposite. My cataphracts charged, forming into an arrowhead formation, and behind them Gallia's Amazons followed, loosing volleys of arrows over our heads and into the enemy's cavalry. Porus, seeing his elephants and then his foot routing, lost his nerve and decided to flee the battlefield. Around him his men, now being hit by arrow fire and seeing their lord turn tail, were in a state of indecision as we hit them. I plunged my lance into a rider attempting to turn his horse around and skewered him on my kontus. Leaving the shaft in his body, I drew my spatha and swung it at the head of a horseman attempting to spear me in turn. But his lance was on his right side and I was on his left, and my sword swing cut into his neck before he had chance to spear me. Then we were hacking at the backs of fleeing riders, chasing them south as they desperately tried to outrun us. Weighted down as our horses were by scale armour and carrying riders similarly protected, many of the enemy cavalry were able to outrun us, but then came Nergal leading two thousand horse archers who overtook my cataphracts and galloped on to hunt down the enemy.

'Keep after them, don't let them reform,' I shouted to him as he passed me.

I halted as hundreds of horse archers streamed past. The other cataphracts also slowed and then halted – there was no use in wasting the stamina of our horses. Gallia's Amazons, retaining perfect discipline, also halted and dressed their ranks. I rode over to her.

'Everything is well?'

She unfastened her cheekguards and pushed the steel plates part. 'All is well.'

The cataphracts formed two lines once more with the Amazons behind them. We rode south to where the legion was following in the wake of the rampaging elephants. Here the battle was also over, as the foot soldiers of Porus were following their mounted companions and fleeing as fast as possible. In front of the advancing cohorts the ground was littered with abandoned weapons, shields and standards. Dead elephants lay scattered among the detritus of battle, while others, horribly wounded, lay on their sides and groaned in agony. No part of Porus' army made any attempt to rally and fight, and aside from killing a few unfortunates who were wounded and unable to flee, Domitus' men had not washed their swords in the enemy's blood.

I found him at the head of the centre cohort in the first line, giving orders to signal a halt to the advance. I dismounted and we clasped arms.

'How did you know about the pigs?' I asked, slapping him on the back.

He took off his helmet and took a swig from his water bottle, as legionaries were detached from the ranks to run to the river and fetch fresh water. 'Old Roman trick that we picked up in the Punic Wars.'

'Punic Wars?'

He spat on the ground and handed me his water bottle. 'The last one was over seventy years ago when Rome finally subdued the Carthaginians, a people who lived in a place called Africa. Anyway, the Carthaginians had elephants but the Romans soon learned that they don't like the squeals of pigs, panics them.'

'So I saw.'

Around us my cataphracts dismounted and legionaries rested on their shields, joking and chatting with their comrades. Domitus looked round approvingly.

'Just what my boys needed, an easy victory.'

'All down to you, my friend,' I said.

I walked with him back to camp with Gallia beside me. Her Amazons formed a rearguard as the legion formed into a long column and marched at a steady pace behind us. Her face and hair were covered in sweat and she looked deathly white, but I put it down to the stress of combat. When we reached camp Domitus ordered a roll call to determine his losses – they totalled five killed and sixty wounded. I had lost two cataphracts killed and three wounded, while Gallia's Amazons had suffered no losses. Three hours later an exhausted Nergal rode into camp at the head of the lords and their men. He reported to me immediately in my command tent as the lords filed in behind him, all of them in good spirits.

'We rode them down and killed them until we ran out of arrows.'

'Then we used our swords until our blades were blunt,' added one of the lords.

Nergal pointed to one. 'Show him.'

The lord threw a bundle of cloth at my feet. 'A gift to celebrate your victory, lord.'

I picked it up, unfolded it and saw the elephant banner of King Porus. There was a mighty cheer as I held it aloft for all to see. Beside me Gallia's eyes rolled back into her head and she collapsed to the floor. I fell to my knees and cradled her in my arms, desperately searching her body for any sign of a wound. I saw none.

'Get a doctor!' I screamed as I held her head to my chest. 'Gallia, Gallia.' I got no response and my heart started to beat wildly in my chest. I began to panic as I held my face next to hers, while around me men just stood open-mouthed. Where there had been joy and cheering there was now concern and silence. Moments later Alcaeus, the wiry, black-haired Greek who had been a doctor in the army of Spartacus, was at my side, examining Gallia.

'Put her on a bed so I can examine her properly, and get these oafs to leave, all of them. The air is foul in here.'

Domitus ushered everyone out while I carried Gallia to a cot in the corner. I gently laid her down and Alcaeus waved me away.

'What's wrong with her?' I asked feebly.

'If you give me some room and stop asking stupid questions, I will try to find out. Wait outside.'

I obeyed his command and stood for what seemed like an eternity outside the tent. A grim-faced Domitus and Nergal looked at the ground while the lords looked at each other and then me, concern etched on their hard faces. Word spread of what had happened and within no time a great crowd had gathered around us – cataphracts, Amazons and legionaries, all standing in silence and unsure what to do.

Then the tent flap opened and Alcaeus walked out into the light. He pointed at me.

'You can go in and see her now. Only you mind.'

'Will she be all right, doctor?' I asked.

He looked at me and screwed up his face. 'Yes, if you get her back to Dura. She should never have left. What were you thinking?'

'I don't understand.'

'Really? Then let me spell it out for you. Bringing your pregnant wife on campaign is the height of idiocy. For a great warlord Pacorus, sometimes you have the intellect of a mule.'

With that he stalked off, pushing his way through the throng.

Domitus slapped me hard on the back, while Nergal clasped my forearm. Praxima threw her arms round me and kissed me on the cheek, while the others started cheering. I was going to be a father. Alcaeus stormed back and ordered me to disperse the crowd of well-wishers as they were disturbing Gallia. I did so and then crept into the tent. She was sitting up in the cot with cushions supporting her, some colour having at last returned to her cheeks.

I held her hand and kissed it. 'Why did you not tell me?'

'I suspected but was not certain. I'm sorry.'

'Nonsense, I am truly happy.' I handed her cup of water from the small table beside the cot. 'Alcaeus is angry with me for bringing you on campaign.'

'It's not your fault, I wanted to be by your side.'

I knelt over and kissed her on the lips. 'I know, but it's back to Dura for you now.'

She was going to protest, but her condition and present exhaustion made her think twice and so she said nothing and fell asleep with me sitting on the side of the cot, gently brushing her forehead with my fingers.

The next day I summoned Praxima to my tent and told her that she and Gallia would be riding back to Dura forthwith, and that I would brook no argument. After changing and eating a hearty breakfast of fruit, salted pork and biscuit, Gallia stepped out into the morning light. Domitus embraced her and showed her a colour party of his legionaries, all washed and arrayed in their finest white tunics and shiny helmets. Nergal gave her the captured elephant standard of Porus as a gift, which she said she would take back to Dura to hang in the throne room. When word spread that she was leaving the army, each of the lords asked permission to escort her back to the city. Had I accepted I would have lost all my cavalry, so I had them draw lots to choose the winner, who turned out to be a one-eyed rascal named Spandarat. He was squat, barrel-chested and had arms as thick as tree trunks and hands the size of a bear's paws.

'Don't you worry, majesty,' he told me as he stood at the head of his two hundred men, 'I'll get her back to the city all right, and be back before you've had chance to slit any more throats.'

'Thank you, Spandarat, I look forward to fighting by your side once more.'

He leaned forward in his saddle and stroked the neck of his horse, an old warrior like him, but as hard as tempered steel. 'I had my doubts about you, especially after we had to put up with that other arrogant young bastard Mithridates, but I have to tell you that

I was wrong. Never seen elephants panic like that. Your man, there,' he pointed at Domitus, 'knows what he's doing.'

'Yes he does,' I said.

Gallia was mounted on Epona at the head of her Amazons, Praxima beside her. Nergal kissed his wife and bade her a safe journey, and I walked over and stood next to Gallia. 'Now, when you get back to Dura make sure you have plenty of rest and food. You are eating for two now.'

'Yes, father,' she replied.

I waved her forward with my hand. She bent down and I kissed her on the lips.

'I love you.'

She smiled that most beautiful smile of hers. 'I love you too, and take care of yourself. Don't do anything idiotic.'

'A charm,' I said, 'I need a charm.'

'What?'

'I need a lock of your hair.'

She took her dagger from the top of her boot and grabbed her long, thick plait that hung down her back, then cut off some strands of her hair and handed them to me. Then she took her helmet from Praxima, put it and tied the cheekguards shut. She commanded Epona to walk forward and then led the column of three hundred riders down the camp's main avenue and then north to Dura. I stood watching them until they were tiny specs on the horizon and then disappeared altogether. It was the first time Gallia had left my side in over three years. Yet I had no time to dwell on my loss, for that same afternoon Malik and Byrd returned to camp bringing a most unexpected gift. They were both dirty and unshaven and their horses needed a good groom. They halted in front of my tent and Malik dumped the body of a dead man at my feet.

'Behold, Pacorus, I bring you King Porus.'

I looked down at the mangled body, covered in filth and dried black blood. Glazed, lifeless eyes stared into the sky, and though I thought I recognised the traces of the neatly trimmed moustache I could not be sure as the face had been cut and bludgeoned. But I did recognise the yellow shirt and red leather gloves that still encased his hands.

I looked up at the tattooed face of Malik. 'Did you kill him?'

He nodded. 'We caught up with him and his entourage and then charged them. They put up a fight at first, but my men made short work of them. We killed them all, none escaped.'

'We also found these,' said Byrd, who reached into his tunic and threw a parcel of parchments on the ground. I picked them up and examined them. They included messages from Narses to Porus and vice-versa.

I nodded at Byrd. 'Excellent, well done. Get some food inside you and your horses seen to. Good to have you both back.'

'What do you want to do with that?' asked Domitus, pointing at the corpse with his cane.

'Cut off the head, stick it on a pole and place it outside the camp's main entrance. Give the rest to the pigs.'

The army of Hatra arrived the next day, fifteen hundred cataphracts and nine thousand horse archers led by my father and Vistaspa. The horsemen established their camp two miles upstream from us while my father and Vistaspa paid me a visit. I had the legion parade in battle array in front of the camp, flanked by my own cataphracts and the horse archers of my lords. Afterwards I gave a feast in their honour in my tent. Domitus sat next to Vistaspa and told him about the defeat of Porus and his elephants, while my father congratulated me on my victory.

'It was not my victory, father, but the knowledge of Domitus that decided the day.'

My father raised his cup of wine to my general. 'My congratulations. This will allow us to march to Ctesiphon and relieve Phraates.'

'We have heard of another force of rebels marching south towards Babylon and Mesene,' I said.

'Then we must deal with them first,' replied my father.

He and his army had passed Gallia and her retinue on her way back to Dura. 'By the way, Pacorus, congratulations on your approaching fatherhood. Your mother will be pleased to be a grandmother at last.'

Everyone banged the hilt of their daggers on the tables in recognition.

'Hopefully Porus has not gone south and added his numbers to those who are threatening Babylon's territory.'

I filled my cup with wine from a jug. 'Porus is dead, father. His head sits on a pole outside this camp.'

The lords banged the tables again and cheered, while my father looked horrified. I saw his look.

'He insulted Gallia, so it is a fitting end for him.'

He said nothing more on the matter, for which I was pleased – I had no regrets that the head of Porus adorned a pole outside my camp.

The next two days were taken up with reorganisation. Domitus had details of men scouring the battlefield and the path of flight of

Porus' army to retrieve anything of use. The hide shields and broken spear shafts were ignored, but swords, spear points, helmets and daggers were piled onto carts and sent back to Dura. There they would be either melted down and turned into javelins and arrowheads or, if they were of decent quality, stored in the armoury. Birds were already picking at the carcasses of dead elephants and men, which prompted a sense of urgency as we did not want to be infected with the pestilence that dead flesh spreads.

I sent Nergal south with a thousand riders to discover the whereabouts of the rebel force that was rumoured to be ravaging Babylonian territory, but he returned with news that it had been dispersed by Vardan and that Babylon's army was now marching north to join us.

'I wouldn't put too much faith in Babylon's ragged band,' said Vistaspa standing in my tent looking at a map of the empire laid out on a large rectangular table. 'A few cavalry and the rest armed with pitchforks and wicker shields.'

'Slightly unfair,' remarked my father.

'But true, lord,' said Vistaspa.

Domitus looked at me and shook his head. Unfortunately, what Vistaspa had said was correct. Babylon had once been a great power, the strongest kingdom in the world, but that was hundreds of years ago. The great Persian king Darius had captured it four hundred and fifty years before my time, and then Alexander of Macedon had seized it two hundred and fifty years ago. Since then it had faded in wealth and importance, and though the kings of Babylon were accorded great respect due to the longevity of their line, in truth their power was much reduced.

'We should move south to link up with Vardan's army,' I said, drawing a finger on the map from our present position and following the course of the Euphrates south towards Ctesiphon.

'Agreed,' said my father. 'We can follow the river until we are level with Ctesiphon, which is only sixty miles north of Babylon, then advance east towards the Tigris and relieve Phraates.'

'If he still lives.' Vistaspa appeared to be in his usual dour mood.

'He's alive,' said my father, 'the reports I've had from Ctesiphon state that Narses is content to sit outside the city and wait for Phraates to offer terms.'

'What terms?' I asked.

My father shrugged. 'To abdicate in his favour, I assume. Narses wants to be King of Kings and he believes that he has the present holder of that office boxed in at Ctesiphon.'

'He will have heard of the fate of Porus by now, lord,' remarked Domitus.

Vistaspa nodded. 'Yes he will, and if he's got any sense he will run back to Persepolis.'

'Or,' mused my father, 'he might want us to attack him. After all, he has to defeat us if he wants to wear the high crown.'

'Do we know the size of his army?' I asked.

Vistaspa laughed. 'I wouldn't worry about that, Pacorus. You have already showed that numbers matter little when it comes to the fight.'

Domitus smiled but my father was not amused by such bravado. 'That may be, but hopefully Vardan will also bring Mesene's army with him.'

Vistaspa raised an eyebrow but said nothing.

The next day we marched south, Nergal riding ahead with the lords in the vanguard in honour of their victory over Porus. I rode beside my father and Vistaspa, the banners of Hatra and Dura behind us, followed by my cataphracts, my father's bodyguard and the legion, with the horse archers and cataphracts of Hatra bringing up the rear. The day was warm and still as we rode at a leisurely pace. Here the land between the Tigris and Euphrates is an alluvial plain, bisected by many dirt roads, fields, irrigation ditches and dams near the rivers to prevent flooding. Usually bustling with trade caravans and farmers working in the fields, today it was a desolate wasteland devoid of activity.

'You appreciate, Pacorus,' remarked my father, 'how war is poison to Parthia. The farmers have all fled north and the trade caravans have taken refuge in the cities. Without farmers there is no food, and without food we cannot fill our bellies. And without trade there are no taxes, and without taxes there is no money to pay for our armies.'

'Then we must crush this rebellion as soon as possible,' I replied.

'You see, Vistaspa,' continued my father, 'how youth always wants to decide matters by the sword.'

'Is there any other way?' I replied.

'Our objective is to relieve Ctesiphon and free Phraates, no more,' said my father. 'There will be no pre-emptive assault against Narses and his army, at least not until we have permission to do so.'

'Narses is a traitor,' I said, 'who deserves a traitor's death.'

'Narses is a king, Pacorus, and you would do well to remember that. He also has the support of other kings. Phraates will want to win them over, not force them into a corner.'

I was unconvinced. 'Destroy Narses and the rebellion will crumble.'

'Perhaps you would like his head on a pole outside your camp as well?'

'Why not? He wants the crown of Phraates, there can be no accommodation with such a man.'

'It is for Phraates to decide such things,' said Vistaspa.

'Exactly,' said my father icily. 'You still have much to learn about diplomacy, Pacorus.'

What was there to learn? Narses had led an insurrection and had to be punished. I could not understand my father's hesitancy, but then I did not have to worry about events in the north of my kingdom like he did, for with the fall of Gordyene to the Romans their legions were now massing on his northern borders. He said nothing of Balas and I did not ask him, but the death of his friend must have weighed heavily on his mind and he obviously had reluctantly marched south to come to the relief of Phraates. I had been disappointed that Vata had not accompanied Hatra's army, but Vistaspa had informed me that my old friend had been given the responsibility of ensuring that the Romans did not encroach upon Hatran territory.

Five days later we met Vardan and his Babylonian hordes. Babylon might not have been the power it once was but Vardan had mustered an impressive number of troops, all dressed in various shades of purple and carrying banners of the same colour, while behind Vardan himself fluttered his banner depicting a great white horned bull called a gauw upon a purple background, the beast being the symbol of Babylon. He rode at the head of his royal bodyguard, five hundred magnificent horsemen wearing so-called dragon skin armour – a leather vest covered with overlapping silver plates protecting their chests and backs. They were wearing open-faced steel helmets, carried large, round wooden shields covered with purple-painted hide, and were armed with swords and lances. Their tunics and leggings were also purple and purple pennants flew from their lances. Next came his horse archers, who wore no armour and who carried swords in addition to their quivers and bows. They numbered around three thousand. The bulk of Vardan's army comprised foot soldiers – slingers and archers who wore no armour and spearmen who carried oblong wicker shields and who wore long purple tunics that covered their arms and extended down to their knees, with purple trousers and turbans. The number of foot soldiers must have totalled an additional six thousand. I rode ahead with my father to greet our ally.

'Hail, Vardan,' said my father, shaking the hand of the king.

'Hail Varaz and Pacorus.' Vardan wore a simple open-faced steel helmet and dragon-skin armour on his body. He also wore thick steel shoulder plates adorned with sitting bulls and at his hip he wore a sword that had a pommel in the shape of a bull's head.

'It is good to see you, my friend,' said my father.

'You too, Varaz.'

'How is Axsen, sire?' I asked.

He smiled at me. 'She sends her love to you and Gallia. Is she with you?'

'No, sire. She has had to return to Dura.'

'She's pregnant,' said my father, 'though she only discovered this after she had fought in battle. It seems I am going to be a grandfather.'

Vardan beamed with delight. 'Excellent news, we will all celebrate in my tent tonight.'

That night the campfires of Vardan's army carpeted the horizon as his men pitched their gaudily coloured tents along the banks of the Euphrates. No neatly arranged lines of tents enclosed in a palisaded camp for the army of Babylon; rather, a disorganised assembly of tents, horses and camels. The only order that existed among the multitude was the king's tent and the tents of his bodyguard circled around it, the horses of the royal bodyguard being quartered in a stable block immediately behind the royal enclosure, the stalls formed by poles and canvas wind breaks. The air was filled with wood smoke and the aroma of roasting meat as I rode with Nergal to the king's tent, our horses being taken from us by purple-clad grooms. The tent itself was a massive structure, actually a pavilion hung with brightly coloured tapestries. Inside, fifty thick wooden columns held the roof in place, oil lamps hanging from each one. Carpets were spread over the floor and couches were arranged in a circle in the centre, while soldiers of the king's bodyguard stood around the circular wall. Incense burned on tables and a host of purple-attired servants ferried silver platters heaped with meats, bread, fruit and pastries to guests. Others poured wine into silver and gold cups. It was a far cry from the austere regime of Domitus and his legion or my palace at Dura.

My father and Vistaspa were already relaxing on couches near Vardan and his senior commanders when we entered. Vardan beckoned us both over with his hand. He was reclining on a large couch stuffed with cushions. Nergal and I sat opposite him.

'King Vardan tells me that Chosroes is also on the march and will be joining us shortly,' said my father.

I accepted a cup of wine from a beautiful servant girl with flawless olive skin, one breast exposed and a gold chain running from her pierced ear to her nose. She smiled to reveal a set of perfect white teeth.

'Excellent,' I said, sipping the wine, which was exquisite. Vardan certainly knew how to travel in style on campaign, I gave him that.

'Pacorus wishes to fight Narses and his army,' remarked my father.

Vardan shook his head. 'I doubt it will come to that. Some sort of negotiated peace seems more likely.'

'That's what I told him.'

I drained my cup and held it out to be refilled. 'There will be no peace until Narses is dead.'

Vardan frowned. 'Killing kings only creates bad blood, Pacorus. Did you know, for example, that Porus had two sons who will seek vengeance for his death?'

I smiled, but Vardan did not know that the sons of Porus had died fighting beside their father.

'And the matter of the killing of King Balas also has to be addressed,' added my father.

'Ah, yes. A tragedy. The Romans have too much arrogance,' mused Vardan. He looked at me. 'Where is your Roman?'

'Attending to his duties, sire.'

'Well, let's hope that he is not the vanguard of a Roman invasion into the empire.'

Chosroes arrived two days later at the head of his army, a ragged band of horse archers dressed in dirty tunics sitting on skinny mounts and foot archers and spearmen attired in a variety of filthy tunics with leather caps on their heads. Though the king's bodyguard of a thousand mounted spearmen had wooden shields and leather armour, the rest of the army was sadly deficient in armoured horsemen. He did bring five hundred archers mounted on camels as well, men whose faces were wrapped in turbans and who wore long flowing robes. In addition to the fighting men, Chosroes brought a horde of camp followers – harlots, beggars, traders and thieves who trailed in his army's wake. I estimated the numbers of his fighting men to be ten thousand, no more, and their quality left much to be desired.

I was standing beside Domitus at the entrance to our camp as the army of Chosroes filed past to set up their tents two miles north of us. I saw the disdain on Domitus' face.

165

'They are our allies, Domitus.'

'I would rather they were our enemies,' he sniffed. 'If we fight a battle in the coming days, try to ensure that they are as far away from my legion as possible.'

'You think they will run?'

'I know they will run. And when they do the poor bastards standing beside them will discover that they suddenly have no flank protection.'

I knew he was right, but that evening Vardan and my father welcomed Chosroes to the army and toasted his loyalty. Dressed in a red flowing gown adorned with gold strips, his eyes were cold and calculating but he was cordial enough if a little curt. He seemed far from enthusiastic at having to muster his army for this campaign, but he too had voted for Phraates and so had a vested interest in seeing him retain his throne. I also learned that Porus had raided his lands.

'I heard about your victory over Porus,' he said, picking at some roasted goat on a silver plate that he held with his long, bony hand. 'A most welcome development.'

'Thank you, sire.' Technically I was his equal, but I was always aware that the rest of the kings were middle-aged men or older and that I was a mere boy compared to their years and experience, so I was more than happy to defer to them, rebels aside.

'Yes, yes,' said Chosroes, 'most welcome.'

Vistaspa, on the next couch to mine, leaned over. 'What he means is that he is glad he did not have to fight them himself.'

'You mean he is a coward?' I was shocked as I watched my father walk over to Chosroes and embrace him, then put an arm round his shoulder in a brotherly fashion and lead him away, the two of them deep in conversation.

'No, no, nothing like that' replied Vistaspa, 'but Mesene is poor. You must have deduced that from the condition of his troops. His kingdom does not benefit from the Silk Road and his people eke out an existence from the land. In the south, where the Euphrates and Tigris flow into the Persian Gulf, there are great marshes populated by a rebellious people, which adds a further drain on his resources.'

'Domitus has a low opinion of his troops.'

Vistaspa nodded. 'He's right in his opinion. But at least Chosroes is here, and for that reason alone we must be grateful.'

'Domitus also believes that if we have to give battle the soldiers of Chosroes will be the first to run.'

Vistaspa laughed out loud, causing Vardan and my father to

look at him quizzically. 'I like your Roman; he's a man after my own heart. And he's right again. Hopefully it will not come to that.'

My father's words had obviously cheered Chosroes up, for he sat back on his couch and raised his cup to Vistaspa and me, smiling as he did so. We raised ours in return.

'Perhaps we could convince him to fight for the enemy,' remarked Vistaspa, smiling at the King of Mesene.

But Chosroes did not desert and so his army formed the rear of a vast column that made its way towards the Tigris and Ctesiphon. Our progress would have been seen miles away, for the thousands of animals and men kicked up a vast cloud of dirt that got in our eyes and covered our clothes, so that after a day we resembled the men of Chosroes' army. We had scouts riding ahead, including Byrd and Malik, but they reported only an empty land and no sign of the enemy. Indeed, when we finally reached the Tigris at Ctesiphon, the city itself on the western bank of the river, directly opposite the large palace complex on the other side of the river, Byrd reported that Narses and his army had hurriedly departed eastwards, towards Susa. Curiously he had left the bridge across the river intact, and there was little evidence of damage to the city itself or the brick wall of the palace compound.

'Of course not,' remarked my father, 'he hoped to make this his home. Why then would he destroy it?'

And so, without raising a sword against him, we had forced Narses to retreat.

Chapter 10

That afternoon I rode with my father, Vardan and Chosroes to the palace. The heavy wooden gates opened to let us enter as soldiers observed us from the walls. Parthian armies have no knowledge of siege warfare and as far as I knew none of the empire's kings had engines with which to batter down fortifications, so unless walls are particularly weak or ill-maintained there is little likelihood of a city falling to an assault. Usually starvation forces surrender, and as I rode through the gates at Ctesiphon the latter seemed most likely had we delayed but a few days more. The wide expanse of open ground between the walls and the palace was filled with tents, horses and camels – troops from Susiana who had remained loyal to Phraates together with the shattered remnants of Elymais' army. Feeding such a multitude would have quickly emptied the palace storerooms. Inside the walled palace complex itself we were greeted by Prince Orodes, who, despite the fact that he had been besieged, still retained his cheerful disposition. He bowed to my father, Vardan and Chosroes and then embraced me.

'It is good to see you, majesty.'

'You don't have to call me that, Orodes. Pacorus will suffice. We are, after all, friends are we not?'

'My father and I certainly need all the friends we can get. Is Gallia with you?'

'I sent her back to Dura. She's pregnant.'

He shook my hand and beamed with delight. 'This is indeed a happy day, Pacorus. Tonight we will celebrate and toast your wife, but first my father wishes to convey his gratitude.'

Our horses were taken from us and we walked up the palace steps and into the cool interior of Phraates' palace. The high ceilings, yellow and blue painted walls and marble columns conveyed power and opulence whilst the immaculately dressed guards gave a sense of protocol and discipline. The ensuing ordered calm was in stark contrast to the disorder that currently raged outside the confines of the royal residence. Clerks and eunuchs scuttled around as Orodes escorted us into one of the throne rooms.

The large white doors inlaid with gold opened and we entered the seat of power, the same throne room where Sinatruces had made me King of Dura over two years before. How long ago it seemed now. That was a happy time, but the atmosphere in the room this time was far from joyous as we walked across the marble-tiled floor and bowed in front of the dais where Phraates sat next to his wife, Queen Aruna. I was shocked by how old Phraates looked. He was in his fifties and his hair had always been flecked with grey, but now there were large streaks of it in his mane, but what was more noticeable was how gaunt he looked. Sunken cheeks, bags under his eyes, his hands constantly fidgeting with the arms of his throne were indicative of the toll the rebellion had taken on him; that and the great weight upon his shoulders of being King of Kings. He did at least seem pleased to see us and raised his right hand in recognition.

'Greetings King Varaz, King Chosroes and King Vardan. You are all most welcome. And greetings to you, King Pacorus, who have added more lustre to your reputation by your recent victory.'

I bowed my head once more. 'Thank you, highness.'

Standing to the side of the dais, dressed in full war gear, was King Gotarzes of Elymais, whose army Narses had defeated and whose forces now sheltered inside the walls of the palace complex. He winked at me and I smiled back.

'Do you intend to march after the rebels, highness?' asked my father.

Phraates shifted uneasily on his throne. 'Well, I was hoping to reach an accommodation with them. The empire needs peace.'

'Peace, I absolutely agree,' added Chosroes.

'There can be peace after we have defeated Narses and his army,' I said.

All eyes were upon me and I soon realised that I had made a mistake to speak thus. Phraates frowned and looked at his feet, while the queen fixed me with an icy stare. It was the first time that I had met Queen Aruna. She was younger than Phraates by about five years, I surmised. Some would call her beautiful, with thick black curly hair that flowed down to her shoulders, a square, olive-skinned face with a perfect complexion and big brown eyes. But it was a harsh beauty, for she had a haughty manner and a condescending attitude, born no doubt of her upbringing in the court at Puta, for she was the sister of King Phriapatus of Carmania, an eastern kingdom that had sided with Narses. And from the first day that I met her she was my enemy.

'I do not wish to see the death of King Mithridates, my son, who currently accompanies King Narses,' she said. 'It is unbecoming for kings to kill each other. This is Parthia, not the barbarian wastelands of the steppes.'

So Mithridates was with Narses. It did not surprise me, the treacherous little snake.

'The current difficult situation will be settled now that you all have arrived,' said Phraates, ignoring his wife's utterance. 'Narses

169

will see sense and return to Persis.'

'Narses should be ordered here to explain his insolence,' added Aruna, 'and for luring away my innocent son from our side. Narses has obviously been bewitched, probably by that vile old hag who corrupted the divine Sinatruces.'

She shot me a hateful look. She was obviously alluding to Dobbai, and must have known that she now resided at Dura.

I caught the look of disbelief on Orodes' face. I had no doubt that whatever the reason for Mithridates being with Narses, it had nothing to do with him being deceived, more likely naked ambition.

'You wish to negotiate with your enemies, highness?' asked my father.

Aruna looked daggers at my father, her eyebrows squeezed together, then at her husband.

Phraates cleared his throat. 'They are not our enemies. They are our subjects, and as such I do not wish to make war upon them.'

The queen regarded us with a smug expression. I felt like we were small boys being chastised. Phraates rose from his throne and held out his hand to his queen, who took it and also stood up.

'You must be tired after your journey.' He gestured to one of his stewards standing by the dais. 'You will be shown to your rooms. Tonight we will have a feast to celebrate your arrival, and tomorrow we will decide what action is to be taken.'

We bowed our heads as the king and queen left the room, after which Orodes and Gotarzes accompanied us to our quarters in the palace.

'You arrived just in time, Varaz,' said Gotarzes, 'another week and we would have been starved out.'

The so-called 'feast' that evening was a dire event, the whole room drenched in an atmosphere of polite iciness. The queen pointedly ignored me, father and Vardan, though she did respond to the obsequiousness of Chosroes, whose mood had brightened markedly now that Phraates had stated his intention to avoid further bloodshed. I spoke to Orodes briefly before he took his place beside his parents at the top table. Then I took my seat on one of the long tables that had been arranged at right angles to the top table and which seated a host of courtiers dressed in bright yellows, greens, blues and reds. I sat next to Gotarzes, who I think was glad of my company.

'Are your family safe, lord?' I asked him.

He was taking large gulps from his silver cup. 'Yes, thank you. I sent them north to Khosrou, they'll be safe at Merv. So what do you think of our queen of queens.'

'You mean Queen Aruna?'

He drained his cup and held it out to a servant for it to be refilled. 'Yes, that's the bitch.'

'You dislike her?'

'Intensely. I did not realise that when we made Phraates King of Kings, we were in fact making her the ruler of the Parthian Empire.'

'Really?' I was unsure whether it was the drink talking.

He looked at me wryly. 'I've been cooped up here in this zoo long enough to know where the real power lies. She's like a hawk and makes sure that she has a say in everything Phraates decides. Bitch!'

He said the last word loudly enough to turn the heads of the high king and his queen, the latter looking hatefully at Gotarzes.

He took another gulp of wine and continued. 'It's easy to see how she could spawn such an evil little bastard like Mithridates.'

'But Orodes is also her son,' I said.

'Her adopted son. Orodes' mother was a concubine of Sinatruces whom Phraates fell in love with. Sinatruces forgave her infidelity, for a son born to a king, even a bastard one, is worth having. The result of his passion sits at the top table, and a fine young man he is, but Aruna's poisonous blood does not flow in his veins, thank God. Aruna never forgave her husband's infidelity, rumour has it, and he's full of remorse, the stupid idiot.'

'What happened to the concubine?'

A wicked smile crept over Gotarzes' face. 'Died of a fever, some say, though others maintain that she was poisoned by queen bitch over there. I am inclined to believe the latter. Bitch!'

He was now quite drunk and full of resentment. Queen Aruna had heard his last word.

'You have something to say, King Gotarzes?'

Gotarzes rose to his feet unsteadily and what little chatter there was died instantly. 'I do.'

The disdainful look on the face of Gotarzes made me realise that he was about to tell the queen exactly what he thought of her. The look of alarm on Orodes' face confirmed this. I therefore stood up and spoke first.

'King Gotarzes and I would like to thank your majesties for a most magnificent feast.'

My father lent back in his chair and regarded me with curiosity, while Vardan looked confused, for even an imbecile would know that this evening was an excruciating affair.

The queen frowned. 'I see. And are those his words or yours?'

'I do not need you to speak for me, Pacorus.'

'Indeed not,' snapped the queen. Her attention now turned to me.

'I have heard, King Pacorus, that you insulted my son at Esfahan.'

I could see where Mithridates got his talent for bearing grudges from. Phraates still said nothing but merely watched with a worried look.

I saw no reason to lie. 'You heard correctly, majesty.'

For a brief moment she was lost for words, but then her disdainful look retuned, her jaw jutting forward.

'You think it wise to insult the son of the King of Kings?'

I was rapidly losing patience. 'I would not have to if he had learnt some manners. But if it makes you feel better, I will apologise to him now. Where is he? Oh, I forgot, he's fighting with the rebels.'

Gotarzes clapped his hands, guffawed and sat back down.

The queen turned to her husband. 'Are you going to let such insolence in your court go unpunished?'

My father stood up to defend me. But before he or Phraates could say anything I walked over the top table and bowed my head to the queen.

'I apologise unreservedly for any offence I may have given. Too much wine, I fear.'

Phraates looked mightily relieved and the queen scowled at me.

'Well, too much wine can certainly provoke a rash tongue,' said Phraates. 'We accept your apology.'

My father looked most displeased as I retook my seat, while Gotarzes gave me a heavy slap on the back.

'I wouldn't have apologised to the bitch.'

'I know, that's what I was worried about.'

The evening deteriorated further when a message was brought to Phraates by one of his stewards, prompting him to shake his head, stand and walk briskly from the banqueting hall, his viper of a wife scurrying after him. We all stood as they did so, and afterwards the kings gathered round my father.

'I wonder what that was about?' said Vardan.

'No doubt we will know soon enough,' replied my father.

'No doubt. Well, Varaz,' Gotarzes was now very drunk, 'the error of our ways in not making you chief over us all is now plain to see. Perhaps we should march out and join Narses. I'm sure his feasts are not such dire occasions, at least.'

My father acknowledged his words with a faint nod, then he turned to me.

'You did not help, Pacorus. You really do need to learn the art of diplomacy.'

'Diplomacy? Perhaps, but being treated like a slave has no appeal, father. I tried it once in Italy and found it most disagreeable.'

Gotarzes laughed and Vardan smiled. A sheepish Orodes joined us.

'I apologise for my step-mother, Pacorus, she can be a little hot-headed.'

Gotarzes put an arm round his shoulder. 'Not your fault, young prince, your father should have taken his belt to that bitch years ago.'

Orodes looked even more awkward, and several of the courtiers who were still standing at their tables looked at the drunken king with contempt on their faces.

'I think,' said my father, 'that it would be sensible to retire to our quarters and put this evening behind us.'

'Better lock your door, Pacorus,' slurred Gotarzes, 'else the queen might creep into your room and stick a knife between your ribs.'

The queen did not try to kill me that evening, I am pleased to say, and the next morning we were all summoned to Phraates' throne room once more. The king looked even paler and more haunted than ever, while the queen, dressed in a stunning close-fitting pure white gown accentuating her voluptuous figure, her arms adorned with gold bracelets, armlets and a necklace of gold at her throat, eyed us warily. I noticed that Phraates held a letter in his right hand. We stood in a line before him – my father, myself, Vardan, Gotarzes, now sober thankfully, and Chosroes – and bowed our heads.

'As if I don't have enough troubles.' Phraates was staring at the floor in front of us as he spoke. 'The Romans have sent this letter demanding a meeting with me to clarify the borders between our two empires. To add insult to injury, they want the meeting to take place in Gordyene.'

'An outrage,' said my father.

'Indeed it is,' replied Phraates, 'but a calculated one. They have obviously heard of our recent troubles and hope to take advantage of them.'

'You should refuse to meet them until they withdraw from Gordyene, highness,' said Chosroes.

'A show of strength is what's needed,' added Vardan.

'That would be my first thought, but unfortunately,' said my father, 'the whole of Hatra's army cannot be sent to face them in Gordyene, not while half of it is sitting here in Ctesiphon.'

I noticed that while this interchange was going on Phraates and Aruna were looking at me, which made me feel uncomfortable. Eventually, the king spoke to me.

'Pacorus, you among us have had close dealings with these Romans. What is your opinion on this matter?'

'They will not respond to threats, not unless they can be backed up with overpowering force. And if they cannot then they will regard you as weak. The Romans only respect strength. They are testing you, highness.' I cleared my throat, aware that my father and the other kings were also listening closely to my words. 'They undoubtedly know about the civil war in Parthia, perhaps they fomented it.'

Aruna was going to object but Phraates raised his hand to still her. He was clearly interested in what I had to say.

'And what would you suggest that I do?'

'Meet them, highness,' I said. 'At the very least it will buy time for Farhad of Media to muster his army and add it to your own forces should it come to war.'

'We need Farhad here,' growled my father.

'Believe me, father, his men are needed where the Romans are. We can beat Narses easily enough, if the efforts of Porus are anything to go by. The Romans are a different prospect.'

'The Romans are barbarians,' sneered the queen.

'Barbarians?' I looked her directly in the eye. 'That may be, but Narses' army contains numerous contingents, not used to working together. The Romans are better equipped and more organised, and Parthia does not want a Roman army rampaging on its western frontier.'

'While Narses rampages in the east,' said Gotarzes.

'Believe me, lord,' I continued, 'the Romans are the bigger threat. I know how they fight. They pose the greatest immediate danger.'

Phraates held up his hand again and sighed. He leaned forward and looked at me.

'I will meet these Romans, and you, Pacorus, will come with me. The rest of you will stay here and prepare to face Narses, should it come to that. Though for now I have sent couriers to him requesting a halt to hostilities and a meeting to discuss how we might resolve our differences peacefully. I will leave for Gordyene tomorrow.'

He waved us away and we departed. I decided to leave the palace and return to my command tent, finding the company there far more agreeable. The camp had been established immediately south of the palace, the neat rows of the tents and the palisade on the earth rampart reassuring me of the strength of Dura's army. Legionaries practised their drills outside the large, rectangular camp and Nergal put my cataphracts, attired in full war gear, through their paces. In the afternoon I called him, Domitus and the lords to my tent and told them of my impending journey to Gordyene. They all wanted to accompany me, but I informed them that I would take only my cataphracts. We would ride directly north to Irbil and then on to Gordyene. It would take about six days. I dismissed the lords and told Nergal and Domitus to remain. I informed them of what had happened in the palace.

'Phraates has no stomach for a fight,' I said. 'He seeks peace when he should be striking at the heart of Narses.'

'The Romans will smell his fear when they meet him,' said Domitus.

'That is what I am worried about.'

'Then you have to convince them that there is steel in Parthia.'

'We should march with you, Pacorus,' said Nergal.

I shook my head. 'No, Nergal, your cavalry and the legion are needed here. If Narses attacks my father will need all the men he can get hold of to beat him.

'There is another thing. I do not trust the mother of Mithridates. She may be in communications with him for all I know. Take orders only from my father, no one else, and certainly not from any commanders in the pay of Phraates.'

I told this to my father that evening in the company of Vardan, Chosroes, Gotarzes and Vistaspa, all of whom I had invited to dine with me.

'We are supposed to be loyal subjects of Phraates,' said my father.

'And so I am, father, but I owe no loyalty to his wife.'

'Agreed,' said Gotarzes, who tonight was drinking water, not wine. 'We should strike at Narses and kill him and Mithridates, for there will be no peace until both of them are food for vultures.'

'I have to concur with your son, Varaz,' added Vardan. 'Phraates wastes his time sending envoys of peace to Narses. The only reason Narses retreated is because we arrived. He may attack when he learns that Phraates has been called away from his palace.'

'How will he learn that?' asked my father.

'Queen bitch will tell him,' spat Gotarzes.

My father held up his hands. 'Friends, idle speculation will get us nowhere. We should concentrate on the here and now.'

Gotarzes looked at my father. 'Have you forgotten, Varaz, that Narses sacked my kingdom and reduced me to the status of a beggar at the court of Phraates?'

My father looked serious. 'Of course not, my old friend.'

'We will restore you to your kingdom, lord,' I said, 'after we have dealt with the Romans.'

'And how will you deal with them?' asked Chosroes, staring at Domitus sitting beside me.

'By trying to convince them that any further incursions into Parthian territory will cost them a high price in blood.'

'And if you don't convince them?' asked Vardan.

'Then we shall have to fight them, lord,' I replied.

The evening thus ended on a sombre note, though I was confident that we could at least buy some time with regard to the Romans. I rose before dawn and assembled my cataphracts, both men and horses wearing full armour. I wore my black cuirass and Roman helmet with a white goose feather crest, my spatha at my hip and my bow in its case secured to my saddle. As the morning sun began its ascent in the eastern sky my father appeared at the entrance to the camp, Vistaspa beside him. An easterly breeze had picked up, which caused my griffin banner to flutter as Vagharsh held it in front of the two hundred horsemen that stood to attention, the steel masks covering their faces presenting a fearsome appearance. Behind them the mounted squires held the reins of camels loaded with spare armour, clothing, horseshoes, lances, bows, arrows, and food for both horses and men. Each squire led two camels – such was the amount of equipment needed to maintain a formation of cataphracts.

Nergal held the reins of Remus as my father dismounted and we embraced.

'Take care, Pacorus.'

'You too, father.'

He placed an arm around my shoulder and led me away from my men. 'You must be careful, Pacorus.'

'Of Phraates?'

'No, of getting the empire involved in a war with the Romans. Phraates, unfortunately, is letting events dictate his actions instead of the other way round. He needs to be firm with the Romans, but not provoke them into launching a war. It will require great diplomatic skill, which I am not sure that he has. In his enthusiasm for preventing conflict he may give the impression that he is weak.'

'The Romans will be looking for signs of weakness,' I agreed.

'Exactly, so you must convey strength without issuing threats, to sow the seeds of doubt in their minds.'

'It will not be easy, father.'

He smiled at me. 'I have every faith in you.'

'Just don't give battle to Narses before I get back.'

'Who said anything about fighting Narses?'

'You think he is going to quietly disband his army and retire to Persis?'

My father said nothing, but the expression on his face told me that he did not think so. We embraced once more and then I rode out of camp at the head of my column of riders, six hundred camels in tow. We rode to the palace gates and waited for the king, who appeared at the head of five hundred cataphracts commanded by Lord Enius, the man who had escorted Gallia and me to the court of Sinatruces over two years before. A thickset man in his forties, his men wore open-faced helmets with blue plumes. Their scale armour covered their torsos, arms and thighs and they each wore yellow cloaks that billowed in the breeze. Their mounts were also covered in scale armour, though some of the scales were made of silver, off which the sun glinted. Together with the blue pennants fluttering beneath the points of their kontus, they presented a magnificent sight. Behind Phraates, who wore a gold crown around the top of his helmet, flew the banner of the King of Susiana – an eagle clutching a snake in its talons. It was an apt standard for Mithridates was indeed a snake, though I wondered if his father would ever have him in his talons?

'A fine morning, Pacorus,' said Phraates, who appeared refreshed and in good spirits.

'Indeed, highness,' I replied.

'Well, then, let us begin our adventure.'

It took us six days of hard riding to reach Irbil, Farhad's capital. As soon as we had left the vicinity of Ctesiphon we took off our armour and stowed it on the camels to speed our journey. We stayed for one day only in the city, enough time to see my sister and her new husband. They both seemed happy enough and I found Aliyeh in a carefree mood, the first time in my life that I had seen my serious sister thus.

'Marriage suits you,' I told her.

'I am happy here, Pacorus. And you look ever the warrior.'

177

I shrugged. 'I do not look for war, but it always seems to find me.'

'And are you here to fight a war?' My serious sister suddenly returned.

'Hopefully not, at least I will try to avoid it if I can.'

'I don't want to be a widow before I have yet to get used to being a bride.'

I laid my hand on her arm. 'I won't let anything happen to Atrax, fear not.'

'Good, because he wants to be just like you.'

I burst out laughing. 'To be like me?'

She raised an eyebrow at me. 'Of course, for do you not know that you are famous? You return from the dead with a foreign princess, you are made a king with the help of a sorceress, you make an alliance with the heathen Agraci and become rich by creating a trade route with Egypt, and you win a great victory against impossible odds in a matter of minutes.'

I have to confess that I was pleased with such acclaim, though I pretended otherwise. 'Surely people have better things to gossip about?'

She shook her head. 'You are wrong, for the news of Pacorus of Dura travels like wildfire to the far corners of the empire. The people here were worried about the Romans massing to the north, but when we heard that you were coming their fears vanished like spring snow.'

'I come to advise Phraates, nothing more.'

She curled her lip. 'Phraates? A man whose own son rebels against him. He is a broken reed.'

I pointed a finger at her. 'He is the King of Kings. I voted for him and will stay loyal to him, whatever happens.'

She smiled a beautiful smile and embraced me. 'Pacorus the strong, Pacorus the unyielding. I think Phraates thanks Shamash every night that he has such warriors as you by his side.'

'Shut up,' I chided her, 'you are being ridiculous.'

Atrax himself then appeared dressed in his leather tunic reinforced with small steel scales. He had the angular face and lithe body of his father. His light-brown hair was shoulder length and his beard and moustache were neatly trimmed. He embraced me warmly.

'We ride out tomorrow to face the Romans?'

I saw Aliyeh looking at me. 'We go to discuss matters with the Romans,' I corrected him.

'You have beaten them many times, I have heard.'

'A few times, yes.'

'Then I'm sure they will run back to Rome when they know that you are with us,' he beamed.

'Perhaps, Atrax, perhaps.'

Farhad had made great efforts to assemble his army at short notice, calling in his lords from far and wide. And so, on the morrow, as we descended from his fortress at Irbil, ten thousand soldiers cheered his dragon banner. He had five hundred cataphracts of his own, to which were added a thousand horse archers of his royal guard. The lords of his kingdom brought their own retinues – horse archers, mounted spearmen with great round shields that protected the whole of their sides from their neck to their thighs, spearmen on foot with long shafts that were tipped with wicked points and had ferocious butt spikes, and foot archers who carried only their bows and quivers. Trumpets and horns blasted as Farhad and his son took their place at the head of their army, while behind them horsemen banged on kettledrums to encourage the troops. These instruments were a pair of hemispherical wooden drums with animal hide stretched over them, positioned either side of the front of the saddle, the rider striking the membranes with wooded sticks to produce a thumping sound that reverberated across the plain. And in front of the host marching north to meet the Roman invaders of our empire flew the banners of Dura, Susiana and Media.

It was fifty miles north to our meeting point at the border between Media and Gordyene, at the Shahar Chay River in the Urmia Plain. The Shahar Chay was one of the rivers that flowed into Lake Urmia, the vast saltwater lake that marked the northern boundary between the Parthian kingdoms of Gordyene and Atropaiene.

The Umbria Valley is wide and fertile, and even though the spring had yet to erupt the area was still covered in green. This was rich country, and despite the fact that Media did not benefit from the Silk Road the kingdom was blessed with rich agricultural lands that produced grapes, honey and apples in abundance. In addition, the lush pastures meant good breeding grounds for horses that were sold throughout the empire; indeed, my father often purchased mounts for his own army to supplement the stud farms of Hatra.

We arrived at the river to find the Romans already formed up on the northern side, row upon row of legionaries dressed in mailed shirts, helmets and carrying pila and shields. I counted two eagles, which equated to two legions, though there was also an abundance of auxiliary troops – slingers, archers and lightly armed spearmen

179

carrying large round shields – deployed on the wings of the legions. Horsemen were stationed on the extreme flanks of each wing, though they were sparse in number, perhaps six hundred in total. I estimated the length of the Roman line to be two miles. In front of the legionaries, on beautifully groomed and equipped horses, were the senior Roman officers, half a dozen in number.

The river meandered lazily towards the great lake, for as yet the spring melt waters from the mountains had yet to flow and swell its torrent. The day was crisp, windless and calm, and were it not for the thousands of soldiers present it would also be peaceful. I smiled to myself when I saw the raft anchored in the water. The Romans, efficient as ever, had secured it in the mid-point of the river. The water itself was shallow at this spot, though the high banks on either side showed how it rose when the melt waters were raging.

The Romans sent over a mounted courier asking if we needed a boat to transport Phraates and his representatives to the raft, but Phraates declined. He did not trust the Romans, I think, though in truth he was in no danger of being assassinated. The Romans liked to defeat their enemies on the battlefield with the world watching, not murder them like thieves in the night. We would ride our horses into the water – I joined Phraates, Farhad and Enius, together with two other men who would take our mounts back to the southern riverbank until our discussions were completed. We relayed this to the courier, who took the message back to his masters. The Romans sent the same number of representatives as us, though they did use a small boat that was rowed across to the raft. Phraates, Enius and Farhad looked magnificent that day in their scale armour of burnished silver plates, shining steel helmets sporting plumes and richly adorned shirts. I too had made an effort to impress, in my black cuirass, Roman helmet with its white crest and white tunic. We all wore our cloaks, for the air was cool on the water.

The Romans, by comparison, presented a more weatherworn appearance, especially their commander, a man in his early forties who was almost bald aside from some hair above his ears. He had a narrow, lean face that looked like a strip of parched rawhide with a slim nose running down the centre. He stood at least six inches shorter than us and had a compact frame. No doubt Phraates took his smaller stature as a sign of inferiority, but I could see that this Roman had a professional bearing whose narrow eyes missed nothing. The officers with him were dressed as he was– helmets with red crests, muscled cuirasses and red cloaks and tunics. Each carried a gladius at his hip. One of them stepped forward and saluted.

'Greetings, my name is Titus Amenius, tribune of Rome. I would like to present to you my general, the consul Lucius Licinius Lucullus, Governor of Asia and Cilicia.'

I heard Phraates take a sharp intake of breath, for to use such a title implied sovereignty over the lands that did not belong to Rome, for 'Asia' was an all-encompassing word.

Lord Enius stepped forward and bowed his head to the Romans.

'Greetings. I am General Enius, commander of the army of Phraates, King of Kings of the Parthian Empire and ruler of all the lands from the Euphrates to the Indus.'

Lucullus raised an eyebrow at this, for his presence here today was a sign that Phraates did not at this time rule all of the area that Enius had just described. Enius then presented Farhad and myself, stating that we were the kings of Media and Dura respectively. Lucullus said nothing, though he kept looking at me as we all sat down in the high-backed chairs made more comfortable by cushions that had been arranged beforehand. A pagoda made from canvas and poles had been erected on the raft, though the sky was clear and I doubted that we would see any rain this day. There were no refreshments on the raft, for protocol dictated that no bread or wine could be shared with potential enemies. Phraates spoke first, looking directly at Lucullus.

'Why do the Romans make war upon Parthia?'

Lucullus leaned back in his chair and regarded this foreign king sitting opposite him. Domitus had once told me that the Romans equated long hair with effeminacy and weakness, and as most Parthians wore their hair long, no doubt Lucullus thought us all inferior. In addition, the other kings sported beards and moustaches, though ever since my time in Italy I had maintained a clean-shaven appearance.

Eventually Lucullus spoke, his voice deep and commanding. 'I am empowered by the Senate and People of Rome to make war upon Rome's enemies. For many years our great republic has been at war with King Mithridates of Pontus and King Tigranes of Armenia. This war is now coming to an end with the defeat of those two enemies. Balas, late king of Gordyene, gave aid to Tigranes and was similarly defeated. As a result, Gordyene has become a client kingdom of Rome.'

'The land you occupy is Parthian,' said Phraates purposely.

'The land we won in battle belonged to an enemy of Rome,' replied Lucullus.

Phraates looked hesitant and cast a glance at me. A strong-willed man like his father would have thrown the Roman's words back in his face, but Phraates was not such a man. An awkward pause followed. I decided to end it.

'How many wars can Rome afford to fight?' I asked.

'King Pacorus,' said Phraates, 'is a man who has knowledge of your people.'

'Thank you, highness,' I said. 'So tell me, Consul Lucullus, are you empowered to wage war on the Parthian Empire, a war that will make your conflicts with Pontus and Armenia seem like mere child's play by comparison?'

Lucullus now studied me more closely. He must have recognised my Roman cuirass and helmet, but I was obviously not a Roman. His officers also focused their attention on me, nodding and whispering to each other.

'I am empowered to make war on all of Rome's enemies,' replied Lucullus.

'But Parthia and Rome are not at war,' I said.

'Not yet,' uttered one of Lucullus' men, which earned him a rebuke from his commander.

'Be careful, Roman,' my blood was now up, 'for I have fought and defeated Roman legions in the past. You think we are weak because we grow our hair long and sport beards, but the soldiers you see arrayed against you today are only a fraction of what the empire can muster. You tangle with Parthia at your peril.'

'Thank you, King Pacorus,' Phraates was clearly worried that I was provoking the Romans, 'but we do not desire enmity, but rather wish there to be peace between our two great empires.'

But Lucullus was not listening to Phraates. 'Where have you fought Romans?' he asked me.

'Did I not say? How rude of me,' I replied. 'I spent three years in Italy campaigning with General Spartacus. I have to confess that I forget how many eagles we took.'

I noted surprise in his eyes, quickly followed by a cold contempt, while behind him his officers became agitated. I decided to add to their discomfort.

'And I remember in particular, consul, entertaining your troops on a beach north of Brundisium once. We killed many that day.'

Lucullus' expression of contempt did not change, but his eyes narrowed as he said to me. 'You're "the Parthian", aren't you?'

My spine tingled with excitement at the mention of that name. 'That is what I was called by my enemies in Italy, and it was a title I bore with pride.' In that moment I felt elated.

'Yes, consul, I am he.'

'I had heard that you were dead.'

'As you can see, consul, reports of my demise were greatly exaggerated.'

To his credit Lucullus did not let his emotions take control of him, though he must have been seething inside. The war that Spartacus waged in Italy was a great insult to the Romans, not least because his army was made up of slaves, who in Roman eyes were like animals that existed only to serve their masters.

'You were once a slave and now you are a king.' He tilted his head to one side. 'My congratulations.'

'I was a prince,' I corrected him, 'before being made a slave by Rome.'

'Do you seek recompense from Rome, King Pacorus, is that why you are here?'

'No, consul. I am here because my high king did me the great honour of requesting my presence at his side. In truth I am just one Parthian king among many. But consider this. If but one Parthian with a handful of horsemen can wreak such damage in your homeland, think what tens of thousands could do to your army, an army that is so far from home.'

'Rome does not respond to threats, Parthian.'

I smiled at him. 'I make no threat, consul, merely an observation. For are we not here to try to avoid conflict? Why look for war unnecessarily?'

'Why, indeed?' added Phraates.

Lucullus regarded us all, weighing up in his mind the options available to him at that moment. And behind us, lined up along the riverbank were our horsemen and foot soldiers, staring across the water at the centuries and cohorts of the Romans. Whatever his thoughts he decided that he would not be drawing his sword this day, for he abruptly stood and raised his right arm in salute to Phraates.

'Great king, I thank you for your courtesy today. Know that I desire no conflict with the Parthian Empire, and that I will be communicating with the Senate in Rome for the resolution of the issue of Gordyene forthwith.'

Phraates bowed his head in gratitude. 'Thank you, consul, I have no doubt that we can maintain a beneficial peace between our two great empires. I look forward to receiving a satisfactory conclusion to the matter of Gordyene.'

Lucullus said nothing further to me, though he did take a last look in my direction before he and his officers departed for the far bank, while Enius signalled for our horses to be brought to the raft. Thus ended the diplomacy on the Shahar Chay River.

Phraates was in jovial spirits on the journey back to Irbil, thinking that he had achieved a bloodless victory.

'You obviously frightened him, Pacorus,' he said, though I doubted that.

'If that is all the men he has,' said Farhad, 'then we have nothing to fear from that particular Roman.'

How they underestimated the Romans. Media alone could put more men into the field than Lucullus, of that I had no doubt, but Roman strength was built on discipline and organisation, something that most Parthian armies lacked. Lightly armed foot soldiers who worked the land for a living and horse archers who fought as a war band for their lord were no match for highly trained legionaries. Every kingdom had palace guards and formations of professional horsemen, but only Hatra had a standing army plus my own kingdom of Dura. If it had come to a fight this day, Lucullus' soldiers would have made short work of Media's army. I kept these thoughts to myself as the host made its way back to Farhad's capital. Atrax was feeling very pleased with himself. He relaxed on a couch in his father's palace eating grapes with one hand while his other arm was around Aliyeh's shoulders.

'The Romans backed down in the face of our strength, darling.' He kissed Aliyeh on the cheek. 'They will scurry back to Italy now.'

A servant brought me a cup of freshly squeezed apple juice. 'I doubt that, Atrax. You must keep a keen eye on your northern frontier. Above all, try to convince your father not to launch any raids into Gordyene, at least until we have had time to deal with Narses.

He waved his hand at me. 'This Lucullus has only a small army, feeble compared to the numbers we can put in the field. He would not dare to provoke a fight with Media.'

I smiled. He had only just turned twenty and wanted to impress his new bride more than anything else. He had never seen the face of battle, and the fact that there had been no fight at the river made him thirst for military glory even more. He had been in the midst of thousands of soldiers, smelt the leather armour, harnesses, sweat and scent of the horses, seen the brightly coloured banners and whetted spear points, and been so close to the enemy. He must have been chaffing at the bit, ready to charge across the river and slay the Romans as a farmer scythes wheat.

'You do not think so, do you Pacorus?' My sister may have been

184

in love, but it had not dulled her sharp mind.

'No.'

She pressed me further. 'Why not?'

I drank from my cup; the liquid was cool and refreshing. 'Because the Romans are a proud and arrogant people, and those two traits will not allow them to yield.'

Atrax was delighted by my answer. 'Then we will fight them.'

'As I said, let us settle the business with Narses before anything else,' I said. 'One war at a time, Atrax. Remember that.'

I doubted he was listening. A new bride, an enemy lying so close to his father's frontier and the promise of fame and glory were too intoxicating to listen to reason. I prayed that the peace would last long enough for us to return and reinforce Media's army.

'Two months, Pacorus, that is how long I will give the Romans.'

After saying our farewells to Farhad, Atrax and my sister, I rode back to Ctesiphon with Phraates and Enius.

It had suited Phraates to be away from the poisonous confines of Ctesiphon. The journey north and the favourable outcome of the meeting with Lucullus had restored colour to his cheeks and made him much more positive. Today, on our way back to Ctesiphon, he was in a bullish mood.

'Two months, that is all, then I shall demand their withdrawal from Gordyene and march at the head of an army to retake it if they refuse.'

'There is the matter of Narses still to be addressed, highness,' said Enius.

'Narses has withdrawn,' replied Phraates. 'He will be seeking an audience with me to beg for my forgiveness, of that I am sure. We have you to thank for that, Pacorus.'

I was surprised. 'Me, highness?'

'Of course, for your defeat of Porus sent a clear message to those who rebel against our royal power. That if they do so they will face certain destruction. I should have had you at court much earlier.'

That thought filled me with dread. In any case Phraates deluded himself, and when we were on the road to Ctesiphon he soon had a stark reminder of harsh reality. Nergal, accompanied by Byrd, Malik and a dozen horse archers, met us fifty miles from the royal palace. Nergal looked resplendent in his white tunic, mail shirt and helmet, while Malik was dressed in his black robes. Byrd looked as dishevelled as ever, made worse by several days' worth of hair on his face.

Nergal bowed his head to Phraates as our column halted on the road. 'Hail, highness.'

'This is Nergal, highness,' I said, 'my second-in-command.'

'Why do you interrupt our journey?' said Phraates.

'I bring news of King Narses, highness.'

Phraates turned to me and smiled. 'You see, Pacorus, what did I tell you. He is eager to atone for his errant ways.'

The look on Nergal's face suggested otherwise. I avoided the king's gaze as Nergal relayed his news.

'King Narses approaches Ctesiphon with a great army, highness. Your presence at Ctesiphon is urgently requested.'

Phraates visibly wilted before my eyes, as if some magic spell had suddenly been cast upon him. He said nothing, then nudged his horse forward past all of us. We followed him, Nergal falling in beside me as Enius rode forward to ride beside his king.

'So,' I said, 'I assume that Narses is moving his army towards Ctesiphon to give battle and not surrender it.'

'Yes, lord,' replied Nergal. 'Byrd and Malik rode east to find out more about his movements. They returned yesterday.'

'Enemy army very big,' said Byrd. 'Many more men than your army.' He nodded towards the stooped figure of Phraates riding ahead of us. 'Might be wise for him to seek peace.'

'Numbers are not everything,' I said. 'Remember when we fought in Italy. We were often outnumbered.'

Byrd looked unconcerned. The affairs of kings probably did not interest him in the slightest, then he nodded again towards Phraates. 'He no Spartacus.'

'We rode towards Susa, Pacorus,' said Malik. 'Narses' army has marched west to the Tigris and then north into the desert. He now turns west again to strike at Ctesiphon.'

'He will be at Ctesiphon in four days,' added Byrd.

When we reached Ctesiphon Phraates resembled the old man whom we had accompanied north to Media. After a short interlude to allow us to wash and refresh ourselves, he convened a war council in his study in the palace's expansive private apartments. The study was large but surprisingly sparse for the King of Kings. It consisted of a large desk, pigeonholes on one wall that held parchments and scrolls, a couch and several well-appointed chairs that had been arranged in a semi-circle in front of his desk. And behind his desk, fixed to the wall, was wood panelling, upon which had been painted a beautifully detailed map of the Parthian Empire, a domain now threatened with being torn asunder. Phraates was sitting behind the desk with his chin in his hands, his elbows resting on the table. His eyes followed each of us as we entered, bowed and sat in a chair. Servants offered us fruit juice or water from silver trays, while others presented sweet meats and pastries. I sat down next to my father, while on my other side Orodes, Gotarzes, Vardan and Chosroes found their places. Enius stood next to Phraates, who at last spoke.

'Gentlemen, you will all know by now that Narses and his army are approaching Ctesiphon. The question is – how will we deal with this predicament?'

Chosroes, much to my surprise, spoke first. 'It is better to seek a peaceful outcome, I think, highness.'

Phraates sat back in his chair and nodded. 'I agree, we will try to come to terms with Narses.'

'I have heard that his numbers have been swelled since he was previously before your palace, highness,' said Vardan.

'Apparently so,' replied the king.

'And you think this predisposes Narses to peace, highness?' My father's words made Phraates shift uneasily in his chair.

'I would hope that he remembers that we are all Parthian at the end of the day.'

'And what of my kingdom?' Gotarzes said.

Phraates looked at him. 'You can be assured, King Gotarzes, that the restitution of your lands will be at the top of the agenda when we sit down and talk with Narses.'

Gotarzes mumbled something in reply which I did not hear, after which there was an awkward silence. I stared at the king's desk, for I believed all talk about discussions to be a waste of time. I was glad that conflict had been avoided with the Romans in Media, but Narses and his band of rebels posed a greater immediate threat to Phraates, for their existence weakened his authority, and a ruler without authority is like a eagle without talons.

'You have no opinion on this matter, King Pacorus?'

I had, but decided to keep my council.

'I concur with your decision, highness.'

Phraates looked puzzled. 'But I have made no decision as yet. Come, speak freely.'

And so I did. 'I believe, highness, that talking to the rebels is a waste of time. We should march out to meet Narses and defeat him, for every day that he and his army exists is a gross insult to you and to the ancient laws of Parthia.'

I was aware at once that my father was fuming at my reply, though he said nothing.

'Well,' said Gotarzes, 'he may be half our age but Pacorus has twice the wisdom. I agree with him. We should put an end to this rebellion here and now.'

Chosroes had gone very pale while Vardan looked contemplative. 'But can we defeat such a host?'

'We can beat him,' I replied, 'if we have the will.'

'And do you agree with your son, Varaz?' asked Phraates.

'The army of Hatra stands ready to obey your orders, highness,' replied my father evasively.

'We cannot remain at Ctesiphon, highness,' I continued. 'There are too many men and beasts to feed and water. Narses knows this. That is why he is marching here. He is forcing your hand.'

'You should not talk to your lord, thus,' said my father. 'It is not your place.'

'It is my duty to speak the truth, father.'

My father rounded on me. 'Is it? Or do you seek a battle for your own ends, to achieve more glory for yourself?'

Enius looked alarmed, Phraates was speechless.

'We should not argue thus,' said Vardan. 'It is for the high king to decide our course of action.'

'We look to you, highness,' added my father.

I purposely ignored my father and looked at Phraates, then Enius. He at least knew what I was saying was true. There were thousands of men, mules, camels and horses camped in and around Ctesiphon. Food and forage were in short supply as it was. We could not withdraw for we could not abandon Ctesiphon, the capital of all Parthia, to Narses. At a stroke that would make us all appear feeble. We had only achieved half of what we had set out to accomplish. We had relieved Ctesiphon, but it would all be for nothing unless we beat Narses. And Narses knew this. Phraates must also have known this. He was no fool, but now he had to show his mettle. He smiled to himself.

'Very well. We will assemble our forces and march east to intercept Narses. This matter must be brought to an end once and for all.'

My father said nothing to me after the meeting ended. He was infuriated with me, but Gotarzes had only praise.

'You did well, Pacorus. We need to give that bastard Narses a good beating, otherwise he'll pick us off one by one.'

'My father doesn't see it as you do.'

'Yes he does. He's angry with himself, not you. He knows that Phraates is lacking as a King of Kings, but what can he do? What can any of us do?'

'Stay true to our oaths of loyalty,' I said.

The area around the palace and the along the east bank of the Tigris resounded with the noise of forges making new arrowheads, sharpening blades and mending armour. Farriers shod horses and veterinaries attended to their health. That afternoon I rode with Byrd and Malik to the east. We travelled twenty miles into the desert and then halted. All around was a barren expanse of flat, parched red earth, upon which nothing grew aside from a few shrubs. The terrain was featureless – perfect for cavalry. In the far distance stood the Zagros Mountains, the direction from where Narses was marching. But here there were no mountains, no hills, not even a hillock.

'Narses is clever,' I said. 'He intends to make his superiority in numbers count, and this is the perfect spot.'

'In what way?' asked Malik.

'If Narses had continued to march north along the Tigris, then we could have anchored one flank of our army on the river, as we did when we fought Porus. But here, in the desert, there is nothing to anchor a flank on, no river, wadi, forest or high ground. That means that we will have to match the extent of his line lest we be outflanked. And that will make our line very thin.'

'You think there will be a battle?'

'Oh yes, Malik, there will be a battle. Narses has not come this far to talk. He did that at the Council of Kings.'

'He expects to win,' said Byrd.

'Of course,' I said. 'And if he does, and manages to kill all the kings who are arrayed against him, then the empire falls into his lap like ripe fruit. What is this place called?'

'Nomads we spoke to call it Surkh,' replied Byrd, 'not know what it means.'

I knelt down and scooped up some of the dry earth. 'It means redness.' I let it fall from my hand. The name was very apt, for this patch of ground would soon be running red with blood.

'Odds not good, Pacorus.' Byrd always did have a knack of summing things up succinctly. We stood in silence for a while. And to the east Narses and his army advanced towards Ctesiphon.

I rode straight to my father's camp when we returned, a vast sprawling collection of tents along the Tigris. He had made sure that he was upstream from the armies of the other kings, especially that of Chosroes. His tent was a great round affair, its roof supported by four giant poles. I left my horse with a servant and was escorted inside by two sentries. I found my father in a conference with Vistaspa and half a dozen of his officers all standing in front of my father's desk. As soon as they saw me the

189

officers bowed their heads, prompting my father to dismiss them. As they bowed once more and filed out, my father indicated to Vistaspa that he should sit in one of the wicker chairs that were placed by one of the tent poles. My father's second-in-command nodded his head slightly at me but said nothing.

'So, the wanderer returns,' said my father, noticing my dust-covered apparel, my shirt tainted red. He gestured to a water jug on a small table to one side. 'You must be thirsty.'

I walked over to the table and drank a cup of lukewarm water.

'Are you well?' asked my father.

'Yes, father.'

'And is this a social visit?'

I slumped down in one of the chairs. 'I need your cataphracts, father.'

He looked at Vistaspa and they both laughed.

'Did I hear you right, Pacorus? You want me to give you my cataphracts, the finest heavy cavalry in the known world?'

'Yes, father.'

'And you wish Lord Vistaspa to command them?'

'Of course.'

My father placed his hands behind his head and stared at the roof of the tent.

'So, not only do you want my cataphracts, you also want the commander of my troops, the man who has forged Hatra's army into the sword of the Parthian Empire?'

'Yes.'

'And am I allowed to know the reason why you make such heavy demands upon me?'

'To defeat Narses.'

He slowly rose from his chair and started pacing up and down.

'Of course, that's where you have been isn't it, mapping out the ground upon which you will fight your battle?'

I must have looked surprised.

'You may be a king, Pacorus, a man whose fame has spread far and wide, but you are still my son. The answer is no.'

Disappointment swept over me, though I tried to remain composed. 'You know that there will be a battle.'

He was still pacing. 'You wish there to be a battle. I wish for the rebellion to be brought to an end.'

I held out my hands. 'Are they not one and the same thing?'

My father stopped pacing and banged his fist on the table. 'No, they are not! Narses has to defeat us to win this war. When he sees the might of Hatra, Babylon, Mesene and Dura arrayed against

190

him, his nerve will falter.'

I stood up and placed the cup back on the table. 'You are wrong,' I said.

I left then without saying another word. But I was not finished yet. I rode to the palace and asked for a private audience with Phraates. In his study once more I requested that Enius and his five hundred cataphracts be placed under my command during the coming march. If it came to a fight I promised Phraates victory, just like the one over Porus. I knew that he regarded me highly at this time and I played on that. When he reminded me that his son, Mithridates, who had been 'tricked' by Narses, was with the enemy army, I lied and told him that I would make it my priority to rescue his son, if I could but borrow his heavy horsemen. And so he gave me Enius and five hundred cataphracts. Gotarzes did not need any convincing and so readily agreed to add his two hundred cataphracts to my own, on the condition that he would fight by my side. He too wanted to find Mithridates, 'So I can chop off the little bastard's head.' I readily agreed to his offer.

The army marched east the following day, each king leading his own contingent with supplies loaded on to camels, wagons and mules following behind. The whole mass resembled an entire people on the move. Dura's horse and foot were to the south, the legion marching behind my cataphracts and Nergal's horse archers. All of the lords had provided their own scale armour for themselves and their mounts, so I added their number to my total of heavy cavalry. They trusted Nergal to lead their archers now – there is nothing like victory to boost confidence and morale, and I reckoned Dura's army to be the best among the disparate elements that had rallied to Phraates. The worst, of course, was the rabble under Chosroes, but it did not matter. In the coming battle the army of Mesene would serve only to make up the numbers. Immediately north of my army was Vardan and his Babylonians. I liked Vardan and his daughter, but he was a close friend of my father so I had not asked him for his heavy horse. In the centre of the columns rode Phraates with the remnants of the army of Elymais and the troops of his own household, including Enius and Orodes. Beyond him were Chosroes and his motley band, while on the northern flank marched the army of Hatra – fifteen hundred cataphracts and nine thousand horse archers. Five thousand of the latter, the professional troops, had scale armour on their chests and helmets on their heads, for my father's kingdom was the richest in the land and could afford to lavish its army with the best equipment. The rest comprised the retinues brought to Hatra by those landowners whose estates were nearest the city.

We marched for most of the day at a leisurely pace until we reached the flat expanse of desert which I had previously visited with Byrd and Malik, and where we would fight the army of Narses.

The Battle of Surkh was about to begin.

Chapter 11

That night we camped under a clear, star-lit sky. A myriad of campfires extended as far as the eye could see as I rode to the pavilion of Phraates for a meeting of his war council. In the distance a red glow filled the horizon – the fires of Narses' army. Palace guards were standing around the royal enclosure every ten paces, while inside a small army of servants attended to the high king's needs. The retinue of the King of Kings for this campaign was large indeed, in stark contrast to the modest expedition made to Media earlier. I was just thankful that Phraates had left his wife behind. The pavilion itself was oblong in shape, its roof supported by four rows of tent poles, each one at least twenty feet high. Beside each one was posted an armed guard dressed in a blue tunic, baggy yellow trousers with a spear and wicker shield. The soldiers wore felt caps on their heads. I smiled when I saw them, for I was sure that Domitus would have been most unimpressed by their uniforms and armament. The pavilion itself was divided into a number of sections: first, the reception area where I left my sword and dagger; this led into the area where the king's throne was positioned on a dais. This section was voluminous and accommodated chairs, couches and tables, and it was here that the kings were assembled. I saw my father and nodded. He nodded back, while Gotarzes and Orodes greeted me warmly. Also present were Vardan and Chosroes, the latter looking most agitated at the thought of the approaching slaughter.

Trumpets blasted, servants drew a large yellow curtain back and Phraates emerged from his private quarters located behind the throne area. He was dressed in a blue silk tunic and leggings with his crown upon his head. We bowed our heads as he made his way to the dais and sat on his throne. Enius and Orodes remained either side of him and we took our places in a line before him.

'Well, gentlemen, here we are at last. Tomorrow we face Narses. I must stress again that it is not my intention to destroy Narses, as he is also a king of the empire. Lord Enius will now give you your battle positions.'

Enius walked over to a table, upon which had been placed carved wooden models of horsemen, each of which carried a flag sporting a different emblem. I saw the banners of Hatra, Dura, Mesene, Babylon, Elymais and Susiana. It was a quaint touch. They had been arranged in a line opposite other models depicting the enemy. We all gathered round the table as Enius pointed to horseman carrying the banner of the white horse's head.

'Here, King Varaz and the army of Hatra will secure our left flank. Next to Hatra's army will deploy King Chosroes and his forces, with King Vardan and the might of Babylon next in line. The army of Susiana will reinforce the centre, led by King Phraates himself.'

Phraates nodded. In truth his was not much of an army as the bulk of it was in the enemy camp under Mithridates. Yet we had the legitimate King if Kings on our side and that was important.

Enius pointed to the right flank. 'The right wing will comprise the forces of King Pacorus and King Gotarzes, and that concludes our deployment.'

After the council my father met me as Remus was brought into the pavilion.

'You take care tomorrow, Pacorus.'

I embraced him. 'You too, father.'

He looked at me with a quizzical expression on his face. 'Do not provoke a fight tomorrow. Narses must be brought to account, but better to talk him into submission. Phraates does not want this war prolonged.'

'Of course not, father. I guarantee that is my desire also.'

'Until the morrow, then.'

'Until tomorrow.'

It was late when I called together the officers of my army. They crowded into my tent and gathered around me in a semi-circle, Nergal, Domitus, Byrd, Malik and my lords. They all accepted the presence of Malik now without question; indeed, they chatted to him as if he was a friend. Domitus, scarred, muscled and eyes full of fire faced me dressed in his tunic and a pair of sandals, clutching his gladius in its scabbard with his right hand.

'I will make this brief. Tomorrow we fight Narses on this ground. Byrd tells me that he outnumbers us two to one.'

'At least,' growled Byrd.

'It doesn't matter,' I continued. 'We will deploy on the army's right flank in the morning, horsemen on the extreme end of the line. Nergal, your horse archers will distract those opposite you while I take the cataphracts around their flank.'

'What about my legion?' asked Domitus.

I smiled at him. 'You, my friend, will deploy your legion in two lines and attack the enemy, straight at their centre.'

'Who will be on my left flank?' Domitus' eyes narrowed.

'The Babylonians,' I replied.

'And they will attack when we do?'

I laughed. 'Domitus, believe me they will have no choice but to follow you.' I looked at their faces in the half-light of the oil lamps that flickered on their stands. 'Remember, we must finish this tomorrow. My father's cavalry is on the left flank of the army and they will easily defeat what is against them. If we triumph on the flanks it does not matter what happens in the centre.'

They murmured their agreement, some slapping their comrades on the back.

'Shamash be with you all. Now get some sleep.'

Dawn came all too soon and with it the sounds of an army preparing for battle. Squires rushed around with swords and armour for their masters, ill-tempered mules and camels spat and growled as their drivers tried in vain to get them to obey their commands, and thousands of soldiers checked their weapons and equipment for what could be their last day in this life. I slept perhaps for two hours before I woke when it was still dark. I held Gallia's lock of hair in my hand and caressed it, praying that I would see her beautiful face again. If not, I hoped for a good death so that she would think of me with pride as I waited for her in heaven. After she had left the army an armourer had fixed her lock of hair onto a chain I kept around my neck. Now I tucked this into the silk vest next to my skin. Over the vest I wore a white shirt and loose, brown leggings, with red leather boots on my feet. My suit of scale armour hung on a stand beside my cot; I would not put it on until I was ready to ride into the battle line.

Domitus shared breakfast with me, a spartan meal of biscuit, porridge, fruit and water. He wore his centurion's mail shirt adorned with discs and his helmet with its white transverse crest. As usual he had brought his vine cane.

I pointed at the cane now lying next to us on the table. 'Going to beat the enemy with that, Domitus?'

'If they are as ragged as the lot that follows Chosroes, I might do just that.'

Outside the tent I could hear the curses and complaints of soldiers being marshalled into their ranks by centurions. Soldiers really were the same the world over.

'Remember, deploy your men in two lines today to extend their frontage,' I said. 'When I give the signal, I want you to charge straight at the enemy.'

'You are going to start the battle?'

'Yes, straight at them. The time for talking is over. I will be attacking on the right flank while you are assaulting their centre.' He nodded.

195

'And Domitus?'

'Yes?'

'Stay alive.'

He stuffed another biscuit into his mouth. 'You too, Pacorus.'

Mercifully, the day was overcast as I rode at the head of my horsemen out of camp an hour later. Domitus and his legion had left earlier and were already moving into their battle positions, five cohorts in the first line and five in the second. Each cohort was made up of six centuries, each century comprised of eighty men drawn up in eight ranks of ten men. I never understood this designation because the Latin word centum denoted one hundred, whereas the century actually numbered eighty men or thereabouts. A cohort's battle formation comprised three centuries in the first line with the other three directly behind.

As our army was forming into line the contingents of Narses were doing likewise. Great numbers of horsemen, both archers and spearmen, were deploying in front of where my cataphracts were lined up behind me. The warriors in front were dressed in leather armour and hide caps. Those carrying spears clasped hide-covered shields to their bodies, while the horse archers wore no armour as far as I could discern. I also spied groups of cataphracts among their ranks dressed similarly to our own. In the centre, between the two wings of enemy horsemen, was the foot. Narses must have emptied the Zagros Mountains of all the hill men who lived there, for such a seething press of men I had never before seen. They resembled a vast black lake that had suddenly been thrust upon the desert floor; hordes of axe men, spearmen, archers, slingers and others carrying clubs and knives. Those who carried shields were banging them with their spear shafts; others were screaming curses at our men opposite, or whooping and cheering at the tops of their voices. Directly opposite my horsemen, kettledrummers were beating their instruments with gusto. The enemy horsemen spread far beyond my flank, perhaps for half a mile or more.

Gotarzes rode up with his cataphracts with Orodes beside him.

'There's thousands of the bastards, Pacorus,' said Gotarzes, who reined in his horse beside Remus as his men formed up on the right of my own.

'Indeed, the combined might of Narses, Phriapatus of Carmania, Vologases of Drangiana, Cinnamus of Anauon, Monaeses of Yueh-Chih and Mithridates himself.'

'Hail Pacorus,' Orodes bowed his head to me. He fell in next to Gotarzes.

'Good to see you my friend,' I said. 'Today we'll get your

kingdom back.'

'My kingdom?'

'Susiana,' I replied, 'you don't think that your father will want your brother sitting in Susa after he has rebelled against him, do you?'

'But my brother is king,' said Orodes.

'Not if he's dead he isn't,' I said quietly.

Gotarzes heard me and smiled, though Orodes was out of earshot. 'I did not hear, lord.'

'It does not matter, the main thing is that you are here.'

A blast of horns announced the arrival of Enius and his five hundred riders who swept around the back of my own cataphracts and formed into line to the right of Gotarzes' armoured riders. Around two hundred paces behind us, sitting on the grass and busily chatting among themselves and consciously ignoring the enemy, were Dura's lords and their two thousand horse archers. Enius trotted up and saluted to Gotarzes and me. His arrival was the signal for Nergal to join us, who rode up and faced us with his back to the enemy. The cacophony of noise coming from the latter showed no signs of abating and I had to shout to make myself heard.

'Nergal, when I give the signal gather your horsemen and assault the enemy opposite. Pepper them with arrows but don't get too close. If they advance, you retreat, but you must keep on annoying them to fix their attention on you.'

Nergal turned in his saddle and looked at the masses of enemy horsemen facing him. 'They will undoubtedly attack us, lord.'

'I know, but if they do, like I said, withdraw but keep on harassing them. Now go.'

He galloped back to his men, who by this time were in their saddles and mustering around their lords. They didn't have the discipline of my cataphracts or legionaries, but it did not matter. As long as they stayed in the field, shooting at the enemy and did not get drawn into a melee, then they would prove their worth.

The wall of noise coming from the enemy's ranks showed no sign of lessening as I rode forward to admire the view, for it was not often that the kings of the empire arrayed their forces in one spot. Next to the legion I spied the purple-clad foot and horse of Babylon, and beyond them the ill-equipped hordes of Chosroes, and in the distance, just visible on our left flank, magnificent in their white tunics and scale armour, the horsemen of Hatra. I saw Phraates sitting on his horse immediately behind the Babylonians alongside Vardan, both kings flanked by mounted spearman and a phalanx of huge axe men standing directly in front of them. Almost exactly opposite Phraates, across the empty space of ground between the two armies, was Narses himself, the handsome, ruthless rebel leader. I could not see his face from this distance but I could see that he was mounted on a large black horse. He wore an armoured cuirass that shimmered in the light, for now the sun's rays were lancing through the breaks in the clouds. Narses wore a steel helmet with a red crest and was surrounded by all the other kings in his army, judging by the standards that were being held behind his entourage. And on his flanks and behind him there must have been at least five hundred cataphracts. Narses and his horsemen looked magnificent and intimidating in the centre of the enemy's front rank, but they were in entirely the wrong place. For which I thanked Shamash.

Then the noise coming from the opposition's ranks began to diminish, until after perhaps five minutes it had completely died away. An ominous silence then descended over both armies as Narses and a group of riders slowly walked their horses forward beyond the front ranks. Immediately behind him his great banner fluttered in the wind – a great yellow flag sporting the black head of Simurgel, the bird-god of Persepolis. So, perhaps he was going to talk after all. I smiled to myself. The time for talking was long past; it was time to fight. I kicked Remus forward to take me about fifty paces beyond our line then halted him. I saw Domitus standing a few paces in front of his legion and lowered my kontus towards the enemy. I kept it there until he raised his hand in recognition of my signal, then I rode back to my horsemen.

Seconds later there was a blast of trumpets and then the whole legion began moving forward. Screams and shouts erupted from Narses' army, while he himself hurried back to the safety of his densely packed soldiers. And then what I had hoped for happened. Their blood up and expecting an easy victory, the enemy foot opposite Domitus and his legion charged. It was not a disciplined advance but a feral rush of maddened men who wanted to wash their weapons in the enemy's blood. And so they ran as fast as they could in a disorganised mob to close the gap between the two armies as ten of my cohorts marched briskly forward.

In such an encounter discipline, not weight of numbers, holds the key to victory. The legionaries in the front ranks of the first line centuries carried no javelins but advanced with their swords drawn, the fearsome gladius held ready to stab upwards into thighs and bellies. The men in the rear ranks behind them carried their javelins at the ready. Then the legion's trumpets blasted once more and the men charged, maintaining their order as they did so. And when the two sides crashed into each other the rear ranks in each century hurled their javelins over the heads of their comrades in front. The front ranks of the legion buckled under the ferocious onslaught of Narses' foot soldiers, but they held. And then the killing began. Legionaries in the front ranks smashed their shields into the enemy, their shoulders behind their shields as men collided at a run. Javelins flew overhead and felled hundreds of the enemy before they even got close to the legionaries, and then the enemy mass thickened as more and more men raced forward to get to grips with Domitus' soldiers, but this worked against them because all it did was push their front ranks onto the swords of the legionaries, who kept stabbing upwards repeatedly. Enemy soldiers, their thighs and bellies oozing blood, fell to the ground and were stepped on by a man behind, whose belly was also soon gushing blood as a gladius found its mark. And so the slaughter went on, but it was entirely one-side as the soldiers of Narses were turned into offal. The mass charge had also entirely negated the influence of the enemy slingers and archers, who were reduced to the role of useless bystanders.

Thus far the battle had unfolded exactly as I wanted. But the day was still young and much was left to do.

'Follow me,' I shouted to my horsemen behind, then wheeled Remus to the right as he broke into a trot.

Much as I would have liked to watch Domitus and his men cut their way through the enemy, I too had work to do. The cataphracts followed me as I cantered away from our centre, Nergal and his horse archers advancing forward to fill the large gap we had left and to begin shooting arrows at the enemy horsemen opposite. The ground was hard and parched, and soon great clouds of dust were being created by the thousands of feet and iron-shod hooves that were trampling the earth. We rode on, keeping parallel to the enemy's left wing, whose members were now preoccupied with returning the fire of Nergal's men. I glanced left and through the haze tried to see any enemy horsemen. I saw none. I continued riding forward for another minute or so then turned Remus left.

'Wheel, wheel,' I shouted as Remus shifted speed and tried to move into a gallop. I restrained him; he would need all his reserves of strength this day. There was no point in exhausting him. I glanced behind; my men were still following me. On we rode, the sounds of battle now clearly audible on our left. I slowed Remus down into a trot, then a walk and then halted him altogether. Those behind me did likewise. Enius, Orodes and Gotarzes fell in beside me.

'We must be behind their battle line now. We will face left and form a line here, on me,' I said. They both nodded and Enius and Gotarzes rode back to their men.

It took some time to form nine hundred cataphracts into an attack formation made up of one-hundred man companies drawn up into wedge formations. Each wedge was made up of fifty men in two ranks that were both widely spaced. I rode up and down the line and told the commander of each wedge not to employ horns for signalling. We would make our appearance unannounced.

My own cataphracts were in the centre of the line and I took up position at the tip of one of the wedges, Orodes on my left and slightly behind me.

'Keep safe, Orodes.'

'You too, Pacorus.'

I raised my kontus, pointed it forward and then nudged Remus to move. He snorted and began walking, while behind me a hundred others did likewise. The clash of steel and cries of men were getting louder in front of us as we broke into a trot and then a canter. I glanced left and right and saw every kontus levelled, ready to strike. I gripped my shaft with both hands tightly on my right side and leaned forward. The sounds of battle grew louder and ahead I could make out figures on horseback moving forward – lightly armed horse archers with bows in their hands and quivers at their hips. We thundered forward, broke into a gallop and screamed our war cries. Directly ahead of me, sitting on a stationary horse, his mouth open in surprise, transfixed by terror, was a bareheaded man wearing a light brown shirt and holding a bow. He did not move as the point of my lance pierced his side and the shaft plunged into his torso. As I released the grip on my kontus he still wore a look of surprise as I raced past him, drew my sword and slashed the rider behind him across the chest, knocking him from his saddle.

We hit the rearmost ranks of the opposition's left flank with the force of a lightning bolt. At first the enemy was surprised, and after several hundred of them had been skewered, slashed, had their skulls caved in by maces, and been run through, they panicked. These men were lightly armed horsemen, mostly archers but some spearmen also, but they had no chance against heavily armoured cavalry. Some attempted to rally and attack us but their blades made no impression on our scale armour and were easily brushed aside. Most turned their horses around and attempted to flee, not to the rear at first, but towards the centre of their own army. They thus careered into other horsemen attempting to advance in the opposite direction to meet us. The result was chaos, and on the edges of the maelstrom, like wolves circling sheep, my cataphracts were picking off their victims with ease. We retained our formations and kept tight to the enemy, hacking and slashing with our blades and maces. We discovered that most of the enemy horsemen did not have swords only long knives, and it was pathetic to see them try to stab us with them, only to be run through or disembowelled because their blades did not have the reach to harm us. These men also wore no helmets and so many of those under the command of Enius put away their swords and used their maces instead, bringing the weapons down on felt caps and splitting skulls in an orgy of slaughter. We pressed on.

I do not know how long we were in the melee, perhaps an hour, probably less, but suddenly, when my sword blade and armour were smeared with blood, the enemy in front of us evaporated. The entire left wing of the Narses' army had disappeared. Many lay dead but most had fled the battle on their horses. It did not matter. Horns blasted around me and our tired ranks reformed. I suddenly felt exhausted but knew that victory was near. Ahead I saw cataphracts clustered around Narses and the other kings, who were still observing the battle to their front. I peered left but all I could see through the dust was a large mass of foot soldiers with their backs to me.

I turned in the saddle. 'Kill Narses, kill Narses.'

Our horses were sweating and grunting and the men were tired, but they fell into their wedge formations once more. I saw Orodes. His helmet was dented and his armour torn, but he grinned at me to indicate that he was fine. I saw Gotarzes some distance away but of Enius there was no sign. Narses and his heavy cavalry were fresh and they still carried their lances. We had to quickly close the distance between them us and to stand any chance of victory. I raised my sword and dug my knees into Remus' flanks. Horns blasted. He reared up onto his hind legs and hurtled forward, the other riders following.

Once more we hurled ourselves against the enemy, only this time they did not break. Narses had noticed us and was desperately trying to deploy his cataphracts to face us. We were upon his men before they could charge us, but they merely threw down their lances, armed themselves with their close-quarter weapons and met us head-on. And so began a grim battle of attrition, sword clashing against sword and mace against mace. I was suddenly beside a great brute whose face was contorted in hate, and who brought his sword down in an attempt to split my helmet. I parried the blow with my sword and then swung the spatha in a scything movement towards his head. I got lucky – the point sliced his neck. He screamed, clutched at the wound and then fell from his saddle. I suddenly felt an intense pain in my right cheek, as if a red-hot iron had been placed on my flesh. I turned and saw a horseman on my right side who had just hit me with his mace, the blow striking my helmet's right cheekguard. He drew his weapon back to deliver another blow but at that moment Orodes severed his hand with his sword. The man squealed like a stuck pig and rode away. I nodded my thanks.

'Are you hurt, Pacorus?' he shouted.

My face burned with pain. 'No,' I lied, 'I'm fine.'

Around us hundreds of men were fighting for their lives. I saw Narses on his black steed perhaps only fifty paces from me, and beside him the serpent-like Mithridates. I clenched my hand tightly around my sword's handle.

'Orodes, with me,' I shouted, and then urged Remus forward.

A group of my Duran cataphracts closed around me as I charged forward once more. I felt nothing but intense loathing for the two rebel leaders as I closed the gap between us, screaming Narses' name as I did so.

Whatever Narses was he did not want for courage. He directed his horse straight towards me and attempted to lop off my head with a deft swing of his sword. I ducked the blow and tried to strike him with a backswing, but he was too quick for me and blocked the strike with his blade. He wheeled his horse around as my cataphracts fought his, and then came at me again with a series of attacks directed at my head and neck, for those were the only places where his sword could cut flesh. I was tiring now and found it difficult to defend his powerful strikes, but salvation came from an unlikely source. I had caught sight of Mithridates, wild-eyed and clearly terrified, before I got to grips with Narses, but now I saw him again, this time turning tail and running away. His flight spread panic among the other kings of Narses' entourage and soon they were doing likewise, taking their bodyguards with them. Narses also saw this undignified retreat. He moved his horse away from Remus and pointed his sword at me.

'Our business is not finished, boy.' Then he wheeled his mount away and galloped after his fleeing allies.

The fight now went out of the enemy. Those who could made good their escape, others threw down their weapons and pleaded for mercy. A blast of horns to my left signalled the arrival of

Nergal and his men. I ordered him to take them and pursue Narses and his entourage, though I doubted that they would succeed judging by the sweat-lathered state of their horses and riders slumped in their saddles. I gave the orders for the cataphracts to reform into line as ahead I spotted the locked shields of the legion coming into view. They were marching at a steady pace, trampling the dead and dying among the enemy. There was no resistance now as the enemy foot, what was left of them, had seen their lords desert them and had either ran for their lives or else dropped to their knees in front of the legionaries and begged for mercy. They were shown none. Those who surrendered and threw down their weapons were killed as soon as the first legionaries reached them. Then I saw Domitus and felt a surge of joy. He was standing next to one of leading centuries, pointing with his gladius for the men to maintain their order. An enemy soldier, a spearman, seeing Domitus cast aside his weapon and fell to his knees, his hands clasped in front of him like a man in prayer, imploring Domitus to save his life. The latter stepped forward and plunged his blade into the man's chest, then walked on. Such is war.

Then I saw the ranks of the Babylonian foot come into view, ragged compared to the legion. But at least they still existed. The side of my face still burned and I could feel blood trickling down my neck. I sheathed my sword and removed my helmet. The cheekguard that had been hit by the mace was dented and its hinge smashed. Around me were men sitting on their horses in a state of exhaustion, the scales on their armour battered and missing, their mounts similarly spent. Orodes appeared at my side and surveyed the view ahead. Dead men and slain horses lay scattered all around. Behind us was a similar trail of carnage where we had cut through the enemy's flank, the earth strewn with slain horse archers. The currency of war is blood and this day the army of Narses had paid a high price.

'You have won a great victory, Pacorus.'

'We have won a great victory, my friend.'

I told him to muster the cataphracts and then I rode over to where Domitus lined up with his men. They had halted now, the legionaries leaning on their grounded shields, grinning to each other – glad to be alive. They cheered as I approached and I raised my hand in recognition of their applause. I halted Remus in front of Domitus and he raised his arm stiffly in a salute. Always the Roman.

He now had his beloved cane in his hand, pointing it at me. 'Nasty wound. You should get it seen to. You broke them, then?'

There was not a scratch on him as far as I could see. 'Yes, we broke them. We hit them hard in their rear ranks and after that they never recovered. How many did you lose.'

He smiled. 'Hardly any as far as I can tell. Once we got tight and cosy with them they couldn't do much apart from be our pincushions. Easy, really.'

'Train hard, fight easy,' I said. 'Narses escaped.'

He spat on the ground. 'That is shame. You will have to fight him again, though I reckon there's not much of his army left.'

A rider thundered up and saluted. He wore the colours of Phraates.

'Hail, highness. King Phraates requests your presence in the company of the other kings.'

I raised my hand in acknowledgement and gladly took the water flask that Domitus offered.

Domitus saw legionaries drinking from their flasks. 'Don't gulp it down! Take sips. You don't know when you will be having your next drink. Save some.'

I put my helmet back on. 'I must pay my respects to the king. Get the wounded seen to and collect anything of use and put it in the carts. And collect our dead. We shall commit them to the fires tonight.'

Orodes and Gotarzes joined me as we walked our horses across the battlefield.

'Where is Enius?' I asked.

'Dead,' said Gotarzes, 'spear straight through his eye.'

'He was a good man,' added Orodes.

'He certainly was. How many more did we lose?' I asked.

Gotarzes shrugged. 'Forty or fifty.'

As far as I could tell Phraates had not moved from the spot he occupied at the start of the battle, and I noticed that Chosroes had now joined him. No doubt he had taken no part in the fighting either, and I assumed that neither had his men. I suddenly grew fearful for the safety of my father, as the army of Chosroes had been deployed on my father's right flank. My fears disappeared when I saw him, white cloak billowing behind him as he too rode up to pay homage to Phraates. I saw no marks on him as he caught up with me a couple of hundred paces from the high king. He rode up beside me and saw my blood-smeared face.

'Are you badly hurt?'

'No, father, I will live, and unfortunately so will Narses and Mithridates.'

He looked ahead. 'Phraates will forgive you that, I think. I am less inclined to do so.'

'Oh?'

'There was no need to fight this day. Narses was ready to yield, or at least discuss matters, but you were determined, weren't you. Could not let it rest. Well, you have your victory.'

'Our victory, surely?'

He said no more and in truth his words did not diminish the sensation of euphoria that I felt, which was increased further when we reached Phraates.

He clapped his hands when we reached him, provoking his bodyguard and the ranks of axe men to begin cheering. Phraates, previously inclined to negotiation, was now basking in the glow of triumph.

'Hail to you, Pacorus, the bringer of victory. First you defeat Porus and now you are instrumental in dispersing Narses. A truly great day.'

I bowed my head. 'The victory is yours, high king.'

This seemed to delight him even more, for he again clapped his hands frantically.

'I hereby make you lord high general of Parthia. Let all those here bear witness to my words, for Pacorus of Dura has today become the sword of Parthia.'

More cheering and applause erupted and the pain in my face seemed to magically disappear. I raised my arms aloft as the axe men started chanting my name. Out of the corner of my eye, though, I noticed that my father was frowning, an expression noted by Phraates, who had the commotion stilled instantly.

'King Varaz, you disapprove of your son's new appointment?'

He bowed his head. 'No, majesty, but there is still much work to be done.'

Phraates waved his hand at my father. 'Nonsense, you are far too serious, just like your father before you. Let us rejoice that God has granted us victory and that He has sent your son to be our deliverer.'

And so it was that I became lord high general of the Parthian Empire. Afterwards, when Alcaeus was stitching my wound as I sat on a stool in camp outside my tent, Domitus brought me the casualty figures.

'Fifteen dead, sixty wounded, none seriously.'

'It is a credit to you, Domitus. You have turned the legion into a fearsome machine.'

He seemed unmoved by my flattery. 'They were trained to do a job and they did it. Straightforward, really.'

'Have you noticed that Domitus doesn't have a scratch on him,' remarked Alcaeus. 'You should take some lessons from him.'

He finished stitching and tied off his handiwork. 'It will heal, but you'll have a scar. Nothing I can do about that.'

'Ha!' said Domitus, 'Gallia won't like that.'

'Indeed,' said Alcaeus. 'Perhaps you should be the kind of king who sits in his palace and sends others to fight his wars.'

I stood up. 'The day that happens, I'll order Domitus to run me through with a sword, for such a king is dead already.'

Alcaeus shook his head. 'A poet as well as a warrior.'

Nergal rode up and dismounted, taking off his helmet as he handed a squire his horse. He looked dirty and tired, his sweat-drenched hair matted to his head. I pointed to a stool and he sat on it. Domitus poured him a cup of water that he drank greedily.

'Lord Enius' body has been conveyed back to Ctesiphon for cremation on the orders of Phraates. Orodes is escorting the body.'

'What are our losses?' I asked.

'Five of your own cataphracts are dead, forty more belonging to Enius and twenty-five of those who fought under Gotarzes' banner were also slain. Of my horse archers, a hundred are dead and a similar number wounded.'

Alcaeus put his instruments back in his leather bag and slung it over his shoulder. 'That's me working through the night, then.'

'There are other physicians,' I said. 'You are, after all, in charge of the medical corps. I would like you to attend the victory feast that is being held at Ctesiphon tomorrow evening.'

He screwed up his face. 'I can't think of anything worse.' Then he was gone.

As the army made its way back to Ctesiphon my father sent out parties of horsemen after Narses. He was convinced that the King of Persis would try to build another army, though I was sceptical. Narses had fled south down the east bank of the Tigris back towards Persepolis, while the majority of my father's horse archers went east with Gotarzes and his followers to reclaim his capital, the city of Elymais.

I rode with my father and Vistaspa on our way back to Phraates' palace. Hatra's army had suffered hardly any casualties during the battle.

'When you took it upon yourself to commence hostilities,' said my father, 'we waited to see what our opponents opposite us would do.'

'And what did they do?' I asked.

'They waited too,' said Vistaspa, 'until they realised that their army's centre and other wing had collapsed, whereupon they decided to run for their lives.'

'You see, father, you should have given me your cataphracts after all.'

'They are mine to command, not yours to throw away.'

'I command all Parthia's armies now, father.'

He remained impassive to my boast, merely remarking. 'Do not get too above yourself, Pacorus.'

In truth it was difficult not to, for at the feast I was treated like a conquering hero. Slave girls, beautiful, young and half-naked, dazzled me with their smiles and enticed me with their oiled bodies. Phraates had bards compose poems about me and harpists sang songs of my victory. Phraates was happier than anyone, I think, and acted as if a great burden had been banished from his life, which in truth it had. He was also delighted that his son still lived, despite my best efforts to send him to the underworld. Even Chosroes allowed a smile to spread across his miserable, narrow face. Nergal and Domitus sat at one of the tables in the banqueting hall with my father, Vistaspa and Hatra's captains, while Dura's lords sat on their own table and were soon very drunk and very loud. The queen and her ladies frowned at them, but they had earned the right to be here for they had followed Nergal unquestioningly. I sat on the king's left-hand side, with the queen on his right and Orodes on her other side.

I may have been a king but I was a poor one compared to the rulers who sat at Ctesiphon. Here, guests ate food from intricately carved gold bowls and drank from silver cups that carried gold figures inlaid on their outsides, each one wearing a crown and Parthian dress and carrying a bow and quiver. Everyone in the hall was drinking from such vessels, an indication of the wealth at Ctesiphon. But then every kingdom in the empire paid an annual tribute to the King of Kings based on how many horse archers it could field. And Sinatruces had hoarded his annual tributes like the old miser he was. I wondered how long it would take for Queen Aruna to spend it.

An army of servants carried food on silver platters from the kitchens, where a similar number of cooks and kitchen slaves prepared the dishes. They brought pistachios, spinach, saffron, sweet and sour sauces, skewers of cooked pork, mutton, camel, goat, chicken and pigeon. For those who liked fish there was cooked sturgeon, dogfish, salmon, trout, carp and pike. Then there were almond pastries, pomegranate, cucumber, broad bean and pea, basil, coriander and sesame. The kitchens had also prepared a myriad of rice dishes, some containing almonds, pistachios, glazed carrots, orange peels and raisins; others laced with vegetables and fearsome spices. Even more dishes included stews, dumplings, sweet meats and stuffed vegetables doused in different sauces.

The queen, beautiful and icy as ever, was at least polite to me, even grudgingly grateful for saving her husband's throne. There was no talk of Mithridates but she would have heard that he had escaped and was, as far as anyone knew, unharmed, much to my regret.

'A most lavish feast, highness,' I said to Phraates as he ate rice and raisins from his gold bowl.

'The least you deserve, Pacorus.' He leaned closer to me. 'Tell me, that man over there, the Roman.'

'Lucius Domitus, highness. The commander of my legion.'

'Why does he fight for you?'

'Loyalty, highness, and a shared bond of comradeship.'

'From your time in the land of the barbarians?'

'Yes, highness.'

Phraates rubbed his chin as he regarded Domitus. 'And now he fights for Parthia.'

'And now he fights for Parthia, highness.'

Phraates looked down at his bowl. 'You are indeed fortunate that you command such loyalty Pacorus.'

I assumed that he was talking of his son, Mithridates, though I did not press the matter. At the bottom of it all he was a father who had been betrayed by his son. That must have wounded him most severely.

Phraates may have been indifferent as a king and he was certainly no warlord, but the years spent running his father's errands throughout the empire were not wasted in the days following. His skill as a diplomat came to the fore and he quickly set about isolating Narses from the other kings who had sided with him. He dispatched messages to the rulers of Drangiana, Carmania, Aria, Anauon and Yueh-Chih asking that they now accept him as King of Kings. He did not demand their obedience, merely requested it. He further stated that the past would be forgotten and that the empire should present a united front against our external enemies. When Phraates told us these things in a meeting of the war council I must confess I was deeply sceptical, but I was proved wrong. The army was prepared for a fresh campaign in the eastern provinces of the empire, but after two weeks couriers arrived from Monaeses, Vologases, Cinnamus, Tiridates and Phriapatus begging Phraates for his forgiveness and assuring him of their loyalty. And as surety for their pledges they would be sending members of their families to Ctesiphon to be hostages. Phraates was beside himself with joy, for at a stroke he had secured the eastern half of the empire and effectively isolated Narses.

'Then, highness,' I said, 'all that remains is to march on Persepolis and destroy the last vestiges of the rebellion.'

Orodes, who had returned from Elymais, having seen Gotarzes placed back on his throne, agreed with me. 'Narses should at least be banished for his treachery, father.'

Phraates, though, thought otherwise. 'No, no, no. I will not have more blood spilt unnecessarily. Once Narses' wounded pride has healed, he will see the impossible situation he is in and renew his allegiance. After all, he cannot fight the whole of the Parthian Empire on his own.'

It was at that moment I realised what Phraates' main failing was – his willingness to believe the best of everyone no matter what their transgression. He should have sent his army south without hesitation to rid the world of Narses for good. Instead he chose inaction.

'Easier said than done,' remarked my father afterwards. 'Persepolis is four hundred miles from Ctesiphon, and I'd bet a great sum that Chosroes for one would find a way of wriggling out of such a venture.'

I shrugged. 'No great loss.'

'You cannot defeat Narses on your own, Pacorus.'

'I would not be on my own, father, for I would have Orodes, Vardan and you with me. More than enough to destroy the remnants of Narses.'

We were riding to his camp along the banks of the Tigris. He suddenly pulled up his horse.

'We are going home, Pacorus. Back to Hatra.'

'Surely you wish to see Narses destroyed?'

'No, Pacorus. I wish to see peace restored to the empire, and it has been. And you will find that Vardan is of the same opinion. Let Narses fester at Persepolis. Phraates has no stomach for more fighting.'

'And you?'

He sighed. 'I have done what I came here to do.'

My father was right, for Vardan came to see me personally and confirmed that he was indeed going home.

'I'm too old to be tramping halfway across the empire to fight Narses. Besides, he'll probably make his peace with Phraates now.'

'You really think so?'

He shrugged. 'He has no army to back up his demands since you have destroyed it. He will sulk for a while and then accept Phraates' offer of friendship. He has little choice. None of the other kings will support him. His credibility has gone.'

'Perhaps you are right.'

He placed an arm around my shoulder. 'If I were you I would get myself back to that young wife of yours. Baby on the way, as well. Far better to be with her than living in a tent in some God-forsaken stretch of desert chasing after a beaten king, if you ask me.'

I smiled. 'You are right. How is Axsen, by the way?'

'Like all daughters, looking for a husband.'

He left the next day, the long column of purple-clad Babylonian soldiers and their horses and camels kicking up great clouds of dust as they marched west. Chosroes and his rabble departed the day after, a move welcomed by everyone as we all thought that we would catch the plague or some other pestilence from the army of Mesene.

'You are being unkind,' remarked my father as I dined with him as a guest of Phraates in his private chambers. It was an intimate affair, just the three of us being served food and drink as we reclined on couches in a small but beautifully appointed room with frescos painted on the walls depicting a lion hunt. And as a bonus, the queen had made herself scarce.

'Chosroes and his army were useless,' I replied.

'But at least they fulfilled their duty.'

Phraates, dressed in a simple blue robe with a red leather belt and pointed red slippers on his feet, was in a relaxed mood. 'How can I thank my two most loyal generals?'

'Serving you is our reward, highness,' said my father.

Phraates smiled at him. 'Well said, King Varaz, but fealty must be rewarded, for it seems to be in scarce supply these days.'

He clapped his hands and four guards, escorted by a captain of the garrison, brought in a large wooden chest carried by means of two poles inserted through metal rings fastened to each corner. It was placed on the floor in front of Phraates, who ordered it to be opened. The captain opened the lock with a key and I gasped as the lid was lifted. The chest was filled with drachmas, thousands of them.

'Enough to pay for your campaign, I think, King Varaz.'

My father rose from his couch and bowed to the king. 'You are too generous, highness.'

Phraates waved away my father's protest then looked at me.

'And for you, King Pacorus, a reward for each of the three times you have come to my aid.' Phraates ordered my father's chest to be taken away, then clapped his hands again.

'Three occasions, highness?' I was confused.

'First you defeated Porus, then you helped me awe the Romans, and finally you were instrumental in beating Narses. All quite simple.'

Three more chests were brought into the room, each as large as my father's, and laid before Phraates who likewise ordered them to be opened. I was truly speechless when the lids were lifted to reveal neatly stacked rows of gold bars in each one.

Without thinking I left my couch and stood beside one of the chests, extending my arm to stroke some of the bars, just to make sure they weren't a mirage. They were cold to the touch.

'They are quite real, I can assure you,' said Phraates, smiling.

I felt myself blushing. 'Of course, highness, I did not mean to imply otherwise. Forgive me.'

Phraates clapped his hands and grinned. 'This is most excellent. You are pleased with your gift?'

'Words cannot convey my gratitude, highness.'

In truth his gift was beyond my wildest dreams. Three chests of gold would go far, and in my mind I was already making plans for the expansion of Dura's army.

'And what will you do with this wealth?' asked Phraates.

'Strengthen my army, highness.'

Phraates rose from his couch and embraced me, much to my surprise.

'I congratulate you, King Varaz, you have raised a most excellent son, both wise and brave.'

My father bowed his head. 'You are too kind, highness.'

I have no recollection of the rest of the evening. I just kept going over in my mind what I could do with such a sum. Dura suddenly seemed too small a kingdom for my ambition.

I found my father's ability to read my mind disconcerting to say the least during his probing of me the next day. Hatra's horsemen had packed up their tents and were heading back west, and so my father took the opportunity to ride over to my camp and bid me farewell.

'I will bring Gallia to Hatra soon, I promise.'

'Good,' he said, 'your mother misses her, as do Gafarn and Diana.'

We were both staring at the opened chests containing the gold that had been placed in my tent for safe-keeping, legionaries standing inside and outside to make sure they did not 'walk' before they were loaded on to a cart for the journey back to Dura. Even Domitus wore an expression of wonderment at my good fortune.

'I have not seen such a haul since Spartacus captured that silver mine in Italy I was condemned to. Do you remember?'

'Indeed I do,' I said, 'only this time all of it belongs to me.'

'Phraates is indeed a clever king,' mused my father.

I was hardly listening. 'Mm?'

'He has paid a high price to secure your loyalty.'

I was annoyed at my father's attempt to spoil my good fortune. 'He had that already. Loyalty has nothing to do with it.'

'Oh I think it does. He knows that you will use this gold to strengthen your army, and a strong Dura means a strong Phraates. He can achieve much with such a weapon as you in his arsenal.'

I really did not see where my father's logic was heading so I merely agreed with him. But we parted on good terms and he reminded me again not to get 'too big for my boots'. After he had gone I told Domitus to bring all the legion's officers to my tent so they could view our bounty, and also had Nergal bring Dura's lords. I told them all that the gold would be used to increase Dura's strength, for a strong kingdom was a safe kingdom. Then we dismantled the camp and headed for home, back to my Gallic queen who was carrying my child.

Chapter 12

It took us ten days to get back to Dura, a leisurely march that turned into something of a victory parade as farmers, traders, shepherds and a host of others lined the roadside to cheer the horsemen and legionaries as we passed by. Everyone wanted to see the legion's golden griffin most of all, though Domitus had to use his cane when some got too enthusiastic and tried to touch it. I saw beggars and cripples implore him to allow them to lay their filthy, misshapen hands upon it, believing that to do so would restore their health and banish their deformities. How strange are the thoughts of men. Domitus was having none of it, telling the colour party guarding the griffin, big men who had served with him in Italy, to use the sharp ends of their javelins if anyone got close, or even to use the unfortunates for sword practice should they so desire, an order I countermanded at once.

'You can't kill people just because they are an inconvenience, Domitus, especially if they are old or infirm.'

He was most unhappy. 'Why not?'

'Because they only want what we all want – a stroke of luck or good fortune. We have become heroes to them, bringing hope to their unhappy lives, if only for a short while. To betray them so basely would be grotesque.'

'No one's going to lay their filthy mitts on my griffin.'

'Well just place more guards around it, but tell them not to kill anyone, and certainly not to draw their swords. That's an order.'

He marched off, muttering to himself. But no one was seriously hurt or killed on the journey back to Dura. The whole of the city turned out to welcome us back, plus many of the farmers who worked on the kingdom's estates who had come to see their lords who had won great victories. It took the legion a full hour to cross over the pontoon bridge and march to its camp west of the Palmyrene Gate. And all order and discipline started to break down as dozens of young women threw their arms around their loved ones and placed garlands over their heads. Domitus had maintained the Roman practice of forbidding legionaries the right to marry, but many had taken women anyway who became their de facto wives, the females living in rented accommodation in the city. And many now held infants in their arms as both mother and child welcomed back their man and gave thanks to whatever gods they worshipped that he had returned to them safely and in one piece. As the legion and its small army of camp followers inched its way back to camp, I rode with my cataphracts and Dura's lords under the Palmyrene Gate and through the city to the Citadel. I bowed my head to the stone griffin above me as I passed through the gates themselves, and then waved to the crowds that lined the main street as I headed towards my palace. Vagharsh held the banner behind me, and Nergal was on my right side as we moved slowly though the throng. Behind us the cataphracts rode bare headed and without lances, their white cloaks around their shoulders. Women threw rose petals at us from balconies and children banged pots with sticks, making a racket that made Remus prick his ears back. The lords left their horse archers outside the city. They dismounted to mingle with their friends and neighbours who had made the journey to the city.

When we reached the palace, guards lined the street outside and kept the crowds back as I rode through the gates and into the courtyard. I had told myself that I was a great warlord returning home as a conqueror, and as such would display no emotion as I greeted my queen. But as I caught sight of her standing at the top of the palace steps I felt tears of joy and happiness welling up inside me, and by the time I had vaulted from my saddle and ran up those steps to embrace her they were streaming down my face. I held her close, my face buried in her hair, telling her that I loved her, then kissed her on the lips. This brought a hearty cheer from the cataphracts now drawn up in the courtyard, while the Amazons standing behind Gallia in front of the palace entrance, Praxima at their head, also cheered.

I stepped back and looked at Gallia, her eyes of deep blue and her hair the purest blonde.

'Welcome back to your home.' She smiled at me and I held her again.

Godarz and Rsan, standing to one side, stepped forward and bowed their heads.

'It is good to see you, majesty,' said Rsan.

'And you,' I said.

'We have been hearing how you have been covering yourself in glory,' Godarz grinned at me.

'And collecting war wounds, I see,' Gallia ran a finger over my scarred face.

'It will heal though not disappear entirely, my love, or so Alcaeus informed me.'

A cart pulled by two testy mules wheeled into the courtyard, escorted by Domitus and a score of his men. I pointed at Rsan.

'Something to fill your treasury, Rsan. Go and look.'

Both he and Godarz walked over to the cart as Domitus jumped on the back and unlocked the three chests that were sitting behind the driver. I noticed that Godarz and Domitus clasped each other's forearms in greeting when they met. They had become good friends. Rsan whooped with joy when he was shown the gold, and even Godarz's usually resigned face displayed excitement. Rsan instantly gave orders to his guards to take the chests into the treasury. I dismissed the cataphracts, whose squires took their horses to the stables. Praxima then dismissed the Amazons and kissed me on the cheek as she and Nergal disappeared into the palace to make up for the time they had been away from each other. I looked at Gallia stroking Remus and talking to him softly, her still lithe figure framed by her leggings and white armless silk tunic. No sign of her pregnancy as yet. A squire took Remus to the stables and I grabbed her hand and pulled her close. I felt my loins stir.

'I've missed you.'

Her eyes lit up. 'Are you going to show me how much?'

Afterwards, as she lay naked on our bed, she ran a finger down my scarred cheek. 'Soon I will be fat and ugly and you will not want me.'

I turned to face her. 'I will never not want you, you are my reason for living.'

'I will hold you to that.'

'I think my father is angry with me.'

She raised an eyebrow at me. 'Have you given any reason for him to be angry with you?'

I sighed. 'He thinks that I lust for glory, and that we should not have given battle to Narses.'

'And do you lust for glory?'

I looked at her and knew that I could not deceive her. 'Yes.'

She smiled. 'Perhaps he envies you and is angry with himself for feeling thus.'

'Perhaps. I think he wishes that we were both back in Hatra under his protection.'

'Or maybe he regrets not putting himself forward to be King of Kings.'

I smiled. 'His pride would never allow himself to admit that he has made a mistake. But yes, I think he does now see that perhaps he, and not Phraates, would have been a better choice. But what is done is done.'

'And now you are Lord High General of the whole Parthian Empire, for a courier arrived from Ctesiphon announcing your appointment before you returned. What does it entail?'

I rose from the bed and stood at the balcony doors, looking at the Euphrates below. 'I do not know exactly, though I have a nasty feeling that I might become Phraates' errand boy.'

Early the next morning I rode down to the Palmyrene Gate. When I arrived I handed a guard the reins of Remus and then climbed the stone steps inside one of the towers on to the arch to look at the stone griffin statue. The sky's purple and pink hues were giving way to blue as the sun began its ascent in the east, while spreading out before me to the west was the great desert plain. The legion's camp was already bustling with activity, the men rising before dawn and then eating their breakfast of porridge, bread and cheese, before assembling for parade. It was at morning assembly that any notices were read out, and I had instructed Domitus to pass on my gratitude to the men for their professional conduct during the campaign that had just finished, and to inform them that each would be receiving a bonus of a week's pay. The legion's clerks meticulously recorded each legionary's pay, the documents being held in the headquarters building in the Citadel. The whole legion was run along Roman lines. 'War is business,' Domitus once told me, and he was right. When I was a boy I used to think that conflict was all colourful banners, shining armour, mighty steeds and personal combat, but the reality was that victory depended on discipline, endless drill, the right equipment and cool leadership in the heat of battle. Bozan, my old tutor in Hatra, had drilled it into me that the key was to make sure you were prepared for war, and that required hours and hours of training and drilling. Train hard, fight easy. And he was right, and so was Domitus, and that's why the Romans were so successful. They didn't care how many men an enemy brought to the battlefield because they knew that every man in every legion knew his task and could carry it out in his sleep. As I watched a century march at double time out of the camp I smiled to myself. Drill, marching and instruction, day after day, month after month, year after year. It was the same with my cataphracts, who every day rode out to the training fields and spent hours honing their formations, obeying the horns that told them when to turn, when to charge and when to retreat. Dura's lords were not disciplined, and though wild and recklessly brave, against determined opposition, such as a Roman army, they would fail. No matter, I now had enough gold to raise a force of my own horse archers and Nergal would be their commander.

'Daydreaming, son of Hatra?'

I was startled by the words, then saw the familiar dishevelled figure of Dobbai ambling towards me.

'Your wife told me that you might be here.'

'We missed you at the meal last night,' I said.

'Of course you didn't. Two young newlyweds want to be on their own after being parted, so I made myself scarce.'

She laid her hand on the griffin statue. 'Afraid he might have been stolen?'

'No, I like the view, and it is also peaceful. Most of the time.'

'Don't be churlish, son of Hatra, it does not suit you. We heard of your elevation to be chief warlord in the empire. Well done, though I had hoped to see the heads of Narses and Mithridates adorning the walls of the Citadel this morning.'

'Unfortunately, they got away.'

Her haggard visage frowned. 'That is unfortunate, for you will have to fight them all over again. Cockroaches are difficult to kill, are they not?'

'I met the wife of Phraates during my stay in Ctesiphon.'

'Queen Aruna?' Dobbai spat over the battlements. 'She possesses the venom of a King Cobra and the malice of a demon from the underworld. She took a dislike to you?'

'An instant one, as far as I could tell.'

'You have won great victories but made powerful enemies. People may forget the victories but your enemies will not forgive you. What are you going to do with the gold that Phraates gave you?'

I bristled. 'That's an impertinent question.'

She pointed a talon-like finger at me and cackled. 'Then have me flogged.'

'Don't be a fool. I will strengthen the army, if you must know.'

'Very wise. You will need many warriors err long.'

'I can command kings to send me warriors,' I declared boldly.

'You can command and they can ignore you. Trust only those who have sworn allegiance to you. Words are worth nothing.'

'Narses and Mithridates cannot conjure up armies out of nothing. Even if they wanted to rebel again it would take them time to rebuild their forces. In any case, the other kings in the eastern part of the empire have sworn allegiance to Phraates.'

She scratched her beak-like nose. 'They have done so because they fear you, that is the only reason. But if you are pre-occupied then they can change their minds. You want my advice?'

'Not really.'

She ignored my words. 'Send assassins to kill both Mithridates and Narses. Persuade Phraates to give you the throne of Persis and Orodes the crown of Susiana. In that way you will secure peace in the empire.'

217

'Flights of fancy,' I said. 'Even if I wanted Persis, which I do not, Phraates would not sanction it, and he would have me executed if he discovered that I had had his son murdered.'

She smiled, her teeth black and foul, turned and shuffled away. 'Very well, have it your own way. But war is coming, son of Hatra, war is coming.'

Despite Dobbai's dire warning the weeks that followed saw a return to normality. Peace within the empire meant a return of trade along the Silk Road and the flow of caravans through Dura to and from Egypt, with more money pouring into Rsan's treasury. The lords returned to their estates and Gallia and I undertook a tour of my kingdom while she had the energy to do so and was not too fat to fit in a saddle. She declared that she would never be transported in a cart, so it was on horseback or not at all. So that summer we visited each lord in his stronghold. I took all my cataphracts with me, though neither they nor their horses wore any armour or carried the kontus. Instead, they all wore white tunics and brown leggings and carried bows and swords. They also left their helmets behind, as the facemasks would terrify the locals. It was a happy time, for the ranks of my cataphracts contained the sons of Dura's lords so each stronghold we visited turned into a homecoming for an eldest son. A great feast invariably followed, at which drunken oaths of allegiance were sworn to me and Gallia, to the amusement of my wife. The other sons of each lord begged their father to allow them to serve in my cavalry. The number of volunteers thus swelled after each visit, especially at the feasts. As the hour grew late Gallia would retire to her quarters. She did not complain but I could tell that her pregnancy was sapping her strength. And so she slept and each lord silenced the music and noise, leaving his eldest son to talk of the campaign that he had just fought in. I always made sure that I was just a face in the crowd at such events, for each man had earned the right to tell his story of the battles that we had fought. Eager faces hungry for news gathered round as he told how we had defeated Porus and his elephants. The logs on the great fires crackled and hissed as a new version of the story was told every time. The elephants, tall as three horses and blood-crazed, charged our lines, only to die on the points of our lances as we abandoned all hope and met the giant beasts head-on. Others told of hundreds of elephants as far as the eye could see, each carrying archers and spearmen who fired thousands of arrows that bounced off our scale armour as we rode among the tusked animals, hacking at their legs with our swords. Occasionally I would catch the eye of our host, invariably

218

surrounded by his lieutenants and giant hunting dogs at his feet, and he would smile at me. He knew the truth, that the elephants had been scattered by a herd of pigs, and so did I, and for that matter so did the storyteller and many of those present. It didn't matter. I smiled back and we both enjoyed the fiction. Then there were stories of our victory over Narses, of our crazy charge into the massed ranks of the enemy, and for once the orator told the truth for there was no need to embellish the tale. The enemy did indeed fill the horizon and we were but few in number.

The lords of Dura were hard frontiersmen, men given lands on the western bank of the Euphrates because only they had the courage and skills to conquer a wasteland filled with hostile Agraci. Dura had belonged to the King of Kings, and the wily fox Sinatruces had sent those who were uncontrollable and rebellious to do battle with the scorpions, snakes and Agraci. Only the strongest and most cunning survived, but those who did carved out their territory with blood and iron and had no time for court etiquette or politics. They still did not kneel to any king and I did not ask them to kneel to me, but I had earned their respect and they now gave me loyalty. And the peace with the Agraci had held, so now their lands were unmolested and turning a profit, which in turn was making them prosperous.

For his part Haytham kept an iron grip on his people and prohibited any incursions into Dura's territory. But old habits die hard and there was the occasional transgression, usually a raid to steal livestock. Haytham always found out and had the livestock returned, along with the severed heads of the thieves as proof that justice had been meted out. Such gestures were appreciated by Dura's lords. For his part, after bidding Gallia and me a fond farewell, Malik returned to his people and took Byrd with him, though after a few days Gallia was harassing me to take her to see Haytham.

'We could invite him here, Rasha too.'

She was insistent. 'No, I think we should visit him. It is only polite.'

I suddenly realised why she was so keen to journey to Palmyra. 'You want to see Byrd's woman.'

She avoided my eyes. 'Nonsense, I had completely forgotten that he had one. In any case...'

'Very well, my sweet, we will visit Haytham and satisfy your curiosity.'

And so we did. I took Haytham a present of a pair of elephant tusks that had been hacked off a dead beast after we had beaten

Porus. On the road I was struck how much traffic there was –
camels carrying great loads, mules weighed down with wares and
even travellers on foot. How different from the first time that we
had made the same journey, when we took Haytham's daughter
back to her father.

Palmyra was a great sprawling collection of tents around a huge
oasis that had turned the arid desert green. There were hundreds of
trees fed by the waters – palms, olives and pomegranates – and
there must have been thousands of people living among the lush
landscape.

'We have set aside a large area to the south for the merchants
and their animals, and we dug irrigation channels to provide men
and their beasts with water, which we charge them for.' Haytham
grinned broadly. He was still an old thief at heart.

We sat cross-legged on the carpets in his tent, eating roasted
goat wrapped in pancakes, dipping them in delicious yoghurt and
washed down by fruit juice. Rasha was cuddling up to Gallia as we
ate and talked.

'Is there any trouble?' I asked.

'Never,' replied Haytham. 'I make sure of that. I provide escorts
from the edge of your territory all the way down to Petra if they so
desire, but most of the caravans have their own guards and keep
themselves to themselves.'

'And you are happy with our agreement?'

He nodded. 'I have no complaints, and Malik does nothing but
talk about you and your army. I think you are turning him into a
Parthian.'

'What do you know of Byrd?' asked Gallia.

Haytham rose and picked up some cushions and placed them
around Gallia. He had obviously heard of her pregnancy. 'Your
scout? He's a strange one. Doesn't talk much but he and Malik
have become good friends so he comes and goes as he wishes.
He's found himself a woman here.'

'Gallia is dying to meet her.'

'I am merely curious, that is all,' she said.

'I'll ask Malik to bring them over tomorrow, if you wish.'

Malik and Byrd had just returned from a journey to Syria, so I
could pretend that my meeting with them was for reasons of
strategy, though I doubt that anyone was fooled, especially as there
was no reason for Byrd's woman to be there. She was a dusky
skinned individual of average height and slim build, wrapped in
her dark brown Agraci robes, her hair braided under her shawl. She
had dark brown eyes, almost black, with a slender nose and full

lips. Her name was Noora and Gallia was delighted to meet her.

'I am a friend of Byrd's,' Gallia said.

'I have heard of you, lady,' she looked at me. 'And you too, sir.'

'Please, call me Pacorus.'

Byrd looked totally disinterested as Gallia took Noora by the arm and bombarded her with questions.

'Sorry about all this, Byrd,' I said, 'you know what women are like.'

'No matter, lord. It is good to see Gallia looking so well. One thing you should know, though. We heard stories of many Romani soldiers marching across the land from Greece into Asia.'

'Going where?'

'Armenia and Pontus.'

That was indeed worth knowing. With reinforcements, Lucullus would be emboldened to make further incursions into Parthian territory, though first he had to destroy the remnants of his enemies in Pontus and Armenia. Perhaps that would keep him occupied and avert his gaze from Parthia. Perhaps, but I was still uneasy. Our stay in Palmyra was an extremely pleasant diversion, though, and I was pleased that Byrd had found a companion after his years of loneliness. Gallia wanted them both to come back with us to Dura to live in the palace, though the look of horror on Byrd's face at such a prospect told me that he would be staying with Haytham and his people.

'I hope I can still call on your services, Byrd,' I said on the morning of our departure. 'You are my best scout.'

'Just send word, lord. I come.'

We did take one person back with us, though – Rasha. She wanted to hear more tales of elephants and in any case Gallia loved having her in the palace, so that was that.

I wrote to Phraates, Aschek of Atropaiene and Farhad of Media telling them about the reinforcements being sent to Lucullus, though I was rather surprised when I received a message back from Phraates telling me that Lucullus had sent a courier to Ctesiphon stating that Rome wished for peace with Parthia and looked forward to amicable relations between our two empires. There was no mention of Rome withdrawing from Gordyene, though. Phraates also informed me that Mithridates had appeared at his court and had begged his forgiveness for being 'intoxicated' by Narses and raising his sword against his father. Phraates had forgiven his son, of course, but had given the city of Susa to Orodes for safekeeping, retaining Mithridates at Ctesiphon to be the commander of the garrison and his 'special advisor', whatever that meant. At least Orodes now controlled the kingdom of Susiana and its army.

'And Mithridates and his mother control Phraates, who controls his son, Orodes. So you see, Mithridates exerts a great influence over the empire still,' said Dobbai as she sat with us on the palace terrace late one afternoon. The day had been stifling, but as the evening approached the heat had diminished and a light easterly breeze made the temperature pleasant. I watched travellers on the road from the east approaching Dura – people on foot, camels loaded with wares and mules pulling carts full of goods. I was always amazed at the volume of people on the road, but Egypt had an insatiable desire for silk and China had a seemingly never-ending supply of the material. And Parthia lay between seller and buyer and grew rich by dint of geography.

'So, Mithridates has crawled back to his mother,' said Dobbai, chewing the last morsels of meat from a rib.

'It appears so,' I replied.

'A viper returns to its nest.'

Rasha stopped eating and looked up at Dobbai. 'When we find a viper we kill it. They are poisonous, you know.'

'You see, son of Hatra, how even a small child grasps the importance of ridding the world of Mithridates.'

I waved my hand at her. 'I am not going to kill Mithridates.'

She grinned at Rasha. 'Not yet.'

'We should visit your parents, Pacorus,' mused Gallia, bored of talk of Mithridates, 'before I am too fat to fit in a saddle.'

'You are right. I will organise it.' And it was also an opportunity to get away from Dobbai's incessant nagging.

'Can I come?' asked Rasha, smiling innocently at Gallia.

'Of course, as long as your father agrees.'

He did, and so we set off seven days later. I left Godarz as my deputy and told Domitus to begin the process of recruiting new legionaries, both to replace the few who had been killed at Surkh and to establish a replacement cohort. I had been toying with the idea for a while of a formation that would act as a sort of permanent garrison at Dura but at the same time would also train new recruits and act as a pool of battle replacements. In this way the legion would always be at full strength because new legionaries could be ferried from the replacement cohort to the legion in the field. I had read that the Persians who had once ruled these lands had a royal guard called the Immortals, whose strength had always been maintained at ten thousand men. I wished the legion to be similar. Domitus thought the garrison cohort a good idea, but raised an eyebrow when I informed him about the Immortals.

'Where are these Immortals now?' were his only words on the matter.

I took Nergal and Praxima with me to Hatra, plus the Amazons, who had been disappointed that they had missed the battle against Narses. I left Domitus and the legion behind, taking only a score of my cataphracts along for the journey, who left their armour behind. Like me they carried only swords and bows, always our bows.

It was good to see Hatra again, its dozens of stone towers glistening in the sun, each one topped by a flag bearing my father's banner. Vistaspa met us with an escort about a mile from the city, two hundred cataphracts in full armour and pennants flying from every kontus, and as we entered the city's south gates Kogan's soldiers lined the streets to the palace.

'A most impressive reception, Vistaspa,' I remarked, 'though my father need not have troubled himself.'

'The visit of another king is a serious occasion, majesty,' he replied sternly. 'Protocol must be observed.' Same old Vistaspa, hard as granite.

My parents waited for us at the top of the palace steps, and I noticed for the first time that my mother had flecks of grey in her hair. She still looked regal and glamorous, her arms adorned with gold armlets and bracelets and a gold braid belt around her waist. My father was dressed in a white robe and looked stern. And standing next to them were Gafarn and Diana. My brother smiled at me, still the irrepressible Gafarn, though Diana looked very different from the plain-looking kitchen slave who I had known in Italy. Now she was dressed in a fine white dress, with gold rings upon her fingers and gold barrettes in her hair, which was now shoulder length. She wore make-up around her eyes and on her lips and exquisite gold earrings dangled from her ears. Her appearance befitted her status as a princess of the empire. And standing beside her, clutching her hand, was a small boy, the son of Spartacus. He was nearly three years old now, and I saw in him the strong jaw and intelligent face of his father, his hair as black as his mother's had been.

After we had all embraced each other, Gallia and Diana sharing a long and tearful reunion, I knelt beside the boy.

'This is your Uncle Pacorus, Spartacus,' said Diana.

He bowed his head to me. 'Hello, your majesty.'

I smiled at him. 'Hello, Spartacus, I was a friend of your father.'

He smiled at me but I think the words meant little to him. All he had known was Hatra's palace, a world far removed from the one lived in by his parents.

'It is good that you tell him of his parents,' I said as I walked beside Diana through the sprawling palace that was Hatra's seat of power.

'I have told him about Spartacus and Claudia but he does not really understand. Why would he? He is being raised as a prince in a far-off land.'

'One day he will understand, I hope. I promised Cannicus that I would tell him.'

Diana stopped and looked at me. 'That's a name I have not heard in an age.'

'Do you remember Castus and his Germans, Diana? All hair, beards and boasting. But they made good soldiers.'

'I remember,' she said. 'I remember it all.'

'I miss those days, Diana. When we were fugitives in a foreign land with a host of Romans after us. But how we gave them a good run for their money.'

She shook her head. 'I think you remember some of those times, not all of them. Besides you should be looking forward, what with a baby on the way. Gallia looks very happy.'

'She is, and so am I.'

My father's frostiness towards me had disappeared and the next day we went to the training fields outside the city to shoot our bows. We all took part in a competition called the 'five targets' – five small packed straw circles mounted on poles that were spaced at one hundred-yard intervals. The rules were simple. Each participant rode up the course as fast as possible, shooting at each target as he passed it. The first target was angled towards the rider, the next two were positioned parallel to the rider as he passed them, but the final two were facing away from the rider, at right angles to the course. This meant that he had to turn in the saddle and fire over the hindquarters of his horse, firing backwards in effect, to hit the targets. Gallia insisted on taking part, as did Praxima, while the men folk numbered myself, my father, Vistaspa, Nergal and Gafarn. All Parthian males learn to shoot the bow before they ride, even before they can walk. They start out on 'baby bows', small affairs that have almost no strength in their strings. They then progress on to more powerful bows, and by the time they reach their teenage years they are shooting full-sized recurve bows made of wood and bone, the same weapons that Parthian warriors use in battle.

As we all took turns to run the course and shoot at the targets, my father sat on his horse beside Remus and told me the news of what was happening to the north of Hatra's borders.

'My scouts report that many Roman troops are marching into Armenia and Pontus. They mean to finish Mithridates once and for all.'

Mithridates, King of Pontus, had been fighting the Romans for twenty years now, and although he was a great general, his kingdom was on its knees. If only his namesake, the son of Phraates, had a tenth of his courage and nobility.

'And once they have finished with Pontus and Armenia, we will be next,' continued my father.

I was shocked. 'You mean Hatra?'

'Hatra, Media, Atropaiene, it's all the same to Rome.'

'They have an insatiable appetite for land,' I said.

'Your Roman.'

'Domitus?'

My father nodded. 'He was right. Phraates appears weak in Roman eyes and that is bad news for all of us.'

His words must have unnerved me, for when it was my turn to shoot I missed two of the targets altogether and finished last behind Nergal and Vistaspa. Gallia and Gafarn agreed to share first place, with my father close behind them in second.

Back at the city I walked with my father and Vistaspa as they made an inspection of the royal armouries. The level of activity was feverish, with men at every forge and anvil. Quivers of freshly made arrows were being ferried to the stores and sword blades were being hammered on anvils and quenched in water. Vistaspa saw the look of surprise on my face.

'We are preparing for the worst. The Romans will find that Hatra is not Gordyene.'

I picked up a mace from a row of racks that lay along one wall, each one filled with newly made weapons. It was a thing of beauty – a wooden shaft with leather strips around the base for grip, and steel flanges at the other end arranged around the shaft in a circular pattern. Primarily a bludgeoning instrument, the flanges could batter their way through mail, scale armour and helmets, especially if wielded from a horse by a cataphract.

'We could always strike first,' I suggested. 'Pre-empt Roman aggression.'

My father took the mace from me and replaced it on the rack. 'You would like that, wouldn't you? Another war to add glory to your name. But I think not. Hatra lies close to the Romans whereas Dura is far away.'

'They will come anyway, father.'

'If they do, then I know that Media will come to Hatra's assistance, and then the Romans will be facing three armies – ours plus Atropaiene's and Media's.'

'And Dura's,' I added.

'You may have to look to your own devices if the Romans attack you from Syria,' Vistaspa's eyes lit up as he considered my discomfort. He had always been a callous individual, a man who took delight in people's misfortunes.

'Have no fear, Vistaspa,' I replied, 'Dura's defences are strong. In any case, Haytham's men would harry the Romans' supply lines while they sat in front of Dura.'

'The Agraci?' Vistaspa's face showed disgust.

'Yes,' I replied, 'the Agraci. Haytham's son, Prince Malik, has fought by my side and the king's daughter is in Hatra's palace as we speak.'

'There's a difference between enemies who have agreed to stop fighting and allies, Pacorus,' growled my father.

'Is there, father? I count Haytham as a friend and have no reason to believe that he does not think of me in the same way.'

'You should have more care in the choice of your friends,' sneered Vistaspa.

I smiled at him. 'Have a care, Vistaspa, one day all this,' I gestured at the armoury with my arm, 'will be mine and those who question my authority will have no place here.'

'Enough!' barked my father. 'Prince Vistaspa is my friend and trusted lieutenant, and I will not have him spoken to thus.'

'My apologies, father, I did not mean to cause offence.'

The rest of the tour was uncomfortable to say the least. In truth Vistaspa had done nothing wrong. Most Parthians were prejudiced against the Agraci, many hated them outright. But still, old ways and attitudes were only useful if they served a purpose, and antagonising the Agraci served none at all. The company of my mother was much more agreeable, especially as she had collected Gallia, Rasha, Diana and Gafarn as well. We all arranged ourselves in her quaint pagoda as Rasha and young Spartacus played with a set of carved wooden farm animals. Servants brought us fruit juice and pastries.

'Been annoying your father again, Pacorus?' asked Gallia.

I shrugged and toyed with my cup.

'I'll take that as a yes.'

'Really, Pacorus,' said my mother. 'We see you little enough, you should not argue when you do come to Hatra.'

'Father refuses to see the bigger picture,' I replied.

226

'Have you been painting?' Gafarn was in an impious mood.

'I was talking of strategy.'

'Which involves you ordering everyone about, does it, in your new role as lord high general? By the way, is there a lord low general?'

I frowned at him. 'It means trying to keep Parthia's enemies at bay.'

'You mean the Romans.'

'Of course,' I said, 'what others are there?'

'Don't you think that you are becoming obsessed by the Romans, Pacorus?' said my mother.

'You should let it go, Pacorus,' said Gafarn. He gestured at Gallia and Diana. 'We all have.'

'Let what go?'

'Your hatred for the Romans, what else? We all escaped, we were the lucky ones. Thousands died in Italy, including our friends, but we escaped.'

'And I should be grateful for that?'

Gafarn looked at me. 'Why not? We all live a life beyond even the dreams of most men. What have we to be angry about?'

'He's right, Pacorus,' said Gallia.

I knew he was, which made it worse, but I could never forgive the Romans for enslaving me.

'My back carries a permanent reminder of the hospitality that the Romans extended to me. As long as they are on Parthia's borders I shall neither forgive nor forget.'

Diana smiled at me, that sweet, disarming smile that could melt the iciest heart. Gallia was more beautiful than Diana, but Diana had a warmth and grace that endeared her to all, from the lowliest slave to the highest king whose aloofness was soon conquered by her charm. Everyone grew to love Diana, myself included, and we all reckoned Gafarn to be among the luckiest men in all the empire. I was the luckiest, of course, but he came a close second.

'Oh, Pacorus,' she said. 'You are still the same proud, defiant young man whom we first clapped eyes upon on the slopes of Mount Vesuvius all those years ago. Unbending, strong and brave. Everything is black and white to you, right or wrong, no middle course. But the world is not like that, my brother, and we must weave a path through life, taking our happiness where we find it. Do not dwell on the past. Spartacus and Claudia knew this, and so do Gallia and Gafarn.'

She walked over and kissed me gently on the cheek. 'Be content with the love of your friends and family, my brave warrior, for

227

they are your source of strength.'

And that was that. There was no more talk of Romans or war and so we sat and laughed and watched Rasha play with young Spartacus, and for a while I forgot about those things that troubled me.

The rest of our stay in Hatra was pleasant enough. I went to Vistaspa's quarters and apologised to him for my rudeness, a gesture that took him somewhat by surprise. He was pleased, I think, for he invited me to stay awhile and we talked of Dura, the Romans and his friend Godarz. I think he missed his old companion, and so I promised that when I got back to Dura I would send Godarz to Hatra for an extended stay.

'So, majesty, we are all agreed that war with the Romans is inevitable?'

'I think we have known each long enough for you not to call me majesty, Vistaspa. And yes, I think war is inevitable.'

Vistaspa never really smiled as such, but a satisfied leer now crossed his face. 'I think you are right and so does your father. Hatra will be ready for it when it comes, though. But what of the rest of the empire?'

'Rome thinks that it can pluck each kingdom in the empire like ripe fruit' I said. 'Phraates made a mistake when he did not retaliate against Lucullus for occupying Gordyene. The Romans will have noted his pusillanimity and will act accordingly. But I think that their underestimation of us may be their undoing.'

He regarded me for a moment with his cold, black eyes, the eyes of a man without pity. 'And yet, they will know, or at the very least will have heard, that you defeated the rebels and placed Phraates back on his throne. I'm sure that the new King of Dura is part of their calculations also.'

'The one thing that I learned about the Romans when I was in Italy,' I said, 'was that they view all other peoples as inferior. We are all barbarians to them, Vistaspa, to be conquered and ruled over. That view above all will be dictating their calculations.'

'Perhaps now you are underestimating them.'

I smiled at him. 'If we can convince the Romans that conquering Parthia is too high a price, then they will think twice before launching a full-scale invasion of the empire. They only respect strength. It would be much easier, of course, if my father sat in Ctesiphon and not Phraates.'

'You want to remove Phraates.'

I shook my head. 'No, we elected him and the decision must stand, for better or worse.'

228

'Then, Pacorus, let us hope it is for the better.'

When a month had passed Gallia decided it was time to make our way back to Dura. Her belly was starting to swell now, not by much, but enough to make her irritable and unhappy with her appearance. I told her every day that she was beautiful and that I would always love her, but though she was thrilled to be pregnant she disliked the inconvenient side effects of her condition. So we said goodbye to my parents at the foot of Hatra's palace steps early one morning, the sky as clear and blue as Gallia's eyes, and made our way south at a leisurely pace. Diana and Gafarn watched us go as well, and standing beside them was young Spartacus, who smiled and waved at us as we rode out of the palace compound.

Life at Dura went on much the same. Domitus drilled his legionaries and I began to increase the number of my cataphracts to five hundred, half a dragon. In addition, Nergal set about raising his horse archers. It was not difficult. Our recent victories had increased the prestige of Dura and men wanted to serve in its army. Recruits came mostly from the estates of Dura's lords, who were happy to send Nergal their men, though others came from as far afield as Gordyene and Armenia. Curiously, a sizeable number of men began to arrive from Pontus. Rome's war against that brave kingdom was coming to an end, and rather than be enslaved many of its soldiers decided to chance their luck in other lands. So they headed south, through Armenia and Gordyene and into Hatra or Media. If they entered Hatra the first city they reached was Nisibus, whose governor was Vata. He fed them, listened to their stories and let them rest their weary bodies in his city, for they would have spent weeks on tracks and roads avoiding Roman patrols, as Hatra was nearly three hundred miles from Pontus. Vata then sent them south on another long trip, to me at Dura. In a letter he told me that Hatra had little use for foot soldiers, being able to raise thousands if necessary from the estates of the kingdom's lords, but that perhaps 'your Roman' might have use of them.

'He's right,' said Domitus, his face and arms now turned dark brown by the Mesopotamian sun. 'I've talked with some of them. All good soldiers who have spent years fighting.'

'How do you know they are good soldiers?' I asked.

'Any man who leaves his homeland, tramps hundreds of miles with his shield and spear to get here instead of giving up and opting for an easy life as a bandit, gets my vote.'

We usually held our council meetings inside the palace, but today I decided that we would all sit on the spacious terrace overlooking the river. It was late afternoon and the sun was casting long shadows, a slight westerly breeze taking the edge off the day's heat. We sat in large wicker chairs, while Gallia, who had taken to attending the meetings now that she rode little, reclined on a couch. She liked to be included in the affairs of the kingdom and no one had any objection to her doing so. Dobbai was also present on this occasion, though only because she found the view agreeable and the temperature bearable at this time of day.

Domitus rubbed his hands over his shaved head and fixed me with his eyes. I knew what he was thinking – two legions were better than one.

'How many exiles from Pontus have presented themselves thus far?' I asked.

'Near two and a half thousand.'

I stared across the river at Hatran territory. 'And more are coming in?'

Domitus nodded. 'Every day. We can increase the size of the camp. We need more tents, that's all.'

I looked at him. 'Very well. I agree, see to it. Godarz, you will organise extra rations, clothes and weapons to be sent to the legion's camp.'

Godarz saw the confused look on Rsan's face. 'The king means to have two legions instead of one. Is that not so, Pacorus?'

Rsan's face went ashen. 'Two legions?'

'That's right,' I replied. 'It would be criminal to waste the opportunity that has presented itself.'

Rsan started shaking his head. 'But the cost...'

'Will be met,' I said. 'The treasury is full, is it not?'

'Yes, majesty, but if it is to remain so then I would advise against such an expenditure.'

'And when the Romans come,' interrupted Dobbai, 'what will you do, tallyman? Throw coins at them from the walls?'

Rsan was now alarmed. 'Romans? We are not at war with the Romans.'

Dobbai cackled like an old crow. 'Not yet, tallyman, but they will come.'

'And when they do we shall be ready, have no fear, Rsan.'

My words did little to assure him.

'So,' I continued. 'Domitus shall raise two legions, Nergal is forming his horse archers and I shall have my additional cataphracts. Due to Gallia's condition, Nergal, it is probably best if you command the Amazons.'

Gallia rose from her couch. 'The Amazons are under my command.'

Nergal looked down at his feet and Domitus stared into the distance.

'Time to reconsider, son of Hatra,' said Dobbai.

Gallia stood defiant and I knew that she would not shift from her position. I shrugged my shoulders. 'As you wish, my dear.'

Gallia smiled and retook her couch. 'Praxima will command my women until I have given birth. She will answer to me and me alone.'

With Rsan still smarting from the news of a second legion, I informed him that I also wanted to establish a school in the city.

'We have schools already, majesty.'

'Yes, but this one will be different. It will be filled with the future officers of Dura, boys who will receive an education in the military arts, so that when they are men they will be able to lead others in battle. They shall be called the Sons of the Citadel.'

'Parthian boys are taught to fight from an early age anyway, lord,' said Nergal.

'To ride and shoot a bow, I agree, Nergal. But I want boys to be taught tactics and strategy, to be able to converse with foreigners in their own tongue.' I pointed at Domitus. 'To know how many miles a legion can march in a day, and how to work in conjunction with foot soldiers on the battlefield.'

'I doubt if there any tutors in Dura who can teach those subjects,' offered Godarz.

I stood and started pacing the terrace. 'Then we will bring them to Dura, Godarz. Greek and Egyptian scholars, Roman engineers, Chinese philosophers and holy men from Judea, Esfahan and Alexandria.'

'But why, majesty?' asked Rsan.

'Dura,' I said, 'is prosperous. But what shall we do with that wealth, Rsan? Squander it on rich furnishings and gold statues, live a life of ease thinking that it will last forever? It will not. So we prepare, Rsan. We lay the foundations for a time when this kingdom will need its people and army to stand as one against adversity. A building with strong foundations stands more chance of surviving an earthquake.'

'You speak well, son of Hatra,' remarked Dobbai. I looked at the blank expression on Rsan's face. He could not see my reasoning. But then, on this beautiful summer's day with the sun slowly sinking in the west, a light breeze to stir the air and peace in the land, it must have been difficult to imagine horror. But I knew that if a kingdom wanted to remain strong it had to prepare for war.

And so it was. Every day exiles from Pontus, hard men with

scarred faces and wounds from a score of battles, made their way to the legion's headquarters in the Citadel. There they signed their names or made their mark agreeing to serve in Dura's army. They served for pay, but it was not loot that had motivated them to walk all the way from Pontus to fight for me, it was revenge. They wanted a chance to kill more Romans. And they were all single men for those with wives and families stayed in their homeland and lived under Roman rule, or most likely were dead or had been enslaved. When they signed up they did so before Domitus, though surprisingly not one objected to serving under a Roman, for like them he too was an exile. In any case all of them had heard the stories of the prowess of Dura's legion and its Roman commander, and they also knew that Domitus had served under Spartacus in Italy.

The armouries continued to work night and day, every day, week after week, month after month, producing swords, javelins, mail shirts, helmets, arrows, bows, maces, axes, scale armour for horses and men and the mighty kontus. Inside the brick buildings men worked with hammers, anvils, grinders, shears, vices and hole punches, while furnaces and bellows heated the steel that was hammered into shape to become sword blades.

Godarz enlisted so many armourers, blacksmiths, steel smiths, artisans, carpenters and saddle makers that we were forced to locate them to a campsite two miles north of the city. A large collection of tents sprang up near the river, and every day hundreds of men and some women made their way to their workplaces within Dura's walls. The original garrison of the city, those score men who had greeted me on my arrival, were either paid off or given the opportunity to enlist in the new legion. Thereafter the guarding of the city, the Citadel and the area around Dura was the responsibility of Godarz. He and Domitus worked out a system whereby cohorts were rotated through the city to perform garrison duties, being replaced every month by a new cohort. In this way no legionary became used to the comparatively soft life of being a garrison soldier, which usually entailed nothing more than spending hours standing on sentry duty or patrolling the streets. With Haytham's permission Domitus took the legion out on manoeuvres deep into Agraci territory, and days later I took my cavalry out of Dura to hunt it down. Malik and Byrd accompanied me, though it did not require any tracking skills to discern the path made by five thousand foot soldiers, nearly seven hundred mules and two hundred carts. We gave them two days' start and then rode out to find them, five hundred heavy cavalry and their squires and a thousand horse archers led by Nergal. Praxima also brought her Amazons and a thousand camels trailed the host burdened with food, water and tents.

These exercises were always an excellent opportunity to keep the legion and my cavalry battle-ready. I always tried to make a mock assault on the legion at the end of the day, when the legionaries were constructing their camp for the night. Hours spent marching in full kit with packs is mentally and physically draining, and I thought that fast-moving horsemen stood an excellent chance of getting in among the legionaries. I was always proved wrong. And no matter how loud we blew our horns or how fast we charged, we always met a solid wall of shields, around which we galloped and hurled abuse at the 'enemy'. And afterwards legionaries and horsemen shared an evening meal and Domitus told me how our approach had been seen from miles away.

'Hundreds of horses kick up a big dust cloud. You never learn, you horse boys.'

The next day the legion and cavalry practised working together amid the heat, dust and flies. At first it was not easy. Roman tactics almost always placed cavalry on the wings in battle, but I wanted Dura's army to be more flexible. So we spent time perfecting drills whereby the cataphracts and horse archers would retreat through the legion's cohorts, who would endeavour to close ranks the moment the horsemen had passed through them. At first it was chaos, as cataphracts and horse archers rode between the gaps in the first-line cohorts, only to come up against a solid wall of shields of a cohort in the second line, as the legion's second line was always drawn up in such a way that the cohorts covered the gaps of the first line. The front rank of riders pulled up and halted and those behind them did the same, so that in minutes there were hundreds of horsemen between and among the cohorts, shouting and cursing at the legionaries. Had it been a real battle the enemy would have had been hacking and spearing stationary riders with ease.

Nergal got very angry and jumped from his horse to confront the commander of the cohort whose men stood like a rock in front of his riders. The centurion strode towards Nergal and I thought they were going to clash swords, until the centurion removed his helmet and Nergal recognised him as one of the Companions, a great burly German named Thumelicus who lifted Nergal off the ground while giving him a bear hug. But the episode had revealed a major problem, which was solved by introducing a new drill whereby each cohort in the second line divided into two halves upon a

233

specific trumpet blast, each group moving left and right respectively to deploy directly behind a cohort in the first line. This meant riders could ride though the first and second lines, which would close the gaps as soon as they were through. It took many weeks to perfect but I knew it would pay dividends in battle.

As the year waned Gallia went into labour. Beforehand Alcaeus moved into the palace to be near at hand when it was time to deliver the baby. Gafarn and Diana also arrived from Hatra. I had written to Gallia's closest friend to ask her to come to Dura, for I knew that her presence would have a calming effect on proceedings, and hopefully would also have a calming effect on me. I confess that as the time approached I grew agitated, more so than before any battle. I knew that women died in childbirth, died screaming in agony as their insides were damaged beyond repair as their unborn child came into the world. Claudia, the wife of Spartacus, had died from loss of blood after giving birth to her son. I had been present on that terrible night, and suddenly I feared for my wife.

'She is in good hands,' said Alcaeus, laying a hand on hand on my shoulder. 'It is normal for a father to feel nervous, especially on the occasion of his first-born.'

Dobbai cackled behind him. 'Greater powers than he wields will determine whether good fortune attends the mother and child.'

'Good medicine and a clear head will help them both, I think,' said Alcaeus, frowning at the unkempt old woman who scuttled around our bedroom with cases in her arms.

'What are they?' I asked.

'The lords of your kingdom may be merciless killers but they fear the gods, as should you, son of Hatra.'

I discovered that she carried gold and silver cases, presents from Dura's lords, each of which contained prayers to protect our child from evil spirits and diseases. Dobbai placed them at the foot of the bed.

Other gifts arrived at the Citadel, including a chest from my parents that contained a large amount of Esfand seeds, which were stored in white silk bags, around which were arranged gold and silver coins. The burning of Esfand wards off evil spirits and curses.

Dobbai nodded her head approvingly. 'Very wise, your mother is very wise. You have made many enemies, son of Hatra, and they would like nothing more than the death of your child and the ruin of your kingdom.'

Dobbai supervised the carrying of the chest into our private quarters, insisting that only those I trusted should be allowed to touch it. So Domitus, Nergal and Gafarn carried it into the palace to our bedroom. This was the first time that Gafarn had met Dobbai, and while Nergal and Domitus said nothing and did what they were told, Gafarn took exception to this ugly old woman giving him instructions. His reward was a fierce rebuke.

Dobbai jabbed a long, bony finger at him. 'Silence, king of Hatra, lest I weave a spell that shrivels your balls to nothing and turns your woman against you.'

Gafarn grinned at me. 'You trust this old hag? She thinks I am your father.'

I said nothing. Dobbai's finger was still pointed at him. 'I did not say you are the current king of Hatra, but the crown will sit upon your head, that is, unless someone lops it off your shoulders before then. Now make yourself useful or go play with the snakes and scorpions in the desert.'

As Domitus and Nergal placed the chest on the floor at the foot of our bed, Gafarn shook his head at Dobbai.

'Silly old witch, my brother is the heir to the throne, not I.'

Dobbai smirked at him. 'How little you know, spawn of the desert, for your brother does not want Hatra's crown. He will never leave the griffin's side.'

Gafarn, clearly bored, waved an arm at her and left the room. At that moment a bird, a stork, landed on the balcony outside the bedroom. It walked on the stone floor for a few seconds, stopped, peered at us all standing like statues looking at it, and then spread its wings. It then flew onto the balustrade, regarded us once more and then flew away.

Domitus looked at Nergal and raised an eyebrow. Alcaeus frowned and I looked at Dobbai for reassurance. She nodded at me and smiled.

'A good omen, son of Hatra, fortune will follow your child. The gods favour her.'

Alcaeus dismissed it as 'nonsense', but I noticed that thereafter he was much more relaxed than he had been, and Nergal immediately went off to inform Praxima about the auspicious sign, who then informed Gallia and Diana, who were in the latter's bedroom avoiding the commotion as Dobbai prepared the birth chamber.

Domitus slapped me on the arm as he departed. 'Venus is smiling on you, Pacorus.'

'Who's Venus?'

'The Roman goddess of love,' he said as he departed.

Two days later Gallia went into labour. Mercifully it lasted only four hours and then I had a daughter. Afterwards Diana washed Gallia and Alcaeus cleaned the baby as Dobbai scooped up the afterbirth and poked it with a needle to frighten away any evil spirits that might harm the child. She then took the afterbirth out of the room and gave it to a waiting Domitus, whom she had ordered to attend, who was instructed to go beyond the city walls and bury it deep in the earth in an unmarked spot, together with a piece of charcoal to keep scavengers away.

I held my daughter in my arms and kissed her gingerly on the forehead. She had blue eyes and fair hair, though not as blonde as her mother's, and her skin was slightly olive in colour. Gallia smiled at us both. Dobbai came back in the room and took the child from me. Her touch and manner was remarkably gentle as she quietly chanted prayers to ward away evil. My daughter was wrapped in a pure white linen gown called a peerahan c ghiyamat, meaning 'dress of resurrection', and on her head was placed a small scarf, in which was fastened a blessed pin to frighten away evil spirits for forty days. Dobbai then opened a small clay pot, inside of which was blessed clay from the city of Karbala. Dobbai touched the clay with her forefinger then placed the finger in the baby's mouth, muttering prayers as she did so. Alcaeus rolled his eyes with contempt, but Dobbai caressed the child's head with her hand and smiled at Gallia.

'All is well.'

That night I slept on the bedroom floor, though in truth I closed my eyes little. Gallia, tired from her exertions, thankfully did sleep. When the morning light crept through the shutters my back ached and my mouth was bone dry. Dobbai entered without knocking attended by Diana, and they both sat by the bed until Gallia awoke. Diana put her arms around me and kissed me on the cheek while Dobbai inspected the child. Assured that my wife and daughter were in safe hands, I stepped outside the room to go to the kitchens. Outside the door were two guards, legionaries in full war gear carrying javelins, while guards also lined the walls of the corridor. There were more guards in the throne room, banqueting hall and on the steps outside the palace. There was also double the number of guards on the walls of the Citadel and at the gates, which were closed.

Domitus, his eyes surrounded by black rings and his face unshaven, walked up and saluted.

'You look terrible.'

236

'No sleep last night. Too busy.'

'Let's get some food,' I said. 'Why all the guards? Are we under siege?'

'Dobbai wanted the whole Citadel ringed with guards to ward off evil spirits.'

'I thought I was king here.'

'Best not to mess with things that we don't understand,' he said, extending his hand. 'Congratulations, we are all thrilled that Gallia and the baby thrive.'

I took his hand. 'Thank you, my friend.'

Dobbai insisted that the Citadel was closely guarded for forty days, during which time the child's ears were pierced on the sixth day, a day that was particularly dangerous for mother and child I was informed. On that day the evil spirits were at their most malevolent, so Dobbai fashioned a long piece of cotton that was blackened at regular intervals with charcoal for protection. Called a mohr, she hung pieces of it around our bedroom. Then the Esfand seeds were burnt in a metal container on a chain, along with camphor, till nothing remained but ash. Then Dobbai took the container and blew the fumes towards Gallia and the baby, and then in the six directions – north, south, east, west, up and down. Once the ash had cooled Dobbai used it to make beauty marks between Gallia's eyebrows, her palms, breasts and feet. Two pieces of thread, one white, the other blue, were twisted around each other to make a bracelet, which was then placed around Gallia's right wrist. Then the baby's eyes were darkened with ash. Thus were my wife and child protected from demons, curses and malevolent influences.

On the seventh day Dobbai permitted mother and child their first bath, though again a strict ritual was observed. Beforehand Gallia's belly was massaged with honey, covered with crushed herbs and wrapped in white linen. Diana accompanied my wife as she was washed, oiled and massaged, and more blessed clay was rubbed on her forehead. This was to invoke the protection of Anahita, the goddess of all waters, war, love and fertility. Then the infant was washed and placed over the mother's head, and as Diana held the baby Dobbai poured water over the baby which then ran down onto Gallia and thus protected her from barrenness.

We named our daughter Claudia in honour of our friend, the wife of Spartacus.

Chapter 13

After the forty days had passed the extra guards were stood down, the charms that had been secreted around our bedroom were taken away by Dobbai and consigned to the fire and everyone finally relaxed and began to feel joyous. The lords came and paid their homage to the kingdom's new princess. I sat in the throne room with Gallia, her health and strength now fully restored, as they gathered before us, grizzled and ruthless men who all knelt before a helpless infant. Each insisted on kissing Claudia's tiny hand and embracing me, usually in an iron-hard bear hug followed by a hearty slap on the shoulders. I was black and blue by the time they had all finished. They laid gifts at Gallia's feet – gold and silver coins, swords, armour, saddles and beautifully crafted horse furniture. Fit indeed for a princess. They all noticed that Claudia had her mother's blue eyes and fair hair and reckoned that it was a good omen. And all the while Dobbai watched over the child with an eagle eye. In truth Gallia had become immensely fond of Dobbai and I had to admit that even I found her tolerable, for the most part.

Two days after the lords had paid homage, Haytham, Malik, Byrd and Noora arrived at the city with an entourage that must have numbered at least three hundred. They also brought Haytham's gift for Claudia – five hundred camels. The entry of Haytham into the city was a sombre affair. This was the man who had formerly brought death and terror to Dura and its lands, and many of the city's residents thought little of his arrival. Most stayed indoors as he and his horsemen passed under the Palmyrene Gate and trotted up the main street to the Citadel. Domitus, sensing the unease of the city, had wanted to line Haytham's route with guards and double those who stood watch in the Citadel itself. I refused his request.

'You don't bat an eyelid when Malik comes and goes, and he is Haytham's son.'

Domitus screwed up his face. 'That's different. He's a friend of ours and everyone knows him. Besides, he has fought beside us so his heart does not contain treachery.'

'So, by that logic, if Haytham made a trip to Dura a regular occurrence you would accept him just as you accept his son?'

'All I am saying is that before we arrived he was killing these people, your people.'

'What is done is done. He is a friend, Domitus, and we shall treat him as such.'

238

Haytham was accorded all the courtesies his rank as a king demanded. We met him at the foot of the palace steps and Domitus arranged for a full guard of honour to greet him and his escort. Behind Haytham rode Malik, who smiled at Gallia and me. Behind him were the turban-clad Agraci warriors, their faces adorned with black tattoos and their bodies wrapped in black robes. They all rode black horses with black saddles and carried round black shields. Long spears and curved swords hung at their hips in black scabbards. They resembled demons from hell sent to inflict tortures upon mortals, but Haytham had them under tight control. We all bowed our heads to him in acknowledgement of his royalty and he reciprocated, dismounting and bowing his head to me and then Gallia. He gestured for Rasha to join him and all protocol vanished as she was helped down from her horse, raced over to Gallia and wrapped her arms around my wife. At once all edginess that had existed evaporated and we escorted Haytham and his men into the palace. He insisted on seeing Claudia before he took rest or refreshment, and smiled in approval when he saw her lying in her cot in the nursery next to our bedroom. He was also aware of the eagle-eyed Dobbai sitting nearby, watching his every move. He nodded ever so slightly at her but her visage of concentration did not alter. We retired from the nursery and I showed him to his quarters, a room located just off the banqueting hall. The latter was given over to his warriors, whom I assumed would want to be near their lord, and in any case we did not have anywhere else to accommodate such a large party. Like our bedroom Haytham's quarters had a balcony with a splendid view of the river.

'That was your sorceress?' he asked me, unfastening his scabbard and leaning it against the wall.

'Some say she is so, lord.'

'And you?'

'Gallia finds comfort in her presence, and in truth she was a great help during the birth of our daughter.'

Haytham gazed at the blue Euphrates. 'She regards me with the same contempt as many in this city.'

'Old hatreds die hard, lord.'

'It matters not, but I thank you for your invitation. I am pleased to be here. Perhaps we can go hunting together.'

The next day we did and he presented me with a beautiful female saker falcon named Najya, meaning 'victorious'. Haytham had brought his chief falconer, and I was in awe of his skill as he directed Najya to bring down a brace of partridges and three bustards. She was a magnificent bird, almost two feet tall with large eyes and a short, hooked beak. Her plumage was a light grey, almost white.

'Your gift is most generous, lord.'

He raised a hand in acknowledgment as we sat down to partake of a midday meal of pancakes and roasted lamb his men were cooking over a fire. Najya sat on a perch nearby with her head covered by a leather hood.

Malik sat beside his father, who stared into the fire then looked directly at me.

'My people have no great love for the Parthians, Pacorus. This you know. And yet you have shown nobility in your heart and have built a bridge between our two peoples.' He placed a hand on his son's shoulder. 'My son has even fought beside you and my daughter thinks of your wife as a surrogate mother.'

'You are too generous, lord.'

He waved away my protest.

'It is thus as a friend, Pacorus, that I have to tell you that I have received ambassadors from the Romans requesting passage through my lands.'

My blood ran cold. 'They mean to attack Dura?'

'They did not say so, but why else would they seek a treaty with me?'

I looked at him. His black eyes betrayed no emotion, though Malik was frowning with displeasure.

'What was your answer, lord?'

'I told them that the King of Dura was a friend of mine and that I do not betray my friends.'

Relief swept through me, these words were indeed heartening to hear. Haytham continued. 'They offered much gold to facilitate my support. Their master must be a very wealthy man.'

'Their master?'

'Yes,' said Haytham, trying to remember the name. 'I think he was called Crassus.'

Haytham went back to his people three days later, assuring me that he would not give the Romans free passage through his land.

'You have my word on that, Pacorus. What kind of king would permit such a thing in any case?'

He offered his hand and I took it. 'I thank you, lord.'

He mounted his horse and looked down at me. 'But they may come anyway. I know they are a greedy people, greedy for land, greedy for slaves. If they invade my lands I will fight them.'

'And Dura will stand by your side, lord,' I said.

He nodded and then bowed his head at Gallia standing behind

me holding Claudia in her arms. Domitus gave the signal, the colour party's trumpets blasted out, the guard century snapped to attention and Claudia began wailing. King Haytham wheeled his horse around and trotted from the Citadel followed by his warriors. I had instructed that the route he took out of the city was to be lined with legionaries standing at attention, as a salute to his friendship. Byrd and Malik stayed behind as there was much work to be done, though Rasha and Noora went with Haytham back to Palmyra. I did not want them in the city if it was attacked.

As soon as Haytham had left I convened a war council in the palace, and asked Byrd and Malik to join us. Gallia, Dobbai, Diana and Gafarn also sat with us, and Claudia was placed in her cot next to Gallia, to the discomfort of Rsan and the amusement of Godarz. Domitus said nothing but sat with his eyes down as he toyed with his dagger.

'It appears that our old adversary, Marcus Licinius Crassus, has decided to come to the East.'

'He is a fool,' sneered Nergal.

'A rich fool,' added Godarz. 'One whose wealth and influence has reached these parts it would seem.'

'If he attacks your father's lands,' I said to Malik, 'then I will take Dura's army west and together we will destroy the Romans.'

Malik beamed. 'We will fight together once more.'

I smiled at him. 'Yes, Malik, we will fight together once more.'

'Brave words, son of Hatra. But you will not have time for such nonsense,' Dobbai could always be relied upon to cast a pall of gloom over proceedings.

'You are wrong,' I told her. 'Byrd and Malik can ride west and give us accurate information as to the Romans' whereabouts. Two scouts can move faster than an army on foot.'

Dobbai walked over to the map of the empire on the wall and ran a claw-like fingernail across its hide surface.

'Last night a cold wind came from the north and in a dream I saw an eagle flying among flames and dead bodies.' She turned and pointed at me.

'You look west when you should be giving your attention to the north.'

Domitus stopped fiddling with his dagger and looked up at her. Rsan seemed decidedly nervous, Gafarn bemused.

'You speak in riddles,' I said.

'Then let me make it plain, son of Hatra. War is upon Parthia and you must act quickly if all is not to be lost.'

'The gods speak to you?' asked Nergal.

Dobbai threw her head back and gave a feral laugh. 'Don't be absurd. Why should they speak to me, much less an idiot whose only talent is to ride upon a horse and shoot a bow? They reveal glimpses of things, that is all.'

Nergal looked confused as to whether she was referring to him or me. Perhaps she was talking of both of us.

'I have heard no word from the northern frontier,' I said, trying to restore some semblance of normality to the proceedings.

'Have it your own way,' she said, and with that she said no more.

It was impossible to continue with her staring blankly at the wall, so I dismissed everyone and left her sitting alone. But her words had fomented an air of foreboding in me that crept through my body like a chill. My mind told me to ignore such outbursts but my instincts told me that she was right. Diana and Gafarn travelled back to Hatra the day after, Diana pleading with Gallia for her and Claudia to go with them. My wife embraced them both but told them that she would be staying, and so we watched our dearest friends and their escort ride from the Citadel. I prayed that we would live to see them again.

Byrd and Malik rode into the desert to keep watch for the Romans, and Malik informed me that he would form a screen of Agraci watchmen to be my eyes. I liked Malik. He was honest, brave and loyal. He would have made a good Parthian king, but one day he would rule his own kingdom and I hoped that he would continue the alliance between our two peoples. After a week he and Byrd returned with news, and it was not good.

'Romani army has marched from Antioch, striking for the Euphrates. They will then march down the western bank to attack Dura.'

'They have decided not to march through my father's lands, Pacorus,' said Malik.

'They are clever,' I said. 'They think to settle affairs with me first. But Antioch is three hundred miles from Dura and it will take nearly three weeks for them to get here; plenty of time to organise a proper reception for them.'

Or at least it would have been had it not have been for the arrival of a courier three days later with news that the combined forces of Media and Atropaiene had been defeated near the shores of Lake Urmia, and that a Roman army was now approaching Irbil. I sat in my chair on the palace terrace and read the latter from Farhad to Gallia sitting beside me. Dobbai was next to the balustrade listening attentively.

242

'So,' I remarked with a heavy heart, 'the Romans are attacking us from the north as well.'

Dobbai rose and faced me. 'Farhad's words do not say that. He states that he has been defeated and now squeals like a little girl for you to come to his aid.'

'And aid him I shall,' I said.

Claudia was fast asleep in Gallia's arms and her serene manner comforted me.

'Farhad is a fool,' said Dobbai.

'What are you going to do?' asked Gallia.

'Reassure Farhad that help is on its way. I am, after all, lord high general and have a responsibility to assist the kings of the empire.'

Dobbai scoffed at this. 'Farhad is beyond hope.'

I sent urgent messages to Dura's lords informing them of the Romans' approach and requesting their presence. When they arrived I assembled everyone in the council chamber, which was barely big enough to accommodate everyone who clustered around the table. Domitus, Nergal, Rsan, Byrd, Malik and Godarz were also present. Gallia left Claudia with Dobbai and also joined us. The room was warm, made worse by the press of bodies, and so sweating servants brought water and fruit juice. Godarz, who had been a slave in Italy for many years and had great knowledge of Roman affairs, addressed everyone first.

'We know that the Roman army approaching Dura's lands is sponsored, perhaps led in person, by a man named Marcus Licinius Crassus.'

A wall of blank faces indicated that the name meant nothing to the lords, though Gallia, Domitus, Byrd and Nergal knew it well enough. Godarz continued.

'Crassus is a very wealthy man who has an eye for a business opportunity. There are two reasons why he would send an army to Dura. The first is to exact revenge on King Pacorus, who inflicted many defeats on the Romans in their own country.'

The lords stepped forward and banged their fists on the table in acknowledgement of my achievements. When they had finished Godarz again continued.

'The second reason is our trade route with the Egyptians. If Crassus takes Dura, then he will control the flow of goods that runs through this city to Egypt.'

'So he's a cheap merchant, then,' said one of the lords, which prompted laughter among the others.

Godarz regained his seat as I stood and raised my hands.

'He may be a cheap merchant but he is no fool. He will have

calculated that he stands a good chance of achieving his aims. He does not spend his own money without great consideration.'

'You know this man, majesty?' asked another lord.

'I stayed in his house as a guest once.' They looked in confusion at me. 'It is a long story and one I do not have time to tell now. Suffice to say he is a dangerous opponent. Byrd, what news have you heard of the Roman army?'

'I hear of three Romani eagles, plus some horse and auxiliaries. Many wagons.'

'Three legions, plus horse and support troops; so slingers, archers and skirmishers. Around twenty thousand men, maybe more,' I surmised.

One of the lords slapped his companion on the arm. 'We can raise more than that among ourselves. We can beat this rabble before they get near Dura.'

The others roared their approval. And he was right. Each of them could raise a thousand or more men from their estates, lightly armed horse archers that could muster and attack the Romans before they bore down on the city. Wave after wave of horsemen crashing against the locked shields of the Romans, just like the horsemen of Farhad and Aschek had attempted to do, no doubt, and just like them they would be slaughtered.

'No,' I said. 'We will not attack the Romans.'

I saw the confusion and disappointment in their eyes as they looked at each other and fell silent, and I smiled.

'That is exactly what the Romans want us to do, and that is exactly what we shall not do.'

'If the Romans engage us in battle, their slingers, archers and javelins will cut us down, and we will be unable to penetrate their wall of shields. You have all seen the damage the weapons of a legion can inflict on the enemy, and I will not permit the same to happen to you. Instead, we will weaken the enemy before we have even raised a sword against him.'

I knew I had them interested now. The kingdom of Dura was a frontier region of warlords. Each of them had as his base a stronghold surrounded by high walls, battlements, towers and thick gates. These great residences were built to withstand attack and were places of refuge, so I told each of them that they must now be prepared to withstand a Roman assault.

'The Romans will march along the river, therefore those of you with lands near the Euphrates must stock up with supplies and send the women, children and those too old or young to fight across the river into Hatra. Those of you whose lands are away from the river must also evacuate the women and the young and old, as the Romans will undoubtedly send out foraging parties far and wide, and will lay waste anything they cannot use. This being the case, those being evacuated must also take their livestock with them to deny the Romans supplies.'

One of the lords was most unhappy. It was Spandarat, the grizzled old warrior who had escorted Gallia back to Dura after we had defeated Porus. 'You wish us to hide behind our walls like old women?'

'No,' I replied. 'I want you to attack the Roman supply lines once the main army has passed. They will establish fortified camps along their route of march to safeguard their lines of communications with Antioch. We offer no resistance until their main force has arrived before the walls of Dura, then I will send word for you to attack.'

'Majesty,' spoke one of the lords, a wiry man with a pointed jaw and eyes bereft of emotion, 'you have your own legion, a formation bloodied in battle and undefeated. Why do you not use it against the Romans?'

'I intend to,' I said. 'But I want the Romans to suffer a grievous defeat here, at Dura, one that will make them think twice before they invade my kingdom again and tangle with its lords.'

They growled their approval of my plan. A thin smile creased Domitus' lips.

'What about the citizens of the city?' said Godarz. 'If there is a siege they will eat up the food quicker than a plague of locusts strips a field of crops.'

'Bring in as much food from the outlying areas, and purchase food from across the river. Once you have done so the city's population will be evacuated across the river to Hatran territory. The city will be populated by its garrison only. The merchants and caravans will disappear quickly once they get wind that the Romans are approaching, so we will not have to worry about them.'

'What about the workers living in tents to the north of the city?' asked Rsan.

'Pay off those who want to leave, the rest will go with the civilians. There are enough oases across the river to water a few thousand people until we can defeat the Romans and get them back to their homes. Godarz, you will have to organise tents to house the civilians.'

Godarz nodded. 'We should have enough, though people won't be happy about having to evacuate their homes.'

'They will be happy enough when they know an enemy army is coming to kill or enslave them,' I replied.

'What of the army?' queried Domitus.

'It cannot remain in the city. Domitus, you will take the legion and the men from Pontus across the river and there wait for my orders. Nergal, you will do likewise with all the horse. Gallia and my daughter will be leaving for Hatra and will be escorted there by the Amazons.'

With hindsight it was foolish of me to presume that my wife would do as she was instructed. When roused to anger, her jaw set solid and her eyes burned with defiance. This was the visage that now confronted me.

'The queen,' she said slowly and deliberately, 'will remain in Dura. She will not flee before a few Romans, to become a fugitive in her own kingdom.'

The lords rapped their knuckles on the table to indicate approval of her words, as did Nergal and Domitus. Godarz smiled wryly and Rsan looked helpless.

'Silence!' I shouted. I turned to Gallia. 'Perhaps we should discuss this further in private.'

She raised an eyebrow at me. 'Further discussion on the matter is useless. I and my daughter will be staying here. The day I flee from my home will be the day that the stone griffin on the gate flaps its wings and flies away.'

I decided that it was futile to argue further, and it was also unbecoming of a king to cross words with his queen in public.

That night I tried to convince Gallia to leave the city but she would have none of it.

'But think of our daughter,' I implored her, to no avail.

'Stop whining, Pacorus. Our daughter is safe behind Dura's walls. Have you not invested heavily in strengthening the city?'

'Yes, but it's not the same.'

Gallia held Claudia in her arms on the palace terrace, while Dobbai remained to one side observing us both.

'Oh, Pacorus, the Romans will never breach these walls.'

'I wish I could share your certainty.'

'I have told her so,' interrupted Dobbai, 'and it will be so.'

I had to confess that the old woman's words, irrational as it may seem, calmed my nerves and reassured me. So I said no more on the matter.

'When the griffin no longer sits upon these walls,' said Dobbai, 'then Dura will fall, but not until then, and certainly will not fall to a red-haired manservant.'

246

She was speaking in riddles again but I was not listening to her words. There were things to attend to. As I left the palace the next morning to ride to the Palmyrene Gate, Praxima and the Amazons were striding up its steps and then disappearing into the interior. I shook my head. For individuals supposedly under my command they were a law unto themselves.

Domitus must have read my thoughts, because when I tethered Remus at the gatehouse and climbed the stone steps to the battlements my legion commander was already there. He stood beside the griffin talking to a dozen centurions, who snapped to attention when they saw me. I told them to carry on. I stood to one side listening to the words of Domitus. He was looking west, towards the legion's camp and the vastness of the desert.

'Now remember, they can only attack the walls from this direction. The wadis on the north and south sides of the city are too deep and their sides too steep for ladders or siege towers. And they can't attack from the river because it's a sheer cliff face. So that leaves the west.' He gestured with his right arm at the area in front of the city.

'Therefore this is the direction they will attack from. First of all they will line up every soldier they have in front of the city, like a giant parade, trying to intimidate you. Expect lots of flying flags, red cloaks and trumpets blasting. Then their commander will send an emissary to demand the city's surrender. Governor Godarz will politely refuse. Resist the temptation to use the emissary for target practice. It is considered bad manners to kill messengers under a flag of truce. There will be time enough for killing. Besides, you need to conserve your missiles for later.'

'Don't give them any easy victories. Keep your men off the walls and inside the towers. Their slingers and archers will be hired professionals from Crete and Greece most likely, and they can shoot. So keep the walls clear until the fighting begins. And watch out for their ballista. They will use them against individual targets on the walls. Taking the head off some poor daydreaming sentry boosts the morale of the besiegers and reduces it among the garrison. Above all do not underestimate your enemy. The Romans have conquered half the world by being determined, disciplined and professional, and they know how to conduct a siege.

'First they will try to soften you up with ballista, both to demoralise you and clear the walls of defenders. As they can't storm the walls on the riverside, or to the north and south, they will concentrate their efforts here. But all the firing with engines, slingers and archers is just a preliminary to an assault, and again it will come from this direction. They may employ a battering ram to smash in the gates or build siege towers to storm the walls, or both. Either way they will not try to starve you out. They don't know the size of the garrison, and in any case as far as they are concerned Dura is garrisoned by Parthians who don't know how to defend a city. All this you can use to your advantage. And finally, remember that you are not alone. The army is just across the river. You are the bait, but you are not expected to fight the Romans on your own.

'Dismissed.'

They saluted and left us, and I noticed that every one of them, now battle-hardened veterans, laid a hand on the griffin as they trooped away.

'So,' I said to Domitus, 'the trap is set. Let us hope they take the bait.'

'Oh, they'll take it all right. You think Crassus is with them?'

'I do not know. Byrd will tell us more when he returns.'

Domitus stared into the distance, across the yellow baked ground that had become his homeland.

'You need to deal with the situation in the north, Pacorus. Otherwise there will be two Roman armies in Parthia, one on each side of the Euphrates.'

'Do not worry, my friend, we faced more daunting odds in Italy.'

He still looked to the desert. 'True, but then we were one army under one general, an army that was well drilled and armed, and using the same tactics as the enemy. But here...'

He stopped, as though fearful to say more.

'If two friends cannot be truthful to each other, then who can? Speak freely.'

He turned to face me. 'The Romans know that Parthia is a collection of kingdoms rather than a unified domain. And they know that the recent civil war has aggravated divisions within its borders, so they seek to take advantage of that.'

'I know this, Domitus.'

'But do you know that they wish to conquer all the lands between the Tigris and Euphrates?'

I did not believe him. 'You exaggerate the threat, my friend.'

'I do not. The Romans are not interested in Media or Atropaiene, though they will seize those lands readily enough. What they really desire is control over the Silk Road, and if they conquer Hatra then they will have it. So I hope that Dura can hold out, for its army may be needed in your father's kingdom.'

His words stayed with me for the rest of the day, and that night I shared a quiet meal with Gallia. A sombre mood hung over me like a dark cloud, though I tried to conceal it from her, to no avail.

'What is the matter?'

'Nothing,' I replied, but she knew me too well.

'I will ask again, then. What troubles you?'

'I am worried that I have made a mistake. Perhaps I should have taken the army and engaged the Romans further north.'

She shook her head. 'It's too late for changing your mind. The die is cast.'

And so it was. In the early hours of the next morning, before dawn had broken, I kissed my daughter's forehead and whispered my farewells to Gallia, then I left them both. I ate a meal of biscuits and cheese washed down with water and went to the stables to saddle Remus. There was much activity as stable hands began the daily chore of mucking out the stalls and the men of my escort went about saddling their own mounts. The air smelt of leather, horse dung and hay. The horses chomped on their bits and scraped the flagstones with their hooves impatiently. Remus moved his head away from me as I grabbed his reins and led him into the courtyard. He was in a bad mood, no doubt resentful at having to be readied at this unholy hour. I pulled him forward and he snorted in disgust. The others followed me into the courtyard and on my signal we vaulted into our saddles to trot through the gates and into the still slumbering city.

The Palmyrene Gate was opened and so we left Dura, swinging right to join the road that would take us across the pontoon bridge. We moved quickly, riding east towards Ctesiphon and the palace of Phraates, taking the same route as I had the year before when we had marched to defeat Narses and his rebels. Once across the Tigris we headed north towards Media.

Media, Gordyene and Atropaiene are forested regions carpeted by beech, yew, juniper, oak, poplar and cypress trees. In the far distance, on our right as we rode, lay the massive, brooding Zagros Mountains, but we rode across lush forest steppe teeming with life. In these lands were bred great herds of horses that carried Parthia's warriors, and which were sold throughout the empire. And there was good hunting in these parts, the rich vegetation being home to leopards, lynx, brown bears, wild boar, wolves, badgers and otters. To the east roamed the mighty Caspian tiger, though I had never seen this magnificent beast, only their pelts lying on the floor of Farhad's palace. Domitus was wrong about this land. Any foreign conqueror would want a land rich in such wildlife.

A week after leaving Dura we arrived at Irbil, which thankfully was not ringed by a Roman army. As we trotted down the main road leading to the city, everything appeared normal in the immediate vicinity. There were no rising columns of smoke on the horizon or dead animals or bodies lying in the fields, though as we got closer I noticed a distinct lack of activity on the road. In fact, we were the only people on it. There was no sign of life either side of it. Nothing. When we reached the huge ramp that led to the fortified city we were met by at least a dozen spearmen at its base who barred our way with their weapons, while on the walls high above archers pointed their bows at us.

One of the spearmen, a tall man with a large belly and long, straggly hair, pushed though his comrades and raised his spear at us.

'That's as far as you go. State your business.'

'My business is not your concern. Tell your king that his brother, Pacorus of Dura, is here to see him, and be quick about it.'

It took a few seconds for his miniscule brain to understand my words, then he grinned broadly.

'Yes, majesty, apologies, majesty.' He turned around and shouted up at the walls. 'King Pacorus is here, King Pacorus has arrived! Salvation is at hand!'

The group of soldiers, their misshapen faces wearing smiles, parted and I nudged Remus forward, walking him up the ramp, through the gates and into Farhad's capital. The streets were crowded with frightened women and children huddled in groups on every corner and in every doorway. As we made our way to the palace I could smell fear, the city was rank with it. It was as if the world's most wretched and hopeless had been gathered up and dumped in this place. All I could see were listless expressions, filthy bodies, unshaven faces, children dressed in rags and men with dread in their eyes. The Romans would not have to lay siege to this city. It was like a rotting apple; all they would have to do was wait for it to decay from within. I was glad to leave the press of refugees that clogged the city and reach the palace gates, which were swung open to allow us to enter. As we did so guards carrying spears and shields raced past us to bar the way of anyone who might try to force an entry into the king's compound. None did, but the tired looks on the faces of the guards who had screened our entry told me that panic stalked these men.

Our horses were taken from us and I told my men to get some food inside them. I had a feeling that we would not be staying long in the city. A steward escorted me into the palace and thence to the great hall where Farhad was sitting on his throne. His wife had died in childbirth giving life to his only child and most precious possession, his son Atrax. Ominously I did not see his son anywhere, though I did see my sister, Aliyeh, standing as straight as a spear on Farhad's right side, her stare cold and unwelcoming.

I bowed before the king, who looked nothing like the proud, confident and strong figure he had been at my wedding. Now he looked a haunted man.

'Pacorus, the gods be thanked that you have come.'

'I came as soon as I could, lord king.' I glanced at Aliyeh. 'Sister.'

She said nothing, merely giving me the faintest of nods.

'How far away is your army, how many men did you bring?'

'Twenty riders, lord,' I answered.

'Yes, I was told. But when will your army arrive?'

I shook my head. 'It defends Dura, lord, for a Roman army is marching on my city.'

Farhad let out a groan and buried his head in his hands. Aliyeh laid a hand on his shoulder and he looked up at me with black-ringed eyes.

'Then Media is lost.'

I was shocked by his reply. 'Surely you have some troops left? What of those from Atropaiene?'

Farhad leaned back in his throne and chuckled. 'Aschek is in a far worse situation than me. Most of his men lie dead on the battlefield; at least I managed to save some to have the luxury of dying at a later date.' The reprieve from his despair lasted only seconds before his dark mood returned and he cast down his eyes once more.

'We will speak later. Go and get some food. Aliyeh will escort you.' He grasped her hand with both of his. 'Your sister is of great comfort to me. It was a mating of eagles when she married Atrax.'

Aliyeh looked upon him with eyes full of comfort, her expression changing back to ice as I walked with her from the hall. She said nothing until we were marching down a corridor towards the kitchens.

I attempted to converse with her, though was afraid to ask about her husband.

'Where is Atrax?'

'Recovering from his wounds.'

'I hope they are not severe.'

'He will live, no thanks to you.'

'How are his wounds my fault?'

She stopped and swung round to face me, jabbing a long finger

251

into my cuirass. 'Because you filled his head with nonsense about honour and glory, and for weeks after you had left he pestered his father about retaking Gordyene, about how the Romans were weak and that it was an insult to Media's honour that the death of Balas had not been avenged. And so Farhad enlisted the support of our neighbour, Aschek, and a meeting was arranged with the Romans at the same spot where you and Phraates met Lucullus. Only this time Farhad and Aschek demanded that the Romans leave Gordyene and pay reparations to Parthia for their gross insolence.'

I closed my eyes. I knew what was coming next. Aliyeh continued, her words as sharp as arrowheads.

'The Romans killed our emissary, and so thousands of our horsemen charged across the river to be felled by their slingers and turn the water red with their blood. And Atrax, my brave and foolish husband, led them. And the flower of Median manhood perished at that wretched river. Atrax kept rallying them and our allies, and again and again he led them against their shields and spears and accursed engines and slingers, and each time they killed more of our men. Our allies from Atropaiene died beside our own until the ground was soaked with Parthian blood. Atrax was knocked from his horse and speared in his leg.'

She said no more but turned away from me, her body shaking with grief.

I laid a hand on her shoulder. 'Sister.'

Quick as a cobra she turned and slapped my face.

'Do not touch me. I do not want your pity. I wish you had never come to Media.'

I held her stare. 'Take me to see Atrax.'

She snorted in disgust and strode away. I followed her and we reached her private apartments in the palace. Before she entered what I assumed was a bedroom she pointed at me.

'Take off your armour and sword and leave them outside.'

I did as she instructed and we entered. It was a small-sized room with a single bed against one wall with a small table next to it. A silver jug, cup and bowl were lying on the table; while on the bed lay the sleeping Atrax. Because the shutters were closed the only illumination came from an oil lamp that hung from the wall. A tall, lean man with a neatly cropped beard and hair, a silver band around his head, was gently dabbing Atrax's forehead with a cloth. He stopped when he saw Aliyeh.

'How is he?' she whispered.

The man smiled. 'Much better, highness. Almost no fever. I have changed the dressing on his leg and the infection is slowly receding. I have reduced the dose of jimson weed and he should start to regain full consciousness very soon.'

Jimson weed was the substance used by physicians to deaden pain in patients, so that even the deepest wound could be cleaned out and sewn up without the patient screaming in agony, though it required great skill to administer the juice of the weed. Too much could induce coma and death. Clearly this man was a skilled practitioner in the healing arts. Aliyeh laid a hand on his arm.

'Thank you, doctor, I am in your debt.'

He bowed his head then looked at me. 'Prince Atrax is too weak to receive visitors, highness.'

My sister allowed herself a wry smile. 'Do not worry, he isn't staying.' She then ushered me from the room and led me away.

'I suppose we had better find some food for you. We cannot have the hero of all Parthia going hungry.'

'I am sorry for Atrax. Alas, sister, being wounded is one of the hazards of being a soldier.'

Once again she spun round to face me. 'You may like playing heroes but I would rather have Atrax as a husband, not some dead warrior in a bard's poem. Thanks to you he will have a limp for the rest of his life. A daily reminder not to follow fools.'

There was no reasoning with her, and once we had reached the kitchens she left me to share a meal with my men. I got talking with one of the cooks, a short, chubby man with stubby fingers and a cheerful disposition, notwithstanding the dire predicament his city was in. He told me that after the battle Aschek and his men had fled for their homeland, leaving Media to the mercy of the Romans. The homes that lay outside Irbil's high walls had been abandoned and the people had taken refuge inside the citadel, though how much longer they could remain was uncertain given the paucity of supplies. Farhad had sent word to his kingdom's lords to attend him at Irbil with what men they could muster, but the injury to Prince Atrax had demoralised them and was seen as an evil omen. The prince was popular among his countrymen, the more so since he had married the tall and stern Princess Aliyeh of Hatra, the sister of King Pacorus the Slayer.

'Slayer?' I said, dipping a piece of bread in a thick vegetable broth that tasted exquisite.

'Yes, sir, that is what they call you in these parts. The king who slays all those who dare to cross him. So we've no need to worry now your here.'

I thought of Narses and Mithridates still striding the earth and smiled.

He was skinning a rabbit, his stubby hands wielding a razor-sharp knife with ease to separate the meat from the skin. 'Anyhow, until Prince Atrax is back on his feet Media's soldiers won't be sticking their arrows in anyone. Some say that the prince is dead.'

'He isn't,' I corrected him.

'I know that, sir, and you know that. But not many others do.'

I realised how much of a talisman Atrax had become the next day at Farhad's war council. His six generals, all of them middle aged and experienced leaders, I had met when we had marched together to parley with Lucullus months ago. Then Media could raise at least twenty thousand horsemen.

'I doubt if we could put five thousand in the field now,' said Farhad without emotion.

'You lost fifteen thousand men at the battle?' I was staggered.

'No, sire,' said one of Farhad's commanders, 'but many men have returned to their homes and may not answer the call to arms if summoned again.'

The situation was worse than I had thought. Panic and fear were obviously sweeping through Media like a plague.

'If only Prince Atrax could ride through the kingdom, majesty, it would give heart to the people and their leaders,' said another commander, to the murmurs of agreement from the others.

'Prince Atrax will not be riding anywhere until his wounds are healed.' My sister's words left her mouth like arrows.

'Aliyeh, daughter,' said Farhad, 'your husband is greatly loved in Media. He is needed to rally our people.'

Aliyeh moved slowly and purposely to take her seat.

'He was close to death. He is far too weak to go on a goodwill tour.' Her eyes narrowed and she looked at each of the commanders, daring them to challenge her. None did.

'That being the case,' I said, 'it is best to prepare this city for a siege, for Lucullus will be here soon enough.'

Farhad looked up. 'You are wrong, Pacorus. Lucullus has departed the Roman army, so my scouts tell me, leaving his subordinate, whose name escapes me, in charge.'

'Aelius Gabinus, majesty,' said one of the commanders.

'Gone where?' I asked.

Farhad shrugged. 'Back to Rome, hopefully.'

I doubted that. Any Roman worth his salt would not let the opportunity pass to follow up his victory. Something more important must have caused Lucullus to leave his army, though I knew not what.

'Shamash has been kind,' I said, 'for now we have an

opportunity to retrieve the situation.'

'We do?' Farhad was surprised and Aliyeh suspicious.

'Yes, lord. You must evacuate your stronghold of all those who cannot fight. Send them to your outlying towns and villages. If the courage of your lords has faltered then at least they can care for Media's most vulnerable. The fact that the Romans have not moved south on Irbil means that their attention has been diverted elsewhere. We must use this opportunity. Keep only foot soldiers in Irbil and send your horsemen to your southern border. I will ride to Ctesiphon and gather what forces I can to come to your aid.'

Farhad was nodding and his commanders were looking at each other and doing likewise. At least now they had something to focus on rather than waiting for the Romans to storm Irbil and put them all to the sword.

Those who were too old, too young or too infirm to shoot a bow were evacuated south, a long line of bedraggled humanity whose abodes and livelihoods they were leaving behind. Their homes still stood, but they lay outside the walls of the citadel and any invading army would use them to house their own troops, either that or burn them. I had suggested to Farhad that he pull them down to deprive their use to the enemy, but he was horrified by the idea and so hundreds of buildings stood intact and empty, hopefully only temporarily. I told Farhad that I would ride south to Phraates with the intention of convincing him to send an army to Media. Before I left I went to see Atrax.

The shutters of his room were still closed though he was sitting up in his bed, propped up by large pillows. Even in the half-light he looked pale but at least he was conscious. I sat on a stool beside the bed as Aliyeh finished feeding her husband a bowlful of soup. She made sure that he finished his meal before she allowed me to speak to him. A servant took away the empty bowl and she sat holding his hand, her eyes like those of a hawk watching me all the time.

'You must stay here until you have regained your strength.'

'I will, lord. Your sister is an excellent nurse.' He smiled at Aliyeh.

'I will send an army to assist your father, of that I promise.'

He seemed cheered by this. 'And then we will crush the Romans and throw them out of Gordyene. Avenge the death of Balas.'

Aliyeh's eyes narrowed to slits. The last thing she wanted was to see Atrax ride off to war once more.

'The Romans have won a battle, Atrax, but they will lose the war. But in war we must be patient to await the right opportunity.'

'And now Pacorus has to leave us,' said Aliyeh forcefully. 'He has a long ride ahead of him.'

I leaned forward and laid a hand on Atrax's arm. His flesh was clammy to the touch.

'Regain your strength, valiant prince. Until we meet again.'

He smiled and raised his hand in salute. Aliyeh kissed his forehead and ushered me out of the room.

Seven days later I stood before Phraates in one of his throne rooms at Ctesiphon. The atmosphere in the palace was drenched in mistrust and sullen resentment. No wonder, because the King of Kings was sitting on his throne flanked by his wife on one side and his son, the reptile-like Mithridates, on the other. I had ignored the latter when I had entered the hall, bowing to Phraates and then his wife but not to his son. The insult was intentional and was noticed by the court officials and courtiers who stood in clusters around the walls like vultures gathered round a rotting carcass. Guards armed with spears and wicker shields stood at regular intervals along the walls and either side of the dais on which Phraates and his family were seated. I was dressed in my full war gear when I presented myself, my Roman cuirass having been cleaned meticulously the night before and my helmet burnished until it shone. I had my boots cleaned and wore my white tunic under my cuirass, my brown leggings and spatha in its scabbard completing my appearance. I stood before Phraates, my helmet under my right arm; its crown filled with new white goose feathers.

'Welcome, King Pacorus, we are glad to see you.'

'And I you, highness,' I replied. I kept my gaze upon Phraates but was aware of the disdainful stares directed at me by Queen Aruna and Mithridates.

'I wish I was here under more agreeable circumstances, highness.'

Phraates nodded thoughtfully. 'Alas, we have heard of the discomfort that has fallen upon Farhad and Aschek. Grim tidings indeed.'

'Yes, highness,' I said, 'that is why I must request that the army of Susiana be sent north to reinforce Media before the Romans lay siege to Farhad's capital.'

'Impossible!' said Mithridates.

'You have something to say, my son?' asked Phraates.

'Great king, it is not for me to offer you advice on matters of state.'

'Indeed,' I remarked.

Mithridates' nostrils flared as he glared at me. 'But if we pander

256

to hysterical demands and send our army north, then who will defend Ctesiphon?'

'Highness,' I said firmly, 'you can call upon the armies of Babylon and Mesene, whose kingdoms lie nearby, their rulers at least are loyal and trustworthy. Though perhaps not Persis.'

There were gasps around the hall as I reminded Mithridates of his recent treachery. Mithridates momentarily appeared as if he was going to take the bait, his face a mask of hatred. But with great difficulty he managed to restrain himself.

'And,' I continued, 'there are also the kingdoms in the east of the empire who will lend assistance to Ctesiphon. Gotarzes of Elymais is a man whom any general would want fighting by his side.'

Now it was the turn of the queen to intercede. 'The armies of those kingdoms have been recently weakened and will be in no condition to lend us aid. Indeed, Sakastan has no king who can lead that kingdom's army.'

This was a sly reference to my having killed Porus during the recent civil war.

'Traitors often suffer a bad end, majesty,' I remarked casually.

'Enough,' said Phraates, 'we will not argue among ourselves, for the laughter of our enemies shall be our only reward. I fear that I cannot send my army north, King Pacorus. To do so would leave the heart of the empire vulnerable.'

I was confused, but then saw the leer on the face of Mithridates.

'Of course, you will not have heard. The Romans have invaded Hatra.'

I felt sick in the pit of my stomach and it was some time before I could utter a response.

'Hatra?'

Mithridates leaned forward, an evil grin on his face. 'That is correct. After he had finished with those imbeciles Farhad and Aschek, Lucullus invaded your father's kingdom with a new army. Even now his soldiers lay siege to Nisibus. So you see, if Hatra falls then a Roman army will be marching from the northwest towards Ctesiphon.'

'It is as my son says,' added Phraates.

I was speechless. The Romans had seized the opportunity offered by Media's aggression to defeat Farhad and use his actions as a pretext for attacking my father's kingdom. Domitus had been right. The Romans aimed for nothing less than the conquest of all the land between the Tigris and Euphrates rivers.

'Susiana has no troops to offer Farhad or Aschek,' said

Mithridates.

I became angry at that moment. I pointed at Mithridates. 'Does this man, who formerly fought in the army of the rebels, speak on your behalf, highness?'

Phraates looked alarmed. 'Mithridates has my confidence, King Pacorus,' he said meekly.

'Last year he was prepared to slit his father's throat.'

The queen stood up. 'How dare you insult my son.'

'How dare he sit there lecturing me.'

Mithridates smirked once more. 'Is this behaviour becoming of the lord high general of the empire?'

'I quite agree,' added his mother, 'such vulgarity in the presence of the high king is unforgiveable.'

In the heat of the moment I then made my mistake. 'If you no longer have confidence in my abilities, highness,' I said, 'I will gladly relinquish my command.'

Phraates looked most uncomfortable and began to babble an incoherent reply, which was cut short by his wife.

'We accept your resignation.'

'We do indeed,' said Mithridates.

Phraates began to say something once more, stopped and then looked down at his feet. The queen and her son regarded me with haughty disregard. And so I lost my position as chief general of the empire. When I bowed and then marched from the hall many of the courtiers turned their backs on me, so disgusted were they with my behaviour. My escort was livid when I later informed them of what had happened, but what could be done? Phraates was completely under the control of his wife and son, and where those two ruled, truth, justice and honour withered. I had little time to brood, though, because a crisis was unfolding in the west that made the affairs of Media seem almost irrelevant. I had to get back to Dura and then see what assistance I could offer to my father. But before all of this, I still had to honour the promise I had made to Farhad. And so I stayed at Ctesiphon to be treated like an outcast once more.

The next day I had another audience with Phraates to see if he would change his mind about sending reinforcements to Media. But it was the same story – the queen and his son made sure my request fell on deaf ears. But then, amazingly, Mithridates revealed a surprising development.

'We have received an offer of assistance from Chosroes of Mesene, who wishes to help his brother Farhad. To this end he is willing to send a large number of horsemen to Media. It seems appropriate that you should lead this force, King Pacorus.' His face still displayed disdain and his words were uttered without emotion, but reinforcements were reinforcements, no matter where they came from.

'We are not unmindful of the predicament Hatra and your own kingdom find themselves in, Pacorus,' said Phraates, 'but you must understand that if Ctesiphon falls the empire would receive a mortal blow.'

I doubted that. Ctesiphon was the capital of the empire, that was true, and it had a full treasury that was also true, but it did not pay for the other kingdoms in the empire. Indeed, it received tribute from them. It had no army that was the backbone of the empire and certainly no great king that could lead it. If it fell the empire would continue, but if Hatra fell then the empire truly would be weakened.

Even though the army of Mesene was not one I would wish to command, any reinforcements would be enough to stiffen the resolve of Media, and it certainly needed stiffening.

'Perhaps Babylon might also be convinced to lend assistance to Media,' I said.

'I doubt that,' replied Mithridates. 'I would have thought Babylon will be looking to the northwest and Hatra, for if your father's kingdom falls then Babylon will be next.'

I disliked Mithridates intensely but he was right in what he said. A Roman army that occupied the kingdom of Hatra would be able to strike at Babylon with ease, to say nothing of Dura, where another Roman army was heading.

Phraates gestured to one of his stewards, a tall, severe man dressed in yellow robes who had a neatly cropped brown beard. Phraates handed him a scroll that had a red wax seal. The steward took the scroll, bowed and then handed it to me.

'That is a personal guarantee from me,' said Phraates, 'that if Chosroes provides you with all the soldiers you need to send to Media, then he will be handsomely recompensed for his loyalty.'

It was as much as I could hope for. The King of Kings ruled because the other kings elected him, but the recent civil war had revealed that his power could often be challenged. If he was a mighty warlord or commanded great respect then the other kings would obey him without question. Unfortunately Phraates was neither. Still, Chosroes had voted for Phraates and had brought his army to fight for him when asked to do so. I saw no reason why the King of Mesene would refuse his request, especially as he would receive gold in exchange for sending his soldiers north. It seemed that even loyalty now had a price.

I bowed to Phraates and his wife, the silent, sullen Aruna. 'Thank you, highness.'

I would never bow to Mithridates, who bridled at my insolence. And he had one last mouthful of venom to spit.

'King Pacorus. We have sent heralds to each of the kings of the empire announcing that you are no longer lord high general. It is better that there exists no uncertainty on the matter in these troubled times.'

'But we will always seek your advice on military matters,' added Phraates, who glanced at his wife. 'We are grateful for your efforts in our service.'

He was truly a broken reed.

I was relieved to depart Ctesiphon, and especially glad to leave behind Mithridates and his mother. I was surprised to see that there were no heightened levels of activity among the garrison as I rode through the gates in the perimeter wall south towards Mesene. In fact there was hardly any activity at all. If the Romans did reach this place they would batter down its crumbling and aged walls with ease. I shuddered at the thought. But the defences of Ctesiphon were no longer my responsibility.

We made good progress south, following the course of the Tigris as it made its way to the Persian Gulf. Keeping to the eastern bank we made at least thirty miles each day, so on the third day we were on the northern border of Mesene. The land either side of the river was green and full of birds and animals. I saw warblers, white-tailed eagles and babblers. The area from here south was dotted with large and small lakes and marshlands – great swathes of wetlands that were inhabited by the Marsh People. I had heard that they lived on small slivers of dry land above the waterline and fashioned their homes from the reeds that they harvested from the waters. They also crafted boats from reeds, which they used to travel throughout the wetlands, or so I was told. From our position on the eastern bank of the Tigris the marshes on the other side of the river appeared vast and limitless, continuing on into the distance.

It was now nearly three weeks since I had left Dura and I knew that the Romans would be near my city, if not already before it. I also knew that Domitus and Nergal were on the other side of the Euphrates by now, ready to spring their trap when I returned. But I worried that my father might request their assistance further north and my mind was filled with thoughts of my two commanders marching north while the Romans assaulted Dura. I went cold at the thought of Gallia and Claudia trapped in the city. But surely Godarz would send them to safety; perhaps they were both already in Hatra? One thing I knew: I had to get back to Dura as quickly as possible.

'Highness.'

I was torturing myself with different scenarios when the commander of my escort shook me out of my daydreaming. Riding beside me he was pointing at dark shapes ahead, which were shimmering in the heat.

'Ready,' I shouted, and we all reached behind to pull our bows from their hide cases fastened to our saddles. We instinctively pulled arrows from our quivers, strung them in the bowstrings and formed into line. The shapes grew larger and I recognised men on horses, a long column of them. I held up my hand and halted the others. I peered at the approaching horsemen, who had made no attempt to change their formation or pace. Indeed, I wondered if they had seen us at all. Then two from the front of the column detached themselves and began riding towards us. As one my men raised their bows and pointed them at the two figures approaching. As they got nearer I could see that neither had any weapons in their hands, and the leader held his right arm aloft. The two then slowed their horses, a brace of mangy looking brown mares, to a walk and they both raised their arms above their heads to show they meant us no harm. I signalled to my men to lower their bows and I returned my arrow to its quiver and slipped my bow back in its case. The two riders halted in front of me and bowed their heads.

They were both dressed like nomads, with baggy brown trousers and light brown shirts with the sleeves rolled up to above their elbows. Their bows were slung over their shoulders and on their heads they wore linen hats.

'Greetings, majesty,' said one, a swarthy man with a long moustache and untidy beard, 'my name is Kaspar. I was sent by my king, Chosroes, to escort you south.'

He led a company of ragged riders, one hundred men dressed in similar attire to their commander. One carried a long staff from which hung a banner sporting the viper symbol of Chosroes.

'How long until we reach the rendezvous?' I asked Kaspar who rode beside me.

He smiled at me, his teeth as brown as his shirt. 'Not long, majesty. Two hours at most.'

'How many horsemen has your king sent to the rendezvous?'

Once again he smiled like an imbecile. 'Many companies, majesty, enough to do you honour.'

261

Eventually we reached a collection of mud-brick huts located a mile from the Tigris, a desolate place that was deserted as far as I could see.

'We are here, majesty,' said Kaspar, who halted his horse and nodded to himself.

'I see no horsemen,' I said.

'They will be here, majesty, that I promise. Would you like to rest out of the sun?'

It was certainly hot and my tunic was drenched with sweat, but I was more annoyed that there were no troops waiting for me. But then, this was the army of Chosroes and it was probably futile to get annoyed with Kaspar, so I gave the order to dismount and led Remus over to one of the water troughs while others gathered round the well in the centre of the village and hoisted up the bucket to quench their thirst. My men took off their helmets and I did the same. It was midday now and the sun was burning the earth, made worse by the lack of any wind. Once Remus had finished drinking I led him over to the shade of some stables located behind one of the buildings. Kaspar followed me and tethered his mare next to Remus.

'Where are the villagers?' I asked.

Kaspar lowered his head. 'I do not know, majesty.'

I turned away from him and stared at his men and mine intermingling in the centre of the village. 'Well, I hope we will not be here long. We have a long journey north ahead of us.'

I suddenly felt a sharp pain on the side of my head and then all was black.

Chapter 14

I slowly came out of unconsciousness to discover that I had been propped up against a wall of one of the village huts with my wrists tied behind my back. At length I regained the focus in my eyes, the side of my head throbbing with pain from where I had been struck. I leaned back against the wall, my wrists burning from the cords that had been wrapped tightly around them. I had been stripped of my cuirass, belt, sword and boots. My mouth and throat were parched, though mercifully I was out of the sunlight. I squinted in its intensity, and then saw with horror the bodies of dead men arranged in a neat row a few feet in front of me. I recognised them as the corpses of my escort, each of which had been stripped of their weapons and armour but not their white tunics. Like me they had also lost their boots. I closed my eyes and prayed to Shamash that they had had quick deaths and that He would be merciful to their souls. Then someone spat on me, causing me to open my eyes.

'Wake up, majesty.'

I looked up to see Kaspar standing before me. He had shed his own ragged attire and replaced it with the items he had stolen from me. I recognised my boots, cuirass, helmet, belt, my spatha in its scabbard and my dagger fastened to the right-hand side of his belt.

'How do I look?' He raised his arms to invite me to admire him.

'Like a thief,' I answered, which earned me a vicious kick in my stomach.

'You should be more polite to me, as you are no longer a king.'

He drew my sword and admired the handle and blade. 'Maybe I should kill you now and save my king the trouble.'

'Why not?' I said. 'Then you can be a murderer as well as a thief.

He replaced my sword in its scabbard and kicked me again, causing me to bend forward in pain. For good measure he also slapped my face hard with the back of his hand. He then stepped back and stood before me with his arms crossed in front of his chest. He looked ridiculous with his ill-fitting helmet and cuirass that was too large for his scrawny torso. Nevertheless, he wore the look of a man who had suddenly won a great fortune in a game of chance. Behind him his men were squabbling over the weapons and clothes of my dead escort, whose corpses were now swarming with flies attracted by the freshly spilt blood. One or two were coming to blows and Kaspar turned and watched the fracas with amusement. Eventually, after a few split lips and black eyes, his men settled down to drinking from their waterskins. Soon most of them were sitting on the ground or leaning against walls, laughing loudly and boasting, and I assumed that the liquid they were drinking was wine not water. Kaspar went among his men and helped himself to their drink, then returned to face me once more.

'Wine?' He spat the contents of his mouth onto me then grinned as his men fell about laughing.

I must have been tied there for at least two hours, during which time several of Kaspar's men stumbled over and directed kicks and punches against my body and face. They split my left cheek and my lip, and soon my face throbbed with pain and blood was running down my neck. As most of them were by now very drunk many of the blows missed their target or were administered half-heartedly, but enough connected to send spasms of pain shooting through my body. Kaspar thought the whole exercise hilarious and he roared his approval and encouragement to his men. My right eyebrow was now cut and blood began tricking into my eye. My breathing was heavy and I was thirsty, so very thirsty. One of Kaspar's men stood before me and emptied the contents of his bladder over my bowed head, then spat on me before he walked away. Then another sauntered up and grabbed my urine-soaked hair, yanking it back so force me to look up at him. With his other hand he pulled a dagger from his belt.

'Let's lop off an ear. He don't need two, do you your majesty?'

He leered at me, his breath stinking of wine. I stared into his eyes, unblinking. I was not going to give him the satisfaction of begging him not to disfigure me.

'Now don't you worry, your majesty, this won't hurt me a bit.'

He laughed aloud and then suddenly released my hair. He straightened his body, coughed and then crumpled on the ground in a heap, an arrow in his back. Seconds later horsemen thundered into the village. Kaspar and his men staggered to their feet as more and more horsemen appeared around them, all of them horse archers with arrows in their bowstrings. Whoever these soldiers were they were superbly equipped and mounted. The horse archers of Dura wore no armour, but these men were attired in scale armour – short-sleeved leather garments reaching down to the thigh and covered with rectangular metal scales arranged in horizontal rows, with each row partly overlapping the row below. Most scale armour was made with iron segments but these men were wearing bronze scales, and on their heads they all wore steel helmets with leather neck guards and embossed metal decoration.

Kaspar's men now stood and grouped around their commander, looking in confusion at each other, and at their dead comrade lying

264

at my feet. I coughed and spat out a mouthful of blood at him. Then I heard the shrill sound of a cavalry horn being blown and yet more horsemen rode into the village. These were cataphracts, each one wearing armour of bronze scales like the archers, though unlike the archers their horses wore armoured skirts that covered their shoulders and hindquarters, though not their necks or heads. The cataphracts slowed and then halted, and from among them rode a large man on a beautiful black steed whose head and neck shone in the sunlight. One of cataphracts dismounted and held the reins of the horse as its rider jumped to the ground. He was dressed in a suit of scale armour of alternating bronze and silver scales that glittered in the sunlight. He was a tall man with wide shoulders wearing a long-sleeved red tunic beneath his armour, baggy red trousers and a steel helmet inlaid with gold leaf whose cheek guards were tied together. The man unfastened the thick leather thongs and removed his helmet. My heart sank and I prepared for death, for Narses himself stood before me.

The King of Persis turned his large round face to gaze down at me. Despite him being Parthian I was surprised at how fair his skin was, and his hair appeared golden in the sunlight. He also saw the dead soldier lying nearby. He pointed at it.

'Remove this piece of carrion.' Two of his men did so as the King of Persis regarded me, then strode over. Like Kaspar had done he too folded his arms in front of his chest, a look of contempt on his face, a glint of triumph in his brown eyes.

'King Pacorus. We meet in far different circumstances from the last time we encountered one another.'

I looked at him with my one eye that remained open, as the other had closed due to the swelling around the wound to my eyebrow.

'I would get up and greet you properly, but as you can see I am tied up and do not have my sword.'

His lip curled into a wicked smile as he unbuckled his sword belt and handed it to a subordinate who stood behind him. He then squatted beside me.

'You smell disgusting. Still, I'm sure you will be made more presentable for your performance in Uruk.'

'Uruk?' Uruk was the capital of Mesene and the residence of King Chosroes.

'Yes, boy, you are to be executed in the palace square so all may see what happens to those who cross me, even the famed young general from Dura who vanquishes his foes. How great will be the fear that I will create when people see your head on a spike.'

'You would not dare?'

'Would I not?' he sneered. 'I did tell you when we met last year that affairs between us would be settled, and so it has proved to be. But unlike you, I will not let my chance slip between my fingers.'

'Kill me now, then, and have done with it.'

He looked genuinely hurt at my suggestion. 'Kill you here, among a collection of hovels in this piece of wasteland? I think not. The death of a king should be witnessed by a multitude so the tale of it will be spread far and wide. And your death will be slow and painful, to give you time to reflect on your insolence towards myself and King Mithridates.'

I chuckled. 'So Mithridates is still betraying his father?'

'He betrays no one,' he said curtly. 'Once we have destroyed those kings who had the temerity to stand against us, we will keep Phraates as high king, as a sort of figurehead. But the real power will be in other hands. And I will make Parthia strong and feared.'

'You will fail.'

Narses stood up, held out his hand and was handed back his sword. He buckled his belt. 'The things that I dislike the most about you, Pacorus, are your ridiculous sense of loyalty and notion of honour. These things have held you back. You could have been the most powerful man in the empire, perhaps King of Kings yourself in a few years. You have a talent for winning battles, I grant you that, but you are sadly lacking when it comes to statecraft.'

'You mean treachery?'

He smiled. 'There you go again, talking nonsense. You seek to make the world a better place, to create heaven on earth. But you live in a fool's paradise. You are blind to the realities around you. Take Chosroes, for example, a man eaten away by jealously. He rules a dung heap and is a pauper among kings, and so I offered him another kingdom if he would but join me, and such is his lust for riches that he readily agreed. I call individuals like him useful idiots. And to think, your father thinks of him as a friend, which is doubly ironic since the kingdom I promised Chosroes was Hatra.'

'You will never take Hatra.'

Narses tilted his head to one side. 'How long can a city hold out against a whole empire? Even now my army is marching with that of Chosroes to lay siege to Babylon. One by one your father's allies are falling. Balas is dead, Farhad and Aschek are broken. So you see, there are none to stand in my way.'

At that moment two of Narses' men threw Kaspar at their king's feet.

'You are the commander of this rabble?' asked Narses.

Kaspar rose unsteadily to his feet and bowed his head, clearly still the worse for wear. 'Yes, highness.'

Narses pointed at me. 'This prisoner is to be taken to Uruk at once. You will commence your journey immediately, and to ensure that he gets there alive a dozen of my soldiers will accompany you and your men on your journey. Now go. Your appearance offends my eyes.'

Behind him the cataphracts and horse archers of Persis were bellowing and cursing at Kaspar's men to get their horses saddled. The men of Mesene, feeling the effects of too much drink, were sluggish and resentful, but eventually they managed to saddle their horses and clamber onto the backs of their mounts. Kaspar sat on Remus and pulled his own horse beside him. He had attached a rope around my neck that was secured to his saddle – my saddle. He looked at me with bloodshot eyes, grinned and then yanked the rope, causing me to lose my balance and fall flat on my face. As I still had my hands tied behind my back I got up with difficulty, spitting dirt from my mouth as I did so.

Narses rode up to me as his men cantered from the village.

'Until we meet again in Uruk, then.'

Then he and his men were gone and I began my journey to Uruk. It was late afternoon now and I comforted myself with the belief that we would probably not be on the road for long, not if Kaspar's men were anything to go by. I stumbled along in the centre of the column, and could see that several of his men were already dozing in their saddles, their chins resting on their chests and reins wrapped around their arms for support. I also saw others lean over to the side and vomit onto the ground. These men were truly the slops of humanity, and I felt ashamed that I had allowed my men to be slaughtered and myself taken by such poor soldiers.

We had not travelled two miles, hugging the bank of the Tigris with a great marsh lying on the other side of the river and disappearing into the distance, when a great herd of water buffaloes suddenly appeared. The beasts with their grey-black coats, their huge heads sporting great backward-curving, crescent-shaped horns ending in sharp points, were nearly the height of a man. Either side of the lumbering beasts herdsmen whacked the animals with sticks, causing them to bellow and grunt with irritation. Within minutes the water buffaloes had collided with Kaspar's horsemen and chaos ensued as horses and buffaloes intermingled. The men from Persis were highly indignant and shouted curses and threats at the herdsmen to get their beasts out of the way, to no avail. Each water buffalo must have weighed two thousand pounds, and from what I could see there must have been at least fifty of them. Soon they had ambled over to where I stood behind Remus, and I had great difficulty in keeping my feet as buffaloes walked past and threatened to gash me with the ends of their horns. Kaspar's men, in stark contrast to the soldiers of Persis, did nothing but shrug, carried on dozing in their saddles or laughed at the vain efforts of Narses' soldiers. Despite my dire circumstances I too found it amusing, but then my instincts told me that something was wrong and the hairs on the back of my neck began to stand up. I looked around and saw the herdsmen gently tapping the beasts, but they were not trying to get them past the horsemen; rather, they were deliberately herding them to get among the column of riders. And then I noticed that there suddenly seemed to be a lot of herdsmen, dozens in fact. Most strange. Then all hell broke loose.

A water buffalo had stopped right in front of me, flicking its tail to swat away the flies that were plaguing it, when suddenly one of the herdsmen raced forward and stabbed Kaspar in the thigh with a knife. The whole column was then assaulted by herdsmen from every direction. The latter, having got close to the horsemen under pretence of controlling their beasts, leapt at Kaspar's men and slashed and stabbed at them with knives. They vaulted onto the backs of the water buffaloes and then threw themselves at the horsemen, aiming the points of their blades at eyes and throats or plunging their weapons deep into unprotected chests. Soon the air was filled with ear-piercing screams as the assailants went expertly to work. Kaspar's men were cut down with ease, those who had been dozing or daydreaming being the first to die. A few managed to resist, but the proximity of their attackers meant they could not use their bows and had instead to rely on their swords, and they wore no armour to protect them from the deadly blades of the herdsmen. Neither did the latter, but Kaspar's men were stationary in their saddles and became literally sitting targets. Most of the Mesenians did not even manage to pull their swords from their scabbards before they were felled. And when they hit the ground their foes were upon them, stabbing in a frenzied bloodlust, turning their victim into dead flesh.

I slapped a huge, stinking beast on its rump, causing it to grunt and amble forward. The wounded Kaspar lay on the ground but I was still tied to Remus' saddle. I shouted his name and he turned his head; I was desperate for him not to bolt forward and drag me under the hooves of the water buffaloes. I reached him and patted his neck, but his eyes were wild and I could see that the events swirling around us had unsettled him greatly. With my hands tied behind my back I was helpless.

A figure appeared in front of me, a youth no more than eighteen years of age or younger. He was slightly shorter than me but with broader shoulders and thicker arms. He had a square, clean-shaven face with a thin nose. His shoulder-length hair was black and his eyes dark brown, and now they regarded me cautiously. He held a long knife in his right hand that was smeared with blood. He wore a simple light brown shirt and frayed leggings that ended just below his knees. He wore nothing on his weatherworn feet.

The killing had mostly stopped now, judging by the absence of screams and shouting. The boy continued to watch me as several of his companions appeared by his side. They were dressed in similar threadbare clothes and armed with a variety of knives or short swords. Together they looked lean, proficient and pitiless, like a pack of hungry wolves. I had the feeling that my fate was about to be decided. One spoke to the youth whose eyes were still upon me.

'Surena, a few escaped. They might be back with reinforcements.' So his name was Surena and I guessed that he was their leader. He turned to the youth who had spoken.

'Gather up anything of use and get the animals over the river and into the marshes. We leave immediately. Go.'

The youth nodded and disappeared, leaving Surena and four others facing me. Then he spoke to me.

'What's your story?'

'Release me and I will gladly tell it.'

'Why should I release you?'

'Because the men you have just killed were also my enemies.'

Kaspar suddenly groaned and Surena looked at him.

I nodded at Kaspar. 'That man stole my horse, weapons and armour and was taking me to a place of execution. He is my enemy, just as he is yours. Does that not make us allies at least, if not friends?'

Surena looked at Kaspar and then me and then laughed to reveal a mouthful of white teeth.

'I will give you the benefit of the doubt, stranger.' He walked over and cut the ropes binding my wrists and neck with his knife.

However old these young men were, they went about the business of stripping the dead and dying of anything that could be of use to them – weapons, food, clothing and horses – with skill and speed. Most of the horses were stripped of their saddles, which were dumped on the ground, and then gathered up into groups. One horse in each group was left saddled and this animal was ridden by one of the herdsmen, who gathered the reins of the others and led them away. By now the water buffaloes were being directed back over the river and into the marshes, the lumbering beasts grunting in disapproval at having to exert yet more energy.

I walked over to the now dead Kaspar and relieved him of my helmet, cuirass, boots, sword and dagger. Surena looked at me in surprise as I put them on.

'They are mine,' I said. 'He stole them from me. That was a well-planned ambush. My congratulations.'

Surena grinned boyishly. 'We had been watching them all morning, but then a great host of other horsemen arrived, and those men were well armed. I was going to cancel the attack, but then the men whose horses wore armour rode north and the odds were better than even once more.'

I finished pulling on my boots and then put on my cuirass and buckled my sword belt. I felt like a Parthian once again, though many of the goose feathers in my helmet's crest were dirty and damaged. I then checked over Remus for wounds. He had none.

'A fine horse,' said Surena.

'He's mine too.' I looked at him. 'You are one of the marsh people?'

'Yes,' he pointed at the expanse of wetlands over the river. 'That is my homeland.'

'Well, Surena, my name is Pacorus and my homeland lies far to the north. I must get back there quickly as it under attack from the Romans.'

'Who are the Romans?'

I smiled to myself. Would that all of us had never heard the name of that race. 'A warlike people who kill and enslave others. I have to get back to my family to protect them.'

Most of the horses and water buffaloes were now wading across the slow-flowing Tigris, which was wide and shallow at this spot. Behind them Kaspar's dead men lay on the ground where they had fallen, flies already buzzing around them. The subordinate of Surena ran up.

'We have collected all that we can carry.'

Surena nodded. 'Good. Keep a watch for any enemy horsemen.'

'What happened to the soldiers who were better equipped than the others, the ones who wore bronze armour?' I said.

The subordinate eyed me aggressively.

'He is not an enemy,' said Surena.

The subordinate, a wiry youth with a long face and brown hair, twisted his mouth in annoyance. 'They beat us off and got away.'

'Then I suggest you make your way home speedily,' I said. 'Most likely they will return with reinforcements.'

'They will catch you again if you ride north,' Surena said to me. 'We have seen many soldiers marching north these past few days. You should come with us.'

'Into the marshes?' The idea did not appeal to me.

He shrugged. 'It is nothing to me, but how far will you get on a tired horse and in your state?'

He had a point. My back, stomach and chest ached from the kicks I had received, to say nothing of the punishment that had been inflicted on my face, and Remus hardly looked fresh.

'Very well, Surena, I accept your offer.'

The water buffaloes were herded into the marshes and after a while were abandoned, much to my surprise. I was informed by Surena that they would make their own way to dry land before darkness fell, and until that time would content themselves with wallowing in the water and eating plants. He also told me that they actually preferred the herbs and grasses found on dry land, but that it was dangerous for a herdsman to take his beasts any distance from the wetlands.

'The soldiers of Chosroes like nothing better than to use us and our animals as targets for their arrows.'

'Are you not the subjects of King Chosroes?'

He and those immediately around us stopped and turned to look at me, appalled at the suggestion. 'We are not under the yoke of any king. We are a free people who have lived in these parts for hundreds of years.'

Surena and his comrades were experts at finding a way through the marshes, keeping to where it was shallowest and avoiding the deep waters. Even so, by the time we reached his village, a collection of large huts built on small spits of dry land, my boots and leggings were soaked. It was late afternoon and very hot and I was plagued by mosquitoes that swarmed around us. But as soon as we emerged from the water to once again set foot on dry land the mosquitoes seemed to disappear.

Surena pointed to small fires burning outside the huts. 'An old marsh-dweller's trick. We mix reeds with buffalo dung and when it dries we throw it on the fire. The acrid smoke keeps the flies away.'

And so it did, and as I sat in the sun with my boots drying beside me I found the scene fascinating. Surena and his comrades were storing the captured weapons in his hut, a large structure constructed from bundles of tall, seasoned reeds that formed the walls and were bent inwards at the top to fashion an arched roof. Surena brought over his grandmother to meet me, a small woman with wiry arms who had an iron grip when she greeted me. Her skin was like old leather. She looked at my swollen eyebrow and scuttled away, returning with a handful of fresh buffalo dung that she slapped on the wound and told me to use my hand to keep it in place. I was so shocked that I meekly submitted to her order. It had come to this, a king of the Parthian Empire sitting on a small piece of dry land in the middle of a marsh pressing cow dung into his head.

The swelling around my eye disappeared after two days and I began to regain my strength. The marshes were rich in wildlife, being home to the ibis, Goliath heron and the smooth-coated otter that feasted on the abundance of fish filling the waters. The grandparents of Surena fed me on the fish they caught each day. Surena himself speared a huge barbel that must have weighed around two hundred pounds. He cooked it in the evening. As the sun descended in the sky many people arrived in boats fashioned from long reeds. They gathered around his large fire that crackled and hissed, and then came the water buffaloes. Surena told me that every night they left their wallowing in the mud and water to spend the night on dry land among the marsh people. I found it very strange the first night I spent with these people, being spied on by the great horned beasts just a few feet behind those of us who gathered round the fire that burned day and night. But the beasts were peaceful and eventually I altogether forgot that they were there. This night was no different as I feasted on roasted barbell, tomatoes, watermelon and rice. I sat next to Surena's grandfather, whose name was Fadil, meaning 'generous', and who was just as wiry as his wife, his hands and arms weathered by many years living in these parts, his face tanned and leathery. There was not an ounce of fat on him and his clear grey eyes were very keen. He missed nothing, not least my sword, helmet and cuirass that were lying on reed mats in his hut.

'You carry a fine sword and wear expensive armour.'

'The sword and armour were gifts from friends, sir,' I replied.

'And your horse is a magnificent beast. Was he too a gift?'

'No, sir, him I acquired when we stormed a city a few years ago.'

He refilled my cup of water from an earthen jug. Around us fifty or more men, women and children sat on the ground eating their evening meal. 'Surena says that you were a prisoner of the soldiers of Chosroes.'

'That is correct.'

He nodded. 'Why were you their prisoner?'

'I was under the impression that their master was going to help me, but he betrayed me instead and has joined the ranks of my enemies.'

His eyes fixed me, unblinking. 'Their master being Chosroes, can I assume that he was once a friend of yours?'

I was aware that these people were the enemies of Chosroes and that I would do well to disassociate myself from the King of Mesene, but I saw no merit in lying. And I was also aware that the other conversations were dying down and that everyone was looking in my direction, not least Surena.

'There was a time when I counted Chosroes as an ally, yes.'

Surena and several of his friends jumped up amid howls of protest.

'You have deceived us,' he shouted. 'You told me that Chosroes was your enemy.'

I suddenly felt very alone and outnumbered. I stood and held up my hands to him. 'I told you the truth, Surena, Chosroes is my enemy.'

His subordinate, the youth who had expressed misgivings about me after the ambush, was enraged. 'We should kill him now. I knew he was not to be trusted.'

There were growls of agreement from the other young men present. The grandfather looked at Surena amid the commotion. 'You are spoiling my meal.'

These simple words were enough to cool Surena's wrath, who looked sheepishly at his grandfather, who in turn looked at each of those who had been calling for me to be punished, daring them to challenge him. None did. And where there had been loud voices and shouting, there was now silence. Fadil looked at me.

'Be seated, Pacorus, please. Continue with your meal.'

'I do not wish to offend you or your people, sir.'

He smiled. 'You do not offend anyone. Your manners are impeccable, unlike those of some of my family and their friends.'

I sat back down beside him, though I had now lost my appetite.

The old man pointed at Surena for him to be seated as well. 'Tell me, grandson, when you first met Pacorus, did you think he was a common bandit who was being taken away to be executed?'

Surena shrugged and looked uninterested. His grandfather continued.

'Did you not see the quality of his sword, his armour or his helmet? At the very least you must have known that his horse is an exceptional creature.'

'I've seen horses before.'

'Sometimes, Surena, your wits are as dull as those of a water buffalo. Even a short conversation with Pacorus reveals that he has received an education. I warrant that he is of noble blood, is that not correct, Pacorus?'

'You are correct, sir.'

He really was quite perceptive and I knew it would be useless to try to deceive him.

'I am the King of Dura Europos, a city that lies to the north of these parts, on the banks of the Euphrates.'

There were a few growls and also some gasps.

'I knew that you were different,' said Fadil. 'Well, the mystery is now solved.'

'You must leave,' snapped Surena. 'We do not have kings here. They are not welcome.' There were murmurs of agreement around him.

His grandfather put down his platter of food and stood up. 'I did not realise that ill manners had become a common custom among our people. Since when did the Ma'adan, the ancient people of the marshes, turn away those who need our help? Since when did we show disrespect to our guests, and turn on those whose only crime is to be different from us?'

'I will leave in the morning,' I said. 'I have no wish to out-stay my welcome.'

'You are our guest, Pacorus,' said Fadil with firmness, 'and can stay as long as you wish.'

Surena looked annoyed and the others cast down their eyes to avert the old man's stare. As in our own culture, the old were accorded great respect among these people.

The rest of the evening passed without further discomfort. Fadil and his wife asked me many questions about my background. I told them how I had been raised in Hatra, captured by the Romans, fought by the side of Spartacus in Italy and returned home with Gallia. I also related the events of the recent civil war and the Roman invasion of Parthia. As I told my tale I was aware that others quietly moved closer to hear what I was saying, even Surena and his wild young followers. And at the end of my talking I had the impression that the hostility towards me had lessened somewhat. Certainly Fadil and his wife were delighted by my tale, and as I yawned and longed for my bed they were still full of vim.

'You see, Surena,' remarked his grandfather as he tossed more dried buffalo dung on the fire, 'Pacorus was once a slave and fought in an army of slaves. Have you been a slave? I think not. And you take exception to him because he is now a king. Surely the lesson to be learnt here is to judge people on their own merits and not condemn them because of their race or position in life. You condemn Pacorus only because he is a king like Chosroes, but does not the King of Mesene make the same sweeping assumptions about the Ma'adan? Are you not guilty of the same prejudice?'

Surena, clearly out-thought by his grandfather, still maintained an air of defiance. But at length he spoke. 'I did not mean to insult you, Pacorus. I apologise.'

'I accept your apology,' I said.

'Tell me,' he replied, 'this Spartacus of whom you have spoken. What was he like? Why did men follow him?'

'What was he like? He was like you, full of fire and rage against injustice. But he had a vision of a world free of slavery where all would be equal. He was also the greatest general who has lived in recent times.'

My answer seemed to please him and yet I did not say the words to flatter him. I sensed that he had a sharp mind and an appetite to learn, though his youthful temper was not far from the surface.

'I think,' mused his grandfather, 'that you could learn much from Pacorus.'

My wounds healed quickly, and two days later I made ready to leave the village. The horses that had been captured in the ambush had already been taken away, to the west I was informed, where they would be traded to the Agraci in exchange for weapons. The marsh people were expert in the use of the spear, which they used to catch fish from their reed boats, and I had seen at first hand how they could kill at close quarters with swords and knives, but they had little proficiency when it came to using the bow. This put them at a disadvantage when it came to fighting the soldiers of Chosroes.

'We do not need bows in the marshes,' remarked Surena when I questioned him about the subject.

'It would be a useful skill to learn.'

'My friends and I know how to use a bow, but my people are herdsmen and fishermen, not soldiers. They have to tend to their animals and put food in their bellies. There is little time for anything else.'

On the morning that I prepared myself and Remus for the journey back to my kingdom Fadil came to me, with Surena tagging along behind him hauling a bulging net of fish he had caught earlier. One thing was certain, the Ma'adan would never starve in these watery lands. Surena dumped his haul on the ground and sat beside it. The day was still young but the temperature was already high as the sun rose in a cloudless, blue sky. Around us villagers busied themselves with the daily chores that were essential to everyday life – catching fish, milking the buffaloes before they disappeared into the cool waters, repairing huts, mending clothes and harvesting reeds to make baskets, spears and boats. Surena was right – these people had no time to be full-time soldiers.

'So,' said Fadil, 'you are leaving us.'

'I have to get back to my own people, sir. I have been away for too long.'

He nodded. 'Of course. But I would ask a favour of you before you depart.'

I checked the saddle straps on Remus. 'If it is within my power to grant it, consider it done.'

He clapped his hands. 'It is indeed, for I want you to take Surena with you.'

The youth spun round and got to his feet. 'Grandfather?'

'You chaff at the bit, Surena,' said Fadil. 'You are a good boy and you work hard, but you have a hunger for knowledge and great ambition that living in the marshlands will not satisfy. I believe that the gods sent Pacorus to us for a purpose, and that purpose is to allow you to fulfil your destiny.'

'I am Ma'adan,' said Surena with pride. 'I do not wish to leave my homeland.'

His grandfather laid a hand on his grandson's shoulder. 'In your heart you do. Ever since the death of your parents your soul has been restless. You must become what you were destined to be, and that is not a farmer.'

Surena was far from happy at the prospect of leaving. 'I do not wish to go.'

'I leave in one hour,' I told him as he walked off, jumped in his boat and rowed it away. 'With or without you.'

Fadil picked up the haul of fish. 'The volatility of youth.'

I took my bow from its case and tested the bowstring, then returned it to its cover.

'He seems set on staying.'

'That is because, like all young ones, he does not like to be told what to do. But I think his sense of curiosity will get the better of him.'

'You do know, sir, that I go back to fight my enemies. Surena will be in danger.'

He unloaded the haul of fish into a large reed basket. 'He is in danger here, we all are, and I do not wish to see him killed in some fight with the soldiers of Chosroes. He has a certain talent for war but he is young and impetuous, and those two qualities will get him killed if he remains here, that much I know. With you he will learn much, not least how to stay alive.'

'You have great faith in me,' I said. 'Perhaps too much.'

Fadil smiled to reveal a mouth of perfect white teeth. 'The one, perhaps the only advantage with growing old is that you acquire a certain amount of wisdom. I believe that you are a man in whom one can have faith.'

'Well, if he does decide to come with me I promise you that I will take care of him.'

'I know that,' replied Fadil, 'otherwise I would not have asked.'

To my great surprise, an hour later Surena appeared at his grandfather's hut with a horse in tow, a rather scraggy looking dun-coloured beast with only a saddlecloth on its back, though it did at least have a bridle and reins. Surena also brought his comrades-in-arms, the youths who had sprung the ambush that had freed me. And then others arrived, men and their families, until each piece of dry ground in the village was packed with sightseers. Surena, dressed in a tan shirt and bleached leggings that ended just below the knee, nodded at me. I nodded back. He had his long knife tucked into his belt and a reed spear in his hand, while over his shoulder he carried a bow and a quiver filled with arrows, no doubt taken from a dead enemy soldier. He walked over to his grandparents standing beside me and hugged them both. I noticed tears in his eyes as his grandfather spoke softly in his ear, and then he brushed the tears away before he turned and faced the crowd. He held his spear aloft.

'Ma'adan,' he shouted at the top of his voice, and they replied in kind, chanting the name of his people as I thanked his grandparents, shook their hands and then led Remus into the marsh. Surena followed me, leaving his family, his friends and his past behind him.

With Surena acting as a guide our journey west though the marshes was relatively easy. He had travelled far and wide throughout his land and knew the location of shallow waters, banks of dry land and how to avoid quicksand, the deadly liquid sand that could swallow a man and his horse in no time at all. He speared fish each day and we ate them at night, the horses being fed on the young shoots that grew in the waters. Surena said nothing to me on the first day and little on the second, but on the third day the walls of his silence began to crumble. He had made a fire after our long journey through the endless waters and reeds, and was cooking fish over it as he began to tell his story. I did not interrupt or question him, for in such circumstances I have learned that it is best to let individuals unburden themselves at their own pace. He did not look at me as he recalled events from his past.

'My parents died when I was fifteen, killed by a patrol of Chosroes' soldiers. They had taken our herd of water buffaloes onto dry land on the far side of the river to eat the herbs and dry grasses. My grandfather has told me that my mother, his daughter, was very beautiful and that was why the soldiers raped her first. They forced my father to watch before they killed him, and when they had finished with her they murdered her too. And then they killed all of their animals. I asked my grandfather how he knew it had happened so, seeing as nobody except the soldiers was present, but he just closed his eyes and told me he knew. Only later, when I had killed myself and had seen the types of wounds inflicted on bodies, did I know that he had told the truth.'

He turned his face to me, his eyes moist at the memory of his loss but also burning with hate. 'I should have been with them, but on that day I was helping my grandfather with the nets.'

We ate in silence and then he spoke some more, again staring into the fire's flames.

'The soldiers of Chosroes have waged a war of annihilation against my people, that is why there are so few men, mostly just the young and the old. But we learned to fight back and now we kill those who come to kill us.'

'Perhaps, Surena, there will be a time when there will be a new king who will be a friend to your people.'

He smiled wryly at the thought. 'I did not realise that you were a dreamer, Pacorus.'

It took us five days to traverse the marshes and reach the Euphrates. We crossed over to the western side of the river because I did not know if Narses or Chosroes would have patrols out searching for me or whether they would be preoccupied with taking Babylon. I prayed to Shamash that Babylon still resisted them. We rode north for two days, keeping watch for any Agraci tribesmen. I counted Haytham as a friend, but there was no guarantee that any of his people would recognise me as the King of Dura. My tunic and leggings were torn and dirty and Remus was covered in dried mud, and Surena in his poor shirt and half-leggings, barefoot and with no saddle, looked like a horse thief. Our luck held, though, and at length we waded back across the wide Euphrates and then rested on the eastern bank under a group of date palms, before heading north once more.

We rode hard to outrun any hostile patrols that may have been in the vicinity, and I often looked back to see if we were being chased, but all I saw was empty and barren land. On the second day I eased the pace and was again looking behind me when Surena shouted.

'Riders up ahead.'

I turned to see half a dozen horsemen heading in our direction, black shapes that shimmered in the heat. Surena grabbed the bow that was slung over his shoulder.

'Not yet,' I said. 'We don't know who they are.'

'They're getting closer,' I detected the worry in his voice.

And so they were, cantering towards us. I could see that they wore helmets and had bows in their hands. I reached behind me and pulled my bow from its case, then strung an arrow in the bowstring. I peered ahead again and saw that the riders wore mail shirts and that the sleeves of their tunics were white. Relief coursed through me.

'You can put your bow away, Surena. They are friends.'

The six riders were some of Nergal's horse archers undertaking long-range reconnaissance duties. Fortunately they recognised me immediately and informed me of what had happened since I had been away. Their commander was a dark-skinned man with a long nose who I was surprised to learn was Agraci.

'Lord Nergal and Legate Domitus took the army across the Euphrates and have set up camp a few days' march from Dura.'

'And Dura?' I asked.

'The Romans took three weeks to march down the Euphrates before they arrived before the city.' He stopped and then glanced at me, as if reluctant to convey bad news. I prepared myself for the worst.

'Go on,' I ordered.

'We have received news from the city each day by carrier pigeon. On the first day the Romans arrayed their forces before Dura and demanded its surrender. Queen Gallia stood on the walls and bombarded them with insults, or so we heard. The next day they assaulted the city with their full might and suffered heavy losses. They have not tried to storm the city again, but sit in front of it like old women.'

So Gallia had stayed in the city despite my pleading. I smiled to myself. The arrogant Romans had believed that they could take Dura with ease, but my city was like a scorpion and its deadly sting

279

was its queen. Still, a city besieged cannot hold out forever and I had to get back to camp quickly.

'You are Agraci, then?'

'Half-Agraci, majesty, though my mother is ashamed that her son was fathered by a desert nomad many years ago. I live in Dura, so when Lord Nergal was recruiting soldiers I put myself forward. He was pleased to accept me, saying that men are judged on their merits as individuals and not according to which race they belong.'

'Lord Nergal is correct,' I replied.

He looked at Surena. 'Is this man your prisoner, majesty?'

'I am no prisoner,' spat Surena, causing the others to turn and look at him.

'This man is an ally,' I said.

The Agraci captain shrugged. 'War brings strange allies.'

I smiled at the irony of his words.

A tiring ride that must have taken us at least thirty miles left both horses and men exhausted. But with a fierce red sun descending in the west I at last saw that sight that never failed to fill me with awe and pride. On the arid ground, as if conjured up by a magic spell, stood the huge camp that housed Dura's army. The giant rectangle was protected by an earth mound on all four sides, on top of which stood a wooden palisade. At each corner stood wooden guard towers, on the top platform of which stood sentries scanning the horizon. And within the camp itself stood neatly arranged rows and blocks of tents, each tent the home of eight legionaries. We rode through the main gate and down the central avenue of the camp, which led to the headquarters tent where Domitus resided. Many men spotted Remus and began shouting my name, others chanting 'Dura, Dura' as our little group made its way to the heart of the camp.

I dismounted in front of Domitus' command tent, who had stepped outside to see what all the commotion was about. I smiled when I saw my old friend, who in turn locked me in an iron embrace. He turned his nose up.

'You smell bad.'

'I've had a somewhat eventful journey.'

He slapped me hard on the back. 'We thought you were dead, but then I remembered that you are under the protection of that old witch of yours, so I stopped worrying. Come inside and have some water.'

'Just a moment,' I said, and then walked to where the standard's pavilion was pitched adjacent to the command tent. The former was a simple square tent, guarded front, sides and rear by chosen legionaries, men who had distinguished themselves in battle. I went inside where four more guards were standing sentry over the legion's golden griffin. They snapped to attention when they saw Domitus and me enter. I indicated for them to stand at ease once more. The griffin on its pole was held upright in a rack, the gleaming gold creature seemingly about to take flight from its silver plate on which it was anchored. I reached out and touched it its cool metal. Behind me Surena, who had also entered the tent, attempted to do the same. His hand was curtly brushed aside by one of the guards, standing in front of him to bar his way. Surena, aghast that he had been treated thus, stepped back and pulled his long knife from his belt. The legionary smiled at him, but before he could draw his gladius Domitus in a flash had drawn his own sword and now held its point at the neck of Surena.

I shook my head. 'Surena, put away your knife and wait outside.'

Surena, feeling the steel at his throat, reluctantly did as he was told. 'I was only trying to touch it.'

Domitus replaced his gladius in its scabbard. 'It's not some cheap trinket, boy.'

Surena jerked his head at me. 'You let him touch it.'

Domitus and the guards began laughing. 'Well, he's a king, boy, and the victor of many battles. When your blade has tasted as much blood as his has, then you can come back and lay your hands on our griffin.'

'What's a griffin?'

'Enough, Surena,' I said. 'Go and get some food in your belly and make sure your horse is attended to.'

We went back outside and I told the Agraci captain to keep his eye on the boy. Then I went with Domitus into his tent.

I flopped down in one of the chairs and drank greedily from the cup of water he offered me. My limbs suddenly ached with frenzy as I stretched out my legs. Domitus sat down next to me.

'Where is the cavalry?'

'Nergal has it scattered over a wide area. There's no need to keep it in camp as there are plenty of your father's bases around here to feed men and their animals.'

He was talking of the small forts that were dotted throughout Hatra. Each one had a tiny garrison, no more than twenty-five men, but they were solidly constructed from mud bricks and had high walls, thick gates and towers at each corner complete with arrow slits. They were both a strongpoint and a place of refuge in times of emergency, and any invader would have to reduce them one by one to conquer the whole kingdom. But to do so would be a lengthy process and would give my father time to muster his army.

'Nergal will be here soon. He reports in every day to hear news of Dura.'

'And what is the news?'

He smiled. 'Gallia gave them a bloody nose and since then they've done nothing except lob a few missiles at the walls. Perhaps they have decided to starve the city into surrender.'

I nodded. 'Good, that is exactly what I hoped for. They do not know that we evacuated the population. Talking of which, where is it?'

'Ten miles north of here. They brought plenty of food with them and there's an oasis nearby, but a few thousand people cannot remain there for any length of time.'

'I know that.' I looked at him. 'They will be back in Dura within a week.'

He frowned. 'We could not persuade Gallia to leave the city, I'm sorry.'

'I knew she would not leave, she told me as much. It is her home, the only one she has ever had. It will take more than a Roman army to evict her from it.'

After I had washed and changed my clothes, I found Surena a new shirt, leggings and a pair of leather sandals. He would have to wait for new boots until we returned to the city. I also found a centurion and told him to take the lad on a tour of the camp. Surena, refreshed and newly attired, was eager to see more of the sprawling tent city and clung to the centurion like an eager puppy.

'Where did you collect him from?' asked Domitus as I watched Surena being scolded for picking up a javelin without asking.

'Would you believe that he saved my life?'

Domitus frowned. 'That's what happens when you go off on wild goose chases without an adequate escort.'

Half an hour later Nergal rode into camp. I was delighted to see the commander of my cavalry, with his gangly arms and legs and infectious smile. I had never seen Nergal downcast, even during our darkest moments. The arrival of Byrd and Malik made for a happy reunion and I was glad to be back among my friends and the legion once more. Byrd and Malik had ridden far and wide since the army had left Dura and they reported that the kingdom's lords were itching to attack the Romans but, true to their word, were waiting until they received orders to do so.

'They are like hungry dogs, lord,' said Byrd, 'they thirst to feed on the Romani corpse.'

As we relaxed around the compact square table in the main section of Domitus' voluminous tent, I told them about the Roman threat to Media and Atropaiene, of the treachery of Chosroes, the return of Narses and his army, and the inaction of Phraates.

'So you see, my friends,' I said, 'all the fighting that we did last year was for nothing, and now the empire faces a greater threat. It is as if the gods have created this situation to test us to the limit.'

Their faces displayed no outward emotion, though each of them must have been wondering what course of action should be taken. I answered their unspoken question.

'Very well. There is no point in sitting here thinking of the most dire outcome. First of all we will destroy the Romans in front of Dura. Byrd and Malik, you will ride to the lords and tell them to attack any Roman supply convoys or bases within easy reach of their strongholds. Hit and run only. Tell them not to get involved in long, drawn-out fights. After their raiding practice, they are to rendezvous with the army at the stone bridge over the Euphrates north of Dura.'

'What of Hatra, lord?' asked Nergal. 'Lucullus has Nisibus besieged. Are we not to aid your father?'

Nergal was Hatran himself, and he had family living in the north of the kingdom, cousins and nieces most probably.

'Hatra will have to wait,' I replied. 'One battle at a time. We beat the Romans at Dura first, then we can march north to aid Hatra.'

Domitus, as usual, was toying with his dagger. He looked up at me. 'And after that?'

'Assuming that Media has not fallen, we will have to leave Farhad to his own devices and deal with Narses. My father can send reinforcements to Media in any case, but Narses is like a viper in the belly of the empire. This time we will kill him, even if we have to march all the way to Persepolis.'

Domitus put away his dagger. 'Well, looks like we will be busy for the next few months. Still, it will give my boys something to do, stop them getting broody.'

'On another subject,' I said. 'Where is Rsan?'

'He decided to stay in Dura, lord,' replied Nergal.

'Wouldn't leave his treasury,' added Domitus. 'Could not bear the thought of all that gold lying there without his protection.'

'I did not think he had the courage to stay in a besieged city,' I said.

'He hasn't,' mused Domitus, 'but his parsimony overcame his fear of being skewered on a Roman javelin.'

I had to admit that I had grown to like Rsan, and I vowed to myself that he would never see death at the hands of a Roman.

'Friends, we march at dawn.'

After Nergal, Byrd and Malik had departed, I sat with Domitus until late into the evening.

'We heard that you are no longer lord high general.'

'It seems that Mithridates applied all his energies to announcing to the world that I no longer have Phraates' favour.'

Domitus began sharpening his gladius with a stone, using long strokes to make the edges razor sharp.

'There is no hope for Phraates,' he said. 'He will meet his death at the end of an assassin's dagger.'

I said nothing but feared his prophecy would come true. Mithridates and his mother had Phraates under their spell and so the living heart of the empire was paralysed. I thought of Balas at that moment. Roisterous, brave, big-hearted Balas. He had been right all along. We should have elected my father King of Kings and then we would have had a strong empire, not one riven by division and weakened like it now was. And Balas would still be alive. Or perhaps events would have turned out exactly the same. I prayed to Shamash that the empire would continue and thrive, but did He listen, do gods listen to insignificant mortals? I did not know. I looked at Domitus whetting his blade and smiled to myself. I did know that he and his men would not let me down, and nor would Nergal's horsemen who were now receiving their orders.

'I had hoped that we would have peace when we all left Italy,' I said idly.

Domitus stopped sharpening his blade and looked at me. 'I think that if you really believed that was true you would have retired to a mountain top and lived out your days as a holy man.'

'No one wants perpetual war, Domitus.'

He shrugged. 'Yes you do. It's the only thing you know, and certainly the only thing I know. We are good at it, and because we are accomplished at it war will always search us out.'

'You make it sound as though it is a living thing, a sort of spirit.'

He carried on sharpening his blade. 'We Romans have a deity called Mars who is the god of war. He was the father of Romulus and Remus, the founders of Rome, and he wears armour, a crested helmet and carries a shield. On the eve of battle I pray to him that he will give me the strength to be a good soldier and will grant me victory. That, or a noble death.'

In all the years that I had known him I had never heard Domitus speak thus, but it cheered me that that he had a reflective side and was not wholly a man of iron.

'You think Mars watches over you?'

He snorted at that notion. 'No. Caring is for women, but I believe that if he is pleased he will protect a soldier so he can watch him again in battle.'

'He did not protect Spartacus,' I said, thinking to catch him out.

'Spartacus wanted to die that day and Mars granted him a good death. I hope one day that he will extend to me the same courtesy.'

'Not yet, my friend,' I told him. 'I need you for a few more years yet.'

I left him keening the edge of his sword and walked outside. The evening was hot and filled with the smell of leather, the smoke of cooking fires and human sweat. Men sat around in groups talking, playing dice or checking their equipment. Mail shirts were being cleaned of any dirt or, most rare in hot desert climes, rust; swords and daggers were being sharpened and helmet straps examined. Every man was trained in the use of the javelin and gladius, but in battle it was his defensive equipment that saved his life. Roman helmets were very practical items, but I had had the armourers strengthen our helmets with a forehead cross-brace. This made them heavier, but Dura's legion was Parthian, not Roman, and that meant having to fight hordes of horsemen on campaign. Even Roman helmets could be split by a man on a horse hacking down with a downward sweep of his sword, but the steel cross-brace offered protection against this.

As I passed near to groups the men stood up, but I ordered them to resume their leisure activities. I did not wish to disturb them; I was just glad to be back among them. I felt relaxed in their company, untroubled by what the enemy might throw at us in the coming days.

A strapping centurion, vine cane in hand, marched up and saluted. He wore no armour or helmet but his cane indicated his rank, that and his broad shoulders, thick chest and muscled arms. I recognised his face. As I wracked my brain trying to think of his name, he saved me the trouble. 'Arminius, sir.'

'Of course, forgive me, I should know the names of all the Companions.'

He grinned. 'I think you have enough on your plate at the moment to be bothering with names.'

I tugged his elbow. 'Walk with me.'

'We are moving out, tomorrow, I hear.'

'Yes,' I said, 'time to remind the Romans whose country it is.'

'I'm glad. I didn't hold with...' he glanced at me.

'Speak freely, Arminius.'

'Well, I didn't hold with leaving the queen in Dura. A lot of us are very fond of her and we want to get back to the city as quickly as possible.'

Neither did I, though I knew that at this moment the queen was exactly where she wanted to be, and that it would take more than a Roman army to evict her from her home.

Chapter 15

I slept for two hours at most as I waited for the new day. Before dawn I dressed and walked to the stables in the middle of the camp to feed and water Remus. Then I groomed him and snatched a mouthful of porridge and water from the stable hands. The area stank of horse and mule dung. Already centurions were barking orders and their men were dismantling tents. The clatter of cooking utensils, the grumblings of mules and the rustle of men donning their mail shirts and personal equipment filled the air. It takes around three hours for a camp to be dismantled and its component parts packed into wagons, loaded onto mules or carried on the shoulders of individual legionaries. Domitus searched me out and we stood watching his men go about their business with consummate ease. They had done this many times before, those who had fought in Italy with Spartacus had done it for years, and I always liked to watch the organised chaos that transformed a heaving camp into a marching army. The first centuries were already forming into column of march, the men six abreast, in preparation for their journey west. By the time the last contingents had departed from where we were now standing, the legion's foremost century would have covered around ten miles.

After an hour Nergal arrived with my cataphracts, who wore only leggings, shirts and helmets. They carried their bows and quivers, but the scale armour for both them and their horses was carried on the camel train attended by the squires, and which waited to the north. It was a hard life for these boys, up before dawn each day to attend to the horses and then learning the art of war around their everyday chores. But at least they would be spared battle, as their task was to stay in camp, ferrying ammunition supplies to the horse archers and to help tend the wounded. Then, at the end of the battle, they would assist their masters in taking armour off men and horses. If the worst happened and we were defeated, the squires were ordered to flee to Hatra and seek the sanctuary of my father.

The day would be hot and already the air was filled with dust thrown up by the thousands of sandal-clad legionaries and the hundreds of mules of the legion. The men of Pontus, my second legion, albeit still in transformation, were also in camp. Thus nearly eight thousand foot soldiers were on the move, and riding on their flanks would be a thousand horse archers and five hundred cataphracts. At the bridge we would hopefully rendezvous with Dura's lords and their horsemen.

'I have scouts riding far ahead, lord, and beyond them are Byrd and Malik,' said Nergal, 'but we have heard of no Romans crossing the Euphrates.'

'Hopefully they still believe that Dura's army is trapped in the city. As long as we are able to cross the river unmolested, then they will have to fight.'

'They could escape west across the desert,' said Domitus.

'Is it in Roman nature to flee from barbarians, Domitus?' I asked.

He winked at me. 'Absolutely not.'

At that moment Surena rode up on his horse, which appeared to have been groomed as it looked decidedly better than when he had ridden it into camp. I vaulted into my saddle.

'You stay with me,' I told him.

'Where are we going?'

'To fight a battle, so keep close and stay out of trouble.'

He smiled at me. 'Are we going to kill Chosroes?'

'No, Surena, we have others to kill first.'

It took us three days to reach the bridge across the Euphrates. When we arrived Nergal, Byrd and Malik were already there, together with a score of Agraci horsemen, black-clad warriors carrying round black shields and armed with long spears and curved swords. As the army marched across the stone arches and engineers mapped out the site for the night's camp on the west bank, I saw dead Romans lying on the riverbank.

'You did well, Nergal,' I said.

'Not me, lord,' he nodded at Malik. 'This was an Agraci victory.'

I nodded to a beaming Malik. 'My thanks.'

'It was easy enough. We pretended to be pilgrims and killed them on the bridge. None escaped.'

Nergal was looking at Byrd. 'Show him.'

Byrd shrugged and reached inside his robe. He pulled out a letter, nudged his horse forward and handed it to me. It was stained with blood.

'It was taken off a dead Romani courier on his way to Dura.'

By the looks on the faces of Byrd and Malik they knew what its contents were. I opened it and read the Greek words.

To my dear friend Lucius Furius

I have received reports of your excellent progress at Dura and the happy news that you expect the city to fall imminently. That you have encountered no resistance does not surprise me, as it is well known that the eastern peoples are effeminate and degenerate.

It would be most desirable if you could capture the so-called King of Dura and his wife, as their parade through the streets of Rome would be a great political boost and would go some way to counter the popularity that Pompey enjoys within the city.

When Dura falls I grant you full authority to do with it as you see fit, though I will retain full control of the dues raised from the tolls levied on the trade caravans, and you are additionally entitled to half of the profits from the sale of its citizens in the slave markets, though what price you will obtain for such wretches I do not know.

Your friend

Marcus Licinius Crassus

I stared at the words after I had finished reading them and felt a rage building within me. It was bad enough that a Roman army was encamped before my city, but it was made far worse by the fact that it was led by Lucius Furius, a tribune whom I had met on several occasions in Italy. A red-haired, arrogant individual whom I had bested in battle several times, though he had always managed to escape. And now he was in Parthia, his army no doubt paid for by Rome's richest man – Crassus. I threw the letter to the ground. Domitus picked it up but he could not read Greek.

'Lucius Furius, that overbearing bastard we fought in Italy, leads the army laying siege to Dura, financed by the wealth of Marcus Licinius Crassus.'

Domitus walked over and laid a hand on my arm.

'Do not let your anger cloud your judgement. It does not matter who leads that army or who paid for it. You still have it exactly where you want it.'

He was right, of course, but for the rest of that day and all morning of the next I was sullen and withdrawn, seething that Furius was in my homeland.

'What difference does it make?' asked Surena, his bow tucked inside a new hide case on his saddle together with a quiver full of arrows. Being inquisitive, he had been asking questions about my time in Italy.

'It just does,' I snapped, not wanting to discuss the matter.

'The commander of the Roman army is an old adversary of ours,' remarked Nergal, 'King Pacorus fought him on many occasions and always defeated him.'

'But now he is here,' said Surena.

'And now he is here,' I mused.

Surena beamed at me. 'You visited his homeland and now he is visiting yours.'

I turned in the saddle to face him. 'Are you trying to be amusing? Because I have to tell you that it isn't working.'

'Well, if you had the chance to kill this Furius and let it slip through your fingers, you now have another chance to finish him. Seems simple enough.'

'Does it!'

'Well, perhaps this time you won't be so careless.'

'Why don't you go and do something useful, Surena. I grow tired of your voice.'

He dug his knees into his horse and rode away. 'The truth always hurts.'

My mood improved, though, when the army halted to await the lords and their followers. This time each one brought around three hundred riders, so that by the time I held a muster of the army we had been reinforced by over six thousand horse archers. The legion numbered four thousand men, the men of Pontus gave us an additional three and half thousand foot, Nergal commanded a thousand horse archers and I had my five hundred cataphracts. That night I held a council of war in the legion's command tent. The lords, Domitus, Nergal, Malik and Byrd all faced me as I explained the plan for the coming battle.

'We are two days' march from Dura. Nergal will throw a screen of riders in front of the army as it marches south. I have no doubt that the Romans know that something is amiss, if only because their supply convoys and couriers have not been getting through. So tomorrow we march south and the day after will give battle.'

'How many men do the Romans have, majesty?' asked one of the lords.

'We have counted three eagles, which means three legions. In addition, the Romans have auxiliaries of foot and their own cavalry. I estimate twenty thousand in total.'

'May be less now, majesty,' said another lord. 'We have destroyed their courier bases and killed their garrisons.'

'It doesn't matter how many they are,' I said. 'I intend to break their battle line before they can make their greater numbers tell.'

They cheered at this statement. I liked my lords; they were like the life they lived – tough and straightforward.

'A fitting plan for the "pitiless one",' shouted one on the right.

'The pitiless one?' I said.

He beamed at me. 'That is what people are calling you majesty – Pacorus the Pitiless. They say that one who uses his wife and infant child as bait to lure his enemies to him makes the devils of the underworld shake with fear.'

My god, is that what people thought of me? I had to admit that I was taken aback, but then they started chanting my name and stamping their feet. Clearly they were impressed by my unintentional ruthlessness.

Having briefed all of the lords, Domitus and Nergal on our plan of battle before we had even caught sight of the enemy, I was confident of victory. I knew the ground we would fight on and I knew the men I commanded.

On the march south towards Dura I was in high spirits, until Byrd rode up in an agitated state.

'Horses approaching from the north, big dust cloud. They are many.'

'Romans?' I was surprised to say the least. I turned to Nergal. 'Go and find out who they are. If they are Romans you must delay them until the army is ready.'

As he galloped away to collect his companies I cursed my luck. I had mapped out the coming battle over and over in my head, considering every imaginable possibility and how I would take all into account to fight the battle exactly according to my wishes. And now I risked being undone by an enemy force that had suddenly sprung up from the desert. As Nergal and his horse archers cantered north a sweating Domitus ran up.

'Problems?'

'Yes, it appears that there may be a Roman army behind us.'

He raised his hand and then raced back to his officers. Then the sound of trumpets resounded across the area as he about-faced his cohorts and their commanders went about marshalling them into battle formation. The cohorts were marched north so that the wagons and mules carrying their supplies would be in the rear of the army if it came to a fight. I deployed the lords on our right flank, next to the Euphrates, while I took my cataphracts out to the left wing. Behind them, the squires struggled with the camels that were burdened with the cavalry's supplies. The cataphracts hurriedly rode back to the camels to get their scale armour, and then began a race against time to put it on, one squire helping his lord, the other dressing his horse in its armour protection. Surena rode up.

'Do you wish me to bring you your armour, Pacorus?'

'No, I will fight as I am.' In truth I found scale armour heavy and burdensome, preferring my Roman cuirass and helmet. 'Get back with the squires. Your knife won't be much use in a battle.'

He rode off. At least that was one less thing to worry about.

I rode out in front of the thousands of men who were deploying for battle to get a better look at what was coming from the north. I could see them, now – horsemen kicking up a vast cloud of dust. Whoever they were they were moving at speed. They obviously wanted to get to us very quickly. Had Furius got wind of our approach and requested reinforcements? I thought it unlikely. Any Roman soldiers in Syria would have to have wings to get here this fast. I was wondering whether it was possible to defeat this new enemy and then fight those in front of Dura, when I caught sight of Byrd galloping towards me ahead of his pursuers. I reached behind me for my bow, pulled it from its case and then strung an arrow. Whoever was chasing him would be felled before they got near him. He was frantically waving his right arm at me and shouting at the same time. I strained to hear his words. I thought he said 'fiends'. Marvellous, we were about to be attacked by devils! But as he came closer I realised that he was actually shouting 'friends'.

He arrived panting and covered in dirt. 'Friends, Pacorus. Orodes and horsemen from Susiana.'

I relayed the news to the army and soon men were standing, cheering and patting each other on the back. The atmosphere, previously tense and uncertain, was now one of elation and relief. Byrd halted beside me and then Nergal and Orodes arrived, and behind them a column of cataphracts in their scale armour. They slowed and formed into a line of two ranks, then halted behind their prince.

Orodes took off his helmet, his sweat-soaked hair matted to his skull, and beamed at me. 'Hail, Pacorus. Hope we haven't missed the fun.'

I nudged Remus forward and shook his hand.

'Welcome, my friend, it is indeed good to see you.'

He looked behind him. 'Five hundred heavy cavalry, my personal bodyguard. All I could bring, I regret to say. My dear brother ensured that my father prohibited any more of Susiana's army coming to your aid. But only I command my bodyguard, and where I go, it follows.'

I smiled at him. I raised my voice so his men would hear. 'I welcome the men of Susiana, and when the enemy learns of their arrival they will tremble, so great is the terror that the warriors of Susa spread before them.' They raised their long lances and gave a mighty cheer. At that moment a panting Domitus arrived, rivulets of sweat running down his face.

'Domitus,' I said. 'Prince Orodes has brought reinforcements. Behold, the finest men in Susiana.'

Domitus took of his helmet and wiped his face with a cloth, then replaced his white-crested headgear. He pointed at Orodes.

'It would have helped if you had sent couriers ahead to warn us of your approach, to save us having to piss around changing direction and formation under this bloody hot sun.'

With that he turned and ran back to his officers.

'My apologies, Orodes, Domitus can be a little brusque.'

'Nonsense, he's right. I'm just glad that he's on our side.'

It took an hour before the army was ready to commence its march south once more, during which time the horsemen from Susiana rested and took off their scale armour, also stripping their horses of the cumbersome protection. Then it was loaded onto the backs of the thousand camels that Orodes had brought with him, ill-tempered, spitting beasts that carried tents, thousands of arrows, spare weapons and armour, food and medical supplies. There were also a thousand squires, each one riding a horse and armed with a bow, quiver and sword. It was actually a small army that Orodes had brought. In temperament he was much like Nergal, being carefree, cheerful and trusting, in fact everything his step-brother was not. You liked Orodes on sight, and when you got to know him better you realised that your initial impression of him was correct. He was also one of life's optimists, which made him popular among his men and people. And, in stark contrast to Mithridates, he was fair-minded and absolutely trustworthy.

Once the army had recommenced its journey south, Orodes rode beside me with Nergal on my other side.

'I heard about your demotion,' he said, 'and then word reached me that you had been killed.'

'Well, one of those rumours was true, and if Narses and Chosroes had had their way my head would be adorning one of the gates into Uruk by now.'

Orodes shook his head. 'I cannot believe that Chosroes has betrayed us.'

'I can,' I replied. 'Narses is clever. He has promised Chosroes great wealth and power in return for his aid, and Chosroes, being eaten away by jealousy and greed, most probably did not take much persuading.'

'Narses must know that he has no chance.'

'I'm afraid, my friend, that he has every chance. The Roman incursions into Hatra and Dura must have seemed like a gift from the gods to him, especially as Media and Atropaiene lie weakened and unable to assist us. What news of Media?'

'The Romans have made no attempt to lay siege to Irbil, but

293

Farhad and Aschek lack the will and soldiers to trouble them. Events in Hatra and Dura will decide Media's fate, I fear.'

I did not look at Orodes when I asked him the next question. 'And what of Mithridates?'

Orodes spat on the ground. 'He and my step-mother control my father, and thus control Ctesiphon and Susiana. No aid will be sent to you or your father, or for that matter to Vardan.'

'So Babylon still defies Narses?' I asked.

'For the moment, yes, but if no aid arrives then Narses will starve it into surrender.'

After that we rode on in silence, but we all knew that Mithridates was still an ally of Narses. He was playing the long game, waiting to see how events would unravel. I had no doubt that he was behind my attempted murder, but the fact that I still lived did not necessarily negate his plans. He knew that I had to defeat the Romans before I could aid Hatra or Media, and that my father was occupied with dealing with the Roman invasion of his own kingdom. I would not put it past Mithridates to have been in communication with the Romans, perhaps even Crassus himself. It all seemed very convenient, too convenient. I should have killed him as well as Narses. At that moment the world seemed full of people that I should have killed but who were still in arms against me. Useless thoughts. I dismissed them from my mind. One battle at a time.

The night was clear and warm, and Domitus had sited his camp near the river so men and animals could quench their thirsts. It had been a hard day's march, and everyone was glad to have the opportunity to rest at the end of it. Malik and Byrd rode into camp late in the evening and reported to my command tent. Domitus was stretched out on the floor, his eyes closed, his gladius beside him. I was sitting in a chair opposite Orodes, whose men and animals were camped two miles to the north. We were now approximately ten miles from Dura.

More of Malik's warriors had arrived during the past two days and he had used them to aid the cavalry screen Nergal had established in front of the army, both to report on the enemy's movements and to keep Roman eyes away from Dura's army. Byrd, true to form, kept his own counsel and went where he wanted, though he always returned with valuable intelligence.

'Romani getting ready to fight you,' he said, filling a cup with water from a jug on the table. 'Much activity in their camp. Romani soldiers not happy.'

I was surprised at this. 'How do you know that they are

unhappy?'

He looked at me as if I had asked a ridiculous question. 'I speak to them, of course.'

This aroused the interest of Domitus, who opened his eyes and propped himself up on one elbow. 'You spoke to them?'

'Of course. They grumble like old women.'

'You rode into their camp?' Orodes was amazed.

Byrd frowned at him. 'No, I take cart and mule and load it with fruit, then drive it into their camp. I say I Agraci and they no question me further. I not look like soldier.'

He was right there, with his ragged, dirty Agraci robe, wild hair and unshaven face. If only the Romans had known that they had been buying fruit from the finest scout in the Parthian Empire.

'They not like Dura, say it is too tough a nut to crack. They were promised an easy victory but have suffered big losses. Say it is insult to their manhood to be held at bay by a woman. They grumble of witchcraft.'

'Witchcraft?' asked Orodes.

'Romani soldiers have been pierced by poisoned arrows shot from Dura's towers. They believed they were at safe distance but arrows found them anyway. Arrows smeared with poison. Romani soldiers who were hit lost use of legs, went blind, then went mad before they died in agony.'

'Well, she never ceases to amaze me,' said Domitus.

'Who?' I asked.

'Your old witch, of course. A few weeks ago she came to me and said she wanted some of my men to go hunting, said it was essential for the security of the city.'

Domitus told us how Dobbai had persuaded him to send a century to hunt down as many Arabian cobras as they could find. They came back with two score of the deadly reptiles. Dobbai had them milked of their poison, then killed and skinned them. The snake poison and flesh were mixed with dung and left to putrefy, after which the Amazons smeared their arrows with the poisonous substance.

'That's what she told me,' concluded Domitus, 'seems to have worked a treat.'

I smiled to myself. Perhaps I should leave these Romans to Gallia, she seemed to be coping very well.

'So Dura still stands, Byrd?' I asked.

He drained his cup and smiled at me. 'No Romani army will take that city.'

After a final council of war, during the course of which I had again explained the tactics that we would use the next day, the lords went back to their men. I had insisted that they and their followers, plus all of Nergal's horsemen and my own cataphracts, should sleep behind the earth rampart of the legion's camp. This made for a crowded camp, as the men of Pontus were also accommodated within its circuit, but I did not trust the Romans not to attempt a nighttimes' assault and I did not want to give them the opportunity for an easy victory Malik and Byrd assured me that their Agraci scouts had the Romans under close watch, but I insisted, and I even requested that Orodes bring in his men as well. He acquiesced, more from not wishing to appear discourteous than because of any sense of danger. Domitus approved.

'Just because we are home doesn't mean we get sloppy.'

It was the first time that I had heard him call Dura home and I was pleased. I always worried that he missed his own people, but if he did he never said so and now I was reassured that he felt one of us. I knew that he was immensely proud of his legion, and had every right to be, and also that he was held in great respect by his men.

That night I wrote a letter to my father and mother, explaining that I would be giving battle tomorrow and that afterwards, Shamash willing, I would march to Hatra's aid. Later I went outside to stretch my legs. I never slept much before a battle, two or three hours at most, but I was seldom tired on the day of action itself. Rather, it was as if my senses were heightened by the prospect of slaughter. My mind raced with ideas, my reflexes were faster than usual and I could almost feel my blood coursing through my body. I put this down to my upbringing, when I had first been introduced to the tools of war as a small boy. By the time I was eight I could shoot a bow from the saddle, wield a small sword, throw a spear with some accuracy and fight with a mace and shield. When I became a teenager I had mastered the use of all these weapons and had learned how to fight as part of hundred-man mounted company, then as a member of a dragon. I had fought my first battle at the age of twenty-two and now, six years later, I stood on the eve of another one. I stared south and saw the black shape of Dura's walls and its Citadel framed against the clear night sky. No lights flickered in Dura. I smiled. Gallia had all the windows barred with shutters and no lamps burned in the city's streets. She knew that a sentry or careless individual framed by light made an easy target for an enemy archer or slinger.

Tomorrow I would be with my love once more.

Surena appeared and offered me a cup of water.

'You should get some sleep,' I told him, taking the cup and emptying it.

'I've tried, but as soon as I shut my eyes a thousand images fill my mind. I will sleep after the battle.'

I hoped that it would not be the sleep of death. He still had his knife tucked in his belt and wore sandals on his feet.

'Come with me,' I said.

We walked among the rows of tents holding sleeping legionaries until we came to the southeast corner of the camp where Nergal and his horsemen were located. The comforting smell of horses, and the not-so welcoming smell of their dung, met my nostrils as I found my cavalry commander sitting on the ground playing dice with his officers.

'I did not know you were a gambler, Nergal.'

They all saw me and made to stand up. I indicated for them to stay where they were.

'I'm not really, lord, but I feel lucky and wanted to take advantage.'

I tilted my head at Surena. 'I came to find this one a sword and some boots.'

Nergal looked at Surena. 'Pity he can't wait until tomorrow. There will be many Roman ones lying on the ground.'

This brought laughter and smiles from his officers.

'I wish to have a sword now,' said Surena sternly, 'so I can kill the enemies of Pacorus.'

Nergal stood up and tugged at Surena's tunic, indicating that he should follow him. 'That's King Pacorus to you, boy.'

Surena mumbled something under his breath and followed Nergal. Two minutes later we were in a fenced-off area containing two- and four-wheeled wagons, the whole park being guarded by a ring of sentries positioned every ten paces. Mules were tethered together in another adjacent area, and further away, though judging by the smell not too far away, was the camel park. Nergal nodded to the guards and we walked up to a small hide-skin tent pitched near one of the wagons. Nergal stood in front of the tent.

'Strabo. Come out, your king has need of you.'

Seconds later I heard a rustling noise and then a large man with long dark hair and a round face shuffled out on all fours.

'Can't a man get a few hours' sleep without being troubled?' He sniffed and then turned his head to me. He obviously knew who I was because he quickly got to his feet and dusted himself down. He wore a simple white shirt and dark leggings. His feet were bare. He squinted at me with piggy eyes.

297

'Well. Apologies, your majesty, but I didn't know you were coming. No one ever tells me anything, it's always Strabo do this, Strabo do that. Well, one day we will have a proper set of procedures for dealing with things.'

'Enough, Strabo. The king needs your assistance.'

'Well, I will be happy to oblige if I can, though all my assistants are asleep. It's late. Well, you are lucky that I was just closing my eyes.'

'The sooner we can have what we came for,' I said, 'the sooner you will be able to return to your slumbers. I need a sword and a pair of boots for my squire here.'

He wiped his nose on a sleeve as he studied Surena. Then he ambled over to one of the carts, mumbling to himself as he did so.

'Like all quartermasters, he is reluctant to part with his supplies. Isn't that right, Strabo?' Nergal called after him.

Strabo ignored the jibe as he lifted the canvas cover on the cart and rummaged underneath. He returned with a pair of boots and threw them at Surena.

'They should fit you nicely. Nice and worn in, they are. Came off a dead one of that lot who fought with Porus last year.'

Surena held them with distaste.

'Now don't you get high and mighty,' said Strabo, 'they're fine boots and the previous owner no longer has a use for them.'

'He's right,' I added.

Strabo scuttled off and began rifling through another cart, then reappeared with a sword in a scabbard. He handed it to Surena, who this time was beaming with delight. He drew it slowly from its scabbard. It was a Roman spatha, exactly like the one I carried, though mine had been a gift from Spartacus himself. The blade was long and straight and finished in a point. Both edges were razor sharp and its hilt was made of dark-stained walnut. It was a beautiful piece.

'Where did you obtain it from?' I asked.

'Malik and his Agraci brought in a load of captured weapons after they had butchered a few Roman horsemen on the road north of here. Seeing as you've got one, I thought it appropriate that your squire should have one as well.'

'A fine sword, Surena,' remarked Nergal, whose own spatha hung from his belt, 'make sure your conduct is worthy of such a blade.'

'My conduct?'

'Of course,' I said. 'Will you use it to further your honour or as a tool to butcher innocents? Will you wield it to defend your family and homeland, or to spread death and misery in furtherance of your own selfish goals?'

He looked at me with a blank expression on his face.

'Well,' I continued, 'these things are for the future. But remember that a man's sword is not just a lump of metal; it is an extension of him. However, it is late and we have troubled Strabo enough for one night.'

'You're not wrong there.'

Nergal froze him with an iron stare so Strabo bowed his head to me and scurried away. I told Surena to go back to the command tent and ready my armour and weapons for the morning, leaving me alone with Nergal.

'Another battle tomorrow, Nergal.'

He grinned. 'Another defeat for the Romans.'

There would be little time tomorrow for idle chatter, so I welcomed the chance to talk to my friend and trusted commander.

'After we deal with this lot we will have to march north to aid Hatra, and after that Media. It seems there remains much fighting left to do.'

'That is what we exist for, is it not?'

'You sound like Domitus.'

He laughed. 'That is a fine complement. You know what his men say about him?'

'No.'

'That his drills are bloodless battles and his battles are bloody drills.'

Now it was my turn to laugh. 'I remember the first time I clapped eyes on him. It was when Spartacus had captured that silver mine near Thurri. Domitus was one of the slaves condemned to work in the mine. But after he had been freed he decided to join us. I am glad he did, for I think that I collected the greatest treasure that was in that mine.'

'The Romans are going to get a surprise tomorrow when they see that there's a legion facing them.'

'By the time they realise,' I said, 'it will be too late.'

I looked at him. 'I am sorry that Praxima is in Dura, I did not wish it so.'

He laid a hand on my shoulder. 'It is not your fault, Pacorus. Praxima would never leave Gallia, you know that. I am proud that she stayed to stand by her friend.'

'If we win the battle,' I said, 'I will have stern words with my wife.'

He raised his eyebrows. 'Good luck with that.'

The day of battle dawned clear and windless. It would be hot later, and for some their last day on earth. Surena had laid out my armour the night before. The heavy hide suit covered in iron scales hung on its wooden frame. My Roman helmet, its crest filled with fresh goose feathers, perched on top. My boots he had placed at the foot of my cot, with my leggings and tunic folded on top of them. I always kept my sword on the floor beside me as I slept and my dagger under my pillow. Before I prepared for battle I knelt beside the cot and held the lock of Gallia's hair in my hand. I closed my eyes and prayed to Shamash that He would give me courage this day, and that my conduct would honour my forefathers.

First I put on my silk shirt, followed by the tunic and leggings. By the time I had pulled on my boots Surena had arrived with a tray of fruit, bread and water. I invited him to join me for breakfast, while outside the racket of an army preparing for battle filed the air.

'Stay with the other squires in camp,' I told him. 'If the worst happens, get your hide out of here as quickly as possible and get across the river.'

He looked surprised. 'I have been told that you have never lost a battle.'

I thought of the last battle with Spartacus in Italy, in the Silarus Valley. All day we had fought the Romans, and though we had not lost, at the end of it Spartacus lay dead and his army broken. It was certainly no victory.

'What has happened up to now counts for nothing. Just do as I ask.'

'I have a sword and would like to fight.'

'And I would like you to stay alive. Fighting Romans is not like ambushing the soldiers of Chosroes and then running back into the marshes.'

He nodded but I could tell that he was far from happy. He was filled with excitement, and being young he never considered that he might be killed. But then, all of us never really thought that we might die on the battlefield. Each soldier knew that battles were bloody affairs, but in his mind it was always the man next to him who was going to die, never him.

And so, once again, I prepared to fight the Romans. In truth there was much to admire about them and their civilisation. For me, their architectural achievements were things of wonder. Parthia had its great temples and palaces, it was true, but nowhere in the empire was there mighty stone aqueducts carrying water to towns and cities or straight, paved roads that connected its cities.

300

The roads in Parthia were dirt tracks, their surfaces baked hard by the sun, which turned to mud when it rained, but Roman roads were a marvel to behold. They were never washed away by rains; rather, they had drainage channels on each side into which rainwater ran. And those same roads carried Roman armies to the far corners of their empire, from where they invaded foreign lands to fulfil the insatiable Roman desire for conquest. The Romans believed that the earth was theirs for the taking, irrespective of what other peoples thought. And in their thirst for conquest they had developed a military system that was the envy of the world. In Italy, no matter how many defeats they had suffered, the Romans always seemed to have an inexhaustible supply of soldiers with which to create new armies. But above all it was discipline and organisation that gave the Romans victory. Ever since I had returned to Parthia I had endeavoured to infuse Dura's army with these same qualities. Today I would discover if I had been successful.

Stripped of its mystery and horror, war is a business, no different to farming the land or constructing a building. There are certain guiding principles that must be observed if one is to be successful. If a farmer plants his seeds and does not water them, his crops will not grow. If an architect does not use the proper materials or ignores the laws of physics, his building will collapse. It is the same with war. The building blocks of battlefield success are training, the right equipment, the correct tactics and good leadership. I knew my men were well trained. Domitus and Nergal had spent countless hours on the training fields putting their men through their paces, endless drills to build stamina and strength and to perfect tactics. Practising over and over so each man knew his place in the century, cohort, company and dragon, practising hard and so often that drills became second nature, performed without thinking, even in the white-hot cauldron of combat. I had beaten Roman armies before, in Italy, but this time was different. In Italy Spartacus had been my commander, but here all eyes were upon me. I was both commander and king. If I lost I would lose my army and my kingdom. It would all be decided in the next few hours.

Many people who have not seen the East believe it to be wholly desert, and whereas vast tracts of Parthia are indeed parched and arid, the lands either side of the mighty Euphrates and Tigris rivers are lush and green. The waters of these two rivers have irrigated the land for thousands of years. It is the same in Dura. The land along the western bank of the Euphrates is the home to an abundance of wildlife, watering thousands of livestock and feeding crops. But the area that we would fight on today is bone-dry and dusty. Dura itself had been built on rock that towers above the Euphrates. Immediately beyond the city's northern wall was one of the two great wadis that flanked the city. Its sheer, high sides made any assault from the north impossible, and it was the same on the city's southern side where there was also a deep wadi. Beyond the northern wadi the ground descends down to the plain in a gentle slope for a distance of around a mile. It was at this spot, on level ground, that caravans and travellers crossed the Euphrates via the pontoon bridge that now lay dismantled and stacked well inland on the far shore. The large caravan park that had been created to provide shelter and food for both men and their beasts sprawled over a vast area, both west and north. Further north still had been the tent city that had housed the workers who had strengthened the city's defences and laboured in the armouries. They had all left now, and there were no longer caravans crossing the Euphrates. But they had all left their mark, for the land all around was flat, dry and barren – a giant dust bowl – ideal for a battle. Ideal for the battle that I intended to fight.

I knew that the Romans would anchor their flank on the river. The Roman war machine is based around their mighty legions of foot soldiers. They have little use for horsemen save for skirmishing and carrying out reconnaissance. But they know the damage that highly mobile enemy cavalry can do, especially Parthia's heavily armed and armoured cataphracts. But if an army's wing is anchored on a river or another impassable feature, then it cannot be outflanked. And so it was today. They would have no need to place horsemen on their right, opposite what would be my left flank. Nor would I place any cavalry there. On this wing I would deploy the foot soldiers of Pontus. They were not yet equipped as the legionaries of Domitus, but it did not matter. Veteran soldiers, they carried spears with long, leaf-shaped blades and large rounds shields faced in bronze after the old Greek fashion. Most had helmets and all wore thick hide armour to protect their torsos. Their officers could be identified by small, overlapping iron plates fastened to their armour. The soldiers also carried a long sword as a secondary weapon, but it was totally unsuitable to fighting as part of a compact body of men. It was a slashing weapon, not one for stabbing. Pontic warriors did not throw their spears at the foe; they were for thrusting into the belly of an enemy soldier while the shield covered the left side of the body. This would all have to change. But not today. Today, the three and a half thousand soldiers from Pontus would advance in their companies against the Roman right flank. They were not unlike the Romans in their organisation, though their largest battlefield formation was a block made up of five hundred-man companies, but if a Roman legion got to grips with them it would cut them to pieces. The Pontic soldiers would form a battle line of five blocks side by side, with two blocks immediately behind as a reserve. Opposite them would stand a Roman legion of ten cohorts arranged in three lines.

The fate of the men of Pontus would hinge on what happened in the centre of the line, to their right. For here Domitus and his legion would assault the Romans. His legion would be drawn up in two lines, six cohorts in the first line, four in the second; there would be no third line. Its job would be to punch through the Roman centre. Normally such a tactic demanded a wedge formation, but in this battle the legion would be working closely with five hundred of Nergal's horse archers. It is extremely hazardous for horse and foot to work closely together on the battlefield. In the confusion of combat the result can often be a tangle of horses and men followed by a rout. But Nergal and Domitus had worked for months to perfect their proficiency when acting together. The horsemen would ride in the gaps between the cohorts, five hundred horse archers divided into five columns, the riders in each column riding one behind the other in a long file. Each column would gallop towards the Romans opposite, the lead rider loosing arrows as he approached the Romans. At a distance of around one hundred paces from the enemy front rank he would wheel his horse to the right and gallop parallel to the enemy for a distance equivalent to the frontage of a cohort, shooting arrows as he did so. He would then wheel his horse right again to begin the journey back to Dura's legion, turning in the saddle as he did so to shoot one last arrow at the enemy over the hindquarters of his horse. During his advance he would ride along the left flank of a cohort in the first line; when he returned he would pass by the right flank of the same cohort, then turn right once again to ride behind the cohorts in the second line to receive a fresh quiver, before galloping towards the Romans once more. When he was riding parallel to the Romans and shooting arrows, how did he know when to wheel his horse right to take him back to Dura's legion, to ride through the gap between cohorts and not crash into one? The answer was countless hours spent on the training field, sweating and cursing under a hot sun perfecting tactics so that they became second nature, almost instinct, so when the day of battle arrived they were performed without thinking, horse archer and foot soldier in perfect harmony.

In this way files of horsemen would maintain a withering arrow fire against the enemy, five hundred men loosing an average of five arrows a minute – two and half thousand arrows flying towards the enemy. The Romans would not fear this arrow storm. In response their centurions would merely give the order to halt and form a testudo, which means 'tortoise'. The front rank would kneel down to form a shield wall, and then the second and third ranks would lift their shields to create a forward-sliding roof over their companions in the front rank. And behind them their comrades would haul their shields over their heads to create a roof impervious to my archers' arrows. The Romans knew that each Parthian quiver held thirty arrows, so if they stood and withstood the hail of arrows my men would soon run out of ammunition. But what they did not realise was that my men could get full quivers loaded onto camels that were positioned behind the second line of Domitus' legion, so they could empty one quiver, then ride back and replace it with another. And all the time the Romans would be stationary, and then Domitus and his men would hit them with the force of a charging bull, and their line would buckle as my men mangled the Roman centuries.

But it would be on the right wing that the outcome of the battle would be decided. Here, I placed my cataphracts – five hundred heavy horsemen whose task would be to smash through the Roman cavalry to allow the lords and their horse archers to sweep behind the Roman army. My father believed that he had the best heavy horsemen in the Parthian Empire, and in terms of numbers he certainly had the edge, but Dura's cataphracts were bloodied, highly trained and straining at the leash to earn more glory. They were mostly young men in their early twenties and they burned with a desire to prove that they were the finest heavy horsemen in the world, not just the empire. My father and Vistaspa recoiled from such ambition, believing that it led to false pride and arrogance, but I indulged my men's thirst for fame and glory. And I knew that this day they would have an added incentive to excel, for the enemy stood on their home soil. I also knew that the Roman cavalry would be unable to withstand my cataphracts. The enemy horsemen were armed with spears, swords and wore mail shirts and helmets. On their left side they carried large oval shields that gave protection from the shoulder to below the knee. But a kontus could go straight through such a shield like a knife cutting through parchment. Nevertheless I wanted the Roman cavalry to be weakened before the cataphracts reached them, so I interspersed five hundred of Nergal's horse archers among them. The cataphracts would charge in two ranks, and in each rank a cataphract would ride beside a horse archer. The latter would begin shooting arrows at the Romans at a range of around three hundred paces, and would continue loosing arrows until the two lines clashed, the horse archers reducing their pace before the impact. At the same time the archers in the second rank, also falling back so as not to collide with the bowmen of the first rank, would shoot their arrows over the first rank into the approaching enemy mass. In this way when the two sides clashed only cataphracts would be hitting the Romans. This drill was most complex but we had spent months perfecting it on the training fields.

Behind the cataphracts would be Dura's lords and their men, six thousand horse archers and a few cataphracts, whose task would be to pepper the enemy legionaries with arrows. By then Domitus and his men would have cut their way through the centre of the Roman line, the Roman army would be broken in two and the battle would be won. Bozan, my old instructor and the man who had led Hatra's army, had once told me that as soon as a battle begins even the best-laid plan falls apart. I prayed that it would not be so on this day.

The arrival of Orodes and his five hundred cataphracts had been a welcome addition to the army, but they had also presented me with a dilemma. They had never worked with any element of Dura's army. I therefore had no choice but to place them on the extreme right of the right flank. I would have liked them as a reserve, but no Parthian lord, much less a prince, would accept such a passive roll on the battlefield.

As the army spread out into a battle line, mounted on Remus I faced Nergal and Orodes, with Domitus standing beside me. Already my throat was tickly on account of the dust that was being kicked up by men and horses.

'Do you have any more orders, Pacorus?' asked Domitus, who clearly wanted to be leading his men rather than standing here.

'No,' I replied, 'as we planned, as soon as I hear your trumpets I will attack their left wing. The rest is in God's hands.'

He nodded and put on his white-crested helmet. 'Well, then, the gods keep you safe.' I lent down and offered him my hand. He took it and nodded, then strode away to rejoin his men. I knew that he would be in the vanguard of the attack. It was useless to suggest to him that he do otherwise as I would do the same. Some kings commanded their armies from the rear, but I had always believed

305

that men respected a general more who led from the front. In any case it was the Parthian way.

'Shamash protect you, Pacorus,' said Nergal, who put his hand to his helmet and then wheeled his horse away to join his men who were acting as a screen in front of the legion. I raised my hand in salute.

'Well, lord prince,' I said to Orodes, 'shall we join our men?'

We had both placed the butt end of our heavy lances on the ground, but we now hoisted them up and rested them on our shoulders as we trotted over to the right flank.

As we passed the lords, their men began raising their bows aloft and cheering. I raised my hand in recognition.

'Your men are confident of victory,' remarked Orodes.

'They are glad that we have the enemy finally cornered, I think. Men don't like foreign soldiers in their homelands.'

Byrd and Malik rode up, halting in front of me, both they and their horses covered in dust.

'Romani army left camp earlier and is forming up next to river, as you told us it would,' said Byrd.

'And Furius?' I asked.

Byrd cracked a smile. 'Riding up and down, shouting at his men.'

'Same old Furius,' I muttered.

'Where do want me and my men, Pacorus?' asked Malik.

'You can choose your own spot, lord prince,' I said.

The whole army had by now deployed into its battle formations and was marching in a southerly direction at a leisurely pace. I rode forward to be at the head of my heavy cavalry, bidding Orodes farewell as he galloped over to be with his own men. Most of my cataphracts were bare headed at this stage. The day was already hot; there was no need for them to sweat buckets unnecessarily. They would put on their helmets when they were needed. Ahead of the front rank rode Vagharsh carrying my griffin banner, though when the charge was launched he would fall back to the second rank, and if he fell the standard would be picked up by another. There was no breeze, though, and so the banner hung limp. Behind him the cataphracts and horse archers shared jokes and exchanged insults. I halted beside Vagharsh and peered ahead. I could see Dura and the Citadel in the distance but strained to see the Romans in the plain below. We were less than ten miles from the city now. To my left four thousand legionaries marched in step towards the enemy and beyond them, out of sight, were the men of Pontus.

So far, so good. The atmosphere was calm, almost serene, and were it not for the fact that we were fully armoured and armed, the horses could have been on a morning stroll. I could make out the enemy now, small black blocks in the distance.

On we went, nearing the enemy ranks. We kept aligned to the legion to our left, the rhythmic sound of thousands of sandals hitting the ground in unison filling the air. Some of the horses, sensing men's nervousness and fear, became jittery and had to be calmed by their riders. Remus, long used to the sights and sounds of battle, showed no signs of emotion. I could see the Roman cavalry now, men armed with lances and shields massing on their left wing, and I could also make out archers on horseback, men who were bare chested and wore no head armour. The Romans had deployed as I had expected them to do.

We halted as the Romans deployed into line, their right flank anchored on the river. I knew that Furius would not wait long before he ordered an attack and so did Domitus. And so my Roman friend launched his assault first, the blast of trumpet calls suddenly filling the air to signal the start of the battle. I glanced left and saw the Duran Legion moving forward like it was on the parade ground, then turned and gave the signal for the cavalry to likewise advance.

I nudged Remus to walk forward as the horns sounded along the line. I urged him to quicken the pace and he broke into a canter. I glanced behind and saw full-face helmets on my cataphracts. Between them, horse archers, their reins wrapped around their left wrist, were stringing arrows in their bows. Vagharsh slowed and let the front rank pass him. I also pulled up Remus momentarily to allow the front rank to catch me up – I had confidence in my men but did not want to be shot in the back by mistake by an archer whose thumb slipped. We were widely spaced as our horses broke into a gallop and as one we levelled our lances at the fast-approaching enemy, holding the thick shafts with both hands on our right sides. I estimated our distance from the Roman cavalry to be four hundred paces.

They scattered before we reached them.

In an effort to break up our charge they had placed mounted archers among their horsemen, but Parthian recurve bows have greater range than Roman ones and our arrows were finding their targets before they had a chance to reply. If the enemy cavalry had reckoned their chances had improved by stiffening their ranks with archers, they disappeared when those same archers began to turn and flee. Some enemy spearmen had advanced towards us in an attempt to mount their own charge, but these now halted in confusion when they saw their ranks thinning. Many turned and joined the archers in attempting to flee, others just sat in their saddles and tried to redress their lines, while a few, a tiny number, levelled their spears and charged us. They were the first to fall, either pierced by arrows themselves or thrown by their horses as iron-tipped arrows slammed into their mounts. The air was rent with the screams of wounded and dying horses as we thundered across the baked ground.

The Roman cavalry was now fleeing back to the safety of its camp. There was little point in chasing after them with three enemy legions still on the field, so I slowed Remus and those either side of me did the same with their own animals. Horns sounded recall and the whole line slowed into a canter, then a trot and finally a walk. I turned and looked up and down the line. There appeared to be no empty saddles. Behind us the lords, as planned, were veering left at the head of their men to attack the Roman legions from behind, the sounds of thousands of iron-shod hooves like thunder to our ears. Orodes rode up.

'That was easy enough.'

I pointed ahead at the Roman cavalry, which had stopped running and was now attempting to reform. 'They'll be back unless we can disperse them.'

I called the commander of the horse archers forward and ordered him to take his men forward to irritate the Roman horse. 'Stay out of range of their bows and drop as many as you can. If they advance, you retreat. But keep shooting at them. Be like flies around camel dung. Above all, keep them away from their foot. Go.'

He saluted and rode away. Seconds later horns sounded and his men were forming into their companies and trotting forward once more. Following on behind were three score of camels carrying extra quivers of arrows.

'And now, lord prince,' I said to Orodes, 'a more difficult task. Follow us.'

'Wheel left and reform the line,' I shouted.

A Roman legion in battle order is usually drawn up in three lines. The one that had been next to the Roman cavalry now had an exposed left flank. I raised my lance and dug my knees into the sides of Remus. He grunted, broke into a canter and headed for the gap between the second and third lines of the Roman legion. It was now a race against time between my horsemen and enemy centurions desperately trying to form a wall of shields on their left flank. The cohorts could stand where they were and form an all-round defence, but that would mean leaving gaps to their front, sides and rear, through which we could pour. Their leaders gambled that they would have time to close these gaps before we hit them. They were wrong.

We broke into a fast gallop less than two hundred paces from the first centuries that were forming the shield wall. Screaming our war cries we crashed into a mass of legionaries, creating a sickening crunching noise as lance tips and horses smashed into them. A horse will not run at a solid object, but the Roman line was still ragged and disjointed and so the horses attempted to lunge through any narrowing gaps. Some failed and tried to turn away, but their momentum was too great so they tumbled over into the enemy ranks, throwing their riders but crushing Romans as they somersaulted and thrashed like rocks careering downhill in a landslide. They carved a path of chaos and broken bodies as the force of horse and rider gouged a path through the enemy. Other horsemen followed, driving their lances into shields and mail shirts, sometimes pinning a legionary to the earth as a kontus was driven straight through a torso and then into the ground behind. A thousand riders hit the flank of that Roman legion, driving deep into its disorganised ranks. Legionaries and horsemen soon became intermingled as the momentum of the charge carried cataphracts deeper into the enemy formation.

I rammed my kontus through the chest of a centurion, let go of the shaft and drew my sword. I swung the blade down to the right and cut deep into the upper arm of a legionary who was running past me. He yelped and fell to the ground. I screamed at Remus and dug my knees into his side. He lurched forward. A Roman attempted to thrust his sword point into his armour, but the iron scales and thick hide defeated his blade. I thrust my own sword at him and penetrated his right shoulder. He squealed in agony and fell to his knees. I rode on, slashing at figures on my right and left. Before battle my scale armour felt heavy and cumbersome; in combat it became as light as a feather as battle frenzy took hold of me. I felt as though the blood of an immortal was racing through my veins. Around me cataphracts were going about their work with a relentless fury. I saw some javelins fly through the air and heard the dull thud of lead pellets launched by slingers hit their target, but in this disorganised melee it would have been almost impossible for missile throwers to have the space or time to launch their weapons with any accuracy.

Roman trumpets blasted and then fell silent as their owners were killed, their skulls caved in by a mace. The din of battle filled my ears and was getting louder. Centurions and officers screamed orders. Remus suddenly kicked out with his back legs. I looked behind me and saw a Roman lying face-down on the ground; he must have been felled by my horse's rear hooves. A javelin glanced off the armoured rings that protected my left arm. A legionary, bare headed and with no shield, blood pouring down the side of his face, ran at me. I raised my sword high above my head and brought it down. He must have been in the grip of delirium, for he brought up his left arm to parry the blow. Perhaps in his mind he believed that he still carried his shield. My sword went straight though his forearm and severed his limb just below the elbow. He made no sound but merely stared at the bloody stump in disbelief. He looked up at me and then died when one of my men rode past him and crushed in the top of his skull with a swing of his mace.

We were herding the Romans before us, slowly and bloodily, and gradually some semblance of order was emerging out of the chaos. The ground lay thick with Roman dead and a few slain Parthians. Cataphracts grouped around the banner held aloft behind me. Ahead I could see a wall of Roman shields forming and javelins arching through the air towards those cataphracts who were still hacking at the Roman soldiers. Then arrows and slingshots began emptying saddles.

'Horns, horns,' I shouted. 'Sound recall.'

It was futile to keep charging the enemy now that they had sealed their flank. The shrill blast of horns bought the rest of the horsemen back to where our own line was forming. In front of us, and all around, the ground was carpeted with enemy dead and dying. Orodes rode up, helmet dented and a cut on his right cheek, his eyes full of fire.

'One more charge and they're finished, Pacorus.'

I shook my head. 'No, we leave them alone for now. They're shaken but will hold what they have. They will not charge horse and we will not charge them.'

He looked disappointed. 'Then what?'

I saw a group of lords riding towards us. I pointed at them. 'We will soon find out.'

They halted in front of me and raised their hands in salute. They all looked dirty and fatigued. One with a full beard whose helmet appeared too small for his over-sized head spoke. 'Your men are breaking through their centre. We've been shooting arrows at them and now we can see that golden griffin.'

A wave of excitement went through my body. I turned to

Orodes. 'We are wasted here. We will move towards their centre.'

I looked at the lords. 'Keep shooting at them, we must help Domitus.'

They galloped away and we followed. We had no lances now and both horses and men were tired from our melee, but we had to aid Domitus. We rode towards the river, behind the Roman lines. We left the legion we had attacked in its all-round defence and galloped to behind the Roman centre. I rode at the head of the column of cataphracts, Orodes beside me and our two banners fluttering directly behind us. Through the dust and haze I could hear the din of battle on my left. This was where Domitus and his men were fighting the enemy. Then I saw the masses of horse archers ahead, riders galloping full-pelt at the enemy shield wall, then wheeling away after they had released their arrows, followed by more riders who did the same, an unending stream of archers making the air thick with their missiles.

I ordered half a dozen of the lords to take their men to harass the Romans who still stood on the left flank, the survivors of the legion we had charged so successfully. This necessitated a reorganisation, as archers were recalled, formed into groups around their lords and then redeployed to annoy the Romans' left flank. The air still resonated with the sounds of battle to the front of the Roman line, indicating that Domitus and his men were still grinding their way through the enemy. I had to aid him, but how?

A blast of trumpets behind made me turn in the saddle. I recognised that sound; it was made by the instruments carried by the legions. I had trumpets in my own legion, of course, but these were coming from behind. Had Roman reinforcements arrived, perhaps from their camp? I turned and rode through the ranks of my cataphracts; Orodes came with me.

'What is it?'

'Roman trumpets,' I said, my stomach knotted with concern.

The cataphracts had also wheeled about and were following us, but then I pulled up Remus sharply. Ahead were two cohorts of legionaries, but these were not Romans. They wore the white tunics of Dura and they were flanked by horse archers wearing helmets, mail shirts and with white cloth showing on their arms. Ahead of them all were two riders, one on a chestnut mare – Epona. The garrison of Dura had come, led by my wife. My men began cheering as they approached, and I must confess that I too took off my helmet and began shouting my praise as the two cohorts and their Amazon escort tramped towards us. The lords and their men also raised a mighty cheer, and momentarily forgot that they were supposed to be attacking the enemy.

Gallia galloped up with Praxima beside her. The cheekguards on their helmets were both fastened shut. She stopped in front of me and cupped my cheek with her hand.

'Did you think I would sit idly by while my husband and my people fought for their homeland?'

I struggled to hold back my tears. It was so good to see her.

'Where is Claudia, my love?'

'Safe in the Citadel protected by Haytham's men.'

'Haytham?'

'I will tell you later. Where is that toad Furius?'

His name refocused my attention back on the battle. I ordered the two cohorts from the garrison to attack the Roman shield wall that had been under arrow fire for some time now. As the men neared the enemy they began banging their javelins on the inside of their shields and shouted 'Dura, Dura' as they dressed their lines. I asked Orodes, who had taken Gallia's hand and kissed it, much to her amusement, to deploy his men on the right of the garrison while my own cataphracts massed on the left.

Another blast of trumpets, this time from the Roman ranks, and suddenly the enemy legion to our left, the one we had assaulted, began moving towards their centre. It was still being peppered with arrows, but its men were now moving crab-like towards the river. Then there was another blast of trumpets from within its ranks, followed by shouts and screams. Its commander, realising that if he stayed where he was the result would be the destruction of his men, had decided to join the legion in the centre, the same legion that was being assaulted by Domitus. With horror I also realised that as he did so his men would in turn hit Domitus in the flank. The discipline of the Romans was magnificent as they shuffled towards their centre, all the time their rear, front and left flank under arrow fire.

I halted my horsemen and the two cohorts from the garrison. Domitus would not be able to break their centre now, not with another legion hitting his flank while his men battled the one in front of them.

I turned to Orodes. 'We must aid Domitus.'

I rode over to Gallia. 'You and your women will come with me.'

'We will not charge them?'

'Have patience, there is still time to dip your arrowheads in blood.'

I galloped back to Orodes with Gallia and the Amazons following. I left orders for the lords to continue their harassing fire, and then I took the heavy horsemen and female horse archers back around the Roman left flank to find Domitus and his legion. Dust was everywhere. It got in our eyes and down our throats, while the sun beat down mercilessly on our backs. Sweat stung my eyes and my limbs ached but I knew there was still much fighting left to do this day.

We had to take a circuitous route to Dura's legion, as the lords and their men hovered around the Romans like flies on a dead carcass. They would have run out of arrows long before had it not have been for the camels that were ridden from camp by squires, each one laden with spare quivers, from which the horse archers could replenish their ammunition.

I found Domitus standing with the legion's colour party grouped around the griffin, just behind the front line. He was having his right arm bandaged by Alcaeus. He looked pale and exhausted as he took a swig from a water bottle and raised his arm in acknowledgement. I halted Remus in front of him and glanced around. The corpses of Roman dead and some Durans lay on the ground.

'We nearly broke them,' he said, 'but then the ones you were supposed to keep occupied hit us on our right flank, so I pulled the boys back. The enemy is shifting left, towards the river. What's happening?'

'We scattered their horsemen easily enough and then mauled the legion next to them, and I thought we had them. We are behind them and I was about to launch an assault on their centre when they started moving.'

As we spoke I could see the Romans slowly moving towards the river, still retaining their ranks and discipline, but as they did so they made no attempt to attack our own foot. Alcaeus finished bandaging Domitus' arm.

'Is it serious?' I asked.

'No,' he seemed more annoyed than hurt.

'I have other wounded to tend to,' remarked Alcaeus, who then sprinted away to where he was needed.

Nergal rode up.

'The men of Pontus have taken heavy casualties, Pacorus. We have been assisting them but the Romans have pushed them back.'

'How far?'

'Not far, two, three hundred paces perhaps, but it is unlikely that they will be able to launch another attack.'

If the Romans next to the river advanced and then swung left, they would hit Domitus in his left flank. I would have to take my horsemen to reinforce our left wing, which was now threatened with collapse.

'Are the Romans still advancing?' I asked.

Nergal shook his head. 'No. They pushed back the men of Pontus, advanced a short distance and then stopped. Most odd.'

'They're saving their eagles,' said Domitus.

'What?'

'They are saving their eagles.'

'You are mistaken,' I said. 'There is no way across the river at this point.'

Domitus thought for a second. 'Any boats?'

'Of course not.'

He looked up at me. 'You sure about that?'

I was wrong. As the Romans redeployed what was left of their forces to form a hollow square with one side open at the riverbank, small boats powered by oarsmen were ferrying the prized eagles to safety upriver. We had been outwitted, but there were not enough boats to evacuate their entire army. And as a continuous arrow fire was maintained against the three sides of the Roman square, I gathered the lords and officers of the army to decide our next course of action. The ground was littered with dead and dying horses and men, while our wounded were being ferried back to camp to be treated. It was then that I saw Surena at the head of a score of horsemen charging the enemy. He galloped up to the Roman front rank, shooting arrows as he did so, then wheeled sharply away as those following him took turns to shoot their bows. He rode well, but I would have words with him afterwards about disobeying my orders.

As we sat on our horses in a large circle the lords were all for finishing the Romans quickly.

'Slaughter them all and then we can go home.'

'Push them into the river and let them drown,' said another.

Orodes' blood was still up. 'We can break them, Pacorus. They have been fighting for hours. One charge at one point with all our heavy horse and we surely break them.' The others cheered him and he beamed in triumph.

I held up my hand. 'I think I will ask them politely if they will lay down their arms.'

There was silence, then spontaneous laughter erupted, indicating that they all thought I was mad. Orodes looked very disappointed.

'You do know who leads them,' said Gallia.

'That is why I think my idea will work.'

I gave orders for all arrow fire to cease as the lords and Nergal pulled back their men out of range of the Romans' slingers and archers. We now formed a huge semi-circle around the Roman square, the men of Pontus next to the river, the Duran Legion on their right, now reinforced by the garrison, Nergal and his men next to them, and the lords and their horse archers deployed next in line extending all the way to the riverbank. An eerie silence descended over the battlefield. I sat on Remus next to Gallia, Orodes on my right. Malik and Byrd came through the ranks behind me.

'Romani have taken their standards away on the river. A dozen boats,' said Byrd.

'They are five miles away now, Pacorus, maybe more,' said Malik. 'You want us to catch them?'

'No, let them go. Our fight is here.'

I nudged Remus forward and walked him into the space between Parthians and Romans. I took off my helmet as I did so and halted about fifty paces from the line of locked Roman shields.

'Men of Rome,' I shouted. 'I am the king of the land you now stand on. I salute your courage. You have done all that honour demands this day and more, but now is the time to listen to reason.'

I saw no movement from within their ranks.

'I call upon your commander to come forward to discuss the terms of your surrender, for to continue fighting will surely condemn you all to death. I give you this promise. If you lay down your arms all of you will walk out of here unharmed. Come forth Lucius Furius.'

I rode back to my men and waited. Domitus strode up.

'Perhaps he left on one of the boats.'

'No,' I said, 'not Furius. His sense of Roman superiority will not let him flee in the face of barbarians.'

And sure enough, a few moments later, he rode out from the enemy ranks. I nudged Remus forward until I stood ten paces from Lucius Furius. He hadn't changed; he still had red curly hair and an angry expression on his face.

'Well, Lucius,' I said, 'we meet again.'

'What do you want?' he snapped, looking down his nose at me.

'I want you to leave my kingdom and I want Rome to stop its wars of aggression against the Parthian Empire. Will those two requests suffice to satisfy you?'

He sneered at me. 'Just like the rabble led by Spartacus perished, so will the Parthian Empire fall.'

I sighed. 'Even now, with death staring you in the face, you still persist in issuing threats.'

He looked immensely smug. 'Armies may fall, Parthian, but Rome is eternal. What is Parthia but a collection of desert nomads and horse stables devoid of culture and learning? It is Rome's duty to bring civilisation to the world. That is why I am here.'

I sighed. 'You are here because you, or more correctly your master, Crassus, wishes to have possession of the trade route into Egypt.'

'Parthia has no jurisdiction west of the Euphrates. King Phraates has given Rome sovereignty over this land.'

This was staggering. 'What?'

He smiled, delighting in my uncertainty. 'It is true. Governor Lucullus has agreed to evacuate the province of Gordyene in exchange for control of all territory up to the west bank of the Euphrates. You see, Parthian, even your own king does not want you.'

I refused to believe that this was so. 'Here are my terms, Furius. Your men are to lay down their weapons and you will become my hostage. Your master, Crassus, will have to pay a handsome price to get you back. We will see how much he values you, which is only fair as he puts a price on everything.'

'I reject your terms.'

'What?'

'A Roman general never surrenders, especially in his own land.'

'You are an idiot,' I replied. 'To continue fighting will result in your certain death.'

'All death is certain.'

A most philosophical answer, I had to admit.

'I give you one last chance to surrender.'

'I reject your offer, Parthian. I do not bargain with slaves.'

I shook my head, pulled on Remus' reins and turned my back on Lucius Furius. I heard a jangling noise behind me followed by a hissing sound. I turned to see Furius directly behind me, sword in hand. He was slumped in his saddle, an arrow lodged in his chest. I looked back at my men and saw Gallia with a bow in her hand. The sword slipped from Furius' hand and then he fell from his saddle. He hit the ground and rolled onto his back. He glazed eyes told me that he was dead.

Mayhem then broke out as horsemen and foot soldiers charged the Romans. Horns and trumpets blasted as thousands of men attacked the wavering shield wall, while the air was thick with missiles as horse archers loosed their bows and Roman slingers and archers replied in kind. Horsemen surged past me led by Orodes, his sword held aloft, while on their flank Domitus and his men hoisted their shields and marched towards the Romans. Around a hundred paces from the enemy they charged, the front ranks racing at the enemy with swords drawn as the ranks immediately behind then hurled their javelins over the heads of their comrades against the enemy. I heard a loud thud as the Durans smashed into the stationary Romans, thrusting their swords upwards into any gaps between the shields. The Roman line buckled and then began to fall back as the impetus of the Duran charge cut its way into the enemy.

The horse archers did not attempt to charge the Romans but merely continued with their harassing fire, pouring volley after volley of arrows into the enemy. Occasionally an arrowhead hit flesh, but mostly it forced the Romans to take shelter behind their shields, but in doing so it prevented them from reinforcing the threatened sections of their line. Orodes and the cataphracts, now wielding swords or maces, rode up to the Roman lines and tried to batter their way through the enemy. But the ranks of the enemy were too dense and they failed. But Domitus did not fail.

Both armies had been manoeuvring and fighting under a hot sun for hours now. The Romans had seen their cavalry scattered, their eagles spirited away and their commander killed, and now they were penned in like sheep against the river. Assaulted once more, their cohesion began to crack as they continued to endure arrow fire from thousands of horse archers, a fire that seemingly never ceased, unlike their own slingers and archers, who soon ran out of ammunition. So Domitus and his men cut their way into the enemy, creating a gap through which Orodes and I led our weary heavy horsemen. The sight of enemy horsemen behind them once again was too much for the weary legionaries. Most of their senior officers, the legates and tribunes who rode on horseback, were now dead, felled by arrows. Soon groups of Romans were throwing down their weapons and giving themselves up. Fighting began to peter out as exhausted soldiers and horsemen disengaged from the Romans and merely watched their opponents submit to them. It was a strange scene – shortly before the Romans had been a tenacious foe, now they were beaten men meekly submitting to their fate. The battle was over.

Chapter 16

The aftermath of battle is never pleasant and this day was no different. As far as the eye could see the ground was covered with the dead and the dying. Injured horses, their bodies gashed open and their limbs shattered, thrashed around in agony. Men whimpered and screamed as the rush of frenzy within them quickly faded and feelings returned to their pierced bodies. Bodies cut open by sword and spear blades, bones crushed underfoot by men and horses during melees, and flesh pierced by arrows and slingshots. And then the stench hit me. In the white heat of battle all sense of smell disappears, but afterwards, when the slaughter has ceased and men's bodies are drained of energy, a rancid aroma hangs over the battlefield. The stench of blood, vomit, human and animal dung and urine, the disgusting combination of men fouling themselves, puking as they saw their friends reduced to offal before their eyes, and the spilling of blood and guts during combat. It is this smell that enters your nostrils, infuses your hair and skin and stays there for days. No amount of water will wash it away. Today it was the same, perhaps even worse than before. Men had difficulty controlling their skittish horses as they dismounted and led the beasts towards the river, for both they and their riders were suddenly possessed by a raging thirst.

I too dismounted and watched Domitus and his men move forward to stand guard over the Roman captives. There was no resistance. Where just a short time before they had been highly trained enemy soldiers operating in formation, seemingly invincible, now they were beaten men, glad to be offered the chance to rest. Glad to be alive.

Domitus ambled over as the legion's colour party escorted the golden griffin back to the city. I raised my sword in salute as it and its escort marched past me. The cataphracts around did the same.

'Another victory, Pacorus. Well done.'

'Yes, another victory.' But it did not feel like victory, not with the words of Furius still in my ears. Had Phraates really handed Dura to the Romans? I dismissed the idea. And yet...

A line of Nergal's horse archers were standing watch as the Romans were ordered to stack their shields, mail shirts, helmets, belts and swords in great piles before being herded under armed guard towards the camp – my camp – they had occupied during the siege of my city. It would now be their temporary prison until their fate was decided.

'If any engineers still live,' I said to Domitus, 'they are to be separated from the rest. I will have need of them and their siege engines.'

'They may not wish to serve you.'

'Better that than death,' I snapped. 'Now go.'

He raised an eyebrow but said nothing, merely saluting and striding away.

Orodes walked up, leading his sweat-lathered horse behind him. 'I salute you, Pacorus, you have won a fine victory.'

I looked around at the broken bodies littering the earth, and heard the pitiful cries of the wounded and dying and the moans of injured animals. 'At this moment, my friend, it is hard to tell the difference between the victors and the vanquished.'

Behind me the cataphracts began to dismount and take off their heavy scale armour, dumping the suits on the ground then relieving their horses of their armoured protection. The squires began arriving from camp to attend their masters, riding on horses and pulling camels behind them. As one squire led his master's horse to the river to drink, the other loaded the scale armour for horse and man on to the camel. Tonight they would be sewing plates of armour back onto the thick hide coats, sharpening blunted swords and maces and knocking dents out of helmets. Others would be building funeral pyres for their lords, for we too had lost men this day.

Surena appeared before me on his horse, his face flush with victory, streaked with sweat and dirt, and his tunic torn.

I took off my helmet and armour and dumped them on the ground.

'Help me with Remus' armour,' I said to him.

He jumped from his horse and began unbuckling the straps that held the armour in place.

'I ordered you to stay in camp,' I said.

'I could not stand idly by while you were fighting.'

'If you had been killed, I would have no squire,' I rebuked him.

'But, surely, you wish for me to learn about war.'

Despite his dirty appearance there was not a scratch on him, and he seemed to be oblivious to the horror around him. 'You cannot learn anything if you are dead.'

'Let the boy be, Pacorus,' said Orodes, who was being assisted by his own squires, 'let us be thankful that we are all still alive.'

I pointed at him. 'I've got a little task for you, Surena.'

He flashed a smile. 'Yes, lord.'

'Go and find the body of the Roman general that the queen killed, then cut off its head and bring it back to me, but not before you have crucified the body.'

He looked perplexed. 'How am I going to crucify the body?'

'You will have to ask General Domitus if you can borrow some of his men to prepare a cross and acquire some ropes and nails. And tell him that you are carrying out my orders.'

I pointed towards the river. 'Erect the cross near the water's edge. Now go, and don't forget to bring me back the head.'

He nodded his head and scurried off to find Domitus.

Orodes looked at me but said nothing. Domitus, however, had plenty to say when he stormed back with a sheepish Surena in tow. He jerked his thumb at my squire. 'This little whelp has just tried to order me to give him some of my men, said he had a very important task to perform for the king, and that he could not waste time explaining to me what it is.'

I shook my head in despair. Surena had a talent amounting to genius for annoying people. I held up my hands to Domitus.

'I apologise, Domitus. I asked him to ask you for your help, not to order you.'

Domitus fixed Surena with his stare, who stared insolently back. I held my head in my hands for I knew what was coming next. Domitus smiled at Surena.

'You know the disadvantage with having long hair?'

Surena looked bemused. 'No.'

As quick as a striking snake Domitus grabbed Surena's hair with his right hand and yanked the boy down onto his knees. He moved his face to within a few inches of Surena's.

'All those pretty flowing locks are easy to get hold off.'

Surena's face was contorted in pain. 'Let go of me, barbarian,' he squealed.

Domitus let go of his hair and stepped back. 'Barbarian, am I? You need a lesson in manners.'

Surena jumped to his feet and drew his spatha. Aghast, I stepped between them.

'Surena put away your sword. Now!'

He looked at Domitus standing before him with only his cane in his hand, then at me, and then reluctantly replaced his sword in its scabbard. I then smiled at Domitus, who was far from amused.

'Whatever you wanted me to do,' he said to me, 'you can attend to it yourself. I'm not some slave to be ordered about by some young dung shoveller.' He then pointed at Surena. 'You stay out of my way, boy, if you know what's good for you.'

He turned and strode back to his legion.

'You had a lucky escape, Surena,' remarked Orodes.

'Come with me,' I said, 'and don't say anything to anyone.'

With Surena trailing behind me I organised a group of my cataphracts to find the body of Lucius Furius and drag it by horse to the edge of the river. Surena decapitated it with an axe and the carcass was then nailed to a cross at the edge of the River Euphrates. I led Remus downstream so he could quench his thirst and gave orders that the head was to be taken back to the city and preserved in salt.

Gallia and her Amazons arrived as I threw my tunic on the ground and stood in my silk vest drenched in sweat, leggings and boots. She vaulted from Epona, took off her helmet and then kissed me on the lips.

'You smell like a bullock,' she whispered.

'A handsome bullock, I hope.'

Gallia untied her plait and shook her long hair free. Praxima and the other women also took off their helmets and Surena's eyes lit up as he beheld the mounted women warriors before him.

'You have won a great victory, lord,' shouted Praxima, to which the others cheered and raised their bows.

'I am glad you are all safe,' I replied, my arm around Gallia's waist.

Surena had probably never seen a blonde, blue-eyed woman before; certainly not one like Gallia and certainly not this close up. He walked up to her and smiled.

'I am Surena of the Ma'adan. I have heard tales of your beauty and they have not been exaggerated.'

Gallia eyed him coolly and then looked at me.

'He is my squire. It's a long story. I will tell you later.'

The arrival of Nergal signalled a touching reunion between husband and wife as he and Praxima embraced each other. I smiled. For a brief moment we were back in Italy. As we chatted and gave thanks for our survival, Surena reached out and touched Gallia's locks. She spun round instantly and held her dagger to his throat.

'Do you not know that it is death to touch the person of your queen, boy?'

For the first time this day Surena looked alarmed, especially as Praxima hissed and drew her sword to protect her friend. I placed my hand on Gallia's dagger.

'He meant no offence, my love. He is from the marshlands many miles from here and his manners require polishing.'

'He is an arrogant puppy,' growled Gallia.

'Perhaps so, but you would not rob my of a good squire, would you?'

Her eyes darted between me and Surena, and then she sneered at him and put her dagger back in her boot. Praxima sheathed her sword.

Gallia vaulted onto the back of Epona.

'We ride back to the city.' She pointed at Surena. 'Teach that one some manners.'

Then she and the Amazons were gone.

'That's the second time you have come close to death today,' I said, 'and whereas for most of us it is the enemy who presents the greatest danger, you appear intent on being killed by your own side.'

'Do you really think that I am a good squire?' asked Surena.

I cuffed him round the ears. 'Shut up. Tonight you will join the burial details to collect the dead.'

After Remus had been watered and rested I rode him back to the city. When I arrived at the Citadel, Gallia, her Amazons, Godarz and Rsan were waiting at the foot of the palace steps, as were a host of black-clad Agraci warriors. Each one had black tattoos on their face in a similar fashion to those sported by Malik. I embraced Godarz.

'It is good to see you, old friend.'

'You too, Pacorus.' He released me and stared. 'You have lost weight and look weary.'

'Now I am home, I can rest,' I replied.

Rsan bowed his head formally. 'It is most excellent to see you again, majesty.'

I looked past him at the doors of the treasury, both of them shut and secured with heavy chains. Domitus was right about Rsan – it would take more than a besieging army to tear him away from his hoard of silver and gold.

I dismissed them all and went with Gallia straight to the palace balcony where Dobbai held the sleeping Claudia in her arms, the old woman gently rocking the child and humming a soft tune to her. It was remarkable that one so foul and ferocious could be so tender. Dobbai saw me and nodded, then handed me my child. I brushed Claudia's face with a finger and kissed her forehead. I said nothing for a long time as I sat holding my daughter, day turning to night, with Gallia and Dobbai seated beside me. I stared into the distance, across the calm, mirror-like waters of the Euphrates and into the black void beyond. To the north of the city funeral pyres burned brightly as thousands of corpses were consigned to the flames. At length Gallia came to my side and whispered that it was time for Claudia to be placed in her cot. I kissed her small cheek and handed her to my wife.

'You do not seem pleased with your great victory, son of Hatra,' observed Dobbai.

I looked at her black eyes. 'I've beaten Romans before.'

'There is something else. What is it?'

I turned away from her. 'It is of no consequence.'

She persisted. 'If it is of no consequence, then why does it eat away at you like maggots in a rotting corpse?'

Gallia returned from our bedroom. 'I know there is something wrong, so you might as well tell us.'

'Indeed,' added Dobbai, 'for it is unbecoming for the king to sulk like a small boy.'

I stood up and pointed at her. 'Remember that I am your king and could have your head for your impertinence.'

Gallia was outraged. 'Do not speak to Dobbai like that. You would not be king were it not for her.'

Dobbai grinned. 'It is all right, child, the king has other things on his mind rather than adorning his walls with my ugly old skull. Is that not so, son of Hatra?'

I slumped back in my chair and told them of Furius' words just before he had been killed, of how Dura had been given to the Romans in exchange for Gordyene. I could not hide my disappointment that bordered on despair.

'And you believed him?' asked Gallia.

'Why would he lie?'

Her eyes narrowed. 'Because he is a Roman. And that particular Roman would say anything to rile you.'

I laughed, the first time I had done so that day. 'That was my initial thought, but now I am not so sure.'

'The Roman spoke the truth,' said Dobbai.

'How do you know this?' I asked.

'Because giving away Dura is a small price to pay to solve a far bigger problem.'

My limbs were starting to ache and I had no time for Dobbai's word games. 'You speak in riddles, old woman. What bigger problem?'

She shook her head. 'For a great warlord you have the brains of a camel. You, son of Hatra, are the problem.'

'Clearly,' I retorted, 'what little sense you had has finally deserted you. In case you have not noticed, I have just defeated an invading army and can now go to Hatra's aid, which is under assault from another Roman army. I hardly think that makes me a problem, more like a saviour.'

'To some, perhaps, but to others your ability on the battlefield is no cause for celebration. You have greater enemies than the Romans.'

'Narses and Mithridates,' the names stuck in my throat.

'Exactly,' said Dobbai. 'Your success here will be like taking a poison for them.

'When the army is rested and has recovered its strength,' I said, 'I will take it east and destroy Narses, and this time I will kill him.'

'Why must you do it?' asked Gallia. 'There are other kings who also have armies.'

I held her face and kissed her on the lips. 'Because it is personal between him and me.'

'You might find it more difficult than you think,' muttered Dobbai.

'What do you know of war?'

She held up her hands to me in mockery. 'Nothing, mighty one, nothing.'

The next day I surveyed the damage the Romans had done to the city's defences. Aside from the minor battering the western wall and gates had taken from stone shot and ballista bolts, the other defences were almost untouched. As Domitus had predicted, the enemy had attempted to take the city by storm after they had first arrived.

I stood with Gallia beside the stone griffin at the Palmyrene Gate looking to the west.

'They came in great waves, the front ranks carrying scaling ladders and their archers and slingers covering their approach.'

She cast me a sideways glance and smiled. 'We had no one exposed on the walls, but as soon as they came within range we threw the Chinese liquid you obtained at them. As we were taught we loaded it into earthen pots sealed with wax and with pitch-soaked rags attached, which we then lit. After the pots had been launched they shattered on impact and sprayed their burning contents on to the enemy. It was horrible.'

'But effective,' I said.

'Yes, the sticky liquid that cannot be put out disrupted their attack, and then my girls began shooting arrows at them from within the towers. That brought their attack to an end.'

'Did they try any other attacks?'

'One more, but again it was stopped by Chinese fire and arrows. Then they settled down to starving us out.'

I ran my hand over the stone griffin. 'Not a scratch on him.'

Gallia smiled. 'Dobbai says that no mortal weapon can mark

324

him.'

I nodded. 'So it seems. Why are Haytham's men here?'

'They arrived two days before the Romans. Their commander brought a message from Haytham saying that as we had protected his daughter, it was only fitting that he should return the courtesy. They even brought their own food so they would not sap our supplies.'

As we stood on the battlements, a procession of wagons ferried the captured Roman arms and armour into the city and transported them to the armoury. Our victory had reaped a rich harvest, though I did not envy the parties that had been selected by drawing lots to scour the battlefield, collecting weapons, stripping the dead and digging arrowheads out of flesh. Iron and steel were too valuable to throw away.

That afternoon I sat in the throne room and heard the reports of Nergal and Domitus. Gallia and Orodes were sitting either side of me, while Byrd and Malik stood to one side and the lords were assembled in front of me.

Domitus' arm was heavily bandaged but he looked in good spirits despite his wound. 'The legion lost two hundred dead and another two hundred wounded, of which around fifty give or take will probably die.'

'And the men of Pontus?' I asked.

'They suffered more than your legion. Five hundred dead and another four hundred wounded. They got well and truly mauled.'

I looked at Nergal.

'We lost only a hundred horse archers and fifty horses. The lords likewise suffered only light casualties. Of your cataphracts, twenty-two are dead.'

'And a similar number of mine were also slain,' added Orodes.

'Your loss will be recompensed, lord prince,' I said.

He grinned at me. 'They died fighting for a worthy cause, my friend, that is payment enough.'

'How many Romans do we hold?' I asked.

'Near ten thousand,' replied Domitus.

'And their engineers have been separated from the rest?'

He nodded.

'What losses did the Romans suffer?' asked Rsan.

Domitus rubbed his injured arm. 'We burned around eight thousand bodies; the rest must have tried to escape into the river. Most probably drowned in the water.'

I waved Malik over. 'Your father is a man of honour, Malik. While other kings did nothing to help Dura, his son fought beside me and he sent troops to protect my wife and child.'

'It is an honour to serve you, Pacorus.' The others shouted in agreement.

'And he will be rewarded, Malik. The Roman captives are to be sold as slaves. They will be transported to Palmyra where King Haytham, your father, will arrange for their sale in Egypt and Africa, or wherever else he can sell them. If he is in agreement, I will share the profits of their sale evenly with him.'

'You are most generous, Pacorus,' said Malik.

'You told them that they would be allowed to walk out of here,' said Domitus.

'And I keep my word, Domitus.'

'You inferred that they would be given their lives.'

'And so they will be. I said nothing of their freedom.'

He raised an eyebrow but said nothing more on the matter.

I had to admit it was a generous offer. Ten thousand slaves would fetch a high price.

'I must protest, majesty,' said Rsan, clearly unhappy. 'Your treasury needs replenishing. The absence of trade has greatly diminished its reserves.'

'The reopening of trade will replenish it soon enough, Rsan. My decision is final. Nergal, we will rest for two days and then you and I will ride to Hatra to aid my father.'

'I will come with you,' said Orodes.

'Should you not return to Susa?'

'I prefer the company here.'

The next day, as long lines of Roman captives began their journey to Haytham's kingdom and a life of servitude, I addressed the Roman engineers gathered in a group next to their old camp, nearly a hundred of them. I pointed at their comrades being escorted into the desert.

'Those men are going to be sold as slaves, for that is the price of invading my kingdom.'

Their faces were downcast as they stood before me, three score of horse archers standing guard behind with arrows nocked in their bowstrings.

'But you have a chance to earn your freedom.' A few looked up at this, their curiosity aroused.

'You men know how to operate the siege engines that were used against my city. I should, by rights, cut off your right hands for such an offence.'

Alarm swept across their faces.

'However,' I continued, 'I have decided to be generous. I make you this offer: serve my army and work your machines for one campaign and I will set you free afterwards. I will even give you an escort back to Roman territory should you so desire.'

One man at the front of the group, who resembled Domitus with his hard visage, if not his wiry frame, spoke. 'And if we refuse?'

I jerked my head at the prisoners filing behind them. 'Then you are free to join your comrades. You have one hour to decide.'

None refused my offer.

Riders were sent to the city's population to announce that it was now safe for them return to their homes, and the pontoon bridge was reassembled across the river to expedite their journey. Couriers were also sent to the representatives of the merchants throughout the empire, informing them that the trade route through Dura to Egypt and beyond was once again open. My mood was lifted somewhat when news reached the city that my father had turned back the Romans who had invaded his kingdom. I informed the others of this news at the first council meeting held after the relief of Dura.

'I will ride to Hatra to see if Dura can lend any help to my father,' I said.

'You can forget about taking the legion or those from Pontus who still live,' growled Domitus, his bandaged arm still obviously causing him discomfort. 'The boys are spent and there's much work to do repairing their armour and weapons. The last fight was a hard one and I want them fully recuperated before they go marching off to god knows where.'

'I realise that, Domitus,' I replied, 'I shall take only horsemen with me, and only a score.'

'That few?' queried Gallia.

'Yes,' I answered, 'Hatra's army is much larger than ours, and with the Romans retreating there is little point in burdening my father with feeding hundreds of horses and men.'

'Speaking of which,' added Godarz. 'How long are the lords and their followers staying here? They are eating up all our supplies.'

'Now that we have beaten the Romans,' added Nergal, 'it would be sensible to let them return to their homes.'

'Agreed,' said Rsan, 'otherwise the cost will be ruinous.'

'Very well,' I said, 'I shall instruct them to return home. But your treasury will be more than full, Rsan, once Haytham has finalised the sale of the Roman prisoners.'

'What use is a full treasury if there are no soldiers to protect it,' mumbled Domitus.

He sat across the table from me with a face like thunder, his eyes cast down.

'What is the matter, Domitus?' I asked.

'Gallia told me what Furius said to you.'

I looked at my wife in annoyance. She merely shrugged with disinterest. 'Did she? Well she should not have.'

'Why? They have a right to know. Tell them.' She stared at me defiantly.

'Very well. Before he died Furius informed me that Phraates,' I shot a glance at Orodes, whose face betrayed no emotion, 'had agreed to cede Dura to the Romans in exchange for their evacuation of Gordyene.'

There were gasps around the table. I held up my hands. 'We do not know if he spoke the truth; he was probably lying.'

'And maybe he wasn't,' spat Domitus, looking up at me.

'We know that Crassus financed the expedition against Dura,' said Godarz, rubbing a hand across his scalp, 'and we know that Dura is becoming rich on the back of the trade between east and west. I would say that Crassus, if not the republic, sees Dura as a jewel that he wants in his crown.'

Rsan was looking decidedly nervous. 'Surely the King of Kings does not wish to see his empire weakened.'

'He has no choice,' said Domitus. 'The recent civil war has sapped his strength. He has already lost Gordyene, and Media and Atropaiene have both been weakened. The defeat at Dura has been a setback for Rome, but only that.'

No one said anything for a while and the silence became oppressive. Rsan fidgeted nervously and Domitus went back to staring down at the table, rubbing his arm as he did so. At length I spoke.

'I say again, we do not know for certain that what Furius said is true. Therefore I will still ride to Hatra while the army stays at Dura.'

I turned to Orodes. 'I would like you to accompany me to Hatra.'

'Of course,' he replied.

I left the next day, taking Orodes and a score of Nergal's horse archers. As far as I knew Babylon was still under siege, though as Parthian kings had no knowledge of siege warfare or engines with which to reduce walls, I felt sure that the city had not fallen to Narses and the rabble of Mesene. Once I had seen for myself that Hatra was safe, I would take the army east and relieve Vardan. The journey to Hatra was uneventful and the city itself had been untouched by war as far as I could tell, the gates being open and caravans still travelling on the roads to and from the city. We entered the city through the northern gates and I went straight to see my father. Beyond the city walls to the west was a great collection of tents and many horsemen milling round. I assumed that my father had raised a general muster of the whole kingdom so great was the multitude assembled.

Orodes walked with me through the palace and into the throne room where my father was sitting listening to grievances concerning land disputes, dowries and a host of other civil problems that have plagued kings since the dawn of time. Stewards and other officials were attending him, Assur standing on one side of the dais and Kogan on the other. Two old men were standing in front of him, each one holding several scrolls, and one was gesticulating with his free hand. My father looked bored to death. His face lit up when he saw me, and he immediately stood and clapped his hands to announce that proceedings were at an end.

'But highness,' implored one of the plaintiffs, 'my neighbour has clearly violated the city's ordinances by building his wall at twice the stipulated height.'

'I would not have had to build it so high were it not for the lewd goings-on that accompany your banquets. My wife and I have no wish to see such depravity.'

'Depravity? How dare you. If I was thirty years younger.'

They began to square up to each other. I smiled. Each must have been in his late sixties. 'Enough!' bellowed my father, causing them both to freeze and one to drop his scrolls.

'I will decide on this matter next week. The meeting is ended.'

He pointed at Kogan, who ordered his guards to usher everyone out of the room.

I embraced my father. 'We heard about your victory,' he said. 'Well done.'

'And your news?'

He smiled. 'We have sent the Romans scuttling back to where they came from. Your mother will be delighted that you are here.' He released me and turned to Orodes. 'Greetings, Prince Orodes, welcome to Hatra.'

Orodes bowed his head. 'It is an honour to be at your court, majesty.'

'Hail King Pacorus, destroyer of Parthia's enemies.'

I recognised the voice but thought that my ears were playing tricks on me. They were not. I turned round to see Narses standing in Hatra's throne room. Narses, the man who had promised that my head would adorn Uruk's walls. Narses the traitor. Narses the liar and thief. He must have been skulking in the shadows along one of the walls when I entered. I blinked in astonishment. He smiled at me as though we were long-lost friends. The large iron-studded doors were closed shut and Kogan returned to stand by the two thrones. Orodes stood speechless.

'King Narses brought his army to assist Hatra, Pacorus,' said my father. 'We have decided to put aside our differences for the sake of the empire's welfare.'

'After all,' said Narses smugly, 'we are all Parthians.'

A deep-thinking man, a philosopher or accomplished politician, would have taken time to compose an appropriate response to this effrontery, but I was not such a man. I strode over to Narses and struck him hard across the face with the back of my hand. The King of Persis is a tall, well-built individual, but he was not expecting such a response and I hit him with such force that he was sent sprawling across the floor. Without thinking I drew my sword and took a step towards the prostrate Narses, who was slowly picking himself up. I smiled; I had no objection to killing him here. I stopped when I felt the point of a blade at my throat.

'What, in the name of all that's decent, are you doing?' It was my father's sword at my flesh.

Narses staggered to his feet, his nose was bleeding. His eyes flashed hatred but then, remembering where he was, his expression softened.

'You dare to draw your sword in my palace,' said my father, 'against my guest?'

'You would not accord him that status if you knew his true intentions,' I snarled.

'Put away your sword,' ordered my father.

'I will not,' I replied.

At that moment my mother appeared, accompanied by Gafarn and Diana. They were shocked at the scene before their eyes. My mother rushed over and placed herself between my father and myself.

'Varaz, what are you doing?'

'Pacorus struck our guest.'

'Not hard enough by the look of him,' remarked Gafarn.

'Silence!' shouted my father. 'Hold your tongue, Gafarn.'

My mother looked at me. 'Pacorus, put away your sword. I will not have such scenes in my home.'

My will weakened in her presence and I slid the spatha back into its scabbard. My father did likewise and then held out his hand. Orodes stared in disbelief at me, while Narses, having composed himself, was now standing to one side with his arms folded and a self-righteous expression on his bruised face.

'Surrender your sword.'

I was mortified. 'This sword was given to me by a friend, one who knew the meaning of honour and loyalty.' I jerked my head towards Narses, whose bleeding nose was being attended to by a servant. 'Unlike him.'

'Very well,' said my father. 'Lord Kogan, have my son escorted to his chambers. He will remain there until he has learned some manners.'

'There is no need, King Varaz,' said Narses, 'I do not wish to come between father and son.'

'There is every need, King Narses,' remarked my father. 'Kings do not act like thieves and beggars.'

'Or slaves,' smirked Narses as half a dozen of Kogan's spearmen, their shafts levelled at me, escorted me from the room.

My mother came to see me later as I paced up and down in my old quarters, fuming. Her words did nothing to cool my temper.

'Narses came to our assistance when the Romans were besieging Nisibus.'

'Narses assists only himself, mother. He covets this kingdom, and now I find his soldiers are camped outside the city walls.'

'He and they will be returning to Persis after the business between him and your father has been concluded.'

'Business?'

Gafarn and Diana entered at that moment, both of them looking well I had to admit. Gafarn now sported a neatly trimmed beard, which gave him an authoritative air. He really did look like a prince of Parthia. I embraced them both.

'Do not trust Narses,' I told them.

'I don't,' replied Gafarn. 'Anyone who smiles as much as he does is bound to be hiding something.'

My mother was not amused. 'Really, Gafarn, don't encourage Pacorus.'

Gafarn flopped down into a chair. 'He doesn't need encouraging. He's more than capable of getting into trouble on his own.'

Still the same old Gafarn under the princely appearance.

'You should not argue with your father, Pacorus,' said Diana sternly. 'Family is important.'

'So is truth and honour,' I replied.

Gafarn laughed. 'Truth and honour? He used to spout the same old rubbish to Spartacus, do you remember, Diana?'

331

'I should have killed Narses when I had the chance, and now he defiles my father's palace. It is an outrage.'

'Enough Pacorus,' implored my mother. 'I want you to apologise to your father.'

'And I want Narses gone.'

My mother's tone changed. 'I would like to believe that the King of Dura has respect for his parents, but it appears I am apparently wrong. Send word to me when you have decided to act like a king rather than a petulant boy.'

With that she turned and left the room. Diana smiled her soft smile and held my hand.

'It is just as well that you are good with your sword, seeing as your tongue makes endless trouble for you,' mused Gafarn. 'Congratulations on your victory over the Romans, by the way. You finally managed to kill Lucius Furius. Perhaps you can now march on Rome and amuse yourself until your father's temper subsides.'

'Did you come here just to annoy me, Gafarn?'

'That and other reasons.'

I shook my head and sat down, while Gafarn ordered the guards standing outside to fetch us food and drink. While we ate I told them both about Lucius Furius, of how I had been captured by Chosroes' men and of Narses' threat against Hatra.

'Well, it may be of comfort to you to know that Babylon is no longer under siege,' said Gafarn, dipping a piece of bread into a pot of honey. 'Chosroes could not take the city and so retreated back to Mesene. Next thing we knew, Narses was here at the head of his army offering to help our father.'

'Narses is clever,' I said. 'Having failed to take Babylon, he has obviously abandoned Chosroes and temporarily sided with my father. But why?'

Gafarn shoved the bread into his mouth, smearing his mouth with honey. 'Sakastan.'

'Sakastan?'

Gafarn licked his fingers. 'In return for laying aside his desire to be King of Kings, our new ally Narses is to be granted the kingless kingdom of Sakastan.'

It made sense now. Narses had tempted Chosroes to strike at Babylon with the promise of an easy victory, and had even dangled the prize of Hatra before the greedy King of Mesene, but his plan had fallen apart when Babylon held out and the Romans had not destroyed Hatra's army. Worse, my victory at Dura had raised the prospect of my father joining with me and marching to the relief of

Babylon. So Narses had abandoned Chosroes and dashed to be at the side of my father.

'Did the army of Persis do any fighting?' I asked.

'No,' replied Gafarn, 'your father had launched raids against the Romans that were besieging Nisibus, which was stoutly defended by Vata by the way, avoiding battle but attacking their supply lines.'

'Gafarn was with his father,' added Diana with pride, nibbling a pastry.

'Eventually,' continued Gafarn, 'the Romans were forced to break off the siege and retreat north back to Zeugma. We harried them all the way, and Narses joined us just as the last Romans were leaving Hatran territory.'

I shook my head. 'He's a slimy toad.'

'But clever. Since then he has been assuring your father that he has the best interests of the empire at heart and similar rubbish.'

'And he wants Sakastan.'

'Yes, Pacorus. He wants Sakastan.'

My father visited me later as the sun was going down in the west.

'Sakastan is a small price to pay for peace and stability, Pacorus.'

'If Narses has Sakastan, then combined with his own kingdom he will have the largest kingdom in the empire,' I said.

My father was staring out of the window at a sky that was now blood red.

'Sakastan has no king and no heirs. Surely you must know that; after all, you were the one that killed them all.'

'Porus offered battle and I accepted.'

He turned to face me. 'Being a king is not all about fighting and glory. It is about dealing with realities and preserving the order of things.'

'The order of things?'

'There was no need to fight at Surkh, but you could not resist the chance for more glory, could you?'

'We did our talking at Esfahan.'

'You killed Porus and then won great fame and glory at Surkh, but in doing so you made enemies of Narses and Mithridates. You weakened the empire, Pacorus, do you not see?'

'I see a traitor at your court, father.'

He threw up his hands. 'Do you think that I do not know what type of man Narses is? He is greedy, cunning and ruthless.'

'Then why tolerate him?'

'Because the empire cannot afford to be fighting a civil war and the Romans.'

'So you give Narses what he wants?'

'He wants to be King of Kings, but he has put that desire aside in exchange for Sakastan.'

'And you believe him?'

He raised his eyes to the ceiling. 'It is irrelevant what I believe. But I know that for now we have seen off the Romans and Narses will not plunge the empire back into civil war. That is the present reality, Pacorus.'

'I have heard, father, that Phraates has come to an agreement with the Romans that they will relinquish Gordyene in exchange for Dura.'

Now it was his turn to be taken aback. 'I have not heard of any such agreement.'

I pointed at him. 'You should have been created King of Kings, just as Balas said. But now, because of your decision, we have Phraates who is wholly under the spell of his wife and son, and it is they who guide his hand. That, father, is the reality that I and Dura have to live with.'

He was momentarily lost for words at this statement, but then composed himself.

'Will you apologise to Narses?'

'I will not.'

'Then I must ask you to leave Hatra immediately.'

His pride would not allow him to bid me farewell when I left with Orodes the next day, though my mother, sister, Gafarn and Diana all embraced me at the foot of the palace steps. Diana held Remus' reins as I said a tearful farewell to my mother.

'Gallia misses you both,' I said to her and Gafarn as I climbed onto Remus' back.

'Tell her that we will visit soon,' promised Diana.

Orodes mounted his horse after bowing to my mother and expressing his regret that his visit had been so brief. My mother, her eyes moist, maintained royal protocol and said it had been an honour that a prince of Susa had visited Hatra. How ridiculous it all was.

I did not look back as I trotted from the city. Passing through the city's northern gates I was gripped by a sudden desire to go back and kill Narses. But as I slowed Remus I heard the sounds of iron-shod hooves behind me. Turning, I saw a few dozen of my father's royal bodyguard approaching, led by Vistaspa. They slowed and then halted behind my stationary horsemen, and Vistaspa then rode up beside Orodes and me.

'Good morning, majesty,' his tone was perfunctory, his face expressionless.

'Am I under arrest again?' I asked.

'No, majesty. We are your escort.'

'Our escort?'

Vistaspa's tone was severe. 'We are to escort you to the borders of your own kingdom, to ensure you do not come to any harm.'

I burst out laughing. 'To ensure that I don't harm Narses, more like.'

Vistaspa maintained his expressionless countenance. 'These are dangerous times, majesty.'

I nudged Remus forward. 'For some more than others, Vistaspa.'

I saw little point in riding to Ctesiphon to hear Phraates' betrayal of me from his own lips. His court was infested with malice and intrigue, and even if I were granted an audience I doubted that I would hear the truth. But then, I had no evidence that Dura had been traded to the enemy aside from the outburst of a dead Roman, but the notion of it gnawed away at me like a toothache.

'I could ride to Ctesiphon,' offered Orodes, 'and if it is true then I can plead your case.'

'You would be wasting your time, my friend, though I thank you for the offer.'

Back at Dura life began to return to normal. The streets once again resounded with the hubbub of everyday life as the citizens went about their business. Work began on repairing the western wall and those houses that had been damaged by Roman missiles. Best of all the mood of Domitus had improved markedly. The legion and what was left of the Pontic contingent returned to its old camp beyond the Palmyrene Gate, with the griffin standard once again placed in its centre. The salted head of Lucius Furius I sent back to Rome so Crassus could see with his own eyes the fate of those who made war on Dura.

One morning, following a hard training session in full armour, I paid the legion a visit with Domitus in tow.

'How's the arm?'

He spat on the ground. 'It's stopped throbbing at least.'

'You should have a nice scar to show off.'

He regarded me with amusement. 'Another couple of inches and the bastard would have sliced my arm off. Then I would have had a nice stump to show off.'

'You know, Domitus,' I said, 'you are supposed to be the

commander of this legion. Aren't legion commanders supposed to be sitting on their horses directing things?'

He winced at the thought. 'Can't be doing with all that. The boys are well trained and every man knows what his task is. For myself, I wouldn't be anywhere else when the fighting begins but at the front. Men fight better when their commander is in front of them, not behind squealing like a little girl telling them to fight harder.'

I slapped him on the shoulder. 'You will get yourself killed one of these days.'

'No more than you. I'm just one among thousands when the battle begins, but you stand out like a boil on a senator's nose.'

'How so?'

'Everyone knows that King Pacorus rides a white horse and fights in Roman armour with white feathers in his helmet. They must be queuing up to put a spear in your belly.'

'Well,' I replied, 'like you said, I wouldn't be anywhere else.'

The camp bustled with activity – centuries marched out to drill, to practise throwing javelins, or to hone their sword skills. Others were sitting on stools cleaning mail shirts and helmets or sewing tunics. And all the time centurions armed with vine canes stalked the tented avenues like wolves, looking for infractions to punish. In general, though, the atmosphere was relaxed and confident. The men had won another victory, boosting their reputation and confidence. For their part the men of Pontus had consigned their dead to the fires, nursed their wounds but did not grumble. Their numbers were depleted but they too were in good spirits. Victory is an amazing panacea for all ills.

The griffin was in its tent as before, guarded within and without by its specially chosen colour party. I chatted to the men outside the tent about the recent battle and then went inside. Next to the griffin I saw another standard, a long, thick shaft surmounted by a silver horse's head. Below it, fixed to the shaft, were three round silver discs.

'What's this?' I asked.

Domitus pointed to the new standard. 'I had it made while you were at Hatra. Take a closer look.'

I walked forward and saw that each disc displayed a different design.

'It is a record all the legion's victories. The staff is made from a kontus, one that we found on the battlefield. And I put a horse's head on top to signify the legion's Parthian heritage.'

I reached out and touched the top disc, which sported an

elephants' head.

'That one is to commemorate the victory over Porus.'

I pointed at the middle one, which showed a group of kings being trampled. 'And this one?'

'Surkh.'

The bottom disc showed an eagle with a spear through it by a river.

'And this must be our recent victory at Dura.'

'That's right.'

I was impressed. 'I did not realise that there was a poet inside you, Domitus.'

He frowned. 'It's good for morale, that's all. I had the idea and Gallia and Godarz agreed, so we had the city's best silver smith make the discs.'

'It must have been expensive.'

He grinned. 'It was, and old Rsan wanted to veto the idea, but you know what Gallia is like when someone tries to contradict her.'

'Indeed. I like it, Domitus. Well done.'

Two weeks passed and messages arrived from Ctesiphon that Orodes was to return to his father's court. He ignored them.

'I can do what I like and only I command my bodyguard,' he said defiantly, tossing the latest missive from his father into the fire.

His men were camped north of the city next to the Euphrates. Those that had been badly wounded and were unable to ride any more had been sent back to Susa. The rest had stayed with their lord.

I was sitting with him and his senior officers wrapped in our cloaks around a raging fire, for the nights were cool now.

'I am going to Media,' I said, staring at the flames. 'I promised Farhad I would aid him. I must honour my pledge.'

'I will come with you,' said Orodes, his face illuminated by the fire.

'I thought you had been ordered back to Ctesiphon.'

'I have no wish to see my step-brother or his mother. Besides, I am the son of the King of Kings, I can go where I will.'

'Perhaps it would be unwise to associate with me further, especially as I appear to be an outcast.'

He looked at me earnestly. 'The day men like you become outcasts is the day the Parthian Empire dies.'

His officers muttered their agreement.

I decided to take a small force to Media; no more than a

thousand riders. Half would be my cataphracts, though they would leave their scale armour and squires behind. The rest would be Orodes and his men, plus a few others to make up the full thousand. Nergal wanted to be one of them and was very disappointed when I refused his offer.

'I am the commander of your horsemen, Pacorus.'

'And that is precisely why you must stay here, my friend.'

He remained unconvinced. 'There is no honour in staying at Dura while you go to campaign in the north.'

I laid a hand on his shoulder. 'If I should fall, you will lead Dura's horsemen. I cannot concentrate on Media if things here are remiss.'

It was a weak argument, but he nodded sullenly and that was that. The fact was that Nergal was my right-hand man and only he knew how to command heavy cavalry and horse archers in battle. Without Nergal Dura's mounted arm would be woefully deficient in leadership. To alleviate his disappointment I told him to take a thousand riders to Babylon as a sign of Dura's allegiance, and I told him that he could raid Mesene if he so chose.

'Just don't get yourself killed,' I told him.

Gallia was also far from happy. 'I see no reason for you to go to Media.'

'I promised Farhad that I would assist him when I could.'

It was early evening and she was brushing her hair. Claudia lay asleep in her cot beside our bed.

'He did not come to your aid when an enemy army was sitting before Dura.'

'That is because he had been defeated and his kingdom threatened. You know all that.'

She stopped her grooming and turned to look at me. 'Let Phraates look after his empire and you take care of Dura. He has not raised a finger to aid Media.'

'I made a pledge, it has nothing to do with Phraates.'

'Good, because he is a coward.'

'You should not say that of the King of Kings.'

'Why not, it is the truth. Or is speaking the truth forbidden in the Parthian Empire?'

'Of course not,' I replied. 'I do not want to argue with you tonight.'

She caught my eye and smiled. 'As you wish. Just make sure you come back.'

I wrapped my arms round her and kissed her on the cheek.

'I always come back.'

'Mmm. I suppose. And take that idiot Surena with you. Hopefully he will get himself killed and save me having to do it.'

Surena had become a good squire. I had enrolled him in the Sons of the Citadel scheme and he had shown great promise. He had a keen mind and learned quickly, but he also possessed a mischievous streak that led him astray. He was insatiably curious about the Amazons and had become obsessed by one of them in particular, a wiry girl who had earned the nickname Viper. She looked like an innocent teenager, with her small breasts and short-cut hair, but she had the strength of a lion and her skill with a bow, dagger and sword made her a formidable member of Gallia's bodyguard. Surena had made a point of sitting next to her in classes, as Gallia had insisted that her most promising women should also be allowed to receive instruction. The tutors, mostly middle-aged or elderly Greeks, Egyptians and Parthians, had strongly objected. But an increase in their pay and a visit from the queen, during which she had used all her feminine charm, had won them over. Out of good manners Viper had smiled at Surena and they had exchanged courtesies, which he had mistaken for an invitation to get intimately acquainted. The upshot being that he had patted her backside and tried to kiss her, whereupon she had slapped his face and stormed off. Word of this reached Gallia, who had ordered Surena's arrest. It had been with the utmost difficulty that I had secured his release. Gallia was very protective of her Amazons, and for the most part everyone treated them like a nest of cobras – with respect and at a safe distance. Surena, on the other hand, believed them to be his personal harem.

'He's just a boy,' I pleaded with Gallia, who wanted to hang him from the city walls.

'No, he's a young man who should know better. Viper is not much older than him yet she does not behave in such a manner. Do you think it is acceptable that men should treat my Amazons like slaves?'

'You know I do not.'

Her eyes burned with fire. 'Then don't insult me.'

'He saved my life once. All I am asking is that you allow me to do the same for him now. What he did was wrong, but I ask you to spare his life.'

I said no more and she still seethed, but at last relented. 'I give you his life. But keep him away from my Amazons and me. If he transgresses once more then I will kill him myself, after Viper has castrated him.'

So Surena had a very lucky escape and he left with me for

Media. I said goodbye to Gallia and my daughter in the Citadel on an overcast autumn morning. Domitus and Godarz were in attendance, and an unhappy Nergal stood beside Praxima, who I think was glad that her husband was staying by her side.

'Now remember,' I said to Godarz, 'to send messages to the craftsmen who worked at Dura previously that they will be offered good wages if they return. We need them back in the armouries.'

He grabbed my arm. 'I know, Pacorus. You have created a system at Dura that is efficient so let it work. You concentrate on staying alive.'

'I will pray to Mars so that he will watch over you,' said Domitus, his new scar adorning his arm.

I said my farewells to Nergal and Praxima and told Nergal that he was in command of the army in my absence. This delighted Praxima but seemed to be little comfort to Nergal.

'I should be coming with you,' was all he muttered.

I held Gallia and Claudia and kissed my wife on the lips. We did not exchange words; there was no need. If the worst happened we knew that we would be together again in the next life. Finally I came to Dobbai.

'You think I go on a fool's errand?'

'I think you must stay true to yourself. Besides, there will be nothing happening here to keep you amused, no enemies for you to kill at Dura. Being an idle king does not suit you.'

'I'll take that to mean that you approve, then.'

'Be gone, son of Hatra.'

I hoisted myself into the saddle, raised my hand to all those present and rode from the courtyard. Orodes was beside me with our twin banners fluttering directly behind. We rode through the city and met the waiting horsemen outside the Palmyrene Gate – a thousand riders, each one leading a spare mule loaded with fodder for his horse and food for himself. There was a rumble of distant thunder overhead and then a light rain began to fall as we began our journey to Farhad's kingdom.

We moved at speed through southern Hatra, then swung north once we had crossed the Tigris and reached Media six days after leaving Dura. At the border of Farhad's kingdom we were met by a small party of the king's guard, mounted spearmen who were led by the commander of Farhad's bodyguard, a dour, pale-skinned individual named Cretus. As we rode north at a gentle pace he informed me of events that had taken place in Media since I was last in the kingdom.

'The Romans sent only small raiding parties into Media,

thankfully.'

'And Prince Atrax?'

'Much improved. He is able to ride now and wanted to lead a retaliatory expedition against the Romans, but Princess Aliyeh persuaded him otherwise.'

I laughed. Cretus did not.

'Your sister has great influence in the kingdom now, highness.'

'Really?'

He nodded. 'It was your sister who organised the defence of the city and vowed to stay there and die if necessary. It is rumoured that the king himself now seeks her advice before making any decision.'

I thought of the cool reception I had received from her the last time I was here. Hopefully, now that the Roman threat had abated, her disposition towards me would be better. I was wrong.

It was raining heavily when we reached Farhad's capital, the city and all around drenched by a relentless downpour that soaked our cloaks. Our horses had their heads cast down as they trotted up the great ramp into the city's stronghold, the raindrops having matted their manes to their necks. Inside the citadel, no longer thronged with refugees, we rode to the palace and there dismounted. Dripping wet, I and Orodes would have to pay our respects to the king while the rest of the men went to the barracks to unsaddle their horses and change into dry clothes. Water ran off roofs in great torrents, creating large puddles in the palace square. Guards stood wrapped in cloaks around the perimeter, their heads bowed down as the rain coursed off their helmets. A court official, accompanied by a servant who held a parasol over his head, led us through the palace to the throne room, our path marked by wet footprints on the stone slabs. Farhad was sitting on one of the thrones, Atrax beside him with his wife standing on Farhad's other side. Farhad was nodding in satisfaction when we entered and Atrax was beaming; no emotion was visible on my sister's face.

'Hail Farhad,' I said, halting before him and bowing my head. 'I have returned, as I promised I would.'

Farhad stood up and embraced me, then Orodes, ignoring our sodden clothes.

'Welcome Pacorus, welcome Orodes. Media is glad that you are here.'

Atrax jumped up and shook our hands, much to the consternation of Aliyeh.

'We heard about your victory over the Romans. I wished I had been there.

341

I looked at my sister's narrowing eyes. 'So do I, Atrax.' I stood back and acknowledged her.

'Sister.'

'Brother,' she muttered without emotion.

That night we ate with the king and discussed our next actions. The rain had finally ceased and the night was clear and cool. A great fire burned in the feasting hall for it was late in the year and the temperature was dropping. The conversation had avoided the matter of Phraates ceding Dura to the Romans in exchange for Gordyene, but my sister could not resist goading me.

'Why have you come to Media, Pacorus?'

'We ride to Gordyene to hasten the Romans in their retreat.'

'Do you look for a new kingdom, brother?'

Atrax was indignant. 'Aliyeh!'

'Why would I want a new kingdom? Dura is my home.'

'We have heard that Dura has been given to the Romans.'

I smiled at her. 'I heard that too. After I have dealt with the Romans in Gordyene, I will visit Ctesiphon to hear that decision from the mouth of Phraates himself.'

'I cannot believe it to be true,' Farhad was shaking his head.

'I am the king of Dura,' I said, 'and as long as I live it will remain Parthian.'

'Well said,' shouted Atrax.

'And does Gordyene also belong to you?' queried my sister.

'Of course not,' I replied.

'Then why do you take soldiers there?'

'To ensure that the Romans leave, as I said.'

'I doubt that they will leave now that they have been denied Dura,' she sniffed.

I shrugged. 'It is of no importance. They occupy Parthian territory and must be thrown out.'

My sister picked at pieces of roasted chicken and lamb in her jewel-inlaid eating bowl, avoiding my eyes. Farhad looked solemn while Atrax was grinning like a small child who has just been given a present.

'Your invasion may provoke the Romans,' said Aliyeh at length, 'and it is Media that will suffer if they decide to retaliate against Parthia.'

Farhad cleared his throat. 'Yes, indeed, we have already suffered grievously at their hands.'

In fact the Romans had not invaded Media or Atropaiene after Farhad's ill-judged invasion of Gordyene, though only because they had been diverted by their campaigns in Hatra and Dura.

'Have no fear, lord king,' I said, 'I shall be showing my own banner in Gordyene so the Romans will know who is visiting them.'

'Mine too,' added Orodes.

I glanced at Atrax. 'I will be making no demands on your forces, lord king, though if there are any warriors among your men who would like to avenge Balas, they will be very welcome to ride with me.'

'No!' Aliyeh rose from her couch and stood before me.

'You have something to say, sister?'

'The soldiers of Media are not yours to command.'

I smiled at her. 'I know that.'

She jabbed a finger in my direction. 'I know your game and it won't work.'

'I play no game.'

She laughed sarcastically. 'The great King Pacorus, the saviour of the Parthian Empire, the man whose legacy is endless war and bloodshed. Media's menfolk are not at your disposal.'

It was amazing that she could speak thus in the presence of Farhad, but his silence confirmed the words of Cretus – Media was now ruled by a woman. Indeed, it appeared that the empire was slowly being taken over by the opposite sex. There was Aruna pulling strings at Ctesiphon, Gallia refusing to obey my orders at Dura and now Aliyeh at Irbil. Where would it all end?

I finished nibbling at a wafer dipped in honey and wiped my hands on a tablecloth.

'If, dear sister, we do not take the fight to the Romans then they will surely return once they have strengthened their forces. That is simple strategy.'

Her eyes flashed with anger. 'You delude yourself, brother. You are merely chasing more glory. Well, I say that is a fool's errand.'

I ignored her and turned to Farhad. 'Lord King, Orodes and I will leave for Gordyene in two days. If there are any that wish to journey with us of their own accord, will you prohibit them from going with us?'

Aliyeh jumped up. 'Majesty, I must protest.'

'No, Aliyeh,' said Atrax, 'this is not your decision to make.'

Aliyeh sat back down, looking daggers at me. I smiled at her while Farhad looked decidedly uncomfortable. At length he spoke.

'I do not wish to embroil Media in another war, Pacorus, I have to say. However, if my son wishes to travel north with you, I shall not prohibit him.'

Now it was Atrax's turn to jump up. 'Thank you, father. I accept

343

your offer, Pacorus.'

Aliyeh looked despairingly at her husband but Atrax had raced over to shake my hand and then he embraced Orodes. Aliyeh, fighting back tears and rage, bowed to the king and then left us. I never saw her again before we left Irbil.

Two days later, our mules loaded down with six months' supply of food and supplies, I led a thousand horsemen north to the Shahar Chay River. The last time I was here, two armies faced each other across its rippling waters. Today the riverbanks were devoid of life as I halted at the water's edge. There was a cool wind blowing from the north and the sky was heaped with grey clouds. It was deathly silent aside from the sound of horses chomping on their bits and the banners of Susa and Dura fluttering in the breeze. I looked at Orodes who nodded at me, then at Atrax on my other side, who was staring across the river determinedly. Looking behind me, a long column of horsemen and mules stretched into the distance. Remus scraped at the ground impatiently. I patted his neck and then nudged him forward. The Romans had invaded my homeland and threatened my family. Even if Phraates had agreed to give up Dura, my experience of the Romans was that they were always looking to expand their empire, never the reverse. As far as Farhad's scouts had gleaned there were still Romans in Gordyene, though his men had not ridden far into the interior of the kingdom for fear of antagonising them. Farhad was clearly frightened of them, though thankfully his son was made of sterner stuff.

As small spits of rain blew in our faces we rode across the river and into Gordyene. It was time to take the war to the enemy.

Chapter 17

We crossed the river and headed north. Gordyene is a mountainous land littered with great mountain steppes and meadows. It is also a fertile country, home to a rich variety of wildlife, such as bears, leopards and the Caspian tiger. High above us, imperial eagles outstretched their vast wings and rode the winds. I hoped that we would not be seeing any silver eagles during our time here. We headed for the country around Balas' old capital at Vanadzor, an ancient city at the confluence of the Pambak, Tantsut and Vanadzor rivers. We saw no towns or villages as our column made its way towards the city. Atrax had visited Balas many times when he had been a boy, and without his knowledge we would have been blind in this strange land. I accompanied him as we rode ahead of the column, leaving Orodes behind in command of the horsemen. Atrax had wanted to go on ahead on his own to act as our chief scout but I dissuaded him. I did not want his death on my conscience and nor did I want the permanent enmity of my sister should misfortune strike him. But he knew this country and led us away from the main road, in truth nothing more than a wide track that led straight from Irbil to Vanadzor, and instead diverted us into a great forest that had been on our right flank. The forest was dank and dim, the canopy masking further the poor light.

'Few people live in this forest,' said Atrax as we moved silently through the trees, 'though it is home to much game. I hunted here often as a boy.'

'And now you come to hunt Romans.'

He halted his horse and looked at me. 'May I ask you a question?'

'Of course.'

He looked troubled. 'When I came to Gordyene with Aschek and my father, our plan was to advance straight to Vanadzor, thinking that if we destroyed the enemy's main garrison we would take the city and they would withdraw.'

I nodded. 'A sensible strategy.'

'But we were beaten and forced to withdraw. My point is, the combined armies of Media and Atropaiene numbered many thousands and still we lost. How, then, are you going to defeat them with only a thousand men?'

I smiled at him. 'By avoiding battle, Atrax. There are many ways to skin a cat. All will become clear.'

Three days later we were camped in the forest vastness to the east of Vanadzor. We had brought eight-man oilskin tents with us from Dura, the same type used by the soldiers of the legion. Eight

345

men and their equipment was a tight fit, but with the days growing colder tightly packed men would keep each other warm. We cut branches from the trees; a collection of cedars, beech, ash and elm, to fashion temporary stables, for if left exposed to the elements, even among the trees, our horses would suffer greatly. And without our horses we would be lost. We all took turns cutting wood to make frames for the stables, then creating wicker panels for their sides. The roofs were also made from wicker panels overlaid with branches. It was hard work and many grumbled that they had come to fight not play at being foresters, but it kept the men busy while we waited.

The camp was purposely spread over a large area and guards were posted beyond its perimeter in every direction. Around the perimeter itself we dug pits and placed sharpened stakes inside them, then covered them with foliage, which was changed on a daily basis. There was only one entry route into the camp and one route by which riders could leave – I was determined that we would not be surprised. Each day the forest was filled with the sounds of chopping as men felled trees and hacked at their branches. I was worried that the smoke from the myriad of fires would give our position away, but we were deep in the forest and in any case the autumn skies were filled with mist and rain.

'The men have to eat, Pacorus,' said Orodes, 'and they need warm food in their bellies this time of year. So we have to light fires.'

Everyone practised entering and exiting the camp, both on foot and horseback, and getting to know the area intimately. We set up shooting ranges to maintain our archery skills, though I also organised hunting parties to track down and kill bears, wild goats, boar and deer. Approaching wild animals stealthily was good training for what was to come. I emphasised that there was to be no wastage of arrows. We were a long way from home and would not be able to replenish our stocks easily.

'I thought we had come here to fight,' whispered Surena as we inched our way towards a magnificent Caspian red deer that was grazing at the edge of a clearing in the trees.

'We are,' I replied.

The deer suddenly stopped chewing the grass and looked up. We froze. Had he seen us? We stood like statues for what seemed like an eternity, our hearts thumping in our chests. He slowly turned his head to stare in our direction, displaying his massive antlers. He must have weighed five hundred pounds, perhaps more. He flicked his ears and then continued with his meal.

'Think you can take him?' I asked.

The distance between us was around three hundred feet.

'Yes,' replied Surena.

I strung an arrow as he did the same and raised his bow. He pulled back the bowstring until the arrow's feathers were against his right ear. I too pulled back my bowstring, just in case he missed. He released the string and the arrow flew through the air, slicing into the animal's neck. I shot my arrow, which went into the stag's chest. The animal jerked in surprise, attempted to turn and flee with the two missiles lodged in its body, then collapsed on to the ground as its strength gave way. We both sprinted forward, Surena throwing himself on top of the jerking beast as its life ebbed away. He pulled his dagger and slit its throat, blood gushing from the wound into the earth. It jerked no more.

'You should have shot him through the chest, to hit the heart,' I said.

Surena smiled. 'Too easy.'

'I used to be cocky like you. It almost got me killed. A big Roman centurion nearly cut me in two. Dig the arrows out; we don't want to waste any.'

Surena screwed up his face, but then shrugged and began using his dagger to work the arrows free from the deer's flesh. Soon his hands and the arms of his tunic were covered in blood. He eventually yanked the arrows free and handed me mine. I wiped the three-winged arrowhead on the damp grass and slid it back into my quiver.

'Why are we skulking around the forest? I thought we were here to fight Romans.'

'You are skulking around because those are my orders. That should suffice. However, as you are my squire and I am in a generous mood, I will answer. But first, let me ask you a question.'

He too wiped his arrow clean before sitting on the dead deer.

'When you were fighting the soldiers of Chosroes, why didn't you meet them in open battle?'

He laughed. 'They would have cut us to pieces. We only had knives and a few bows and spears. And we were too few.'

'Exactly, Surena. Now go and fetch the horses so we can haul this magnificent feast back to camp.'

We had been in camp for ten days when one of the sentries came running to my tent. I was sitting on the ground sharpening my sword with a stone, while Surena was grooming his horse. Orodes was replacing the feathers on one of his arrows.

'One of the out-riders reports two men approaching the forest, majesty.'

Orodes and Surena stopped what they were doing. I rose to my feet.

'Good, we will go to meet them.'

I pointed at Surena. 'Saddle your horse.'

Orodes had already thrown the saddle on the back of his mount as I walked over to Remus and did the same. Minutes later we were riding out of camp heading west. I told the officer on duty that we would return shortly.

'Do you require an escort, majesty?'

'That won't be necessary.'

We followed the path out of the camp as the out-rider met us at the perimeter. I ordered him to show me the two strangers approaching and so we rode through the trees. Eventually we came to the edge of the forest and rode on to a wide mountain steppe. A chill wind was blowing from the north as I peered ahead and saw the two riders ambling towards us, now no more than a mile away.

'Who are they?' asked Orodes, leaning forward in his saddle.

'Friends,' I answered, then dug my knees into Remus.

We galloped across the grassland until we reached the mystery riders. I pulled up Remus and halted before the two now stationary men.

'You found us, then,' I said.

Byrd looked as unconcerned as ever. 'Of course, you told me of your plans before we left Dura.'

'Even so, this is a foreign land.'

'Simple enough,' replied Byrd. 'Get to Vanadzor, then look for hiding place large enough to conceal a thousand men and their horses, not too far from the city. You getting predictable.'

'Not too predictable, I hope.' I looked at Malik. 'Hail, prince. I trust your father is well.'

'And in your debt,' he replied. 'He is most appreciative of your generosity.'

Orodes smiled at them both. 'Good to see you again, Byrd, and you too, Malik.'

The spirits of the men rose when they saw the new arrivals. Byrd had become something of a legend among us, the man who travelled like a ghost among the enemy. His status was enhanced by his remoteness; he gave his time only to those who had been with him in Italy, or those few others he liked. Everyone else he largely ignored. Malik was liked because he was a fearless warrior who had served Dura of his own volition. No one gave his race a second thought; he was one of us now. That night we skinned the

348

deer, cooked it over a great fire and then Surena cut strips of meat from it for us to eat.

After we had filled our bellies we sat round the fire as it slowly died, Byrd speaking as he stared into the red glow. He and Malik had journeyed to Vanadzor and I wanted to know about its garrison.

'Garrison was stripped for campaign in Hatra, but still strong.'

'How many men?' I asked.

Byrd shrugged. 'There is a legion camp outside its walls, though many empty spaces where tents should be, plus whatever within.'

'They have horsemen as well, Pacorus,' said Malik, tossing a rib into the fire, 'we saw a few dozen while we were there.'

I shook my head. So much for the Romans giving up Gordyene. They had duped Phraates and had had no intention of yielding any territory. The only question remaining was how long would it take for those soldiers who had invaded my father's kingdom to return to Gordyene. If they were in Syria, then hopefully they would stay there for the winter.

'Not easy to move around city,' said Byrd.

'You are usually able to blend into your surroundings,' I told him.

'City half empty,' he replied.

'The plague?' asked Orodes.

Byrd's eyes narrowed and he smiled. 'No. Romani take away half as slaves.'

I should have guessed. Any land unfortunate enough to fall into Rome's lap is punished for its temerity in resisting, and the slave markets of Italy had an insatiable demand for new merchandise. I was going to say something philosophical about how we are fighting for freedom, but then I remembered that I was not in Italy serving under Spartacus. In any case, I had given the Romans we had taken at Dura to Haytham to share the profits when they were sold as slaves. At that moment I suddenly realised that I too was a slave trader. I hated the Romans even more for reducing me to their level. But then, I did not have to sell the Romans, I could have let them go. So that they could get new weapons and return to kill more of my people? I had made the right decision. I said nothing in response to Byrd's news, merely avoided anyone's gaze and stared into the fire.

The next day I called the officers together and told them of my plans. They were quite simple. I intended to ride up to the city walls and insult the Romans, who would hopefully send out a cavalry patrol to apprehend me. I would take Surena and Vagharsh with me, no one else, and would show my banner to the enemy to let them know who was paying them a visit. The rest of the day was spent checking horse harnesses, saddles, bows and swords. We wore no armour aside from our helmets, just two layers of long-sleeved tunics with silk shirts next to our skin. The winters of Gordyene are generally mild, but each man had brought a thick woollen cloak treated with lanolin oil to keep out the cold. My cataphracts did not have their scale armour or the kontus, but they kept their full-face helmets, while the men from Susa had open-faced models. Surena did not have a helmet so he wore a padded felt cap on his head, complete with ear and neck flaps.

It was a three-hour ride from the camp to the capital, a journey across empty steppe land, past fast-flowing streams and through steep-sided valleys covered in trees. Eventually we reached Vanadzor itself, nestled in a narrow valley and straddling the river of the same name. Atrax had told me that the city had originally been a small settlement on the west bank of the river, no more than a collection of wooden huts protected by a stake fence, but in time the wood had been replaced by stone as trade with Armenia and its southern neighbours had brought a degree of prosperity to the kingdom. That had been over a hundred years ago. Now the city looked sad and forlorn, with crumbling walls and no King Balas to sit in its palace. After his defeat and death the Romans had just walked into the city and occupied it without a fight.

On the plain there were some travellers on the wide track that followed the course of the river north to the city gates, two hauling a small cart loaded with animal pelts, another bowed down with a large sack on his back. Two squat towers flanked the gates. We halted to take stock under some trees by the side of the track where the valley narrowed, around a mile from the city itself. The air was damp and the sky grey, with the tops of the hills wreathed in mist. Balas' old capital looked a miserable place indeed.

We followed the track that hugged the eastern riverbank and then crossed a wooden bridge over the river itself. The waterway was not wide at this point, around forty feet or so, but the water was dark and fast flowing. Then we headed towards the city's main entrance, once again following the course of the river. The gates were open, though aside from two guards standing sentry I saw no other signs of life. Then I spotted two helmets on the walls either side of the gates, then more as legionaries came out of the towers to peer at the three mystery horsemen approaching. We trotted on until we were around three hundred paces from the gates, the walls above now crowded with around a score of Roman soldiers all staring at us. I nudged Remus forward a few paces and then stopped. I spread out my arms.

'Romans,' I shouted at the top of my voice. 'My name is Pacorus, King of Dura, and I order you to leave the city you now occupy and return to Italy.'

Nothing happened, aside from a few legionaries looking at each other in bewilderment. The two sentries turned to face us and instinctively lifted their shields to protect their left sides. I drummed my fingers on my saddle. After a few moments a burly centurion appeared at the gates, instantly recognisable by the transverse crest on his helmet, and began to stride towards us. The sentries followed him.

'Surena,' I said. 'Do you think you can drop the big fellow in front with the fancy crest?'

He gave no answer, but seconds later I heard a twang and saw the arrow fly through the air, to hit the centurion in the centre of his chest. He immediately doubled over and fell to the ground. I pulled my bow from its case, strung an arrow and released the bowstring. One of the sentries had dropped his javelin and was bending down, trying to assist the centurion. My arrow went into his shoulder and he crumpled onto the ground. Surena shot another arrow that hit the remaining sentry in the thigh, who screamed and collapsed on the ground, clutching at his wound. I rode forward and shot three more arrows at the men standing on the walls, my arrows clattering off the stone, then I heard a great clamour as they raised the alarm. More Roman soldiers ran from the city and formed a line of locked shields in front of us, those behind using their shields to form a roof as protection against falling arrows.

I turned in the saddle. 'Vagharsh, time for you to leave.'

He nodded and then wheeled away, galloping back towards the bridge, my griffin banner fluttering beside him. Surena came to my side.

'Should not we be leaving, too?'

'Not yet. It's time to see if you have been keeping up with your training rather than pestering young Viper.'

He was indignant. 'I wasn't pestering her. She likes me.'

'I doubt that.'

'I was wondering if you could put in a word for me.'

I transferred my eyes from the Roman testudo to Surena. 'What?'

'She is in the queen's bodyguard.'

'What of it?'

'Well, you must know her personally.'

I shook my head. 'This may come as a surprise to you, Surena, but I do not know every person who is in Dura's army. Even if I did know her, it is not my task in life to provide you with young girls.'

I heard a blast of horns and seconds later horsemen thundered out from the city, a column of Roman spearmen in two files heading straight for us.

We turned tail and galloped back towards the bridge with the Romans hard on our heels, then raced across the aged wooden beams onto the eastern side of the river. Moments later the enemy thundered across the bridge and then swung right to catch us. I leaned forward and urged Remus on, Surena beside me. There was no bravado on his face now as he continually glanced behind him at the enemy horsemen straining every fibre to catch us. We galloped along the track, the edge of the forest a green blur as we made our escape. There were trees on either side of us as we followed the course of the river south through the valley. The Romans were still chasing us as we rounded a bend in the track and came to a fork in the road, taking the track that veered to the left that led away from the river. We headed into the forest, the Romans at the head of their column screaming at us to halt. Then I heard another sound, a series of whooshing noises followed by screams and the shrieks of wounded and rearing horses. I slowed Remus and looked behind, to see a heap of riders and their horses on the track. My men had positioned themselves at the edge of the tree line, giving them an uninterrupted field of fire. They loosed their arrows as soon as the Romans came within range, pouring a devastating volley at the head of the column. There was no need to shoot at the middle or rear of the group – disable the head and the body will crumble. As arrows hit the first files, horses lost their footing and fell to the ground and those following collided into them. Those further back tried to veer left and right or halt, but their momentum was such that though their horses came to a sudden stop the riders were catapulted forward from their saddles. The rear of the column managed to slow their horses and avoid the mounds of men and horses to their front, but as they slowed they came under a withering arrow fire from my men in the trees. Arrow after arrow came from the forest, each one finding a fleshy target. Some of the Romans tried to turn and flee, but my men lined the track for half a mile and there was no escape. And then, where there had been shrieks, squeals and shouts, the only sounds were the low moans of the wounded.

Riderless horses scattered as my men walked their mounts out of the trees. Romans that had been thrown from their horses staggered to the feet, dazed and confused, only to be felled by one or more arrows. Some raised their arms and endeavoured to give themselves up but there was no pity shown to the enemy this day. When all had been dropped, I pointed at Surena.

'Make yourself useful.'

He nodded, jumped from his horse and went among the enemy. Others of my men did the same, all the time covered by the bows of their comrades. Slitting the throats of a disabled adversary is not a pleasant business, but wounded men can recover to fight another day. A handful of Romans had feigned death, hoping that they would go unnoticed. But not today. While this necessary measure was being carried out Orodes and Atrax rode over to me.

'That was easy enough,' said Orodes.

'The next part will take longer,' I replied.

'You ride back to the city?' enquired Atrax.

'I do indeed, brother. This time perhaps you two would like to accompany me.'

And so the three of us rode back to the gates of Vanadzor, this time with a hundred riders behind us. We did so at a gentle pace; there was no point in tiring the horses unnecessarily. This time the banner of Susa fluttered beside my own. Atrax has wanted to fly Media's standard in Gordyene but his father had forbidden him to do so. Farhad clearly feared the Romans, but I did not tell his son this. We arrived once more at the gates, which were now slammed shut. I told the others to keep well out of bow range as I once more goaded the enemy.

'Romans,' I hollered. 'Were those horsemen the best you could offer? Their blood now fertilises the earth. Surrender now and save your skins, for to fight further is to invite death.'

I saw no movement on the towers or walls, and so after a few minutes waiting I returned to the men.

'Why don't they attack us?' Atrax was plainly itching for another fight.

I shrugged. 'They will come in their own time. I suggest we withdraw and get some food inside us.'

'I want to insult them.' Atrax made to ride forward but I reached over and laid a hand on his arm.

'No Atrax, we have done enough.' His face was a mask of disappointment but I did not want him to get shot for the sake of mere bravado.

We camped five miles south of the city in the forest, though I made sure that I had sentries posted all around. There were other gates out of the city, and just because the Romans had not shown themselves at the southern entrance did not mean that they would not send soldiers from another gate to sweep around our rear and catch us unawares.

After two hours Byrd and Malik rode to where we were camped, our horses tethered to branches and their saddles dumped on the ground. Parties had been sent to the river to fetch water for them, and while we waited for the enemy we checked their iron shoes and groomed them.

'Romani marching out of city,' said Byrd.

I was standing in front of Remus holding a waterskin to his mouth. 'How many?'

'At least two thousand legionaries, plus light troops and more horsemen.'

I gave the order to reform and the sound of horns filled the forest as the companies were assembled. I called their commanders together and they stood in a semi-circle around me.

'Our plan is simple. We goad the Romans, annoy them, and then fall back. We wear them down.'

'We could surprise them, attack from the trees, like we did with the last ones,' suggested one of my officers.

'No, they outnumber us and there is no point in charging legionaries. You might kill a few, but once we get close to their locked shields we will ride into a hail of javelins.'

'What about their horsemen, Pacorus?' asked Orodes.

'We can kill them. They will be acting as scouts and riding ahead of the foot. Kill them with arrows. But remember that our aim is to lure the Romans further away from the city.'

'To what end?' queried Atrax.

'Attrition, lord prince. Grind them down, just like the Romans like to grind down their enemies.'

And so it was. We saddled our horses and then rode south, letting the enemy horsemen see us but always keeping a safe distance between them and us. The road we were on led south to Media, but after an hour we left it and made our way back to the camp we had constructed among the trees. As we moved we left small parties of riders, half companies, in the trees either side of the track we travelled along. These men would ambush the Roman cavalry, empty a few saddles and then gallop way. Once they had recovered the enemy cavalry would give chase, only to run into another ambush set further along the track. I took part in these ambushes, as did Surena, Atrax and Orodes, and they were immense fun. We would wait in the forest some hundred paces from the tree line, so anyone on the track would see only darkness if they stared into the trees. Once the enemy horsemen appeared we would shoot at the front and rear of the group, which would sow confusion and terror, then we could pick off those in the middle as men tried to calm their frightened horses. Then we would ride away through the trees, leaving the survivors to deploy against an enemy that was no longer there.

By dusk the Roman cavalry no longer pursued us. We had killed most of them and the rest had retreated to take refuge with the foot. The latter had been under the observation of Byrd and Malik, who rode into our camp after dark, having dismounted at the edge of the forest adjoining the wide steppe where the Romans had built their camp. I forbade the lighting of any fires lest they give our position away, even though we were deep in the forest. It therefore took Byrd and Malik some time to weave their way in the dark through the traps that had been laid among the trees. Eventually they found their way to my tent where Orodes, Surena and Atrax were sitting on the ground eating biscuits washed down with water.

'There must be four thousand Romans in that camp,' said Malik, flopping down on the hard earth.

'Tomorrow we will entice them into the trees,' I said, 'but tonight perhaps we might ruffle their feathers.'

'Ruffle their feathers?' asked Byrd.

'Why not? Get close to their camp and kill a few sentries. Keep them all on edge.'

Byrd was unimpressed. 'Romani camp in middle of grassland. Uninterrupted view in all directions.'

'We'll just have to crawl, then.'

Two hours later I was impersonating a snake as I crawled on my belly towards the enemy camp. Like all Roman camps it was a neat rectangle surrounded by an earth mound that was surmounted by a palisade of stakes. Inside the legionaries slept eight to a tent, the latter arranged in neat rows and blocks. The night was overcast; if there had been moonlight we would not have attempted our raid because any sentry would have had a clear view of the illuminated steppe. With me were Orodes, Surena and Atrax. Farhad's son has immediately volunteered to come with us and I had initially refused his offer, but he had made such a protest that I changed my mind just to shut him up. In truth I regretted that he had come on this expedition, not least because I did not want anything to befall him. On the other hand he was brave and loyal, two qualities that seemed to be in short supply in Parthia at present.

Before we left camp I had borrowed a dark brown shirt to wear instead of my white tunic, and we all left our helmets behind. So we crawled for at least an hour across the steppe, inching closer to the Roman camp that was illuminated by the lighted oil lamps and braziers within. We carried no swords, axes or maces, only daggers attached to our belts, full quivers and our bows. No one spoke as we shuffled in a line towards our target. It was a miserable night: cold, damp, the air filled with spits of rain carried on a cool northerly wind. Hopefully the Roman guards would be wrapped in their cloaks with their heads down. On we crawled. I could hear muffled noises now. Straining my ear I thought I caught the sound of laughter. Perhaps a group of men was playing cards or throwing dice, the universal pastimes of soldiers the world over. Around two hundred paces from the camp we halted and then did not move for at least ten minutes. There appeared be a guard every ten paces, and if any of them had seen movement ahead their first instinct would not be to raise the alarm but to look again to confirm what they thought they had seen. So we remained dead still and the guard would have seen no further movement; he would shrug it off as being a lapse in concentration or a trick of the mind, nothing more.

I rolled onto my back and reached into my quiver. The arrows had been bound together to stop them rattling during the journey. I slowly untied the twine and pulled an arrow out and placed the nock in the bowstring. Then I very slowly assumed a kneeling position, my right knee on the ground. I peered head and saw a guard's head and shoulders directly in front of me. I drew back the bowstring, keeping my eyes on the target. It would be a difficult shot because the only real target was his face. I slowed my breathing and focused entirely on the target; nothing else existed at that moment. Subconsciously I had already made allowances for the wind and distance. The bow was not a weapon; it was a part of me, at one with my senses and instincts. Time slowed as I released the string. I heard a twang and low hiss, then a dull thud as the arrowhead struck the sentry and he fell to the ground. The others took their shots as I strung another arrow and loosed it. The air was filled with hissing noises as my companions searched out targets, and then other sounds were carried on the wind – trumpet blasts and shouts as the camp was awoken from its slumber.

'Time to go,' I said, releasing another arrow at a centurion, his telltale crest betraying his rank, who was standing behind the palisade barking orders.

We ran as fast as our legs would carry us, my heart pounding in my chest as I strained every muscle to get back to the safety of the forest. We must have covered that two-mile stretch of ground in a time that a Greek Olympian would have been jealous of, because when we entered the trees we all collapsed on the ground, gasping for air. Some of my cataphracts had been posted there as a rearguard should we be pursued, and now they helped us to our feet. For a while I had difficulty standing upright and it was painful to breathe, but eventually our hearts returned to normal and anxiety and stress were replaced by boyish enthusiasm as we congratulated ourselves on a job well done. Back at camp we sat on the ground until the grey light of dawn came, exaggerating our feats wildly. Once again we had given the Romans a bloody nose.

In the morning we broke camp and rode to the edge of the forest. The Romans had also left their camp and were forming into ranks on the steppe in front of us. We moved out of the trees and faced them, though they were well over a mile away and we were beyond the range of their archers and slingers. Their cohorts were arrayed in the centre and the light troops – spearmen with shields but no armour, archers and slingers – were deployed on the flanks. A blast of trumpets signalled their advance. Thousands of men began a steady march towards us. I saw few horsemen among their ranks save a small group behind their centre wearing red cloaks and surrounded by standards. The commander and his senior officers, no doubt.

There were only two hundred of us arrayed before the Romans, deployed in one long line at the tree line. But we raised a great clamour and hurled insults at the enemy as we fell back into the trees.

The Romans followed us, sending forward their lightly armed spearmen and archers first. Those of us on horseback withdrew into the vastness of the forest, but always letting the enemy see glimpses of us as we did so. The enemy thought that their light troops, used to operating in open order, would be more than adequate to deal with a few horsemen among the trees. The spearmen entered the trees gingerly, the archers and slingers positioned on their flanks to offer them protection. They shot a few arrows at the fleeting shapes of horsemen among the trees, but the day was overcast and the foliage diminished the light still further. The spearmen kept moving forward, their shafts levelled and their round shields held in front of their bodies. The archers and slingers, carrying no shields to protect them, crouched low in an effort to reduce their silhouettes. Those of us on horseback put away our bows as we kept out of range of the enemy bows and slings. Further we retreated into the forest, back towards our camp.

Then our trap was sprung.

Hidden among the trees were the rest of my men, seven hundred archers behind cover waiting for the enemy. The remaining hundred Parthians remained in camp tending the horses and mules, and would form a reserve if we needed them. A Parthian recurve bow has a greater range than its Roman equivalent with its straight limbs, but today my men let the enemy archers get close to them. On horseback a Parthian horse archer can shoot between five and seven arrows a minute; on foot this increases to up to ten arrows a minute. When the enemy had closed to within fifty paces a horn blew and Parthian bows began shooting. My men were hidden and stationary and their first volley was deadly accurate – seven hundred arrows sliced through the air and buried themselves in flesh and bone. After half a minute three and a half thousand arrows had been shot at the Roman archers and slingers, who suffered horrendous losses. Most had been hit and either killed or wounded by the first two volleys, but my men kept on firing until the survivors fled. Two horn blasts signalled that the enemy was now running. I turned and gave the order to sound the advance. Now it was our turn to move forward.

The plan was for those on foot to stay where they were as the horsemen counterattacked. We drew our swords and moved forward, cantering through the trees. The enemy spearmen had been left alone while their archers had been dealt with, but now my archers began directing their arrows at them. Ahead I could see the spearmen, their ranks being thinned by arrow fire, then I signalled the charge. Horns blasted and we screamed our war cries as we galloped at the enemy. Gaps had already appeared in their ranks where dead spearman lay on the ground, and in any case among the trees it was difficult to form an unbroken shield wall. A few threw their spears at the onrushing horsemen and one or two found their target, but many had already turned tail before we made contact. And then we hit them like a thunderbolt.

Had they stood firmed in solid blocks we would not have been able to defeat them, but these men were auxiliaries, not legionaries. They were not trained to stand shoulder-to-shoulder with shields locked facing the enemy, to withstand arrow fire and spear storms and the charge of enemy horsemen. And the rout of their archers and slingers had shaken their morale. I slashed left and right at heads and torsos, taking care to avoid spear points, for neither our horses nor we wore armour. On we rode, hacking and thrusting, splitting thin shields with swings of our swords. Many of the enemy had thrown away their spears and shields and were running as fast as they could to escape us. We pursued them to the edge of the forest and beyond, catching some as they fell to the ground and began retching due to their exertions. They just had time to look up before a swing of a sword blade ended their life. Dozens fled back to the safety of the cohorts deployed on the steppe, which were now advancing towards the forest. I chased after one man who still carried his shield. I held my sword arm straight as I closed on him, then brought it up as I rode past him and slashed down, knocking him off his feet as my blade bit deep into the left side of his skull. I slowed Remus and then wheeled him right, then heard a hiss as a javelin flew past me. In concentrating on my quarry I had ridden dangerously close to a Roman cohort that was closing on me. I yelled at Remus and urged him forward, out of javelin range.

'Sound recall,' I shouted, as some of my riders got too close to the enemy and were felled by javelins.

I rode back to the edge of the forest, to be joined by Orodes and Atrax. As the men reformed either side of the royal standards I saw Surena riding up and down in front of the Roman front line, loosing arrows at them.

'Stay here,' I shouted to Orodes and Atrax, then rode back towards the advancing enemy. I halted when I was within shouting distance of Surena.

'Get back, you young idiot. Obey orders for once or I will shoot you myself.'

I turned and galloped back to the men, followed by Surena. His eyes were wild with the excitement of battle.

'Listen for the horns next time,' I said. 'I was nearly killed because I got too close to them.'

In front of us five cohorts of legionaries were getting ready to attack. We had won one relatively bloodless victory; the next fight would be much harder.

'Back into the trees,' I said, 'same tactics as before.'

Except this was not the same as before. These Romans were obviously veterans, because they seamlessly advanced into the forest and then deployed into their centuries, shields locked to the front, overhead and sides.

They moved slowly to maintain their formations and our arrows could make no impression on them. Eventually I gave the order for those on foot to get back to camp as quickly as possible while those of us on horseback maintained a steady fire against the Romans. We did manage to inflict some losses on the Romans when some of them fell into the traps that we had dug, men screaming as they were impaled on stakes in the pits. Their testudo

359

formations were momentarily broken, allowing us to shoot at exposed bodies, but then the Romans would lock shields once more and continue to advance. As they were doing so the rest of the men were evacuating the camp via the other side. Thus ended our fight with the garrison of Vanadzor.

We lost fifty men killed in the action and a further forty wounded, and had shot a great many arrows. We carried on moving east through the forest until we came to a vast expanse of grassland. It was now nearly dusk, but we rode across the plain for another two hours until it was dark and then made camp. We kept the horses saddled in case we had to make a quick escape, for I did not know if there were other Roman garrisons in the area. Fortunately we were not pursued, and so the next day we moved further east once more and pitched a new camp in another great forest that bordered Lake Urmia.

We stayed in Gordyene for six months, operating around Vanadzor and Lake Urmia, launching raids against the Romans and fending off the parties of horsemen they sent against us. After a while we split into three groups, Orodes leading one, Atrax the other and myself the third, riding far and wide to attack isolated Roman outposts and sometimes putting their small garrisons to the sword, at other times being beaten off or unable to storm the wooden towers that had sprung up all over Gordyene. We ambushed supply columns, taking any food the wagons carried. We killed the guards and drivers and torched the wagons, but when the snows came the tracks became impassable and there was no traffic on the roads. As it grew colder we were forced to build huts in the forest to house men and horses and rarely ventured out. We became unshaven, lice infested and filthy. My helmet lost its feathers and rusted, our boots were holed, but we kept our bows and arrows dry and our swords clean and sharp. During the winter we forgot about the Romans and concentrated on keeping our horses and ourselves alive. At the turn of the year Byrd and Malik actually travelled to a small town and purchased fodder from a corrupt Roman official, no questions asked.

When spring came the Romans once again sent out cavalry patrols to hunt us down, so we moved further east out of Gordyene and into northern Atropaiene. The Romans followed us. We were down to six hundred men by this time and were woefully short of arrows. We had eaten all of our mules and many of the men had sores on their faces and bodies due to the cold that we had endured during the winter. Occasionally we laid an ambush for our pursuers, killing a score or more before riding away. But such minor victories only reduced our numbers and ammunition still further. In truth we had become nothing but a group of bandits trying to stay one step ahead of our hunters. My plan to wear down the Romans had turned out to be a flight of fancy – it was we who were being ground down. As we moved further east we reached the shores of the great Caspian Sea, part of the northern frontier of the Parthian Empire. We continued our retreat, striking southeast but still pursued by the Romans.

To save the horses' strength we were forced to spend days walking them instead of riding, the lack of good fodder having weakened them considerably. Most of them, including Remus, had become skin and bone. Only the horse of Byrd remained unchanged as it had always been a scrawny, thin beast. One day, as we were resting in a canyon by a shallow stream under a warm sun, Byrd and Malik rode into camp. Many of the men had stripped off and were washing or lying in the cool water, their first soak in weeks.

Byrd was agitated. 'Romani cavalry very close.' He pointed to the direction from where they had ridden.

'How many?' I asked.

'I estimate two thousand,' said Malik, now sporting a thick black beard, his robes torn and holed.

'How long before they get here?'

Byrd shrugged. 'An hour, perhaps less.'

I called everyone together – five hundred tired men and their equally tired horses. Some were lame and could not carry a man anyway, so I knew that this was the end. They all gathered round me in a big semi-circle; Orodes and Atrax were beside me. The prince was no longer the fired-up youth of last year; rather, he had become a more sober individual, thoughtful though still brave and loyal. I told them what Byrd and Malik had told me. A show of hands revealed that fifty of them had lame horses, which meant that they would not be able to ride to safety, and I also knew that none of us would abandon our comrades.

'We have failed to stay beyond their reach,' I said, 'so the only course of action is to stand and fight them here.'

'Well,' said Orodes, 'I for one am tired of running.'

There were murmurs of agreement.

Atrax smiled at me. 'We've beaten them before.'

'So we have,' I replied.

We had no armour, many had lost their helmets and we averaged three arrows per man. Nevertheless, we saddled our horses and formed up into three groups, each one numbering a hundred and fifty and led by myself, Orodes and Atrax respectively. The remaining men and their lame horses were positioned to the rear. All our remaining arrows had been distributed among those who were in the front ranks. Our tactics were simple – we would charge the enemy and kill as many as we could before going to work with our swords. And after that... I smiled to myself. There would be no 'after that'. I look around. So this is the barren place where I would breath my last. I reached inside my vest and touched the lock of Gallia's hair. Together for all eternity.

I rode over to Atrax. 'My apologies, lord prince.'

'Apologies?'

'I promised your wife that I would keep you safe. I have failed in that promise.'

'Much as I love my wife, I would not be anywhere else at this moment. It has been an honour serving with you, Pacorus.'

Honour. How much blood had been spilt in name of that word? It had seemed so simple when I returned from Italy. I had always carped on to Spartacus and anyone else who would listen in his army that the only life worth living was an honourable one. He had smiled wryly and I thought that he was mocking me, but I now knew that he was much wiser than me and realised that in their hearts most men are corrupt and greedy. They talk of honour when it suits them and then ignore it when it is an inconvenience. But then, it was easy for me when I was riding with Spartacus. I had no kingdom to protect and I did not have to deal with other kings, whose ideas concerning how to conduct diplomacy were very different from mine. I had tried to be true to my beliefs and myself. At the end, that is all that matters.

The sound of horn blasts further down the canyon brought me back to reality. The Roman cavalry was deploying into line. I could see a forest of spear points and a great line of green shields that spanned the canyon. They were in no hurry to charge us. There was no need; we were few and they were many. They would take their time. Though we matched their line in length we could only muster a paltry three ranks.

I turned to Vagharsh. 'Unfurl the standard, Vagharsh. Let them see it.'

He slipped off the waxed sleeve that protected the banner and then held it proudly on his right side. There was a slight breeze that ruffled the material but was not enough to display it fully. Orodes likewise commanded that the standard of Susa be unfurled. Ahead of us the Roman horsemen at last began to move forward. They were around half a mile distant. I looked around. Beside me Surena was placing an arrow in his bowstring, while Orodes was cutting the air with his sword and Atrax was sharing a joke with his men. I could see why his people liked him. He had an amiable manner and quiet courage that never faltered no matter how dire the circumstances. These qualities did not falter now.

'Surena, it probably does not matter now, but I want you to know that you are no longer a squire. You are a cataphract.'

He smiled with delight. 'Thank you, lord.'

He looked round and grinned at the men behind. Those within earshot raised their weapons in salute.

'I'm sorry that it has ended this way.'

He suddenly looked serious. 'It does not mater. I was, am, a poor boy from the marshes. But because of you I have seen great cities and rubbed shoulders with mighty warriors, kings and queens. Why should I regret that I have experienced such things? Besides, everyone has to die sometime, lord.'

In that moment he was ridiculously proud and sat ten-foot tall in his saddle. At least he would die happy. I rode forward to place myself in front of the men; Orodes and Atrax did the same. I drew my sword and held it aloft. The men raised their bows and began cheering, and then, coming from behind our ranks, I heard a low rumbling noise that began to shake the earth. The cheering died away as men turned in their saddles to peer behind them. I rode back and through our thin line to get a better look. Had more Romans swept around us? I halted and saw a great mass of horsemen filling the canyon and riding towards us. There were hundreds of them; no, thousands. Some riders were hitting the skins of great kettledrums with thick drumsticks, others were blowing horns, and above the approaching mass flew the sun banners of Margiana and the Caspian Tiger standards of Hyrcania. The armies of Khosrou and Musa had come.

Momentarily stunned by this gift from the gods, I rode up and down our line shouting like a mad man.

'Let them pass, let them pass. Move aside.'

My men did so as a great block of cataphracts swept past us and then halted a hundred paces or so in front of where we had previously been positioned, men and horses in scale armour, rank upon rank of them as far as the eye could see. Khosrou and Musa galloped up, while in front of us the Roman cavalry had halted upon seeing the horde that they now faced.

I bowed my head to the two kings. 'Majesties, I thank you for your timely arrival.'

Musa, his big round face encased in a helmet that had a black horsehair crest, smiled. 'The King of Dura is a welcome guest in my lands.' He jerked a finger down the canyon. 'Romans are not.'

Khosrou's narrow eyes regarded me and then my horse. 'Well, young Pacorus, it would appear that you have had a long campaign. I think you and your men deserve a rest.'

Musa waved his hand at one of his officers, who galloped to the head of the great mass of horsemen and gave the signal to advance. I sat in awe as the thunder of thousands of hooves reverberated around the canyon and hundreds of cataphracts moved forward as one. Seeing this tidal wave of men and horseflesh approaching, the Romans beat a hasty retreat, pursued by a torrent of Parthian cavalry.

The camp of the two kings was located five miles due east of the canyon, on a large grassy plain that was crisscrossed by small streams. The camp was a sprawling collection of brightly coloured tents of varying shapes and sizes, the largest being the two royal pavilions that stood side by side in the centre. Behind them was a vast fenced-off area that housed the horses of the royal bodyguards, a myriad of wood and canvas windbreaks forming stalls and stables for the animals. A host of squires and servants scurried around like an army of ants, tending to their masters and the horses, digging latrines, cooking food, feeding and mucking out horses, and repairing armour and sharpening weapons. The armies' other horses were corralled in fence-off areas beside the tents of their owners, men and horseflesh as far as the eye could see. And beyond the tents parties of horse archers established a screen of scouts ten or more miles away in all directions from the centre of the camp. It was as if a great tent city had suddenly sprung from the earth.

We spent several days as the guests of the two kings, during which time both we and our horses rested and consumed great quantities of food. We burned our threadbare clothes and were given new robes, in my case a fine pair of leather boots, baggy red leggings and a purple shirt with gold trimmings. I was offered a new helmet but asked if my own could be repaired instead. I gave it to one of Musa's chief armourers, a squat, stocky man with forearms as thick as tree trunks and a neck to match. He examined my helmet with its dents, broken cheekguards and battered crest.

'You'd be better getting yourself a new one.'

'It was a gift from a friend,' I said, 'and I would prefer to keep it.'

He ran his fingers on the inside of the helmet and then held it at arm's length.

'It's a nice piece, I'll grant you that. I suppose I can fix it. Won't be cheap, mind.'

'I will give you gold to repair it.'

This obviously discarded any doubts he may have had about the task. He placed the helmet down on his anvil and rubbed his hands.

'Well, then, I'll get started. A gift, you say? Mmm, doesn't look Parthian. Persian, perhaps?'

'No,' I replied, 'it is Roman.'

'Weren't those the lot that we chased off a few days back?'

'Indeed they were,' I replied.

He nodded. 'Come back in two days.'

On the sixth day I was invited to a meal by the two kings. They had already been generous hosts, giving us new saddles, horse furniture and replacing our arrows as well as our clothes. The men's spirits soared when they learned that our Roman pursuers had been tracked down, engaged in battle and defeated. A great many had been killed and the rest had been captured. No doubt the meal that was being prepared was in celebration of this victory.

The heavy cavalry of Musa wore scale armour like my own cataphracts, but the armoured horsemen of Khosrou wore bands of hardened leather laced together for protection or suits of black horn scales. They also wore leather armour on their arms and thighs. They carried long spears that were lighter than the kontus and on their heads they wore helmets fashioned from thick hide. Each man also carried a bow and quiver, plus a sword and dagger. Their horses were smaller than our own mounts but they were swift and hardy beasts, born and bred on the endless northern steppes. Only the men of Khosrou's royal bodyguard wore metal scale armour and helmets. What struck me was the sheer number of Khosrou's men – there were swarms of them.

I made my way to partake of the kings' hospitality but was taken aback when I arrived outside Musa's pavilion. Khosrou and Musa were seated cross-legged on top of a large square, wooden platform made up of two layers of thick planks lashed together. Carpets and cushions had been piled on top of the platform, and a procession of servants stood around its edge with platters heaped with food and jugs holding drink. But my eyes were drawn to what was underneath the platform, for I could see feet protruding from beneath the planks, and then I spotted the top of a head between the feet, and then another and another. With horror I realised that the platform was resting upon a host of bodies.

'Pacorus, welcome,' Musa, dressed in a flowing white robe edge with red and gold, rose and beckoned me over. Khosrou was dressed in a simple white shirt and black leggings. He bowed his head and said nothing, but noticed my startled reaction.

'Welcome. Sit, sit, enjoy my hospitality,' said Musa, as though feasting on top of dead men was the most natural thing in the world. As I stepped onto the platform I thought I heard a groan from underneath.

I sat next to Musa and opposite Khosrou. A servant offered me a small silver eating bowl, others brought cooked lamb and hare. My appetite had greatly diminished.

'Thank you, lord,' I said. 'Your hospitality is most generous.'

He nodded and smiled. 'It is not often that we have a hero of Parthia in these parts, isn't that right, Khosrou?'

I heard another groan and put down my bowl. I beckoned over a servant proffering a cup, and then ordered a second to fill it with wine. Another groan. I took a large gulp.

'Pacorus does not approve of our eating arrangements, I think,' said Khosrou, a small grin creasing his lean face.

Musa pushed a handful of meat into his mouth. 'In their haste to catch up with you, the Romans gave no thought to the lands they were crossing. I cannot have armed bands roaming freely in my kingdom. What sort of king would that make me?'

'A weak one,' said Khosrou, his eyes still on me.

'Exactly,' retorted Musa, eating more meat. 'And I deal harshly with bandits in my kingdom, as I'm sure you do in yours.'

'Margiana and Hyrcania have an alliance,' said Khosrou, 'so I was more than glad to lend my friend Musa assistance.'

'To cut a long story short,' continued Musa, 'my men scattered the Romans and took some prisoners. They lie underneath us. And I have sent a message to Rome that I will not tolerate any incursions into my kingdom.'

My appetite did not return, though I warmed to their company. Musa was gruff and plain speaking, while Khosrou was more measured in his talk. He had eyes like a hawk and missed nothing. As we talked at least the groaning beneath me ceased.

'I must apologise for my unannounced entry into your kingdom, lord,' I said to Musa. 'I meant no offence.'

'And none was take,' replied Musa.

'Though we did wonder why you were so far from home,' added Khosrou.

So I told them about my promise to Farhad and my expedition into Gordyene. Of how we had battled the Romans and then had been pursued by them.

'I believed that the Roman garrison in Gordyene was smaller

than it was. I was wrong,' I said.

'We have heard that the Romans have been reinforcing their forces in Gordyene,' said Khosrou, 'not reducing them as they promised Phraates.'

'So you know about the agreement between Phraates and the Romans,' I said.

Musa nodded. 'Of course, we are well aware of the machinations at Ctesiphon.'

Khosrou pointed a finger at me. 'You should have killed Mithridates and Narses when you had the chance. It will harder for you to do so now.'

I also told them about the agreement between my father and Narses concerning the latter giving up his claim to be King of Kings in exchange for the crown of Sakastan. Even Khosrou smiled at this.

'Clever, very clever. At a stroke Narses becomes ruler of the largest kingdom in the empire.'

'That is what I told my father,' I replied, 'but he would not listen.'

'He had no choice,' mused Khosrou, 'not with the Romans at his throat and Narses and his army nearby. How's your woman?'

The mood suddenly changed as I told them about Gallia and my new daughter, of how she had defended Dura against the Romans while I had been away from the city.

Musa interrupted me. 'We heard that you used her and your child as bait for the Romans to take.'

'No, lord, that is untrue. I told her to seek refuge in Hatra but she ignored me.'

'Your reputation increased greatly when the story spread. Pacorus the Pitiless is your name in these parts,' said Khosrou with approval.

'And what will you do now?' asked Musa, holding out his cup for a servant to fill.

'Go to Ctesiphon,' I replied, 'so that I may hear from Phraates himself of the agreement he made with the Romans.'

Khosrou exchanged glances with Musa. 'We are coming with you. Affairs in the empire need settling.'

The two kings did not take their armies south to Ctesiphon, their royal bodyguards, their wagons and spare horses sufficing as escorts. The combined royal retinues still numbered over four thousand men, plus my own party of five hundred, now refreshed and re-equipped. My helmet had been repaired and once again it sported a crest of white goose feathers. Remus had a new saddle

367

and iron shoes and his constitution had benefited greatly from a plentiful supply of good fodder. I rode beside Khosrou and Musa, with Atrax and Orodes immediately behind, followed by the royal standards. Musa sent couriers ahead requesting passage through Atropaiene, which was freely given by Aschek. Indeed, he himself insisted that we journey via his capital. He was a much-changed man since the last time I had seen him, with dark-rimmed eyes and sunken cheeks. He looked as though he carried the weight of the world on his shoulders. The defeat at the hands of the Romans had obviously shaken him to the core, but he seemed genuinely glad to see us and even smiled when Musa informed him that he would fight to preserve the territorial integrity of his own kingdom and that of Atropaiene. And when Khosrou said that he too would lend Atropaiene assistance if required, Aschek was temporarily relieved of his black mood. But gloom and despondency hung over his palace like low cloud, and I could tell that the fight had been knocked out of him.

'You should have taken your whole army into Gordyene, Pacorus.'

'It needed rest and replenishment after our fight with the Romans,' I replied.

He shoulders slumped. 'Is there no end to these Romans?'

Ctesiphon – grand, sprawling, slightly ramshackle and decadent. The first time I had visited the royal residence it had been a centre of power. The aged Sinatruces had maintained its defences and garrison, had kept the numbers of his courtiers and staff at a minimum, and had not abused the office of King of Kings. I had seen him in his autumn years when his body was feeble and giving up on him, but his mind was still sharp to the end. He knew that empires crumble from within, and had sought to keep the petty jealousies and ambitions of the empire's kings in check. When he first became King of Kings he had done this by force, leading armies to crush his enemies and laying waste their lands to set an example. His reputation was fierce, but he was also a fair ruler who forgave his truly repentant enemies and never bore a grudge. He stamped down on any signs of treachery ruthlessly, however, and was careful not to abuse his high rank. In return the kings gave him obedience and the empire flourished. Above all, Sinatruces was a good judge of character. How different was his son.

Ctesiphon was now a place of catamites, whores and debauchery. Incense filled our nostrils as soon as we entered the palace, its corridors filled with gaudily dressed courtiers and their capricious wives. Men walked arm-in-arm with other men while eunuchs with shaved heads and dark make-up around their eyes regarded us warily. Even the guards looked decadent, dressed as they were in red boots, bright yellow baggy leggings and tops with bright red felt caps on their heads. They carried wicker shields painted white and carried spears with brightly polished blades.

'They wouldn't last five minutes on the battlefield,' Khosrou mumbled to me in disgust.

The throne room had undergone a transformation since the last time I was here. There were several throne rooms in the palace but this was the largest. Under Sinatruces they had always been sombre, foreboding places designed to intimidate guests, but now their purpose was to awe visitors. The stone pillars had been cased in gold leaf and the walls had been painted white. White marble tiles covered the whole of the floor, while the royal dais was covered with small red tiles. Phraates and his queen sat side-by-side on the dais, with Mithridates hovering like a vulture on the high king's left and a portly court official standing behind the King of Susiana. A group of beautiful, haughty women dressed in expensive white robes and dripping with gold jewellery stood next to the dais near the queen, while clustered around the great columns were groups of courtiers.

I stood before the dais, Khosrou on my right and Musa on my left, Atrax and Orodes completing the line. All chatter died away as we bowed our heads to Phraates. Aruna displayed her usual icy beauty, though Phraates looked withered and withdrawn, bewildered even. He waved his hand at us but his eyes were blank and his stare vacant. I wondered if he was drugged.

'Welcome to Ctesiphon.' Phraates' voice was feeble.

There was an awkward silence. Courtiers looked at each other and the queen's serpent-like eyes fixed me. I decided to grasp the cobra by the neck.

'Lord king, I have come to your court to seek clarity on a most pressing issue.'

Phraates' brow furrowed. 'Issue?'

'Yes, highness, for I have heard that you have traded my kingdom for Gordyene. If so, I have to report that the Romans have not evacuated Gordyene. I know, for I was there not long ago.'

Phraates looked alarmed and cast his eyes down. Musa then spoke.

'What King Pacorus says is true, great one. I and King Khosrou were forced to defend our realms again these Romans who wandered uninvited into our domains.'

'And why was this so, King Musa?' asked Mithridates.

369

Musa frowned. 'Why? Because they sent soldiers into my kingdom, that is why.'

Mithridates nodded gravely. 'But surely, lord king, if they had not been provoked they would not have strayed into your kingdom.'

The queen was nodding. I knew where this was leading.

'The fact is,' continued Mithridates, 'that King Pacorus' ill-judged adventure provoked the Romans into retaliating.'

'Are we to let Rome dictate to us?' I asked. 'Are its armies free to roam at will throughout the empire, to burn and loot with impunity?'

'Of course not,' said Phraates, looking at me, some fire in his eyes at last, 'but you have provoked them as my son says, Pacorus. It is a most disagreeable situation.'

'You should demand that the Romans retreat from Gordyene, great one,' said Musa.

Mithridates smiled. 'Alas, we are not in a position to demand. The recent civil war has weakened the empire.'

Musa turned on Mithridates. 'I was not addressing you. Be silent.'

For once Mithridates was lost for words, though his mother was not.

'Is that how you speak in the presence of the King of Kings, Musa?' Her voice was filled with venom. Musa ignored her and glared at Mithridates.

'I must ask again, highness,' I said, 'if these rumours of the agreement to trade Dura for Gordyene are true.'

'Well,' muttered Phraates, 'you must understand, Pacorus, that our position was and is most delicate.'

'The answer is yes,' spat Mithridates, 'Dura was ceded to the Romans in exchange for the return of Gordyene to the empire.'

I felt a surge of anger course through me. So my kingdom had been traded like a cheap trinket in the marketplace. In that moment any respect I might have had for Phraates evaporated. He was beneath contempt, while his son and mother were not even worthy of thought.

'Dura is my kingdom,' I said slowly, 'and none may decide its fate except its king.'

'Except that it is not your kingdom,' said Mithridates.

'What?'

Mithridates turned and ordered the portly man who had been standing behind him to step forward. He had pale skin and a wispy light brown beard, with small piggy eyes that darted left and right nervously. He held his effeminate hands in front of his body, his fingers short and puffy.

'This is Ashlen,' continued Mithridates, 'my father's chancellor and considered something of a legal expert when it comes to the affairs of the empire.'

My patience was fast running out. 'Is there any point to this?'

Mithridates sneered at me. 'Ashlen, explain to "King" Pacorus the legal status of Dura.'

Ashlen shuffled forward a few more steps. 'Well,' his voice was slightly high pitched, 'the lands on the western bank of the Euphrates, that were and are administered by the city of Dura, have always been part of the Kingdom of Susiana, not a separate kingdom per se.' He looked at Mithridates.

'Please continue, Ashlen,' said Mithridates.

'Yes, well, Dura was technically a region that was used by the Great Sinatruces as a place of exile for undesirable elements.'

'What point is this idiot trying to make?' I said in exasperation.

'The point,' retorted Mithridates, 'is that my grandfather gave you Dura, which at the time was actually part of my father's kingdom, that is, Susiana. That being the case, he is only too pleased to exchange it for Gordyene.'

This was ludicrous. 'And what of the thousands of Parthians who inhabit Dura and the thousands more who live on its lands.'

Mithridates held out his hands. 'What of them? They were sent there in the first place because the empire did not want them. Thieves and beggars, most of them. I should know, I had the misfortune of ruling over them for a while.'

Mithridates stood with a smirk on his face, while the courtiers and the queen's ladies looked down their noses at me.

'So be it,' I announced. 'But I will defend my kingdom and all those who live in it, legality or no.'

Mithridates guffawed. 'Dura is tiny. What chance will you and it stand when the Romans send a larger army against you, standing all alone against their host of legions?'

'Not alone,' it was the first time that Khosrou had spoken. 'Pacorus is my friend and I will stand by him, even if others will not.'

'As will I,' announced Musa.

'And I,' said Orodes.

'Media also stands with Dura,' said Atrax.

Mithridates looked alarmed, as did Phraates. They may not have cared about me, but when a ruler such as Khosrou spoke men listened. It was rumoured that he could raise an army of a hundred thousand men, and Margiana was a power that could certainly make the empire tremble.

Phraates rose from his throne, his face gaunt and pale. 'Musa and Khosrou, we do not wish to stir your anger, but we must bring Gordyene back into the empire.'

'Then take it back, high king,' replied Khosrou, 'for you have only to give the word and my army is at your disposal.'

Phraates managed a wry smile and then sat back down. 'There is no point in shedding an ocean of blood when a mere document will achieve our aims.'

'Lord king,' said Khosrou, 'you cannot sacrifice Dura just for the sake of averting war.'

'Cannot?' snapped Mithridates, 'my father is the King of Kings.'

Khosrou turned on Mithridates. 'I was not addressing you, boy.'

'Mithridates is a king like you,' said the queen.

'Not like me, lady,' said Khosrou, 'for I do not crawl on my belly as he does.'

I laughed and the hall erupted in anger, courtiers jabbing their fingers at Khosrou and the queen's ladies chattering in alarm like a gaggle of geese. The guards around the hall moved menacingly towards us. Eventually Mithridates raised his hands to still the commotion.

'King Khosrou, we are all friends here, or should be.'

Khosrou was unmoved. 'Friends do not abandon each other.'

'I must have Gordyene back,' said Phraates.

'Then take it back, highness,' I said. 'Dura's army is at your disposal.'

'No,' for once Phraates' voice was firm. 'You have caused too much war, Pacorus. You are no longer welcome at Ctesiphon.'

He waved to the guards who levelled their spears and moved to circle me. So it had come to this – all the blood that my men had shed keeping Phraates on his throne and now I was being treated like an outcast, a common criminal. In that moment I despised Phraates and his whole family. No, not his whole family; for as I bowed and then turned to walk from the hall, Orodes accompanied me.

Phraates stood up once more. 'Those who leave with Pacorus will likewise be unwelcome here.'

'Orodes,' said Mithridates, 'would you turn your back on your family?'

'I have no family,' he replied, marching beside me.

Seconds later I was joined by Khosrou, Atrax and Musa. Outside the palace we collected our horses and rode from Ctesiphon to our camp pitched ten miles north of the palace. I never saw Phraates again.

The next day the two kings struck camp and headed back to their homelands. I decided to ride north with them, before heading west to Media to deliver Atrax back to his wife. Khosrou seemed unconcerned by the recent events.

'Alas for Phraates, an innocent in a nest of vipers.'

'Things will get worse while he's high king,' said Musa, 'we'd better keep our sword blades sharp and our bowstrings taught.'

'What will you do, now, Pacorus?' asked Khosrou.

'Go home, lord, back to my family.'

He nodded. 'A wise choice. You and your wife are always welcome in Margiana. I would like to see your blonde beauty again.'

'Thank you, lord. I will bring her north to see you, I promise.'

'The same goes for me,' added Musa.

We said our farewells to the two kings at the eastern border of Media. I, Orodes and Atrax then rode west to Irbil. Byrd and Malik rode ahead to announce our arrival, and some miles from the city we were met by a large party of Farhad's bodyguard. They were glad to see their prince in one piece, as was his wife when we reached the palace. When we marched into the hall I noticed that there were now three thrones on the dais. My sister's power and influence in Media was obviously growing. The reunion between husband and wife was tender and touching, and afterwards as Atrax sat between Farhad and his wife he held her hand and grinned at her like a small child. Farhad himself seemed happy and relaxed now that his son and heir was back at his side. That evening he gave a feast for all of us who had returned from Gordyene in his great hall. I sat on the top table on the left side of the king, with Orodes, Malik and Byrd beside me. Atrax sat on Farhad's other side, next to Aliyeh. As the evening progressed and more wine was consumed, many of Farhad's bodyguard grumbled that they should have been allowed to accompany their prince, whose reputation for valour had increased markedly during his absence. Farhad told them they obeyed orders and were not free to go on personal crusades, but I could tell that he was pleased with his son and the outcome of our expedition north.

'The Romans have been keeping very quiet in Gordyene of late. I receive reports that they are reducing their garrison.'

I said nothing but doubted the accuracy of those reports.

'We also received news from Ctesiphon that the high king is

displeased with you, Pacorus, and that you are banished and your kingdom has been given to the Romans.' There was a triumphant tone in my sister's voice.

I decided not to rise to the bait. 'It is true, sister, I have displeased Mithridates and his mother, it seems. It is of no consequence.'

'Really?' she was positively gloating now. 'But have you also heard that King Narses has been made lord high general of the empire?'

My heart sank. 'No, I had not.'

'It would appear that you have made yourself an enemy of the whole empire.'

'You are wrong, Aliyeh,' said Atrax, 'Pacorus has many friends, Media among them.'

But my sister's news had dampened my appetite and I did not enjoy the rest of the evening. All I desired was to get back to Dura. It was now seven months since I left, too long to be away from Gallia and Claudia in the service of a king who was no longer my friend.

Chapter 18

Seven months and ten days after I had left Dura I rode across the pontoon bridge over the Euphrates and returned to my kingdom. It was good to be back and I inhaled the rich aroma of horses, camels and spices coming from the heavy traffic on the road going east and west. Indeed, so choked was the road leading to the bridge that I ordered my horsemen to dismount and walk through the throng. We removed our helmets. Our bows were in their cases affixed to our saddles. Ahead of us was a fat man bellowing at the drivers of his camel train, who were allowing too wide a gap to develop between each beast.

'Keep them together,' he shouted, 'if we get separated in this crowd it will take hours to get you all together again. And we are on a tight schedule. Use your sticks!'

I walked up behind him, Remus following. 'A busy day, friend?'

He turned to look at me, shielding his eyes from the sun as he did so. He had a dirty brown turban on his head and grey stubble on his chin. 'I blame the idiot who built this bridge for all this mess.'

'But surely,' I replied, 'it is quicker crossing here than further upstream?'

He looked at me as though I was a simpleton. 'Of course, but they should have built two bridges, one for eastern traffic and one for western traffic. Quite simple, though I suppose that king in his palace up there,' he gestured at the Citadel sitting atop the escarpment, 'thinks it's great fun to see us all struggle like this. Charges us for the privilege as well.'

By this time my men had made the congestion worse, as mules, horses, camels and dozens of men and women tried to get on the bridge. It was chaos, and soon people were arguing and pushing and shoving each other as tempers ran high.

'You see?' said the merchant, shaking his head, 'if he had built two bridges we wouldn't have all this. Keep those camels together, you sons of whores.'

Then we heard a blast of trumpets and whistles, which startled the beasts and briefly made everyone forget their grievances. Remus flicked his tail nonchalantly – he had heard those sounds many times before. Seconds later a century of Dura's legionaries pushed its way through the crowd, the men ordering some to retreat back down the road and others to continue with their journey over the bridge. They used their shields to herd people back, while the centurion at the front employed his vine cane to 'persuade' the more recalcitrant to move aside. Then they were in front of me.

The centurion frowned and then his eyes widened as he recognised me. He stopped and bowed his head.

'Majesty, forgive me, I did not know that you were back at the city.'

'Why should you? A lot of people on the road, I see.'

He shook his head. 'It is easier fighting than keeping control of this mob, majesty.'

He turned around. 'Clear a path, clear a path for the king.'

The merchant's mouth opened as I mounted Remus. 'I will think on your suggestion of a second bridge. Shamash keep you safe on your journey.'

I raised my hand to the centurion as his men cleared a path on the bridge and we rode across it and back to the city. The watchouts on the towers saw us coming and sent word back to the Citadel, so that when we rode through the Palmyrene Gate a guard of honour was waiting for us, as was another in the Citadel itself. And there, on the steps, in boots, leggings and a white shirt edge with blue, her long blonde hair shimmering in the light, stood Gallia, my gorgeous Gallic queen. I vaulted from Remus, ran up the steps and embraced her, locking my lips on hers. The Amazons arrayed behind her began rapping the ends of their bows on the flagstones in salute and my men began cheering. Claudia, in the arms of Dobbai, began crying due to the din. I released Gallia and scooped up Claudia kissing her forehead, then wrapped an arm around Gallia's shoulders.

'You have been gone too long,' said Gallia, struggling to hold back the tears.

I too was choking with emotion. 'Yes. I have done with the empire and politics. This is my home and this is where I stay from now on. No more adventures for me.'

We held each other closely as I dismissed the men and went into the palace with Claudia in my arms and Gallia beside me. Dobbai trailed after us. I had hoped that I could spend some time alone with my family, but Rsan arrived after dealing with a trading dispute in the city, followed by Godarz.

'It is good to see you again, majesty,' remarked Rsan, bowing his head, spreading his arms out wide in front of him in homage. 'The financial affairs of the city are in order, you will be glad to hear.'

'I don't doubt it,' I said, one leg drooped over the arm of my throne. 'Trade appears to be thriving if what I saw on the road today is anything to go by.'

'Indeed, indeed,' smiled Rsan, 'though our overheads are still high.'

I embraced my old friend Godarz when he arrived, who likewise expressed his happiness at my return.

'Last we heard you were in some god-forsaken hole near the Caspian Sea.'

'No place is god forsaken,' I replied.

Later Domitus and Nergal arrived at the Citadel, the former giving me a hearty hug.

'You are forbidden to go away again without the army at your back.'

He noticed my purple top. 'What's this, gone all oriental on us?'

'No, Domitus, it was a gift from a friend.'

'You should burn it,' he sniffed, 'the lads will think you've gone soft.'

'And how are they?'

He grinned. 'Lean and mean and ready for another fight.'

The next day, after I had spent the night hours and the morning alone with my wife, I called everyone together on the palace terrace. In the early evening the heat of the day had abated. Dobbai attended, as did Orodes, now a prince without a home, Malik and Byrd. I told them what had happened in Media and how we had been saved by Musa and Khosrou. Of how we had journeyed to Ctesiphon, where the rumours about Dura being given up to the Romans were confirmed to me by the high king himself.

'What of it?' said Gallia, 'we are here and will defend our home no matter what an idiot king says, no offence meant, Orodes.'

'And none taken, lady,' he replied. 'Would that there were more kings in Parthia who had your courage and determination.'

There were murmurs of approval from all present. Even Rsan managed an enthusiastic nod.

'Phraates is not long for this world,' said Dobbai, suddenly. She looked at Orodes.

'You were lucky to escape with your life; your father will not be so lucky.'

Orodes was outraged. 'You are wrong. No one would dare strike down the King of Kings.'

Dobbai laughed. 'What is the King of Kings but the guardian of a meaningless title who sits in his palace at the behest of the other kings? You think your brother...'

'Half-brother,' Orodes corrected her.

Dobbai ignored him. 'You think your brother will wait until your father is dead before he wears the high crown? And you think that viper of his wife cares about Phraates, whose weakness is apparent throughout the whole world? Mithridates wishes to sit on Ctesiphon's throne.'

'So does Narses,' I added.

Dobbai stood up and began pacing the terrace. 'You are right in that, son of Hatra, though the only thing you have been right in of late. Narses and Mithridates are united in their ambition, but their alliance is only temporary.' She stopped and jabbed a bony finger at me. 'You should have killed them long ago. Now they will return to haunt you.'

'I have more urgent things to think about, the Romans for one.'

She raised her eyes to the heavens in despair. 'The Romans, what of them?'

'They will be marching on Hatra again soon enough,' said Orodes, 'now that my father has ceded Dura to them.'

Dobbai waved a hand at him. 'The desert will rise up and see them off. You should look to the east.'

'Speaking in riddles again, Dobbai?' I queried.

'The only riddle is why you let your enemies live?' She then walked over to Gallia, kissed her on the cheek and shuffled from the terrace.

We resumed discussing matters at hand. It was agreed that Malik and Byrd should ride to Syria to discern the movements of the Romans, and to gather news of any new army that they were raising to throw against us. Rsan reported that Haytham had sent a large amount of gold to Dura's treasury, half the proceeds of the sale of the Roman prisoners that we had taken at the battle near the city last year.

'What about their engineers?' I asked Domitus.

'Growing fat and lazy on the food we give them,' he replied.

'And their siege engines?'

'All safe and in working order.'

Nergal reported that he had visited Babylon as ordered and that Vardan and Axsen were safe and their city unharmed.

'The walls of Babylon are high, Pacorus. Chosroes could not take it and so retreated after burning all the outlying villages.'

'Will Vardan march against Chosroes, Nergal?' I asked.

Nergal shook his head. 'Not unless Dura marches beside him, but even then I suspect Babylon has no appetite for war.'

'Chosroes will have to wait,' I said, 'we must look to our own defences first. Especially as we have a new lord high general who might just be tempted to try his luck against us.'

'The last we heard,' remarked Nergal, 'he was preoccupied with subduing rebellious tribes in Sakastan.'

'Perhaps someone will stick an arrow in him,' said Gallia.

'Alas, my love,' I replied, 'I doubt that we will be that lucky.'

'The Romans won't take kindly to have been given a good thrashing here, Pacorus,' remarked Godarz. 'They will be back.'

He was right, of course, but the question was – when would they return? It was late spring now, and I estimated that there would be no campaigning until the fierce heat of the summer had disappeared.

During the days that followed I went to see Dura's lords to tell them the news of developments at Ctesiphon. I could have ordered them to attend me at Dura, but it gave me an excuse to visit them and to take Gallia and her Amazons with me. They liked entertaining their queen and I liked to show her off to the kingdom. Her blonde hair and her women warriors endlessly fascinated them, the more so since her exploits in defending Dura against the Romans. No Parthian woman had done such a thing before.

'But I'm not Parthian,' she whispered to me one evening as we were being entertained by a group of jugglers throwing swords above their heads as though they were scrolls.

'You are now, my love. They have adopted you.'

My own escort included Surena, now a fully fledged cataphract, and Orodes, whose banishment from his own kingdom had been announced throughout the empire. It was a terrible slight but one which he took in his stride. Everyone made him welcome at Dura and Gallia wanted him to stay with us permanently. But though he maintained his jovial, endearing manner, I think his father's abandonment of him cut him to the core. Surena, on the other hand, walked around without a care in the world, though I noticed that he always gave Gallia a wide berth. He never let an opportunity slip to be near Viper, though, and his boyish charm and confidence began to weaken her defences, just as a besieging army grinds down a city.

On the way back to Dura we diverted our journey to pay Haytham a visit. We found him at a much-enlarged Palmyra, which had become a veritable tent city. Trade was excellent and the Agraci had obviously profited handsomely from it. Indeed, there was even some discourse between Dura's lords and Haytham's people, a thing previously unheard of.

'Trade means profit and while there's money to be made there's no point in slitting each other's throats.' Haytham may have been a king but his tent was austere and his clothing functional. No decadent comforts for him.

'You should erect some buildings, lord,' I suggested. 'I can send you some of Dura's architects if you wish.'

He shook his head. 'We can pack up and disappear into the desert if the need arises. The whole of Palmyra can vanish like a mirage.'

'Why would you wish to do that?' asked Gallia, Rasha snuggled up in her arms.

'We still have many enemies,' said Haytham. 'Romans to the west and Parthians in the east.'

'The Parthians are not your enemies, lord,' I said.

Haytham smiled wryly. 'I like you, Pacorus, I really do, but sometimes my Rasha has more common sense than you do.

'The Romans are like ravenous wolves. They will not be satisfied until they have conquered the whole world. And there are many Parthians who see the Agraci as cockroaches, to be stamped on.'

'Not this Parthian, lord.'

'No, not you. But few have your foresight. We have heard that your new lord high general has vowed to rid the earth of the Agraci.'

'I would not worry about him,' I said, 'he would not dare venture near my kingdom, not unless he wants another mauling.'

'Well,' he said, 'the Agraci know who their friends are and we know how to survive.'

Our stay in Palmyra was extremely pleasant and we took the opportunity to visit Noora, Byrd's woman. Once again Gallia asked her to come back with us to Dura but again she refused. I said that I was sorry that I was responsible for her husband being away for long periods. She just shrugged and said that Byrd came and went as he pleased.

'It does not matter, lord, for we will be together when we are old and frail, and then the days will be filled with nothing but each other's company.'

Gallia was moved by these words.

'I hope that we are still together when we are old.'

'Why wouldn't we be?' I asked, as we were riding back to Dura.

'Because it seems that you are always away fighting on behalf of the empire.'

I smiled. 'I told you, I am done with all that. Now I shall stay in the Citadel and become fat and indolent and sire lots of children.'

She looked at me. 'Is that right? A queen's duties are endless, it seems.'

I smiled at her. 'Duty? I thought it was a pleasure.'

'Don't flatter yourself, Pacorus.'

I had hoped that Dura would go unnoticed while Narses and Mithridates played their games of intrigue at Ctesiphon, and that the Romans would stay away after they had been given a bloody nose at the gates of my city. But when I told Domitus this he merely laughed and said that Mars had not finished with me yet. He himself seemed happy enough. The Duran Legion had been brought back up to strength, the Pontic contingent had been replenished with exiles from Armenia and more from Pontus itself, so that we now had nearly ten thousand foot soldiers, all trained and equipped in the Roman style. In fact we had so many legionaries that we were forced to billet them along the Euphrates in small mud-brick forts, each one having a watchtower and a small barracks for half a century – forty men – together with stables for four horses. We built fifty of these forts; the legionaries themselves carrying out their construction, each one spaced at five-mile intervals along the riverbank both north and south of the city. In this way two thousand soldiers were garrisoned outside Dura who also provided eyes and ears right up to the kingdom's northern and southern borders. Not that they needed to do so, as the lords and those who lived on their lands kept a close watch, but it alleviated the crowded conditions in the camp outside Dura.

Nergal's horse archers now totalled eleven hundred men and by promoting the most promising squires we had brought the cataphracts up to five hundred in number. Orodes had only two hundred and fifty out of his original five hundred heavy cavalry, but there was nothing that could be done about that. With his banishment he was forbidden to have any contact with his homeland or the other kings and princes of the empire; indeed, his men were free to leave him and travel back to Susa, though none did. I felt guilty that I was the cause of his misfortune but Gallia dismissed the notion, saying that he would not have stayed with me this long had he not wanted to. Nevertheless, in an effort to make him feel at home I hung his banner beside mine in the throne room.

With the horse archers that the lords could muster, Dura could now field an army of around twenty thousand men, a most respectable number given the modest size of the kingdom.

I had had no contact with my father since our argument the previous year, though there had been a flurry of letters between Gallia and my mother over the issue. My mother also wrote to me, usually begging me to visit Hatra, and I always wrote back expressing my love but evading her invitation. But no word came from my father and I would not budge on the matter. If he did not

381

apologise then I would not contact him. I found it all rather tedious, but then a happy interlude occurred when Gafarn and Diana visited us and brought with them the welcome news that she was pregnant. They had left little Spartacus at Hatra but assured me that he was thriving.

'He acts more like a prince every day,' said Diana as we relaxed one evening on the palace terrace. Below us, small boats with lanterns at the prow were night fishing on the marble-smooth waters of the Euphrates.

'Well, that is what he is,' I replied, refilling Vistaspa's cup with wine.

'Thank you, majesty,' he replied.

'There is no need to be so formal, Vistaspa,' said Gallia, 'we are all friends here.'

Gafarn laughed and Vistaspa looked awkward. A lifetime of strict adherence to protocol was difficult to put aside. I had been most surprised that Vistaspa had come to Dura, but he must have missed Godarz. Diana told me that he had been delighted with the invitation to accompany them. Rather than billet him at the palace I had lodged him at the governor's house with his old friend.

'It is so good to see you, Diana,' Gallia was smiling as she held Diana's hand.

'When are you two going to visit Hatra?' Diana looked at me.

'When my father apologises, of course,' I replied.

Gafarn was shaking his had. 'Same old Pacorus, stubborn as a mule.'

'If you had been arrested,' I said, 'you would think the same as me.'

'No I wouldn't. I would be grateful that I had a father.'

'I will visit Hatra,' announced Gallia, 'with or without Pacorus.'

'Do as you wish,' I said.

'I will,' she replied.

Vistaspa was staring down into his cup, no doubt highly embarrassed by the conversation.

'It is not good that Dura and Hatra do not have warm relations. Is that not so, Lord Vistaspa?' asked Diana.

Vistaspa cleared his throat. 'I think that Narses fears a united Dura and Hatra, especially as King Pacorus worsted him in battle. A divided father and son plays into his hands.'

'Well said,' remarked Gafarn, 'though perhaps we should write it on the wall in big letters so Pacorus can understand it better.'

Gallia and Diana laughed. Vistaspa looked more embarrassed.

'Did you come all this way just to annoy me, brother?' I asked.

'Of course not, it's far too easy and therefore no fun at all.'

I toyed with the idea of riding to Hatra and making amends with my father. Everyone urged me to do it, even Dobbai, who usually took no interest in emotional matters.

'You are Hatra's heir, though you will never wear its crown.'

'I do not understand,' I replied.

'Of course you do not. The gods made you useful with a sword not with your brain. The future king of Hatra is at this moment within your walls.'

Her ramblings became worse by the day and in truth I took what she said with a pinch of salt. The visit of Gafarn and Diana was over too soon, and on the morning of their departure they again both urged me to make amends with my father. Finally relenting, I promised them that I would, and that Gallia and I would be journeying to Hatra soon after they had departed. This pleased them immensely and they both left Dura happy, as did Vistaspa. As Gafarn, Diana and their escort were leaving the Citadel, the commander of my father's army halted his horse beside me.

'Your army is a credit to you, Pacorus, well done. The empire is all the stronger for having a king such as you serving it.'

With that he bowed his head to Gallia and then me and rode away. Strange as it may seem, his few words of praise meant the world to me.

It was just two days after our friends had departed that Malik and Byrd arrived at the Citadel, both unshaven and covered in dust from what had obviously been a hard ride. The look on their faces told me the news they brought was not good.

Byrd gulped down a cup of water that was offered to him. 'Romani army marching from Syria.'

I grew alarmed. 'Marching to where?'

'To Dura, Pacorus,' replied Malik, holding out his cup to a servant to be refilled.

Two hours later the war council was gathered at the palace, where Byrd told them the news that another Roman army was marching on Dura.

'At least eight legions, plus cavalry and light troops. Also siege engines,' reported Byrd.

'I estimate around fifty thousand men in total, perhaps more,' added Malik.

'That's a lot of men,' commented Domitus, 'they obviously mean business this time.'

'Does Crassus lead them?' I asked.

Byrd shook his head. 'No, they are commanded by a man named

Pompey.'

The name meant nothing to me, though the fact that he led fifty thousand men indicated that he had great power and influence. In the next few minutes, though, I became more acquainted with Pompey, the new Roman commander in the East. He had certainly been busy of late. Byrd informed us that it had been Pompey who had destroyed the power of the Cilician pirates. In this I was not displeased, for they had betrayed the army of Spartacus when it had been trapped in southern Italy. A vision of the pirate leader we had dealt with suddenly appeared in my mind, a slippery fellow named Shirish Patelli. He had flattered and deceived us with his false smile and deceitful promises, and then suddenly vanished with the gold that Spartacus had given him. I hoped that this Pompey, who had apparently destroyed the pirate scourge in a matter of months, had nailed Patelli to a cross.

Byrd continued to relate how Pompey had gone on to finally defeat King Mithridates of Pontus. Next, Pompey had turned his attention to Antioch, the sad rump of what had once been the mighty Seleucid Empire. Nearly two hundred years ago that empire had ruled from the Mediterranean Sea to the Indian Ocean, but now it had vanished. Its last ruler, Antiochus XIII, had been a Roman puppet who had ruled Syria on their behalf. But now Byrd told us that Pompey had expelled Antiochus from Antioch and then had him murdered.

'A lesson for you all,' said Dobbai, holding each of us with her eyes, 'Once a mighty empire, ruled by the heirs of Alexander, turned into a plaything of the Romans and now vanished from the earth.'

Her eyes narrowed as she fixed her gaze on Domitus, who returned her stare.

'And yet it seems that the gods have earmarked Dura as a special place, that much is certain,' she said at length. 'Why else would they gather Parthian, Roman and Agraci together, were it not for a specific purpose?'

'And what purpose would that be?' I asked.

She pursed her lips. 'How should I know? I am not a god.'

'You are right, there,' remarked Domitus casually.

Dobbai turned on him. 'Have a care, Roman, your gods have no power here. "The Follower" will stop your kin.'

'Follower?' asked Gallia.

Dobbai waved a hand at us. 'I have said enough, go back to listening to the ramblings of the Cappadocian pot seller.'

She shuffled from the room, leaving us none the wiser. I told

Byrd to continue, who informed us that Pompey had declared the whole of Syria a Roman province.

'Can he do such a thing?' asked Rsan.

'With eight legions he can,' answered Domitus, who looked at me. 'What will you do?'

I suddenly felt the weight of expectation bear down heavily on my shoulders. They were all looking at me, waiting for my speech of deliverance. My next words would probably decide my own fate and that of the kingdom of Dura.

'We have no choice, we must march north to meet the Romans before they set foot on Duran territory.'

'We will be outnumbered by more than two to one,' said Godarz with alarm.

'If we do not engage them at the border,' I continued, 'they will destroy all the villages and lords' strongholds as they march south. Each lord will fight them and be defeated in turn, and by the time this Pompey sets down before the city we will have lost half our army.'

'We could harry them as they marched south,' suggested Nergal, 'launch hit-and-run raids on their army and attack their supply lines and garrisons they leave behind, like we did last year.'

'If we had time on our side I would agree,' I replied, 'but we do not. And there are a lot more of them than last year. Hit them hard before they set on Duran territory, that is the only option.'

Domitus looked up. 'And then?'

He knew as well as everyone else that we would not be able to defeat eight legions plus auxiliary troops and horsemen. We might scatter their cavalry easily enough, but when it came to fighting their legions we did not have enough men. There was an unbearable silence as each of us created what would happen in our minds. Domitus would lead his men against the Roman line while Nergal and I defeated their horsemen, but in the centre Domitus would be forced back as the sheer weight of numbers began to tell. On each wing our horsemen would wheel inwards and strike at the enemy's flanks and try to get behind him, but we would be met by unbroken shield walls and would be forced to call off our attacks. And in the centre the Roman legions would be grinding down the foot soldiers of Dura into dust.

'There is no alternative,' I said at last. 'That is my plan. We march in two days.'

Messages were sent to the lords to muster their men and then link up with the army as it marched north to Dura's northern border. As the city and the legion's camp outside the city burst into activity, I went to see Godarz. I found him in his residence issuing orders to a group of city officials concerning the collection of food from outlying areas. I stood outside his study until he had finished.

'Collect as much as you can. We will slaughter the livestock and salt the meat. Don't bother with fruit, but bring in enough wheat so we can produce biscuit in the bakeries. It keeps for months and is reasonably nutritious.'

He dismissed them and they filed out of the room, some of them slightly startled by my presence. I went into the room.

'Expecting a long siege, Godarz?'

He stood up. 'Pacorus? I didn't expect you to be here.'

I sat down in a chair opposite his desk. 'Take a seat, my friend.'

'I wish I was marching with the army,' he said, taking his seat across the table.

'Your place is here, and I have an important mission for you.'

He wore a confused expression. I continued. 'We both know that Dura will not be able to hold out for long against a large army, especially if there is no hope of relief.'

'But surely?' I held up my hand to still him.

'I do not intend to sacrifice the people of this city needlessly. If you receive word that the army has been destroyed, I want you to evacuate the city. Seek refuge in Hatran territory. Better that than death or slavery.'

'That is an order that only you can give.'

I smiled. 'If the army is beaten then I shall be dead, my friend, in which case you will command the city, so please do as I say.'

'What of Gallia?'

'She is marching with the army.'

He was horrified. 'And Claudia?'

'Will remain here with Dobbai. If the worst happens make sure they both get to Hatra. They will be safe there, or as safe as anyone can be in this world.'

'Gallia will fight?'

I nodded. 'Of course, she and her women are itching to get to grips with the enemy. You know what they were like in Italy.'

'You could evacuate the city now and leave it to the Romans.'

Now it was my turn to be horrified. 'No, Godarz, what sort of man would that make me? I do not intend to run from the Romans. Remember what Spartacus told us – it is better to die on your feet than forever to live on your knees.'

'He still casts a shadow over us all,' mused Godarz.

'Indeed he does.'

'You know, I always believed that he would fail in the end. The world was not ready for a man such as Spartacus. But I have a feeling that his memory will outlast us all and will reverberate through history.'

'I would like to think so, Godarz, I would like to think so.'

'Well,' he stood up, 'I can't sit here chatting to you; I have a city to organise.'

The rumour of the approaching Roman army spread like wildfire and soon the volume of caravans on the road diminished to a trickle and then stopped altogether. This cast Rsan into the pit of despair but I told him there was nothing to be done, and in truth I was glad for it was one less thing to worry about. Not that there was any alarm in the city. The citizens had already been evacuated once, albeit for a short time, and they must have expected the same this time. After all, the Romans had been defeated here once, why not again? This result had given them a false sense of optimism; but then, that was better than panic.

It is around three hundred miles from Antioch to Dura, though the journey can be shortened by striking southeast from Antioch, across the desert, to reach my city. But that involves crossing vast stretches of wasteland, and whereas a lone traveller or a small group may attempt it, especially if they have a local guide to plot their course from waterhole to waterhole, no commander would lead his army into such a desolate vastness. Instead, Pompey would lead his legions directly west to the town of Aleppo, a centre of Greek learning and culture, and then west again until he reached the River Euphrates. He would then march down the west bank of the river, thus ensuring his men and animals had plentiful supplies of water, until he eventually reached Dura. It would take him just over three weeks to reach the city, which meant that I had a week to get the army to the kingdom's northern frontier to meet him before he set foot on Duran territory. Preparations had gone smoothly, however, and the army was ready to march north when an agitated Domitus arrived at the Citadel. I was in the treasury explaining to Rsan that he must box up the city's reserves of gold and silver for transportation across the river to Hatra in the event of my defeat.

'I will leave sufficient soldiers behind to act as a guard for the treasure, but it is imperative that it gets to my father's city. You are one of the few who know about the city's evacuation and you must not tell anyone else.'

He was delighted that I had entrusted so big a secret to him, though perturbed about what it meant for his precious treasure.

'But, majesty, I, you, have a great deal of gold and silver stored here, and if word got out that it is being moved.'

'That is why it must remain a secret, Rsan. Tell no one, not even your most trusted official. On pain of death.'

He went ashen faced, but then recovered when I laid a hand on his shoulder. 'Just keep it to yourself and liaise with Godarz, who also knows of my plan.'

Domitus came in unannounced and threw his helmet on Rsan's table. 'You need to keep that bitch under control.'

Rsan frowned at such rude behaviour but said nothing. He knew to stay clear of an angry Domitus.

'What bitch is that?' I asked.

'Your sorceress, that's who.'

'Dobbai?'

'Yes, and lucky for her that she has your favour, otherwise I would have slit her throat there and then.'

'Calm down,' I said, 'and tell me what she has done.'

Dobbai usually restricted herself to the Citadel, occasionally going into the city to purchase herbs and spices for her concoctions, usually potions to cure Claudia's teething problems and other minor ailments or to produce incense that she burned in her private quarters. She had endless arguments with Alcaeus concerning medicine and the treatment of illnesses. Alcaeus accused her of being a charlatan who took advantage of people's fear and ignorance, while she accused him of being an ill-educated foreigner who had no business telling her about things he did not understand. But now she had commandeered a cart and driver and had visited Domitus' camp, whereupon she had begun to order the soldiers to stop what they were doing immediately and seek refuge in the city, otherwise the desert sands would bury them. These men were battle-hardened veterans but they knew of Dobbai's prophecies and her words had spread alarm throughout the camp like wildfire, much to Domitus' fury.

'Please go and get her,' he said to me through gritted teeth, 'otherwise I swear by Mars that I will cut her head off.'

So I rode from the Citadel to the camp where Domitus had confined Dobbai to his tent and placed her under armed guard. When I arrived she was sitting behind his desk, her hands resting on the polished surface. She leaned back in her chair when she saw me.

'Where is your Roman pet, son of Hatra?'

'Your words are not helping, Dobbai, we are preparing to march north.'

She shook her head. 'You need to get everyone into the city, a

388

storm is coming.'

'Storm?'

'I told you,' she continued, 'but you chose to ignore me.'

The day was hot and airless, like every other day of late, and the sky cloudless.

'I have eyes, Dobbai, and the sky has no clouds. There is no wind, so I see no reason to believe that any storm is on its way.'

She rose from her chair and began pacing. 'You have eyes but cannot see. As for your reason, it is deceiving you.' She stopped pacing and looked at me, her expression one of almost pleading. 'Do you trust me, Pacorus?'

A shiver went down my spine. She never called me by my name but she did so now. There was no mockery in her eyes, only a deadly seriousness that made me apprehensive.

'I trust you.'

'Then give the order to get everyone into the city. All the buildings must be boarded up and everyone must stay inside. You must give this order today or all will be lost.'

Reason told me that this was idiocy, that to disrupt our plans was foolhardy in the extreme. Yet my instincts screamed at me that it was the right thing to do. So I gave the order.

Domitus was at first enraged by my decision and then dumbfounded, but he carried out my order. I told Nergal to call in all his patrols as thousands of men and horses, and hundreds of carts and wagons filed into the city. The men were billeted in barracks in the city and Citadel, and fortunately there was enough room in the stables to accommodate the horses of the cataphracts, their squires and the horse archers, though it was a squeeze to say the least. But eight thousand foot soldiers could not be housed in the barracks, even with men sleeping on floors, and so they had to be billeted on the city's citizens. I was thankful that two thousand more were safely housed in the forts that we had built up and down the Euphrates. The citizens grumbled but acquiesced – they had no choice – and the soldiers assisted each household in boarding up and securing the properties. The carts and wagons were stored in the city's squares and along the sides of roads, and the supplies, spare clothing, tents, weapons and utensils they held were secured in homes, temples, offices and storerooms. Then the carts and wagons were themselves covered over with canvas.

In the Citadel itself soldiers were allocated to any spare rooms and bedded down in the feasting hall, throne room and even in the corridors. The Amazons filled the rooms next to our bedroom, though no one wanted, or dared, to bed down in Dobbai's room.

389

That night I held a grand meal in the feasting hall, though Domitus sat with a face like thunder and ate next to nothing throughout. He was close to despair, I think, and avoided my gaze all evening. Eventually he slammed his fist on the table and stormed out. I think he believed that I had taken leave of my senses and that we had let any chance of meeting the enemy at the border slip through our fingers. And then the storm struck.

Al-Dabaran, they call it, 'The Follower', one of the great sandstorms that sweep down from the north, caused by a prevailing northwesterly wind that kicks up the fine desert sand and dust and carries them south. Where there had been quiet and no wind, suddenly there was a dark sky as a wall of sand descended on the city, accompanied by a howling noise and a fierce wind, a wind that at first rattled the shutters and doors and then, as it grew in intensity, produced a banging noise at though huge fists were hammering on the shutters and doors, demanding entry.

'It is the storm demons,' shouted Dobbai, 'they wish to enter and spread their desolation.'

For five days the storm raged. Such was its fury that no one could venture outside, with visibility reduced to nothing and skin and clothes running the risk of being sand-blasted after even a few seconds of exposure. On the third day the wind increased in intensity, a ceaseless roaring noise surrounding the Citadel and driving everyone inside to distraction. I thought the roof and doors would be ripped off such was its rage. I saw fear in men's eyes as the wind and sand assaulted our fortress. Claudia screamed and wailed and people began to pray to their gods. I too prayed to Shamash that He would spare us, or at least my wife and daughter. Even Domitus looked alarmed. No, not alarmed, helpless, something I had not seen in his eyes before. This in turn made me alarmed. Nergal held Praxima close and I held Gallia and Claudia, while Dobbai paced up and down, seemingly oblivious to the terror that was spreading among us. Only one person seemed truly unconcerned, happy even, and that was Surena, who held a pale Viper in his arms, her face buried in his chest. And then, after the fifth day, when our nerves had been frayed to breaking point, when we had despaired of getting solace from the pounding noise that filled our world, the wind stopped. There was suddenly absolute silence. At first I thought that my hearing had given out after the days of howling and roaring, but then Dobbai laid a hand on my arm.

'It is over, they have returned to the underworld once more.'

We sighed with relief and embraced each other. Some fell to

their knees, wept and thanked their gods. Domitus caught the eye of Dobbai and nodded in acknowledgement that she had been right. She nodded back. Then it was back to normality.

Domitus called together his officers and began the task of preparing the march north once more. Men were recalled from the outlying forts. Thanks to Dobbai's warning the army and its supplies were unharmed, and soon men and materials were moving out of the Palmyrene Gate to assemble once more in camp. Shutters and doors had been pummelled by the storm and some roofs had been torn off, but in general the city was relatively unscathed. Then I remembered the stone griffin statue at the Palmyrene Gate. High and exposed, it would have taken a terrible beating from the sand and dust – if it was still there at all. I rode down to the gate and raced up to the battlements, to find the statue untouched. I ran my hand over its contours. It was as if it had just been carved; there was not a mark on it. How could this be?

It took two days before the army was ready to move. I was still concerned that the Romans had stolen a march on us but Dobbai scoffed at my worries.

'You think the Romans were able to march through Al-Dabaran? They will be in a perilous condition. It will take them many days to recover from the punishment they have received.'

'Thank you,' I said.

'It is of no consequence.'

'If it is of no consequence,' I said, 'then why did you bother to warn me of the storm?'

'Because I am fond of your wife and daughter, son of Hatra, that is why. If anything happens to you then they will suffer, and I do not wish to see that. And the gods have not yet finished with you, so go and play at being a general.'

Byrd and Malik rode ahead as the army began its march from Dura, the legionaries marching six abreast and Nergal's horse archers forming a flank guard for the foot, wagons and mules. Domitus, as always on foot, marched at the head of his men in front of the colour party carrying the gold griffin and the standard of victory. I rode at the tip of the army with Gallia and Orodes. Behind us came the standards of Dura and Susiana, and behind them Gallia's Amazons. The cataphracts, their squires and camels were in the centre of the column, Domitus and his legionaries trailing behind. Nergal also had two hundred horse archers acting as a rearguard. I left five hundred foot and fifty horse archers behind at Dura, plus the Roman engineers that we had captured.

We marched north at a steady pace, covering around fifteen

391

miles a day, and each day our numbers were increased when we linked up with one of Dura's lords and his retinue. Many of their sons were members of my cataphracts and each day brought a happy reunion of father and son, sons in some cases. Each lord brought at least five hundred horse archers, so that by the time we reached the northern boundary of the kingdom the army totalled over twenty thousand men. How absurdly proud we all were, for we were unvanquished and rated ourselves among the best warriors in the empire. And we all also knew that our numbers were too few to take on the might of Pompey. We travelled under an intense clear blue sky, the army strung out over many miles as it hugged the Euphrates. Camels grumbled and spat, mules brayed and men sweated. Each night we slept in tents in a large camp erected in the Roman fashion, surrounded by a ditch and rampart surmounted by a wooden palisade, and each day it was disassembled ready for its erection on another site at the end of the march. As men spent between three and five hours a day disassembling the camp, Nergal sent his scouting parties far ahead into the surrounding desert, and ahead of them all rode Byrd and Malik.

We kept close to the Euphrates as we passed a mountain called the Jabal Bishri, a massive limestone and sandstone plateau with huge basalt outcrops that some said were fifty miles in length. We halted in the large expanse of land between the Jabal Bishri and the river, in the irrigated strip beside the Euphrates. At first I thought I might anchor one flank of the army on the river itself, as I had done at Dura last year, but Pompey had so many foot soldiers that he would be able to outflank our own legionaries with ease, and then herd them into the river while he fended off our own cavalry. So I decided to fight him inland on the plain, where at least our advantage in horsemen would keep his own cavalry at bay, and where the hard-packed dirt surface made excellent ground for charges and flanking manoeuvres. But eight legions against two was still sobering odds.

This was the furthest extent of Dura's lands. Further north there were no fields or homes – just flat desert, the Euphrates disappearing into the distance.

On the final day of marching, with the sun beating down on us with relentless savagery, Surena came galloping up to the head of the column. Since the sand storm he had been in a ridiculously happy mood and today was no different. Like all of us he wore only his white baggy shirt and loose leggings and boots, a floppy hat on his head – helmets were carried on our saddles until the fighting began, unless you wanted to roast your brain. Gallia and her Amazons wore wide-brimmed floppy hats to keep the sun off their necks, and they let their hair fall freely about their shoulders. Some, such as Viper, cut their hair short to save them having to plait it when they donned their helmets, but Gallia and Praxima kept their hair long, which I was glad of. But it was Viper who was the topic of conversation today.

Surena halted his horse beside Remus and bowed his head. 'Lord, I have happy news.'

'Excellent, Surena. Have the Romans retreated?'

'No, lord, I don't know anything about them, but Viper has agreed to see me when we get back to Dura.'

I looked at Gallia on my other side, who rolled her eyes. 'My congratulations.'

'I knew I would win her round in the end. Bit of luck that storm blowing up when it did, though'

'I'm sure the gods arranged it especially so you could woo her, Surena,' I said.

'Yes, lord,' he beamed. 'I was wondering, lord, if I might have some leave after the battle.'

'Leave?' The idea that he might be killed during the next few days had obviously not entered his mind.

'Yes, lord, so I can take Viper to meet my people.'

I thought of the reed huts of his people, the marshes, the dried dung they used for firewood and the water buffaloes sharing the dry land with the villagers. 'I'm sure she will enjoy what will be a unique experience. You have my permission. Now kindly rejoin the ranks.'

He whooped with joy, bowed his head and then galloped back to the cataphracts.

'Idiot boy,' remarked Gallia.

'He's not so bad, and he is a good soldier.'

'I don't know why you indulge him. He has a rebellious streak as wide as the Euphrates, and I don't like the way he pesters Viper.'

'You mean he reminds you of yourself.'

She was outraged. 'He is nothing like me.'

'Not in looks, obviously, but as for a rebellious streak, what can I say? Anyway, young Viper seems happy enough with him.'

She wore a look of mischief. 'I could forbid her to see him.'

'That would be cruel, and cruelty is not one of your vices.'

'Do I have any vices, Pacorus?'

'Aside from stubbornness, rebelliousness, volatility and a refusal to obey orders, absolutely none.'

'Well, perhaps Surena will be killed when we fight the Romans,' she said happily.

I laughed. 'We may all suffer that fate, my love.'

On the seventh night Byrd and Malik returned to camp and brought with them a tall, wiry man riding a camel. The man's name was Martu. He was one of the people who lived on the Jabal Bishri, the descendents of an ancient race called the Amorites who had possessed a great empire many hundreds of years ago. Now these people lived a semi-nomadic existence on the desert steppe of the great mountain. Byrd and Malik had made contact with them two days before, and Martu had agreed to accompany them to our camp. He brought with him desert truffles the size of a man's fist, which he roasted in the dying embers of our fire and then served them to us with a sauce called Samneh, which was fomented butter made from goat's milk.

'This is delicious, Martu,' I said, 'you honour us with your presence.'

Martu sat cross-legged near the fire, his weather-beaten face resembling a piece of old leather, his eyes dark brown and his teeth brilliant white.

'Martu has knowledge of the Romani,' said Byrd.

'It is true, lord,' Martu's accent was strong and I had to concentrate to understand his words.

'Where are they?' I asked.

'We heard that they left Aleppo and marched east, but were then hit by the great storm.' His eyes were on Gallia as he spoke, his stare fixed on her long blond locks. 'Last I heard, lord, they were at Tabaqah.'

'That is a small town on the Euphrates,' said Byrd, 'three days' march from here.'

'It is a great army that marches against you,' remarked Martu casually, still staring at Gallia. 'Are all your women like her?'

I smiled at him. 'No, she is unique. She is my queen.'

He laid his right palm on his chest and bowed his head at Gallia. 'You are indeed fortunate, lord.'

'He is indeed,' answered Gallia.

The next day Nergal and a hundred horse archers accompanied Martu, Byrd and Malik into the desert. I did not want any Roman patrols getting close to our position and reporting back to their commander. I wanted to retain the element of surprise at least. The next day Byrd and Malik returned.

'We had a fight with about fifty Roman horsemen,' said Nergal, 'killed about half of them but the rest got away.'

'Romani army is close, only five miles away,' said Byrd.

'And they will know that we are here by now,' remarked Malik.

That night was subdued as the next day's battle grew ever closer. The morale of the army was still high, which made my mood darken even more. Most of them would be dead by this time tomorrow. I glanced at Gallia; perhaps she too would also be lying dead beside me. I had brought them all to this place and the burden of responsibility weighed heavily upon me. But what was the alternative? There was none. At least here, in the open, we could try to maul the enemy. To sit in Dura was to invite certain death. But then, as my old adversary Lucius Furius had said, all death is certain. As usual, Gallia stayed with her Amazons on the eve of battle, each woman checking her quiver, sword, bow and dagger. I went to the stable section and ensured Remus was comfortable for the night. He rested his head on my chest as I stroked his neck.

'Well, old friend,' I said to him softly. 'We have ridden far together and shared many great victories.' His ears twitched as I spoke the words.

'And now we have to fight again. I thought that we would live in peace once we got back to Parthia and that you would grow old and grey beneath its blue skies. It appears that I was wrong.'

His head rose and he looked at me. I stroked the top of his head.

'The Parthians are horse lords, Remus, but I think that of all the horses that have carried the kings of the empire you are the finest. I pray to Shamash that if I should fall tomorrow, He will keep you safe and direct you to a new master, one worthy of you. But as He is merciful then perhaps I will ride you again in the next world for all eternity. I would very much like that.'

He nodded his head and I stroked his neck. 'Until tomorrow then, old friend.'

I walked back to my tent, clasping the arms of Companions who were gathered round fires, talking of the old times, and acknowledging others who had joined me after my time in Italy. Back at my tent Domitus sat sharpening his sword.

'The night passes too slowly,' I grumbled.

He looked up. 'Eager to die?'

'Eager to get to grips with the enemy, more like.'

'There is no point in fretting. The morning will come soon enough.'

'Do you think that god of yours?'

'Mars?'

'Yes, that's him. Do you think he will favour us tomorrow?'

He put down his stone and regarded me for a few seconds. 'I

think all gods admire courage in mortals, and you have it in abundance. But as to whether he will show us any favours.' He held out his hands. 'Who knows?'

I sat down in a chair. 'Well, it's all in God's hands now.'

Malik appeared at the entrance to the tent, Byrd following him.

'Good,' said Domitus, 'perhaps you two can cheer him up. He thinks he's going to die tomorrow.'

'Never say that, Pacorus,' said Malik, looking alarmed, 'to say such a thing can sometimes make it come true.'

They both sat down beside me, stretching out their legs.

'This isn't your fight, Malik, you can return to your people if you wish. You too, Byrd. Go and make Noora a happy woman.'

They both looked at each other and then at me. 'I thought we were friends,' said Malik.

'So we are,' I replied.

He smiled. 'Well then, I will be staying. I will not abandon a friend in his hour of need.'

'Me too,' was all Byrd said.

In all the years that I had known Byrd I had never seen him fight. Indeed, the only weapon he carried was a long knife, and I doubted that he had used that in anger. Still, it was reassuring that he would be with us tomorrow to face the Romans.

Domitus was right, the morning came soon enough, and with it the sounds of trumpets and horns as men were mustered into their companies and centuries. Today I decided not to wear my scale armour. Instead, I wore my Roman leather cuirass over my white top. My helmet had a new crest of white goose feathers. I pulled on my boots, secured my belt that carried my spatha on my left hip and my dagger on the other hip, and then went to the stables.

Nergal sent out riders before the first rays of the sun announced the dawn, and they reported back that the Romans were leaving their camp and deploying on the plain. As Dura's foot soldiers were marching out of camp I called the commanders of the army together in my tent. We had already visited our horses to saddle them and ensure they had been fed and watered. The only thing left was to ensure that everyone knew what to do.

'The legions will deploy side-by-side in two lines, not three. In this way we can present as broad a front as possible in the centre of our line.'

I looked at Nergal. 'Your horse archers will be with me on the right wing, interspersed between the cataphracts, just as we did at Dura last year, but you yourself will be on the left wing leading the lords and their men.'

This would give Nergal ten thousand men to command, a massive number to deploy on one wing.

'No reserve?' queried Domitus.

'A small reserve,' I replied. 'I will come to that. Nergal, you must extend your line as far as possible, so the Romans will have to place troops in front of you. Hopefully this will dissipate their strength in the centre.'

'What about me and my men?' asked Orodes.

I smiled at him. 'I would consider it an honour if you joined me on the right, Orodes.'

'Or you could stand beside me,' said Domitus, 'see a bit of real fighting for a change instead of galloping around waving your sword in the air like Pacorus does.'

They all laughed and Nergal slapped Orodes on the back. Even facing great odds their morale was unshakable.

'Have no fear, Orodes,' said Gallia, 'I and my Amazons will be riding beside you.'

'I had hoped, my love,' I said tentatively, 'that the Amazons might form a reserve behind Domitus' men.'

'Well, you thought wrong.'

More laughter as Gallia stood before me, unbending. I held up my hand. 'Very well. May Shamash protect us all and give us victory this day.'

They gave a hearty cheer and then we departed for our commands. Though it was early morning it was already warm; it would be a hot day. The legionaries were marching across the plain and deploying opposite the enemy, while on the wings the horse was also forming up. Each lord led his own followers, which meant that there were twenty blocks of horse archers, each numbering around five hundred men. They looked imposing and were spread over a great distance, but these horsemen lacked the discipline of my cataphracts and Nergal's horse archers. They were essentially hardy farmers who could ride and were expert in using a bow in the saddle. Their only advantage was their numbers. On the right wing it was very different. Here we only had seventeen hundred men, plus Gallia's Amazons, a further one hundred, but these men were, I liked to think, the best-trained horsemen in the empire. We would first deal with the Roman cavalry we faced by placing horse archers among the cataphracts. The archers would ride beside the heavy cavalry, shooting their bows as the two lines closed. Even if the Romans matched our tactics their bows did not have the range of our recurve type. When it came to the melee, those enemy horsemen who still lived would stand no chance against my armoured horsemen. And then we would reform and wheel left to attack the exposed left flank of the Roman foot.

It took two hours to get the army into its battle positions, and shortly afterwards the enemy came into view. No, that is incorrect – we heard them first, a great rumbling noise that came from the horizon. Straining my eyes to peer at the distant haze at first I saw nothing. Then, as if by magic, the horizon was filled with a long black line. It shimmered in the heat and seemed to just stand still, not getting larger or smaller. But the noise increased, a loud rasping sound as thousands of sandal-clad feet tramped towards us. And then the black line dissolved to become rows of shields and a forest of javelins, the sun glinting off their points. It was a seemingly unending line of legionaries marching towards us, cohort after cohort moving in perfect unison.

Directly opposite us was the cavalry of their left wing, spearmen with oval shields protecting their left sides. And beside them was a remorseless tide of wood, leather and steel, red banners dotted along the line and trumpet calls rending the hot air. I nudged Remus forward so that I moved ahead of the first line of our horsemen, most of whom had their helmets pushed up on their heads. Dura's cataphracts were a ferocious sight in their full-face helmets, but for the wearer it could become unbearably hot very quickly.

Then the Romans halted and there was silence, an oppressive silence as thousands of men stared at each other across the thin strip of ground, no wider than four hundred paces, that separated the two armies. Horses scraped at the earth and chomped on bits, others flicked their tails to rid themselves of the flies that buzzed around them. Some legionaries were standing ahead of the front ranks beside their scorpion bolt throwers, while the vast majority of their comrades rested their shields on the ground as they waited for the killing to begin. I had seen scorpions in Italy and how effective they were. In appearance the scorpion looked like a large bow lying parallel to the ground on a wooden bolt carrier, the whole on a wooden stand. Just under the height of a man's chest, the scorpion was a complex piece of equipment, the two arms that fired the two-foot-long bolt being pushed through ropes made of animal sinews, which are then twisted to create hugely powerful tension devices that push each arm forwards. The arms are then pulled back by means of a bowstring, the bolt is placed on the carrier and then the bowstring is released. The bolt has a range of around five hundred feet and can inflict terrible damage on the densely packed ranks of an enemy.

And then, behind me, I heard horn blasts and drums. I looked round and saw no movement in my ranks, aside from others peering behind them. Then the sounds from behind us grew louder and suddenly to our right, from the desert vastness, came similar sounds. Suddenly I saw a rider, and then another and another, until the horizon was filled with horsemen. And I saw banners flying and windsocks. Then I caught sight of a banner I had not seen in a long time. A great scarlet square embossed with a white horse's head – the standard of my father. The army of Hatra had come.

As rank upon rank of cataphracts formed up to swell and extend our right wing, my father and Vistaspa galloped to where I was sitting, halting their horses beside me. They were accompanied by wild cheering from Dura's army as the news of their salvation spread through its ranks.

Vistaspa bowed his head to me and then wheeled his horse away to oversee the proper deployment of his companies.

'Well, Pacorus,' said my father, gazing at the Roman masses opposite, 'you know how to pick a fight, I give you that.'

For a moment I was speechless, hardly believing what I was seeing was real. And then other riders came from the desert, and I knew that Shamash had performed a miracle for me. Gotarzes trotted over to halt before me, and behind him came Vardan of Babylon and Atrax of Media, brave Atrax who never stopped grinning. And the line of horsemen on my right was extending ever further into the distance as the soldiers of the kings of the empire filled the desert.

'I don't understand,' I stuttered, 'how?'

'How?' replied my father. 'It is quite simple. The water level of the Euphrates drops considerably this time of year, so it was relatively easy for horsemen to ford.'

'I did not mean that.'

He laughed. 'I know. Do you think that I would allow my son to stand alone against his enemies?'

'But Phraates has given Dura to the Romans.'

'Poor Phraates. He is so deceived by his own family members that he has lost all sense of reason, I think.'

'You risk banishment for aiding me, father.'

He laughed out loud. 'Look around you, Pacorus. You can see horsemen from Babylon, Elymais, Hatra, Media and Atropaiene. If Phraates wants to make war on all of us, so be it.'

'Aschek is here?' I was most surprised to hear that the King of Atropaiene had come to assist me, seeing as all the fight had seemingly been knocked out of him.

'Musa and Khosrou persuaded him. They have formed an alliance with him, which has given him back his courage somewhat. By the way, Khosrou sent a thousand of his wild horsemen as well, said they were a gift for Gallia. Where is she?'

As my father sought out my wife I looked at my heaven-sent reinforcements. The kings had brought only horsemen with them to quicken their journey, but it was enough to match and then outnumber our Roman opponents. My father had brought his fifteen hundred cataphracts and a further seven thousand horse archers; Vardan had brought five thousand Babylonian horse archers and five hundred cataphracts, Aschek a thousand cataphracts and three thousand horse archers, Atrax another five thousand horse archers and seven hundred cataphracts, and Gotarzes rode with a thousand of Elymais' cataphracts and eight thousand horse archers. Added to this number was Gallia's gift of a thousand of Margiana's spearmen come horse archers. Our numbers had been swelled by over almost thirty-three thousand horsemen, and now we outnumbered the Romans, albeit by not a great number. But more importantly, we possessed nearly five thousand cataphracts, a mighty steel fist that would be able to crush the enemy horsemen with ease, leaving their legions to face an endless storm of arrows on all sides as our horse archers swarmed around them like angry bees.

As these reinforcements were being marshalled into position by an increasingly fraught Vistaspa, who had been selected to act as general-in-chief for the day, the kings assembled around my father and me, while Gallia left the ranks of her Amazons to greet each of them in turn. Thus far the Romans had made no movement but I suspected that it would not be long before they attacked, as the one thing that I had learned about them was that they liked to draw the first blood in battle. Hopefully, though, my unexpected reinforcements would have made their commander pause. We now outflanked the Roman army greatly, especially on the right wing where the cataphracts were deployed, and beyond them the tens of thousands of horse archers extending the line far into the distance. A rider on a black horse came through the ranks and cantered over to where we were sitting on our horses. His horse had no armour but he himself wore a leather helmet with ear and neck flaps and his body was protected by leather armour. He carried a bow, quiver, sword, dagger and a long spear. Sensibly, given the heat in these parts, he wore a white surcoat to stop his armour getting too hot in the sun. He halted in front of us and snapped his head forward in a salute. He had a squashed nose and narrow eyes that

400

were almost like slits. His small mouth was topped by a tidy moustache and had a neatly trimmed beard underneath.

'Hail, majesties. My name is Kuban. My king, Khosrou, has sent me to serve Queen Gallia of Dura. Where is she?' His tone was terse bordering on aggressive.

'The gift for Gallia I was telling you about,' remarked my father.

'I am she,' Gallia nudged Epona forward so that she was facing the fierce warrior from the northern vastness of the empire.

He took off his helmet and lowered his head. 'I and a thousand others are here to serve you, majesty.'

Gallia took off her helmet and stared at him. I could tell that she was delighted with Khosrou's gift. 'You and your men are most welcome, Kuban.'

'Kuban,' I said, 'you and your men are to form a reserve around the queen and her warriors.'

Gallia swung in her saddle to look at me. 'Reserve?'

'Don't worry,' I replied, 'there are enough Romans to go round today, I think, you will get your turn to fight.'

'As you wish, Pacorus. Kuban, follow me.'

Gallia wheeled Epona around and rode her back followed by Kuban to where her Amazons were standing. The line was then reordered as the Amazons and Kuban's men were formed into a block behind the cataphracts. I had no doubt that when the fighting began Gallia would be leading those men against the Romans soon enough.

'Where is your Roman, Pacorus?' asked Vardan.

I pointed to a lone Domitus standing around fifty paces in front of Dura's two legions. 'Over there, lord.'

'He does not mind killing his own kind?' asked Gotarzes.

'No, lord,' I replied, 'he'll kill anyone given the chance.'

At that moment Nergal arrived. He bowed his head to the kings.

'The lords are most eager to attack the enemy, Pacorus. They are chafing at the bit, especially now we have greatly increased our strength.'

'I have no doubt,' I said, 'but you must restrain them until the heavy cavalry strikes first.'

I turned to the kings. 'Lords, and friends, I think it is time to take up our positions.'

'What is your plan, Pacorus?' asked my father.

I had thought to let the Romans attack us, but now we possessed so many cataphracts I saw no reason not to hit the enemy first.

'The plan is simple. The cataphracts will scatter the Roman

401

horse opposite to allow the horse archers to surround the Roman foot. When you see Dura's heavy cavalry move forward, that is the signal to attack.'

With over forty thousand horse archers even eight Roman legions would have their hands full dealing with us. I decided to ride over to Domitus and inform him that he would now be the army's reserve, and would be held back until the Romans had been sufficiently weakened.

'What is that?'

Aschek was pointing to the south and soon everyone else was peering in that direction. I too turned to look, and saw that another army had come to northern Dura. The southern horizon was filled with black-clad figures riding camels and horses, many armed with spears and carrying round shields. There were thousands of them. A lone horseman left their ranks and galloped towards us, passing by the ranks of Dura's lords. The latter began cheering as he did so and I knew then that yet more allies had come. The horseman kept on riding until he reached me, his mount careering to a halt in a cloud of dirt and dust.

'Greetings, Malik,' I said.

'Hail, Pacorus.' He pointed at the seething black mass to the south. 'Behold, my father, King Haytham, brings his army to fight by your side.'

I reached over and laid a hand on his shoulder. 'You and he are most welcome. This is a great day, when our two peoples are united in the face of a common foe.'

In truth, the other kings sitting in silence were facing an awkward moment. The Agraci had been the sworn enemies of the Parthians for many decades, and yet, even though there had previously existed open warfare between Haytham and Dura's lords, the latter were now cheering the arrival of their former foes. Nothing lasts forever, it seems. Eventually my father broke the silence.

'Hail, Prince Malik, you and your father are true friends to my son, and as his father I thank you both for your aid.'

'Well,' grunted Gotarzes, 'what now?'

The Agraci had halted at right angles to our own left wing and faced the right flank of the Roman army, which was now vastly outnumbered. Once again a silence descended over the plain.

'Now, my lords,' I said, 'I think it is time to see if the tongue can achieve more than the sword.'

I nudged Remus forward and began to walk him into no-man's land between the two armies.

'Is this wise, Pacorus?' I detected concern in my father's voice behind me.

'Have no fear, father, we have the Romans' attention. I'm sure they will be most interested in what I have to say.'

As I moved closer to the enemy I raised my right arm and then halted some two hundred paces from their front ranks.

'Romans,' I shouted, 'my name is King Pacorus and I would speak to your commander, General Pompey.'

I received no answer in reply, just the steely gaze of hundreds of helmeted legionaries who stood in their ranks holding their pilum in their right hands and their shields on their left sides. I sat there for what seemed like an eternity but was probably only a couple of minutes, and then a burly centurion shoved his way through the ranks and strode up to me. He could have been the twin brother of Domitus, with his lean face and stern countenance, his transverse crest on his helmet and his mail shirt adorned with round discs.

'You must dismount, sir.'

'What?'

'You must get off your horse, sir, and then the Great Pompey will speak with you.'

'Does he not own a horse?'

The centurion frowned. 'He does, sir, but you might try to kidnap him and ride away with him.'

I burst out laughing, which increased his frown. This was absurd.

'Very well, centurion, I will do as you ask.' Then I added mischievously. 'I hope you are not thinking of kidnapping me.'

For a split-second I thought I saw a hurt look on his face. 'Of course not, sir.'

I dismounted and stood a few paces from him.

'There you are.'

'Thank you, sir.' He cleared his throat. 'I will also need to hold your horse, just for security reasons, you understand.'

I shook my head and handed him Remus' reins. 'There he is. Don't frighten him, say something nice to him, stroke his head. He likes that.'

As soon as he took Remus' reins he raised his right arm and then stood to one side, standing statue like. A few seconds later the ranks opened again and a tall, stocky individual appeared and walked towards me. He was bare headed and had a round face with small lidded eyes. His nose was slightly bulbous and he had a thick mane of hair on his head. His clothing marked him out as a man of some importance. He wore a large red cloak that was fastened at

403

the right shoulder by means of a large silver broach. On his feet he wore red leather enclosed boots tied with black leather laces. Over his white tunic he wore a black cuirass not dissimilar to the one I wore. I estimated his age to be around forty.

I took off my helmet and bowed my head to him. He bowed his head in reply and smiled.

'So, at long last I meet King Pacorus, the Parthian who dresses like a Roman and,' he looked past me to where my legions were lined up, 'fights in the Roman fashion.' His tone was serious though not mocking.

'I like to think that I have combined the best of Parthia and Rome, lord.'

He looked at the army arrayed against his own. 'I had been informed that Dura's army was small and insignificant, but it seems that I have been deceived.'

'There are other kings of the empire present, lord, and they will fight to preserve Dura's territorial integrity.'

'I do not doubt it.' He then looked to the south where they Agraci were gathered. 'And those?'

'More friends of Dura, lord.'

He turned to look at his own men and then once again fixed his eyes on the Parthian host standing opposite.

'Do you think you can win, Pacorus?'

I looked directly at him. 'Of course.'

He looked thoughtful. 'I have claimed Syria for Rome, and vowed in the temple of my forefathers that I would make the Euphrates the eastern border of Rome's domains.'

'Tabaqah is on the Euphrates, lord, so you have fulfilled your oath. But I have to tell you that you will have to destroy the army behind me if you wish to advance any further.'

'But where is Dura's border?' he asked.

I stepped away from him and raised my hand at the cataphracts opposite, specifically Surena. I pointed at him and beckoned for him to ride over to me. The centurion looked alarmed and drew his sword.

'I attempt no ruse, centurion. You can easily strike me down before he arrives.'

Pompey indicated that his subordinate should put away his sword. Surena trotted over and I ordered him to give me his kontus. I took the long lance and then dismissed him. I turned it upside down and then drove the point into the ground with all my strength.

'This is where the kingdom of Dura ends.'

Pompey nodded and then held out his right hand. 'Your sword, centurion.'

The centurion saluted and placed the handle of his gladius in Pompey's palm, who then rammed the blade into the earth next to the upright kontus.

'And this is where Roman Syria ends.'

I looked at him suspiciously.

'You do not trust me?'

'I meant no offence, lord, it's just that my experience with Romans has not been a happy one.'

His lips creased into a smile. 'I believe that you were once a guest in the house of Marcus Licinius Crassus.'

I thought back to that opulent home on one of Rome's hills. 'That is correct, lord. His hospitality was beyond reproach, and then he led an army against me.'

'I think my great rival bears you a grudge.'

His rival? That was a positive sign, at least.

'He has taken your escape from Italy as a personal affront and is determined to rectify it. Your killing his protégé will not have helped, I might add.'

'And you?' I asked.

'I, Pacorus, serve the interests of Rome. Looking at the army arrayed against me, I think that Rome's best interests will be best served by a diplomatic solution to this situation.'

'I will never yield Dura to anyone while I live.'

'I can see that,' he said. 'Tell me, out of curiosity, is your queen here?'

I smiled. Gallia's fame had certainly spread far and wide. 'She is here, lord.'

He nodded. 'You may be interested to know that in Rome Queen Gallia has become something of a celebrity among the fine ladies of the city.'

'I find that difficult to believe.'

'You are wrong,' he reproached me. 'They say that she was the real reason Spartacus managed to survive for so long, that she led his horsemen and that she even told him what to do. They like the idea of a determined woman, and one of royalty too. I believe she was a princess of Gaul?'

I laughed. 'I thought I was the commander of his horsemen. But yes, she was a princess of Gaul, now a queen of Parthia.'

'Myths spread quicker than the truth, Pacorus, and I have to admit I have encouraged and indulged these stories.'

I was confused. 'Why?'

'To annoy Crassus, of course. His triumph against Spartacus diminishes somewhat if people believe the slaves were led by a woman.'

It comforted me to learn that Rome was riven with rivalries just as Parthia was.

'This all very interesting,' in truth it was not, 'but what about Rome's intentions here, today?'

'I decide Rome's intention, and today I have settled the eastern border of Roman Syria.' He held out his hand. 'Do you trust the word of a Roman?'

I had just cause not to trust any Roman, and yet I felt that this Pompey was a person in whom one could place confidence. The fact that he was no friend of Crassus was a recommendation in itself. I took his hand.

'I trust the Roman who stands in front of me.'

'Good, that is settled.' He looked at Remus. 'A fine horse.'

'Remus? Yes, we have travelled far together.'

Pompey eyed me quizzically. 'Remus? You are a strange one, Parthian.'

He turned smartly and ordered the centurion to follow him back to his army. The Roman soldier handed me Remus' reins and marched behind his commander. I vaulted into the saddle and rode back to the kings.

'What now?' asked my father.

'Now we see if I have made a miscalculation,' I replied.

For what seemed like an eternity nothing happened, and then a cacophony of trumpet calls rang out from the Roman ranks. As one the cataphracts to my right and left lowered their lances in preparation for a charge, but then the Roman cavalry opposite us wheeled about and began riding away, showing their backs to us, while in the centre the legionaries about-turned and also began to retreat. It was the same on the opposite flank where Nergal commanded the lords. The Romans smartly wheeled about and rode away. I sensed a tide of relief sweep through me and my body began to relax. Around me men began shaking hands with their neighbours as the realisation that there would be no fighting this day rippled through the ranks.

'Hail, Pacorus,' said Vardan.

Gotarzes put his own unique slant on the day's events. 'Whatever you said must have scared him shitless.'

My father reached over and laid his hand on my arm. 'This is your greatest victory, Pacorus.'

'But no blood has been spilt,' I said.

He smiled. 'Exactly, my son, exactly. Well done.'

Gallia came from behind me and stopped by my side.

'So how did you do that?'

In front of us the Romans were disappearing into a great cloud of dust kicked up by thousands of hobnailed sandals and horses' hooves.

'I like to think that my charm had something to do with it.'

She raised an eyebrow. 'Really?'

Domitus came running over, sweat pouring down his face and neck.

'We're not going to fight them, then?'

'Not today, Domitus,' I replied.

He looked at Pompey's army gradually diminishing in size to the west. 'It's not too late to attack them, given that all these fine lords have made the effort to get here.'

I looked at him, then at my father, who wore an alarmed expression.

'No, Domitus, I shook hands with Pompey and we agreed each other's border.'

Domitus took off his helmet and wiped his brow with a cloth. 'Spartacus was right, that honour of yours will get you killed one day.'

I smiled. 'But not today, Domitus, not today.'

He put his helmet back on and pointed at the Romans. 'They will be back, Pacorus, you can be sure of that.'

He saluted us and returned to his men, then gave the order that they were to return to camp. Around us the kings likewise instructed that their horsemen were to withdraw to the river and make camp for the night, all except my father. He pointed at the seething black mass of Agraci warriors gathered to the south.

'What are you going to do about them?'

'Invite them to eat with us, of course.'

The next few hours were an exercise in logistics as around eighty thousand men, the same numbers of horses, thousands of camels and hundreds of mules made camp for the night along the Euphrates. Vardan insisted that all the kings, princes and Gallia dine with him in his royal pavilion that took dozens of slaves a few hours to erect. Babylon may not have been the mighty power it was in the time of the Persians, but its king still knew how to impress. The pavilion was at least two hundred paces in length and fifty wide, its enormous canvas roof supported by rows of poles and secured by dozens of ropes secured to long iron stakes that were driven into the earth. It made my own tent look paltry to say the least.

'Big tents don't make a good army,' growled Domitus when I told him of Babylon's encampment.

'Do you feel robbed, Domitus?'

He shrugged. 'There's always someone else to fight, so we'll keep our blades sharp.'

I poured myself a cup of water and sat down opposite him. Outside the legionaries were going about their business of checking their equipment, sentry duty and sharpening their swords.

'Do you think we could have beaten Pompey, Domitus?'

'Do you mean before or after your father and his friends turned up?'

'Before, of course.'

He tilted his head to one side. 'We'll never know now, but I like to think that we would have given a good account of ourselves.'

I rode from my camp with Malik and Byrd to the black tents of Haytham that extended far into the desert. The Agraci warriors were a mixture of camel riders armed with spears and bows and horsemen who carried spears, swords and small round shields. They all wore flowing robes and turbans that they used to cover their faces and shield their eyes. As far as I could tell none wore armour either on their heads or around their bodies. Malik escorted me to his father's tent located in the centre of the camp, where we found Haytham with his tribal chiefs. They were like him, big men with unyielding expressions and skin like tanned leather. All carried great swords at their hips and daggers tucked into their belts. The chiefs looked at me suspiciously when I entered, but then relaxed when they saw that I was with Malik, a few even greeted Byrd.

I halted in front of Haytham and bowed my head. 'Great king, I came to thank you for bringing your mighty army to this place.'

He walked over and embraced me. 'Don't be so formal, Pacorus, we are all friends here.'

He looked round at his chiefs, daring one of them to contradict him. None did.

'So,' continued Haytham, 'we were all wondering why you didn't launch an attack when they turned tail and ran?'

'I had made an agreement with their commander, lord, which made bloodshed unnecessary.'

He released me and smiled. 'No bloodshed is unnecessary, Pacorus. Still, it is what it is. How's that wife of yours?' He looked at his chiefs. 'You should see Queen Gallia, long blond hair, blue eyes and the body of a goddess. But even I would not want to get

408

on the wrong side of her.'

'You will all see here tonight,' I announced, 'for I would like the king of the Agraci and all his chiefs to come to the feast being held in honour of our uniting against the Romans.'

The chiefs looked at each other and then at me.

'Will Parthians sit down to eat with Agraci?' said one condescendingly, a great brute with a thick beard and black eyes.

'You forget yourself, Yasser,' growled Haytham.

'My apologies, lord,' Yasser placed his right palm on his chest and bowed to his king, 'but I have had experience of Parthian hospitality.'

There were mumbles of agreement. I held up my hand.

'I am Parthian, you all know this, but I esteem Prince Malik, son of your king, as one of my closest friends. I also count your king as a friend, and I say to you that you will all be welcome to the feast tonight, when Parthian and Agraci will sit side by side in peace and friendship.'

I thought it a fine speech that would not be out of place among the great speakers of ancient Athens, though a line of blank faces told me that I would have to sharpen my skills greatly if I wanted to be an orator.

'Well said, Pacorus,' barked Haytham. 'We shall be glad to attend.'

'We shall?' said an incredulous Yasser.

'We shall,' replied Haytham with such force that there was no further discussion on the matter.

As the sun began its descent in the west, Malik, his father and a dozen of the Agraci chiefs arrived at our camp, all attired in black and riding black horses. I entertained them in my tent while we waited for Gallia. She had brought no fine clothes with her on this journey, but when she finally appeared she made a great impression as usual. Her hair hung loose around her shoulders and tumbled over her white satin shirt edged with blue. She wore gold at her neck, long gold earrings and around her waist she wore her sword. Her slim legs were encased in tight black leggings and on her feet she wore red leather boots. I smiled when I noticed that she had her dagger tucked in the top of her right boot. Haytham smiled, took both of her hands and kissed them, while Gallia kissed Malik on the cheek. I introduced Orodes to Haytham and then we set off for Vardan's great tent. I told Gallia of Yasser's hostility to the Parthians, so she insisted that she rode beside him on our short journey to the Babylonian camp. She explained to him of the journey that had led her to Dura, and within no time his wall of hostility had crumbled as they talked and laughed together. I think that he was delighted that she had seemingly picked him at random to be her escort.

Babylon's pavilion was ringed with guards when we arrived and our horses were taken from us. A captain and a detachment of purple-clad spearmen escorted us inside, where a wall of noise greeted us. The floor was covered in red and yellow carpets and oil lamps hung from every pole. Guards stood around the sides and a small army of slaves served food and drink from silver platters. The kings and their senior officers were gathered in a great circle in the centre, where they were lounging on couches piled high with red and gold cushions. I saw my father, Vistaspa, Vardan, Atrax, Aschek and Gotarzes, who by the look of his rosy cheeks had already had too much to drink. Musicians played in one corner, half-naked girls danced in another and fire-eaters and jugglers went about their craft largely ignored.

We stood at the entrance and the noise suddenly began to fade as Parthians cast their eyes on a party of Agraci in their midst, and not just any Agraci. This was Haytham, the scourge of Parthia's western frontier, the devil of children's nightmares, the man whose name inspired both loathing and terror throughout the western half of the empire. All eyes were suddenly upon our group. Some of the officers put down their food and wine and stood up, while I saw the guards posted around the tent look at each other nervously. Vardan slowly rose from his couch. The King of Babylon was dressed in a rich purple robe edged with gold, a jewel-encrusted crown on his head and gold rings on his fingers. He spread his arms wide.

'Welcome Haytham, King of the Agraci, and his brave lieutenants, new allies of Parthia. Take freely of my hospitality. Be seated, please. Let us forget our animosities and begin a new era in the relations between our two peoples.'

Haytham bowed his head ever so slightly at Vardan and then walked over to Babylon's king, ignoring the hateful stares that were being directed at him. The silence was deafening. Haytham halted before Babylon's king. The Agraci king was big and stocky, Vardan also solid. Haytham held out his hand, Vardan smiled and they clasped each other's arms, then Vardan gestured for Haytham to sit beside him on the royal couch. He did so and the noise slowly returned to the royal tent. We were shown to our couches and suddenly the pavilion was once again alive with sound and activity.

I embraced my father, who then hugged Gallia. He also shook Malik's hand.

'Good to see you, again, Malik.'

'You too, lord,' smiled Haytham's son.

'Another victory, Pacorus,' said my father, 'bringing Agraci and Parthian together. I think that you will make a worthy king of Hatra.'

'Not for many years I hope, father, not for many years.'

It was a most excellent evening and for once I allowed myself to drink a fair quantity of wine, though nothing compared to Gotarzes, who was striking up an unlikely friendship with Yasser, also revealing himself to be a hearty drinker. At the end of the evening they were both singing at the tops of their voices with their arms around each other, before collapsing into a deep stupor. They were both carried from the pavilion to sleep off their indulgence.

Vardan excused himself in the early hours and returned to his private quarters in the royal compound behind the pavilion, and then the other kings, save Gotarzes, did the same. I bid my father and Vistaspa farewell and rode with Haytham and his chiefs back to my camp, the sleeping Yasser strapped to the back of his horse. At the entrance we said goodbye to the Agraci king and his entourage.

'An interesting evening, Pacorus,' said Haytham.

'Hopefully it will be the start of a new chapter in the story of our two peoples, lord.'

He reached over and slapped me on the arm. 'Perhaps. Take care of yourself.' He bowed his head to Gallia. 'Lady.'

Then they were gone and I was alone with my wife. Guards snapped to attention as we rode up the camp's central avenue to my tent. I felt immensely smug. I had secured Dura's frontiers without having to fight, several kings of the empire had made a show of force in my favour and the king of the Agraci had even brought his army to fight by my side. As I collapsed onto the floor of the tent after Gallia had assisted me inside, my last thoughts before sinking into a deep sleep was how it had been a most satisfactory day.

I was awoken sharply by a boot being kicked into my side.

'Get up,' I had difficulty in focusing but was aware of Gallia's voice.

There was another sharp pain in my side. I opened my eyes to see my wife standing over me. I smiled at her.

'Get up, Pacorus.'

I still felt groggy. 'What?'

I jumped up with a start when a bucket of cold water was thrown over me. I saw Domitus holding the bucket.

411

'Is this some sort of joke?' I snapped.

Gallia pulled me to my feet. 'Dura is under siege.'

Chapter 19

Gallia's Amazons were already armed and mounted when I stumbled out into the early morning sun, shielding my eyes as the light stung them and intensified my headache. Domitus offered me a cup of water, which I drank in one gulp. Gallia vaulted into her saddle and beckoned Praxima forward.

'Where is that heathen from the north, what was his name, Kuban?'

'He and his men are camped a mile away.'

'Go and fetch them, and tell him that we are riding south immediately.'

Praxima saluted and galloped off.

'Wait,' I shouted, 'you cannot just ride off without any plan.'

'He's right, lady,' said Domitus.

Gallia snapped her fingers and held out her right arm. Viper rode forward and handed Gallia her helmet.

'You stay here and sleep off your hangover, Pacorus. I will ride south to save our daughter and your city.'

She put on her helmet and then tugged on Epona's reins to turn the mare around, digging her knees into the beast and galloping away down the camp's central avenue, followed by her Amazons.

I threw the cup on the ground. 'In the name of all that's holy Gallia, wait,' I shouted at the top of my voice. It was useless; my wife was disappearing in a cloud of dust. My head felt as though a herd of horses was stampeding through it.

Nergal and Orodes ran up, followed by Surena. 'Get my horse,' I said to Surena.

'What's happening?' he asked.

I could have run him through at that moment. 'Just get my horse, idiot!'

He momentarily froze, saluted and then ran off to the stables.

'Easy, Pacorus,' muttered Domitus, 'remember you are on display. It's not a good idea for the king to show he has lost control of things.'

I looked at him, and then took a deep breath. 'Very well. Sound assembly, you will take all the foot back to Dura as quickly as you can.' He raised his arm in salute and then began barking orders at his officers who had gathered behind him. Orodes and Nergal looked at each other in confusion.

'Dura is under siege,' I said to them.

'Under siege?' they looked even more confused.

I threw up my hands. 'You know as much as I do.'

Then Byrd and Malik arrived on their horses. I pointed at Byrd.

413

'What is going on?'

'We received news from a courier sent from one of your forts earlier. Dura under siege.'

'Who is besieging the city?' asked Orodes.

'The Romans?' I said.

Byrd shook his head. 'Chosroes.'

'Chosroes?' I did not believe it.

'That was the message,' said Byrd flatly.

Surena arrived on his horse with Remus in tow. I went inside the tent and began donning my equipment. I felt sick, tired and confused. I strapped on my sword, leather cuirass and picked up my helmet. Nergal and Orodes stood waiting for orders.

'Orodes, assemble the cataphracts and bring them south. I will ride ahead with the horse archers. Nergal, how many of your men are already mounted?'

'No more than two hundred.'

'It will have to do,' I said, 'I ride at once. Nergal, you will follow with the rest, and bring the lords as well.'

They nodded and left.

'Orodes,' I called after them.

'Pacorus?'

'Before you leave, be so kind as to inform my father and the other kings of what has happened.'

He nodded and then followed Nergal.

'Byrd and I will be riding with you,' said Malik.

Half an hour later we were heading south along the Euphrates, two hundred horse archers plus me, Byrd and Malik. I thanked Shamash that we had built the forts along the river; otherwise we might not have received the terrible news until it was too late. Perhaps it was already too late. Do not think that! Chosroes, the miserable rat. He had obviously been watching events carefully, no doubt encouraged by the nest of cockroaches at Ctesiphon. He must have believed that the Romans would defeat me, perhaps even kill me, leaving Dura defenceless. But still, even if that had been the case, he would have had to deal with a victorious Roman army. His ragtag forces were no match for the Romans and he must have known that. Unless, of course, he had allies. I suddenly saw the hands of Narses and Mithridates pulling the strings of their puppet.

Gallia set a cruel pace. We had thrown some food and fodder in sacks and tied them to our saddles and then followed her. She had collected Kuban and his men, whose camp stood empty and deserted. A horse can comfortably cover around thirty miles a day, but that first day we travelled over thirty and still did not catch up with my queen. We halted for the night at one of the mud-brick forts where the commander, a fresh-faced centurion on crutches, told us that she had visited them earlier.

'They took all the fodder but left most of our food, sir.'

I pointed at his crutches. 'What happened?'

'Got crushed under a testudo during training, sir. Occupational hazard.'

'Indeed,' I said. 'How was the queen when you saw her?'

'Like a snake that has just been stepped on, sir.'

The garrison of each fort had been greatly reduced when the army had marched north, but a small number of men had been left behind, including any that were infirm or generally unfit for duty. In this way the fort's stores would be secure and communications maintained between the city and the army. We slept under the sky outside the fort that night and, after what seemed only five minutes of sleep, saddled the horses before dawn and were riding south again as the first red shards of light were seen in the eastern sky. Unwashed and unshaven, we picked up a quick pace once more and thundered ahead. There was no conversation as we headed for Dura, but throughout the day I began to worry what we would find when we got there. If the city had fallen... Do not think, keep moving, stay focused.

The second night our bodies ached and our horses were lathered in sweat. So we halted, unsaddled them and led them into the cool waters of the Euphrates. Once more we grabbed a pitiful amount of sleep and rode south again in the pre-dawn light. After three hours of hard riding we finally caught up with Gallia. Her horses were tied together in the shade of a large group of date palms a hundred paces from the Euphrates. Most of Kuban's fierce warriors were similarly in the shade, many lying asleep on the ground beside their leather armour. But Gallia had also ensured that she would not be surprised and had thrown out parties of guards to keep watch, and a dozen of Kuban's men had ridden up to our column before we arrived at the main body, escorting us down the road to where Dura's queen was standing with a group of the Amazons. I dismounted, handed Remus' reins to Surena and walked over to them. They parted when they saw me, bowing their heads as I walked up to my wife.

'You took your time,' was all she said, looking at a semi-naked man spread-eagled on the ground in front of her. His wrists and ankles had been lashed tightly to wooden stakes that had been hammered into the ground. The figure of Kuban was kneeling

415

beside him, a bloody knife in his hand.

'This wretch has told us that the army of Mesene is besieging Dura,' she snapped her fingers and one of her Amazons handed her a round shield. She then passed it to me. 'But this carries the bird-god symbol of Persis.'

'Narses is at Dura?' I said.

Gallia smiled and then nodded to Kuban, who ran the blade of his knife across the victim's chest, drawing blood as he did so. The man's body contorted with pain and Kuban stopped cutting. The man turned his head and spat at him. Kuban wiped his face and then cut off the man's left ear, causing him to scream and thrash wildly at his bonds.

'You heard his majesty,' barked Kuban. 'Answer his question.'

The man's eyes were full of fear as they looked at me, blood pouring from his ear socket.

'No Narses,' said weakly, 'he sent us to reinforce Chosroes. Water, please.'

Gallia walked away. 'Kill him, Kuban.'

I winced as Kuban drew his blade across the man's throat. He passed from this life as blood gushed from his neck onto the earth. I followed Gallia.

'We ran into a patrol earlier and killed all of them except that one. Kuban has some very useful skills when it comes to extracting information.'

I stopped her and placed my hands on her shoulders. There were black rings round her eyes and she looked very tired.

'You must rest.'

She shook off my hands. 'I will rest when my daughter is safe.'

Gallia looked at my men leading their horses to drink from the river. 'Is that all you brought?'

'More are coming. More to the point, how many do we face?'

'Fifteen thousand, according to that piece of carrion we captured.'

'When did they arrive?'

'Five days ago. They have yet to assault the city but it cannot be long before they do so.'

Fifteen thousand was a big army, but I was not as worried now as I was when I first heard that Dura was under siege. Parthians have no knowledge of siege warfare, save surrounding a city and starving it into surrender. Then Gallia dashed my hopes.

'He told us that Chosroes knew that the city would be weakly defended because its army had marched north, and he has brought siege towers with him.'

'Siege towers?'

'Yes,' she said, 'but they had to be dismantled and then reassembled once at the city. He told us that the assault would take place tomorrow. We have to get to Dura today.'

I grabbed her arm; she wrenched it free.

'Wait, Gallia, please wait. We cannot attack fifteen thousand men with just over a thousand. We must wait until Nergal and Orodes arrive. That at least will even the odds.'

Her blue eyes narrowed. 'I don't care about odds, all I care about is my daughter.'

'So do I, but getting ourselves killed will not help her.'

Her eyes misted with tears and I held her close. 'Have no fear, remember that Godarz is in command of the city and he has engines at his disposal.'

Byrd and Malik rode further south with a score of horsemen to try to discover more information, but I forbade them to take any risks or engage any enemy they might encounter. I did not want them to be staked out in the sun and tortured, or worse. While I waited for them to return the men and women took the opportunity to rest, fill their bellies and tend to their horses. Several of the latter were lame due to the exertions of the journey and so they and their riders would have to be left behind. This further reduced our numbers, and though Kuban and his officers wanted to attack the enemy without waiting, I knew that our only hope lay with Nergal and Orodes. Nergal arrived that evening with his horse archers and the lords and their retainers. I was delighted to discover that Atrax and Vistaspa accompanied them, along with two thousand of Hatra's horse archers and another three thousand of Media's horse archers.

'The rest of Hatra's army, together with the forces of the other kings, are marching down the east bank of the Euphrates, majesty,' he said formally. Same old Vistaspa. Then he added. 'Your foot under Domitus are following in our wake on this side of the river.'

It was a happy reunion and as the men relieved their horses of their saddles and prepared an evening meal, the senior officers gathered under a gnarled old date palm to decide what to do. The mood was relaxed as we drank water and chewed on hard biscuit. I estimated that we now numbered over seventeen thousand men, excellent odds for the morrow. And crucially, Orodes' own and Dura's cataphracts were following close behind.

'The heavy cavalry will be here tomorrow, Pacorus,' reported Nergal, 'together with the camel train carrying armour, arrows, fodder and food.

'Are you planning to wait for their arrival before you attack?' asked Vistaspa, his long black hair now streaked with grey.

'Wait?'

The atmosphere changed suddenly with Gallia's arrival.

'Wait for what, wait for my city to fall or for my daughter to be skewered on the end of a spear?'

Vistaspa tried to maintain his sense of decorum, bowing his head to Dura's queen. 'I was merely endeavouring to ascertain if...'

'Useless words,' she spat, 'we attack tonight.'

A look of horror crossed Vistaspa's face, though I was unsure whether it was caused by him being spoken to in such a manner by a woman or the thought of tired men and horses fighting a battle in the dark. To his credit he retained his composure.

'Majesty, it would be unwise to attack now.'

But Gallia was in no mood for arguments. 'Unwise? Is it wise for a soldier to contradict a queen?'

Vistaspa's face hardened and his eyes flashed with anger. He had, after all, been royalty himself in a former life.

'Gallia,' I interrupted, 'the horses are exhausted after a long ride. They will not perform well in combat in such a state, and night battles are confusing affairs at best.'

'It is not the Parthian way to fight in the darkness,' added Atrax.

The prince of Media was a brave men and a good friend, though his notion that fighting enemies face to face in daylight was more honourable than killing them at night made little impression on my wife, who now spun round to face him.

'Not the Parthian way? What is the Parthian way, boy, to sit under a tree and do nothing while my people are butchered?'

Atrax's eyes were wide with alarm as Gallia advanced upon him, the ferocious Kuban backing her up.

'Enough!' I shouted. 'If we argue among ourselves the victory of Narses will be our only reward. Gallia, we wait until Byrd and Malik return, and then we will make our plans. Until then the men and horses will be rested.'

Gallia sneered at me, turned and strode off into the night followed by her loyal hound. I excused myself and went after her, catching her up and then walking beside her as she went back to the Amazons.

'You know waiting till it's light makes sense,' I said.

'Do I.'

'More men will be arriving tomorrow.'

She stopped and faced me. 'Men? I'm beginning to wonder if there are any men in Parthia.'

'That is unfair.'

She eyed me coolly. 'I remember a time in Italy when we fought at night to rescue the army of Spartacus.'

'That was different.'

She would have none of it. 'No it wasn't. If Claudia dies then her blood will be on your hands.'

I tried to put my arm around her but she brushed away my affection and went back to her women.

An hour later Byrd and Malik returned and reported that the army of Chosroes had made no assault on the city. I thanked Shamash for that. But they suspected that the attack would be made imminently as four siege towers had been placed before the western wall. This made my heart sink – Dura's walls were stout but not particularly high; siege towers meant soldiers could be placed on top of the city's walls with ease. We had to attack in the early hours. They also told me that the pontoon bridge had not been destroyed and that there were in addition enemy soldiers on the eastern bank of the Euphrates. This offered some hope as it meant that the enemy had dissipated his strength by dividing his forces. I thanked them both and told them to get some food and rest, although it was now only a couple of hours before the dawn.

It was still dark when I assembled the senior officers and told them of my intentions. I had not slept a wink, partly because I had been formulating a plan of attack but mostly because Gallia's words were still ringing in my ears. I had not shaved since leaving the kings and I felt dirty, but no worse than the tired individuals gathered around me. We stood in a circle next to the old date palm once more, Gallia's eyes boring into me. Kuban once more attended her, who looked no different from the first time I had met him. Perhaps he was a demon from the northern steppes that required no food or sleep. Atrax kept glancing at his sister-in-law but avoided her gaze when she looked in his direction.

'Very well,' I said. 'We will break camp immediately and ride south to Dura. Nergal, you remain here with the lords and wait for Orodes and the heavy horsemen and the camels. I have learned that the enemy has soldiers on the eastern side of the river as well as camped in front of the city. Therefore, if we can seize and hold the bridge across the river we will divide his army and make the odds more favourable.'

We broke camp and headed south. I threw a party of scouts led by Byrd and Malik ahead to ensure we did not run into the enemy on the way, but as the dawn broke and light filled the world we saw no activity ahead. We halted and waited for them an hour after

419

dawn, though Gallia once again vented her frustration at the lack of action. However, when they returned and reported the road ahead was clear for the next five miles we once again commenced our journey. Ten miles from the city we divided our column. Vistaspa and the bulk of Hatra's horse archers would keep to the road so they could seize the pontoon bridge and hold it, while I took the Amazons, my own two hundred men, Kuban's thousand warriors and Atrax's horsemen into the desert. This would take us more time to reach the city but would allow us to deploy into line and attack the enemy from the west. I still worried that we were too few and had insufficient ammunition but the die was cast.

I could see Dura's Citadel shimmering in the distance now; we were only around half an hour away from our destination. I slowed the column and then halted it, and called together the commanders. Kuban may have been good at torturing the helpless and he certainly looked like a warrior, but he and his men were an unknown quantity when it came to the battlefield, so I placed them on the right wing. My own men and the Amazons I deployed in the centre, with Atrax and the Medians on the left. I wanted Gallia close to me when we attacked so I could keep an eye on her and try to prevent her from doing anything rash when we reached the city. Then we moved forward at a canter.

Dura was plainly visible now, its yellow walls and towers set against a blue sky. Rising above the walls was the Citadel standing defiantly. I could see the enemy camp as well, scores of brightly coloured tents of various sizes filling the plain directly in front of the city, plus hundreds of camels that transported provisions for the army of Chosroes. Hundreds more horses were tethered in compounds. Curiously, they had made no use of the walled camp that usually housed Domitus' legionaries and which now stood empty.

'Open order,' I commanded, which was passed along the line. We would have to move through the horses, camels and tents before we reached the enemy's troops. And then I saw the siege towers looming above the tents. It was difficult to tell, but it appeared that their sides were covered in hide as protection against arrows. Not that there appeared to be any arrows being fired from the walls.

We flanked Domitus' camp, then rode into the enemy's compound and threaded our way between the camels, horse compounds, wagons, campfires and tents. The enemy army may have been drawn up in front of the city but there were still many people milling round, mostly camp followers – wives, whores, the deranged and hawkers – a veritable army of non-combatants who trailed every army, though I tried to discourage such hangers-on in Dura's army. A half-naked woman, a whore no doubt, came out of a tent with her breasts exposed. She froze when she saw us, and then died when one of my men put an arrow through her throat. It was a good shot.

'Ignore them,' I shouted, 'save your arrows.'

I nocked an arrow in my bowstring as we left the camp, infirm enemy soldiers and civilians scattering before us. We rode on towards the rear of the enemy army. I saw few horsemen save officers riding up and down with swords in hand berating their men to move forward. The army of Mesene was as ragged as I remembered it, but it made for an imposing sight. Archers, spearmen with shields, slingers and men armed only with axes and clubs filled the area in front of Dura's western wall. We fanned out into a long line of two ranks and moved into a canter, then a gallop. I saw the towers ahead, archers packed on their top platforms searching for targets on the walls or towers, but I could see none of Dura's garrison.

At a range of five hundred paces we began loosing our bows, firing at a rate of five arrows a minute as we quickly closed the distance between ourselves and the enemy's rear ranks. The shouts and war cries of the Mesenians, expecting the walls to be conquered by the siege towers, drowned out the sounds of our horses' hooves, so that the first they knew of our arrival was the sight of their comrades collapsing on the ground, their bodies pierced by arrows. Most wore no armour and more than a few had no helmets, so our arrows easily found flesh and bone. Around twenty thousand arrows had been fired before they realised what was happening. Then we were less then fifty paces from them, loosing arrows as we abruptly wheeled our horses' right and then retreated, shooting a final shot over the rear quarters of our animals. A line of Mesenian dead bore testament to the success of our first charge. As we had done a hundred times in training, we halted five hundred paces from the enemy and then wheeled right once more, before commencing another charge against them. By this time the enemy had realised what was occurring and their officers were frantically trying to realign their ranks to form a wall of shields and spears against us. I strung an arrow and shot it, and then shot another and another as we hurtled towards them, then yanked Remus to the right once more, but this time enemy arrows were being shot back at us. Horses and riders went down as we pulled back. I felt a knot in the pit of my stomach as I desperately

421

sought out Gallia. There she was, leading her Amazons, shooting arrows and for the moment safe.

Relief.

Back we went, loosing arrows and taking more casualties, and then we fell back once more to regroup. I reached into my quiver. Empty! I looked left and right and saw other riders similarly out of missiles. In front of us the Mesenian line, battered and littered with dead, still held. I ordered a halt to be sounded and considered our next action. And then I saw a wondrous sight. From within the city what appeared to be black rocks arched into the sky and fell on and around the siege towers. One, two, three and then a fourth, hurtling into the sky and then smashing into the wooden towers. When they struck a tower or crashed onto the earth they turned into a fireball. How was this possible? Then I realised that they must be clay pots filled with the Chinese liquid that was kept in the armoury. But how were they being launched? In minutes one of the siege towers was ablaze, burning figures hurling themselves from the top platform, then a second caught fire and exhilaration swept through me.

'What is causing that?' Gallia was at my side, pointing at one of the burning towers with her bow.

'I have no idea,' I replied. 'But I thank Shamash for his miracle. I am out of arrows.'

She shoved her bow back in its case. 'Me also.'

Around us men and women began cheering as a third tower was hit by two Chinese fireballs and erupted into flames. We might have failed to break the enemy line, but the attack on the city had been stopped in its tracks.

Then I heard frantic horn blasts and looked to my left, to see a line of horsemen armed with spears, protected by round shields and wearing helmets hurtling towards Kuban's men. The latter in turn charged them and they smashed into each other with a sickening crunching sound that echoed across the battlefield. Enemy cavalry had hit us with a devastating counterattack against our left wing. I placed my bow in its case. I forgot about the enemy foot soldiers in front of us – we had to help Kuban or our flank would be rolled up.

'Form column,' I shouted, 'follow me.'

I tugged on Remus' reins with my right hand to turn him left, then shouted at him to move. He knew every inference and tone of my voice and broke into a gallop. I wrapped his reins round my left wrist and drew my sword with my right hand. Horns blasted and Gallia, the Amazons the rest of the horsemen careered after me. We formed a loose wedge as we closed the gap between the enemy horsemen that were going to work with their spears, parrying the swords and spears of Kuban's men with their shields. Already they were cutting their way through the northern horsemen, who to their credit were fighting back and giving ground reluctantly. Then we hit the flank of the Mesenians and in no time a frantic melee erupted. I swung my sword at the neck of a passing horseman, the blade biting deep into his flesh and knocking him from his saddle. I felt a searing pain in my left arm and turned to see a spear blade had brushed my flesh. I yanked on Remus' reins and he turned away from my assailant, who directed his own mount in an attempt to skewer me with his lance. I raised my sword and brought it down to cut through the wooden shaft, then brought it up and thrust the point into the man's thigh. He yelped in pain and turned his horse away to beat a retreat. And so it went on, stabbing, slashing and thrusting at fleeting targets as they came within range. Screams, shouts and obscene language filled the air. My men tried to stay close to me, tried to maintain some semblance of discipline, but it was hard as individuals became locked in combat and absorbed in their own private battles. Riderless horses, wild-eyed and bleeding, bolted from the carnage while others, too hurt to move, stood still and then collapsed on to the ground.

There was a blast of horns and the Mesenians began to disengage and fall back. They obviously had had enough, for the moment. Other horns sounded, our own, and we too fell back to regroup. Gallia and the Amazons appeared mercifully unhurt. We reformed into our companies, the ground in front of us sprinkled with dead and dying men and horses, though in truth, considering the great effort that had been expended hacking and stabbing, there were fewer casualties than I expected. But there were many wounded, men with wounds to their bodies, arms and legs, and also horses that had been gashed by blades. I checked Remus over; I could not see any wounds.

Smoke was now drifting across the battlefield from the four siege towers, which were all burning brightly. To our front the enemy foot soldiers, plus those horse archers whose mounts we passed in camp, had now turned away from the city and were marching towards us. I looked left and right. No one had any arrows left and arrows were now flying from the enemy ranks towards us. There was nothing left to do. I turned to the nearest signaller and ordered him to sound retreat. He blew his horn, a sound that was soon echoing down the line. Gallia galloped over to my side as horsemen wheeled their animals away to ride back from where we had come from.

'We are falling back?' She had a nasty dent in her helmet and her left sleeve was gashed, though I could see no blood.

'Are you hurt?' I enquired.

She ignored my question. 'The city is still besieged, Pacorus.'

'Their siege towers are destroyed and their foot are marching towards us. They will attempt no further assault on Dura today. Now get your women back.'

Kuban and his men acted as a rearguard as we fell back through the enemy camp. I ordered that any enemy horses and camels were to be untethered and scattered into the desert, and the tents, wagons, supplies and compounds to be torched. The next few minutes were not the proudest of my life as my men and the Amazons went about firing the camp cutting down any unfortunates they came across. Panicking women ran around screaming and were either trampled under horses' hooves or killed with swords. I saw one woman, with rouge on her cheeks and gold in her hair, perhaps no older than twenty, fall to her knees in front of a group of Amazons, imploring them to show mercy. Perhaps she was a whore or a slave taken against her will to serve the soldiers of Chosroes. It did not matter. Gallia rode up to her and almost severed her head with a swing of her sword. Tents burst into flames, their occupants running into the sunlight with their clothes alight. They too were killed. Sick and wounded soldiers limped from hospital tents, only to be cut down without mercy. I was worried that the bloodlust would distract my men and so rode among them, ordering them to fall back, smoke stinging my eyes as the camp was engulfed in flames. Terrified horses and camels were herded into the desert and scattered far and wide as we finally left the Mesenian camp and moved back into the desert.

Recall was sounded and once more the men formed into their companies as Kuban's men emerged from the smoke and again formed up on our right wing. Atrax, Gallia and Kuban joined me, their eyes red from the smoke, their faces streaked with dirt and their blades smeared with blood.

'We must get back to reinforce Vistaspa.'

So we rode to the bridge, our wounded carried behind other riders. Fortunately the enemy cavalry did not pursue us as we cantered across the plain to the river. We arrived to discover that Vistaspa had seized the bridge intact and had erected a protective barricade of wagons on the eastern bank, facing the enemy on that side of the river. He had established his command post next to a small cart on the western side of the river, around two hundred paces from the pontoon bridge.

'There is no point in holding one end of a wooden bridge if the enemy can set fire to the other,' he said.

He told me that when he arrived there was only a light guard manning the bridge, whose members had been speedily killed, allowing him to send men across the river and secure the eastern end. Then he manned the barricade with archers and threw a cordon around the bridge on the west bank of the river. As I spoke to him my cavalry filed past his horsemen sitting in their companies ready to beat off any attack. My men dismounted and threw themselves on the ground, exhausted. He looked at our tired faces and ripped attire.

'We could not break through to the city,' I said despondently.

He nodded and handed me a waterskin. 'Is Queen Gallia well?'

I managed a smile. 'She is well.'

I looked across the river to see a great mass of horsemen approaching from the north.

'Hatra's horsemen, plus those of the other kings,' remarked Vistaspa. He looked at me. 'Your city will soon be free of any threat.'

More horn blasts came from our side of the river and I mounted Remus once more. I saw the banner of Orodes fluttering in the hot air and behind it a column of cataphracts, the sun glinting off the whetted points of their great lances, followed by Nergal, Dura's lords and their horse archers. My tiredness started to recede as I rode to greet them. The enemy's army had now been split in two, but we still had to force a way through to the city. Dura was difficult to see clearly now because the whole plain was wreathed in smoke caused by the burning enemy camp. I now realised that torching it was a mistake. Gallia rode over to me as Vistaspa joined us on his horses.

Orodes, dressed in his scale amour, raised his left arm. 'Hail Pacorus, hail Gallia.'

'We can push our way through to the city now,' said Gallia impatiently.

Across the river the shouts and cries of thousands of men signalled that the two sides had now clashed. I looked at the smoke obscuring the city, horses and camels bolting and injured men limping past us.

'What are we waiting for?' snapped Gallia.

'Very well,' I said. 'Orodes, get your heavy cavalry into line on the plain behind that burning camp. Nergal, get your men on the plain in front of those of Orodes.'

Gallia nodded her head enthusiastically and Vistaspa raised an eyebrow but said nothing. Across the river the din of battle increased.

'You disagree, Lord Vistaspa?' I asked.

He was aware of Gallia's animosity towards him so he chose his words carefully.

'It might be prudent to wait for your legions to arrive.'

'They are two hours' march away at least,' said Orodes.

'Two hours is too long,' said Gallia. 'We must attack again.'

They were both right, so I decided to compromise.

'Orodes, your men will form a reserve in case the enemy mount a charge against us at the bridge. Nergal and Atrax, take the horse archers and annoy the enemy deployed in front of the city.'

They saluted and rode off to organise their men.

'What are you doing?' said Gallia, clearly annoyed.

'We use the horse archers to pepper the enemy with arrows. They will not storm the city now.'

Vistaspa nodded and Gallia rode off to refill her quiver. Orodes had brought camels loaded with arrows with him, and now these were distributed among the horse archers of Dura and Media. Surena also went and brought me back a full quiver. Nergal and Atrax then deployed their men across the plain to the west of the city and led them forward once more. This time, however, they operated in their hundred-man companies, moving forward, shooting at the enemy and then retreating. Orodes deployed his cataphracts behind the archers, well back from still-smouldering enemy camp. If the enemy's horsemen showed themselves again the horse archers were to fall back to let the cataphracts deal with them. And so, while we waited for Domitus, the enemy was once again assaulted by an arrow storm. The enemy also had arrows, but because they had used many when we had first assaulted their ranks earlier that day, their fire soon lessened and then stopped altogether. Nergal reported that they had fallen back from in front of the city's walls and were grouped in a solid block on the plain between the city and their own destroyed camp. Our horsemen did not ride through the charred remains of the camp, but rather skirted it by riding north to south, shooting arrows at the enemy ranks on their left side. Then, once a company had ridden beyond the southern flank of the enemy, it wheeled right and rode back north behind the camp. In this way there was a continuous chain of companies loosing arrows at the enemy. The ammunition expenditure was prodigious, and after it had made two circuits each company had to ride back to the camel train for fresh arrows. We could not maintain such expenditure indefinitely, for soon our own supplies would be exhausted, but we did not have to. To the north the shrill sound of trumpet blasts could be heard – Domitus had arrived at last.

His cohorts began deploying on the plain as he reported to me. He looked remarkably fresh after his forced march, but then he and his men were in peak physical condition. The tents, mules and wagons had been left behind and were being escorted by the rest of the Median cavalry. The legionaries had slept under the stars after each day's march with guards posted every ten paces. It would have irked Domitus to disregard a habit of a lifetime, but there was no time to erect a camp each night.

'It will take the boys a couple of hours before they are in their battle formations and after they've had some water to drink,' he said, taking off his helmet and wiping his sweating forehead with a rag.

Even as he spoke legionaries were filling water bottles in the river and ferrying them back to their comrades. It was early afternoon now and the heat was intense. A canvas awning had been erected next to the wagon that was Vistaspa's command post, and several stools had been placed under it. Gallia, Vistaspa and I joined Domitus as he placed his helmet on the ground and sat down on one of the stools.

'So,' he said, 'what is the situation?'

I told him about our attack with the cavalry earlier and how the siege towers had been destroyed by fire.

'Lucky for you that you kept those Roman engineers,' he said. 'It was undoubtedly their machines that threw those fireballs. Did the enemy fire their own camp?'

'Er, no,' I replied.

'Then which idiot set it alight?'

Gallia pointed at me. Domitus shook his head. 'I worry about you, Pacorus.'

He stood up and put his hands on his hips. 'We can't march through it, so we'll have to split our forces and launch our attacks from the flanks, straight at their centre.'

I told him about the enemy horsemen that had counterattacked us.

'Where are they now?' he asked.

'I do not know.'

He smiled. 'They will be covering their foot, most likely.'

'Orodes and his horsemen will deal with them,' I said

The sounds of battle could still be heard across the river, though Domitus made no mention of what was happening on the other side of the Euphrates. His attention was focused on this side of the river. He replaced his helmet on his head and strode away to join a knot of his officers who were waiting nearby, then they all marched off to rejoin their units.

A lull descended over the battlefield as Domitus arranged his cohorts for the next attack on the enemy. Nergal's horse archers were pulled back and drawn up on both flanks of the legions, while behind the foot Orodes' cataphracts roasted in their scale armour. With Gallia I rode over to where the legions were deploying for battle, each one drawn up in three lines on either side of the still-burning camp. This meant that there was a large gap between each legion and I was worried that the enemy could escape through this space.

'Escape to where?' asked Domitus, watching his officers arrange their cohorts in close order. 'If any do manage to escape, all that awaits them are the scorpions of the desert and Haytham's warriors.'

Those of Nergal's horse archers who were drawn up on the right flank I sent across to the left, for Gallia had brought her Amazons with her. Behind them came the leather-clad horsemen of Kuban, who now formed themselves into a long line extending south. I could see the enemy mass clearly, a great brown block of Mesenian foot, which included the horse archers who had left their mounts in camp. I wondered what they were thinking as the legionaries made their final preparations. They were about a quarter of a mile from Dura's walls and had been standing there for some time now, with no food or water and under a blazing sun. I glanced at the Pontic Legion drawn up on our left.

The constant drills and training that the legionaries had performed over the preceding months meant that their deployment into their battle positions was as smooth as silk. The forthcoming clash would be a mere formality, but then the unexpected happened. I never considered that the enemy opposite us would attack, but that is precisely what they did. Not a measured approach followed by a disciplined rush at our ranks, but a wild charge against the Duran Legion positioned to the north of the burnt camp. Whoever the general was who led those forces, and I hoped it was Chosroes himself so I could kill him with my own sword, he had obviously realised the hopelessness of his situation. Having retreated from before the walls of Dura, he and his men were now trapped between the city and two legions that were each flanked by horsemen. I estimated by the extent of the enemy line that there were still around six or seven thousand men arrayed against us, though many of those were dismounted horse archers who had been used to sweep Dura's walls and towers of guards as the siege towers approached the city. Now those same men were largely without arrows. The rest were a motley collection of spearmen and other foot armed with axes, clubs and swords. Some of our horsemen had been hit and killed by lead balls, which meant that there were also some slingers among their ranks. But their commander knew that to stand and wait to be attacked was to invite certain death, so he threw all his men against the Duran Legion standing to the north of the charred camp. He could see that the latter divided the forces formed up against him, and probably gambled that he could smash his way through our lines before our forces deployed to the south of the camp could reach him. It was a bold gamble.

The two sides were around five hundred paces apart when there was a mighty cheer and the whole of the enemy mass began moving towards the Duran Legion. I was standing beside Domitus, finalising the plan of attack, when I heard and then saw the charge of the enemy. For a moment I was stunned; I could hardly believe that they would attempt such a thing. Then alarm swept through me. If they broke through the legion then they would reach the bridge, and if they reached the bridge they might escape across the Euphrates.

'Brave but stupid,' remarked Domitus nonchalantly.

Already trumpet blasts were coming from the legion's centuries as the frontline cohorts prepared to receive the enemy's charge. As they had done countless times on the training field, the men would close up and then advance against the seething mass that was now running towards them. When they were within thirty to forty paces of the opposition the front ranks would hurl their javelins, draw their swords and then charge the enemy. The storm of javelins would cut down their front ranks and then the legionaries would go to work with their short swords, stabbing with their points at their opponents.

'Don't worry,' said Domitus, 'the boys will hold. You had better deal with those, though.'

He was pointing at a long line of horsemen heading in our direction from south of the city, no doubt the same ones that had attacked Kuban's men earlier in the day. I vaulted into Remus' saddle.

'The enemy must not be allowed to reach the bridge, Domitus.'

He raised his hand. 'They won't, but you had better keep those horsemen away.'

'Don't worry about them,' I replied.

I galloped back to my horse archers, who were already stringing arrows in their bows, while Kuban's men levelled their spears in preparation for a charge. However, I decided that this was a task for Orodes. I sent a rider to fetch the Prince of Susiana and his men, and at the same time I ordered our whole line to fall back. This would temporarily expose the right flank of the Pontic Legion, which dismayed Gallia. As horns blew and the horsemen about-faced and pulled back she was at my side, her Amazons behind her. She pointed at the approaching enemy horsemen, who were still at least half a mile away.

'Why are you running away from them? We should be attacking them. You are leaving your own foot soldiers exposed.'

My patience was fast running out. 'If you were one of my officers I would have had you clapped in chains for your insubordination by now.'

With hindsight this was the wrong thing to say. 'Don't you dare speak to me that like,' she bellowed. By now those horsemen within earshot had stopped their rearward movements and were sitting in their saddles observing their king and queen bickering.

'Get back and obey my orders,' I insisted.

'I will not let you abandon our soldiers. Amazons,' she shouted, 'face front and prepare to charge.' Her women nocked arrows, while Kuban's men began moving their horses forward.

I swung in the saddle. 'Stay where you are!'

I turned back to Gallia, but at that moment the low rumble of horses' hooves came from the rear and I saw the banner of Orodes coming towards me. He and his cataphracts rode through our horsemen and began forming into two ranks in front of us. Ahead, the enemy was breaking into a canter.

'I desire you to deal with those horsemen opposite, my friend,' I said.

'Consider it done.' He smiled and rode forward and as one the two lines of cataphracts began moving towards the enemy, at first trotting and then breaking into a canter. Each rider then levelled his kontus and grasped it with both hands on his right side as the cataphracts broke into a gallop. Moments later there was a scraping noise as the two sides collided. As the horizon disappeared in a cloud of dust and our ears were filled with the screams of men and horses, to our left the Pontic Legion was moving forward prior to wheeling left to attack the flank of the Mesenian foot that had failed to break through to the bridge.

It was time to remove Gallia from the battlefield.

430

'Gallia,' I shouted, 'take your Amazons and Kuban's men and ride to the city gates. Reinforce the garrison while we mop up here.'

She was in no mood to be told what to do, but a mother's desire to ensure that her child was safe overrode all other emotions. With the enemy foot trying to save itself and Orodes driving back the enemy horsemen, the way to the city now lay open. It would take some time for the rubble and braces that would have been placed behind the city's gates to be removed, but at least Gallia would have something to occupy her mind.

She nodded and ordered Praxima and the rest of the Amazons to follow her towards the Palmyrene Gate. Behind them Kuban and his men followed in a long column. I also sent Vagharsh and my banner with Gallia to ensure that the garrison knew who was riding to the gates. This left me with around a hundred Duran horse archers, including Surena.

'Feisty, the queen!' he beamed.

'Be quiet.''

'Did you see Viper when we were shooting arrows at them earlier? Beautiful. Do you think she would marry me?'

'Not if she has any sense. Now stop daydreaming and concentrate on the task in hand.'

Orodes was cutting the enemy cavalry to pieces. A kontus can go straight through a wooden shield with ease, and through leather armour as well, and after the initial impact the cataphracts would go to work with their swords and maces, while the enemy would not be able to pierce scale armour or steel leg and arm armour. I rode forward with my greatly diminished command before encountering Orodes himself, who joined me with an escort of a dozen men. He raised his left hand, a blood-smeared mace held in the other.

'Most of them are dead, the rest have fled south.'

'Your own casualties?' I asked.

He shrugged. 'Insignificant.'

'Well done. Get your men back to the city, they've earned their pay today.'

As Orodes rode back to his men I journeyed across the battlefield to join the Pontic Legion that was now marching at right angles to the enemy's camp. Dura's legion was still locked in combat with the Mesenians, but it was obvious that the latter had failed in their efforts. And from the other flank Atrax, Nergal and their horse archers were attacking the Mesenians. Soon Chosroes' men would be assaulted on both flanks as well as fighting the

Duran Legion to their front.

Seeing the Pontic Legion approaching from the south, the Mesenians attempted to form a line on their left flank. To their credit there was still a semblance of order within their ranks, but their fate was sealed when the Pontic centuries smashed into them. Assaulted on two sides by legionaries and on another by horse archers, they were slowly being squeezed into a densely packed square, from which there was no escape when I led my own horse archers against its rear. Those equipped with shields turned to face us and formed a front rank, ramming the ends of their shafts into the hard earth and levelling their points at us, daring us to ride forward and impale ourselves on the long spears held at an angle of forty-five degrees. We did ride forward, but loosed our arrows at them and then turned our horses away before they could get to grips with us. We were few and they were many, but it did not matter because they were stationary and in ranks – easy targets for our missiles. But then, after hours standing under a hot sun, having failed in their bold attempt to break through our lines, and now assaulted on four sides, their will suddenly collapsed and the Mesenians suddenly turned into a mass of refugees. Unfortunately, the only route in which they could flee was in my direction.

The enemy mass seemed to dissolve as men started running towards us, thousands of them. Our only choice was to get out of their way – we could mop them up later. I gave the order to join Atrax's men when a burning sensation engulfed my left leg. I looked down to see an arrow embedded in the flesh, and then an enemy soldier ran straight into Remus. He was obviously gripped by a wild panic, and in his desperation to escape the slaughter had been looking behind him when he hit a wall of horseflesh. He tumbled to the ground before scrambling back to his feet and continuing his flight, but Remus reared up on his back legs and I tumbled from the saddle and fell to the ground. He bolted away as I tried to get to my feet, but the pain in my leg made this difficult and I had been also badly winded by the fall. I drew my sword and used it as a crutch to haul myself to my feet. I felt nauseous and saw that there was now a large patch of blood on my leggings around the arrow wound. Enemy soldiers were fleeing in all directions but not all had lost their minds. To my front one approached me with his spear levelled and his shield covering the front of his body. I tried to limp out of his way but it was impossible to put any weight on my left leg. He leered in delight as he ran towards me with his spear, but suddenly pitched forward as he was shot in the back. I collapsed on the ground in great pain.

Surena rode up, slipped his bow in its case and jumped from his saddle, kneeling by my side.

'You must get on my horse, lord.'

I weakly pointed at two enemy soldiers advancing towards us with axes in their hands. Surena pulled his bow from its case and shot them both in quick succession. Yet more of the enemy, seeing Surena's horse as a means of escape, bore down on us. Surena calmly shot at them until his quiver was empty. He threw down his bow and drew his sword.

'Save yourself,' I ordered, weakness engulfing my body, 'get out of here.'

A man lunged at him with a spear but Surena deftly jumped aside, grabbed the shaft and ran his blade through the man's body.

'Can't do that, lord. My grandfather would never forgive me.'

A Mesenian tried to split him in two as he held his sword above his head with both hands and brought it down with all of his strength. Surena blocked the blow with his own sword and thrust his dagger into the man's guts, then stood over me as a ring of enemy soldiers formed around us like a pack of wolves. I thought I heard strange whooshing noises as I drifted into unconsciousness.

I awoke in my bed in the Citadel with Gallia sitting beside me holding Claudia. I felt the wonderful caress of my wife's fingers on my cheek as I slowly came out of my deep slumber. Claudia smiled when I opened my eyes and I managed a faint smile back. She then crawled onto the bed and snuggled up to me and in that moment I experienced true happiness.

'How long was I asleep?'

Gallia leaned over, kissed my lips and smiled, her long locks falling about my face.

'A day and a half. Atrax and Surena carried you here and we have been watching over you ever since.'

I felt very weak but deliriously happy, surrounded as I was by my loved ones. There were no noises of battle, no stench of death, just a gentle breeze that ruffled the cotton nets hanging at the entrance to our balcony.

Alcaeus appeared by the side of the bed.

'How do you feel?'

'Weak,' then I was aware of an aching sensation in my left leg. I noticed my bandaged left arm and then instinctively felt for my lower limb.

Alcaeus smiled when he saw my concerned look. 'Don't worry, you still have your leg. You were lucky, the arrow did not smash the bone, and once we had stopped the bleeding it was just a matter of sealing the wound and binding it tightly.'

'I was worried that you might sleep forever,' he continued, 'but now we can all rest easy.'

I looked at Gallia. 'The battle?'

She gripped my hand. 'Was won, Pacorus, you have saved our city.'

'Nearly got yourself killed in the process, though,' Dobbai suddenly appeared at my bedside, a cup containing white liquid in her hand.

'What is it?' I asked, seeing Alcaeus' disapproving look.

'Poison, of course,' replied Dobbai, 'I thought I would achieve what Mithridates and Narses could not. Now drink it and stop whining.'

'Remus,' I said, 'he bolted during the battle.'

'He's safe and being treated like a lord in the stables. Unlike you,' replied Dobbai, 'he hasn't a scratch on him, so drink the liquid.'

Claudia had fallen asleep beside me as Dobbai handed the cup to Gallia, who held it to my lips. It tasted of nuts but had the texture of thick milk. Most strange.

'The kings are still here,' said Gallia. 'They will be most relieved that you are recovering, as I am, my love.'

Dobbai took the cup and shuffled away. 'I'll fetch some more. It will soon get you back on your feet.'

'I will decide when he gets back on his feet,' insisted Alcaeus, to which Dobbai merely waved her hand dismissively at him and left the room.

'You will have another scar,' said Alcaeus, 'and you may have a slight limp.'

'Limp?'

He shrugged. 'It's too early to tell, but better that than having no leg at all.'

The rest of the day I spent slipping in and out of sleep with Gallia and Claudia beside me, interrupted only by Alcaeus applying a fresh dressing to my arm and leg and Dobbai giving me more of her concoction to drink. She would not tell me what was in it, only that it was frequently used by the people of the northern steppes as an aid to recovery. That night I slept like the dead and in the morning awoke to discover that my strength was indeed slowly returning, just as she had promised. Alcaeus scoffed at such nonsense but did accept that I looked healthier than the day before. I agreed that my father could visit me in my bedchamber, but no one else. I did not want anyone to see the King of Dura incapacitated. The height of vanity, perhaps, but the Romans had taught me that you should always project an image of strength to the world, never weakness.

'So,' my father stood at the entrance to our bedroom balcony, 'how is the hero of the hour?'

'Weak and helpless, if truth be told.' A dozen well-stuffed pillows propped me up.

'Your doctor told me that you should be up and about in no time. Curious fellow, treats royalty like something he's scraped off his sandal.'

'He's Greek,' I said. 'They are a people who believe that everyone is more or less equal.'

'Ah. I can see why he likes it here.'

'You do not approve of my kingdom, father?' It was the first time he had visited Dura.

He walked over and sat down in a bedside chair. 'It has a certain rustic charm, I'll grant you that. And that Roman of yours.'

'Domitus?'

'Yes, he has forged a fearsome weapon in his foot soldiers. He reminds me of Vistaspa. Uncompromising, like a rod of iron, but as for Gallia's women...'

I was more interested in the battle that had taken place than discussing Dura's army. 'Was the fight on the other side of the river a hard one?'

My father stretched out his legs. He was dressed in a white baggy shirt and loose blue leggings and looked very relaxed. 'Not at all. The Persien heavy cavalry put up a fight but Chosroes and his bodyguard scarpered after our first charge. The rest lost heart after that.'

'Was Narses present?'

My father laughed. 'No. He has better things to do than lay siege to Dura, I think, no offence meant.'

'None taken.'

'Anyway, the kings await your pleasure.'

'I will see them all tomorrow,' I replied.

My father stood and offered his hand. I took it. 'Thank you, father, for your support.'

'What sort of father would I be if I stood by and did nothing when my son was in danger?'

'Is Haytham here?'

He nodded. 'He's here. One of his lords and Gotarzes have renewed their friendship.'

'Who would have thought it,' I said mischievously, 'Parthian

435

and Agraci making friends with each other?'

'Who indeed, Pacorus, who indeed.'

The next day I felt well enough to get dressed and hobble to the throne room, where I received a succession of visitors. Gallia sat beside me and Dobbai hovered around, making unwelcome comments and taking delight in annoying people, mostly Alcaeus who insisted that I should not tire myself out. Already the armies of the kings were heading for home, my father's horse archers having left the day before for Hatra, his cataphracts remaining with Vistaspa to escort their king home. I insisted that while they were in Dura all the standards of the kings should fly side-by-side from the ramparts of the Citadel, so that all may see our great alliance. So the griffin flew beside the white horse's head, the bull of Babylon, the dragon of Media, the shahbaz of Atropaiene, the eagle of Susiana, and the four-pointed star of Elymais. I also insisted that the black standard of Haytham should be accorded a place among the banners, Gotarzes declaring that it should stand next to his own just as he had stood next to Haytham in battle.

'Next to each other by the wine jug, more like,' whispered my father.

Before the great feast to celebrate our victory, I had a private gathering of those whom I trusted the most to thank them for their conduct during the preceding weeks, especially Godarz, the man who had been in charge of the city during two sieges and whose calm demeanour had inspired confidence in everyone around him. That the city had not fallen was due in no small measure to him.

'I had hoped that your time in Parthia would be one a peaceful one, Godarz,' I said to him after we had all come together on the palace balcony.

'Fate has a way of interfering with the best-laid plans of men, Pacorus, but hopefully now we will have no more bother.'

'No more armies will come to Dura,' announced Dobbai, who insisted that I drink another cup of her milky elixir. In truth I had come to like it and I had to admit that the pain had largely disappeared from my left leg.

'But Dura's wrath will soon be known to all. What do the minds of men know about anything?'

No one understood what she was talking about so they ignored her as she held Claudia's hand and the two of them ambled around the balcony.

'Well,' said Orodes, 'perhaps we can all look forward to a period of peace.'

'Not while Narses and Mithridates still live,' growled Domitus, who today was dressed in a plain grey tunic, sandals and black leather belt.

'The Roman's right about that,' added Dobbai, who was smiling at Claudia as my daughter clutched her hand and squealed with delight. 'They will be most aggrieved that you are not dead, son of Hatra.'

'Let us not talk about those two,' I said. 'Let us instead talk about rewarding those who have shown themselves to be courageous.'

I gestured to one of the guards standing by the entrance to the balcony, who disappeared and then came back with Surena by his side. My former squire looked very different from the rebellious youth I had first encountered in Mesene's marshlands. He had grown in stature and maturity. Today he was dressed in a long-sleeved white shirt, beige leggings and brown leather boots. He wore a black leather belt from which hung his spatha. He bowed to Gallia and me and stood to attention before us. He still had that self-assured air that bordered on cockiness, but over the past months he had proved himself to be a brave and resourceful soldier.

'Well, Surena,' I said, 'you are to be rewarded for your valour in the recent battle, not least for saving my life. So, to repay my debt, what would you ask of me?'

'To be an officer in your cataphracts, lord.'

It was a reasonable request. He was well liked among the men and I believed that he would be able to win the respect of the hundred men in the company under him. He was young, it was true, but age should never be a barrier to talent.

'What is your opinion, Nergal,' I said, 'do you think Surena would make a good officer?'

Nergal was sitting next to Praxima on a couch, his long legs stretched out in front of him.

'He's a little headstrong, sometimes has difficulties obeying orders, but I think some responsibility will do him good.'

'So do I,' I added. 'Your request is granted. Well done.'

Surena beamed with delight. 'Thank you, lord. I will not let you down.'

I waved him away but he still stood there, something obviously on his mind.

'Is there anything else?'

For once Surena was hesitant. He looked at Gallia, who frowned at him. 'I would like to ask the queen something.'

She regarded him coolly. 'Spit it out, then.'

437

'I would like to ask your permission to marry Viper.'

Domitus rolled his eyes and Praxima laughed. Godarz shook his head while Nergal nodded approvingly.

'To ask for the hand of an Amazon is no small thing,' replied Gallia.

'I realise that, majesty.' Surena was certainly trying his best to please her.

'I wish to know what Viper has to say about this,' said Gallia.

'Is that really necessary?' I asked, my question being met by a steely blue-eyed stare. 'Very well, very well. Guard, go and fetch Viper.'

He bowed and left. I just hoped that the Amazons were not on the training fields otherwise we could be here for hours. Surena stood like a statue, staring ahead.

'Sit down, Surena,' I told him, 'you are making me feel uncomfortable.'

He perched on the end of a chair. Now he looked like a sitting statue.

'Good job he's not as nervous as this in battle,' remarked Domitus, 'otherwise Pacorus would be having his bones picked clean by buzzards by now.'

Some ten minutes later Viper arrived, with short-cut hair and her shirt clinging to her girlish figure. It was hard to believe that she was one of my wife's most accomplished killers. I had to admit that she had a certain beauty. Her skin was flawless and she had large brown eyes with a small nose and chin. Surena stood up when she entered and stood by her side, Viper smiling at him.

'Viper,' snapped Gallia. 'You know that I love you and the Amazons like sisters.'

'Yes, majesty,' even Viper's voice was like that of a young girl.

'And you know that you will always have a home here, at Dura.'

Viper smiled at Gallia and nodded. I began to see why Surena was so attracted to her. She was certainly disarming.

'Marriage is a union of equals,' continued Gallia, 'not the possession of a woman by a man. You must not feel that you are being coerced into anything.'

'I would never...' protested Surena.

'Silence!' barked Gallia.

'We love each other, majesty, we truly do,' said Viper.

Gallia sighed and then walked over to Viper and embraced her. 'Then you have my blessing. May you both be happy.'

She waved them away. They both bowed and then left us, arms round each other and their laughter filling the air. Later, when we were alone, I asked Gallia why she had been so opposed to their union.

'I was being selfish, I suppose. This will be the beginning.'

'The beginning?'

'Viper's marriage will be like a small stone that starts a rockslide. Soon more of the Amazons will wish to marry.' She suddenly looked sad. 'I suppose that I wanted things to stand still, that is all. Time moves on relentlessly and I sometimes think … it doesn't matter.'

I pulled her close. 'Alas, my love, only the gods have the power to make time stand still. But you must admit that Surena and Viper are happy. And I think he will make a good husband.'

She kissed me on the cheek. 'You are probably right.'

Another group of individuals who were also happy were the Roman engineers that we had captured the previous year. At first they had been confined to a large house in the west of the city that had belonged to one of Mithridates' cronies during his brief reign in the city. They had been placed under guard and their siege engines had been placed in a secure warehouse on the other side of the city as a precaution against them being sabotaged by their former owners. At first the Romans were surly and uncooperative, but after a few weeks, when it became clear that they were not going to be abused or sold into slavery, their attitude slowly improved. Domitus and Godarz visited them frequently and gained their trust, and after a while they were permitted to leave their lodgings and venture into the city. During my time away in Gordyene they had frequently dined with Godarz in his house, talking about Rome and Italy no doubt, and gradually they came to accept their situation more readily. As the months passed their guards were reduced and then removed altogether and they were even allowed outside the city. During the recent siege they had worked their engines to destroy the Mesenian siege towers that had assaulted Dura. This had turned them into heroes in the city, and afterwards they had been deluged with invitations to banquets and had been sent many gifts from a grateful populace.

A week after all the kings had departed I went to see them. They now came and went as they chose, and because they were not part of the army their time was largely their own. The first thing I noticed when I walked down to their accommodation with Domitus was how they had all put on a few pounds in weight, more than a few pounds in some cases. Their leader was a man named Marcus Sutonius, the same individual I had spoken to directly after the defeat of Lucius Furius all those months ago. Then he had been lean and surly, today he was stockier and much more agreeable. The rest of his men gathered behind him as I spoke to them in the courtyard that fronted their living quarters. Their home was surrounded by a high wall with a large gate directly opposite the house's main entrance, with its stables and store rooms along the walls either side of the courtyard. Its security had made it an ideal prison, but now the gate was open and there were no guards. I stood next to the fountain that was in the middle of the courtyard.

'I wanted to thank you all for your help during the recent siege,' I said.

'Just doing our job, sir,' replied Marcus. 'Lucky you had that Eastern liquid. We just poured it in some clay pots, sealed them and tied rags doused in pitch round the tops, which we then lit. When they shattered it burned nicely. No wonder you keep it under lock and key.'

'Indeed. Well, your actions helped to save the city and my daughter, so I have come to tell you that you are all free to leave Dura. I had desired that you aid me in another venture, but in all conscience I cannot hold you here any longer after what you have all done.'

Marcus turned and looked at his men, who all seemed remarkably underwhelmed that they were now free men. One or two looked almost distraught. Marcus cleared his throat.

'Thank you for your kindness, sir, but the fact is that me and the lads, well, we wouldn't mind staying around for a while longer if you have a use for us. Like you said.'

There were murmurs of agreement behind him and his men were nodding to each other. Clearly their pleasant confinement at Dura was more agreeable than service in the Roman army.

I looked at Domitus, whose face betrayed no emotion.

'Well,' I said, 'your offer is gladly accepted. Your services will be indispensible for the coming campaign, so I thank you.'

'Thank you, sir, we won't let you down,' replied Marcus.

Afterwards, as we were walking back to the Citadel, Domitus questioned me.

'The first I've heard of any campaign.'

'That's because it is the first time that I have mentioned it.'

I could tell by the tone of his voice that he was unhappy. 'If you are planning a war you should have told me and you should also have persuaded the kings to stay at Dura.'

'We do not need them, Domitus. What I have in mind will not take long and Dura's army will be more than sufficient.'

He was still far from happy. 'May I ask the nature of this new campaign?'

I smiled. 'All will be revealed at the meeting of the war council.'

Chapter 20

I summoned the council that afternoon and it convened on the palace balcony five hours after midday. It had been nearly two months since we had defeated Chosroes outside the city wall and my leg had now healed fully, though I had a nasty scar where the wound had been, as had my arm. Fortunately I also had no limp, though Alcaeus informed me that I still might develop one in later life – something to look forward to in my old age!

The army had recovered its strength after the battle and once more trade had returned to normal, an endless stream of carts and camels filling the road to and from the East and Egypt. No word had come from Ctesiphon and my father had also heard nothing from the court of the King of Kings.

'They are replenishing their stocks of malice,' was Dobbai's comment on the ominous silence.

I had hoped that Narses himself, now in possession of the command that I had held when I had the favour of Phraates, would lead an army against me so that I could destroy him once and for all.

'Narses has been burned by you before,' remarked Godarz. 'I doubt he will try again in the near future, especially since now you have an alliance of other kings behind you.'

'Exactly,' I said, 'and for that reason the time is ripe to strike while I have an opportunity to do so.'

Domitus, as was his wont, often fiddled with his dagger during these meetings. Now he stopped and looked at me. 'Strike where?'

'Uruk, of course.'

'Is that wise, majesty?' asked Rsan, no doubt already alarmed at the expense of yet another campaign.

'Very wise, Rsan, and long overdue,' I replied.

'I see the reason why you were so keen to retain the engineers now,' said Domitus.

I told them of my plan to strike southeast and assault the city of Uruk, the capital of Mesene and the stronghold of Chosroes.

'He thinks he is safe behind his walls,' I said, 'but he has reckoned without my siege engines that our Roman allies have agreed to operate.'

'You would storm the city?' Nergal looked alarmed.

'Of course,' I replied. 'I do not intend to just sit in front of his walls.'

'To what end, son of Hatra?' Even Dobbai was intrigued.

'To the end of removing Chosroes and sending a message to his allies that Dura is not to be underestimated or insulted.'

'I think they know that already,' commented Godarz.

'I would have a friend sitting on Mesene's throne,' I said.

I gave no further details but ordered Domitus to prepare his legions for the march south, which would commence in two weeks, and for Nergal to ready his horse archers. Orodes had been made commander of all the cataphracts, leaving me free to command the whole army, and I asked him to ensure that the heavy cavalry was fully armed and equipped after its exertions in the last battle. I told Godarz that we would be away from Dura for no longer than three months. I also sent word to Palmyra that I would like to see Byrd and Malik and they duly arrived three days later. They were informed of my plan and I asked Malik if he would like to accompany us; he agreed, of course, as did Byrd. Malik, because he liked being a warlord, and Byrd because he liked the company of his friend Malik. I was very pleased to have my old companions with me once more. I also asked Gallia and her Amazons to march with us.

'What are you up to?' she said suspiciously.

'I don't know what you mean.'

'Usually you try to keep the Amazons and me for that matter, as far away from your army as possible, but now you wish us to march alongside you.'

'Of course,' I replied, 'is it not natural for a husband to want his beloved wife by his side?'

She was far from convinced. 'I know that something is afoot, Pacorus, so you might as well tell me.'

I placed two fingers on her lips.

'All will be revealed, my love, all will be revealed.'

I decided to leave five hundred horse archers behind to stiffen the garrison of five hundred legionaries. I doubted that Dura would be attacked a third time but it was better to be safe than sorry. Nergal was far from happy but his mood lightened when I told him that he would be commanding the lords and their retinues once more.

'We do not need all their men,' I told him, 'if each lord brings a hundred men that will suffice. Kuban will also be coming with us.'

'Gallia commands his men,' said Nergal.

'Not in battle. When it comes to a fight you will lead our friends from Margiana. And get a new shirt and leggings, Nergal. You are, after all, the commander of all my horse.'

'Yes, lord.'

Nergal had never been one for gaudy uniforms, but it was time he dressed according to his rank. To that end I had the armourers

443

make him a new helmet, a beautiful piece with steel neck guard, cheekguards and silver strips inlaid in its crown. I also ordered him a white cloak edged with silver. He was delighted with these gifts when I presented them to him, though also confused.

'You are too generous, lord.'

'Nonsense,' I replied, 'you are a great warlord of Parthia now, Nergal, and people need to be reminded of that.'

Praxima was also delighted and said it was about time that her husband was attired according to his rank. After we had finished entertaining them both in the palace, Gallia, still suspicious, questioned me further.

'Nergal does not need fancy clothes to win the respect of his men,' she said, 'he has that already.'

'I know that,' I replied, avoiding her eyes.

'And since we have been here you have cared little how Nergal dresses. So why now?'

'I just feel that he should look the part, that is all.'

She shook her head. 'I don't trust you; I can tell that something is brewing.'

But I would say no more on the matter and that was that. The next day I had an invitation to attend Dobbai in her private chambers. Her room was down the corridor from our own bedroom, though no one ventured past its doors, mostly through fear that they would not come out alive. But I never heard any strange noises that indicated that sorcery was being practised and we never broached the subject of what was in her room out of respect for her. The palace staff had grown quite fond of Dobbai despite her uncouth ways and fierce tongue, and Claudia of course loved her. It was a source of comfort to me that she lived with us, though I knew that at any time she might leave and never be seen again. That said, I liked to think that she was happy here.

I swallowed and then knocked on the doors.

'Enter.'

I opened one of the doors and walked in. I had expected to be met by a room covered in cobwebs, filthy and with a foul odour. Instead I found a neat and tidy space with a single bed along one wall, two rows of shelves opposite holding neatly arranged scrolls and jars of what I assumed were herbs of some sort, and a table and chair next to the twin doors that opened onto her own balcony. Light and airy, a slight smell of incense entered my nostrils.

'Why did you summon me?' I asked.

She smiled. 'I know what you desire, but I have to tell you that if you march to Mesene the empire will be engulfed in flames.'

'Chosroes must be punished for his attack against me.'

She shrugged. 'Is not his defeat and the destruction of his army not punishment enough?'

'No.'

'I would advise against it.'

I was in no mood for her games. 'Why, have the gods spoken to you, threatening divine retribution against me for daring to fight for my kingdom's freedom?'

She said nothing for a few seconds. 'Why do you speak of the gods with such disrespect? Has your thirst for revenge dimmed your wits? The gods have been kind to you thus far; it is unwise to insult them.'

'There is no honour left in the empire,' I said with disgust.

She doubled up with laughter, placing her hands on her knees.

'Since when has there been any honour in Parthia, or anywhere else for that matter? What a foolish man you are at times.'

'Narses and Mithridates must be removed. They will destroy the empire if they are allowed to go unchecked.'

'Ah, now we come to it. You wish to see Ctesiphon purged of the family of Phraates and its supporters.'

'I wish to see order and honour restored to the empire,' I said grandly.

'And you think marching on Mesene will achieve that?'

'It is a start,' I replied.

She looked directly into my eyes.

'Perhaps Dura is too small for King Pacorus, perhaps he wishes to sit on the throne at Ctesiphon.'

'Don't be absurd.'

She still fixed me with her stare. 'Absurd is it? No more absurd than returning from Italy like a dead man returning from the underworld, or making peace with the Agraci, or defeating your enemies before Dura.'

'I do not wish to be King of Kings,' I said firmly.

'Then I say this to you again, son of Hatra,' her voice had an ominous tone, 'if you embark upon the path of retribution you will plunge the empire into chaos, the outcome of which may not be to your advantage or liking.'

'No,' I shouted, 'Chosroes will be held accountable for his actions, even if it means all the demons of the underworld are unleashed upon the world.'

'You go to kill Chosroes.'

'Yes.'

She shrugged. 'It is of no concern to me. Do what you will.'

445

'I will.'

She pointed a bony figure at me. 'The gods love chaos and they love you, son of Hatra, for you give them what they desire most.'

'And what is that?'

'An endless river of blood.'

'Well, then,' I said smugly, 'if the gods love me then I cannot lose.'

She nodded and smiled. 'You cannot outwit the gods, son of Hatra.'

'As long as they are not against me, then I will settle for that.'

I was little troubled by Dobbai's warning, and in any case I had no desire to take control of the empire. Just a short, sharp campaign in Mesene and then things would return to normal. My father wrote to me saying that still no word had come from Ctesiphon but that he had heard from Babylon, Media, Elymais and Atropaiene and even from Khosrou and Musa. They all pledged their allegiance to him and Dura, which further stiffened my resolve to punish Mesene. I was careful not to mention my plan to him, as I knew that he would try to dissuade me. I was not to be denied on this matter.

Practical matters pushed Dobbai's musings aside as the final preparations were made for the campaign. Haytham sent a thousand horsemen to accompany Malik and Gallia told Kuban that he was to obey Nergal for the duration of the expedition. Kuban was delighted to be marching once again. No doubt the prospect of more slaughter filled him and his men with glee. The area around the legionary camp began to fill with tents, horses and camels as the lords and their followers rode into Dura. Kuban's men had established their own camp south of the city, a sprawling collection of tents, each one domed, circular and made from a wooden frame covered with felt. The felt itself was made from the hair of camels, sheep, goats and horses and was remarkably resistant to the wind. The whole structure was tied down with straps that crisscrossed over the tent. They varied in size from those accommodating five men to Kuban's command tent, which could billet up to fifteen people. Each tent took around an hour to set up or take down, though on campaign he and his men usually slept in the open beside their horses, though Kuban told me that they also slept in the saddle when the need arose. They numbered just under a thousand men now, having suffered some casualties during the battle with the Mesenians. Domitus grumbled that they were ill disciplined, which meant that they would not take his orders, but they were fierce warriors and a welcome addition to the army. Besides, technically they were under Gallia's command.

The cataphracts had suffered greatly during our venture in Gordyene, but with the promotion of squires and the induction of new ones from the sons of the kingdom's farmers their strength was brought up to eight hundred men. Of the five hundred heavy cavalry that Orodes had brought with him from Susiana, only two hundred and fifty were still alive, but they still rode under the banner of their prince and were accorded equal status with the Durans. Before we marched Domitus added another disc to the staff of victory, bearing the image of a burning camp.

'I thought your decision to choke everyone with smoke should be immortalised,' he said as I stood beside him in the tent that also held the gold griffin standard.

'That is most considerate of you,' I said. 'Are the legions ready?'

'They are ready, and they know that they are going to wreak vengeance on the Mesenians.'

'How is their mood?' I asked.

'Excellent, the boys like the idea of visiting death and destruction on the bastards who threatened their families.'

I looked at him. 'And how do you feel?'

'I obey orders.'

'I know that, Domitus, but as one friend to another, what is your opinion?'

'Men respect strength,' he replied gruffly, 'so if we give those Mesenians a good hiding then that will send a message to anyone who's thinking of tangling with us again.'

He had confirmed what I believed, though I was determined to give Chosroes more than a good hiding.

We set off on an overcast morning, a slight drizzle in the air, marching south on the western side of the Euphrates. As the legions tramped out of their camp and Byrd and Malik rode at the head of a large party of Agraci scouts, I said goodbye to my daughter in the Citadel's courtyard. Dobbai held her hand. She cried when she realised that her father and mother were leaving her. It was heartbreaking to see her in such a condition, and Gallia had tears in her eyes as she embraced her daughter. Rsan stood on the steps beside Godarz, his head bowed in reverence. Dobbai wore a resigned expression – she was still obviously perturbed by my course of action.

'Take care of yourself, son of Hatra.'

I scooped up Claudia in my arms and kissed her on the cheek. 'Have no fear, I will be back in no time. After all, the gods love me, do they not?'

I put Claudia down and she grabbed Dobbai's hand. Behind me Surena was sitting in his saddle holding Remus' reins. I nodded to Godarz who nodded back; then I vaulted onto Remus' back and rode from the Citadel, followed by Gallia and her Amazons. It was just another busy day in Dura as the long line of legionaries, marching six abreast, snaked south towards Mesene. To their front and on their right flank hundreds of horsemen filled the horizon. We marched with nine thousand legionaries, a thousand Agraci cavalry, just over a thousand cataphracts, Kuban's nine hundred horsemen, five hundred of Dura's horse archers and another two thousand horsemen that the lords had mustered. It was more than enough to defeat the remnants of the army of Chosroes that had scurried back to Mesene. We also had the Roman engineers and their siege engines with which to batter the walls of Uruk.

The quickest route there was to head east from Dura and then march down the east bank of the Euphrates, but that would entail traversing Hatran and Babylonian territory and I did not wish to antagonise my father or take advantage of Vardan's friendship, so we marched on the opposite bank. In former times this would have been suicidal with open war between Dura's rulers and the Agraci, but now it was a pleasant enough journey. We maintained a brisk pace, covering twenty miles a day. Domitus insisted that we built a camp every night and that everyone slept within its ramparts. During the day those horsemen who were not undertaking scouting duties dismounted and walked their horses, not only to save their mounts but also to maintain their physical condition. Men sitting in saddles on long marches with nothing to do are apt to go to sleep, especially if in friendly territory, and this was certainly that. Nevertheless, we still maintained our standard marching order. Far ahead of the army were Byrd, Malik and his Agraci warriors, riding far and wide to ensure our safety and to collect any useful information. The tip of the army comprised small parties of horse archers. If they came into contact with the enemy they were to instantly disengage and ride back to the army to pass on their information. Next came a vanguard of a hundred fully armoured cataphracts followed by the senior commanders of the army and their standards. The Amazons also rode with this assembly. Behind this group came the rest of the cataphracts and their camels carrying their armour and supplies and then mules and carts pulled by oxen carrying the battering rams and other siege equipment of the Roman engineers. Behind them came the colour party of the Duran Legion with its gold griffin and guards. The trumpeters followed them and then came the cohorts of legionaries divided into their centuries. The men marched six abreast and were accompanied by centurions with their trusty vine canes. The Pontic Legion, the Exiles, followed the Durans. It now had its own standard, a silver lion representing the revered beast of Pontus that had also been the standard of Balas. It had been cast from the silver taken from the armour and helmets of the dead Mesenian soldiers recently slain before the walls of Dura. The tents, spare weapons, armour and other supplies for the two legions came after them, carried by hundreds of mules and dozens of wagons. The lords and their followers trailed after the legions, with a body of Duran horse archers forming the rearguard and more horse archers acting as flank guards and scouts. As the day wore on the drizzle ceased as the sun burnt away the clouds, warming the earth. Soon the thousands of feet and hooves tramping across the baked ground had produced a dust cloud hanging over the whole army, stretching for ten miles.

Dura's territory extended south of the city for a distance of a hundred miles and after that came the empty vastness of the Arabian desert; an endless wilderness of sand that the Agraci called the Rub'al-Khali, the Empty Quarter; yet it was far from empty. It was home to the Agraci and the striped hyena, jackal, honey badger, sand gazelle and white oryx. Within Dura's borders the land next to the Euphrates was fully irrigated and cultivated, but as we marched beyond my kingdom's southern border the land turned into a red sand wasteland with great sandstone plateaus in the distance. It was as if we had entered a land devoid of life. On the fifth day, however, a group of Agraci riders joined us; black-clad figures mounted on camels armed with long spears. They were led by the hulking figure of Yasser, one of Haytham's chiefs I had met when the king had brought his army to face Pompey. The day was waning when he and his men appeared and so we invited him to stay with us for the night.

Gallia and I entertained him in my command tent, along with Byrd, Malik, Orodes, Nergal and Domitus. Gallia sat next to Yasser flattering and teasing the grizzled old warrior. His previous suspicion of us seemed to have evaporated, though he saw no reason for our fortified camp.

'Haytham rules all this land, there is no enemy here.'

'We have our procedures, Yasser,' I said, 'we stick to what is tried and tested.'

'You march to make war on Mesene?' he winked at Gallia.

'You are well informed,' I replied.

He smiled. 'We knew that you would strike at Mesene as soon as you had defeated its army.'

'You approve of my course of action?'

'Of course, you cannot allow Chosroes to live after such base treachery.'

'We do not go to kill Chosroes, Yasser,' said Gallia, 'we go to show him that Dura is not a toy to be played with.'

I said nothing but Yasser caught my eye and smiled knowingly. I also saw Domitus smile to himself.

Yasser accompanied us south to the ford across the Euphrates some fifty miles from Uruk. Of the enemy we saw nothing, though Yasser told me that after his losses at Dura Chosroes would have few soldiers left.

'Prince Malik told us of the great fires that were used to turn the dead Mesenians into ashes.'

'My men counted near nine thousand enemy dead,' I said.

'I doubt that there are any soldiers left in Uruk,' was Yasser's approving comment.

The next day I summoned Surena to my tent.

'I want you to ride south to your people and spread the word that the time of Chosroes is over,' I told him. 'Take a company of horse archers and recruit any who can carry a weapon. You can start by enlisting that little group of bandits that you belonged to. Bring any that join you north to link up with the army at Uruk.'

Surena was shocked. 'They will be slaughtered, lord. My people have no weapons aside from what they have taken from the enemy.'

'I know this, Surena. But it is not my intention to get your people killed.'

'I do not understand, lord.'

'Neither do I,' added Domitus, who was seated nearby.

'It is quite simple,' I said. 'If Chosroes learns that the marsh people are in revolt, he will send troops to crush them. But we will intercept them before they reach your people, Surena. Yasser is wrong when he states that Chosroes has no troops left, so I want to entice some of them out of Uruk where they can be dealt with in the open.'

When Surena had left I called together Nergal and Orodes and worked out how we would spring our trap. I sent Byrd and Malik ahead to scout the land and ensure that there were no enemy forces approaching our location, which was still on the west bank of the

Euphrates. We had actually marched south of the Mesenian capital to reach the ford.

At night we set no fires, which meant the men grumbled, wrapped their cloaks around them and chewed on cold food. Their moaning was a small price to pay for our veil of secrecy. For the fires of twenty thousand men would be seen for miles, even by the sentries on the high walls of Uruk. Five days after Surena had left, Byrd and Malik returned to inform me that a large group of marsh people had left the safety of their watery domain and were heading north as requested.

'They have a collection of old shields, spears, a few swords and long knives,' said Malik with disdain.

'They no soldiers,' added Byrd.

'That is our job,' I said.

I told them to return to Surena and inform him that he would be receiving reinforcements shortly, but that he must keep heading in the direction of Uruk. I then ordered Domitus to send two cohorts to support Surena. Domitus was most unhappy.

'I thought we were here to take Uruk.'

'And so we are, Domitus.'

'Then why are we wasting two cohorts of good men playing nursemaid to a bunch of vagrants?'

'I too do not understand,' said Orodes.

'Listen, my friends,' I replied. 'Chosroes hates the marsh people, so when he learns that they are marching on his capital he will send troops to destroy them. Only when he does, they will be running into a trap.'

'If he's got wind that we are here,' replied Domitus, 'he'll barricade himself inside his city and won't take the bait.'

Domitus, as ever, saw everything in purely military terms, and he was right. Having lost the majority of his army in a recent battle no commander would further weaken his forces on dispersing a band of marsh people. But I knew that Chosroes despised the Ma'adan and would relish the opportunity to slaughter them. In any case, as far Chosroes was concerned Dura's army was still in its homeland. My gamble paid off, for Byrd and Malik brought news that a body of horsemen had indeed left Uruk and were riding south to intercept Surena. Chosroes had no system of forts such as existed in Hatra, to pass on information to neighbouring strongholds or watchtowers. Sitting in his capital he was effectively blind.

Mesene is mostly flat, with a highly cultivated strip on the eastern side of the Euphrates, extending inland for a distance of around two miles. As in Hatra there is also another belt of rich agricultural land on the other side of the kingdom, along the River Tigris. Byrd and Malik had reported that there was little activity on the opposite side of the river, no doubt because many of the farmers who had worked the land had been killed at Dura. Their families must have taken refuge in Uruk. It was now time for us to cross the river.

As the Euphrates begins the final leg of its long journey before it enters the Persian Gulf, the depth of the river lessens and there are many fords that will allow an army to cross. Nevertheless, it took two days to transport the men and beasts and the hundreds of wagons over to the other side. Nergal sent parties of horsemen many miles ahead of the crossing to ensure that we were not surprised, but there were no hostile moves against us. When everything and everyone was across the river, Domitus made camp and I rode with Orodes at the head of five hundred cataphracts and their squires to intercept and destroy the Mesenians who had been sent from Uruk. We rode across cultivated land and then arid, featureless desert as we headed south. At midday on the second day of our journey we saw a great dust cloud on the horizon – we had found the enemy.

Byrd and Malik joined us as we were equipping our horses with scale armour from the camel train that accompanied us. It was mercilessly hot and I knew that horse and rider would not be able to spend many hours encased in steel armour, thick hide and iron scales. Byrd told me that the enemy was five miles south of our position.

'They made camp hereabouts last night and wait for their prey.'

'Where are Surena and his men?' I asked.

'Ten miles south of the Mesenians,' said Malik. 'Your foot soldiers are also with them.'

'Did you count the Mesenians, Byrd?'

He squinted in the sunlight. 'Not more than a thousand, mostly spearmen and horse archers. No problem for your horsemen.'

We left the camels under a guard of squires and then began our journey. My plan was hardly subtle. We would ride south in two lines and strike the enemy while they were attacking the marsh people. I thanked Shamash that the cohorts had linked up with Surena. I was unconcerned about the legionaries, they could handle cavalry easily enough, but if the marsh people had been intercepted before my men had linked up with them, then the desert would be littered with their corpses by now.

On we rode, the dust cloud filling the horizon where men were fighting and dying. At around two miles from our target we broke into a canter, my kontus resting on my right shoulder. The sounds of battle were pulling me, making my heart race as the lure of combat made my blood race through my body. Remus strained at the leash to break into a gallop, for he too knew the sounds of battle. Not yet, my friend, have patience. On we rode, now less than half a mile from the bloody maelstrom. I could see figures ahead, men on horseback riding parallel to a line of shields – Duran shields!

I brought down my kontus and grabbed it with both hands on the right side of Remus.

The enemy spotted us as we broke into a fast gallop, hurtling across the iron-hard earth towards them. They desperately tried to form a line as we closed on them, riders lowering their spears and then moving toward us. But we had the momentum and when we hit them their thin line disintegrated. My kontus felt as light as a feather as I clutched it hard, drove it into the chest of a horsemen then let it go. I drew my sword and slashed left and right at figures as I thundered through the enemy formation and then wheeled Remus around and went back to the melee. A figure lunged at me with his spear but the point glanced off the metal rings protecting my arm. I brought my sword down and hacked at his shoulder as he rode past me, the blade cutting into flesh. These riders had shields and helmets but wore no armour protection over their torsos. Many had been speared in our first charge and now my horsemen went to work with their swords and maces. The enemy could find no way through our scale armour and metal leg and arm protection. A figure dressed in an ornate helmet and scale cuirass came at me with his sword, driving the point towards my face. I parried his blow and then swung at him with my spatha but he deflected my blade. He used his sword with great dexterity, thrusting and then withdrawing it, always looking for a gap in my defences. I raised my blade above my head and brought it down against his neck but he blocked the blow and then drove his sword point into my arm. The metal rings fortunately deflected the blow. We fought for what seemed like an eternity and I forgot about what was happening around me. Once more he raised his sword above his head, and then an arrow slammed into the side of his chest. He froze, looked down at the feathered shaft protruding from his flesh and then slowly lowered his sword. Another arrow hit him in the back and he pitched forward in the saddle, dropping his sword. I looked past him and saw Surena on his horse with a bow in his hand. He nocked another arrow and then shot my opponent in the back once more. The man gently slid out of his saddle and fell to the ground. Surena rode up to me.

He spat at the dying figure beneath us. 'That is Chosran, the eldest son of Chosroes who has persecuted my people for many years.'

The son of Chosroes lay on the ground face-up, blood oozing from his mouth as he tried to gasp for air. Around us the last remnants of the Mesenian horsemen were being killed, while their horse archers, who had been trying to break the square of legionaries, turned tail and ran. I gave orders to let them go – most likely they would flee to Uruk and we would have another chance to kill them soon enough.

Surena strung another arrow in his bowstring to shoot at the prostrate figure of Chosran.

'No,' I ordered, 'slit his throat and have done with it.'

But Surena merely sniffed, spat on the ground once more, replaced his arrow in his quiver and wheeled his horse away. I slid off Remus' back and knelt beside Chosran. He was already more than half dead, his eyes wide and vacant and his breathing very shallow. I pulled my dagger from its sheath and drew it swiftly across his throat to send him into the next life.

'Know that it was your father's treachery that led you to this place.'

Orodes rode up as I began to take off my arm and leg armour and dump it on the ground. Others were doing likewise, for the heat was intolerable.

'That was easy enough, Pacorus.'

'How many did we kill?'

Orodes looked around. 'Difficult to say at this juncture, but our first charge must have cut most of them down.' He looked at the dead figure at my feet. 'Who is that?'

'One of Chosroes' sons. I'm hoping that when he learns of his death Chosroes himself will march out to exact vengeance on me.'

'I doubt that,' mused Orodes.

In the battle's aftermath the squires brought us water and helped us take off the horses' scale armour. It may have saved them from missiles and blades in combat but it caused them to sweat horrendously. Our own losses amounted to five dead and a similar number wounded, while we counted over three hundred enemy bodies. Not as many as I would have liked, but it was three hundred less men who would be defending the walls of Uruk.

We burnt our own dead and left the Mesenians to rot. The cohorts that I had sent to link up with the marsh people were commanded by a grizzled Thracian named Drenis, a man who had not only served under Spartacus in Italy but had also been a gladiator in the same ludus in Capua. How long ago that time seemed now.

'They tried to charge through us at first. They must have thought we were just a bunch of ill-armed savages. So we formed into line and then emptied many saddles with our javelins. They were a bit more wary of us after that.'

'Did you lose many men?'

'No, about ten or twelve wounded, none killed. Our main problem was keeping these people,' he jerked his head towards the great crowd of Ma'adan, 'from trying to run after the enemy horsemen when they fell back to reform.'

'Well done, Drenis, you have helped a great deal today.'

'I don't think those marsh people will be much help against Uruk,' he said, 'they have hardly any weapons and no discipline.'

'They are the future of Mesene, Drenis.'

'Really?' He looked long and hard at the long line of bare-footed, scruffy individuals tramping after his cohorts. 'No wonder it's a shit-hole.'

Surena, though, was delighted and on the way back to camp was full of grandiose plans about how he would form all the marsh people into a great army.

'These are only the ones I was able to muster in a short amount of time.'

'I think that most of your people would like to remain in their homeland, Surena.'

'I don't,' he announced.

I had to smile. When we had met he had been a wild boy from the marshes, content to live among water buffalo and cane and mud huts. Now he was on his way to being an accomplished officer in what I liked to think was the finest army in the Parthian Empire. For him it was impossible to go back to his former life.

'I think, Surena, that the point of the matter is that your people should be allowed to live their lives unmolested.'

'What king in Uruk will allow that, lord?'

'An enlightened one, Surena; one who will respect your people and their way of life.'

'Kings have always persecuted my people, lord.'

'You must have faith that things will change. I predict a new dawn for your people.'

'I hope so, lord, I hope so.'

The mood of Domitus noticeably darkened when our guests

455

arrived at camp. He was less than impressed by a couple of thousand more mouths to feed.

'We'll be on half-rations in a week,' he complained. 'I don't suppose they brought any food with them?'

'They are our new allies, Domitus. Make sure they are fed and well treated.'

'I'll make sure anything valuable is guarded, more like.'

'It is important that they take away with them a favourable impression of us,' I said. 'Surena once looked liked them, and you will agree that he has turned into a fine soldier.'

'There's always an exception, but I will do as you command.'

The marsh people were allocated a corner of the camp and were given food and tents to sleep in. Surena was placed in temporary command of them and he took to the task with relish. It helped that some of them had been his fellow associates in crime, and so he soon had officers of sorts to assist him. Domitus wanted them to sleep outside the camp, but that would have been an obvious insult and would have left them very vulnerable to any attacks against us. Not that there was any sign of the enemy, or indeed any signs of life at all. Byrd and Malik had ridden far and wide and reported people fleeing towards Uruk with their meagre belongings, no doubt hastened in their flight by the sight of Agraci warriors in their homeland. The latter had even approached the walls of the great city itself but had seen no enemy patrols on the roads.

'Chosroes must be keeping what soldiers he has inside the city,' remarked Malik as he was relaxing in my tent after he and Byrd had returned from their scouting.

'Uruk has high walls,' remarked Byrd.

I had called a war council when they had returned for I was eager to get to Uruk.

'That is why we have brought the Romans and their siege engines,' I said. 'High walls make good targets.'

'Sieges take time,' muttered Domitus. He was still unhappy about the presence of the Ma'adan inside the camp.

'Not this one, Domitus,' I replied. 'I have been talking to Marcus and we have hatched a plan to bring it to a speedy conclusion.'

'Will you give Chosroes an opportunity to surrender, Pacorus?' Orodes was a true friend, but I knew that he was uneasy about attacking the capital city of one of the empire's kings. I would have liked to dispense with the formalities but I valued Orodes' friendship too much to upset his sense of protocol.

I smiled at him. 'Of course. I would prefer it if we could enter the city without shedding any blood.'

'Ha,' Domitus had a mischievous grin on his face. 'There's more chance of a mule pissing gold than that happening.'

Gallia frowned at his coarseness. 'Perhaps you could persuade Chosroes to surrender, Domitus, as you have such a way with words?'

'We will have to storm the city, of that I'm sure,' said Domitus. 'And it will take a long time.' He looked at Malik. 'The walls are high, you say?'

'Very high, and there are many towers.'

'Archers could inflict much harm on an attacker,' added Byrd.

'Then you are looking at between three and six months to take the city, though you might starve them out before then.'

Domitus folded his arms and sat with a smug expression on his face. Gallia frowned once more and Byrd looked disinterested. I had asked Praxima to join us, which caused something of a surprise among the others.

'What do you think, Praxima?' I asked.

All eyes fell on the wife of Nergal, who was dressed in her leggings and mail shirt, her wild hair about her shoulders. Fearsome and fearless in battle, she was now very uncertain.

'I know nothing about strategy, lord.'

'Nonsense,' I said, 'you have fought in nearly as many battles as I have. What would you do, attack or sit around doing nothing?'

Domitus looked away in disgust, while Nergal looked perplexed.

'I would attack, lord,' she replied.

'And so we will,' I announced. 'We break camp in the morning.'

Gallia cornered me after the others had left.

'Since when did Praxima have a voice on the war council?'

'Since today,' I replied.

'And you are suddenly interested in her opinion?'

'Of course, why not?'

She was unconvinced. 'Because you usually listen to no one but yourself, that is why.'

'I have to say that is unfair.'

'But true,' she retorted.

I said no more and eventually she threw up her arms and left. I would reveal my plan when we stood in the royal palace at Uruk. Until then it would remain a secret.

The march to Uruk was uneventful, though as usual Nergal threw a screen of horsemen all around the army. Domitus placed Surena and the Ma'adan in the very rear of the army, which ensured that they were covered in the dust thrown up by those that went before them. This appealed to his cruel streak. After two days of marching and seeing no enemy we arrived before the southern walls of Uruk.

Uruk, famed city of history. It was rumoured to be five thousand years old, or at least there had been people living on its site for that long. High, mud-brick walls surrounded the city with towers at regular intervals. They had been built over four thousand years ago by a great warrior king named Gilgamesh. The city was located some five miles from the Euphrates and was connected to the great river by a series of canals that brought water to Uruk. One of the reasons for these was to irrigate the great gardens inside the city that had been created by its kings for their recreation. The gates into the city were located at the four points of the compass, though the main gates were those that faced south. These were flanked by two high, square towers from which flew the viper standard of Chosroes. He had hoped to plant his banner on Dura's walls but I promised myself that soon the griffin would be atop those towers. The gates were slammed shut as the army surrounded the city and the Roman engineers positioned their siege engines. Marcus thought it would be straightforward enough.

'A city this size, filled with refugees and with no relief army to march to its aid – might as well starve them out. Tedious, but effective.'

'But if we starve them out you will not be able to demonstrate your machines,' I said, 'and I was so looking forward to seeing them in action.'

He looked at me as though I had gone mad. 'Starving them will save you a lot of blood.'

'You let me worry about that.'

I walked with him towards the southern gates while Domitus and Nergal organised their commands. The Duran Legion set up its camp to the south of the city and the Exiles were positioned on its northern side. Kuban and his wild men were ordered to form a defensive screen to the east and Nergal established company sized camps up to twenty miles from the city in all directions. Beyond them all rode Byrd, Malik and their Agraci scouts. In this way I would have plenty of prior notice if any enemy relief force approached, such as Narses.

'Narses won't come,' said Domitus bluntly. 'He won't risk being beaten just to save Chosroes.'

'Alas for Chosroes,' remarked Orodes, 'he chose his allies unwisely.'

'Don't waste your pity on him,' I said. 'He would have none if the roles were reversed.'

At the end of the first day, when the army had settled into its positions around Uruk, I convened a meeting of the war council to determine the next day's course of action. I had invited Marcus to attend after we had finished our inspection of the city's defences.

'This is the plan,' I said, smiling at Marcus. 'The attack will commence tomorrow when we begin battering the main gates and the towers next to them. We will keep shooting at them until we have effected an entry.'

'Those walls look very thick,' mused Nergal.

'And very strong,' added Domitus.

'May I speak, sir?' said Marcus, raising his right hand.

'Be my guest,' I replied.

He stood up and bowed awkwardly to me and Gallia, then Praxima. Orodes grinned and Domitus raised his eyes to the ceiling. Gallia nodded back to him courteously while Byrd looked bored by it all. Malik raised his hand in greeting.

'Well,' said Marcus, 'I have given the matter careful consideration and believe that my engines can break those gates.'

'And if you can't?' Domitus was unconvinced.

'Then we will find another way,' I said. 'The point is that we are here and will not be leaving until I we have taken the city. Thank you, Marcus.'

'Will you still try to convince Chosroes to surrender, Pacorus?' Sometimes I found Orodes' sense of protocol extremely irksome. I bit my lip.

'Of course, as I promised.'

Chapter 21

The dawn came soon enough, an orange glow in the east that illuminated the white walls of Uruk in a ghostly glow. I smiled to myself – the last day that it would know peace under its present king. Marcus and his men had risen early and were already assembling their siege engines, watched by a curious Domitus. I ambled over to him as he munched on a handful of biscuits and sipped from his water bottle. I could tell that he was fascinated.

There were six of the giant ballista, each one weighing several tons, being three times the height of a man and around thirty feet long. The ballista works like a bow, with a strong wooden frame holding two skeins of animal sinew in place vertically. Two horizontal wooden arms pass through each skein and are linked by a strong bowstring. As the arms are pulled back the sinews become twisted to create a great tension for propelling a missile forward, the latter resting in a groove in the horizontal stock of the ballista. The bowstring is pulled back using winches and held in place by a rotating trigger.

Marcus was bellowing orders at his men, ten of them working on each large machine. And on either side of these were smaller ballistae, which could throw a metal-headed bolt, solid metal balls and stones over great distances. A team of two men worked these smaller machines, similar to the scorpions I had encountered in Italy. Marcus had ensured that his men and their machines were out of range of the archers who were now lining the walls facing us. When he saw us both he stopped shouting and sauntered over.

'Morning! We shall soon be ready.'

Domitus nodded towards the machines. 'You think they will be up to the task?'

'Oh yes, they are the latest in military technology,' replied Marcus. 'Crassus had them made specially to knock down....' He stopped and looked sheepishly at me.

'To knock down Dura's walls,' I continued for him. 'It is quite all right, Marcus, you are a soldier who was obeying orders, a professional. You have nothing to be ashamed of.'

'Anyway,' he said, 'he had these specialists brought over from Greece and they built the big ballistae and then trained us to use them. It took half a year to get us ready. This is the first time the big ones have been used in anger.'

'They were not used at Dura?' I asked.

Marcus shook his head. 'The army's commander wanted to take the city by storm, thought my machines were a waste of time. I pleaded with him but he would not have it. We did some damage with the smaller ballista, and after he was repulsed from the walls he said he would think about employing the big ones. But then your army arrived and, well, he had other things to think about.'

'Indeed,' I said.

'How long will it take before they are ready?' asked Domitus.

'About two hours.' Marcus rubbed his hands. 'After that we'll soon have a nice fire going.'

'Fire?' I asked.

'Oh, yes, we will be shooting half and half.'

Domitus looked at him. 'Half and half?'

Marcus looked at us as though what he had said was the most straightforward thing in the world. 'Half stone and iron shot and half incendiaries. Anyway, I best get back to make sure they are assembled right. If you will excuse me?'

Marcus saluted and strode back to his machines. More wagons began to arrive carrying the ammunition for them, great round stones, smaller stones, iron balls, clay pots and bolts. The pots would be filled with naphtha and then sealed, with a burning, oil-soaked rag wrapped around the top. Upon impact the pot would smash and the flaming rag would ignite the naphtha.

The walls were lined with many soldiers now – so much for Yasser's claim that Chosroes had no more troops – observing Marcus and his men going about their business. The latter were beyond the range of the Mesenian bows and the soldiers of Uruk would have never seen Roman siege engines in action before, so they just stood and watched, thinking themselves safe behind their big gates and high walls. Behind the siege engines the Duran Legion began forming up in its cohorts. They were widely spaced so that they extended towards the river. Next in line, to the right of the legion, came the Amazons and Dura's cataphracts commanded by Orodes, with his own men on the extreme right of the heavy cavalry's line. Nergal's horse archers then formed a great line that extended north to run parallel to Uruk's eastern wall. On the northern side of the city were deployed the Exiles in their cohorts and centuries. Thus was Dura's army arrayed for the garrison of the city to see.

True to my word, and while Marcus readied his machines, I tied a white cloth on the end of a kontus and rode towards the city gates to ask for a parley. I had not ridden fifty paces beyond the siege engines when two arrows were shot in my direction from the walls. Fortunately they both fell short. I wheeled Remus around, walked him out of range and then faced the gates once more. I untied the white cloth from the lance and spat in the direction of the city. The time for talking was over.

I purposely rode over to where Orodes was sitting in his scale armour at the head of the bored cataphracts.

'They would rather fight than see reason, lord prince.'

He nodded solemnly. 'You have done all that honour demands, lord.'

I bowed my head to him and rode back to the engines, the cataphracts jeering and whistling at those on the walls.

'That was rather foolhardy,' said Domitus.

'I have fulfilled my promise to Orodes. How is Marcus progressing?'

'They will be ready in about half an hour. I hope you are not going to keep the men standing for hours in this sun.'

I looked into the clear blue sky. It was going to be another hot day. Most of the horsemen had already taken off their helmets or had pushed them back on their heads. The horses were swishing their tails to keep the flies away. Then I heard a noise coming from the walls and saw the Mesenians jeering and throwing insults. Some jumped on to the wall itself and lifted their robes to expose their genitals. I glanced at Gallia and her Amazons who were sitting emotionless on their horses, their faces enclosed by the cheekguards of their helmets. The other horsemen and the legionaries did not respond to the taunts but remained standing in their ranks in silence.

I dismounted and stood beside Domitus as the taunts and insults were flung in our direction. Gallia rode up on Epona.

'What are we waiting for? Are we going to sit here all day while they ridicule us?'

'We are waiting for the engineers to ensure that everything is in place.' I cocked my head at the walls. 'Are they upsetting your girls?'

She took off her helmet, her hair plaited behind her neck. 'Nothing they have not heard before. But they may be frightening your cataphracts. Or perhaps your legionaries, Domitus?'

'Don't worry, Gallia, when the city falls I will get some of the boys to slice off the balls of those on the walls and present them on a silver tray to your girls.'

She frowned. 'You are all heart, Domitus.'

At that moment Marcus sauntered up, looking very pleased with himself. He bowed his head to Gallia and raised his hand to Domitus and me.

'All is ready, sir.'

'Excellent,' I said, 'please begin.'

462

Marcus looked at Gallia and then at me. 'Actually, sir, I was wondering if the queen would bless the first shot, for luck you see.'

I looked at Gallia. 'Well?'

She smiled at him. 'I would be delighted, Marcus.'

She dismounted and handed me Epona's reins. 'Make yourself useful.'

I led Remus and Epona after Gallia and Marcus as they walked over to one of the machines; one of the giant ballistae that fired stones. A member of its crew lifted up one of the large missiles stacked in a great pile behind the machine and stood holding it. It was obviously heavy as he was straining from the effort.

'If you would lay a hand on it, lady,' said Marcus, 'then we can begin.'

Gallia, clearly delighted, placed her palm on the stone. The crew cheered and then the stone was placed on the wooden channel from which it would be launched. Marcus raised his hand, lowered it and the ballista was fired. The stone shot through the air and slammed into the gates with a loud crunch. And then the other machines opened fire.

Large stones and pots filled with naphtha flew through the air and smashed into the gates, shaking them and then covering them in flames as the clay pots burst and the naphtha ignited. The missiles of the smaller ballista – stones and iron bolts – were directed at the walls and towers that flanked the gates; the stones striking the torsos and skulls of those lining the walls. The crews worked like frenzied ants, loading and reloading their contraptions and sending a hail of stone, fire and metal at the enemy. Marcus had sited his machines well. They did not shoot haphazardly but were directed against where the two gates met and against the walls where their hinges were located. I did not know how old those gates were, but they appeared ancient and would not withstand such an onslaught for long.

The crews sweated and cursed as they loaded the missiles and then loosed them at the gates and the walls. Great gaps began to appear in the latter as chunks of brickwork were ripped out. The gates themselves shuddered every time they were hit and the flames continued to eat away at the ancient wood. I and thousands of others looked on in awe at the devastation that was being unleashed upon Uruk. There was no one on the walls now, no jeering soldiers, only the dead and the dying. The rest had fled for their lives. Then the cheering began, a great wall of noise coming from behind me as the Duran Legion raised their javelins and began beating them against their shields. The men chanted 'Dura,

463

Dura' as the city's defences were pounded without mercy in front of them. Then the horsemen joined in, raising their weapons and shouting the name of their own city. I hoped that Chosroes, wherever the miserable wretch was cowering, could hear the voices of those who had come to repay him for his treachery.

The hail of iron and stone continued. One or more of the naphtha pots must have got wedged in the arch above the gates, because suddenly there was a loud crack and then that part of the wall erupted in flame and caused a great part of it to come crashing down on top of the gates. Marcus immediately ordered his men to halt firing their machines and came running over to me.

'The wall's collapsing around the gates, see there,' he pointed at the gap where the bricks had fallen to the ground. 'I will direct the missiles above the gates, we can chip away until the whole lot comes down.'

'How long?' I asked.

He looked back at the torn section of wall and the smashed and burning gates. 'Two hours, I'd say.'

I slapped Marcus on the arm. 'You are truly a craftsman. Two hours will do fine.'

Marcus smiled and ran back to his machines to reposition them.

'Domitus, send a rider to the Exiles to bring them here to the southern gates.'

He saluted and called over a courier. I gave the order for the horsemen to stand down except for the scouts that were carrying out reconnaissance, and I also ordered that the legion stand down, the men taking off their helmets and lying on the ground, leaving only a cohort to guard Marcus and his men. Then I called a council of war.

'The gates will soon be breached,' I said, 'and when they come down we will storm the city. This day Chosroes will rule in Uruk no more.'

'When we go in,' said Domitus, 'most likely there will be a reception party waiting for us, archers and slingers, no doubt. Casualties might be heavy in the first wave.'

'I will instruct Marcus to keep sweeping the walls with his ballista,' I said.

'Just make sure they don't start shooting wild. I don't want my men cut down from behind,' added Domitus

'What about my horsemen?' asked Nergal.

'They won't be able to ride over the rubble,' I replied. 'In any case there will be columns of legionaries going into the city so you and your men will have to sit and watch, I'm afraid.'

'We could fight on foot to support Domitus and his men,' he suggested.

'Not a bad idea,' remarked Domitus, 'archers are always useful to have around.'

'Very well,' I said, 'Nergal, dismount half your men to support the attack. But they are to go into the city behind the first cohort. We don't know how many enemy soldiers we are facing yet.'

'Not many,' mused Orodes. 'Chosroes lost thousands at Dura and I doubt he has enough men to man his defences fully.'

'Perhaps,' I said, 'but your saw the number on the walls. In any case cornered men often find a courage born of desperation. I don't want to give them any easy victories. If I am killed then Gallia will command the army.'

They all looked at each other in surprise.

'Why should you be killed?' asked Gallia.

'Because I shall be leading the cohort that storms the city.'

They tried to dissuade me but my mind was made up. I had brought the army to this place. It was my decision to storm Uruk and it was therefore only proper that I should be in the first formation that broke into the city. I dismissed the council and afterwards, when we were alone, I held Gallia close.

'You understand why I have to do this, don't you?'

Her eyes were filling with tears. 'Not really.'

'I cannot sit on my horse and watch other men go where I should be. There is no honour in that.'

'Who cares about honour? Honour will get you killed.'

I kissed her on the lips. 'I care about honour. I must do this, Gallia.'

She stepped back and wiped her tears away with her sleeve, then composed herself.

'Go then, and may the gods protect you.'

She turned and left me without looking back. I followed her outside where Praxima was waiting on her horse holding Epona's reins. Gallia vaulted into the saddle, placed her helmet on her head and rode away back to her Amazons without giving me a second glance. Orodes was at my side as I walked out of the camp towards where the cohort was forming up to storm the gates. Marcus' machines were still pounding the gates and the surrounding masonry, which was now full of gaping holes.

'Are you sure about this, Pacorus?'

I smiled at him. 'Quite sure. Can I ask you a favour?'

'Anything, my friend.'

I laid a hand on his shoulder. 'If I fall, please take care of Gallia and my daughter. It would comfort me to know they will be in your safekeeping.'

He looked extremely solemn. 'On my life, Pacorus, I shall do as you ask.'

'Good. Now I must ask you to take charge of the cataphracts once more. If the enemy proves to be stronger than we thought we might be pushed back, in which case we will be looking to you and your horsemen to save us.'

It was unlikely that we would be pushed out of the city, but it focused Orodes' mind and stopped him from offering to stand beside me in the cohort, which I knew was going through his mind. We shook hands and he left me to go his cavalry. I walked over to where Domitus was organising his men. The first century, ten men in the front rank and seven ranks behind them, stood at the head of the cohort of five centuries formed into a column. The front five ranks had no javelins – they would go in armed only with the gladius. In front of us stone and iron continued to smash the enemy gates and brickwork. I stood beside the legionary on the end of the front rank, on the right. Domitus stopped issuing orders and stomped over to where I was standing.

'What are you doing?'

'As I said, Domitus, I will be accompanying your men during the attack.'

He looked me and shook his head. 'First of all, I command this cohort, so you do as I say. So take that helmet and cuirass off and we will find you a pot like the men wear and a mail shirt. And take that cavalry sword off, it will be bloody useless when we go in.'

I was going to protest but Domitus was wearing that iron-hard visage that struck terror into friend and foe alike, so I took off my helmet, cuirass and unbuckled my sword belt. An orderly took them away and a member of the commissary brought me my new fighting gear – mail shirt, shield, belt, gladius and scabbard and felt-lined helmet.

'That's better,' said Domitus, 'any enemy archer worth his salt would have seen your fancy helmet with its feathers and your expensive armour and would have dropped you first. Now you stand as much chance as any of us staying alive, which isn't much.'

The legionaries around us started laughing at their commander's black humour. Domitus bundled me to the centre of the formation and pointed at two of the men in the front rank, who saluted and made their way to the rear of the century. Domitus pushed me into one of the vacated places and then put himself on my right in the second spot. I drew the gladius and jabbed it forward.

'Know how to use one of them?' asked Domitus.

'I think I can manage.'

'Well,' he said, 'we are about to find out.'

At that moment there was a great crashing sound as the masonry above the gates collapsed on to them and caused them to fracture and then collapse onto the ground. There was a great cloud of dust, which cleared slowly to reveal a yawning gap where the gates had once been standing. The defences of Uruk had been breached.

Domitus raised his sword. 'Advance!'

As one we marched forward towards the great pile of smashed wood and rubble standing four hundred paces away. The smaller ballista continued to shoot at the walls but the larger engines had ceased their barrage. We quickened our pace, breaking into a trot and then a run as we neared the rubble. The men maintained their formation, battling the urge to sprint ahead. Then we were at the rubble, which forced us to slow our pace as we scrambled up and over the smashed bricks and shattered and smouldering wood. Dust still hanging in the air caused us to cough and spit and got in our eyes as we scrambled down the other side of the debris and saw a great mass of the enemy coming towards us – spearmen with large oblong shields in a long line, and behind them I could see the sun glinting off more spear points.

'Don't stop, straight into them!' screamed Domitus as he charged towards the enemy. The men gave a great cheer and followed him. My heart was pounding in my chest as I held the shield in front of me and ran at the enemy. Arrows hissed through the air and felled some of our men, but not enough to halt the momentum of our charge. I screamed my war cry as our rear ranks threw their javelins and I ran at a man who had his spear pointed at my chest. I barged the point away from me using the metal boss on my shield and then rammed my gladius over the top rim of the shield into his face. The sword point went through his mouth and out through the back of his neck. I shoved him back into the man behind, who staggered back. I lunged forward and thrust the gladius through his wicker shield and into his arm. I jerked back the blade and stabbed it into his thigh, then thrust it again, this time into his belly. I charged on, treading on men slain by javelins, smashing my shield boss into a man's face and then driving the point of my gladius upwards into his guts. I was elated. I screamed and with all my strength pushed the entire blade into his body up to the handle. I could not extract it! I pulled and yanked but it was stuck fast! Out of the corner of my eye I saw an axe blade coming

467

at me. I parried the blow with my shield and Domitus severed the hand that was holding it with one blow. I finally freed my blade, which was now covered in blood.

'Stop being a hero and concentrate,' shouted Domitus, bloodlust in his eyes.

On we went, stabbing at enemy bellies, thighs and groins. Around us more and more centuries were pouring into the city and forming into line, then charging the enemy ranks, which were being pushed back. We stepped on and over the bodies of the enemy dead and dying as we pushed them back away from the gates. Some were running now. Others were trying to give themselves up. One man threw away his sword and fell to his knees, clasping his hands in front of him as a sign of surrender, but just as at Surkh Domitus thrust his sword into the man's chest and then kicked his body to the ground with his right foot. On we went. Suddenly a hail of javelins flew over our heads and hit the thinning ranks of the enemy, felling dozens. Trumpets sounded. We halted and reformed our ranks and charged once more. We were killing boys and old men now, the dregs of Chosroes' army, but we killed them anyway. There was no mercy in Uruk this day.

The threadbare ranks of the enemy fell back. Now Nergal's dismounted archers came forward and poured volley after volley into them as all around me men were suddenly gripped with a raging thirst and drank greedily from their water bottles. Domitus, his tunic and mail shirt splattered with enemy blood, shared his bottle with me as other legionaries brought full bottles forward for the men and took away empty ones to be refilled. The ground in front and behind us was covered with enemy dead. How many more Mesenians were there?

'Thirsty work,' said Domitus. He slapped me on the arm. 'Not a scratch on you. Well done.'

'Well done to you, my friend.'

Behind us the rest of the Duran Legion was filing into the city and forming up, followed by the Exiles.

Uruk is divided into four main areas, the palace quarter, the temple quarter, the royal gardens, called the Royal Orchard, and the working quarter. The latter is located in the southern part of the city, a vast collection of mud-brick homes and businesses not unlike those found in Dura, Hatra and a host of other towns and cities throughout the empire. These were now ransacked as the army moved through the city. The Exiles and the Duran Legion maintained their discipline and formation as they marched through the streets, searching for enemy soldiers. But after them came the

Ma'adan led by Surena and they were looking for vengeance. They smashed anything that could be broken and killed any unfortunate enough to cross their path. Marcus and his men cleared away the rubble from the smashed gates to allow horsemen to enter the city. Nergal ordered his dismounted archers to get on the walls and in the towers to prevent any enemy archers or slingers shooting at us, but he and his men found no one on the walls. They had all fled to the north of the city. At the northern end of the working quarter I called a halt and retrieved my armour, helmet and sword, handing back my legionary's kit that had served me so well. The legionaries took the opportunity to sit or lie on the ground as Nergal formed a screen of horse archers in front of the army and the Amazons joined me. Behind us I could hear screams and shouts as the Ma'adan slaughtered those who had failed to find refuge in the temple compound or the palace.

'Are you going to do something about that?' asked Gallia, gesturing with her arm to where houses burned and innocents were dying.

'Not until the city has fallen.' I replied curtly.

Orodes rode up at the head of the cataphracts.

'The people are being slaughtered, Pacorus,' he said.

'You must do something,' said Gallia.

Half the city had fallen but there was still some fighting left to do. Still, I had enough foot soldiers to do the task.

I pointed at Gallia and then Orodes. 'Very well, take the Amazons and the heavy cavalry and stop the Ma'adan in their slaughter, but do not kill them, however tempting it may be. We need those people.'

Orodes raised his hand and wheeled away. Gallia was about to do the same when I called after her.

'And Gallia.'

'Yes?'

'Do not kill Surena, that's an order. I need him too.'

I heard no reply as she galloped away. A wide canal bisects Uruk, separating the homes of the citizens and the city's businesses from the royal quarter and the great White Temple that was on my left as I looked across the canal. Several bridges spanned the waterway, the widest of which stood directly in front of us; white stone viper statues sat on pedestals either side of it. These were the only guardians to the last bastions of Chosroes' kingdom.

'We had better get across the bridges before they decide to make a stand,' said Domitus, who had walked over to where I was sitting on Remus.

'Very well. The Exiles are to take the temple and the Durans are to assault the palace.'

He saluted and ran back to his officers. After a short conference the first centuries sprinted across the bridges and formed up on the opposite bank. Dismounted horse archers stood on the edge of the canal to provide covering fire should it be needed. It was not; there was no sign of the enemy. I trotted over the bridge and joined the foremost centuries, which were now forming into great columns ready to advance against the temple and palace. I made my way to the head of the Durans and we began to move through the royal gardens; a great expanse of date palms, fountains, orchards and flowerbeds. Nergal joined me on his horse, a host of horse archers behind him.

'We will scout ahead,' I said, 'bring your men.'

The Royal Orchard was not only a place of flowers, trees and watercourses, it was also a large park used for hunting. It covered many acres and contained an abundance of wild animals, such as deer, antelope, onager, boar, bulls and panthers. The noise of thousands of hobnailed sandals would have frightened away any wildlife nearby, but I passed the word for the men to take care and watch the trees for any panthers that might be in the branches, ready to pounce.

In the centre of the royal gardens was a large pool with a temple on a small island in its centre. This was a shrine to the goddess Anahita, the goddess of all waters, war, love and fertility. I gave orders that no one was to desecrate this temple surrounded by stone columns plated in silver. Anahita had been good to Gallia during the birth of our daughter and I had no wish to offend Her. We moved past other rectangular pools that had steps leading into their waters, and around the edges were terraces filled with water plants. The waters themselves were teeming with brightly coloured fish, with ducks swimming on the surface. Around the ponds were acres of trees – date palms, doum palms, sycamores and fig trees – planted in straight lines. The Royal Orchard was truly a sanctuary of peace and beauty, and I said a silent prayer to Shamash, asking for His forgiveness for marching an army through its sacred avenues.

I urged Remus forward and we rode through the gardens towards the palace. Nergal's men filled the trees, bows at the ready, looking for any enemy soldiers that might be in the foliage. We emerged from rows of ancient cypress trees to reach the mud-brick palace walls covered in plaster that had been painted white. There was a well-tended cobbled road that led from the gardens to the palace gates, which were shut. Arrows flew at us from archers standing on the walls either side of the gates.

'Back into the trees,' I yelled.

There was no point in sitting on our horses shooting at men standing behind a wall, so we retreated back to the trees and there waited for Domitus and his men to arrive. I ordered a rider to fetch Marcus and to tell him to bring a means of breaching the gates. Some of the dismounted men were standing at the edge of the trees, losing their arrows at the enemy but I ordered them to desist. There was no point in wasting arrows. I too dismounted and walked to the last row of trees to look at the palace, rising up behind the walls; a great whitewashed two-storey stone building with a wide frontage. It appeared to be set back some distance from the walls that protected it, no doubt with a great square before it. No doubt the square where Narses and Chosroes had planned to put me to death.

Byrd and Malik appeared and informed me that there was another set of gates into the royal compound on the other side of the palace.

'They too are guarded,' reported Byrd.

'Will you storm the palace, Pacorus?' asked Malik.

'Yes,' I replied.

Domitus arrived a few minutes later, his men halting among the trees. Guards were posted and the rest took off their helmets, stacked their shields and then lay in the shade. Domitus joined us as we studied the palace walls.

'I have ordered Marcus to bring some of his engines so we can gain entry via the gates,' I said.

'How many men are on those walls?' asked Domitus.

'Hard to tell,' I replied, 'but they are the palace guard and they will put up a fight.'

Domitus took off his helmet and wiped his brow. 'It doesn't matter, we'll kill them easily enough.'

It took Marcus an hour to arrive with the means to get into the palace, a great battering ram that was loaded on to half a dozen wagons. It took him and his men another hour to assemble it, during which time there was no activity on the walls. A strange silence descended over the area as the Duran Legion rested and Marcus and his men assembled the battering ram. I asked Byrd and Malik to ride over to the western side of the city and report back on what was happening at the White Temple, and they took all the Agraci warriors as an escort just in case there were any roving bands of enemy soldiers still at large. I prayed to Shamash that

Gallia and her Amazons were safe.

The battering ram was truly a wondrous thing, a huge tree trunk suspended by chains from a thick overhead beam that formed the top of its arched frame. The beam and the ram itself were under protective screens laid over the frame, the screens being composed of wooden boards overlaid with iron plates with clay underneath and then an inner layer of thick hide. No enemy arrow would be able to pierce that thick roof of iron, while the clay formed a fireproof barrier. The whole ram was mounted on four great wooden wheels so it could be pushed forwards and backwards. The ram itself had rope handles at regular intervals along its length. This was to enable those manning it each side to pull it back and then hurl it forward against the target. And on the point was a massive iron head cast in the shape of a snarling ram, complete with horns.

'I like your ram, Marcus,' I said, stroking the massive iron head.

'Yes, sir, it cost Crassus a great deal of money.'

I smiled. 'I have no doubt. He is a man who likes quality in all things.'

A mischievous grin spread across Domitus' face. 'Tell him what your men have nicknamed it, Marcus.'

Marcus cleared his throat and looked sheepish. 'I don't think the king would be interested in such trivial gossip.'

'Nonsense,' replied Domitus.

'Yes,' I added, 'please tell, Marcus.' I looked at the snarling image; they probably called it Crassus. I smiled to myself.

'Pacorus, sir, begging your pardon.'

'What?' I said.

Marcus avoided my eyes. 'They nicknamed it Pacorus.'

Domitus and Nergal thought it hilarious.

'It looks like you,' said Domitus.

'The mirror image,' added Nergal, creasing up with laughter.

Marcus was blushing while my two senior commanders were giggling like young girls. I decided to maintain my dignity. I laid a hand on Marcus' shoulder.

'It is quite all right. When these two have finished with their childishness we will put my namesake to work.'

The smaller ballista had also been loaded on to carts and driven to the royal gardens where they were re-assembled by their crews. Once in position they began sweeping the walls with bolts and iron balls, just as they had done before the city gates. After a few enemy heads had been caved in, the palace walls were soon empty of archers, allowing the ram to be pushed forward. I insisted on being a member of the party that grabbed the beams inside the ram's protective cover and hauled it forward. Domitus and a century of his men followed immediately behind the ram, the legionaries' shields held above them and on their sides as a defence against enemy missiles.

There were twenty of us pushing the ram, including Marcus, and even with all our efforts it was slow to move so heavy a beast. I began sweating heavily as I pushed on one of the beams, the iron-headed ram swaying slightly with every forward effort. Iron plates mounted at the front of the ram provided additional protection for those manning it, but also added more weight to the machine. Marcus coordinated our efforts, telling us when to push forward, but it was painfully slow progress. I heard the crack of the ballista balls and bolts hitting the walls, though the sounds gradually died away, presumably because there were no targets to aim at. Occasionally there was a dull thud on the ram's roof as an enemy archer diced with death and shot at us, followed by more cracks as ballista missiles flew at him and struck the walls.

Domitus was directly behind the ram and delighted in making fun of our efforts.

'Come on, push it. We want to get into the palace before dark. Perhaps I should knock on the gates and ask to be let in.'

We had no energy to reply, all our strength being used to push the ram forward. My heart was pounding in my chest and sweat ran into my eyes as I heaved it forward. The others, veins bulging in their muscled arms, groaned as they threw their weight behind each effort, with the voice of Marcus constantly in our ears.

'Heave; heave; heave.'

Then, finally, we were at the gates. We shoved the ram's roof right up against the gates just in case the enemy above decided to throw rocks or burning oil down upon us. Each man grabbed one of the rope handles that had been nailed to the trunk and pulled it backwards, then on Marcus' command we hurled it forward. The great iron head smashed into the gates, splintering the wood. Again we pulled it back and then sent it hurtling into the gates once more. More cracking and splintering as the ram's head fractured the gates and wrenched them from their hinges, forcing them back. Again and again we propelled the iron head into the wood until one of the gates lay twisted on the ground and the other had been smashed in two.

'Grab the ram, pull it back,' shouted Domitus to the men behind him as he picked up one of the ropes fastened to the rear of the ram for just such a purpose. Then we were pushing the ram back so it no longer blocked the broken gates. Domitus drew his sword and ran past the battering ram and through broken gates into the palace grounds, his men following. They barely had time to form a wall of shields before being attacked by Chosroes' palace guards.

These men were well armed and no doubt knew their craft. They wore bronze helmets, red tunics covered with bronze scales and carried large round shields that had bronze facings sporting a black viper motif. They were armed with spears that had leaf-shaped blades, which they used to thrust at the legionaries, keeping the shields tucked tightly into their left sides. They advanced in a compact line with several ranks behind, not charging wildly but moving as a disciplined body. Their front rank tried to thrust their spears into the bellies of my men, jabbing the points forward. Our line of shields held in the press but my men could not make any headway against them. Worse, they were actually being forced back towards the gates and the walls. Domitus and his legionaries tried to thrust their swords over the top rim of their shields, into the faces and necks of their opponents, but the enemy's spears kept them out of reach. More legionaries were flooding into the palace, but this only resulted in a great crush of men in and around the gates as the palace guards began herding the legionaries back. I was going to order a retreat when I saw archers on the walls. For a moment a feeling of nausea swept through me, believing them to be Chosroes' men. But then I realised that they were Nergal's archers. He had ordered his men to ride up to the walls, stand on their saddles and then haul themselves up onto the walls. The latter were no more than twice the height of a man so it was easy enough. Those who reached the top of the walls first then hoisted up the others, until there were dozens of archers either side of the gates. They then began pouring a withering fire into the enemy ranks, their arrows striking faces and necks.

The advance of the palace guards faltered and then stopped as they were hit by the arrow storm, men instinctively raising their shields to deflect the missiles being shot at them from the walls. But in doing so they lost the initiative, and a blast of trumpets preceded a charge by the Durans. The front ranks rushed forward into the now stationary palace guards and hacked their first line to pieces. Nergal's archers were shooting arrows like men possessed until their quivers were empty, but their efforts were enough to tip the scales of the bloody melee below. Disorganised, their rear ranks thinned by arrows and their first two lines now destroyed, the guards began to fall back while the legionaries cried 'Dura, Dura' as they cut their way into the enemy. Back the guards went, towards the palace where archers were filing out from the building to form a phalanx at the top of the stone steps.

The legionaries pressed on, stabbing at their opponents, but then a volley of arrows brought their advance to a halt as the front ranks closed their shields together and those behind hoisted their shields above the heads of those in front to form a testudo. The arrows slammed harmlessly into leather and wood as the command was given to retreat and trumpet calls rang out across the palace square. The royal guards also fell back and regrouped at the foot of the stone steps, covered by the archers behind them. These men were good soldiers, that much was true, but they faced certain death if they continued fighting.

A temporary lull descended over the battle as the legionaries held their shields in place and the Mesenians took no further action. Of Chosroes there was no sign.

Domitus came trotting back to where I was standing just inside the broken palace gates, and where Nergal joined us a few moments later. Domitus embraced him.

'I knew your horse boys would come in handy one day,' he grinned.

'I never thought they would fight as well as they did,' remarked Nergal, looking at the royal guards. 'What now?'

Around us more legionaries were flooding into the compound and taking up position on the flanks of the first men who had fought their way into the palace grounds. Fresh javelins were ferried to the men facing the palace guards. Soon there would be nearly five thousand men facing what I estimated to be under a thousand palace guards and around two hundred archers.

Nergal looked towards the palace steps. 'They must know that they are going to die.'

Domitus spat on the ground. 'They know, but they are good soldiers and are prepared to die for their lord.'

'And where is their lord?' I asked.

'Skulking inside his palace no doubt,' replied Nergal.

'Let's get it over with, then,' said Domitus.

'No, go and tell Marcus to bring his smaller ballista inside the palace grounds,' I said. 'I don't want to lose any more men than we have to.'

Domitus nodded and ran back to where the engineers stood with their machines. He took a hundred men with him, who helped the Romans carry their ballista into the square and position them around three hundred paces from the royal guards arrayed at the foot of the palace steps. They loaded spears with long iron heads into the machines as I tied a white rag to the end of my sword and walked forward with it held aloft.

'Don't be an idiot,' Domitus called after me.

I turned and smiled at him. 'Is that any way to speak to your king?'

I walked to where the legionaries were standing in their ranks, shields still hoisted above their heads. They parted as I made my way to the front and then strolled beyond the front rank to face the enemy, their shields forming a wall of bronze to my front, the spears of the front ranks levelled towards me. Behind me Marcus' men dragged forward the ballista as the legionaries shuffled their tightly packed centuries sideways to create gaps for the ballista to shoot from. I raised my sword so all could see the white rag tied to its point. I carried on walking towards the enemy until I was around a hundred paces from them.

'That's far enough,' called out one in the front rank, their commander I assumed.

I lowered my spatha and untied the white rag.

'I would ask that you lay down your weapons. I guarantee your lives will be spared.'

I slid my blade back in its sheath. There was no answer from the Mesenian ranks.

'You have done all that honour requires,' I said to them. 'It is senseless to die for no purpose.'

Silence greeted my plea. I tried once more.

'I ask you once more to lay down your weapons. I will not do so again.'

The enemy stood like stone statues before me.

'Go back to your blonde whore,' shouted one.

I turned and walked briskly back to my Durans and then to where Domitus, Nergal and Marcus stood near the gates. I pointed at Marcus.

'Kill them all.'

He saluted and then rushed off to begin his work.

'One day,' said Domitus, 'you will get an arrow through your heart or a spear in your guts while you stand in front of the enemy trying to sweet-talk them. If they didn't want to fight any more they would have run away or thrown down their weapons already.'

I nodded. 'You are right, it was a waste of time.'

Seconds later a score of ballista began shredding the enemy ranks. The first volley of iron-tipped missiles cut down the front rank with ease, slicing through shields, armour and flesh. Men were not only hit but also thrown back by the force of the blow, knocking those behind off their feet. Half the ballista fired solid iron balls the size of a fist at the archers at the top of the steps, smashing skulls and bodies with ease.

As the balls careered through the enemy's ranks the archers loosed one volley against us, the arrows slamming harmlessly into the locked shields of the Duran ranks, but that was the only volley they shot. Seeing their comrades' skulls being caved in and the spearmen of the royal guard being skewered by iron-tipped bolts, the archers ran. They suddenly disappeared into the palace. Domitus was standing beside me as we watched the archers melt away. I heard Marcus bark some orders and all the ballista were then directed against the spearmen, who to their credit were still standing in their ranks. But the missile fire was mercilessly thinning those ranks.

'Finish them,' I said to Domitus.

He walked forward to a group of his officers, who sprinted to the trumpeters standing behind the cohorts. The instruments blasted and Marcus turned to look at me. He raised his hand at the signal and then shouted at his men to cease their shooting. The testudo formations broke up as legionaries brought their shields down to cover the front of their bodies. Another trumpet blast signalled the advance. The cohort that had forced its way into the palace grounds faced the royal guard now and began to advance. Just as they had done a hundred times on the training ground, the men trotted forward to within thirty paces of the enemy and then hurled their javelins. The missiles flew through the air and lodged in the shields of the enemy, the soft metal bending after impact to make it impossible for its user to pull it out. After throwing their javelins the legionaries drew their swords and charge headlong into the royal guard. As the two lines clashed the rearmost ranks in each century also hurled their javelins into the enemy. This time the Mesenian formation buckled. Already weakened by the fight at the gates and being cut to pieces by ballista missiles, they were at first pushed back as the Durans used their swords to stab with frenzy. On their flanks more centuries cut into the guardsmen so that in no time they were being assaulted on three sides. Incredibly they did not fall back but stood and died in their ranks. It did not take long, more legionaries sweeping up the steps and then assaulting them from the rear. The piercing screams of the dying cut the air as the guardsmen were scythed down by hundreds of gladius blades. No quarter was asked for or given, and then there was only a pile of dead men where the best of Chosroes' soldiers had once stood.

The Durans then poured into the palace. I walked with Domitus and Nergal in the wake of the slaughter. My soldiers were disciplined, but they had earned this victory and I was in no mood to prevent their excesses as bloodlust gripped them. We walked up the palace steps, skirting the piles of dead that were scattered all around. Already Marcus' men were walking among the corpses looking for ballista missiles that could be retrieved. We had a century as an escort as we made our way through the stone columns at the top of the palace steps and then went into the building itself. Ahead I could hear shouts, screams and whoops as the Durans vented their wrath upon anyone who still resisted. A total of three cohorts had entered the palace, which I soon regretted.

The palace consisted of a great vaulted main hall leading to the throne room, which was flanked by two smaller rooms opening into three larger, domed halls. These in turn led to the rear of the palace where numerous private apartments were located. Everywhere there were smashed statues, wrecked furniture and torn curtains and tapestries. I ordered Domitus to go back outside and bring more soldiers into the palace to control the ones who were already inside and running amok. Nergal and I continued through the main hall to the throne room and then the private apartments. We came across corridors littered with dead servants and court officials, with Durans lounging around on furniture or hacking at desks and valuable ornaments with their swords. As soon as they saw me they stopped and stood to attention. I ordered them to leave the palace immediately and assemble on the square outside. We continued our journey, stopping when we heard the screams of women at the end of a long corridor on our left. We ran down it and came to two red doors inlaid with gold that had been forced open. Four gaudily dressed servants lay dead immediately inside the doors, their torsos ripped to shreds by repeated sword thrusts. This was Chosroes' harem. Its floor was covered with white marble tiles, white and red curtains were hanging from the ceiling; the air was filled with the aroma of sweet incense. No doubt the dead at the doors were eunuchs charged with guarding the king's wives. The women themselves, around twenty in number, were huddled in a frightened group in the middle of a great columned room, surrounded by at least a hundred leering, raucous legionaries. Many of the women, some young girls, had been stripped naked before being herded together. They were clinging to each other, terrified, weeping and pleading for mercy. The escort formed into close order as I marched through the throng and stood in front of the women.

'Stop this at once,' I bellowed at the top of my voice.

The din ceased immediately as the soldiers recognised me.

'The finest soldiers in the empire are not rapists or murderers of young girls,' I said sternly. 'Leave this place and assemble on the square outside the palace.'

I drew my sword as they looked at each other. 'Any man who wishes to touch any of these women will have to come through me first.' Nergal likewise drew his sword and stood beside me.

The next few seconds confirmed my belief that these men were indeed Parthia's finest warriors as they saluted and tramped from the harem with their heads down, not one of them protesting against my decision. I placed a guard outside the harem and left the king's wives alone to compose themselves. My only wish was to find Chosroes; I had no interest in his women.

Domitus returned with more troops, who were divided into parties to carry out a sweep of the palace, halt all further looting and order the soldiers to assemble on the palace square. The palace may have been ransacked, but Domitus had ensured that the armoury, treasury and royal granary had all been secured before anyone had a chance to loot them. Order was quickly restored as the Duran Legion was assembled on the square where a roll call was taken. On the outside of the square Nergal's horse archers were sitting in their saddles waiting for their commander. He and I stood at the top of the palace steps. I heard marching feet and turned to see Domitus leading half a dozen legionaries carrying a corpse. They halted in front of me and dumped the body on the stone slabs.

'Behold King Chosroes,' said Domitus. 'We found him lying on his bed. Looks like he took poison.'

I stared at the corpse. The eyes were wide open and there was white froth around the mouth. Nergal laid a hand on my shoulder. 'Your victory is complete, Pacorus.'

I nodded and thanked him, yet I felt cheated. Narses said that I was to be executed on this very square, and I had wanted so much to see Chosroes executed here instead, to see the terror in his eyes before he died. But now he was gone and only a pile of carrion remained. I spat on the corpse.

'Put it on a cart,' I said.

We left the legion to guard the palace compound and also left Marcus and his men there. It was late afternoon now and the soldiers were tired after their exertions. I also instructed Domitus to stay at the palace.

'Where are you going?' he asked.

'To make sure my wife is safe.'

'I should come with you,' he growled as I mounted Remus.

'You must stay here, my friend. Get some rest and food, you have earned them. I'm sure the palace kitchens can provide something agreeable to eat.'

The bodies of the palace guard were being loaded on to carts to be carried to the fires that were already burning outside the palace compound, the nauseating smell of burning flesh filling the air.

I raised my hand to Domitus. 'I will return later.'

He raised his arm in salute as I rode from the palace at the head of Nergal's horse archers. We rode back through the Royal Orchard to the White Temple located on the other side of the city. The White Temple was one of the wonders of the world. The temple itself was a ziggurat, a pyramid built in five receding tiers that sat on a massive square stone platform. Constructed of sun-baked bricks, it was faced with white stone. As we approached the temple I could see the great outside ramps that led to the pyramid's summit. And yet the ziggurat was not a place of worship, it was a dwelling place for the gods; in the White Temple's case the sky god Anu. Having His own house, Anu could be close to His worshippers who gathered around the temple's base. Only priests were allowed inside the temple. The extensive temple grounds were surrounded by a white stonewall twice the height of a man. When we arrived at the walls themselves we found Gallia, Orodes, Kuban, Surena, Byrd and Malik gathered in a richly appointed house directly south of the main entrance to the White Temple's grounds. Gallia rushed over and threw her arms around me when Nergal and I appeared. Nergal and Praxima also had an emotional reunion.

Orodes embraced me. 'Thank the gods you are safe.'

'Of course,' I replied, 'the palace has fallen. Chosroes is dead.'

'Yes,' hissed Surena, clenching his fists in triumph.

'What is happening here?' I asked.

'The people have taken refuge in the temple compound,' said Gallia, 'those that haven't been butchered, that is.' She shot a disdainful look at Surena.

'We have surrounded the temple,' said Orodes, 'but decided against ordering an assault.'

'There are no soldiers guarding the temple, only priests,' remarked Surena. 'We can take it easily.'

'Your opinion does not count,' retorted Gallia.

'You were right not to order an assault,' I said. 'We cannot begin the city's new era in blood.'

'Then what do we do?' asked Orodes.

'We show humility, Orodes, that is what we do.'

I ordered that the Exiles fall back to the south, out of site of the temple. There may not have been any soldiers inside the compound, but there would be eyes on the walls that would have seen the thousands of troops encircling them. I also ordered Kuban, Malik and Surena to withdraw their men; Surena especially as his followers had been involved in excesses in the working quarter. Even Gallia's Amazons and Orodes and the cataphracts were pulled back out of sight of the walls.

'What if they scorn your appeal?' asked Gallia.

'The troops can be summoned back easily enough,' I replied. 'We have to gain their trust.'

'That might be difficult after the killings by Surena and his swamp people.'

'Marsh people,' I replied.

'You indulge him far too much, Pacorus.'

'Perhaps,' I said, 'but if my plan works it will be worth it.'

I approached the main entrance to the temple without weapons or armour.

I had forgotten how many times I had done this – that is, walk up to the enemy's stronghold alone and vulnerable. I always comforted myself with the notion that the enemy would not strike down an envoy seeking a parley, but in many ways this was a foolish notion. What did honour or rules mean to most kings and generals in the world? I myself had been betrayed more than once and yet still clung to the notion that right and wrong were woven into the very fabric of the world. As I approached the white gates I could hear the laughter of Spartacus in my mind, Domitus too for that matter. The gates were not large or particularly strong; rather, ornate and an ostentatious display of wealth, being inlaid with silver and gold, with grilles over the two spy holes, one positioned in the centre of each gate. There was no one on the walls so I banged on one of the gates with my fist and then stepped back. Silence. I banged on the gate again and waited. Nothing. This was ridiculous.

'I am Pacorus, King of Dura,' I shouted at the top of my voice. 'I am alone and would speak to your leaders.'

I looked left and right for any signs of life but saw none. Then a thought flashed through my mind. Perhaps the temple compound was empty. But if that was the case, where had all the people gone? Perplexed, I turned to walk back to my men when I heard a sliding noise behind me. I turned around to see a face at one of the grilles.

481

'Are you alone?' a voice asked.

I held out my arms. 'I am alone and unarmed.'

The spy hole snapped shut. A few seconds later one of the gates opened and a man came from the compound, a tall individual with a long stride and broad shoulders. In his late fifties, he wore a white robe with long sleeves edged with gold and gold earrings. He had a long face and nose and dark brown eyes and was completely bald. His eyebrows had also been shaved. He halted a few paces from me and looked around to see if I had told the truth about being alone.

'As I said, I am alone.'

'So it would seem,' his voice was deep and commanding. 'I am Rahim, high priest to Anu.'

I bowed my head. 'It is an honour to meet you, sir.'

He studied me for a few seconds. 'So you are King Pacorus, the great warlord whose infamy is known throughout the empire.'

'I like to think of myself as a man who was wronged and who has searched for justice.'

His brow creased. 'Perhaps you confuse justice with revenge.'

I smiled. 'If I was intent on revenge I would have ordered my soldiers to have stormed the temple compound. I assume the people are within.'

His nostrils flared. 'They are under the protection of Anu. He watches us now, especially you young warlord.'

'I have no desire to harm the people, Rahim.'

He maintained his defiance. 'You have already killed some innocents.'

'I deeply regret that. I did not desire it.'

'Who else have you killed this day?'

'Only those who desired to kill me,' I replied casually.

He looked to the east, where the Royal Orchard lay. 'You have taken the palace?'

'Yes.'

His eyes narrowed. 'And you have killed the king?'

I sighed. 'He killed himself, took poison I believe.'

'It is a terrible thing that you have done.'

'No more terrible than assaulting my city with the intention of killing my family,' I replied. 'Did Chosroes believe that I would forget such a gross insult, that I would not seek redress for his crimes?'

He looked away from me. 'The affairs of kings are of no concern to me. I serve Anu and all those who follow Him.'

'I have no wish to offend Anu, Rahim.'

'Then keep your soldiers out of his temple,' he snapped.

I raised my arms. 'Do you see any soldiers, Rahim? I wish to bring peace to Uruk.'

'By slaughtering its king and his people? A curious stratagem.'

'By ensuring that there is a friend of Dura on its throne.'

He pointed a long finger at me. 'So you wish to make yourself king in Chosroes' place. I detect ambition to be your chief motive rather than to redress any wrongs done to you.'

I feigned a hurtful expression. 'I? Of course not, I already have a throne.'

He was confused. 'Then who?'

I looked up at the sky. 'It is late, Rahim. We will talk more in the morning. Please come to the palace at your convenience where I shall explain all. And tell the people they can return to their homes if they wish.'

He shook his head. 'They are fearful and will remain in the temple compound until they feel safe.'

I bowed my head to him. 'Very well. Until tomorrow, then.'

I turned and walked back to the house where Gallia and Orodes were waiting. The light was fading as I ordered the Exiles and the horsemen to march to the palace of Chosroes. It had been a most satisfactory day.

When we arrived at the palace Gallia became most annoyed. Not only was she appalled by the existence of Chosroes' harem, she also learned that the women had come close to being mass-raped. And to compound her fury some of the walls were splattered with blood from where servants and court officials had been killed by the first Durans who had swept through the palace. She insisted that the Amazons stood guard over the king's wives and prohibited any man from entering that part of the palace where the harem was located. She also wanted those men who had stripped the women to be publicly flogged in the palace square, a demand that I talked her out of with great difficulty. In the end I told her that I was responsible for the looting of the palace and therefore some of the blame for what happened in the harem was my fault.

'Those women are under my protection,' she hissed.

'Of course.'

'And any who wish to join the Amazons will be free to do so. Those who do not wish to ride with me will be free to go where they will, and will have gold to start their new life.'

'As you wish.'

We had all gathered in one of the rooms in the palace's private chambers, a small feasting hall near the kitchens with the walls decorated with scenes of hunting. Domitus had posted guards on the city's walls and at the gates where we had forced an entry. He had also organised patrols to enforce the curfew that had been put in place. The Ma'adan had been brought into the palace compound where they could be watched and prevented from committing any more mischief, while the horsemen of Nergal and Orodes were also camped in the palace grounds, their mounts finding fresh bedding and food in the royal stables. As the palace servants had either been killed or had run away, we were served a meal of roasted lamb that had been prepared by some of Domitus' legionaries. Gallia sat at one end of the long table flanked by Praxima and Nergal, while I sat at the other end. Domitus and Orodes sat next to each other on one side of the table, facing Surena and Marcus on the other side. I had asked Marcus to join us because it had been his machines that had made our victory possible.

The wine that had been found in the cellars beneath the palace was excellent, and soon Domitus was in high spirits. He rose and held his silver cup aloft.

'Here's to you, Pacorus. A great victory.'

The others rapped their knuckles on the table.

I stood and acknowledged their acclaim. I held up my cup to Marcus. 'Without Marcus and his men we would not be sitting here, so I thank him and them for their splendid work this day.'

The others toasted our Roman ally, who blushed and avoided our eyes.

Domitus drained his cup and refilled it with more wine. He stood once more. 'Hail to Pacorus, King of Uruk.'

More rapping on the table. I held up my hands. 'Thank you, Domitus, but I shall not be king of this city.'

Domitus looked confused. 'You won't?'

'No.'

He sat down, shrugged and drank more wine.

Gallia leaned forward and focused her eyes on me. 'Then who will rule Uruk?'

'Who, my love? The two people sitting either side of you, that's who.'

Gallia leaned back in her chair and eyed me suspiciously, while Nergal and Praxima said nothing. Indeed, Nergal appeared not to have grasped the meaning of what I had said, but Praxima certainly did. She looked at Gallia, then at Nergal and then at me. I smiled at her.

'That is correct, Praxima, you two shall rule Uruk.'

'So,' said Gallia, 'this is the little scheme that you have been plotting all this time.'

'Hardly a little scheme, my love. More like a great scheme'

Nergal had finally grasped the significance of my words.

'And do Nergal and Praxima have a say in this?' asked Gallia.

'Of course,' I replied.

'You hear that, Praxima,' said Gallia, 'Pacorus would make you a queen and your husband a king.'

'It is a great honour,' said Nergal.

Gallia's eyes were still on me. 'Is it, Nergal? You will be alone without an army when Pacorus returns to Dura. What will happen then when Narses and Mithridates march against you to avenge their ally's death? Do you think so little of our friends, Pacorus, that you would sacrifice them so easily?'

I jumped up. 'Of course not. Uruk will have an army. Surena will stay and train his people to be the garrison, and Kuban and his men will also stay to serve Nergal. Babylon lies to the north of Mesene, and so I will ask Vardan to send soldiers to reinforce the garrison. I think he will be glad to have a friend to the south of his borders rather than an enemy.'

'I accept the charge, lord,' said a partly drunk Surena.

'Be silent,' hissed Gallia.

'Surena will raise more men from the Ma'adan,' I said, 'and the citizens of Uruk will accept their new rulers.'

'They will?' said Gallia, incredulously.

'Of course. Chosroes and his sons are dead. His line is ended. Dura needs an ally on Uruk's throne. So what say the both of you, will you accept? I promise that you will never stand alone.'

I could see that Gallia still had reservations, but Praxima was grinning with delight and Nergal was bursting with pride. They looked at each other and Praxima nodded at her husband.

Nergal looked at me. 'We accept, Pacorus, you are a most generous friend.'

He and Praxima went to bed in high spirits that night. I told them to meet us the next morning in the throne room. Gallia was far from happy.

'It is a ridiculous plan, hare-brained. You think the people of this city will accept Nergal and Praxima?'

'Why not? They accepted Chosroes and all he brought them was war and misery.'

She was brushing her blonde locks near the gold inlaid wicker doors that led on to the balcony. Her beauty still took my breath away. We had taken one of the bedrooms near the quarters of the new king and queen.

485

She stopped her grooming and turned to look at me. 'And what of Mithridates and Narses, do you think they will accept your little arrangement?'

I walked over to her and kissed her on the head. 'No, but who will they send against me? Mithridates will not leave Ctesiphon and his doting mother and Narses will have to raise a large army before he dares to march against me. And to raise an army will take time.'

'You have it all worked out, don't you?'

I cupped her face in my hands. 'Of course. But enough of politics. Let us talk of giving Claudia a brother or sister, if my queen is agreeable to the notion.'

She placed her hands on my hips and looked at me with her big blue eyes and her mood softened. 'She is agreeable.'

It was truly a most wonderful end to a great day.

The morning came soon enough, and with it the sound of hobnailed sandals on the flagstones of the palace square. The voices of centurions barking orders and trumpet and horn blasts signalled that it was just another routine day in the life of Dura's army. After a breakfast of fruit, honey, yoghurt, bread and water, Gallia and I went to the throne room where we found a nervous Nergal and Praxima. Gallia embraced her friend and I laid a hand on Nergal's shoulder.

'You are not going into battle, my friend.'

'I wish I were,' he said, his face slightly pale. 'Are you sure about this, Pacorus?'

'Quite sure. How many years have we fought together? Remember, you have Dura's army behind you.'

And I made sure that the army's strength was on show that day. The city walls were lined with legionaries and Nergal's horse archers made a sweep ·through the Royal Orchard looking for any remnants of the garrison. They found a large group of them who promptly surrendered themselves in exchange for their lives. I asked Orodes to take the cataphracts attired in their scale armour to the White Temple to act as an escort for Rahim. I kept Surena and his Ma'adan out of the palace and thus out of the way of Gallia, but he approved of my plan to make Nergal king.

'An excellent choice, majesty. Lord Nergal is a great warrior. Will he expel the population from the city?'

I was horrified. 'Certainly not.'

'They have oppressed my people for many years.'

'That may be, but today is the beginning of a new era for Uruk,' I said, 'one in which Ma'adan and Mesenians will live in peace.'

'Old wounds take time to heal, lord.'

'But they do heal, Surena, eventually. So I will have no more talk of enmity between your people and the Mesenians.'

He remained sceptical but was nevertheless delighted that Chosroes, the murderer of his parents, was dead. And as the late king's army had also been put to the sword I foresaw few difficulties in uniting the kingdom under Nergal. The only potential obstacle to the whole project was Rahim, who arrived mid-morning, escorted into the palace by Orodes and accompanied by a dozen other priests dressed in white robes. Also bald like him, they trailed a few steps behind him with their heads bowed. We waited for Rahim in the throne room, Nergal and Praxima sitting on the dais. Nergal sat on Chosroes' old throne but we had to find another seat for Praxima, as the old king had not shared his power with any of his many wives. We fetched the most richly decorated chair we could find and draped it in a red cloth to give it a mask of authority. Praxima wore her white top under her mail tunic, leggings and boots, her trusty dagger at her hip. Her sword in its scabbard rested against her chair. Nergal wore Chosroes' crown and kept touching it, more from nerves than anything else. I stood beside him on the dais on his right-hand side, while Gallia stood next to Praxima. Both women let their hair hang free, Gallia's pure blonde, Praxima's a fiery red. To me Praxima would always be the wild, fierce warrior who killed with relish on the battlefield with the Amazons when we had been in Italy, but looking at her today I could see that she was also a very striking woman. Not a beauty, perhaps, but proud, strong and uncompromising. She would make a fine queen for her king.

Nergal touched his crown again. 'Don't worry,' I whispered, 'it won't fall off. It suits you, Nergal, it really does.'

Around the outside of the room legionaries lined the walls and Amazons in their helmets and clutching their bows were either side of the dais. Rahim may have been surrounded by a host of soldiers but he retained his haughty demeanour, standing proudly in front of the dais with his arms folded. His stance could have been interpreted as a sign of disrespect but I gave him the benefit of the doubt.

'Welcome Rahim, I trust you and the people are well.'

'They are well,' sniffed Rahim, his eyes darting from me to Nergal and then Praxima.

I held out a hand towards Nergal. 'Behold, King Nergal, ruler of this city, and his queen, Praxima.'

I thought I saw a flash of awe in Rahim's eyes, but then it was gone as the priests behind him started whispering frantically among themselves. One walked forward and uttered some words into Rahim's ear. The high priest nodded and then looked at Nergal and then Praxima. Then they turned their backs on us all and conferred together. Gallia looked across at me and frowned while Domitus looked bored. Nergal and Praxima both looked confused. Then Rahim and his priests stopped their chattering and went down on bended knees in front of Nergal. Rahim spoke, his voice echoing around the room.

'Hail, holy one. Your coming was foretold many generations ago. We beg your forgiveness for doubting you. Please accept our humble apologies and our devotion.'

I was stunned. It was certainly more than I expected. I had hoped for Rahim's acquiescence, a grudging acceptance would have sufficed. But this? I slapped Nergal on the shoulders, which earned me a glower from Rahim when he spotted it. No matter. Dobbai had been right; I must be beloved of the gods.

'Get up, please, get up all of you,' said a rather surprised Nergal.

Rahim and his priests rose and bowed their heads at Nergal and Praxima. A priest took two paces forward and whispered into Rahim's ear once more.

Rahim nodded. 'Excellent idea.' He bowed his head to Nergal. 'Would your highness and Queen Allatu care to visit the temple and inspect your people assembled there?'

Allatu? What nonsense was this? Praxima looked at Gallia, who shrugged.

'Your idea is an excellent one, Rahim,' I said.

He glowered at me again. 'Only the king and queen may enter the temple itself.'

Nergal stood up, which caused Rahim and his priests to gasp in wonderment and once again go down on bended knee.

'There is no time like the present,' said Nergal, who now appeared much more confident. He held out his hand to Praxima, who rose from her chair and took it. They both then walked from the throne room with Rahim and his holy men following.

'Go with them, Orodes,' I said, 'make sure they stay safe.'

Rahim turned sharply to face me. 'I can assure you that they will be quite safe.'

He then scurried after Nergal and Praxima with Orodes walking briskly after them. When they had left Domitus dismissed the guards from the room and Gallia stood down her Amazons, leaving the three of us alone in the great chamber.

'Does either of you understand what just happened?' asked

Gallia.

'Pacorus has obviously bribed that head priest,' said Domitus.

'I don't think any amount of money would have produced that outcome,' I replied. 'But whatever the cause of Rahim's change of heart I give thanks to Shamash for it. It has made things much easier.'

'He obviously saw something in Nergal and Praxima that reminded him of something sacred,' remarked Gallia.

Domitus slapped me hard on the arm. 'Whatever it was, Jupiter has smiled on you this day. You are one lucky bastard.'

'Who is Jupiter?' asked Gallia.

'King of the gods,' said Domitus.

'The king of the Roman gods,' I corrected him.

'Roman, Parthian, they are all the same,' said Domitus, 'they demand endless grovelling and buckets of blood. Well, whatever the reason, I have an army to run. How long are you thinking of staying here?'

In fact we stayed for two weeks, during which time we learned more about Rahim's change of heart. When Nergal and Praxima returned to the palace I was delighted to learn that Rahim had ordered the people to return to their homes. The new king and his queen had been taken on a tour of the White Temple, during which Rahim had taken them to the shrine at the summit of the ziggurat. Inside they had been shown ancient clay tablets and stone carvings on the walls.

They tablets told of Nergal, the god of war who was the eldest son of Anu. As Nergal related what Rahim had told him, I realised why he and his priests had reason to believe that Nergal was the reincarnation of his namesake. As well as his name, Nergal resembled the god in other ways. He was a gangly individual and the tablets told of a god who was a man having the legs of a cock, thus when Nergal stood up in the throne room the priests would have seen his long legs. Rahim had said that Nergal would come to the city at the head of an army for he was the god of war and pestilence and the lord of the half-human demons of the underworld. Rahim interpreted Dura's legions as demons and, more importantly, worshippers of Shamash accompanied him, for Nergal was the brother of the sun god. Rahim then showed them a stone carving of Nergal on his throne with his wife, the goddess Allatu, a deity of the underworld, seated next to him. Allatu had the head of a lion, and seeing Praxima's fiery mane Rahim and his priests had interpreted this as further proof that they were indeed the ones that the ancient tablets had spoken of.

489

Marcus and his men, having been responsible for the destruction of the city's southern gates, oversaw the rebuilding of the walls and city life began to return to normal. The body of Chosroes was taken outside the city and reduced to ashes on a pyre, the ashes then being tossed into the Euphrates. I left a cohort under Drenis in Uruk to train the Ma'adan recruits that Surena had raised, who was sent back to his people to spread the news that there was a new king on the throne of Uruk. He took Viper with him to show her off to his family. He would stay with Nergal, as would Kuban and his Margianians. Gallia also left half the Amazons with Praxima, the two of them having a tearful farewell in the palace as the Duran Legion and the Exiles were already on the march out of the city. We would take the same route back to Dura that had brought us to Uruk. Orodes said his farewells and then departed the palace square at the head of the cataphracts and horse archers. At the end only Gallia, I and those Amazons who were returning to Dura remained, plus half a dozen new recruits, former members of the harem, now in my queen's bodyguard. To one side, observing the proceedings, stood the brooding figure of Rahim.

I extended my hand to Nergal. 'It has been an honour serving with you, my friend.'

He took my hand and we embraced. 'You too, Pacorus. I owe everything to you.'

'He would have been proud of you, of both of you.'

'Who?' he asked.

'Spartacus.'

'You think he watches over us, Pacorus?'

I smiled. 'I like to think so.'

'Me too.'

I embraced Praxima and kissed her on the cheek.

'Remember,' I said, 'you are not alone. Dura stands with you always.'

Gallia was silent as we rode from the city and rejoined the army that was winding its way south and then west to the ford across the Euphrates. Byrd and Malik rode ahead to ensure there were no hostile groups in our path, but it was unnecessary. Even before we had left Uruk those lords of Mesene who were still alive had ridden to the city to pay homage to their new king. It would take time to rebuild the kingdom's army, the more so because Mesene was not rich, but Nergal and his officers were up to the task and when they had finished Dura would have a valuable ally.

The march back to Dura was uneventful, though it was made at a hastened pace as Gallia wished to be with Claudia as soon as possible. Domitus used her desire for hurry as an excuse to push the army hard, the legionaries marching over twenty miles a day and grumbling like fury as they did so. They did not mind hard marching at the beginning of a campaign, but thought that they were entitled to take it easy after they had won another great victory. The oxen pulling the wagons that held Marcus' siege engines could not maintain such a pace without collapsing in the heat, so I was forced to detach Orodes and half the army's horse archers to protect them as the rest of the army sped north. After four days the gap between the wagons and the rest of the army had become too great and I called a halt, informing Gallia that the army would march as one. We waited for Orodes to catch up and then proceeded at a more leisurely pace. On the seventh day we bade farewell to Malik and Byrd, who both returned to Palmyra with Malik's men.

Ten days after we had crossed the Euphrates to head back to Dura, Gallia and I rode through the Palmyrene Gate and into the city. Domitus and his legions returned to their camp and the lords and their retinues continued on to their homes. Crowds lined the streets and cheered as we led the cataphracts and their squires to the Citadel. Orodes rode beside us, the banners of Dura and Susiana fluttering behind. At the Citadel Godarz, Rsan and Dobbai, the latter holding Claudia's hand, greeted us. Gallia jumped down and raced over to our daughter, then scooped her up in her arms. Godarz and Rsan looked solemn, and then I saw my father at the top of the palace steps. Somewhat taken aback, I dismounted and handed Remus' reins to a waiting stable hand. Behind me the cataphracts and squires were likewise dismounting and leading their horses to the stables. I walked over to Gallia and embraced my daughter, one eye on my father who still stood at the top of the steps.

'How long has my father been here?'

'He arrived this morning, son of Hatra,' said Dobbai.

I kissed Claudia once more and strode up the steps to where my father stood.

'Greetings, father.' I walked forward and embraced him. 'This is an unexpected pleasure.'

'I waited on the other side of the river until news arrived that you were near the city.'

'Is mother well?'

'She is well. We need to talk.'

My instincts told me that something was wrong, which was confirmed half an hour later as we sat on the terrace taking refreshments. I sent a rider to fetch Domitus and also asked Orodes, Godarz and Rsan to attend us. Dobbai, though not asked to be present, invited herself anyway. My father paced up and down the terrace in front of us as we waited for Domitus, frequently glancing at Orodes. Eventually Domitus arrived and the doors were closed.

My father stopped pacing and looked at Orodes. 'Prince Orodes, I regret to inform you that your father is dead.'

There was a stunned silence.

Orodes went pale. 'Dead? How, are you quite sure, majesty?'

'We received word from Ctesiphon a week ago.'

'What was the cause of his death?' I asked.

'A broken heart, we were told. Brought on by the murder of Chosroes at your hand.'

I was dumbfounded. 'What?'

'My sincerest condolences for your father, Orodes,' continued my father, 'he was a good man.'

Orodes' eyes were cast down. 'Yes, he was.'

'Mithridates blames you for his father's death, Pacorus, and has sworn vengeance against you,' said my father. 'Moreover, because the empire is in a state of war Mithridates has become temporary King of Kings until the present emergency is dealt with.'

'What war, what emergency?' I asked.

'Do not you see, son of Hatra,' said Dobbai, 'that you were the instrument by which Mithridates has gained the high crown?' She looked at the wilted figure of Orodes. 'I grieve for you, young prince, for your father was surely murdered by Mithridates and the queen, poisoned most likely, and now your brother rules in Ctesiphon.'

'How can he become King of Kings without the agreement of the other kings of the empire?' I asked.

'It is simple arithmetic,' replied my father. 'Gordyene has no king and is no longer part of the empire.'

'That is only temporary,' I spat.

My father frowned and held up his hand. 'Gordyene has no king, and neither does Sakastan, thanks to you, or for that matter Mesene, also thanks to you. You have been banished, which means Dura has no vote in the matter. This means that the kingdoms of Susiana, Carmania, Drangiana, Aria, Anauon, Yueh-Chih, Persis and Sakastan support the election of Mithridates as temporary King of Kings.'

Now it was my turn to pace the terrace. 'But Narses rules both Persis and Sakastan, those kingdoms cannot have two votes.'

My father shook his head. 'He rules his own kingdom and is protector over Sakastan.'

'Mere semantics,' growled Orodes, still looking down.

My father sighed. 'That may be, prince, but Narses can still muster two votes on this issue.'

'But the kingdoms in the western half of the empire,' I said.

'Are out-voted, Pacorus,' interrupted my father. 'And even if they were not they have no stomach for another civil war. Atropaiene and Media have been weakened by conflict with the Romans, while potential enemies surround Gotarzes at Elymais. The kings are tired of fighting Pacorus, and many of them blame you for the cause of much of it.'

I stopped pacing and looked at him. 'And Hatra?'

He smiled, the first time he had done so today. 'Hatra will stand by you.'

'But the only one that will,' said Dobbai. 'Your enemies increase in number, son of Hatra. I did warn you, but your thirst for glory blinded you. You should have marched on Ctesiphon instead or Uruk. You had the armies of other kings with you then.'

'They would not have supported an attack against the high king,' said my father sternly.

Dobbai cackled. 'Now you will face the wrath of two empires.'

'Two empires?' I said.

An evil grin spread over her old face. 'You did not think that Rome had forgotten about you, did you?'

'Careful old woman,' I replied, 'one day you will talk your head off your shoulders.'

'But not before two mighty armies will march against you, son of Hatra, one from the east and one from the west. Not before then.'

My father left for Hatra the next morning. He told us that we would always have refuge in Hatra. Gallia embraced him in the courtyard as his bodyguard waited for their king.

'We will not leave our home,' she said.

He picked up Claudia and kissed her on the cheek. 'Don't leave it too long before you visit us. Your mother misses you all.'

He put Claudia down and offered me his hand. I took it.

'Take care of Orodes, he has suffered a heavy blow.'

'I shall, father.'

He suddenly looked old and careworn. 'And take care of yourself. You have, unfortunately, made powerful enemies who have no understanding of the virtue of forgiveness.'

'Dura's walls and its army are strong, father.'

He mounted his horse and managed a smile for Gallia and Claudia.

'You cannot fight everyone, Pacorus. May Shamash protect you.'

He rode from the Citadel with his bodyguard following him. Gallia and Dobbai took Claudia back inside and I stood alone in the courtyard. Guards stood on the walls and at the gates and squires busied themselves tending to their masters' horses. A party of cataphracts in full war gear, a kontus resting on every right shoulder, trotted from the stables, across the courtyard and through the gates, raising their left hands in salute as they rode past me. The routine of military life went on, oblivious to the machinations of kings.

That afternoon I wrote a letter to Mithridates at Ctesiphon. I am no scribe, but I think it summed up my feelings succinctly. I sat alone on my bedroom balcony, Najya perched on a stand beside me.

To King Mithridates

Word has recently reached me that your father, King Phraates, has died of a broken heart. It indeed breaks my heart to think that such a good man has departed this world, and sickens me greatly that the one who was the cause of his death has stolen his crown and now dares to call himself the King of Kings.

I have also heard that you hold me responsible for your father's death, and have used this lie to deceive numerous other kings of the empire into electing you to your present high office. And now you seek to make yourself master of all the Parthian Empire, but I have to tell you that while I still live you will never know peace. For you are a poison at the very heart of the empire, and every day that you sit upon the throne Parthia dies a little. The only cure for the empire is to remove this ulcer, this rottenness, and that includes your lackey Narses, another traitor who fouls the empire by his mere existence. I will not rest until you and he have suffered the same fate as those other traitors Porus and Chosroes. This I swear by all that is sacred.

I remain, your most implacable enemy.

Pacorus, King of Dura.

Thus was the die cast. The falcon suddenly stirred and spread her wings, and made at harsh kak, kak, kak noise while looking to the east, obviously sensing an ill wind. I stroked her head.

'Easy, little one.'

I gave her a morsel of meat and she stopped fretting. I walked to the balustrade and gazed across the blue waters of the Euphrates to the east. So Mithridates was King of Kings with Narses as his right-hand man. They would soon be gathering an army to march against Dura, for they realised that neither of them would know peace while I was still in the world. And that would mean they would have to fight me. It would come down to one great battle, one final clash to decide the fate of the empire. I smiled. Good. Let them come; I would be ready.

Epilogue

The view was certainly impressive; Crassus conceded that. As the most powerful and wealthy man in Rome he normally never left the centre of the Roman Empire, but this spring had been different for Gnaeus Pompey Magnus was returning to Rome. He had been away from the city for five years, during which time he had destroyed the Cilician pirates and defeated Mithridates of Pontus and Tigranes of Armenia. These triumphs had made him extremely popular in Rome, much to the annoyance of Crassus. Pompey was already a hero to the common people of the city and these victories would only serve to increase his prestige and therefore influence. Pompey had a talent amounting to genius for getting under Crassus' skin, and the past few years had provided a perfect example. Not only had Pompey used his political influence to gain extraordinary powers to deal with the pirate threat in the eastern Mediterranean, he had also used his influence to gain command of the entire Roman war effort in the East. And to cap it all Pompey had sent one of his toadies, a legate by the name of Quintus Caecilius Metellus, to Rome to persuade Crassus to meet him in Asia Minor. He knew why he had made the request, of course. Pompey would receive a hostile reception from a Senate packed with Crassus' allies, which would make honouring his word to his soldiers about granting them land upon their demobilisation extremely difficult.

So Crassus found himself in the luxurious splendour of a villa overlooking the town of Ephesus on the Aegean coastline. Pompey had invited him to dine with him as soon as he had arrived at the port, the villa nestling in the hills above the bustling town. Crassus was a frugal man – he had only one house in Rome – whereas Pompey was the exact opposite, flaunting his wealth and power at every opportunity. Tonight was no different, with the food being served from plates of gold and wine poured into jewel-encrusted silver cups. There were mosaics on the floor depicting images of Greek gods and hunting frescoes on the walls. Crassus reclined on a large couch that was set against the back wall of the dining area, facing the open side of the room that gave a panoramic view of the port and sea below.

Pompey reclined on his couch propped up on his left elbow, Crassus next to him. Servants first served them mulsum, a delicious chilled white wine with honey, and then served the first course of eggs, salad with asparagus and salted fish.

The formalities out of the way, Pompey got down to business.

'I assume that the Senate is still hostile towards me.'

'You are right in that assumption,' gloated Crassus.

'The Senate is ungrateful to its faithful sons.'

Slaves began serving the second course of meat, game and poultry.

Crassus saw no point in playing word games with his host. 'What do you wish of me, Pompey?'

Pompey laughed and clapped his hands together. 'Blunt and to the point, as ever. Is it not obvious? I wish to return to Rome without having to endure the tedium of censure by the Senate.'

Crassus picked at some cooked peacock brains. 'You also want land for your returning soldiers?'

'Of course, those who have shed blood for Rome should be rewarded.'

Crassus was prompted to ask where the gold and silver that Pompey had looted in Cilicia, Armenia and Pontus had ended up. Such wealth would be more than enough to purchase land for his veterans, but he thought better of it. He knew Pompey was very familiar with the phrase, 'to the victor, the spoils', and interpreted it very literally.

'I have friends in the Senate who can calm troubled waters,' said Crassus, 'though such services are difficult to arrange.'

'And very expensive, no doubt,' added Pompey.

Crassus said nothing but smiled at his younger rival. Pompey continued.

'I have been away from Rome for too long, but Rome still has unfinished business in the East. The man who leads the Roman invasion of Parthia will become very rich and very powerful, perhaps the most powerful man in the whole world.'

Crassus was now very interested. He knew the Parthian Empire was rich from its control of the silk route from China and its vast stockpile of gold that had once belonged to the ancient Persian Empire. But Crassus was slightly wary of his host. He was, after all, probably more ambitious than himself.

'But do you not covet Parthia yourself?'

Now it was Pompey's turn to smile. 'My friend, there are other lands in the world to conquer. Besides, as I said, I have been away from Rome for too long.'

Crassus then brought up a subject designed to wipe the smile off his face.

'Tell me, why did you retreat in the face of the Parthian rabble at the Euphrates?'

Pompey may have covered himself in glory in the East, but his withdrawal from the Euphrates without a fight had puzzled many in Rome and had cast a shadow over his military reputation.

Pompey seemed unconcerned by the question. 'Why? I will tell you why. Prior to facing "the rabble" as you call them, we had been battered for five days by a sandstorm the like of which I had never seen before. We lost half our supplies and the men had no sleep for at least four nights.'

'A sandstorm?' Crassus was most sceptical.

Pompey's smile had now disappeared. 'Unless you have been in the midst of one you will not know their power. When we arrived at the river we did not find a rabble but a well-disciplined army of horse and foot led by a king called Pacorus.'

'Pacorus?' Crassus was startled by the name. Pompey's smile returned.

'That is correct, the same Pacorus that led the cavalry of Spartacus during the slave rebellion in Italy. Well, he is a king now and has raised two legions of his own. Can you imagine that, a Parthian king with Roman legions? But you know this, of course, because he destroyed your man, what was his name, Lucius Furius, at Dura.'

'But you had eight legions, did you not?' snapped Crassus.

'I did, but other kings brought their armies to support Pacorus until the horizon was filled with Parthian horsemen, and then the Agraci hordes came to add their numbers against us.' Pompey waved a hand in the air. 'Besides, I have secured Rome's eastern frontier on the Euphrates, as I vowed I would do. I had not planned for an invasion of Parthia. But I tell you this, the Parthians are not to be underestimated, especially Pacorus at Dura.'

'He needs to be dealt with.'

'It will take more than eight legions to destroy King Pacorus,' remarked Pompey. 'Remind me, how many men did you lose at Dura?'

All conversation stopped as Crassus toyed with his food and mulled over what Pompey had said. During the latter's absence Crassus had strengthened his spider's web of political and business allies, though if he left Rome then Pompey would no doubt set about trying to unravel them. He would have to give the Parthian question careful thought.

The rest of the evening was pleasant enough, with dancing girls and poetry readings saving the two men having to make polite conversation. Pompey never mentioned Parthia again and Crassus did not press the matter, but as Pompey was bidding his rival goodbye he reiterated that in return for his assistance in the matter of land for his veterans he would throw his weight behind securing

Crassus a command in the East.

The next morning, while sitting in the study of his rented villa three miles south of Ephesus, Crassus pondered his next move. Ajax, his faithful slave, brought him water and fruit as he sat at his desk. He usually took breakfast in his study to allow him to get through the bulk of his work before the afternoon. Ajax was about to leave when Crassus stopped him.

'Do you remember that Parthian whom you brought to my house in Rome some nine years ago, I think it was?'

Ajax stood still searching his mind for a few seconds. 'Ah, yes, sir. I rode to the camp of the slave leader with your letter addressed to him, then escorted him back to Rome. He rode a white horse if my memory serves me right.'

Crassus sat back in his chair. 'That is correct. Well, it appears that young man escaped from Italy after I crushed the slave rebellion and returned to his homeland. He is now a king who halted Pompey's advance in the East.'

'He did appear to be a most resourceful young man,' offered Ajax. 'Not to be underestimated.'

Crassus looked at Ajax, who wore a blank expression. Perhaps he had also heard of the defeat of Lucius Furius at Dura. Did he know that his master was thinking of a campaign in the East, was he warning him against such a venture? He dismissed such thoughts. Of course he could not know. Still, Ajax was an old companion, a trusted servant who had much responsibility in the house of his master. He was still a slave, of course, but one that Crassus was immensely fond of.

'Thank you, Ajax, you may go.'

Ajax bowed his head and made to depart but then stopped and turned around. 'Some letters have just been delivered; do you wish to see them now, sir? One of them is from Gaius by the look of the seal.'

'Yes, bring them to me.'

Crassus had always taken an interest in sponsoring promising young men, in both politics and martial affairs. Grateful protégés made useful future allies. It was a gamble, though, and often ended in failure. Crassus shook his head as he remembered Lucius Furius, a man who had cost him a great deal of money and had ended up as a corpse in Mesopotamia. Too hot-headed by far, and losing three legions and expensively assembled siege engines and engineers to work them was unforgivable. At least Furius had saved his eagles. The shame would have been unbearable had those precious objects fallen into the hands of barbarians. Well, at least Furius had had the good manners to die a hero's death. Crassus hoped his latest protégé, a certain Gaius Julius Caesar, would do better. And so far Gaius had proved himself to be most able, though only time would tell.

Crassus fingered the letter knife on the table in front of him. There were many reasons to mount a campaign against Parthia, not least the attraction of succeeding where Pompey had failed. Sandstorm indeed! He would not have turned back just because of a strong wind. No, Pompey had obviously lost his nerve. A war against Parthia would be an opportunity to put Pompey in the shade. What's more, the wealth that would be captured would more than pay for the expense of raising an army and maintaining it during the campaign. He had heard that Ctesiphon, the Parthian capital, was filled with gold. But he would leave nothing to chance. He would raise his army and prepare it thoroughly for a campaign in the East. And afterwards the eastern frontier of the Roman Empire would no longer be the River Euphrates, it would be the Tigris. Though what would prevent a capable commander marching his army as far as the Indus? What was certain is that the whole of the western half of the Parthian Empire would become Roman territory, its inhabitants conquered and sold into slavery, and that included the citizens of Dura Europos and its troublesome king.

Made in the USA
Lexington, KY
27 March 2018